D1118633

THE RUIN
OF KINGS

THE
RUIN
OF
KINGS

JENN LYONS

TOR

**A TOM DOHERTY
ASSOCIATES BOOK**
New York

THE RUIN OF KINGS

Copyright © 2019 by Jenn Lyons

Map by Jenn Lyons

A Tor Book
Published by Tom Doherty Associates
175 Fifth Avenue
New York, NY 10010

www.tor-forge.com

Tor® is a registered trademark of Macmillan Publishing Group, LLC.

Library of Congress Cataloging-in-Publication Data

Names: Lyons, Jenn, 1970– author.
Title: The ruin of kings / Jenn Lyons.
Description: First edition. | New York : Tor, 2019. | "A Tom Doherty
    Associates book."
Identifiers: LCCN 2018045774| ISBN 9781250175489 (hardcover) |
    ISBN 9781250175496 (ebook)
Subjects: | GSAFD: Fantasy fiction.
Classification: LCC PS3612.Y57525 R85 2019 | DDC 813/.6–dc23
LC record available at https://lccn.loc.gov/2018045774

Our books may be purchased in bulk for promotional, educational,
or business use. Please contact your local bookseller or the Macmillan Corporate
and Premium Sales Department at 1-800-221-7945, extension 5442,
or by email at MacmillanSpecialMarkets@macmillan.com.

First Edition: February 2019

Printed in the United States of America

0 9 8 7 6 5 4 3 2 1

For David, who gave me the first seed, and
Mike, who helped me nurture that seedling into a whole world.
And for Kihrin's three fathers: Steve, Katt, and Patrick.
He wouldn't be the same without you.

Your Majesty,

Enclosed within is a full accounting of the events that led up to the burning of the Capital. Much of the first section is based on transcripts derived from a conversation between two of the most pivotal individuals to the events; other sections consist of my own reconstruction. I used eyewitness accounts whenever possible, and tried to remain true to the essential spirit of events when I was forced to go afield. I've annotated the text with observations and analysis I hope you may find helpful.

I pray your forbearance for when I lecture you on subjects on which you are the greater expert, but ultimately, I decided it safest to assume on your ignorance rather than the reverse.

It is my hope that if you possess as complete a picture as possible of these events that led up to these matters, you will show leniency regarding the Lord Heir; the Council members who are recommending charges of treason and a death sentence surely do not have the whole story.

Your servant,
Thurvishar D'Lorus

PART I

A Dialog Between a Jailer and Her Prisoner

"Tell me a story."

The monster slouched down by the iron bars of Kihrin's jail cell. She set a small, plain stone down on the ground between them and pushed it forward.

She didn't look like a monster. Talon looked like a girl in her twenties, with wheat-gold skin and soft brown hair. Most men would give their eyeteeth to spend an evening with someone so beautiful. *Most* men didn't know of her talent for shaping her body into forms crafted from pure terror. She mocked her victims with the forms of murdered loved ones, before they too became her next meal. That she was Kihrin's jailer was like leaving a shark to guard a fish tank.

"You must be joking." Kihrin raised his head and stared at her.

Talon picked at the mortar of the wall behind her with a wicked black nail. "I'm bored."

"Knit something." The young man stood up and walked over to the line of iron bars. "Or why don't you make yourself useful and help me escape?"

Talon leaned forward. "Ah, my love, you know I can't do that. But come now, it's been so long since we've talked. We have all this catching up to do and ages before they're ready for us. Tell me everything that's happened to you. We'll use it to pass the time—until your brother comes back to murder you."

"No."

He searched for somewhere to rest his gaze, but the walls were blank, with no windows, no distractions. The room's only illumination shone from a mage-light lamp hanging outside the cell. Kihrin couldn't use it to start a fire. He would have loved to set the straw bedding ablaze—if they'd given him any.

"Aren't you bored too?" Talon asked.

Kihrin paused in his search for a hidden escape tunnel. "When they return, they're going to sacrifice me to a demon. So, no. I'm not bored." His gaze wandered once more around the room.

He could use magic to escape. He could change the tenyé of the bars and rocks to soften iron or make stone fragile as dried grass. He could do that—if Talon wasn't watching his every movement. Worse, if she wasn't capable of plucking thoughts of escape from his mind the moment they entered.

And she never slept.

"But I do *eat*," she said, answering his thoughts with a gleam in her eye, "especially when I'm bored."

He rolled his eyes. "You're not going to kill me. Someone else has that honor."

"I don't consider it murder. I'd be saving you. Your personality would be with me forever, along with—"

"Stop."

Talon pouted and made a show of examining the clawed tips of her fingers.

"Anyway, if you can read my mind, you don't need *me* to tell you what happened. Take my memories—the same as you've taken everything else."

She stood up again. "Boring. Anyway, I haven't taken everything from you. I haven't taken all your friends. I haven't taken your parents." Talon paused. "Well, not your real parents."

Kihrin stared at her.

She laughed and leaned back. "Should I leave then? If you don't tell me a story, I'll go pay your mother and father a visit. *They'd* entertain me. Though the visit might not be so much fun for them."

"You wouldn't dare."

"Who would stop me? They don't care about your parents. All they care about is their little scheme, and they don't need your mother and father for that."

"You wouldn't—"

"I would," Talon growled, her voice inhuman and shrieking. "Play my game, Bright-Eyes, or I'll come back here wearing your mother's skin cinched by a belt of your father's intestines. I'll reenact the moments of their deaths for you, over and over, until your brother returns."

Kihrin turned away, shuddering, and paced the length of his cell. He examined the empty bucket and the thin blanket tucked into a corner. He searched the walls, the ceiling, and the floor. He studied the iron bars and the lock. He even checked himself over, in case his captors had missed something, anything, when they'd taken his weapons, his lock-picks, the intaglio ring, and his talismans. They'd only left the necklace they didn't care about, the one worth a fortune.

"Well. When you put it that way . . ." Kihrin said. "How can I refuse?"

Talon brought her hands together in front of her face and made a tiny clap of delight. "Wonderful." Then she tossed him the small rock she'd put between them earlier.

Kihrin caught it. "What's this?"

"A rock."

"Talon—"

"It's a *magic* rock," she said. "Don't tell me a man in your position doesn't believe in magic rocks?"

He studied the stone again, frowning. "Someone's changed this stone's tenyé."

"Magic. Rock."

"And what does it do again?"

"It *listens*. Since you're telling the story, you hold the stone. Those are the rules." She grinned. "Start at the beginning."

1: The Slave Auction

(Kihrin's story)

When they brought me up to the auction block, I looked out over the crowd and thought: *I would kill you all if I had a knife.*

And if I wasn't naked, I amended.

And shackled. I had never felt so helpless, and—

What? You don't think this is the beginning, Talon?*

What do you mean by "beginning" anyway? Whose beginning? Mine? I don't remember it that well. Yours? Talon, you're thousands of years old and have stored the memories of as many people. You're the one who wanted to hear this. And you will, but under my terms, not yours.

Let's start over.

The auctioneer's voice boomed out over the amphitheater: "Lot six this morning is a fine specimen. What will I hear for this human Doltari male?† He's a trained musician with an excellent singing voice. Just sixteen years old. Look at that golden hair, those blue eyes, those handsome features. Why, this one might even have vané blood in him! He'll make a welcome addition to any household, but he's not gelded, so don't buy him to guard your harem, ladies and gentlemen!" The auctioneer waved his finger with a sly grin, and was answered with a few disinterested chuckles. "Opening bid is ten thousand ords."

Several members of the audience sniggered at the price.

It was too much.

I didn't look any prize that day. The Kishna-Farriga slave masters had bathed me but the scrubbing only made the raw whip wounds on my

---

*It seems Talon was serious about that "magic rock," for it records the words spoken by its holder. I could have fabricated the other side of the conversation, but the gist seems clear enough through context and so I have let the words fall where they may.

†Having known Doltari slaves, I can only assume the auctioneer was blind. Then again, perhaps the good citizens of Kishna-Farriga have become experts at accepting the labels given to slaves without question.

back stand out in angry red stripes. Copper bangles on my wrists did a poor job of camouflaging sores from long months spent in chains. The friction blisters on my left ankle were swollen, infected, and oozing. Bruises and welts covered me: all the marks of a defiant slave. My body shook from hunger and a growing fever. I wasn't worth ten thousand ords. I wasn't worth one hundred ords.

Honestly, I wouldn't have bought me.

"Ah, now don't be like that, my fine people! I know what he looks like, but I promise you, he's a rough diamond who only needs polish to shine. He'll be no trouble either—see, I hold his gaesh in my hand! Won't someone here pay ten thousand ords for the gaesh of this handsome young slave?" The auctioneer held out his arm and revealed a tarnished silver chain, from which dangled something that glittered and caught in the sun.

The crowd couldn't see the details, but I knew what he held: a silver hawk, stained black from salt air. A part of my soul, trapped in metal: my gaesh.

He was right: I would cause no more trouble. Never again. Controlling a slave via a gaesh was as effective as it was terrible. A witch had summoned a demon, and that demon had ripped part of my soul away, transferring that essence to the cheap tourist bauble the auctioneer now held in his hand. Anyone who carried that damn gaesh charm could command me to do anything they desired. Anything. If I ignored those orders, my reward would be my agonizing death. I would do anything that the holder of my gaesh asked of me, no matter how objectionable, no matter how repugnant.

Obey or die. There was no choice.

No, my body may not have been worth much, but in Kishna-Farriga the going price for a man's soul is ten thousand ords.

The crowd stirred and looked at me with new eyes. A troublemaking teenage boy was one thing. A teenage boy who could be healed and perfumed, forced to obey every whim his owner might command, was quite another. I shivered, and it had nothing to do with the warm breeze that prickled the hairs on my skin.

It was a fine day for a slave auction, if you're into that sort of thing. The weather was hot, sunny, and the air tinged with the stink of gutted harbor fish. Paper umbrellas or canvas awnings obscured the bidders as they lounged on cushioned seats.

Kishna-Farriga was one of the Free States, border city-states that owed no fealty to their neighbors but relied on shifting political tensions* to

---

*I have heard a great many theories to the effect that the Free States are a vassal of some other nation. So Doltar believes the Free States are in league with the Manol and the Manol believes

keep themselves off anyone's leash. Countries who didn't want to deal with each other used Kishna-Farriga as a halfway entrepôt for trade goods and commodities—commodities that included slaves such as myself.

Personally, I was used to the slave markets of the Quuros Octagon, with its endless mazes of private chambers and auction theaters. The slave pits in Kishna-Farriga weren't so elaborate. They used just one open-air stone amphitheater, built next to the famous harbor. At maximum capacity, the rising stone steps seated three thousand people. A slave might arrive by ship, visit the holding cells underneath the amphitheater, and leave with a new owner the same day—all without clearing the smell of dead fish from their nose.

It was all quite charming.

The auctioneer continued to speak. "Do I hear ten thousand?"

Reassured that I was tame, a velvet-clad woman of obvious "professional" talent raised her hand. I winced. I had no desire to go back to a brothel. A part of me feared it would go this way. I was by no means homely, and few are those who can afford the price of a gaeshed slave, without means of recouping their cost.

"Ten thousand. Very good. Do I hear fifteen thousand?"

A rich, fat merchant leered at me from the second row and raised a little red flag to signal his interest. Truth be told, he raised all kinds of red flags. His ownership would be no better than the whorehouse madam's, and possibly quite worse, no matter what my value.

"Fifteen thousand? Do I hear twenty thousand?"

A man in the front row raised his hand.

"Twenty thousand. Very good, Lord Var."*

Lord Var? Where had I heard that name?

My gaze lingered on the man. He appeared ordinary: of medium height and weight, nondescript but pleasant, his dress stylish but not extravagant. He had black hair and olive-brown skin—typical of Quuros from west of the Dragonspires—but his boots were the high, hard style favored by Easterners. Jorat, perhaps, or Yor. In addition, he wore a shirt of the Marakor style rather than an Eamithon misha or usigi wrap.

No sword.

No obvious weapon of any kind.

---

the Free States are in league with Zherias, and of course Quur thinks the Free States *are* Doltari and thus must be protected by the Manol. If large-scale war ever breaks out, I fear it will go poorly for these Free States people trapped in the middle.

*There is no record to indicate that Relos Var has claim to a noble title or order of merit. On the other hand, there's scarcely any record of Relos Var at all. The earliest mention of that name I have been able to locate is from the book *History of the Raevana Conquest* by Cilmar Shallrin, which mentions the name once. Since that book was published five hundred years ago, the idea that this might be the same person is troubling.

The only remarkable qualities about Lord Var were his confidence, his poise, and the fact the auctioneer recognized him. Var didn't seem interested in me. His attention focused on the auctioneer; he barely glanced at me. He might as well have been bidding on a set of tin plates.

I looked closer. No protection, hidden or otherwise, and not even a dagger in one of those unpolished leather boots. Yet he sat in the front. No one crowded him, though I'd spotted plenty of pickpockets working the crowd.

I'd never been to Kishna-Farriga before, but I didn't have to be a native to know only a fool came to this auction house without bodyguards.

I shook my head. It was hard to concentrate. Everything was noise, flashing light, and waves of cold—which I suspected were from a fever. One of my cuts had become infected. Something would need to be done about that soon, or I would be the most expensive paperweight some poor gull had ever purchased.

Focus. I ignored the crowds, the bidding, and the reality of my situation as I slipped the First Veil from my eyes and looked at him again.

I've always been skilled at seeing past the First Veil. I had once thought this talent would be my redemption from the Capital City's slums, back when I was naïve enough to think there was no fate worse than poverty.

There are three overlapping worlds, of course, each ruled by one of the Sisters: the world of the living, the world of magic, and the world of the dead.* We live in Taja's realm, as do all mortals. But I'd learned from a young age that my talent for seeing past the First Veil, into Tya's magical domain, was a terrific advantage.

Only the gods can see past the Second Veil, although I suppose we all do when we finally travel to what lies beyond, to Thaena's realm—Death.

The point is that wizards always wear talismans. They stamp such trinkets with their own auras to guard against the hostile sorceries of other mages. Talismans can take any shape. A smart wizard conceals their talismans from casual observation by disguising them as jewelry, sewing them into the lining of their clothes, or wearing them under robes. You might never know if someone is a wizard . . .

. . . unless you can see past the First Veil yourself, in which case that talisman-enhanced aura always betrays a wizard's profession.

That's how I knew Relos Var was a wizard. He wasn't wearing any

---

*This is . . . so wrong. So wrong. The odd number alone should have been the giveaway. This is what happens when you neglect to have a proper education. Two worlds. Just two. Magic is not a "realm"; it is a metaphysical river separating two parallel shores.

obvious talisman, but that aura was terrifying. I'd never seen an imprint so strong before, nor an aura stamped so hard, sharp, and crisp.*

Not with Dead Man, not with Tyentso . . .

And no, lovely Talon, not even with you.

I couldn't remember why Lord Var's name was familiar, but I could sum the man up in a single word: dangerous. But if I was lucky . . .

Who was I kidding? There was no luck left for me. I had angered my goddess, lady of luck both good and bad; her favor was gone. I did not even dare to hope that Lord Var would treat me better than the others. No matter who won me this day, it didn't change that I was a slave, and would be so until the moment of my death. A normal slave might hold out some faint hope of escape or buying his or her freedom, but a gaeshed slave can't run, and no one would ever free them. They are worth too much.

"The bid is twenty thousand. Do I hear twenty-five thousand?" The auctioneer wasn't paying attention anymore: he thought the sale all but over. He'd done well to fetch twenty thousand. That price exceeded his expectations.

"Twenty thousand, going once, going twice. Fair warning—"

"Fifty thousand," a clear voice said from the top of the seats.

Murmurs spread through the crowd. I strained to see who'd placed the bid. It was a large stadium. I couldn't see the speaker at first, but then I noticed who the rest of the crowd had turned to watch: three seated figures in black hooded robes.

The auctioneer paused, surprised. "The Black Brotherhood bids fifty thousand. Do I hear fifty-five thousand?"

The man they called Lord Var looked annoyed. He nodded at the auctioneer.

"Fifty-five thousand. Do I hear sixty thousand?" The auctioneer was awake now that there was a bidding war.

One of the three black-clad figures raised their red flag.

"Sixty thousand." The auctioneer nodded at them.

Half the crowd looked at Lord Var, the other half stared at the robed figures. The auction had just become an entertainment sport.

"Do I hear seventy-five thousand?"

Var nodded again.

"I have seventy-five. Do I hear one hundred?" The auctioneer saw the

---

*Having personally met Relos Var on several occasions, including at public baths, I have to say that I have never been able to figure out where the man keeps his talismans either—or if he even wears any. Relos Var has the power and aura of someone who wears a great many talismans without seeming to wear any at all.

black-clad figures' flag rise again. "I have one hundred from the Brother-hood. Do I hear one-fifty?"

Var nodded.

"One-fifty. Do I hear two hundred?" The red flag rose. "I have two hundred. Do I hear two-fifty?" Var frowned, but made a quick wave of his fingers. "I have two-fifty from Lord Var. Do I have five hundred from the Black Brotherhood?"

He did.

The desire to vomit hit me hard, and not just because of sickness. Had a slave ever sold for so much? There was no use that justified such a price; not as musician, not as catamite. Unless—

My eyes narrowed.

I wondered if, against all reason, they somehow knew who I was, knew what I carried. I almost reached for the gem around my throat. The Stone of Shackles was worth such a price, worth any price, but I had used the only spell I knew to hide what I wore.

I might be gaeshed, but I couldn't be ordered to hand over what no one knew I possessed.

"The Black Brotherhood bids a half-million. Do I hear seven hun-dred fifty thousand?" The auctioneer's voice broke. Even he seemed stunned by the price rising from his throat.

Lord Var hesitated.

"Lord Var?" the auctioneer asked.

Var grimaced and turned to glare over his shoulder at the three figures. "Yes," he said.

"I have seven hundred fifty thousand ords from Lord Var. Do I hear one million?"

The figures in black didn't hesitate.

Lord Var cursed aloud.

"I have one million ords. Final warning." The auctioneer paused for the required time. "Sold to the Black Brotherhood for one million ords. Ladies and gentlemen, we have a new record!" The end of the staff pounded down on the floor.

I fought the urge to join it.

2: The Kazivar House

(Talon's story)

—that back.

Of course, I took the stone back; it's my turn to tell your story now.

Why yes, I do so get a turn. Why should I not? It amuses me, and you're in no position to argue. Since you don't wish to start at the beginning, I shall do so for you. There's no point in you trying to keep parts of your tale from me. You aren't protecting anyone's memories, not even your own. So, I will tell you your story, because I want you to remember how it went, seen through someone else's eyes. Indeed—through many eyes, from many points of view; for that is what I am now. No one can change that. Not even you, my love.

Stop struggling. The bars are stronger than your skull.

Let me tell you a story about a boy named Rook.

Ah. I thought that might catch your attention.

As you know, his real name was Kihrin,* but he liked the name Rook because it was both his aspiration and occupation. Rook was a burglar: a very special burglar, a Key. He loved to perch, fingers clamped to the highest ledges, alone with the birds, his thoughts, and his crimes. He dreamed of soaring, freedom, and a world where no one would ever chain him.

Ironic, considering.

Alas, we rarely get what we want, do we?

He was fifteen years old: not yet an adult in Quur, and yet too old to be properly called a child. Like all people caught between two worlds, he hated and longed for both. He hadn't considered himself a child since he was twelve, when his teacher had died and he paid his first dues as one of the Shadowdancers's Keys.†

---

*I find it highly unlikely his real name is Kihrin, but without confirmation from his birth mother, it would be difficult to know for certain. Perhaps Kihrin is a misspelling.

†*"Found a witch in the City today, a burglar in the process of robbing a mansion through the use of her*

Perhaps Rook was even right, for no one stays a child in the slums of the Lower Circle for long. Those poor waifs who hitched themselves to gangs like the Shadowdancers grew faster still.

Rook's methods possessed one flaw, one misstep that would spell his doom.

He was curious.

Rook had spent almost a week planning the best way to rob the house of a wealthy merchant in the Copper Quarter. The merchant would be away for two weeks, attending his youngest daughter's wedding, giving Rook all the time he wished to explore the vacant house.*

Except when Rook arrived, he discovered someone was already there, someone with motives very different from his own.

If you asked me today if there was a single action, one event, that might have changed the course of what followed, I will unfailingly point to this: the day you broke into that Kazivar House and let curiosity bid you stay, when a wiser man would have fled.

But you did not, and so I call *this* the beginning.

The young man stifled a curse, balanced himself on the edge of the windowsill, and scanned the bedroom in the faint light. There was no sound save that of screaming coming from inside the house. After a pause, Rook remembered to breathe. He dismissed the tingling in his fingertips as fear and finished sliding through the narrow opening of the villa's upper window.

As he entered, he tucked the key ring of strips back into his belt. Most of the strips were made from wood—bamboo, mahogany, cypress, even distant, exotic woods like pine and oak—but a few rectangles were also crafted from glass and ceramic tile made from local clay. Using those strips as a guide revealed if a house was enchanted, if someone had spent metal to hire Watchmen to spell windows and doors against intrusion. Keys like him practiced no magic of their own, but they could see beyond the First Veil and divine if a door, a lock, or a chest was more than it seemed. For a thief, such knowledge was the difference between success and an ugly, short end to a criminal career.

The window frame was carved teak, the panes made of cloudy glass. Perfectly normal. No traps, no enchantments.

---

witch gift. While questioning her, she revealed that she was something called a 'Key.' Must investigate if there's a secret organized group practicing illegal magecraft right under the noses of royalty."—Journal of Kolban Simus, Watchman, found under his pillow after his body was discovered. His death was ruled a suicide.

*Aidin Novirin, a merchant of minor means associated with the Gatekeepers. After returning from personal business, he reported a burglary to the Watchmen, but said he could not determine what, if anything, had been stolen.

The screaming though. The screaming from inside was not normal.

Someone inside was in pain, such that even a Key-thief like Rook had never known in all his fifteen street-smart years.

The young thief closed the window behind him and let his eyes grow accustomed to the dim light. He wondered who was being abused. Was the current resident (that merchant what-was-his-name?) the one being beaten? Or was he the one handing out the awful punishment, his trip north to Kazivar nothing but a convenient alibi for satisfying a fetish for torture or worse?

The bedroom Rook entered was large and daunting, filled with the ostentatious filigree and tile work for which imperial craftsmen were famous. Cotton sateen covered the massive bed, tapestries lined the walls and divans, and elegant figurines of heavy bronze and jade sported across the boudoir countertops.

The north wall was open and a giant balcony overlooked the covered courtyard in the center of the villa. The screams came from the courtyard garden, on the ground floor.

Rook relaxed as he realized he couldn't be seen from below. This was important, because tonight anyone but his blind father would be able to see: all three moons were out, adding their glow to the violet, red, and shifting green aurora of Tya's Veil. It was a sorcerer's night. A night for working magics or sneaking past them, because Tya's Veil appearing in the night sky meant it was easier to "see" past the First Veil into her realm.*

The bedchamber had been used recently. Perfume lingered in the air and on sheets tossed back and rumpled. Discarded clothing spoke to an assignation gone very wrong.

None of his business.

His expert eyes sought out the money and jewels tossed on a bedside table. He placed each item into his belt pouch while he listened.

There were voices.

"It's so simple. Just tell us where the Stone of Shackles is and your pain will end," a velvet-smooth male voice said.

Sobs filled the gaps between speech. "I . . . oh goddess! . . . I told you . . . I don't KNOW where it is!"

Rook wondered if it was a woman's voice. His eyes narrowed. If they were beating a woman . . . he stopped himself. So what if they were beating a woman? he thought. He told himself not to be a fool.

"The stone was last seen with the Queen Khaeriel, upon her death. It was never recovered." A different voice spoke: a colder voice. "Her serving girl ran off with it, but it's no longer in her possession. Did she smuggle the stone back to the new king?"

---

*Oh, how I lament the lack of education in the world. This is nothing but superstition.

King? Rook thought. Queen? Quur had princes and princesses in plenty, but no king, no queen. Quur was the greatest, largest, mightiest empire that had ever existed, that would ever exist. Quur had an Emperor—immortal and powerful as a god. He suffered no "kings."

"I don't know! No one's seen Miyathreall in years. If she's still alive, how would I know where she is?"

Rook changed his mind: the victim was male but his voice was high-pitched. The thief almost dared to steal a glance, but forced himself back. It would be insanity to intervene. Who knew who those men were? They didn't sound like folk to be trifled with.

"Do you take us for fools? We know who you work for." The first voice growled, heavy with anger. "We offered you money and power beyond your wildest dreams. You refused our generosity, but you'll tell us every-thing. We have all night . . ."

Rook heard an odd gurgling noise before the screaming resumed. A shudder passed over him, then he shook his head and continued his work. It wasn't any of his business. He wasn't there for charity.

He continued looking beyond the First Veil. It muddied his normal vision with rainbows and bright scintillating lights, as if he'd pulled the aurora down from the sky. He had no talent for reaching past that bar-rier and forcing change, as wizards did, but looking was often enough.

Seeing past the First Veil allowed him to distinguish materials from each other with great accuracy, even in the dark. Gold had a particular aura; silver, a different one; diamond, yet a different aura still. Gemstones shone as if reflecting a light even when in darkness. A Key could walk into a dark room and unerringly find the single gold coin hidden under a pillow, every time, which was the other reason mundane thieves so cov-eted their skills. There was nothing to keep him from tripping over a rug and breaking his neck, but that was remedied by watching his step.

Rook's eyes picked out the rainbow glimmer of mineral wealth from a dark corner of the room. A few treasures had been tossed and forgot-ten in a corner: a drussian dagger, a pouch of herbs, an intaglio-carved ruby ring.

Rook also found a large rough green stone on a silver chain. Some-thing like silver wire wrapped around the unfinished green gem, but his sight told him the metal was not silver and the stone was not emerald. The thief stared at the green stone in surprise, and then looked over his shoulder to where he imagined the three men were having their "talk." He left the herbs, but snatched up the necklace and ring before tuck-ing the dagger under his belt.

And there it was again: Rook's curiosity. In all his years of thieving, all the jewelry stolen, he had never seen a necklace like that one . . . except once.

He pulled its mate out from under the collar of his shirt. The stone he wore was an indigo blue that looked like sapphire but was not, wrapped in a yellow metal that looked like gold but was not. Both faux-sapphire and faux-emerald were rough and unpolished, with sharp crystal edges and smooth facets. The two necklaces were different in color, but in theme and design, they were identical.

He could no longer resist the urge to satisfy his curiosity.

Rook inched himself over to the balusters, crawling on his stomach, until he gazed into the courtyard garden. He let the Veil fall into place and waited for his eyes to adjust to the change.

Two men stood. The third sat, tied to a chair. At first glance Rook wondered if he had been wrong to think the victim was male, and even more wrong to think him human. The seated figure had tightly curled hair, layers of fluffy spun sugar. The color was completely unnatural: pastel violet, like the edges of clouds at sunset. The victim's features were wide and delicate, but contorted in pain and smeared with blood. Still, he was piercingly beautiful.

Rook almost cried out when he realized the victim was a vané. He had never seen one before.

However, the vané's torturers were very much human. Compared to the vané, they were ugly and unclean. One had the grace of a dancer, solid muscle under watered blue silk. The other dressed in strange, heavy black robes that contrasted with his odd skin—not the healthy brown of a normal Quuros, but pale and ugly as scraped parchment. They made an odd pair. From the embroidery on his shirt and breeches to the jeweled rapier at his side, the first man was a devotee of worldly comfort; the second man a follower of ascetic reserve.*

The hairs on Rook's neck rose as he watched the pale man: something was wrong with him, something foul and unwholesome. It wasn't his crow-black eyes and hair, which were normal enough, but something intangible. Rook felt as if he were gazing at a dead thing still walking—the reflection of a corpse with the semblance of life, not the truth of it.

Rook dubbed the two men Pretty Boy and Dead Man,† and decided if he never met either of them face-to-face, he might die happy.

He dreaded what he might see with his sight, but after a second's hesitation he looked beyond the First Veil again. He winced. It was worse than he'd feared.

Both men were wizards. They both had the sharpened auras that

---

*A flattering observation, but you and I both know perfectly well that his lack of vanity had nothing to do with monastic discipline. Thank the gods for the house servants, or I likely would have starved to death before he remembered that children need regular meals and baths.
†Far better names than their legal ones, in my opinion.

Mouse had taught him was the hallmark of magi–men to be avoided at all costs. Pretty Boy wore plenty of jewelry–any of which might serve as his talismans.

Dead Man's aura matched his appearance: a hole in the light around him.

Rook's skin prickled as the urge to run hit him hard.

Pretty Boy picked up a stiletto and plunged it into the vané's stomach. The prisoner arched up and tore against his restraints, screaming in such anguish that Rook gasped in sympathy.

"Wait," Dead Man said. He motioned Pretty Boy aside and pulled the stiletto out of the vané, who collapsed into desperate sobbing.

Dead Man cocked his head, listening.

Rook began the mental recitation of the mantra that had saved his life on more than one occasion: *I am not here. No flesh, no sound, no presence. I am not here. No flesh, no sound, no presence. I am not here . . .*

"I don't hear anything," Pretty Boy said.

"I did. Are you sure this house is empty?" Dead Man asked.

The young thief tried to melt back into the shadows, tried to quiet his breathing, to still it, to be nothing to see, nothing to hear. How had Dead Man heard him over the screaming? *I am not here. No flesh, no sound, no presence . . .*

"Yes, I'm sure. The owner is marrying off his daughter to some fool knight in Kazivar. He's not due back for another two weeks."

This seemed to satisfy Dead Man, who turned his attention back to the vané. "I believe this one has told us all he knows. It is time for our contingency."

Pretty Boy sighed. "Must we?"

"Yes."

"I was rather hoping we might save our new friend for a rainy day and I wouldn't have to do the blood ritual again. Talon can't be everywhere–or imitate everyone–at once. People will ask questions if too many of my family members go missing without explanation."

"Then you're lucky you have a large family to sacrifice. Do you have enough information to find it?" Dead Man directed his question toward the shadows in a corner of the courtyard.

Horrible, nightmarish laughter echoed through Rook's brain.

OH YES. I HAVE SEEN IT IN HIS MIND.*

Rook bit his lip to keep from making noise. That voice hadn't spoken aloud, but thrust, unbidden, inside his thoughts.

---

*Whose mind, I wonder? I find it highly unlikely that the demon wasn't fully aware that Rook was in the house the entire time. So, it seems quite possible that he pulled the information, not from the prisoner but from Kihrin himself.

That voice . . .

Dead Man's expression didn't change as he reached out a hand toward the vané. Somehow, his gesture was more menacing than Pretty Boy's actual torture. A fine flow of energy began to leak from the vané's eyes, from his forehead, and from his chest—flowing through the air to form a glowing ball of pale violet fire in Dead Man's fist.

As the last bit of the vané's soul was pulled from his body, his eyes widened and then stared, unseeing.

Dead Man tucked something hard, amethyst, and sparkling into his robes.

"What about the body?" Pretty Boy asked.

Dead Man sighed and gestured one last time. There was a crackling, crashing noise as energy flowed *from* the Dead Man's fingertips this time, radiating out toward his victim.

Rook gagged as he watched the flesh melt off the vané's body like water, leaving only bloody clothing and a strangely clean skeleton.

The gore whirled in a red miasma and hovered around the bones for a few eternal seconds. Then it flowed toward the shadows, swallowed whole by the gigantic mouth of the demon that stepped out of the darkness.

"Shit!" Rook cursed between shaking teeth, and knew he'd made a mistake—probably a fatal one.

Dead Man looked up at the balcony. "There's someone up there."

"He'll get them," Pretty Boy said. "You. *Fetch.*"

Rook dropped all pretense of stealth and ran for the window.

3: THE BLACK BROTHERHOOD

(Kihrin's story)

I'd ask how you could know what I was thinking that night, but . . . never mind.*
  My turn? How generous of you, Talon.
  Where was I? Ah, yes.

After the auction, I was sick and injured enough that my new owners reached the sale room first. They waited for me like a trio of judges for the dead in the Land of Peace. They were silent shadows, with robe hoods pulled so far down by all rights they should have been blind.

The figure on the right was female; tall for a western Quuros, but average for most Doltari, or eastern Quuros. The figure on the left was tall—very tall. He or she towered above the others, at least a half-foot taller than the next tallest person (which was me). The center figure, the one who seemed hunched and old, hobbled forward toward my escort, a Kishna-Farrigan eunuch slave master named Dethic. The stooped figure held out its hand, gloved in black silk.

For a moment, no one spoke.

"The gaesh," the smallest figure demanded.

I startled at the voice, so distorted it didn't seem real. That voice was the harsh rasp of glacial ice breaking apart mountains, the tossing of waves against sharp rocks.

All things considered, that voice was a bad sign.

Dethic swallowed. "Yes, of course. But . . . the house rules. You understand. Payment in full before transfer of goods."

"Yes, I'd like to see this," Relos Var said as he walked up to the gathering. "I find it unlikely they can pay in full."

The figure on the left side (the tall one) reached inside its cloak. It removed a necklace from a black velvet pouch and held it up with two fingers. The value of the gold chain paled in comparison to the twelve

---

*There is a pattern to the people that Talon impersonates in these dialogs. They tend to fall into two categories: those she has eaten and those she has spent long periods of time around, such as Kihrin. Clearly she's been using her telepathic abilities to learn a great many secrets.

gems attached. Each diamond was the size of a fingertip, pear-shaped and midnight blue with a flaring white star in the center.

I felt even more lightheaded. A necklace of star tears. How many such gems even existed? Twelve star tear diamonds? Of equal size and coloring?

Dethic was stunned. "Star tears! Gods. Those are priceless."*

"So is the boy," the harsh voice snapped.

"You broke the auction record." Dethic was giddy thinking of his percentage.

Lord Var said, "Make sure it isn't counterfeit."

At this interruption, the figure looked sharply at Lord Var, before it reached up and flipped back the hood from its face.

I should have known from the height: he was vané.

Before this, I had seen damn few vané, all of them flower-colored Kirpis. He was different, resembling a vané who had played in too many fires. His skin was a field of dark ashes, his long hair matte black, his eyes shadowy emeralds. He possessed all the prettiness of the vané race, but was a creature of angles and sharpness. His beauty was that of the razor and not the flower.

I couldn't guess his age. For all I knew, he'd witnessed the founding of the Quuros Empire. He only looked a few years older than me, but that meant nothing. The vané are an ageless race.

My Quuros ancestors probably needed no more reason than that to hate them, to push the Kirpis vané out of lands we claimed as our own. Confronted by Emperor Kandor's invading armies, the Kirpis vané had folded, fled their forest homes, and watched in horror as Kirpis became yet another Quuros dominion.

Then again, this was not a Kirpis vané.

To the south of Quur lay the *other* vané kingdom, the Manol. The Manol vané—dark jewels in contrast to Kirpis's bright flowers—had not been so easily conquered. Quur's unstoppable expansion had come to an abrupt and unexpected halt with Emperor Kandor's death, by Manol vané hands. The fabled Quuros sword Urthaenriel—better known as "Godslayer"—ended up lost somewhere on a jungle floor, along with a generation of Quuros men. Quur would conquer two more dominions through later Emperors, but it never recovered its momentum.

The Manol vané went right on ignoring us after that; we were no threat to them.

---

*Besides the Dana Jewels, one of the only recorded sales of a star tear was from a retired Quuros military officer named Duvos. He somehow acquired one and traded it to House D'Kard in exchange for the construction of what is now Sileemkha Palace in Khorvesh. By such standards, this exchange is rather extravagant: just a single star tear would have been an adequate stand-in for one million ords.

"The star tears are real, Relos Var. But you don't think I'm stupid enough to let you handle them, do you?" The Manol vané raised one eyebrow.

A faint smile played across the wizard's lips. "One can always hope."

"You. You check the necklace." The Manol vané man thrust the necklace and its bag at me.

Dethic looked perplexed. "But sir . . ."

"It's all right," I murmured, not taking my eyes from the black-skinned vané. "I have experience appraising gems."

I was going to lie about the necklace. I was Quuros; he was Manol vané. Whatever he wanted with me couldn't be good. The fact that he was paying for me with a necklace of star tear diamonds wasn't just excessive, it was creepy. I'd heard about that necklace my whole life. To me, those diamonds were as infamous as the sword Urthaenriel or the Crown and Scepter of Quur.

Suddenly, I knew which side to root for: this Relos Var fellow seemed very much the lesser evil. I held the diamond necklace up with shaking fingers, moving the stones back and forth so they caught the light.

"You know your gems? Excellent." Dethic's expression turned to a thoughtful frown. "No lying now. Tell me true. Are those star tears?"

I repressed a sigh. It all might have ended right there. I would have lied and told him the stones were fake, taken my chances with Relos Var. But Dethic held my gaesh, held a piece of my soul trapped in the metal charm in his hands. That only meant I had to obey his spoken commands. Like most gaeshed slaves, I followed a slew of orders that were perpetually in effect; I was forbidden to escape, kill my owner, or disobey commands from my owner (although that last seemed redundant). I wasn't under any obligation to anticipate my owner's needs or look out for their interests. Loopholes could be exploited.

This whole sordid tale would have crashed to an early end if I hadn't been *ordered* to tell the truth.

I looked at the diamonds again. They were flawless, perfect, cut into refracting shapes by ancient, skilled hands. It was as if you stared at a real star, captured and trapped in diamond.

I opened the velvet bag. Everyone heard the necklace hitting the bottom with a clink of chain. No one noticed the copper bangles no longer hung around my wrists.

I am *very* good at hiding things.

"They're real." I handed the bag to Dethic. I scratched at the nape of my neck as far as the shackles allowed. I used that motion to hook the stolen jewels to my own necklace, hiding the mass under my hair.

There. As long as Dethic didn't discover my deception, I'd just been sold to the Brotherhood for the cost of a few copper bracelets.

It's not that I don't think my soul is worth more, but I was damned if I wouldn't make metal off my own sale.

Lord Var addressed my new owners. "Members of the Brotherhood, we have always had good relations. Don't jeopardize our friendship over one slave."

The vané was expressionless as he replied, "You have nothing we want." He said to Dethic, "You've been paid. Hand over the gaesh."

"Don't give him the gaesh," Relos Var ordered.

Dethic hesitated.

The Manol vané said, "This is no longer your concern."

"I want the young man," Relos Var said.

The vané sneered. "Perhaps you should send courtship gifts first."

The air simmered between the two men. I wondered if the Black Brotherhood had bought me for no other reason than to keep me out of Relos Var's hands. That option seemed likely unless they knew who I really was, knew about the Stone of Shackles around my neck.

Unless . . . That "unless" was all too plausible. My stomach knotted. The last thing I needed was to be the middle of a power play. Gods, more politics. I was sick to death of politics. If only I could leave. I didn't dare use the word "escape," even in the quiet of my thoughts. The gaesh would tear me apart for thinking about escape.

Var said, "Do you have any idea with whom you speak?"

The vané smiled. "I used your name, didn't I?"

"Then you should know better than this insolence."

The vané shrugged. "He's not yours and he never will be. Why don't you go back to looking for Yorish virgins? There must be a fast eight-year-old somewhere in the mountains who's escaped the attention of your minions."

A sound like granite rocks being scraped against one another issued from the cowled robe of the smallest Brotherhood member: he or she or it was *laughing*.

Dethic reached forward, hesitantly, holding the hawk medallion containing a piece of my soul in his hand. Both men facing him stared at the pendant as if either one would grab it away from the slave-trader, sale or no sale.

"You've made a serious mistake, young vané," Relos Var cautioned. "I'll remember you."

The vané grinned, sharp and feral. "Not 'young vané,' please. Mortal enemies should be on a first-name basis."

"That's what you think you are? My mortal enemy? Suckling at

Thaena's teats has made you so hungry for a short, ugly death?" Relos Var seemed to find that thought amusing. "What is your name then?"

"Teraeth." The vané's eyes glowed,* mocking satisfaction played across his features. I didn't know why the vané hated this man so much, but he was emphatic. I started to back away, not to escape, but simply to stay out of the splatter zone.

"Teraeth?" Relos Var said. "You have not the coloring of that line, unless . . ." His eyes widened in triumph. "Not just arrogant, but foolish. Your father Terindel isn't here to save you, vané child, and you are no match for the likes of me."

"Terindel isn't here," the vané with the terrible voice said, "but I am. And I'll protect my son, wizard."

The mage looked at the figure, his forehead creased with anger and then recognition. "Khaemezra. Clever. Very clever."

"It has been some time, Relos." The words might have been friendly save for the harsh iciness of the voice.

"We could help each other, High Priestess. Our goals are not so different."

"Poor child, you think so? Foolish—but then, you always confused death with annihilation."

The man's eyes narrowed. The expression on his face verged on a growl. "You, of all beings, should understand inevitability."

"Perhaps the real problem is I understand it better than you."

There was no way for Relos Var to make eye contact with the old woman, who had never pulled back her hood, but I imagined the two were staring at each other. Relos Var seemed intent on a contest of wills, and his gaze never left her.

He shuddered and looked away.

A tsking sound emanated from underneath her hood, chasing down a dry chuckle and gobbling it whole.

Relos Var glanced back at Teraeth. "This isn't over between us."

"I sincerely hope not," Teraeth agreed. He wore a wolf's grin, showing no fear.

Relos Var turned to me.

His expression wasn't what I expected: not frustration, pity, lust, or even resignation. Hate raged in those dark eyes. His malice burned. His eyes held no promise of rescue, no offered salvation. Whatever his interest in purchasing me, that interest circled around a core of malevolence.

He was not my friend.

"I have found you now," he told me in a whisper. "I have seen the color of your soul."

*One presumes not literally.

A dozen snappy comebacks thought about crossing my lips, but under that baleful stare they all huddled at the back of my throat.

Relos Var turned on his heel and walked out of the room.

Even amongst the members of the Black Brotherhood, there was an almost visible release of tension as he left, as if the clouds parted to reveal the sun.

The seconds crawled by as no one spoke.

Teraeth shook off the dread first. He snatched the medallion from Dethic's shaking fingers. "Take those things off him."

"I . . . what? Things?" Dethic stood blinking in the direction of the door. He had a look of horror on his face—the terrible fascination normally reserved for the damage path of a rampaging demon.

Teraeth pinched the eunuch's shoulder. "Shackles, Dethic. Shackles. A gaeshed slave has no need to be in irons."

Dethic jumped out of his reverie. "What? Oh yes, sorry. Right away." He fumbled the keys from his belt pouch and unlocked me.

I winced as the shackles fell away. I had been in chains so long their release was simply a different kind of pain.

"Relos Var isn't angry at you, Dethic. Stay out of his way for a while and he'll soon forget," Teraeth cautioned. "See if your masters will let you take a leave of absence."

"Right, right." Dethic still looked dazed. "I'll fetch your carriage." He stumbled as he ran from the room.

The three members of the Black Brotherhood turned their attention to me.

"Who are you people?" I asked.

Teraeth snickered. "You weren't paying attention?"

"I heard names. Black Brotherhood. It doesn't mean anything to me."

The third figure finally spoke with a silky female purr. "If you're in Quur and want something stolen, or someone beaten, there are plenty you may hire for the task. But if you want someone dead, quietly and without fuss, and you wish to be sure they will stay that way . . ." She left the end of the sentence hanging in the air.

I was weak and upset, but I felt argumentative. "The priests of Thaena might have something to say about whether someone stays dead."

The hooded old woman pulled at the robe covering her neck, revealing an amulet: a rectangular black stone, framed with red roses and ivory—the symbol of Thaena's disciples.

I felt a chill. There are those who don't think of the Second Veil as a diaphanous shroud, but an unknowable portal to Thaena's realm. A final portal one never enters, only exits; a journey most only Returned from to start the cycle over as a mewling babe. The church of Thaena boasted the fewest devout worshippers, but was universally respected to either avoid its attention or beg the favor of its mistress. *Bring my baby back to me. Return my family. Give me back the people I love.*

Such prayers go unanswered. Thaena is a cold goddess.

And Relos Var had called Khaemezra her "High Priestess."

"Thaena's priests—and priestesses—do influence who stays dead," Teraeth explained. "For some reason, the Pale Lady rarely agrees to Return those we have taken."

"But Thaena's priests wear white, not black . . ."

Okay, I admit it: as arguments go, it wasn't my best work.

Teraeth's only answer was harsh laughter.

Khaemezra turned away from me without comment and raised her arms. She flicked her fingers outward and strands of light spun out from her fingertips and coalesced into a large round portal made up of complicated skeins of glowing magic. The lights shimmered, then shrank. Through the opening I saw a yellow, twisted land with steam erupting from vents in the ground and bilious fog hugging the dank earth.

I waited, but Khaemezra didn't step through. Teraeth walked forward, but stopped when she raised her hand. The old woman ticked off a dozen or so seconds on her fingers, then grabbed at the air like pulling a curtain closed. The portal collapsed and vanished.

Teraeth turned to her. "Why aren't we using the gate?"

"Because Relos Var is expecting us to." Khaemezra addressed the third Brotherhood member. "Kalindra, once we're gone, take the coach and lead Relos Var's dogs on a chase, just in case he decides to protest the sale. Meet up with us later."

The woman bowed. "As you wish, Mother." She, too, turned and left.

The Manol vané who held my gaesh, Teraeth, looked me over. He wasn't happy with what he saw. "You don't blend in, do you?"

"When was the last time you looked in a mirror?"

He scowled, and then unfastened the front of his robe. Underneath he wore black trousers and a cross-tied tunic of thin silk that was almost, but not quite, a Quuros misha.

Teraeth handed me his robe. "Can you walk with that wound on your ankle?"

"If I have to." Even as I said the words, I felt myself fighting to keep my balance.

The vané gave his mother an exasperated look. The tiny figure hobbled over to me and placed her hand on my leg.

The pain and the fever faded.

That quickly, the wound on my leg and the whip marks on my back healed. A number of minor scrapes and bruises I'd suffered during the three-month voyage from Quur to Kishna-Farriga also vanished. My head cleared of fever and my vision returned to normal.

"I . . . Thanks."

"Save your thanks. You're no good to us hobbled."

I scowled. "Where did you find that necklace? It can't have a twin . . ."

Teraeth grabbed my arm. "I will only explain this once. That man, Relos Var, doesn't want you as a toy in his seraglio, and he doesn't care who owns you. He wants you dead. He will do whatever he has to—kill whoever he has to—to make that happen. Being near you puts all our lives in danger."

"Why? I've never met the man. I don't understand!"

"And I don't have time to explain. So I need you to follow my orders without question."

"You're holding my gaesh. I don't have any choice."

He stared at me for a moment as if he had forgotten what the silver hawk he clenched between his fingers meant, then grimaced. "Good. Let's go."

4: BUTTERBELLY

(Talon's story)

Pre-dawn light tinged the sky with amethyst, and turned the wisps of Tya's rainbow veil into half-imagined phantoms. Most shops closed at night, but the pawnshop owner and fence the locals nicknamed Butterbelly* paid no heed to the time. Two lanterns lit his cramped shop, while Butterbelly's most precious possession, an oil lamp filled from the sacred Temple of Light,† sat at his right hand. His oil paints were spread over the battered old teak dining table he used for a desk; his canvas and brushes rested on an easel beside that.

When Butterbelly painted, he strayed into a world of beauty and light far from the ugly realities of the Lower Circle. He painted from memory and he painted all night.

His customers came to him at night anyway.

Butterbelly had just put away his paints when the alley gate bell rang. Rook entered, looking as though an army of Watchmen followed close behind. Butterbelly frowned.

He'd never seen the young man so scared.

Rook stepped into the shop, looked behind him, and shuddered as he closed the door. He stopped only long enough to rub the head of Butterbelly's bronze almost-twin—his Tavris statue, fat god of merchants and profit. The gesture was habitual, done for luck.

"You got the guard chasing you, boy?" Butterbelly called out.

Rook stared at the pawnbroker, shocked, then laughed nervously. "Nooo. No, nothing like that."

"You sure? You're awfully pale and acting like you got a hell-hound

---

*Every record of dues or fees paid to House D'Erinwa lists this particular pawnshop owner's name as . . . Butterbelly. I can find no record of any other identity.
†The Temple of Light is dedicated to the Vishai Mysteries, which are considered something of a heterodox faith dedicated to a solar deity named Selanol, who dies and is resurrected with the passing seasons. The religion is extremely popular in Eamithon and looked at oddly everywhere else.

on your ass." Butterbelly frowned. "You're not bringing bad business into my shop, are you, boy?"

Rook glanced around the pawnshop filled with strange tidbits, found artifacts, cases of jewelry, weapons, clothing, and furniture. Seeing it empty of customers, he crossed over to Butterbelly's desk. Halfway there, his mood changed. Between the old carved mermaid scavenged from a Zheriaso pirate ship and the cabinet of secondhand Khorveshan silver, Rook's fear turned to anger. By the time he reached the desk, he was livid with it.

"Butterbelly, I swear if you've set me up I'll string you up from the rafters by the ropy guts in that big fat stomach—"

"Woah! Boy! What's wrong?! I'd never cross you!" Butterbelly raised one hand in a gesture of surrender. He put his other hand on the crossbow he kept under the table to deal with difficult "negotiations," just in case.

Rook moved his hands, flicked them over his sleeves, and suddenly held twin shivs. "I mean, you told someone else about the Kazivar House. Someone was there first."

Butterbelly eyed the daggers. "Put those away, Rook. We've been good business for each other, ain't we? The Kazivar job was your claim. And my tip came from a good source—"

"What source? Who told you about that house?"

"I can't tell you that! It's a good source. A trusted source. Never let me down. Why would I ring you out to someone else anyway? I make no profit that way. 'Sides, I know what the Shadowdancers would do if they even thought I was snitching."

Rook scowled, but he lowered the knives. "Someone was there when I showed up," he said.

"Shadowdancers?"

"I . . ." Rook bit his lip. He pulled his ring of key tiles from his belt, fidgeting with the strips. He counted past cypress, teak, tung wood, and bamboo as the samples clicked against each other. "No. Not one of ours."

"What then?"

"I don't know. They were killing someone, but I didn't get a look at any of them."

"You sure? You were white as the city walls when you walked in here." *And awfully shaken up for somebody who didn't see nothing,* Butterbelly thought to himself.

Rook shrugged. "The screams were something else. Didn't want to see what made them."

The fat man stopped and cocked his head in the teenager's direction. "If you ain't seen nothing and you ain't got nothing, whataya doing here?

I ain't running a charity for orphaned boys, and even if I was, you've already found yourself a pa."

Rook grinned and tucked his key ring away again. "Oh, I didn't say I found nothing. Mouse trained me better than that." He pulled a small bag from his belt and jingled it.

"That's my boy," the fence said. "Come bring that swag round here and let me feel the weight of its metal."

Rook walked around the desk, saw the easel and canvas painting, and gave a low whistle. He set the small bag on the table.

Butterbelly smiled at the boy's reaction. "You like her?"

The pawnshop owner was surprised to see pink color the boy's cheeks. "Yeah. She's . . . umm . . . she's great."

"That one's going up at the Shattered Veil Club. Not finished yet. I want at least one more sitting with the new girl. What's her name? Miria? Or something . . . ?"

"Morea," Rook said as he stared at the painting.

"That's it," Butterbelly said. "Cute girl."

"Yeah." Rook continued staring as if he'd never seen a pair of titties before, which was unlikely, considering.

Butterbelly chuckled as he produced a jeweler's loupe from his stained robes. This was better than Rook's usual loot, much better. The intaglio-carved ruby ring alone was worth several thousand thrones if he could find the right buyer.

Butterbelly said, "Not bad. I'll give you four hundred chalices for the lot."

"Four hundred? Only four hundred?" Rook looked skeptical.

"It's a good price." It was a lousy price and Butterbelly knew it, but better and safer than Rook would find anywhere else. "Ain't I always straight with you?"

Rook raised an eyebrow. "That's a *ruby,* Butterbelly."

Damn, he needed to stop thinking the boy was one of those roughs who couldn't tell the difference between a ruby and a chunk of pink quartz. Rook was a Key. And as Rook's late teacher, Mouse, had once explained to Butterbelly, every substance in the world had an aura distinct from every other. A Key could use their sight to tell if a coin was painted lead or real gold, and if gold, what purity. If a certain teenage ragamuffin had been smart enough to keep master samples, he could also use it to identify just what sort of precious gem he'd stolen.* Damn the boy for his

---

*The implication here is that the Shadowdancers are sophisticated enough to train those they find with talent, but not advanced enough to train their students to memorize tenyé signatures. Just enough knowledge to be useful, and not a shred more.

smarts, they had been no help to Butterbelly's business. "Not ruby, but spinel," he corrected. "And warm to the touch, like."

Rook cursed and half-turned away. "Taja! That matches pure, Butterbelly. Raven has a ruby earring, a real one, so don't rain me."

Butterbelly rubbed the corners of his mouth and looked at the boy. Rook was tall, taller than anyone Butterbelly knew and not full-grown. Prettier than anything a local would encounter outside a velvet house too. His whole body was a walking advertisement of foreign ancestry. Sure, Rook dyed his hair black—either because he thought black hair would fit the name "Rook" or because of some fool notion he'd fit in better—but Butterbelly thought it looked stupid. The funny thing was, despite his looks, Rook did have a talent for vanishing on a man if he wasn't paying attention. Butterbelly never figured out how a boy so out of place could be so damn good at the sneak.

Maybe some people were born to be thieves.

"If you don't mind me being nosy," Butterbelly changed the subject, "you been working with me since Mouse went south, what, three years?"

Rook shrugged. "So?"

"So, what gives most kids away is you spend the money too fast. Even the Watchmen are smart enough to know something's up, when some urchin too young for service burns a path through Velvet Town. But not you. You never spend a coin, so the guards and the witch-hunters ain't ever come looking. By my count, you have a bundle tucked away somewhere. What does a boy your age need so much money for, anyway? You thinking of getting out?"

Rook crossed his arms over his chest and didn't answer.

Butterbelly waved his hand in front of his face. "Never mind. None of my business anyhow."

"It's not for me."

Butterbelly stopped and looked at Rook for a long minute. He'd had a good idea it wasn't for Rook. Folks in the Shadowdancers weren't supposed to know each other's real names, but even in a city with one million people during the dry season, the residents of a quarter were bound to run into each other. Since Butterbelly scouted out the models for his paintings from the velvet houses of the quarter, there were few houses he had never visited. He knew Rook's given name was Kihrin. He knew Rook's adopted father was a blind musician named Surdyeh who eked out a meager living performing at the Shattered Veil Club. And he knew Rook wanted the money not for himself, but so Surdyeh could retire to a life spared from the toil of nonstop performances on arthritic fingers. It made Butterbelly all maudlin if he thought about it too hard.

Sometimes he was tempted to give the kid a break, but Butterbelly always got over the impulse.

He ducked his head once and nodded. "All right. Yeah, okay. I see it. You're a good kid, Rook. Don't let no one tell you different just because your ma weren't no local girl. You want me to send you the money the normal way?"

"Wait. We haven't settled on a price yet. There's something else I want to show you—"

The street bell rang as someone stepped into the pawnshop. Butterbelly saw who it was and groaned.

A voice called from the front of the shop as a teenage boy swaggered forward. "Well hell. If it ain't my favorite velvet boy. You trading favors for metal, Rook? I got a spear that could use polishing." He grabbed his crotch just in case Rook missed the innuendo.

Rook didn't turn his head to acknowledge the newcomer, but Butterbelly saw the boy's knuckles turn white as he squeezed the edge of the table.

Rook said, "Butterbelly, next time Princess has kittens do you want me to bring you a couple? Your shop seems to have a problem with rats."

The bell rang again as several more teenagers entered the pawnshop behind the first.

"You boys remember where you are. No fighting," Butterbelly admonished all of them.

"Oh, I was just having fun. Right, Rook?" The leader of the newcomers was a hardened, creased street tough a few years older than Rook. Butterbelly had seen a hundred like him in the course of his career: bullies and sadists who thought membership in the Shadowdancers was a sure amnesty against all crimes. Sooner or later, most learned their lesson, often in chains. Some never did. The street tough moved his left hand toward Rook's back.

He had no right hand.

"Touch me, Ferret, and you'll lose the other hand too," Rook said. He'd pulled the knives back out of his sleeves.

"How many times do I have to tell you? It's Faris!" However, Faris drew back his hand.

Rook didn't smile. "That's okay. You'll always be a weasel to me."

"No *fighting*!" Butterbelly shouted as both teens readied weapons. "Remember where you are."

Faris and Rook had history. Worse, they'd once been friends. Although something had soured that friendship, turned it into a seething hate, Butterbelly never knew the specifics. Maybe it was as simple as jealousy: Rook had grown up handsome and singled out for special training as a Key, and Faris had not. There were darker rumors of what had happened, involving Mouse and her death. Rumors that Butterbelly wasn't sure he wanted to believe.

Faris laughed and held up his good hand and the stump of his other arm. "Yeah, sure. No fighting at all. We just want to do business. Took some great metal off a few merchants one of my boys drugged up over at the Standing Keg."

Rook glared. "Great for you. Why don't you finish your business and go?"

Faris smirked. "Ladies first."

"I'm done." He looked at Butterbelly. "The usual will be fine." The boy turned on his heel to leave, but two steps toward the door he stopped with one hand to his belt, his expression angry.

Butterbelly looked over to see Faris dangling Rook's belt pouch from his fingers, a wicked smile cracking the hard leather of his face.

"Lookie what the velvet boy dropped!"

"Give that *back,* Rat!"

"NO FIGHTING."

One of Faris's boys interposed himself between Rook and Faris, who laughed and opened the small pouch. Rook's key ring spilled out, along with an uncut green gemstone wrapped in silver.

"Ooo . . . look what we have here, a pretty necklace. Saving this for your next boyfriend?" Faris taunted as he held the green stone above his head.

Rook kicked Faris's thug in the groin and pushed him out of the way. Another teenage boy pulled a wicked club from under his sallí cloak and moved in to take the first one's place.

Butterbelly decided he'd had enough.

"Arrgh!!" The boy with the club screamed as a crossbow bolt sank into his arm.

Everyone stopped what they were doing.

"Bertok's balls!" Faris screamed at Butterbelly. "You *shot* him."

"I SAID NO FIGHTING!" Butterbelly shouted again, waving the crossbow above his head like a flag.

Faris glanced over at Rook. "He started it."

"I was here watching, you addle-brained fool of a cutthroat. Stealing from Shadowdancers? Are you out of your MIND?"

"I was joking . . ."

"My arm! My arm!" The boy was moaning on the floor.

"Oh, quit your whining," Butterbelly scolded. "I ain't hit nothing important. Now go get yourself to a blue house for healing, before you have to explain how you was injured."

Faris growled and stabbed a finger at Rook's chest, as if it was something much more lethal. "You better watch your back, Rook. I've made friends. Important friends. Don't think I've forgotten what you've done."

"Likewise, Weasel," Rook sneered. He beckoned toward Faris with two fingers. "Scabbard isn't as nice as the City Guard. He won't just take your hand for stealing from the Shadows. Those are mine."

The tough growled and threw the stone and key ring at the desk. Faris hurled the leather pouch to the floor and stomped on it as he exited with his friends.

Butterbelly didn't say a word. He reloaded the crossbow and placed it under his desk again. Then he noticed the necklace. He reached for the stone with trembling fingers, hardly daring to breathe, not believing his good fortune.

"Laaka in the sea, Rook—where did you get this?" He held up the green stone and let it sparkle and glimmer in the light.

Rook picked up his belt pouch and recovered his key ring. "You know."

"Really?"

"Yeah. That was the other thing I wanted to talk to you about. Wish the Rat hadn't seen it. Looks valuable."

Butterbelly nodded. "Very valuable."

The teenager chewed on his lower lip. "Is it something you can move?"

Butterbelly grinned. "Can I move it? Oh, can I ever! This, my boy, THIS, is a tsali stone, a special magical vané gem. Only thing worth more'd be if you came back with a star tear, but nobody's got enough metal in their vaults to buy one if ya did."

"Yeah? Raven owned a whole necklace of star tears once."

Butterbelly snorted. "You know better than to listen to Raven's god-king tales. Raven will have you thinking she's the long-lost Queen of Kirpis if you give her a chance." He waved a hand. "Anyway, this is better than a star tear. This is something I can sell."

"It's not wrapped in silver. I checked for that," Rook admitted. "I don't recognize that metal."

"Platinum, I'd wager," Butterbelly said. "You don't see it much down here. It takes a Red Man to make a fire hot enough to melt the ore. Just like drussian. Expensive stuff, and that's just the findings—the stone though—"

"It's not emerald. It's like the metal—nothing I've ever seen before."

"Boy, if you came in here and told me you could identify what this stone is, I'd have known for sure it was fake. I've always had my suspicion that tsali stones just can't be found outside vané lands, but I'm not a Key like you. Most folks just assume it must be diamond.* Hard as diamond, anyway."†

"Diamond? That big?" Rook looked impressed.

---

*It's not diamond.
†Harder.

"Yes, yes, yes. And there are collectors in the Upper Circle who will not only pay for such a stone, but ain't gonna question the source." Butterbelly's grin faltered for a minute as he realized he was being an idiot. He'd shown the boy how excited he was, shown him that this was no common whore's bauble. "But they are traceable, distinctive. Each stone's unique, with its own history. I'd have to be careful."

"How would you trace it?" The amused smile and raised eyebrow on Rook's face told Butterbelly he'd ruined his chance to buy the rock for a pittance.

"Well . . . they say every single one of them stones is magic. Each with their own auras and marks. I'm surprised you didn't figure that out on your own."

Rook blinked and seemed to take a step back without moving. "Must have missed that."

"Anyhow, the vané take objection to us mortals owning their stones, and I sure as hell ain't going to ask them how they know." The fat man reached a mental decision. "I'll give you two thousand for everything. The tsali stone plus the rest."

Rook seemed to make his own calculations. "I want five thousand . . . thrones."

"What? Are you daft?"

"You'll sell this one to a buyer you've already lined up for ten times that."

"Hmmph. Twenty-five hundred, but only because you're not going to just blow the money on wine and whores."

"Three thousand, and I don't mention this sale to Scabbard."

Butterbelly chuckled. "You're learning, you're learning. All right, we've got a deal. I'll send it through the usual way." The fence stopped and leaned over toward the boy. "Or . . . I'll give you six thousand for the lot if you throw in both of them."

Rook stared at Butterbelly. "What?"

"Ah, come on, boy. I've known you since you were a downy-haired fellow, nothing more than a bit of golden fluff that Raven would parade around like chum for the sharks. You think I wouldn't notice a little babe like you wearing a vané tsali stone around your throat? I offered to buy it from your Raven. She told me it wasn't hers to sell. Can you imagine that? Raven passing up the chance to make metal? Well, you're old enough to make your own decisions now, aincha?"

Rook's jaw tightened. "I didn't . . . it's not for sale."

"I see what you're trying to do for your old man. I'll give you five thousand for the green diamond, and another five thousand for that blue one wrapped in gold that you're wearing. That's enough money to get your father out of here, and be rich besides."

Rook put his hand to his neck, fingering something under the cloth of his shirt. "Why so much?"

"Them vané stones is rare, and if I'm reading the signs right, that one you're wearing is old. Fifteen thousand. You won't get a better offer than that from anyone, anywhere. Come on, some trinket from a momma who ditched you can't be worth more than getting out of this hellhole, can it?"

The teenager stared at him. Something in that stare made Butterbelly uncomfortable. Something in that stare wasn't natural, wasn't healthy. It made him feel small and petty.

He wondered if maybe those rumors were true.

"My necklace isn't for sale," Rook repeated. "Five thousand thrones for the rest. I'll take payment the usual way." Without another word, he left.

Butterbelly cursed and stared after Rook, irritated with himself for letting the boy take advantage of him like that. Eventually he sighed and started to cover his work before closing shop. Soon he was singing to himself.

He had a vané tsali stone, and he had a buyer. Oh, did he ever have a buyer. He knew a man who'd burned a path through the Capital looking for vané jewelry-craft of all sorts, and money was no object. He would be interested in what Butterbelly offered.

Very interested indeed.

5: LEAVING KISHNA-FARRIGA

(Kihrin's story)

Outside the auction house, a carriage squatted in the middle of the street like a rotted gourd. The theme continued with black lacquered enamel and matching metalwork. A long black fringe hung from the black undercarriage like a skirt. A black-robed figure (possibly Kalindra) sat up front, holding the reins of four impressive large horses.

They were black too.

"Don't you ever grow tired of that color?" I asked.

"Get in," Teraeth ordered.

There was no resisting. I pulled myself up into the carriage. Teraeth helped his mother follow me before entering the carriage himself.

"I thought that other woman was going to—"

"No one cares what you think," Teraeth said.

The blood flowed to my face.

Six months prior, I would have done something, said something. I'd have cut him a little, verbally or otherwise, but six months ago—hell, two weeks ago—bah. I saw the silver hawk and chain wrapped around his wrist. He could say whatever he wanted, give me whatever order he wanted, as long as he held my gaesh.

He surprised me then by pulling up the flooring in the middle of the carriage and unfolding a rope ladder.

"Climb down," he ordered.

I didn't argue. The trapdoor didn't exit to the street as I expected. Rather, the coach had been positioned over an open grating, which led to an ancient but still serviceable sewer system. The small tunnel led straight down with a ladder built into the side. With the grating open, we enjoyed free access to an escape route.

Only the sound of hands and feet on rungs above me let me know Teraeth followed. Someone closed the grate above us, and then I heard the staccato clap of hooves as the black-clad driver drove the carriage away.

I couldn't tell how long I climbed or which way we went once we reached the bottom. My eyes adjusted to the inky blackness of the sewer tunnels, but for a long, long time my only operating sense was olfactory. I gagged on the stench. Seeing past the First Veil wouldn't have helped either: the blurry auras of second sight wouldn't have stopped me from tripping over a sodden branch and slamming face-first into rotting waste, as it drifted sluggishly past.

Teraeth tapped my side to signal when I should turn.

The sewer tunnel widened until I found myself able to stand. Here lichen glowed with phosphorescence, casting subtle shimmers over the otherwise disgusting walls. I couldn't read by that light but it was bright enough to navigate.

I would have given anything for a smoky, badly made torch.

Eventually, I rounded a corner and saw sunlight. A sewer opening lay ahead at the end of the tunnel. The odor of saltwater and decaying fish—the charming perfume of the harbor—mingled with the stink of the sewer.

Teraeth brushed past me and grabbed the large metal grating. He yanked the bars without releasing them, preventing a clumsy, loud clank of metal. At this point, I realized his mother Khaemezra was still with us. Teraeth motioned for us to follow.

We exited into an alley by the harbor. No one noticed us. Any eyes that strayed in our direction didn't seem to find our strange little group unusual at all.

Khaemezra had also tossed aside her robe. I'd already seen Teraeth, but this was my first chance to examine the frail "Mother" of the Black Brotherhood.

She was a surprise, as I had always thought the vané were ageless.

Khaemezra was so bent and shrunken from age she stood no taller than a Quuros woman. If her son Teraeth was the color of ink, she was the parchment upon which it had been spilled. Bone-white skin stretched thin and translucent over her face. Her fine hair, pale and powdery, showed the old woman's spotted scalp. Her quicksilver eyes—with no irises and no visible whites—reminded me of the eyes of a demon. I couldn't tell if she'd been ugly or beautiful in her youth: she was so wrinkled that any such speculation was impossible.

I fought the urge to ask if she kept a cottage in the darkest woods, and if she preferred rib or thigh meat on her roasted children. If she'd told me she was Cherthog's hag wife, Suless, goddess of treachery and winter, I'd have believed her without question.

Khaemezra noticed my stare and smiled a ridiculous toothless grin. She winked, and that quickly she was no longer vané, but an old harridan fishwife. She wasn't the only one who changed: Teraeth wasn't vané either, but a swarthy Quuros, scarred of face and possessing a worn, whipped body.

I wondered what I looked like, since I was sure the illusion covered me as well.

Teraeth and the old woman stared at each other as though speaking without words. Teraeth sighed and grabbed my arm. "Let's go." His voice revealed the flaw in the illusion, and I hoped no one would notice that his voice originated from somewhere above the illusion's "head."

"Where are we going?" I asked.

Teraeth scowled at me. "We're not out of danger yet." The vané walked out into the main throng of the crowd. After a few steps, I realized the old woman, Khaemezra, hadn't followed. I lost sight of her and wanted to ask if she would be coming along too, but I would have to ask Teraeth.

I hadn't had a lot of luck with that so far.

Teraeth pulled me through the crowd at a dizzying speed. My sense of direction became fuddled, until I only knew we were heading to one of the ships. Teraeth shuttled me up a gangplank, past sailors and a row of chained slaves. I fought back the desire to kill the slave master leading them onboard—and I didn't have a weapon, anyway.

Then I heard a familiar voice say, "What can I do for you?"

I turned toward it in angry surprise.

It was Captain Juval. I was back on board *The Misery,* the slave ship that had brought me from Quur to Kishna-Farriga. Captain Juval was the man who had ordered me soul-chained in the first place. Quuros might be made slaves, usually to repay debts or as punishment for crimes, but those slaves were not supposed to be sold outside the Empire's borders. Quuros were definitely never taken south and sold in Kishna-Farriga. Quuros didn't go south at all.*

I'd been unconscious for my sale to Juval and my departure from Quur. I'd never known the details of why Juval had broken Quuros laws to buy me, or how much he'd paid. I suspected Juval had paid nothing, that he'd been the one given metal in exchange for putting me in the rowing galleys and working me near to death. A feat he had gleefully tried to accomplish.

Captain Juval wasn't on my favorite-people list.

But the Captain's eyes slid over me without recognition.

Teraeth bowed to the man and said, "Thank you, Captain. I was told you're the person to see about a quick passage to Zherias."

Preoccupied loading the newest cargo, Captain Juval spared the briefest glance at the disguised vané. "How many?"

---

*"Going south" is a Quuros euphemism for dying. I suspect the saying goes back to Emperor Kandor's ill-fated attempt at southern expansion into the Manol.

"Three," Teraeth said. "My family. My mother is frail. I've been told the springs of Saolo'oa in Kolaque might have a chance of—"

"I charge two hundred ords for a cabin." Juval was still paying more attention to his cargo than to their conversation. "You fit in however many you want. Food is twenty more ords a person for the trip."

"*Two hundred* ords? That's robbery! . . ."

I walked away as they haggled over the price, and found a quiet corner of the ship, far out of the way of the sailors. No one recognized or even looked at me. I guess that was fortunate.

I couldn't believe I was back on board *The Misery*. Of all the dumb luck . . .

No, not dumb luck.

I didn't for a moment think that this was an accident. It was deliberate luck. Directed luck. This reeked of Taja's meddling hands.

My goddess. Taja. I could have worshipped Tya, or Thaena, or any of a thousand gods or goddesses for which the Empire of Quur was famous. But no, I had to worship the goddess of random, fickle, cruel chance. I always thought she pushed the odds in my favor, but that assumption now seemed the height of naïvety.

I was overcome with a paralyzing sense of foreboding.

Closing my eyes, I breathed in the stinking sea air of the harbor, gathering my strength. If anyone recognized me, if Teraeth or the old woman asked me any questions about *The Misery* or its crew, I was dead. Juval hadn't wanted me talking about how I'd ended up a slave: it was the whole reason he'd had me gaeshed. The specter of the chains lashed around my soul, the gaesh that allowed my owners to control my every moment, hovered over me, waiting to strike.

I clenched the tsali stone at my neck. I'd been allowed to keep it only because the slavers hadn't been aware I possessed it. I knew just enough magic to hide my most valuable possession (okay, fine, second-most valuable) in plain sight. Maybe Relos Var had seen through what was (I suspected) a simple, basic illusion.* Maybe that's why he'd been so eager to buy me. I knew the damn thing was valuable—more valuable than the star tears I'd just stolen. I knew all too well the lengths men had been willing to go to possess the Stone of Shackles (a name, by the way, that I found less and less amusing now that my soul was itself shackled).

And as I had suspected, no one checked me when I left with the Brotherhood—I had been naked, after all.

I sighed and fished under my hair, freeing the necklace of diamonds

---

*This is a common mistake. In fact, the first spell one learns can be quite sophisticated. Not knowing one's limits is occasionally a marked advantage.

I'd snagged on the back of my tsali stone's chain. Star tears weren't mag-ical, something I could now confirm. No, not magical, just rare and valu-able, worthy of crown jewels.

If I was right about this necklace's provenance, that's exactly what these were too. Crown jewels from the treasury of the mightiest Empire in the whole world, stolen from the hoard of a dragon, gifted to a god-dess, and lastly, used as a payment to a whore in what must surely have been the most expensive night of earthly pleasure ever purchased.

The same whore turned madam who'd raised me.

Maybe, once I returned to the Capital, I'd give her the necklace a second time. Ola would think it hysterical. With a fortune in star tears she'd be able to free all the slaves at the Shattered Veil Club and . . . I don't know. Maybe Ola could actually afford to pay them, if that's what they wanted to do for a living.

I refused to think about the fact that Ola was probably dead—along with many others I loved. Even the idea that Thurvishar D'Lorus was probably dead filled me with grief, though he was responsible for my present predicament.*

I tried not to think about it. Tried, and failed.

I bounced the necklace in my palm, thinking of other necklaces, the one wrapped around Teraeth's wrist in particular. Funny how he hadn't worn my gaesh around his neck. My grandfather Therin hadn't either, wearing Lady Miya's gaesh on his wrist too. It was as if both men wanted to distance themselves from the reality of their atrocities by treating the control charm as a temporary accessory.

I wondered when Dethic would look inside that velvet bag and real-ize he'd sold me for a few jangling copper bracelets—ones that he already owned. He probably already had, but with all the precautions Teraeth had taken to prevent being followed, the auction house's chances of track-ing us down were slim.

Maybe Dethic's life would be forfeited for his mistake. I smiled at the idea. I knew I was being a hypocrite; I'd known people associated with slavers back in Quur, but they hadn't owned *me*. Dethic had: I hoped he rotted.

Teraeth's black robe served as my only clothing, so I fastened the star tear necklace over my own and hoped the high collar and Khaemezra's illusions would prevent discovery. I would spend the journey studying the star tears until I could add them to the list of materials I knew how to conceal—and keep myself out of sight in the meantime.

---

*Obviously, I am not dead. I also reject the idea that I'm responsible for his situation here. I am at best an accessory.

When I returned, Teraeth and Juval were finishing their negotiations. Teraeth's mother Khaemezra now stood by Teraeth's side. Money changed hands, and one of the sailors showed us a tiny cabin filled with four bunk beds where we could sleep (in theory)* for the voyage.

Within a half hour of our arrival, the slave ship called *The Misery* weighed anchor and set out to sea.

---

*The beds on board an average Zheriaso-built slave ship can comfortably accommodate a person under 5'2" tall. By comparison, the average Quuros is 5'6" tall, the average Zheriaso is 5'8", and the average vané is 6'2" tall. So in answer to the question "Who could possibly find such accommodations comfortable?" the answer is "No one." This only highlights the desire of Zheriaso slavers to squeeze every possible bit of space, even from their paying passengers.

6: THE ROOK'S FATHER

(Talon's story)

Thirty-five paces from the fountain at the center of the flowering courtyard to the steps in the back. Two steps, then a hallway. The door on the left was Ola's, and the door on the right led to another set of stairs. Ten more steps, a small turn, another ten steps, then a door.

Surdyeh knew the route by heart, which was convenient, as he had never seen it.

The blind musician opened the door, frowned, and sighed. His son snored—

Is this bothering you, Kihrin?

Oh, such a shame. You must have realized Surdyeh is part of my memory collection. You are too, to a lesser extent.

You didn't know? Oh.

I guess you know now, ducky. Surdyeh's an active part of me. He wants so badly to protect you. A father's love is so powerful.

You're adorable when you're angry.

As I was saying—

His adopted son snored, still asleep on one of the cots crammed into the storeroom turned living space. The situation hadn't been so bad when Kihrin was a pup, but as the lad had grown older he'd grown larger. Now there was barely room for the two of them.

Better than nothing though, Surdyeh thought. Better than being tossed out into the street.

If only he could make his ungrateful wretch of a son understand.

Sadly, he suspected his son understood too well. As much as Surdyeh pretended they walked the razor's edge with the whorehouse madam's good grace, the threat was idle. Madam Ola would never evict them. He would have preferred, though, if Ola didn't sabotage his efforts at every turn. The boy needed to have a little respect shaken into him from time to time.

Surdyeh pulled himself out of his reverie for long enough to smack the end of his cane against his son's backside.

"Kihrin, get up! You've overslept."

His son groaned and turned over. "It's not time yet!"

Surdyeh banged the stick against Kihrin's bamboo cot this time. "Up, up! Have you forgotten already? We have a commission with Landril Attuleema tonight. And Madam Ola wants us to break in her new dancer. We've work to do and you've been up all night, haven't you. Useless damn boy, what have I told you about stealing?"

His son sat up in bed. *"Pappa."*

"If I wasn't blind, I'd beat you until you couldn't sit. My father never put up with such foolishness. You're a musician, not a street thief."

The cot creaked as Kihrin jumped out. "You're the musician. I'm just a singing voice." He sounded bitter.

Kihrin had been bitter about a lot of things lately, but he'd been such a sweet boy. What had Surdyeh done wrong?

"If you practiced your lessons . . ."

"I do practice. I'm just no good."

Surdyeh scowled. "You call that practice? You spend more time helping yourself to Ola's velvet girls and prowling rooftops than you do learning your chords. You could be good. You could be one of the best if you wanted it enough. When I was fifteen, I spent all night in the dark learning my fingerings. Practiced every day."

Kihrin muttered under his breath, "When you were fifteen, you were already blind."

"What did you just say?" Surdyeh's hand tightened on his cane. "Damn it, boy. One of these days, you're going to run afoul of the Watchmen, and that will be it, won't it? They'll take one of your hands if you're lucky, sell you into slavery if you're not. I won't always be here to protect you."

"Protect me?" Kihrin made a snorting sound. "Pappa, you know I love you, but you don't protect me. You can't." More swishes of cloth: Kihrin grabbing loincloth, agolé, sallí cloak, and sandals to dress.

"I protect you more than you know, boy. More than you can imagine." Surdyeh shook his head.

His son headed for the door. "Don't we need to be somewhere?"

He wanted to say so much to the boy, but the words were either already spoken or could never be spoken. He knew better than to think his son would listen too. Ola was the only one Kihrin paid attention to anymore, and only because she told the boy what he wanted to hear. Surdyeh was tired of being the only one saying what the boy *needed* to hear. He was tired of arguing, tired of being the only whisper of conscience in this sea of sin.

Six more months. Six more months and Kihrin turned sixteen. And it would all be over; Surdyeh would find out just how good a job he'd done of raising him.

The whole Empire would find out.*

"Move your feet, son. We don't want to be late."

Surdyeh picked up his cane and poked his son in the ribs. "Quit daydreaming!"

Kihrin stammered through his verse. The crowd in the main room booed, although the audience had thinned out once they realized it was just a rehearsal session.

Most of the customers weren't patrons of the arts, anyway.

"Start over," Surdyeh said. "My apologies, Miss Morea. You'd think my son had never seen a pretty girl before."

"Pappa!"

Surdyeh didn't need to see to know his son was blushing, or that Morea was the cause. She was the newest dancer at the Shattered Veil Club, as well as being Ola's newest slave. She would remain a slave until she earned enough extra metal from her service to pay back her bond price. To earn her freedom, she would need to be both an accomplished dancer and a successful whore.

Surdyeh didn't much care, but from the way Kihrin carried on, he could only assume Morea was more beautiful than a goddess. At least, his son didn't normally make quite this much of a fool of himself around the girls.

Morea grabbed a towel from the edge of the stage and wiped her face. "We've run through this twice. Once more and then a break?"

"Fine by me, Miss Morea," Surdyeh said, readying his harp between his legs once more. "Assuming certain boys can keep their damn eyes in their damn heads and their damn minds on their damn work."

He didn't hear Kihrin's response, but he could imagine it easily enough.

"Stop scowling," Surdyeh said as he nudged Kihrin in the ribs again.

"How—?" Kihrin shook his head, gritted his teeth, and forced a smile onto his face.

Surdyeh started the dance over. Morea had asked him to play the Maevanos. If Morea had come from a wealthy house, the Maevanos was probably the best compromise she could manage. She'd have had no time to learn anything bawdier.

The story to the Maevanos was simple enough: A young woman is sold into slavery by her husband, who covets her younger sister. Mistreated by the slave master who buys her, she is purchased by a high lord of the

---

*I can't help but wonder just what Surdyeh thought would happen on Kihrin's sixteenth birthday. A more distressing idea: what if it all happened exactly as Surdyeh had originally planned?

Upper Circle. The high lord falls in love with her, but tragedy strikes when a rival house assassinates her new master. Loyal and true, the slave girl takes her own life to be with her lord beyond the Second Veil. Her devotion moves the death goddess Thaena to allow the couple to Return to the land of the living, taking the life of the philandering husband in their place. The high lord frees the girl, marries her, and everyone lives happily ever after who should.*

While the Maevanos was meant to be danced by a woman, the accompanying vocals were male. The story was told by the men the girl encountered rather than the girl herself. The scenes with the high lord and the slave trader were provocative, the whole reason Morea had suggested it as a compromise.

Surdyeh hated the dance for all the reasons it would probably do well at the brothel, but it hadn't been his decision.

The crowd was larger than when the dance had begun; the first of the evening crowds had started to filter inside. Hoots and clapping greeted Morea as she gave a final bow. Kihrin trailed off his song. Surdyeh allowed the last notes to echo from his double-strung harp, holding his finger-taped picks just above the strings.

Surdyeh smelled Morea's sweat, heard the beads as she tossed her hair back over her shoulders. She ignored the catcalls of the crowd as she walked back to his chair.

"What are you doing here?" Morea asked him.

Surdyeh turned his head in her direction. "Practicing, Miss Morea?"

"You're amazing," she said. "Does every brothel in Velvet Town have musicians as good as you? You're better than anyone who ever performed for my old master. What is Madam Ola paying you?"

"You think my father's that good?" Kihrin's step was so quiet that even Surdyeh hadn't heard him approach.

Surdyeh resisted the urge to curse the gods. The last thing he needed was Kihrin wondering why Surdyeh played in the back halls of Velvet Town, when he could have played for royalty.

"Hey there, pretty girl, leave off those servants," a rough voice called out. "I want some time with you." Surdyeh heard heavy footsteps; whoever approached was a large man.

---

*There are many variations of the Maevanos, but they all follow the same basic story: the hero dies, travels to the underworld, is judged by Thaena, and is allowed to Return to life again. *The Archetype of the Dying God,* by Qhadri Silorma, plays on this theme in detail—further elaborating a theory in which Thaena is just one part of a cycle of spiritual reincarnation vital to all existence. This is along with goddesses Taja and Tya, each ruling one of three coexisting realms of reality. These conform to Physical, Magical, and Deathly metaphysical states. Silorma's book is hugely hated by followers of the Goddess of Life, Galava, who object to being pushed aside in favor of the triplet goddesses.

Morea inhaled and stepped backward.

"Can't you see she's tired? Leave her alone." Kihrin's attempt to intimidate would have gone better if he'd been a few years older and a lot heavier. As it was, he was too easily mistaken for a velvet boy himself. Surdyeh doubted the customer paid much attention to his son's interruption.

Surdyeh placed his harp to the side and held out his ribbon-sewn sallí cloak to where Morea stood. "Lady, your cloak."

While Morea covered herself, Surdyeh rewove the spell shaping the sound in the room so the Veil's bouncer, Roarin, heard every word. Morea's would-be customer might be large, but Roarin had morgage blood in him—enough to give him the poisonous spines in his arms. Surdyeh knew from experience how intimidating the bouncer could be.

"My money's as good as the next man's!" the man protested.

Another voice joined him. "Hey, it's my turn!"

"Oh great. There's two of you," Kihrin said. "Miss Morea, you're not taking customers right now, are you?"

The beads in her hair rattled as she shook her head. "No."

"There you are, boys. She's not open for business. Shoo." Only someone who knew Kihrin would have noticed the tremble of fear in his voice. The two men must have been large indeed.

"Bertok's balls. You don't tell me what to do." The man stepped in close.

Even from the stage, Surdyeh smelled the stench of liquor on the man's breath. Surdyeh clenched his hands around his cane and prepared himself for the possibility he would have to intervene.

"What's all this?" Roarin asked. A hush fell over the crowd nearest the stage.

"I, uh . . . I want to reserve a bit of time with the young lady. Uh . . . sir."

"Kradnith, you're a mad one. I was here first!"

"Of course, fine sirs, of course," Roarin said, "but this is just a dancing girl. Pretty slut, to be sure, but useless for a good lay. Too tired out. Come with me. Madam Ola will show you some *real* women! They'll drain you dry!" He slapped his thick hands on the men's shoulders and escorted them elsewhere in the brothel.

Surdyeh exhaled and turned to pack up the harp. "Some days I really hate this job."

"Are you all right, Miss Morea?" Kihrin asked.

The young woman groaned and stretched her neck. "I can't believe—" She cut off whatever she'd been about to say. "It was nice of you to stand up for me like that." Then her breath caught in her throat. "You have blue eyes."

Surdyeh's heart nearly stopped beating.

No. Damn it all, no.

"I only wear them on special occasions," Kihrin said. Surdyeh could tell his son was smiling. Of course, he was smiling. Kihrin hated it when people noticed the color of his eyes, but now the attention came from a pretty girl he wanted to notice him.

Surdyeh racked his brain. Where had Ola said the new girl was from? Not a Royal House. Surdyeh had forbidden Ola from ever buying a slave from a Royal House. Too risky.

Morea said to Kihrin, "I'm going to lie down in the Garden Room. Would you bring me an iced Jorat cider? I'm parched."

"We're leaving," Surdyeh said. "We have a commission."

"I'll fetch you a cider before we go," Kihrin said.

She slipped out of the room, now emptying as customers who had stayed for the rehearsal looked for a different sort of company.

"No, Kihrin," Surdyeh said. "We don't have time."

"This won't take long, Pappa."

"It's not your job to play hero, swoop in, and save the girl. Leave that to Roarin." He knew he sounded peevish, but he couldn't stop himself.

"She took your cloak," Kihrin reminded him. "I'll bring it back. You wouldn't want to show up at Landril's without your Reveler's colors, would you?"

Surdyeh sighed. Unfortunately, the boy was right: Surdyeh needed the cloak. That it was just an excuse didn't mean it wasn't a good one. He grabbed his son's hand and squeezed. "Don't help yourself to the sweets for free. We need to keep in Ola's good graces. It's her goodwill that keeps us off the streets. There's a dozen musicians better than us who'd give their eyeteeth to perform at the Shattered Veil Club. Remember that."

His son pulled his hand away. "Funny how Morea doesn't agree with you."

"Don't scowl at me, boy. You'll put wrinkles on that face that Ola tells me is so handsome." His voice softened. "We have to be at Landril's at six bells, so you have a bit of time, but don't linger."

Any resentment his son might have harbored vanished in the face of victory. "Thank you." Kihrin gave Surdyeh a quick hug and ran out of the room.

Surdyeh sat there, fuming.

Then he called out for someone to find Ola.

7: THE MISERY

(Kihrin's story)

—don't want to hold the damn rock. I don't want to keep talking about this, Talon. I don't even remember where I left off.

Right. I was on board The Misery. *Thanks so much.*

Fine.

I don't remember much about those first hours back on the ship. Sailors made their knots, raised their sails. The men shouted, yelled, and cast off. I paid little attention. I waited in our cabin.

Or rather, I hid there.

I found it eerie to watch these normal, humdrum-looking people enter the cabin and yet know that their appearance was a lie. It was odder still to know they had disguised me in the same way; if I looked in a mirror, my real face wouldn't stare back.

"What do you people want with me?" I asked Khaemezra when they returned. "Don't tell me it was a coincidence that you paid for me with a necklace of star tears. My grandfather used a necklace just like that to pay for his vané slave Miya, a slave he bought from 'an old vané hag.' Someone told me once, after I was finally reunited with my darling family. I always thought that was just a story, since there's no such thing as an old vané, but here you are, an old vané hag."

She raised an eyebrow.

I cleared my throat. "No offense."

"None taken," Khaemezra said. She looked amused, even though I'd called her a hag to her face, twice.

"Is the reason you bought me something to do with my grandfather?" I demanded.

She looked at me kindly but said nothing.

"Enough of this," Teraeth said. "It's a long trip back to Zherias. Find the Captain and ask him if he keeps a weather witch. I'd like to know when we'll arrive."

This was what I'd been waiting for, what I'd been dreading. An order from my new master, directly contradicting a previous gaesh order from

Captain Juval. I already knew the answer to Teraeth's question: yes, Juval had a weather witch. But talking about her, and talking about Juval, would disobey the orders he had given me when he had me gaeshed. As soon as I returned from my errand, Teraeth would demand an answer. If I gave him that answer, the gaesh would kill me for disobeying Juval's earlier command.

But if I didn't give Teraeth an answer, the gaesh would *still* kill me, this time for disobeying Teraeth.

The edges of pain surged inside me as I hesitated too long.

I figured it had been a short, weird life. Maybe Thaena would laugh when I told her about it past the Second Veil. "The gaesh won't–"

"Go!"

I gritted my teeth as the pain washed through me. My only chance of survival was if I could somehow communicate the problem quickly enough for Teraeth to countermand Juval's order, or get him to change his own. Maybe. If Taja still liked me. "Juval's–orders–"

The old woman stood. "Teraeth, quickly!"

"Juval–gaeshed–" The commands rolled over me with smashing waves, drowned me in my own blood. The gaesh tore into my body, roared its way through my veins, ate me away from the inside, burned, seared.

I collapsed on the floor, convulsing.

8: THE ANGEL'S BARGAIN

(Talon's story)

Morea fretted over the best place to present herself in the Garden Room. On this couch? No, too easily seen. That one? Yes, that one was better. Morea removed the ribbon-covered sallí cloak, draped it over a chair, and splashed water to freshen herself. She ran a hand over her braids and reapplied her perfume, rubbing scented oil over her body until her skin gleamed. She hurried to her chosen couch and lay down, acting ever so weary.

It wasn't entirely an act.

A few minutes later, the harper's son walked into the solarium with a mug in his hand. Morea knew he couldn't be Surdyeh's actual get. Surdyeh might be an extraordinary musician, but he was recognizably common, and his son—well, his son was no farmer's brood.

The teenager stopped and stared when he spotted her. Morea almost smiled. She wondered how any brothel child could have stayed so inno-cent that they could still be aroused by simple flesh. All children of the seraglio she had ever known were jaded beyond measure, hardened to any normal sensual allure.

"Here's your drink, Miss Morea." Kihrin handed the cider to her.

Morea looked up at him. An angel, surely. He had dark skin somehow more *golden* than the olive hue of most Quuros. The black hair made his skin look paler than it really was, while his skin made his blue eyes shine like Kirpis sapphires. Those blue eyes . . . Morea clicked her tongue and smiled, sitting up on the couch and taking the offered drink. "Not Miss, surely. Just Morea. Madam Ola calls you Angel?"

The young man snickered. "Ola calls me a lot of things. Please, call me Kihrin."

"I'd think you were from Kirpis, except for the hair." She reached out to touch it. "Like raven feathers." She leaned back against the cushions to look at him again. "But you're not from Kirpis, are you?"

He laughed, blushing. "No. I was born here."

Her face wrinkled in confusion. "But you don't look Quuros at all."

"Ah." He squirmed. "My mother was Doltari."

"What?"

"Doltar's a country to the south, far south, way past the Manol Jungle. It's cold there. They have blue eyes and light hair. Like me."

She resisted the urge to roll her eyes. "I know where Doltar is." She reached out to touch his hair once more. He dyed his hair. She could see that now. "A lot of slaves are shipped north from Doltar. But you don't look Doltari."

He frowned. "Really?"

"All the Doltari slaves I've known have been stocky people, wide and large, built for labor. Big noses, thin lips. You're slender. Your nose, your lips—just the opposite of a Doltari." She tried to imagine him with brown hair, tried to imagine him dressed in blue. She found it easy, and even though the room was stifling warm, she shivered.

"Are you cold?" the young man asked.

Morea smiled. "No. Sit with me."

Kihrin cleared his throat, looking embarrassed. "I shouldn't. It's, uh . . . there's a rule."

"I have heard how Madam Ola speaks of you. Surely she lets you spend time with whoever you like?"

The blush graduated to a red flush. "It's not Ola's rule. It's my rule. I don't force myself on the women here. I don't think it would be right."

"It's not force if I *want* you here." She patted the cushion next to her. "Sit with me. Let me brush that beautiful hair. Please?"

"I—" He moved over to the bench. "I suppose a few minutes wouldn't hurt."

"It's a crime to see such lovely hair so neglected. Why do you wrap your agolé around your neck like that? You'll strangle yourself." Morea unwound the long cloth, letting it fall to the couch. She reached for a brush another slave had left behind and pulled it through Kihrin's hair, untangling the knots. Unfastened, his hair reached past his shoulders. The black dye hadn't been kind. She found spots of gold where he'd missed a strand, or patches of violet where the dye had faded. When she finished brushing out his hair, she began massaging his scalp, gently kneading with skilled fingers. She leaned close as she massaged, pressing her breasts against his back. His breathing quickened. Morea smiled.

Kihrin sounded uncertain. "I always thought my hair looked strange."

"Golden? People would kill for such hair. You must not work here."

"You know I do. What was that at practice?"

"No. I mean you don't—you're not a velvet boy. I've known musicians who did the same duty as the dancers."

Kihrin frowned and turned his head away. "We rent one of the rooms in the back. Ola gives us a good rate because we play for the dancers, but that's it."

"With your looks, you could make a lot of metal."

"No offense, but I prefer to make my metal a different way."

Morea felt the skin on his back shiver as she ran her fingers over his shoulder. "Are you Ogenra then?"

The mood broke. Kihrin turned to stare at her. "I told you I'm Doltari. Why would you think I'm one of the royal bastards?"

She tried to make her response idle, tried to make it seem like she didn't really care. "Blue eyes are one of the divine marks. The only other person I've ever seen with blue eyes, with eyes as blue as yours, was royalty, one of the god-touched. You remind me of him, so I assumed you must be related."

His voice turned icy. "I told you I'm not Ogenra."

"But—"

"Please drop it."

"Are you so sure? Because—"

"I'm not."

"If you were Ogenra though—"

His face contorted with anger. "My mother was a Doltari who left me to die on the garbage heaps of Gallthis. Happy? She was too stupid to know she could buy a fix from the Temple of Caless, or any blue house, for ten silver chalices to keep her from taking with child. And so she abandoned me at birth. I am *not* an Ogenra. Yes, blue eyes are one of the god-touched marks, but there are plenty of people with eyes all colors of the rainbow. Hell, Surdyeh's eyes were green before he went blind. It doesn't mean he's related to whichever Royal House controls the Gatekeepers,* it just means he's from Kirpis. I've never seen the inside of a mansion in the Upper Circle and *I never will.*"

Morea flinched and drew back. His anger—Caless! She whispered, "But . . . you look just like him . . ."

She started to cry.

After a few seconds, his hands wrapped around her, his voice whispering as he stroked her hair. "Oh hell . . . I'm so sorry . . . I . . . I didn't . . . was he important to you? Someone you cared about?"

She drew back. "No! I *hate* him."

His expression turned stony. "Wait. I remind you of someone you *hate?*"

Morea wiped away her tears. This wasn't going the way she'd wanted *at all.* "It's not like that. I just wanted—"

---

*I don't think it should be assumed that Surdyeh wasn't trained by the Gatekeepers, although it's possible that the Revelers were responsible for Surdyeh's musical training. He seems to have known spells that aren't officially in the Reveler repertoire. Let's simply say that it would not surprise me to discover Surdyeh had ties to the Gatekeepers, or rather House D'Aramarin.

"What? What did you want so badly you'd make a play for someone who reminds you of a man you hate—someone you hate so much, that the thought of him sends you to tears? Because now I'm curious."

She edged away from him on the divan. "It's not like that!"

"Explain it to me then."

"If you were Ogenra, you could find out where the Octagon's slave auctioneers sold my sister Talea. You could ask for a favor from your family, if they were noble. I thought you had to be Ogenra. You're even wearing his colors . . ." She pointed to his chest.

He touched the blue stone wrapped in gold around his neck. "*His* colors. I see." He nodded, his expression hard. He wasn't looking at her with tenderness anymore.

"Kihrin, I like you—"

"Really."

"I do! I didn't know who else to turn to."

"Who you should have turned to was your new owner. Ola's friends with half the people in this town, and she's blackmailing the other half. She could have found what you needed from the Octagon. She could probably buy your sister too. But Ola would want something, and you didn't want to owe her any more than you already do. Me? You thought you could rook me on the cheap."

Morea's throat dried. "I don't know Madam Ola like you do. I've never had a master who wouldn't beat me for asking a favor like that. But you . . . you're sweet, and you're beautiful, and you stood up to those men . . . why do my motives have to be any more sinister than that?"

His expression didn't soften. "Because you're selling something, and you thought I was eager to buy."

Morea tried to slap him, but he ducked away from her. He was quick.

He ignored her attack and stood. "I'll ask Ola. She used to be a slave. And she still knows people in the Upper Circle. Someone will know what happened to your sister." There was no smile in Kihrin's eyes. He no longer looked at her like a lovesick youth pining after his latest crush.

Morea looked down at the floor, hating the way she felt, hating what she knew came next. "What would you expect in return?" she finally asked.

He grabbed his father's sallí cloak and tossed it over his arm.

"Nothing," he said. "I know this is the Capital, but not everything has to be a business deal."

Kihrin bowed, the graceful flourish of a trained entertainer, and left the room without a backward glance.

Kihrin stalked into the main room of the Shattered Veil Club, and scanned the room for his father.

"So how'd it go, my little Rook?" Ola's voice whispered from behind him.

"Ugh. I don't want to talk about it." He wished she wouldn't call him Rook at the Club. He didn't call her Raven here, did he?

The large woman raised an eyebrow. "That house last night didn't have a guard out, did they?"

He stared at her for a moment, blinking. She wasn't talking about the rehearsal. She'd meant the Kazivar House burglary. "Oh! Um. . . . no. No, that went great. Better than great. Best yet."

The woman grinned and gave him a hug, ruffling his hair while she trapped him in her arms.

"Ola—" Kihrin gave his standard protest, habitual by this point. He straightened himself up as Roarin led Surdyeh toward them. "I'll tell you about it later. We need to talk."

Surdyeh reached them and said, "We must hurry. Landril is very wealthy; it would be ill if we were late to our first commission from the man."

Kihrin picked up the harp in its cloth case. "Sorry. I was delayed."

"I'm sure you were, little one." Ola winked at him.

Kihrin grinned back at her, shameless. "No, it's not like that." Then his expression grew serious. "I need to talk to you about that too."

The whorehouse madam tilted her head to the side. "One of the girls giving you grief? Which one?"

"Morea," Surdyeh said. "It couldn't be anyone else."

"Pappa, I can answer for myself."

Madam Ola pursed her lips. "I wouldn't be too hard on her, Bright-Eyes. That one's still a bit of a mess from her last owner. Give me a few months to soften her up a bit. Why don't you play with Jirya instead? She likes you."

Which was true. Jirya did like Kihrin, mostly because Kihrin used afternoons spent in Jirya's crib as an opportunity to catch up on his sleep after all-night treks on rooftops. She'd also proven to be a fantastic alibi. Of course, the alibi was needed for his father Surdyeh, and not the Watchmen. Surdyeh may not have approved of what he erroneously thought Kihrin was doing with Ola's slave girls, but he approved of burglary even less.

"No, it's not—"

Surdyeh shook his head. "You spoil him, Ola. You'd think he was a royal prince from the slave girls you let him take his pick from."

It had been Surdyeh's favorite argument of late, and it made Kihrin scowl even more than normal. Ola noticed, and raised an eyebrow. Kihrin pressed his lips together, shook his head, and said nothing.

The madam stared at Kihrin for a moment.

Then Ola laughed and chucked Surdyeh under the chin. "Men need to have good memories from their youth to keep them warm in their old age. Don't try to tell me you don't have some good ones, because I know better, old man. And you didn't have no owner's permission, either. Now get going, before you're late."

She shoved them both out the door.

9: Souls and Stones

(Kihrin's story)

I woke to pain and the rhythmic seesaw of *The Misery* under sail. I had been jammed into one of the child-sized bunks, naked again, with Teraeth's black robe draped over me as a makeshift blanket. The man himself leaned against the cabin wall, his expression sullen. His mother, Khaemezra, sat next to my bunk, pressing a wet cloth against my face.

"Ow," I said. Khaemezra had healed my wounds, but everything hurt—a sore, achy, pulled-muscle hurt.

"You'll be happy to know you'll live," Khaemezra said, sounding amused about the matter.

"At least for now," Teraeth said. "No telling what the future holds with your talent for getting into trouble."

"Right, because I asked for this." I swung my feet out of bed and wrapped the robe around my middle, although it was a bit late for modesty. I attempted to ignore Teraeth and concentrated on his mother. "I should say thank you for saving me from that gaesh attack, but I have to go back to my favorite question: what do you people want from me?"

She smiled. "A better question: how did you survive disobeying a gaesh when no one ever does?"

I hesitated. "What? Wait, but I . . ." I cleared my throat. "I thought that was your doing?"

Khaemezra shook her head. "Oh, no."

"Then how—" I put my hand to my throat. The necklace of star tear diamonds was missing, probably reclaimed when they had removed the robe. The Stone of Shackles, however, remained.

She saw the gesture. "Yes, I suspect it was the stone too. It protects its wearer, although it doesn't do much to mitigate pain. You might wish you were dead." Khaemezra continued, "Juval was the one who gaeshed you, wasn't he?"

Yeah, I wasn't going to fall for that twice. "Don't be silly."

Teraeth frowned. "Then why—"

Khaemezra held up a hand. My gaesh charm dangled from her fingers.

"You may answer honestly, dear child. I've removed the previous prohibitions."

Teraeth must have given her the gaesh while I was unconscious.

"Oh, well in that case, sure, Juval had someone summon up a demon and *that's* who gaeshed me." I waited for a second, but I didn't seem inclined to go into convulsions, so I continued. "Juval was furious when he realized he'd been tricked into committing high crimes against the Quuros Empire. It's not like they'd just smile and dismiss putting a Quuros prince in the rowing galley for a season as 'just a misunderstanding.' I convinced him that if he killed me, the priests of Thaena would just lead the Quuros navy to his sails even quicker. He figured ripping out my soul also solved the problem."

"Being gaeshed doesn't rip out your soul," Teraeth snapped.

"Oh, I'm sorry," I replied. "Is that personal experience talking? You've been gaeshed? Or have you just gaeshed a whole lot of people? I bet it's the latter one, huh?"

"The Black Brotherhood doesn't engage in slavery."

I couldn't stop myself from laughing. "The kind auctioneers back in Kishna-Farriga might beg to differ. Didn't you have reserved seats?"

"We buy vané slaves to free them, not to gaesh them," he retorted.

"Is that so? Is that what your mother here did with Miya? Freed her? And how do you finance an operation like that? Good intentions? Or do you have a couple dozen more star tears back home?"

"No, but if you'd like to keep stealing them back, we could work something out."

"Quiet, both of you." The old woman clucked her tongue. "Teraeth, go upstairs and ask the Captain how many days until we reach Zherias."

He glared at me a moment longer, his expression righteous. "We don't sell slaves."

"Whatever you say, *Master.*"

"Teraeth, go."

He nodded to his mother, his brow furrowed. He spared me one last parting glare and left.

I looked sideways at Khaemezra. "He's adopted, right?"

The corner of her mouth twitched. "He has chosen to take after his father."

That stopped me. I'd asked rhetorically. Teraeth was *clearly* not Khaemezra's blood kin. "Night and day" was an apt metaphor for the pair. He was one of the Manol vané. She was a Kirpis vané.

At least, I thought she was. A woman who lived and breathed illusions could look like anything she wanted.

I grimaced, rubbing damp palms on the fabric of my robe. "I can't trust you. I know where those star tears came from."

"As do I: the hoard of the dragon Baelosh."

I blinked. "Excuse me?"

"The hoard of the dragon Baelosh," Khaemezra repeated. "Where they were stolen by Emperor Simillion. After he was murdered, the jewels were locked up with all the other priceless artifacts, in the center of the Arena in the Quuros capital. Centuries later, Emperor Gendal gave the necklace of stars to a striking Zheriaso courtesan whose beauty matched the night sky, and she used the jewels to buy her freedom. When her former owner, a man named Therin, was off having adventures with his friends, he used the necklace to save the life of a vané woman who was about to be executed. He offered to trade the necklace for ownership of the woman's gaesh—and his vow that she would never return to the Manol." She smiled. "That's how the necklace came to me."

"So you don't deny that you sold Miya—" I halted. "Execution? She was going to be *executed*?"

"We call it the Traitor's Walk. The condemned is gaeshed and forced into the Korthaen Blight. It may sound like exile, but trust me, it's a death sentence. No rebirth. No Returning."

"And you thought, 'Why not make some metal on the side?'"

She scoffed. "I'd have sold her for a handful of glass beads and a broken twig if it meant she didn't end up spitted on a morgage pike, while demons feasted on her soul. I was there when she was born. I watched her grow up. Watching her die would have broken my heart." The sadness in Khaemezra's eyes seemed too heartfelt to be anything but genuine.

"You . . . you know Lady Miya then?" I had assumed their relationship was more . . . professional. I mean, Dethic the slaver back in Kishna-Farriga "knew" me, but I don't think he'd have gotten broken up by the idea of my death.

She didn't answer at first. She turned away and looked to the side and I . . .

I recognized that gesture, that look. I'd seen it before, even if the two women looked nothing alike. Khaemezra didn't look like Miya any more than she looked like Teraeth, but something about their manner was so alike, that I recognized the connection immediately.

"Holy thrones, you—" I gaped. "You're related to Miya."

She blinked and turned back to me. "How observant. Yes. She was my granddaughter."

Oh. OH. "How could you? To summon up a demon and watch as it ripped out part of your granddaughter's soul . . ."

"Oh, no. I'm not like your Captain Juval. I didn't order some lackey to summon a demon," she said. "I gaeshed her soul myself. I used *that*." She leaned over and tapped the Stone of Shackles at the base of my throat.

I stared at her in horror. "No, you can't—this can't—"

"You probably thought that bauble was a tsali stone, assuming you understand what a tsali stone is. It is not." She flicked her hands away as if brushing away evil thoughts. "There are eight Cornerstones. Two stones for each of the four founding races. Each different, each with a different awful set of powers, each meant to usurp one of the Eight Gods." Khaemezra chuckled, low and evil and without any warmth. "They failed in that at least. I'll take my comforts where I can."

"I don't understand. Are you saying I could use this to gaesh other people? But I *am* gaeshed!"

"So? The Stone of Shackles cares not if your soul is divided or whole, only that it is here on this side of the Second Veil. Listen to me, because this is important: that glittery rock on your chest embodies a concept, and that concept is *slavery*. Every slave who has ever crawled or squirmed or died at the end of a lash feeds it, just as every death feeds Thaena. You wear an abomination around your neck and it makes the world a more terrible place by the fact of its existence."

I felt light-headed and dizzy. People had tried so hard to get me to remove that damn stone. At that moment, I wanted to take it off and throw it across the cabin—more than I had ever wanted anything in my life. I reached for the knot at the back of my neck, fingers scrambling in a panic. "And you used this on your granddaughter? I want it destroyed. I'll smash it. I'll break it—"

"As easy to kill a god, dear child. No weapon you own is up to the task. Besides, it protects you. The Stone of Shackles saved your life just a few minutes ago. Your enemies believe they cannot kill you so long as you wear it; that the power of the Stone of Shackles would twist such an act to mean their deaths and not yours. Why do you think I gave it to Miya? As for why I used it on her, I had my reasons. Leave it at that."

That stopped me cold. Khaemezra was right, of course. The necklace couldn't be taken by force; it had to be freely given.

Also, she'd just given an order.

I forced my hand away from the stone. "Is this what Relos Var wants? The Stone of Shackles?"

Khaemezra sighed. "No. I doubt he cares for that particular trinket. He seeks something other than a magic necklace—your destruction."

"But why does he want to kill me? I've never met him, or done anything to him."

She smiled at me in a grandmotherly sort of way. "Dear child, I did not say he wants to *kill* you."

"But you said—" I stopped and felt cold. As a priestess of the Death Goddess, she wouldn't be imprecise with any phrasing concerning murder.

"Killing you would be a sloppy mistake, one that puts you back in the Afterlife, to be reborn or Returned." She reached over and patted my knee. "Understand, it was pure luck . . ." She nodded at me. ". . . pure luck, that we had any idea about this auction. A source overheard Relos Var discussing the sale, and relayed that information to us without understanding its significance. However, I don't know how *he* knew you would be there."

"He could have heard about my kidnapping. I'm sure half of Quur knows I'm missing by this point." I grimaced. "How he knew to go looking for me in the Kishna-Farriga slave pits though . . . if Darzin knew where I was–" I paused. "Darzin's found me before. Could he have ordered this Relos Var person to collect me once he knew my location?"

She blinked at me and then laughed, awful and loud. "No."

"But–"

"Darzin might be Relos Var's lackey, but never the reverse. Prior to this you have met small men with small ambitions. But Relos Var? Relos Var is a Power, one of the strongest in the whole world."

"Thanks for telling me. I'll sleep so well tonight." I swallowed. "Why me, again?"

"There's a prophecy."

I stared at her.

Khaemezra stared back.

I blanched, looked away, and reminded myself not to get into staring contests with High Priestesses of death cults. "I don't believe in prophecy."

"Neither do I. Unfortunately, Relos Var seems to take these prophecies seriously, so I must as well. And in the meantime, I would like to train you and make sure that the next time you run into trouble, you will be better prepared." She smiled. "I'll think of it as a favor to Miya."

"No thanks, I already have a–" I started to say, *I already have a goddess.* I couldn't spit out the words.

She noticed the pause and her eyes narrowed. "Yes, Taja is your patron. But despite our origins, worshiping the Death Goddess is not a requirement for admission into our order. I seek a soldier, not a priest or fanatic. The Goddess of Luck will not object to your training at our hands."

I closed my eyes and shuddered. "I don't give a fuck what Taja wants with me."

When I opened my eyes again, Khaemezra stared at me with open contempt.

"Fool," she whispered. She'd used much the same tone with Relos Var.

Blood warmed my cheeks. "You don't understand what I've been through–"

"What is it about the idiot men in your family that you are all such fools? Stubborn. Mule-headed! If one of the Sisters chooses to give you her grace, do you think you can walk away from a goddess? That you can say 'Bah, a bad thing has happened to me, fie on my goddess forever'? Taja walks with you as much now as she ever did. She protects you and comforts you, and if you will not see it, that is not her doing."

I rolled my eyes. "Exactly what I'd expect a priestess to say. Easy words when you don't sit here gaeshed, with the dried blood from flayed skin still staining your back. She . . . She . . ." I realized I shouldn't say the words, but the damage hurt. What happened to me still hurt. Khaemezra may have healed the damage to my body, but the damage to my emotions, my soul, still festered, hot and raw.

I leaned forward and finished the sentence. "She betrayed me."

Khaemezra's nostrils flared. "You're mistaken."

"The Quuros navy had *found* me." I gestured toward the hull of the ship. "I'd spent months huddled in the rowing galley downstairs, praying the slave masters didn't remember I was there, and then the navy arrived, looking for me. And what happened? They couldn't see me. The one time in my life I didn't want to be invisible. I watched as that navy captain looked right through me, even though I was exactly who he was looking for—the only yellow-haired bastard in the room. That was the moment I realized that my goddess didn't want me rescued."

"Of course not. Going back to Quur would have been a disaster."

"A disaster?" I tried to keep my voice a careful neutral.

Khaemezra glanced at me, narrowing her eyes, and I knew I'd failed. She saw the anger as clearly as if I'd lost my temper outright. "Return to Quur and you die."

"You don't know that."

She raised an eyebrow. "Oh child. You think so?"

"I do. I had a plan. It would have worked. Instead, people I love are probably dead."

"Yes. Some are. Far more would be dead if you had stayed. I know that. I know that far better than you."

I looked at her.

"What was it you said, not five minutes ago? About how you convinced Juval not to kill you outright? The dead keep no secrets from the Pale Lady."

"Yes, but I was lying to Juval. The lady's priests weren't looking for me—my grandfather hadn't been an active priest of Thaena since before I was born."

"He's not the only one who speaks to her." She paused, as if deciding to change tactics. "I am well familiar with Darzin D'Mon, the one you call 'Pretty Boy.' Do you know why?"

Without waiting for my answer, she continued. "He once sought access to our order. He once sought to be part of the Black Brotherhood, to seek solace from his imagined pains and injustices in the embrace of the Lady of Death. She refused him as an unworthy suitor and, like an unworthy suitor who would force himself on a lady who does not love him, he obsesses over her. He glories in murder, each one an offering to a goddess who does not seek them, each innocent life a rotted rose left before Thaena's gate. Had you been able to go through with your grand plan, he would have added another flower to his macabre bouquet."

"You still don't know that."

"Oh, I do." She shook her head. "At least once a week, sometimes more, your 'Pretty Boy' goes to the Winding Sheet in Velvet Town. As someone who grew up in that part of the Capital, I trust you are familiar with that particular brothel and its reputation?"

My mouth tasted like ash. "I know what they sell."

"Once a week, 'Pretty Boy' makes a special request, one difficult to fulfill, so it requires the services of a priest of Caless to make sure that the young men provided are exotic: gold-haired and blue-eyed. Just like you. Temporary, but the illusion need not last for more than a few hours. Would you like to know what 'Pretty Boy' does with his pretty boys? How many mangled flowers he has left on the lady's doorstep?"

I looked away. "No." Damn me though, I imagined well enough. The catamites and whores of the Winding Sheet aren't rented, but purchased.

One does not rent something whose purpose is to be destroyed.

I shuddered.

Khaemezra stood up. "Please think on my words. We are not your enemy, and you are in dire need of friends. Sooner or later, you will have to trust someone."

After she left, I sat there with my fist wrapped around the Stone of Shackles and thought about my options. I had no way to tell what had happened to my real family, if Ola still lived. I had no way to tell what had been done to those I loved while I traveled in chains to Kishna-Farriga, or what might still happen while I was under the Black Brotherhood's control. Training, Khaemezra had said. Maybe they would train me. Maybe not.

More than anything, I wondered how much of what I had just been told was truth, and how much was lie, and if I had any way to know the difference.

10: Demon in the Streets

(Talon's story)

The sights, smells, and sounds of the City assaulted Kihrin the moment he and his father left the shaded comfort of the Shattered Veil. The late afternoon sun was a red ball of fire in the summer sky, heating the white stone streets of Velvet Town to an oven's warmth.

Those streets were empty. The afternoon was too hot for whores and drinking. Anyone with sense was sequestered in whatever shade they could find. Wispy clouds teased the teal sky, but it would be months before those clouds exploded into the monsoon season's fury. Until then, the Capital City roasted in its own juices.

Kihrin enjoyed the heat himself, and he preferred to travel when few people were about: early morning before the dawn or late afternoon when everyone napped. In the first case, it meant less chance of witnesses to Kihrin's burglaries, and in the second case, the empty streets made navigating with Surdyeh easier.

Surdyeh was quiet as they turned down Peddler's Lane, a shortcut to Simillion's Crossing,* where their patron Landril kept his penthouse and his mistresses.

Kihrin knew something was bothering his father, but he could only guess at the cause. Surdyeh did hate it when he thought Kihrin was spending time in velvet-girl cribs. He always made a point of reminding Kihrin that the girls at the Shattered Veil Club weren't there of their own free will. Surdyeh would then follow that by stating—with a significant look in Kihrin's direction—that any man who exploited such circumstances for his own pleasure was no man at all.

Surdyeh was a hypocrite. His father had no problem taking Ola's metal or performing in front of the men who came to the brothel. He passed judgment on every customer without giving any consideration to

---

*Believed to be named because the road marks the spot where Simillion killed the god-king Ghauras. In fact, it's so named because it marks the spot where the First Emperor's murdered, mutilated corpse was put on display by the Court of Gems as an "object lesson" to anyone who would defy them.

the fact the velvet girls and boys *needed* that business to earn their freedom. And Ola was even worse: for all her talk about how she had been a slave herself once, she still bought slaves and she still whored them out to anyone willing to put enough metal in her pockets.

And Butterbelly had wondered why Kihrin wanted to get out.

Kihrin scowled as he remembered his father's taunt, that Ola spoiled him like a prince. Kihrin couldn't be Ogenra. It wasn't possible. He knew it wasn't possible because he didn't look Quuros, which meant he didn't look like Quuros royalty either. He knew it wasn't possible too because someone—a friend, or enemy of his "royal" family—would have come looking for him.

Mostly, it wasn't possible because if Ola had had the slightest inkling he originated from a Royal House, she'd have turned him in for the reward years ago. She may have helped raise him; she may have taught him everything he ever knew about tricking a gull; she may have been his introduction to the Shadowdancers; she may have been his closest thing to a mother—but he would never underestimate her greed. Ola Nathera's number one priority in life was Ola Nathera, and anyone who failed to remember that deserved everything they got.

He wished he were Ogenra though, if just for Morea's sake.

Kihrin cringed when he thought of Morea. He hadn't wanted their conversation to turn out like that. He'd meant to be suave, to be charming. Instead, he'd turned on her at the first sign her interest was in any way ulterior. He'd lashed out at her when he liked her. He really liked her.

She hated him now and he deserved it.

He snapped back to awareness as he felt his father release his arm. He turned to see what was wrong. Had a pickpocket been foolish enough to try something? As he turned, he continued walking—and slammed into a wall.

A wall? In the middle of Peddler's Lane?

Kihrin heard shocked gasps from the few pedestrians still on the streets. His eyes focused on the white wall suddenly before him. Its stone bricks were rounded from age and tinged with green moss. Kihrin stared, not understanding how a wall had materialized in the middle of his shortcut. The wall stank too: seaweed and sulfur and old, stale sex.

A purple vein throbbed over the surface of a brick, pulsing where the rock burrowed in to form a small round recess. Then the stone rippled.

He inhaled sharply and looked up. He wasn't looking at a wall; he was looking at a stomach.

A *demon's stomach.*

The demon was enormous, twice as tall as Kihrin himself. Along his stomach (and the demon was clearly a "he"),* the demon's flesh was white. This turned to a sickly yellow-green along his massive bulging legs. His arms were bright red, slick and shining as if the creature had just plunged them to their pits in a vat of blood. The demon's face featured a wide grinning mouth that stretched from ear to pointed ear. The eyes were black voids with no whites, and it lacked a nose. The creature's hair was long, glowing white, but the ends had also turned scarlet as if they too had fallen into gore. A thick purplish-green tail, much like a crocodile's but longer and more flexible, thumped and twitched on the cobblestones with a mind of its own.

But more importantly than any of that, Kihrin *recognized* him.

It was the demon from the Kazivar House burglary.

"PAPPA, RUN!" Kihrin shoved his father into an open doorway.

The demon looked down at the teenager and grinned. His white teeth were sharp and jagged and there were far too many of them: they jutted from the demon's mouth like maggots escaping a wound.

HAIL TO THEE, LAWBREAKER.

"Oh Taja . . ." Kihrin prayed under his breath. He slid his knives into his hands even though he was certain they would be useless.† There was no question Pretty Boy had sent this demon after him, no question the demon had found him, and no question Kihrin was about to die. That thing looked big enough to bite off his head.

HAIL TO THEE, THIEF OF SOULS.

Kihrin decided his only chance was to run for it. He feinted right, dodged left, ran, and kept running. And for a few seconds, he thought he might make it, but then he felt a sharp slap against his ankles. He looked down to see the demon's purple-green tail wrap around his feet and lift him into the air.

He did what anyone would do when lifted into the air by a rampaging demon about to tear them apart on a public street: Kihrin screamed his head off.

HAIL TO THEE, PRINCE OF SWORDS.

"Let me go! Let me go! FUCK! Let me go!" Kihrin tried cutting the tail with his knife, but as he suspected, he might as well have been trying to chip stone with a silk handkerchief.

The demon lifted his whole body as easily as Kihrin might have lifted

---

*Probably not. Demons are not natural creatures, although they can, temporarily, take on physical forms. As such, demons do not possess any gender beyond which is assigned to them, or sometimes, the gender they decide has the most utilitarian value.

†Demons are, naturally, poorly understood entities, and despite the amount of research that has gone into deciphering these creatures, huge gaps in our knowledge remain. *The Lesser Key of Grizzst* is an obvious beginner's treatise, but I also find *The Cold Invasion* by Killus Vornigel to be an excellent perspective on these monsters and their interactions with the physical world.

a kitten by its scruff, and held Kihrin high in the air. This left Kihrin close to the demon's face, and far too close to that enormous maw. It was all too similar to a pose he might have struck before popping a grape in his mouth.

Just as Kihrin decided that he had nothing to lose by sticking a shiv in the demon's eye, the creature grabbed both his arms, holding them outstretched and helpless.

The demon laughed, a sound that would haunt Kihrin's nightmares for months afterward. He dangled close enough to the beast's mouth to see it was not empty, but filled with a writhing red tongue and white, crawling grubs. The stench was beyond description, a combination of blood, offal, and rotted sexual fluids that made Kihrin fight to keep from retching. The demon shook Kihrin by the feet.

Kihrin's tsali stone slid out from under his cloak and caught on his chin. The stone felt cold.

LONG DID I SEARCH FOR THE LION, BUT NOW I HAVE FOUND THE HAWK.

The demon's mouth drew close, and Kihrin closed his eyes rather than see what was about to happen. He tensed in expectation of his death.

There are some who would claim what came instead was more horrible. It was certainly more lingering.

He felt the demon's tongue move against his face, touch his cheek, the necklace, the indigo stone. As the demon did this, thoughts flowed into Kihrin's mind.

I OFFER THIS TO THEE, MY KING: A SMALL TASTE OF HORROR TO WHET THY APPETITE FOR THE FEAST OF SUFFERING.*

The mental images grew more intense: Kihrin with his old teacher Mouse, with Morea, with any number of girls and boys from the Veil velvet house. Kihrin saw himself doing things to them—terrible, nonconsensual things. The demon showed Kihrin image after image of himself as a cruel, sadistic monster of a man, a demon clothed in human skin who delighted in the pain and terror of those around him. He fed on it the way crocodiles feed on anyone foolish enough to come too close to the river. The demon dove deep into Kihrin's mind and pulled up the memories of everyone he'd ever known and loved, and then had Kihrin tear them apart—or murder, torture, or rape them. Even in the Copper Quarter, even for a boy who had grown up in Velvet Town, sins still

---

*Compare with the following prophecy from *A Study of Demonic Possession in Quur:* "Hail to the Lawbreaker; Hail to the Thief of Souls; Hail to the Prince of Swords. Long will we search for the lion, Until at last we find the hawk, Our king who will free us from ruin, The long suffering of our souls unlocked."

existed beyond his experience or comprehension. The demon emptied one atrocity after another into the boy's head until he had seen them all.

Kihrin screamed and screamed.

He had no way to gauge how long he hung there while the demon poured horrors into his mind, a seemingly unending orgy of filth and perversion.

Too long, by any account.

When Kihrin's voice tore and collapsed into gasping sobs, the pressure on his mind vanished, and he heard footsteps running toward him. He looked down the street. Fear warred with relief as he saw the Watchmen running toward them, swords drawn.

The demon threw back his head and roared, the sound of a lion accompanied by a thousand screaming cats. The demon let go of Kihrin's arms and let the boy dangle upside down from his tail. Then the demon picked up Surdyeh's harp.

"No—!" Kihrin's throat was rough and broken; the protest barely more than a whisper.

The demon grinned and swung the harp, case and all, down on the first Watchman to come within reach. Rather than braining the soldier, the man's head broke through strings and case fabric while the wooden frame trapped his arms. Had the demon let go of the harp at that point, the man would have spent the next five minutes freeing himself from the tangle of wood and string, but the demon did not let go. Rather, in one smooth, fluid motion, the monster pulled the struggling man closer. The demon opened that impossibly wide mouth wider still.

Kihrin flinched and looked away as the demon bit off the man's head with no more difficulty than Kihrin might bite into a mango. The dead man's blood splashed over Kihrin even as the body fell to the city street.

"Xaltorath. Your presence here is unwelcome," a loud voice proclaimed.

Kihrin thought that was a profoundly unnecessary statement of the obvious. He turned his head to see who would die next.

His perspective was skewed because he was upside down, but Kihrin didn't think the man was a member of the Watch. The newcomer was older, in his forties, with peppery hair and beard. A bear of a man, he was almost as wide as he was tall—and all of that shoulder, sinew, and hard muscle. He looked none too happy to see a demon prowling the City streets.

That made two of them.

Kihrin had never paid much attention when Surdyeh had lectured him about Quuros military ranks, but the man wore armor. The shiny metal cuirass on his chest glittered and flashed in the orange light of the sun. Behind him, a veritable legion of City Guard and military soldiers hung back to let the newcomer take point.

Xaltorath snarled and whirled on the man, while Kihrin swung from his tail like a lantern in monsoon season.

IMPUDENT MORTAL, YOU DARE TO CHALLENGE MY RIGHTS? I AM XALTORATH. I AM THE RAGE OF BATTLE, THE SIN OF LUST. I AM THE MOAN ON THE LIPS OF THE DAMNED.

The demon's mental "voice" raised to a cacophonous howl as he grew, literally grew, larger and more menacing.* Fresh, wet blood ran down the sides of his mouth, painting his white torso crimson.

"Go on. Keep talking." The soldier glanced at Kihrin only long enough to frown and note his presence before he returned his attention to the demon.

Unexpectedly, the demon's fury abated, although his grin was worse. ***I KNOW YOU.***

"Yes," the soldier agreed. "We've met before. You hid behind a child then too. Will you do so now as well?"

THIS BOY MEANS NOTHING TO YOU, BUT SHE WAS EVERYTHING. The demon chuckled. ***HER SCREAMS WERE SWEET TO MY EARS.***

The soldier's knuckles whitened around the pommel of his sword, but his voice stayed even. "Why this young man? Tired of hurting little girls?"

HIS TERROR TASTES AS SWEET AS THE HONEY FROM YOUR DAUGHTER'S THIGHS.

A tic started up on the soldier's face. He circled, never moving his eyes from the demon. "You weren't freed from your prison to molest little boys. Why are you here, Xaltorath?"

The demon's expression turned contemplative, as if he were catching up on old times with a friend he hadn't seen in years. ***I AM HERE BECAUSE I MUST BE. I AM HERE BECAUSE THE ANCIENT BINDING STILL HOLDS ALL MY KIND. I AM HERE FOR AS LONG AS YOU FOOLS CONTINUE TO SUMMON ME, UNTIL

---

*Demons are not generally locked into a single form, although they are not the same as mimics such as Talon who shape-change with disconcerting impunity. However, once a demon enters the physical world, they seem to keep their form for the duration of their stay. A demon's form may be dictated by the sorcerer who summons it, who might declare that a demon should only appear with "a seemly and handsome form" or demand that a demon appear "hideous and terrifying to scare his enemies." *The Lesser Key of Grizzst,* for example, recommends demanding a form the demon would find unpleasant, as a way of determining if the demon is truly under control. (I don't put much stock in this personally, since a demon is more than capable of putting up with a few hours as a cuddly puppy—if it means ripping his summoner to tiny pieces later on.)

THE DAY ALL OATHS ARE BROKEN, THE DAY ALL SOULS ARE FREED.*** He smiled. ***SOON NOW.***

"And which fool summoned you this time?"

WHY, THE– The demon stopped. ***WHY DO YOU TALK, AND NOT FIGHT?***

"I'm content to let you do the talking. You enjoy it more."

YOU SEEK TO DISTRACT ME!

"No, rot-breath, I seek to delay you." With that, the soldier closed in, the sword in his hands a glowing bar of reflected sunlight.

Xaltorath grinned wide, swung his deadly clawed arms back for the attack–and screamed as Kihrin shoved his knife up to the hilt in Xaltorath's left eye.

Kihrin missed the rest of the fight. Xaltorath's tail flicked out and tossed him aside like a broken doll. He crashed headfirst into the whitewashed wall of a local store.

Everything was fuzzy after that.

He heard Xaltorath's roaring bellow, the clanging clash of weapons, the screams of men, and the low chanting of a clear tenor voice. It all came from a faraway place.

Shaking, shuddering, Kihrin climbed to his feet. His eyes wouldn't focus. His hair felt wet and sticky. The blood on his face was his own. He was burning up too–the sapphire around his neck felt scalding.

He knew (in a distracted it's-somebody-else's-problem kind of way) that he was injured, maybe mortally injured. Part of him wanted to sleep. Another part of him wanted to throw up. The rest of him though–the rest of him was filled with a kind of searing white-hot rage that Kihrin had only experienced once before in his life. The desire for vengeance was so strong it overrode all other instincts. That anger gave him the strength to stand and the strength to stagger back to the intersection where he had been attacked.

The soldier was still there, along with lots of guards and a newcomer: a man in a patchwork brown sallí cloak. He looked as out of place as a Shadowdancer thief at a Watchmen retirement party. Kihrin had no idea who the newcomer was, but since he wasn't a demon and he wasn't a guard, Kihrin decided to ignore him until he became important.

There was no sign of the demon besides the lingering traces of unnatural red light and the odor of filth.

"How did you make it here so quickly?" the large soldier with the sword asked the man with the patchwork cloak, as Kihrin staggered toward them. "I only just dispatched a man to find you."

"Taja was smiling on us. One of my agents alerted me–dear Tya, are you all right, young man?" The newcomer turned toward Kihrin as he approached.

Kihrin ignored the question. It was a stupid question. He would never be all right again. He blinked at the fellow in the patchwork cloak. The newcomer was a plain-looking man in his twenties, although he had the chestnut skin and high cheekbones of a Marakori to provide a small amount of exotic flair. He had dark eyes and straight black hair that wanted to wander in every direction, kept in check by a plain brass circlet worn on his forehead. Kihrin wondered if he was with the Revelers Guild, and if he attracted much work with a cloak so threadbare. He seemed more like a farmer than a performer. Kihrin decided he was probably some kind of servant or valet of the soldier. "Is he dead?" Kihrin ground his teeth together to keep from listing.

"Qoran, catch him. He'll fall," said the smaller man.

The soldier reached for Kihrin, put a hand on his shoulder, and Kihrin jerked himself away, fighting the most awful flashbacks. "Don't touch me!"

The soldier sheathed his sword and held up his hands in a way he no doubt meant to seem nonthreatening. "Son, you need to calm down—"

"Don't call me son," Kihrin hissed. "Is he dead?"

The two men blinked at him, surprised. The soldier glanced back at the gory mess that used to be one of the guards, the shattered remains of a double-strung harp wrapped around his upper torso. "Very."

"Qoran, he means the demon," the smaller man corrected. His gaze lingered, eyes still narrowed, on Kihrin, as if the young man reminded him of someone he couldn't quite place. "Xaltorath isn't dead, no. You did, however, help send him back to Hell for a while."

The soldier stepped forward, although he didn't make a move to touch Kihrin a second time. "We need to know what Xaltorath said to you, young man. Every detail, every word could be of vital importance. How much can you remember? What did he want from you? Why did he let you live?"

"He ruined my knife." Kihrin saw it lying in the middle of the street, twisted and warped as if someone had returned it to the forge and left it there. *Ruined my knife. Ruined my life.* He laughed out loud at the rhyme, but then he quieted again. Stupidly, all he could think of was how upset Landril Attuleema would be when they didn't show up for their scheduled performance.

The soldier was less amused. "Argas, take your knife! Do you have any idea how many will die if some fool summoner starts another Hellmarch? When demon princes get loose from Hell, they don't just throw a party. They summon more demons! Answer my questions, boy." The soldier reached out to grab him, but let his hand fall short at the last second.

Kihrin flinched back anyway, but his jaw clenched in a stubborn line.

Something snapped inside him, some better sense that might have kept him from saying something stupid to a man who could have him thrown into a pit—just by snapping his fingers. Kihrin drew himself up without wobbling, without listing, without throwing up, even though the need to do all those things lurked in waiting ambush. "That monster destroyed my father's harp. How are we supposed to make a living? How are we supposed to eat? That may mean nothing to you, but it means a lot to me."*

"General, wait." The man with the patchwork cloak held up a hand before he focused his attention on Kihrin. "That was your father's harp? You're Surdyeh's son?"

Kihrin meant to keep yelling, but the soft question cut the strings of his anger. "How did you know . . ." He blinked. "You know my father?"

"Indeed." Fond remembrance wrestled with old pain behind the man's eyes. "We were friends, once." He examined Kihrin, his expression unreadable.

"Wait, my father! Where is he? He was right here—" Kihrin hadn't seen him since he pushed Surdyeh through the doorway. He hadn't been injured, had he? Kihrin could imagine his father slumped up against some alcove, leaking his life away into a gutter while no one paid him the least attention. He turned back to the soldier—wait, general—who seemed like the one with the authority to help. "You have to find him. He's blind. He probably didn't get very far."

The General stared at him, unfriendly and hard as drussian. Then he snapped his fingers and gestured to one soldier nearby. "Captain Jarith, have your men search the area. See if they can find a blind man, possibly hiding, named Surdyeh. Please escort him back with every courtesy. We must reunite him with his son."

The young soldier saluted. "Yes, General. Right away."

"Thank you," Kihrin said. "Thank you." He closed his eyes in relief.

Closing his eyes was a mistake, however. The anger that had been keeping him conscious retreated. His world tilted as darkness wrapped around him.

"Quickly—" he heard the General say.

Kihrin might have paid more attention to what happened next, but he was too busy fainting.

---

*One wonders if Kihrin occasionally forgot that he had a great deal of money saved up, or if he just lost himself in a role, that of a musician's young apprentice. I suppose the easiest way to keep from spending that money would be to forget he had it.

11: THE COMING STORM

(Kihrin's story)

Eventually, I went up on deck. Staying in our room felt like being trapped in a wooden crate: the passenger cabin on board *The Misery* was smaller than a water closet. It fit four people, in theory.

I was in a mood to find whoever had come up with this "theory" and beat their head against the railing.

A bulky, Zheriaso-built ship, *The Misery* shuttled slaves bought in Kishna-Farriga and Zherias to Quur, where the good citizens of the Empire bought them for a variety of unsavory uses. The ship possessed the usual number of masts and sails, and a deck of slave-rowers in the bowels— to speed passage in poor wind or navigate tricky port dockings.

I am more familiar with the rowers' galley on *The Misery* than I care to remember, even now.

The slave holds were further divided into levels, or 'tween decks, by thick iron gratings. These quarters housed the majority of the slaves with ceilings so low that a small woman wouldn't have room to stand. The 'tween decks made our passenger cabin seems like the height of grand privilege.

The cargo deck had been emptied of all but trade goods (maridon tea, sugar, barrels of sasabim brandy, Eamithon pottery) when *The Misery* had brought me to Kishna-Farriga as a slave, but no longer. Captain Juval had stayed in port only for as much time as was necessary to drop off his cargo and pick up the next batch of victims. He probably planned to buy more in Zherias* before the trip across the Galla Sea to Quur. I wondered how many times he'd made the trip, how many lives he had bought and sold.

I took perverse pleasure in putting myself where the Captain could see me. Watching his eyes slide right past me without recognition helped

---

*One hundred and twenty-five years ago, the King of Zherias, Shogu, attempted to outlaw the practice of slaving, traditionally one of the primary Zheriaso tradecrafts (along with piracy and mercantilism). He survived less than five days past his declaration, and his eldest child, Sinka, promptly legalized it again.

smooth the occasional impulse to use a dagger to sever his spine. Juval was in a sour mood too, growling and snapping at every crew member who came near.

Perhaps he'd heard the news of my final sale price. He'd been in such a hurry to get rid of me that he'd taken a flat fee instead of staying in Kishna-Farriga for a percentage. Juval didn't realize he'd gotten the better end of the bargain.

Teraeth sat on one of the grates covering the slave holds, fingers laced around the iron bars as he stared down. The sailors gave him a wide berth.

I wasn't surprised. He might look like a Quuros and sound like a Quuros, but the illusion wrapped around him couldn't hide his menace.

Teraeth looked up and saw me watching.

We stared at each other for a few moments. He motioned me over.

I avoided looking into the hold.

"I'm sorry when I said you were nothing but a slaver. Khaemezra explained things, and—"

"Look." He pointed through the grating.

I felt no compulsion to follow his orders, a reminder his mother carried my gaesh. "I know what slaves look like, thanks. I just wanted to say—"

"Look, damn you!" He reached up, grabbed the corner of my robe, and dragged me to his level. "This is what you are."

I pulled at his fingers with my hands. "You don't need to remind me I'm a slave."

"You think I mean you're a slave?" He scoffed with a whispery sharp voice. "*They* don't care that you're a slave. Look at them. Really look. Do you see them? Men, women, children. Some of them won't live to see the end of this journey. Others will start their lives of concubinage early and rough. They come from a dozen nations, some from villages so small they didn't know they had a 'nation.' Most of them don't speak Guarem, or any language you know. They would gladly give their souls to be where you are, too valuable to be thrown in a cell like rotting meat. Instead they'll die of starvation, or flux, or not have enough air to breathe during a storm. Look at them. There is no hope in their eyes. They don't even have the strength to cry, or ask why this has been done to them. They can only whisper the question, the way a madman shouts the same phrase over and over, growing soft and quiet until there is only silence . . ."

I choked off a sob and tore his hand from me. "I don't need—"

"You're Quuros. This is your legacy. This is your gift to the world: ship after ship of pain, sailing the seas to sate your people's lust and cruelty and your thirst to conquer everything. Don't you dare look away from your birthright. This is what the wizard Grizzst created when he bound the demons. This is what your Emperor Simillion brought to the world when he claimed the Crown and Scepter. This is the way of life Atrin Kandor died to save."

I sat down on the grating, numb.

"How many slaves have you known? How many have you taken for granted, dismissed as just another unchangeable facet of Quuros life?" Teraeth settled back on his heels, fingers pressed against the bars to balance himself. "You asked who we are, and I will tell you who we are *not*. We are not people who would ever *do this*."

I didn't answer for a long time.

Finally, I whispered, "That doesn't make what you do right."

"No, but for every life I take, I give others their lives back. When I meet Thaena in the Afterlife, my head is held high and my conscience is clean."

"I can't do anything to free these people."

"That's true if you believe it, but make no mistake—it is *only* true because you believe it."

I stared out at the sea. Seagulls had followed us from Kishna-Farriga. They would stay with us for a few miles yet before they decided the scraps weren't coming fast enough. The salt air filled my nose and the sound of rigging stretched and groaned against my ears. If I listened, I could just make out the muted sound of crying. The ship didn't smell of anything but salted wood and tar. More awful smells would come later.

I thought long and hard on the irony of being lectured on freedom by the assassin who owned me.

"Juval used a cat-o'-nine-tails on you, didn't he?" Teraeth asked after a long silence.

"He had questions. He got all cranky on me when I wouldn't answer them."

"Do you want me to kill him?"

I looked sideways at the vané. "Don't you think that might delay our arrival in Zherias, just a little?"

"His first mate looks capable enough."

The idea made me shudder. If I had nightmares anymore, first mate Delon would haunt them. "Delon's worse than Juval. Much worse."

Teraeth stared at me. The line of his jaw turned rigid and he looked away. "I'll remember that."

"Besides, Tyentso will take it personally if you start killing off her crew. Even you might have a problem with her."

"Tyentso?"

"The ship's sea witch. Remember how you wanted to know if the Captain keeps one? The answer's yes. Tough as drussian. She's the one who gaeshed me. I haven't seen her yet, but she's around here somewhere.

She spends most of her time by herself. She's like a hermit in a cave, except her cave is on a ship."

Teraeth smiled in a way that reminded me of tigers scenting the air for prey. "If my mother can handle Relos Var, I don't think a hedge witch will be much problem." He flexed his fingers around the bars.

"Show me around the ship," he said after a pause. "I want to be familiar with the deck plan when things go wrong."

"Why? You think something's going to happen?"

"I think Relos Var gave up on you too easily." He turned to stare out at the water. "That's not his reputation."

"So, he'll make another attempt?" I didn't need to ask. In my heart, I knew Teraeth was right. Relos Var wasn't finished with me yet.

He chewed on the end of a finger. "He'd have to know where we are. My mother shields us both against scrying, and you've always been hidden from magical attempts to locate you. No one is tracking you down using magic."

I scowled. "It's been done."

"Not easily."

"They had to summon a demon prince to do so, so yeah. We should be fine. Unless Var's into that kind of thing."

"He's been known to dabble." Teraeth looked nervous.

That made me nervous. If there was going to be trouble, the last place I wanted to be was trapped on a slave ship, a thousand miles out at sea.

As Taja would have it, that's exactly where trouble found us.

12: Behind the Veil

(Talon's story)

Morea poured herself a glass of water from the pitcher at her bedside, swished the water around in her mouth, spat it back out again. She repeated the process until the tang was gone.

The small room was barely furnished once one looked past the tapestries, lewd sculptures, labial mosaics of Caless, and the priapic offering dishes of her lovers. There was a bed, a sideboard, and an armoire. A pitcher, ceramic mugs, and a washbasin rested on the sideboard. The armoire held the few clothes Madam Ola had given her.

The bed held a drunken merchant named . . . Something. Hallith? She didn't remember. He'd been too intoxicated to do much, and the smell of his boozy breath on her face had set her skin crawling. She'd cooed and stroked him and prayed he'd be content with suckling.

Fortunately, he was.

It wasn't easy for Morea to come to a place like this. She knew her lot was better than many, but she still remembered a time when a room this size wouldn't have been fit for her use as a water closet. Baron Mataris hadn't been handsome, or charming, or even young, but he had been rich, and not so unkind to his slaves that she didn't regard his memory with fondness. If she and her sister hadn't been happy at least they had been pampered, and the men and women that Baron Mataris gave them to believed in daily baths.

Unlike some. Her eyes flickered over to the form of her customer, already snoring.

Madam Ola told her that on nights when Morea did not dance, she might expect to make two or three thrones in tips. The madam allowed her people to keep their tips, although she was under no obligation to do so. That meant, if Morea saved up every throne, every chance, every chalice, she might have enough to pay off her slave price in five years. Five years of this. Five years of taking all comers, of lying on the mat under the grunting, thrusting attention of drunken sailors, miners, merchants, and anyone else who paid Ola Nathera enough metal.

Morea had one consolation: the possibility there might be an end to this. Ola allowed for the potential of buying her freedom. Baron Mataris had never done so.

Ola herself was an enigma to Morea. The woman was a legend with a dozen stories about her origins, all of them probably lies. Ola didn't use the veils so many Zheriaso wore outside the borders of their island home, so it was obvious to all that she had once been a wild beauty. Her skin was midnight, her eyes like the ocean depths, her soft curled hair tied in elegant knots. Yes, a great beauty—or she would have been if time and a fondness for sweets had not rounded out all the edges.

Morea had already heard a dozen stories during her brief stay at the Shattered Veil. How Ola Nathera had been a Zheriaso princess, and had run from an unwelcome marriage. That Ola was in fact an infamous witch, banished from her country for enchanting the king. Or, Morea's favorite: that Ola has once been a slave girl herself, who'd earned her freedom and her fortune in a single night unwittingly spent with the Emperor. Her beauty so charmed the man that he'd bestowed a necklace upon her of impossibly rare star tear diamonds. With such treasure, she purchased her slave price, bought the Shattered Veil Club velvet house, and never slept with a man again.

Morea didn't know about the necklace or the Emperor, but she was sure the last part was true. Ola looked at her the same way most men did. And Morea had spoken to the others enough to know that when Ola helped herself to her own slaves, it was not the boys she ordered into her bed.

Halith? Harith? Halis? Whatever-his-name snored, turned over, pushed his arm up over his head like a cat, and started to drool into his beard. He was her first customer of the afternoon, and she wondered if he had come in for sex or just to get out of the heat. Morea stared at him for a moment before deciding she needed fresh air in the worst possible way.

Morea stepped out of the crib into the courtyard. The heat was a tangible beast, a monster that stalked and hunted everyone in its path. Very little breeze penetrated the opening in the central courtyard; it was an afternoon set to broil on an open flame. The soothing color of the teal-green sky overhead mocked her, vibrating against the red-orange heat of the sun.

The servant's entrance at the back of the Club swung open as Morea heard the voice of the old musician, Surdyeh, raised in anger.

"Careful! Careful!! Don't trip on that third step."

"Pappa, I'm *fine*."

Morea inhaled sharply when the pair came into view. A soldier supported Kihrin, while two more guided the blind harpist. Despite his protestations to the contrary, the young man didn't look at all fine. Dried

blood matted and clumped his black hair in ugly snarls. Crimson splattered his sallí cloak. Other unwholesome stains lent their aspect to the
air of a man with serious injuries. His father appeared uninjured, but the
look of anger, frustration, and worry on his face was clear from across
the courtyard.

Morea ran inside to fetch Madam Ola, and when they returned, they
found two of the soldiers standing stiffly at attention. The third, the one
who had been helping Kihrin, was talking to the blind musician.

"I told you," Surdyeh snapped. "We thank you for your courtesy, but
we'll do fine. We don't need charity."

"Pappa, you're being rude."

The soldier, tall and dark and beautiful, smiled as if he found the old
man's ire adorable. He started to say something.

"Bright-Eyes . . ." Madam Ola rushed across the courtyard. She threw
her arms around Kihrin and pressed him close. "My baby!"

"Mmm, mmm mmmm," Kihrin said, his voice cut off by the flesh of
Ola's bosom. He struggled to escape her embrace.

Ola pushed herself away, putting her hands protectively on Kihrin's
shoulders. "What did you do to my angel?" she demanded.

The soldier spread his hands in a gesture of helpless innocence. "It
wasn't me, ma'am. Your, uh . . . angel . . . ran into a demon."

She stared at him, blinking, and then looked at Kihrin. "Was Faris
causing some kind of—"

"No, Ola," Surdyeh said. "Not a metaphorical demon. A real one."

"What?"

The old man shook his head. "The blasted monster was waiting in
the center of the street, Ola. I've never heard of anything like it. If I
hadn't smelled it up ahead, I might have run right into the damn thing.
I heard it kill one of the guards. We were lucky to escape with our lives."

Kihrin gave Surdyeh a look so filled with venom that Morea flinched.
"One of us *did* run into it."

"At least it didn't kill you, boy," Surdyeh said, his face and voice peevish.

"A small favor," Kihrin said. Then he shook his head, and a shudder
passed through him. He gestured to the guard. "Madam Ola, this is Captain Jarith."

Jarith took Ola's hand and kissed it, smiling roguishly. He looked
nineteen or twenty years old, and far too young to be a captain of anything. "A real pleasure, Miss Nathera. My father's told me a lot of stories
about you."

The smile froze on Ola Nathera's face. "Oh?" She looked wary.

The Captain's grin widened. "Why, yes. He used to say you were the
most beautiful courtesan who ever stepped foot in the Upper Circle, that

once there were a thousand men lined up just for the right to be ignored by you." He paused and winked at the whorehouse madam. "Of course, he never says it where Mother might hear."

She laughed, hearty and full. "Ah! Well, the joys of youth, yes? You should come by sometime. I'll find a special someone for you." She turned, realized Morea was still nearby, and gestured toward her. "This one is new, and quite lovely, yes?"

The Captain smiled, shrugged. "My apologies, Miss Nathera—"

"Ola. You must call me Ola, you handsome devil."

He grinned. "Ola then. No offense, but I'm afraid the kind of woman I prefer doesn't tend to end up in a brothel." His eyes nonetheless slid over Morea's form. "You are lovely, though. I don't suppose you know how to use a sword?" He questioned her directly, and improperly, with nothing in his manner to suggest he realized how he was breaking slave etiquette. No doubt, he was aware that Ola wouldn't dare call him on it.

Morea swallowed and shook her head.

The Captain sighed. "Pity." He dusted himself off and turned to Kihrin, whose gaze of thankful admiration had turned to something suspiciously like a glare. "The invitation stands. If you're still interested, come by the House of the Red Sword at eight bells. It's in the Ruby District, two streets out from the Great Forge. I'll leave word with the Watchmen."

"Don't expect him," Surdyeh growled.

"I'll be there," Kihrin said, glaring at his father.

"What's going on?" Ola demanded.

"I have to return to my duties," Captain Jarith apologized. "It was a pleasure to meet you, Ola, Miss, Surdyeh, Kihrin." He tilted his head in Kihrin's direction. "You did well back there. If you ever want a job, we are always looking for soldiers with your kind of instincts. A man could do worse than starting service with a recommendation for valor from a general."

"Thank you, but umm . . ." Kihrin grimaced and looked toward his father.

"I understand. Oh, before I go. What was that slave girl's name?"

Kihrin glanced at Morea, worried at his lower lip a little, then smiled. "Your sister's name, Morea?"

Morea's heart beat frantically when she heard that, and she put her hand to her mouth. "Talea—"

Kihrin looked back to the Captain. "It's Talea."

"I have a few friends at the Octagon. I'll see what I can find out."

"Thank you, Captain."

Jarith nodded and left, taking his guards with him.

Madam Ola waited until the soldiers were gone and then turned on Surdyeh and Kihrin. "By all the gods! What just happened?"

"Qoran Milligreest, the High General of the Great and Holy Empire of Quur," Surdyeh began with a mocking, angry voice, "has just invited our pride and joy to come over to his *house.*" He inhaled deeply. "He wants to replace my harp the demon smashed up. At least, that's the official story." Surdyeh's tone said he didn't believe it for one minute, for one second. He expected his son would put one foot inside this General's house and be set upon by a hundred guards with crossbows and pikes.

"General Milligreest?" Ola's eyes were wide and shocked.

"Ola, would you knock some sense into him?" Kihrin hooked a thumb in his father's direction. "The General saved my life. The demon would have killed me if he hadn't stepped in. Then he orders his man to heal me and he even offers to replace Surdyeh's harp with one of his own. He'll probably want to commission a performance. How is that bad? Taja! Pappa's been telling me for years how I should try to make influential contacts—'never let an opportunity pass, boy'—and when I finally do, he doesn't want me to go!"

"We don't need his charity."

"It's not charity, damn it. It's a *reward.* I helped fight off a demon. I put a knife in its eye! Come on. His man said he was an old friend of yours."

Surdyeh looked confused, then frustrated, and finally angry. "*What* man? There wasn't anyone there that I'd trust."

Ola swallowed hard, and she looked from Kihrin to Surdyeh and back again. She was breathing through her nose—flat, shallow breaths—and her eyes were wide. Her mouth pressed into a thin line, and behind her back, where no one could see it but Morea, the woman's hand slowly bunched the fabric of her skirt into a tight knot, so hard that Morea could see the white of Ola's knucklebones through her black skin. The hand shook.

At first, Morea thought the woman was scared, but she quickly revised her opinion. Morea had been a slave for most of her life, sold along with her sister by a mother who couldn't support them when their father ran off. Like most people who grew up as slaves, she was adept at reading the emotions of her owners, a survival skill.

No, Ola Nathera wasn't scared. She was *angry.*

Ola smiled as if trying to cheer a small child who'd banged his knee. "Sweetheart?"

Kihrin looked at her with suspicion in his blue eyes.

"Pay no mind to your pappa. He's had a fright. How could he not, what with you almost getting killed out there today? I mean, Bright-Eyes, look at you. Is that your blood?"

The young man tugged at the cloth of his sallí cloak. "Most of it isn't. They healed what was."

"Well now, no wonder he's upset."

The old man shook his head. "Ola, don't do—"

"Hush, honey," she cautioned him. "You just let Momma Ola take care of everything." Ola gestured toward Kihrin. "You gonna go see the General like that? Covered in blood and muck and dressed like a gutter rat under that ripped cloak? Your clothes all torn and looking like you just crawled out from under the garbage dump?"

"I—" Kihrin shifted uncomfortably.

"No, I didn't think so." Ola smiled. Morea watched her warm to the role of attentive mother. "You been through a lot, Bright-Eyes. A lot. You need to take care of yourself." Ola turned to shout something, and stopped. "What are you still doing here, girl? And what was that business about a sister?"

"I thought—"

"Never mind. You take Kihrin here back to my private bath and clean him up."

Morea chewed her lip, looking at Kihrin. He wouldn't return her stare. "I have a customer . . ." She pointed back to her crib.

"Never you mind. I'll take care of that. Don't you worry about your customers for tonight. My angel could use a little cheering, so that's what I want you to do. Cheer him."

Kihrin glanced up. "Thanks, Ola, but I don't need it. I know where the bath is. I don't need any help taking one."

"Who said you needed help? Sweet cheeks, when you need help taking a bath it stops being any fun. I never met nobody who didn't like to have their back scrubbed by someone cute and willing.* Now you two scoot. I'm gonna tell your pappa he's being a fool and then I'll fetch you some dinner." She was the definition of attentive, loving care.

Morea watched Kihrin stare at Ola for a moment, then he smiled a dazzling white grin that would have melted glaciers in the Dragonspires. "Yeah, I guess you're right, Ola. Thanks." He hopped to his feet and walked to the back. Halfway there, he turned and looked at Morea. "Coming?"

She looked from Kihrin to Ola. The brothel madam smiled at her, making shooing motions toward her apartment in the back of the courtyard.

Morea followed Kihrin, but he didn't wait for her. He already had the door open and was holding it for her when she arrived.

---

*"Willing" is a debatable term given Morea's status as a slave.

The smile on his face vanished as soon as he closed the door. He leaned against the wood and shut his eyes as if he was tired or in pain.

"Is there something wrong?" Morea asked, then bit her lip. "Oh, how stupid of me. Of course, something's wrong."

He opened his eyes and smiled at her. At least the corners of his mouth turned up. She didn't consider it a real smile; there was too much pain in his eyes.

"Yeah," Kihrin agreed after a moment, then he straightened. "Do you think I oversold the 'little boy who believes anything his mother tells him' routine out there?"

"I'm not sure . . . Maybe a little at the end."

"That's what I thought too. Let's hope she's too distracted to notice."

"Kihrin, what is going on? What happened?"

He held up his hand as if to ward off the question. "I'll explain. I promise I'll explain. Just give me a minute." He crossed the room.

"As you say, but—" Her voice faltered as she tracked his movement. Her mouth fell open as she stared at the apartment interior.

Ola's front room was large enough to fit six or seven brothel cribs. Bright murals of verdant jungle, birds, and sky painted the walls. There were animals Morea was familiar with and snake creatures Morea had only heard of in stories. Striped carpets of exotic patterns and lush colors lined the floors, woven from deep garnets and emeralds, amethysts and sapphires, rubies and bright glittering ribbons of gold. Sequins sewn into the weave made the rugs look jeweled in the light. Chests of carved dark woods served as tables to hold vases of peacock feathers. Lanterns of stained glass and thin mica hung from the ceiling, along with crystals and bells and little glass trinkets. Masks of every description hung from the ceiling: paper masks and clay masks, carved wooden masks and stone masks, cloth masks and metal masks.

A stuffed raven perched on a fake tree limb that jutted from the wall, above a cauldron filled with twigs and branches and bones. The scent of spices hung thick and heavy in the air: myrrh, cinnamon, and rose. Opposite the door they had entered, a curtain of jade beads served as a privacy screen for the room beyond.

A large table sat in the center of the room on top of a jaguar skin. The table's three legs resembled ravens attempting flight, each bird prevented by the python encircling its lower body. A sheet of solid glass rested on top of the base. On top of that rested a silk pouch that appeared to hold something square, a mirror of black obsidian, and a low-rimmed leather platter used in high-end dice games. Two chairs sat on opposite sides of the table, but not much else in the room was useful for sitting. There were no lounge chairs, no couches, and no beds. This was not a room for romantic liaisons.

She wanted to ask Kihrin about this room: what it was for, why it looked this way. She took one look at him and decided the questions could wait.

Kihrin walked over to a cabinet and found an earthenware jug. He brought it and two goblets back to the table, before sitting and covering his face with his fingers. His whole body, Morea realized, was trembling.

"Kihrin?" She smiled at the young man. "Would you like to have me? If it would make you feel better, I would gladly–"

"No!" Kihrin raised his head. "No. Please. I don't–I can't–"

She frowned. A part of her wanted to feel hurt and offended at the rejection, but his shame was directed inward. He was still shaking, his eyes wet, on the verge of tears. She was familiar enough with the signs. Morea poured his cup of wine and took the liberty of finishing the second cup for herself. "Do you have anyone you can talk to about what happened?"

"Ola–but I can't tell Ola. She wouldn't understand–"

"She might. But anyone can see she's a mother to you, and that's not the right kind of person for this. You need a friend, not a parent."

He grimaced, picked up the wine cup, and drank deep. "I don't really have any then. I guess–well, it turns out they were all Faris's friends. We don't speak anymore."

"You should talk to someone. This sort of hurt festers inside the soul if you ignore it. Ignore it for long enough and you will begin to convince yourself that what happened was your fault, that you deserved to be treated this way–"

He stared at her with wide, frightened eyes. "What if it *is* my fault? Gods, how could I have been stupid enough to think I could outrun a *demon*. I am the world's biggest idiot. Those wizards will summon it again, find out it didn't kill me, and they'll send it back to finish the job. Oh, Taja, help me, what if next time it finds me here at the Veil?"

"Wait. I thought it was an accident? Just some monster you ran into on the street?"

"No. It was hunting me. It was looking for me. It's going to come back, Morea. I know it will."

"Then you'll have to do something," Morea reasoned, fighting her own fear. "Why doesn't your father want you to see the High General?"

"I don't know. It makes no sense at all. There was another man there who claimed he was a friend of my father's, but when I woke up, he was gone. Maybe . . ." Kihrin frowned. "I guess the idea that they used to be friends doesn't mean much. Faris and I used to be friends too, and look how well that worked out."

"What was his name?"

A helpless, defeated look came over Kihrin. "He didn't say. And you heard my pappa. He denied he knew anyone there."

"Even so, if the General fought that demon, he'd take the threat seriously, wouldn't he? I've heard of the High General. My old master used to say that the Milligreest family have been soldiers in the service of the Empire for almost as long as the Empire has existed."

Kihrin grimaced. "Xaltorath—the demon—knew him, Morea. Knew him well enough to taunt him while they fought." He shuddered. "I think that demon murdered one of Milligreest's daughters."

"Then you know Milligreest won't turn you away. Ask the High General for help."

He ducked his head. "I'm not used to thinking of the guard as people I can run to for help."

"Those aren't guards, Kihrin. Those are soldiers. Army. And the army takes the threat of demons very seriously."

"I guess . . . I wasn't thinking."

"Be thankful you have me around to set you straight." She laughed, and he chuckled.

Then his eyes clouded as he looked at her, and he shuddered and turned away.

"It's not your fault," Morea told him. "It's the fault of those wizards who summoned that thing. It's the fault of that demon. You didn't do anything—" She raised her hand when she saw him about to interrupt. "Nothing you could've done deserves this."

Kihrin reached for his wine cup with unsteady hands. "You talk like that demon raped me."

Morea blinked. "Didn't he? I assumed—"

Kihrin flinched, and almost dropped the cup. He set it down awkwardly on the table and drew his legs up onto the chair, so his arms wrapped around his thighs, his head resting on his knees. He hugged himself and trembled.

Morea stretched a hand toward him.

"Don't touch me," he said with a muffled voice. "Please don't. It's not safe."

"I won't hurt you."

He looked up at her with wet and shining eyes. "Morea, I didn't say it wasn't safe for *me*."

She sat back in her chair in surprise. "Tell me," she finally said. "Tell me what happened."

"He . . ." Kihrin inhaled, shut his eyes, and started over. "He put thoughts into my head. Terrible thoughts. Memories. Some of them mine, but twisted. Others not mine at all. No one hurt me. I was the one

hurting everyone else. I was hurting people I know and people I've
never even met before. Doing things to them. Killing them and worse. I
liked it." His voice was rough with horror. "Those thoughts are still there.
Those memories lurk. I can't–I don't trust myself."

"No," Morea said. "No. That's the lie. He was tricking you. That's not
you. You're good. You could never enjoy anything like that."

His laugh was half a sob. "Morea, you've known me for a few weeks,
and only done more than exchanged stares with me today. Have you
forgotten this afternoon already? You don't think I have it in me to be
mean? To be petty?"

She looked away.

"What if it wasn't a trick? What if my reactions were my own and I
really do enjoy hurting people? What if he only showed me what I truly
am?"

"No," she protested. "Someone like that wouldn't have ordered me to
not touch them–for my own protection. I have known evil men. I have
known men who love no sound so much as the screams of their victims.
They don't feel guilt about the hurt they cause. They don't obsess about
whether or not they are good people. This demon wasn't trying to show
you the truth about yourself. He wanted to hurt you. What could cause
more lingering pain than this?"

His smile was awkward. "I pray you're right."

Morea looked at the rim of the wine cup. "You said he showed you
doing terrible things to people you've never met?"

He nodded. "Yes. Except there was a girl–" He scowled and didn't
finish.

"I'm so sorry."

"It's not what you think." Kihrin shook his head. "She probably wasn't
real. She looked so strange. I don't think she was human."

"What did she look like?"

"She had red hair," Kihrin said, after an uncomfortable silence. "Not
hennaed red hair, like yours. Her hair was either black or the color of
blood, depending on the angle, and she only had a single stripe of it
running from her forehead to her neck. Her eyes were fire, all flickering
red and orange. And her skin was odd. Most of her body was normal
enough, but her hands and feet were black, like she wore gloves and
stockings."

A strange thing happened to Kihrin as he talked about the phantom
girl; a faraway look caught in his eyes. He released some of the tension,
some of the horror, that had kept him a trembling prisoner. He didn't
seem to notice.

Morea frowned. *Just exactly what had that demon done to this poor boy's
mind?*

"From the hair I'd say she sounds like a girl from Jorat," Morea said. "My old master bought a slave girl from that dominion once. Everyone told him not to; they make poor slaves. The old bloods–the ones who trace their ancestry back to the Jorat god-king–they aren't human anymore. There's something in them that's wild, and stays wild, and will not be broken."*

"What happened?"

"She ripped out my master's throat with her teeth and took her own life. My master's daughter didn't want to own a seraglio, so she sold us off. That's how my sister and I were separated."

"I'm sorry."

"Now you know not to ever buy a Joratese slave." Morea leaned forward. "Is she beautiful, this demon-brought Jorat-girl?"

His expression faltered for a moment before he smiled. "Not as beautiful as you."

"You're lying. I can tell."

"Jealous?" He was trying to tease, and not succeeding.

"Can't I be? She is, isn't she? Very beautiful, I mean."

"Maybe a little," he said, looking away.

"Ah, and to think just this afternoon I was the girl who made you blush."

He looked guilty then, and Morea chided herself for teasing him when he'd had so much horror in his day. "Is that some sort of game?" she asked, looking at the silk-clad block and the dice cup on the table.

"Not at all. Fate cards. Ola uses them." He picked up the silk pouch and withdrew a deck of cards. Kihrin pulled a card off the top and showed her an intricately drawn miniature of a silver-haired angel flipping a coin: Taja, Goddess of Luck.

"I don't understand."

"Ola sells more than sex here." He shuffled the cards with one hand, flipping them in front and behind each other with nimble fingers.

"You're good at that."

"Ola's better. She's the one who taught me." He paused. "She didn't mean it, you know. About letting me see the General. She's as set against it as Pappa. I know her too well." He offered her the deck, fanned out so he couldn't see the faces. "Take a card. Don't tell me what it is."

---

*The Joratese culture, and particularly their god-touched nobility, survive in large part because they were created as a servitor race to the centaurs that ruled that area. When Quur invaded, the Joratese eagerly sided with the Empire to overthrow the god-king Korshal. The Joratese were quick to offer their sons and daughters to Quuros soldiers, who were entitled to landholdings in the new dominion. Eventually, this resulted in the current Jorat dominion. It takes a dim view of outsiders, or the magic that resulted in their original enslavement.

She smiled and plucked a single card from the deck. "She did seem upset."

"Mad as old Nemesan.* And I don't know why. But I know her. Hell, I was her apprentice when I was a kid. She'd never tell me not to do something, not if she was serious about it. She'd just fix the odds. You picked the Pale Lady."

Morea laughed and flipped the card over, revealing Thaena. "How did you do that?"

"I fixed the odds."

Kihrin shuffled the cards and dealt, this time dealing cards on the table in a cross pattern with a card in the corners to form a square. He started turning over cards, the scowl on his face only increasing as he did. She studied the pictures with interest, but she didn't know enough about fate cards to understand what they meant.

"That good?" she finally asked.

Kihrin stared at the cards blank-faced. "You know, I think that's the worst reading I've ever seen. With a day like this, I shouldn't be surprised."

"But what do the cards say?"

"Oh, you know, the usual stuff. Death, loss, pain, suffering, slavery, and despair." He started gathering the cards back up. "Not even a nice reward at the end of it, just this." He picked up the card in the center: a solid rectangle of blackness. "The cold void of Hell. Nice." He snorted and put the cards back into the bag. "Now I remember why I hate these things." He refilled his wine goblet, stood up, and put the wine jug back in the cabinet.

Morea examined the cards for a moment longer. "How do you think Ola is going to fix the odds?"

Kihrin glanced down at his cup of wine. "We'll find out soon enough if I'm right. Come on. Ola's bath is through that curtain. We'd best get this over with."

---

*Speaking of old, dead god-kings . . . but I really don't need to provide a history lesson on old Laregrane's god-king, do I? It's been a mandatory class at the Academy for the last two centuries.

13: The Determined Wizard

(Kihrin's story)

I jumped up onto the railing and kept myself from falling overboard by grabbing the rigging. "Are those whales? I've never seen whales before."

"Oh, those?" Teraeth looked over the side of the ship with a bored expression. "Nothing but several dozen sixty-foot-long limbless blue elephants going for a swim. Pay them no mind."

"I've never seen so many."

"Apparently you haven't seen any, so that's not saying much."

I looked out over the ocean, watching the long, elegant forms breaking the surface, hurling themselves into the air to come crashing back down. After a few minutes, I stopped smiling.

"Are they always this jumpy?"

"It's called breaching."

"And the blood?" I asked. "That's normal too?"

"What?" Teraeth turned around. I pointed behind the ship to where the whales jumped and churned. A streak of dark red spread out against the blue tropical water. The whales were racing, panicking, trying to overtake *The Misery* and swim past her.

They were trying to escape.

The vané knelt on the deck and put both hands against the wooden planks. He cocked his head to the side and closed his eyes.

"What are you doing?"

"Listening." He opened his eyes again. "Damn it all. Go bring my mother here. The whales are screaming."

"Screaming? But what could—" My voice died. A tentacle wrapped around one of the whales and pulled it under the waves. The water nearby churned a fresher crimson.

I started to do as Teraeth ordered. He may not have been carrying my gaesh anymore, but just this once I was willing to make an exception. His mother was on a first-name basis with the Goddess of Death herself; she could only be an asset on an occasion like this. Then I stopped, because a second problem had manifested.

"Tyentso's headed right this way." I stood caught between the approaching witch and the monster lurking in the ocean behind us.

"I don't care if she wants to ask me to dance, she can wait—" Teraeth looked up and paused.

The ship's witch, Tyentso, was marching aft, with Captain Juval close behind her. Sailors scattered as they advanced. It wasn't the Captain's presence that made them jump back as if they were about to touch a diseased corpse.

Some women are worth staring at because of their beauty. When men stared at Tyentso, it was not admiration or lust but shock that the gods would be so unkind. She was a dark, thin woman, scarecrow-like, who dressed in a shapeless robe of layered rags and stained sacking. Her eyes were hard and arrogant; she held herself with the straight-backed poise of an aristocrat—one who could order the death of anyone who displeased her. Her tangled, unwashed nest of hair was the color of dirty sand and bleached driftwood; her nose and chin long and sharp enough to polish on a grindstone; her lips little more than a razor's gash across her face.

It would be impossible to guess at her talismans, not because she had none showing, but because she had too many. Bones, dried kelp, seashells, and bird beaks hung from her staff of ocean-washed, twisted pine. Similar flotsam found a home in that tangled hair. The staff made a noise like a rattle as she walked, as if to warn people to get out of her way.

Which they did if they were wise.

No, she did not radiate beauty. Instead, her aura was fear. She took the superstitious dread most people felt for the idea of a witch and wore it like a crown. No one who saw her doubted her profession, or that she could curse—would curse—any man who crossed her.

The first mate, Delon, liked to use the threat of a night spent in her bed as insurance on good behavior from the crew.

I liked her.

Yes, she was the one responsible for summoning the succubus who gaeshed me, but only under Juval's orders. She had been my single and only ally on board *The Misery*. Her spells were the only reason I'd survived Delon's attentions. When not otherwise occupied, she'd spent the voyage locked away from the rest of the crew, studying her books, casting the myriad minor spells designed to keep the ship safe or detect danger.

This was why the purposeful strides she made toward us, her storm-cloud eyes giving hard examination to the blooded ocean, made me so uncomfortable. She wouldn't have left her cabin—worse, dragged the Captain with her—if the situation wasn't every bit as serious as I feared.

She saw me and stopped dead in her pace. "Just what in Tya's name are you doing here?"

"Never mind them," Captain Juval said. "They're passengers. They can walk the deck if they stay out of the way of the sailors. You two—" He gestured toward Teraeth and me. "Get out of here. We've business."

Tyentso ignored the Captain and continued to stare at me. She was, I realized, waiting for an answer.

I looked over at Teraeth. *Taja,* I thought. *The illusion isn't working on her. She recognizes me.*

"I—" What could I say? How could I answer her with Captain Juval right there?

"Never mind. Later." She waved away any chance of response and moved to stand above the rudder. She paled as she looked out over the bloodied waters.

Tyentso raised her staff into the air and spoke in a language that tugged at the back of my mind—something almost but not quite comprehensible. She moved her free hand in the air, and I couldn't so much see as feel the faint traceries left behind. Complicated skeins of mathematics and arcane notation lingered behind my eyelids before releasing, with a rush of imploding air, out the back of the ship. The energy trails arched into the water: dozens, no, hundreds of tiny pulses created visible splashes.

Teraeth joined me at the railing as we both watched the water. For a long pause, nothing happened. Every sailor on the ship was holding their breath. Then the waters around the whales began to fleck and boil with new bodies: smaller, silver flashes that converged on the blood smears growing faint in the distance as *The Misery* continued her trek. Another tentacle flipped out of the water, and the whole ship seemed to gasp. Hundreds of white water trails rolled over the waves toward the monstrous form.

"Dolphins . . ." Teraeth whispered.

Tyentso proclaimed, "THUS will I destroy the creature!" Her theatrical gesture was overdone, performed for the audience behind her.

There was an audible sigh of relief, a sense of reprieve. The first mate, Delon, began snapping at the men to get back to work.

Only Teraeth, the Captain, and I saw Tyentso's expression held no such promise. She lowered her arms and glanced at Juval. "It's a delay," she said, "and nothing more. That is a Daughter of Laaka in those waters, not any mortal being."*

---

*There have been any number of servitor races created by the god-kings during their supremacy. Some, such as the centaurs of Jorat or the snow giants of Yor, are extinct or nearly so. The Daughters of Laaka have flourished, in large part because Laaka invested them so heavily with resistance to magic, but mostly because their preferred habitat, the ocean depths, is far from the dominion of man.

I felt ill. I was enough a minstrel's son to know the songs and stories of the great kraken, the cursed daughters of the sea goddess. They were immortal beings and deadly foes of any ocean creature large enough to be prey, including ships. I had wanted to believe they were nothing more than stories.

"We'll outrun it," Juval said. "By the time it's done with your sea dogs, we'll be long gone."

"I'm afraid," Khaemezra said, "that would only work if the whales were ever her true quarry."

Captain Juval looked annoyed at the interruption. He didn't notice how Tyentso's eyes widened as she saw Teraeth's mother, or the way the sea witch's knuckles turned white as she gripped her staff. Tyentso's gray eyes moved to Teraeth, then to me, and finally back to the Mother of the Black Brotherhood.

She saw all of us for who we really were. No illusions for her.

"Blooded shells!" the Captain snapped. "What is it with the passengers on this run? You three got no business here. Now get back to your damn cabin and leave this business to folks who know what's what."

The rest of us looked at each other. I felt an unexpected sympathy for the Captain. I had been so scared of him once. He had been so angry with me; done terrible things to me in the heat of that anger. He was a towering figure, full of brooding violence that had never been just for show. Now—he was unimportant. He was all but dismissed, and just didn't realize it yet. Tyentso and Khaemezra would decide who was in charge. The slave captain possessed no power to decide his destiny.

"Juval, these are not normal passengers. It would be best if you leave this to me." Tyentso's tone belonged to a queen and allowed no room for argument.

"Witch—"

"You must trust me," Tyentso hissed. "We are not yet out of danger."

I watched the battle going on under the waves. Even though the ship outpaced the original site of the whales and their attacker, I saw shapes moving in the water, sometimes jumping above it. Through it all, the long slithery tentacles slammed up above the waves to come crashing back down. The creature that owned those arms had to be enormous.

I felt bad for the dolphins. I doubted Tyentso had politely asked them to throw their lives away fighting that thing, that they had volunteered.

Tyentso turned to Khaemezra. "What did you mean about quarry?"

"She comes for the ship," Khaemezra explained. "It was Taja's good fortune that she crossed the path of her favorite meal, and so gave us warning."

"She chases you." The nest-haired witch stopped and narrowed her eyes. Then Tyentso turned to me. "No. The Laaka's Daughter chases *you*."

"Me? It's not me. They're the ones that upset the wizard." I pointed to Teraeth and Khaemezra. "He didn't like being outbid."

Juval scowled. "You lot are the cause of this? I've a mind to throw you all overboard and let the damn sea monster take you."

"That would be stupid," Teraeth hissed. His whole body tensed. He had the look of a man mentally fingering his knives.

"Enough!" Khaemezra said. "It does not matter why the kraken chases or whom it seeks. What matters is that she was summoned. I underestimated the resolve of the wizard responsible. I was sure the gate would lead him astray."

"I'll have to destroy it," Tyentso said. She surprised me by smiling, the first time I recalled her doing so. "I've never killed a kraken before."

"Aren't they immune to magic? Isn't that what all the stories say?"

Tyentso smiled at me with grim, dark humor. "So is a witchhunter, but I learned a long time ago that everyone needs to breathe air or walk on land or swim in water. Those elements are mine. Let's see how our kraken likes acid." She pushed her sleeves up her arms.

"No," Khaemezra said. "You cannot."

"Oh, I very much can." Tyentso raised her hands.

"You *should* not then. You would be making a horrible mistake."

Tyentso sneered. "If you have a better plan to deal with this bitch, by all means share."

Khaemezra sighed with exasperation. "The wizard who did this was ignorant as to which ship we used to leave port. He didn't summon a single Daughter of Laaka: he summoned one for *every* ship that left Kishna-Farriga. He knows I can destroy a kraken. He is counting on this very thing. Now he sits like a bloated spider, linked to each monster by a thin line of magic, waiting for the right thread to snap—for the kraken who does not survive her hunt. He knows that on the other side of that thread, he will find his prey. He will find us."

Tyentso stared at Khaemezra.

Juval scowled. "I don't understand, over a dozen ships left port—"

"And he summoned a dozen kraken, one for each," Khaemezra said.

Tyentso shook her head. "Tya bless me. Relos Var. There's no other wizard it could be."

"You know him?" I asked, surprised.

"Oh, of course. He used to come visit my late husband for a cup of tea and a nice human sacrifice. We were terribly important people, after all." Tyentso raised her hand in a showy, sarcastic wave. Then her voice lowered to a throaty growl. "He's only the most powerful wizard in the whole world, inches from being a god. If all he's waiting on is our location before he strikes, then she's damn well right—we don't dare destroy that monster."

I turned to Khaemezra. "But he'd still have to deal with you. He obviously doesn't think he can take you. You stared him down. He's *scared* of you."

Tyentso stopped moving. Hell, she might have stopped breathing. She looked at Khaemezra as if she were a rearing cobra. "You—"

"We don't have time for this," Teraeth said. "The kraken's on the chase again." The Manol vané was keeping one eye on the Captain and another on our monstrous pursuer.

"You're good," Tyentso told Mother. "I can't even tell you're a wizard."

Khaemezra's smile was maternal. "I've had years of practice, my child."

"Help me," Tyentso pleaded. "We could do this together."

"I can't," Khaemezra said. "There are rules, and consequences. If I, one of the people who made those rules, break them because they are inconvenient I would win this battle and lose the war. I do not wish to return to the chaos of the old times before the Concord.* Do you understand, child?"

"No. No, I don't. There's a sea monster gaining on the ship," I said. "Anybody remember the sea monster? Hard to kill, gigantic, lots of arms? *Hungry?*"

Khaemezra looked angry. "Damn it, child, I cannot do anything. If I kill that beast, Relos Var will be on us in minutes. And he will not arrive alone. He will have an army of shadow and darkness with him—demons of the cold, frozen Void. In saving you from that, we would lose everything. At least if you are killed by the kraken, you keep your soul and you can be Returned . . ."

I felt faint. Trapped in the hands of a demon for all time—

No, anything but that.

Even death, rather than that.

"Gods below, you are not talking about letting that monster tear up my ship?" Juval said, screaming even though his voice never rose above speaking level.

"We could go north," Teraeth said. "Steer the ship north."

"Are you insane?" Juval said. "There's a reason every ship that sails these lanes takes the long way around Zherias. You try to take a shortcut through the Straits and you'll hit the Maw."

---

*She means the Celestial Concord, perhaps? Very little is known about the Celestial Concord, save that it was a binding agreement between the Eight Immortals and certain god-kings. They all decided it was better to play nice and promise to behave than be hunted down and slain by the Emperor—using his preferred weapon for such, Urthaenriel. Presumably it was some kind of treaty on acceptable behavior. And afterward, the Concord gods did not physically rule on earth. This had previously been a common occurrence during the Age of God-Kings.

"There's a safe passage through the Maw," Teraeth replied. "I know it."

"Child," Khaemezra snapped.

"Whale puke," Juval said. "I'm Zheriaso and I can't sail the Maw. No man can."

Teraeth ignored him and turned his attention to Tyentso. "There is a safe passage through the Maw, but I have to steer. Your people must obey my orders without question or hesitation. They call you a witch, but what you just did smacks of something else. Formal training or self-taught?"

"A little of both," Tyentso admitted. "I had excellent private tutors." She looked back over her shoulder at the waves. "I can turn the currents against her, the winds in our favor. It should get us to the Straits before she can catch up to us. She won't dare enter the Maw itself." She stopped and looked back at Juval.

"I was wondering when someone would remember whose bloody ship this is," the Captain growled. "Are you all insane?"

"Or, we could stay here and be ripped apart," I said with a smile. "Completely your call, Juvs."

He stared at me, his eyes widening with recognition. "I know that voice. You *brat*. What are you doing back on my ship?"

"Enjoying your fine hospitality, of course." I grinned at him. "Trust me when I say you've come out of this better than you would've if we hadn't come back on board. Then Tyentso would've killed the Daughter and you'd be facing Relos Var all alone. Oh, and not even able to say you don't know who I am, when he started asking the fun questions."

"Captain–" Teraeth said. More than a small trace of urgency strained his voice.

Juval scowled. "Fine. *North*."

14: BEDTIME STORIES

(Talon's story)

When Ola looked through the green beaded curtain into her bathing room, she found Kihrin stripped of his torn, stained clothes and lounging in her special copper tub. Lantern light flared off motes of dust and sparkled on the bathwater, which soap, fragrant oils, and blood had colored milky pink. Kihrin had scrubbed his bronze skin to a bright red, pressing so hard with the sea sponge he had scratched himself in places. His neck was ruddier than the rest of him, contrasting with the blue tsali stone.

Her baby boy was talking with the new dancer. To Ola's surprise, the girl was still dressed. She hadn't helped with the bath at all, which Ola thought strange, given how Kihrin had been mooning after her.

Ola scowled, her thoughts troubled by dark memories of an ill-spent youth. She pushed the expression from her face, straightened her shoulders, and inhaled. Ola entered with all the flamboyance of a Reveler-trained circus performer. "Ah! Yes! Here is a feast for my poor darling boy."

Ola gathered a small folding table, which she set up next to the tub.

Kihrin laughed. "Don't you think that's too much food?"

The whorehouse madam smiled. "I brought a little of all the day's specials from the kitchen." She waved her hand over the tray of food like a waiter presenting the meal. "We have hot peppered goat with strips of fresh voracress, mutton with leado sauce wrapped and grilled in the traditional banana leaf, nakari marinated yellow fish with mango, fried bezevo root fingers, coconut rice, heart of palm, and pieces of bitter melon with chocolate." Then, as if she'd forgotten, she added, "And some of my Kirpis grape wine. It will relax you."

Morea gave Ola a startled look, so the whorehouse madam added, "I know, I know. I mostly save it for rituals,* but I've always liked grape wines more than the local rice or coconut wines when I'm trying to relax."

---

*Citizens of the Kirpis and Kazivar dominions like to insist that only wine made from grapes should be called such. The presence of the Academy in Kirpis means that generations of wizards have returned home with a taste for grape wine and the quirk of preferring it for rituals.

Kihrin lay back against the tub. The window light reflecting in his eyes danced and skipped. "I don't eat this good on my naming day, Ola."

She chuckled. "You might if you ran into demons more often. You should try the yellow fish. That's nakari powder from Valasi's, not from Irando." Ola cast a knowing glance at Morea, and the girl blushed and looked away. Everyone knew nakari powder was made from aphrodisiacs.* That was the whole reason a place like the Shattered Veil Club served it.

Ola teased the girl for Kihrin's benefit but he never so much as glanced at Morea when Ola mentioned Valasi's. She frowned. Surdyeh had been upset, but for the first time Ola wondered just how bad it had been out there.

Kihrin picked up the goblet from the tray, paused with it at his lips, and then lowered it. He reached for the fried bezevo fingers, long deep-fried wedges of sweet root, and leaned back against the copper rim again. "Tell me about the day you found me, Ola."

Ola blinked. Of all the . . . why did he want to hear *that* story? Why did he want to hear that story *now*? She flicked her fingers at him and snorted. "You know this story."

The boy grinned as he ate. "Morea hasn't heard it yet."

"You want me to tell tales? At a time like this?"

Kihrin set his goblet on the floor, on the opposite side of the tub from Ola. He cast a meaningful glance in Morea's direction. "You always used to say that times like this are the best times to tell stories. Good luck, remember?"

The look told Ola everything. She knew Kihrin liked the girl, but she had no idea he liked her that much. And yet, here he was, obviously enchanted, for the first time in his life holding back. A girl like Morea had probably never known a man who gave her any consideration or courted her feelings. He was trying to impress the girl, and so, he was letting her set the pace. Her smile for her adopted son was warm and sentimental.

"She hasn't heard it yet," Ola repeated in a teasing mock. "She don't need to hear it, either." Ola looked up at Morea, whose eyes were uncertain and clouded. "Well, child? Do you need to hear a story while you give him a bath? And why the hell aren't you bathing him, anyhow?"

While Ola never attended the Academy, she must have picked up this association from her time spent in the Upper Circle.

*And poisons. The heart-pumping, excited state nakari powder is famous for inducing can be created through poisonous mushrooms, aconite, and the thorax of the red dragon beetle. In small quantities, these are harmless, but I would be careful to buy nakari powder from a trusted source.

"Because I told her not to," Kihrin said, and gestured to the plate of food. "Morea, this is too much for me. Eat something."

"Bright-Eyes . . ."

"Go on, Ola, give us a story. Tell me about my mother." He paused. "I suppose I could tell it . . ."

"You'd never tell it right. You weren't there."

"I was there," Kihrin corrected. "I may not remember it, but I was most definitely there."

"You are an uncontrollable rogue. I don't know what I was thinking the day I picked you up from that park."

"Tell me the story anyway," Kihrin teased. "Even though I don't brush my hair and I don't obey–"

"And you don't do your chores–" Ola added with a huff.

"And I'm never up and dressed by the first bell–" he agreed.

"And you're a thief–" she accused.

"And I drink too much–" he confessed.

"And you're far too young to be such an incorrigible womanizer–" she yelled with increasing volume.

"And I'm a terrible burden on my father!"

They both shouted the last line together, ending in hails of laughter that resulted in Kihrin leaning forward, coughing. Ola whacked Kihrin a few times on the back when it seemed like he might choke. Finally, Kihrin reached for his goblet of wine and took several long gasping droughts before his lungs settled.

Morea had her hand over her mouth too. She looked like she was trying not to laugh.

"All right," Ola said, as much to Morea as Kihrin. "I'll tell you the tale." To Morea she said, "He'll be sixteen years old this New Year's, and it will be sixteen years ago, this New Year's, that the old Emperor of Quur died."

"What was his name?" Kihrin asked, with a wink to Morea, who looked startled as a lamb upon realizing the tigers were not going to eat her after all.

"Gendal," Ola answered. "Do you want me to tell this story or not?" She straightened her agolé for emphasis. "Yes, it was sixteen years ago, and Gendal had been murdered. We knew it was murder, because murder, my dear girl, is the only way an Emperor of Quur can die."

"No risk of an accidental death?" Kihrin asked. He leaned his head against the copper side of the tub, smiling.

"Not even if he tripped on a rock and fell over Demon Falls," Ola replied with grim authority.

"He can't catch the pox?" Kihrin asked.

"Quite immune," Ola answered.

"Could he have eaten something poisonous?" Morea asked. She bit her lip but the whisper of a smile played at the corners there.

"That's the spirit, girl. No, he could not. Not even Manol black lotus could hurt him," came Ola's firm reply.

"And when he grows old?" Kihrin pretended to be skeptical.

"From the moment the Emperor places the Great Crown of Quur on his brow"—Ola raised a solitary finger upward and poked at the heavens—"he is immortal. He will never age, he will never be sick. No, the only way the Emperor can die is by violence—by murder."

"So how did you know he was dead?" Kihrin asked. He scrubbed himself with one hand while holding his goblet of wine with the other.

"We knew because inside the Arena, where the contest itself is held, past the great invisible barrier that surrounds it—came a great shining light. It was the light of the Crown and Scepter of Quur. They return to the Arena when the heart of their owner beats no more. And they wait there for the next man who dares claim them. You can believe me, child, when I say men wasted no time spreading the word that the old Emperor was dead. It was time to choose a new Emperor. Everyone came to see."

"Everyone?"

"Oh yes," Ola said as she nodded her head. "Everyone. Rich, poor, old, young, fat, thin, freemen, slaves, citizens, and foreigners came to the park that very day. Some folk go their entire lives without seeing the choosing of the Emperor. Gendal himself lived for two hundred years. The opportunity to see the Choosing happens at most once in any person's life, and no one wanted to miss it: least of all the men who hoped to become the next Emperor."

She smiled at the memory. "Ah, you should have seen it, my lambs. There was barely room to stand in Arena Park—barely room to breathe! There was no rank or status at such a time. Commoners bumped shoulders with High Lords. Guild masters found themselves boxed in by street thugs. Velvet girls were felt up by Ivory District priests! More purses were cut than ever before or ever since." She paused significantly.

"But worse crimes than purse-cutting were committed that day."

"Like what?" Kihrin raised an eyebrow at Morea, as if she might know the answer. Morea smiled and held up her hands.

"The contest itself, some would say," Ola explained. "For thousands of years the Great Empire has chosen its highest ruler in the same way—by contest of blood. They lowered the invisible wall surrounding the Arena, and all those men rushed in to claim the Crown and Scepter—and kill anyone who might seek to claim it first. I watched the best and brightest wizards of a generation go up in brightly colored patches of smoke on that day. Believe me when I say that with a little magic, human flesh can burn any color you can imagine and a few you probably can't. The land inside the Arena was a cooking pot: it melted, it boiled, it flowed, and it steamed. And out of the crucible was born our Emperor."

"So, who won?" Morea asked.

Ola was thrown aback for a moment as she realized the slave girl genuinely didn't know. Ah, but what need for a sex slave to know the name of the Emperor? She probably didn't know how to read or write either. Not everyone's master was as liberal as Ola's master Therin had been. The madam swallowed bile, shook her head, and continued the story.

"To the profound embarrassment of the royalty, a commoner won," Ola told Morea. "A peasant from Marakor named Sandus. But to win the Great Tournament is to become Emperor, no matter what your previous status, and so Sandus became our ruler. He still is to this day. When he finally exited the Arena, the crowd screamed so loud that you could hear nothing but a roar. And that, my girl, is when I found Kihrin."

"Yup, it sure is." Kihrin nodded in agreement, splashing water.

"I saw his mother first, noticed her through the crowd." Ola's voice turned at once sad and passionate with longing. "She was an extraordinary beauty with golden-wheat skin and a shimmering brown curtain of hair. Her eyes were as gentle and kind as a fawn's. She was lovely enough to be a princess, dressed in an agolé of fine ivory satin. She carried a small package in her arms, no larger than a few pieces of firewood."

Morea paused. She looked at Kihrin. The young man frowned and stared at the cloudy water as if it were a scrying glass. He was silent.

Morea turned back to Ola. "So, what happened?"

"I saw a man rush up toward her, place his hands around her neck, and choke the life out of her. There was nowhere for her to run to, you understand? And no way for me to reach her, because I was so crushed in with the others I couldn't move. Still, she made a great showing for herself and fought valiantly, not that it did any good in the end."

"Didn't anyone try to help?" Kihrin whispered the question this time, his voice bitter.

"It is Quur, is it not? No one lifted a finger to help that lady. I saw the woman fall just as the roar of the new Emperor's victory covered her screams, and by the time I reached the spot where she lay, her murderer was gone. Only her body and my darling, the babe she carried, remained. When I picked him up, I discovered, much to my amazement, that he was alive. He still had his birthing blood on him, and it was obvious little Kihrin had only come into the world that day. So if I had left him for someone else to find he would have surely died." She grinned impishly as she finished the tale. "Kihrin is my one and only act of charity, which means that it's true what they say about virtue."

Kihrin stifled a yawn. "And what is it they say, Mamma Ola?"

"It never goes unpunished!" She snapped the edge of a towel at him and howled. He splashed bathwater at her. Morea quickly stepped out of the way.

Morea looked at Ola and then back at Kihrin, her expression wondering. "So, you really are an Ogenra then?"

"Garbage. Fewmets!" Ola sputtered. "What nonsense is this?"

Morea shrank back under the onslaught of Ola's volatile anger. "I didn't mean . . ."

"It's just a story, Morea," Kihrin said. "A god-king tale. In this part of town there are a thousand orphans—ten thousand orphans. And if you got us drunk enough, every single one of us would admit to a dream that we're a long-lost prince, that ours is a romantic tale of betrayal and woe. The truth is what I told you earlier: Surdyeh found me on the trash heaps. I was abandoned by a mother who didn't want me." He shrugged as if it didn't matter.

Morea would always wonder, though. Ola knew that had been Kihrin's whole point—as well as the only reason Ola had played along.

Ola chuckled. "Can you see me naming a child 'Kihrin' anyway? Surdyeh picked out that one when he adopted the boy."

"Captain Jarith said it was a traditional Kirpis name," Kihrin said, drowsily.

"Did he now? You and he get all friendly?" A faint tinge of menace crept into Ola's voice. She had no love for the City Guard or the army soldiers, but most of all—*most of all*—for the sons of men who had known her when she was a courtesan herself.

"He's not so bad for a soldier. I don't think he'd be so friendly if he knew what I do for a living—" Kihrin closed his eyes and began to slide down the side of the tub, the remaining wine spilling out of his goblet into the water like fresh blood.

"Quick girl, get his arms. Don't let him go under," Ola ordered.

Morea, used to following orders, grabbed at Kihrin. Ola roughly hauled the naked young man from the tub, a reminder that she was larger than most Quuros men, larger even than Kihrin.

"You . . . you . . ." Morea blinked in shock.

"Relax, child. He ain't poisoned, just drugged up a bit." She shifted his body into a position easier to carry.

"Now come on. Help me get him into bed."

Morea did as Ola ordered and tucked the young man into the large cotton-stuffed bed normally used by Ola alone.

The brothel madam retreated into the bathroom and brought back the tray of food, which she placed on a small table. She ate noisily, with great appetite, and motioned for Morea to do the same.

"I ain't never called myself the boy's mother," Ola explained, "but

I am his mother in all the ways that matter. I love him like he was mine. Just like he was born out of my own womb. And I'm proud of him. Proud as any mother could be of her son. I don't want him coming to no harm. I'll protect him, even if I have to protect him from himself."

"I don't understand."

"I wouldn't expect you to. Let's just say that he's stubborn. He gets that from me. Oh, he might act all flighty sometimes, but that ain't how he is really. Truth, he gets something into his head, he don't ever let it go. He'll just keep worrying at it, coming back to it, until he's worn it down, like the winds tearing down a mountain. Damn, but I wish his father had more sense. You can't tell a boy like Kihrin to stay away from an invitation to the High General's house and expect the boy will do it. Demons, no. Surdyeh's gone and made that just about irresistible.* Being told he can't just makes it all the worse." Ola wrapped some fish up in a flat piece of sag bread and munched. "Mmm . . . good sauce today."

"Would meeting the High General be so bad?"

Ola stopped in midbite, and gave Morea such a glare that the girl yelped. "Yes, it would, and I ain't going to explain why that is. You need to trust that I know what I'm about. He can't go." Her expression softened, and she said, "He'll sleep tonight, sleep deep, and he'll have rowdy dreams because of what I gave him. In the morning, he'll wake up with you in his arms and he'll think missing the meeting with the General was his own damn fault. And everything will be okay."

Morea didn't answer, but her expression was skeptical.

"He likes you," Ola said, "so you can help me. There's a big reward in it for you if you do."

"What sort of reward?"

"My boy has some money saved up. Don't ask where he got it from. Never mind that. I figure he's got a tidy sum stashed up with the priests of Tavris up in the Ivory District. He's planning on buying his pappa a tavern in Eamithon, someplace nice and peaceful to retire to. Nice people up there. I found the perfect tavern a while back and I went ahead and bought it. Kihrin don't know I done it though. So I figure tomorrow I'll let Kihrin buy that tavern from me, on the cheap, and I'll send Kihrin there with his father and his pick of a couple slave girls to do waitress duty and the like. They take a dim view of slavery over in Eamithon,† so

---

*Is it paranoia I suspect that was the whole point?
†Eamithon is home to some curious exceptions from Quuros law, due to the fact that of all the dominions of the Empire, Eamithon (under the reign of the god-queen Dana) was the only one to join the Empire willingly, with the full cooperation of its ruler. Technically speaking, slavery is legal in Eamithon, but since virtually no one in Eamithon seems to realize this, slaves brought into the dominion have a habit of "vanishing" and turning up in isolated villages

it wouldn't be long at all before you found yourself a free woman. You'd end up being paid–legitimately–for your time and trouble, and with that boy just as crazy about you as crazy can be."

"What do I have to do?"

"Nothing you don't want to. Don't think I ain't seen how you stare at him. Just keep the boy distracted, keep him from thinking too much about crazy ideas of rubbing shoulders with his betters. We ain't nothing to people like them. They chew us up and spit us out as easy as eggnuts."

Morea nodded. "Of course, I'll help."

"Good! Good. Now you get out of them clothes and make all warm and cuddly with my boy so he's not thinking clearly when he wakes up." Ola wiped her greasy fingers on the front of her agolé and stood, crossing over to where Kihrin lay on her bed. She stared at him. Her eyes were haunted.

"I've made a mistake," Ola whispered.

"Mistress, did you say something?"

Ola almost smiled. "I said . . . oh veils, never mind. You get to be my age, girl, and you look back over your life and sometimes you don't like what you see. I've done plenty I'm not proud of, but I always had a good reason for it. Survival, mostly. Just trying to get by, to protect myself, just like every other damn bastard in the Lower Circle. They're all jackals down here, just waiting for you to make a mistake." Then she laughed, hard and cynical. "I guess that ain't much different from how things are in the Upper Circle, is it?"

Her expression sobered, and she said, "I ain't done much in my life that was just pure maliciousness, pure spite. Save one thing. Just one. And it's come looking for me. I can feel its breath on my heels . . ."

Ola Nathera closed her eyes, for just a moment, and shuddered. "You can look at someone your whole life and never see them. But Qoran, that damn General. Those damned eyes. Those Milligreest boys were never blind. He'll know just what he's looking at, assuming he ain't seen it already."

After a moment, Ola gestured toward the bed. "Well? Get in there and take good care of my boy."

Morea nodded and unwrapped her agolé. Ola stared at her and then grunted. "At least he's got good taste," she said. "Must get that from me too." Without another word, she turned and left.

Several moments later, Morea heard the sound of the front door opening and closing.

---

where the natives swear that the person has lived there for their whole life. There is also enormous peer pressure on anyone settling in Eamithon with their slaves to free them.

The dancer tiptoed out to the front room and looked around carefully to make sure no one was there, that Ola really had left.

"She's gone," Kihrin's voice said behind her. "That woman weighs close to three hundred pounds. She's good at a lot of things, but sneaking isn't one of them."

Morea turned to see Kihrin had stood up from the bed. Candlelight outlined his body in golden pink highlights. The rim light made him look otherworldly and unreal—beautiful but alien. He looked too beautiful to be human.

Morea reached for her clothing. "You switched cups, didn't you? You knew she would drug the wine."

"I couldn't have done it without your help. You were the perfect distraction. Anyway, it was a safe bet. She likes using riscoria weed, and grape wine is the best way to hide the taste. She'll feed it to a mark if she wants them to wake in a compromising situation, with the vague memory that maybe they did things the night before that they shouldn't have." He sounded disappointed.

"Stay with me," Morea said. "Don't go."

Kihrin shook his head. "I have to."

"You heard what she said. Eamithon sounds nice, doesn't it?"

He looked at her, blinking with surprise. "I have to warn the General about that demon. Besides, Captain Jarith said he'd meet me tonight with news about your sister."

She felt as though she'd been slapped across the face. "Oh."

The expression on the young man's face softened, became something that was almost tenderness. "I'll go and meet with General Milligreest, take his reward and talk to him about the demon, then find Captain Jarith and come back here. Ola will never know I left and tomorrow morning we'll pretend that everything went exactly as Ola planned. She's always a lot easier to deal with if she thinks she got her way." Kihrin began looking around, rooting through wardrobes and cabinets. He pulled out a pair of baggy kef trousers and a matching vest with slippers, all in bright, festive colors.

"Let's hope these still fit. They were large last New Year's Festival, but I've grown since then."

Morea helped him with the clothing and his hair, worrying over him. She was careful not to touch him, although her fingers shook and she suspected the nakari powder was having an effect. She wanted to touch him, hold him, and thank him with the only thing of value she thought she possessed, but she didn't. Instead, she helped him dress and watched him leave out a back window.

She then turned her attention to making sure the bed looked like it held two bodies instead of one.

15: The Zherias Maw

(Kihrin's story)

Surdyeh's repertoire had always included sea tales, essential for a port town like the Capital. I was all too familiar with stories of the Desolation, an area of reef, broken islands, shoal, and becalmed sea that ate up ships the way Yoran witches ate children. From the north side, calm seas without wind or current left ships stranded. A southern approach meant conflicting currents, giant waves, and rocks for ships to dash themselves upon.

Some said the vané crafted the Desolation to keep the navies of Quur off their shores. Others said a forgotten god's death was to blame. The Desolation interfered with shipping lines and caused panic in the hearts of seasoned sailors. The Daughters of Laaka, the kraken: those were a god-king tale, something a man who sailed all his life might never see. The Desolation was a certainty that waited to trap the unwary. I'd heard rumors of Zheriaso pirates who used the Desolation as refuge, but most scoffed at these stories—anyone fool enough to sail the Desolation would only end up as one of its victims.

Whether we would ever reach the Desolation was a matter of debate. On the Quuros side, to the north, the Desolation itself was the most pressing danger, but we were approaching from the *south*. Before we reached the mists, we faced the Zherias Maw, the result of the strong southern current hitting the rocks of the Desolation's island chain. With no outlet, the current turned in on itself, creating a churning brine capable of smashing ships against the hidden reefs of the Desolation. The Maw waited long before *The Misery* reached the dead waters on the other side.

Teraeth hoped that the kraken would find passage through the Maw too difficult and would turn back.

I thought the assassin was being naïve.

For this stretch of the journey, I didn't growl as I heard the shouts of Magoq the galley master, who was whipping the slaves to row faster. Even with a strong wind in our sails, we needed the speed. Tyentso manipulated the currents to slow our pursuer, but if I looked out behind us using my second sight, I could see the glowing spectral outline of the monster gaining on us.

We sailed for three days but weren't losing the creature. I knew—knew in my heart, in my bones—that if it caught us, it would kill every person on board, freeman or slave. Any who survived would either drown, be picked off by sharks, or devoured by the Maw. Already, the water surrounding the ship was turning choppy. Worse, the ship was starting to turn, to sail at an angle counter to the direction of Tyentso's summoned winds.

It would be poetic to say it was a stormy, dreary day, but the sky was bright and beautiful. Even the increasingly jerky water was an intense blue. It didn't seem like a day for dying, but then again, Surdyeh never once told me a story where Thaena the Death Goddess paid any attention to the weather.

For the first time in many months, I gave serious consideration to praying.

I spotted Khaemezra standing against the railing, talking to Tyentso, who looked more wan and frightened than I ever imagined possible. She hadn't flinched at summoning a demon, but this? If the kraken didn't kill us, the Maw would, and she seemed aware of the realities. Khaemezra, on the other hand, was as calm as if seated in a restaurant waiting for the waiter to bring her a second cup of tea.

"May I speak with you two ladies for a moment?"

Khaemezra smiled at me, but Tyentso snorted. "Lady? Good to see you haven't lost your sense of humor."

I bowed to her extravagantly. Fortunately, she was looking for anything to distract her from thinking about our situation, and laughed instead of turning me into a fish. Although, I thought it might be handy to be a fish when the kraken showed up.

Preferably a small one.

I gestured back toward our pursuer. "She's not fallen back, even with the time we're making, and I have a feeling she's playing with us. She'll attack before we can reach the Maw."

Tyentso's expression twisted, and she looked green. "Too late for that."

"No, I think we—what?"

"We entered the Maw several hours ago," Khaemezra whispered. "The outer edges are calm, so the crew doesn't realize yet. Our only chance is to approach the fangs in the correct order, sail around the Throat, and hit the safe passage perfectly, without waking the Old Man."

"Could you repeat that in a way that makes sense?"

She clicked her teeth together in annoyance. "The main vortex is called the Throat, but there are eddies, little currents, spiraling off the main whirlpool. We call those fangs. Most ships are ruined by the fangs before they ever reach the Throat."

"And what's the Old Man?"

"There are worse things than kraken in these waters." Khaemezra cocked her head, examining me with those strange blue-green eyes. Looking at them, I thought they were the color of the sky, then decided that no, they were the color of the sea. Then I had the peculiar thought that the vané hag's eyes were a mirror reflecting the light of ocean and firmament; that indoors, underground, at night, Khaemezra's eyes would have no color at all.

In any event, she had spooky eyes.

"What can we do?" I found myself matching her whispers. "If this ship crashes, those slaves will drown."

Tyentso rolled her eyes. "Think to your own skin. Even a Zheriaso will drown in the Maw.* If this ship goes down, we *all* drown."

I continued staring at Khaemezra. "I don't think so. If you didn't want Teraeth to reveal the safe passage, you could've shut him up. We're going where you want us to go."

The old woman smiled. "Clever child. You're wondering: Is Relos Var truly responsible for the kraken behind us, or did I summon it? Is this all a ruse to convince the Captain to willingly change course and take us directly to where we want to go? Will I sacrifice all these people for a quicker, untraceable passage?"

I swallowed. She hit all the right points.

"You couldn't! If we lose the ship—!" Tyentso's voice started to rise, but Khaemezra gestured to her and her speech stopped. I couldn't tell if she had used magic or simple intimidation. Khaemezra's gaze never left me, but I found it difficult to meet her stare.

"Will you?" I finally whispered. "Will you let them all die?"

"What do you think?" she asked.

I remembered what I knew about Thaena. I remembered the look on Teraeth's face as he stared down at the slaves in the hold. I remembered Khaemezra's concern when I almost died because of the gaesh. I would've thought cultists of a death goddess more callous, but they defied my attempts to pin them with an easy label.

"No, I don't think you'd let them die here," I finally said, "but that doesn't mean you didn't call in the kraken. You'd do it if you thought you could free those slaves."

"So now a kraken is a weapon of emancipation?" The corner of her mouth twitched upward. "I must admit I've never heard that one before.

---

*"Like trying to drown a Zheriaso" is a colloquial expression for attempting something impossible. The phrase's origins are believed to be tied to one of the many Quuros pirate wars, when Zheriaso were often seen to simply jump overboard and abandon ship rather than fight the superior Quuros navy. They later turned up whole and hale back on Zherias, even in instances where ships were scuttled miles from the coast.

But I didn't do it, and I believe Relos Var did. You may choose to doubt me, but it remains the truth."

"That puts us right back at being destroyed by the kraken, devoured by the Maw, or dashed apart on the shoals of the Desolation."

"You forgot about the Old Man," Tyentso added. "She hasn't explained that one yet."

"Pray I never have to." The old vané woman turned to me. "You want to help? Watch my son's back. When things go wrong, someone will try something stupid. He's going to need to keep his concentration."

"Wouldn't you do a better job of that? I don't even have a weapon."

"Tyentso and I will be directing our energies to keeping the ship intact as it suffers forces far beyond its normal capacity to endure," Khaemezra said. "You may not have mastered all the skills that are your birthright, but the ability to pass unnoticed is very much your own. I suggest you make that the key to your goals." She pushed a dagger into my hands. "And now you are a man with a knife. Woe to the Empire."

As I turned to leave, I looked over at the ocean water and frowned. Khaemezra saw my expression and turned as well.

"It begins," she said.

Tyentso made a whimpering sound, and moved toward the stairs. Khaemezra grabbed her arm.

"Be strong, daughter," she told Tyentso. "I am with you this day." Then, to me: "Go, while you still can."

We sailed on the lazy edge of what looked like a slick of oil. The perfectly smooth water was shiny as glass and stretched for three hundred feet. Everything looked serene and safe and calm.

Then a rumbling noise filled the air. The center of the slick erupted in a column of thrashing steam and water. When the water spilled back down, it sank as though draining through the bottom of the world. In seconds we were staring at three hundred feet of spinning gyre, a maelstrom of ocean water spilling down into unfathomable darkness.

We rode on the edge, balanced on the precipice of a cliff. The ship listed, staying in place by what magic—hmm . . . now that I think about it, I'm sure I *do* know by what magic. *The Misery* sailed faster than row or sail could account, racing along at unholy speed.

The crew couldn't help seeing this. They were silent for a moment before shouts and cries and even orders to help were drowned by the scream of the whirlpool.

I looked around. No one was in a blind panic yet, and Teraeth could handle himself. It would be a while yet before the chaos transformed into screaming frenzy—likely when the crew realized this was a minor "fang" and not the Throat itself.

There was one other detail I wanted to take care of first.

16: The General's Reward

(Talon's story)

Kihrin skipped saying goodbye to Surdyeh, although his thoughts were on his father the entire time he navigated the winding streets to the Upper Circle. Under other circumstances, Surdyeh would have been overflowing with supposedly helpful advice on how to behave around nobility. Under other circumstances, Surdyeh would have lectured endlessly on etiquette in his quest to ensure his son's future as a musician. This always struck Kihrin as hypocritical, when Surdyeh knew perfectly well his success in the Revelers Guild depended on a magical aptitude that the old man refused to let his son legally pursue.*

And Surdyeh had offered no advice for his son except "Don't go."

Kihrin never once considered that Surdyeh and Ola's reasons for keeping him from this meeting might have been legitimate. All he could see was he'd been given a chance: a chance to impress Morea, a chance to win a reward gained on his own merits instead of his father's, and a chance to shake off the curse of a demon he was sure still hunted him. A chance to escape Velvet Town and the Lower Circle forever.

Besides, he was curious.

The night air cooled the wildfire temperatures left over from the Quuros summer day. The rainbow scintillation of Tya's Veil and the soft glow of all three moons lit the sky. The shadows staggered over the white-washed cobblestones like drunk men more afraid of coming home to their wives than the dangers of passing out in an alley. At night, the streets of Velvet Town were more crowded than during the day; this was an entertainment district after all, and not one where the customers wished to be recognized. Sallí cloaks paraded silently, with hoods up—a field of muddy phantoms making the rounds from home to brothel and back again.

His feet slowed as Kihrin climbed the great Stair of Dreams. He'd never passed this way before. There'd never been a need. On those few occasions Surdyeh had taken him to the Ivory District (or later, when

---

*Since he was never licensed, this technically makes Kihrin a witch.

Kihrin had come by himself), they'd always used the Praying Gate entrance. By contrast, the switchbacking marble steps of the Stair of Dreams were the only public access to the maze of manicured hedges, estates, villas, and palaces Quur's elite called home. Halfway up, Kihrin realized the long, steep stairs were purposefully intimidating. Royalty traveled by litter or carriage, and would use private gates. Only commoners ever made this climb. They would arrive at their destination gasping for breath and humbled.

He suspected he might be in trouble when the Watchmen at the top of the stairs recognized and were expecting him—exactly as Captain Jarith had promised. They dispatched an escort to show him the way to the Milligreest estate, eliminating any possibility he might become "lost." Normally he'd have resented the babysitting, but this once he was grateful. Without it he'd have arrived late or never found the place at all. Unlike the guards he was used to, these were polite, clean, and professional, and Kihrin didn't quite know how to deal with that.

The Milligreest estate was in the Ruby District, which Kihrin could tell because all the mage-lights on the street (there were mage-lights on the streets!) were red. He knew enough about the Royal Houses to know the Red Men—the Metalsmiths Guild—owed their allegiance here. He didn't know enough to remember the House's name.*

He knew the Royal Houses of the Court of Gems were god-touched, knew they alone had been blessed by divinity. While each of the twelve houses was identified by some meaningless bit of heraldry, they could also be recognized by the color of the gems the houses used as tokens.

He knew House D'Jorax's mark was rainbow-hued, their Royal Family had eyes like opals, and they controlled the Revelers. Surdyeh paid them a yearly guild fee for membership and his license to perform. Kihrin also knew House D'Erinwa was amethyst, because D'Erinwa owned the Collectors, to whom Butterbelly paid his guild fees. Pretty much everyone assumed the Collectors were the ultimate authority behind the illegal Shadowdancers.

Kihrin knew many, if not most, of the guilds ultimately took their cues from a Royal House, but he'd never learned which ones.

The blue-eyed nobleman Morea had assumed was his relative was almost certainly one such member of royalty. However, Kihrin found himself at a loss to remember the specific house to which the villain owed fealty. Did blue mean he was a physicker? Kihrin had no idea which Royal Family controlled the Blue Houses, where one traded metal for healing.

---

*House D'Talus.

For the first time in his life he wondered why his father, who made such a show of chiding him to practice and study—if he wanted to play before anyone important—had so thoroughly neglected his education in this regard.

17: Waking the Old Man

(Kihrin's story)

We swung round the fang at top speed, the ship tilting at an angle she was never built to endure, racing at a speed she was never meant to sustain. Maybe a sleeker warship could've handled the strain, but *The Misery* was a clunky slaver. She groaned, and I wondered if she would break up before we reached the real hazards, even with Tyentso and Khaemezra's magic. We spun twice around the whirlpool before it spat us out. The ship's planking and mast screamed as another fang formed on our port side, spinning us in the opposite direction like a horse's rider changing leads.

I bumped against Captain Juval's first mate Delon while crossing the deck. Walking on a boat pitching like a velvet girl in bed was hard work. Hardly my fault if I had an attack of clumsiness right next to him, right?

"Gods be damned, boy!" Delon cursed at me.

"Sorry," I said.

"Fool boy. Go hang onto something!" Delon pulled himself up to the wheel deck. I grinned and bounced the keys to the slave hold in my hand as I watched him go.

Maybe we wouldn't make it, but I'd be damned if I would let all those slaves die trapped in tiny cages like fish in a net.

This fang wasn't any smoother than the last, but we were traveling faster than before and *The Misery* wasn't happy about it. The deck bucked under my feet. The mast began to warp.

"Come on, Taja, keep her together," I muttered. "And keep Delon from looking this way."

I knelt on the deck. My hands were cold as I unlocked the massive iron padlock that held shut the grating hold-door.

The rest was easy. The crew of *The Misery* were focused on impending doom and the spinning vortex. None of them had any concentration to waste on a teenage boy roaming through the hold, unlocking cages. The sound of our crazy, mad spinning muffled the reactions of the slaves inside. Some of them stared at me in disbelief. A depressing majority shied away from the door, as if they thought this must be some kind of trap. I shouted at them to get out, but I doubt any understood me, assuming they heard me over *The Misery*'s screams.

The real test wasn't the slave hold, but the rowing galley. Every slave there was shackled to their bench. Every slave there was individually chained. The ship's crew had taken in the oars, just as they'd taken down the sails—both interfered with the sharp turns *The Misery* needed to make to stay afloat. They'd left the slaves down there though. In the months I had been a guest of *The Misery*'s delightful rowing galley, I had only left my bench at the very end, when they had pulled me out to be interrogated, whipped, and gaeshed.

I shivered from the cold in the small passage leading to the rower's galley. The heavy iron door creaked as I opened it. Inside, slaves clutched at their oars in the dim light. They had no knowledge of what terror faced them—simply the certainty it would be awful.

I was surprised to see Magoq, the galley master who had so freely whipped and abused any rower who dared lag in their pace, curled fetal in a corner. The hulking giant was crying, shaking.

I had told myself I'd kill Magoq. I'd meant to do it, but I couldn't bring myself to murder the man when he was grabbing his knees, all but soiling himself in terror. I ignored him as I unlocked the people at their benches. The wind outside howled, or we were just moving at terrific speeds, or both, and I found it hard to stand upright against that momentum. The people chained to their benches could barely stand either. Others slipped in the effluvia of months spent shackled in the ship's bowels. We didn't say a word to each other. It wouldn't have mattered if we had: the roar of wind snatched away any conversation before it could be deciphered.

As I finished unlocking the men, I realized the cold was neither fear nor the weather. I reached for the Stone of Shackles with a nervous hand. I might as well have been feeling a block of ice. One of the men gestured, giving me the warning I needed as Delon swung a cutlass through the space where I'd stood a moment before.

Delon shouted at me, but I couldn't make out the words. He wasn't happy with me. That was clear enough.

He swung at me again, and as he did, the ship shifted violently. The room darkened as something massive flashed by the portholes. Delon's cutlass swung far off the mark and embedded itself in one of the wooden benches. There was noise and shuffling and (although I thought it hard to know for sure) the sound of screaming.

Something moved away from the porthole. A tiny wedge of light illuminated the room. I saw one of the galley rowers had picked up his chains and wrapped the metal links around Delon's throat.

Funny thing. Their leg strength might be atrophied by disuse, but a galley rower's upper body strength is nothing to mock. Few of the "permanent" slaves on board *The Misery* had any love for Delon. They hated him more than they hated Magoq.

I didn't stay to see what they'd do with him. I'd recognized the object that had briefly covered up the porthole, and knew we were in serious trouble.

It was a tentacle.

As I ran back on deck, I noticed the tentacles wrapped around *The Misery* didn't have suction cups. Not a one. Instead, they had teeth. Sharp, angry, curved points of bone or chitin or some other razor-sharp material that cut into wood like khorechalit axes.

I mention this detail because, like axes, those tentacles did no favors to the ship's integrity as they wrapped around mast and hull.

Under other circumstances, I'm sure the sailors would've attacked those tentacles with sword and harpoon. Instead, they grabbed onto the railings and whimpered with all their might. The ship tilted precipitously. I looked up, thinking we must be passing close to a particularly nasty fang.

We weren't: this was the Throat.

The ship tilted so far over that half the sky was now a spinning vortex. The gyre was a mile wide and spun into a fathomless abyss, probably opening up into Hell itself.

"Oh Taja," I whispered.

We were spinning around too fast, and it appeared that at any second we would lose our balance and fall screaming into the deep. The wind tore at me as if it wanted to toss me in personally.

I dragged myself along, holding on to ropes as I pulled myself up to the main deck. Teraeth balanced on the crux of the wheel, one foot against the main post, the other foot steering. He had one hand behind his back, and held the other one up in the air, counting upward. He looked no more bothered by the wind or the whirlpool than a fish is bothered by water.

Teraeth was getting on my nerves.

"I don't know if you've noticed," I shouted over the noise, "but a kraken's hanging off the back of the ship!"

He nodded. "She's catching a ride. She knows the whirlpool would tear her apart. She thinks her only chance is to ride it out with us!"

"She knows? She THINKS?"

"Of course. She is the daughter of a goddess!"

"I was trying to forget that." I looked around. Captain Juval was pressed against the wall of the stairwell down to the crew quarters. I thought he might have been praying. "Can we make it?"

"Three." He counted and held up another finger.

"There's got to be something we can do. We come out of this vortex and that kraken's going to tear us apart!"

"Sing."

"WHAT?" I screamed.

"That auctioneer said you were trained as a musician!" Teraeth shouted. "So *sing*. Sing as though your life depends on it!"

"How's *that* going to help?"

"Four!" Teraeth raised another finger.

The ship was spinning faster, and rode higher around the edge. At some point, it would spit us back out. While that should have been reassuring, I knew the rocky shoals of the Desolation waited for us to the north. If we didn't exit perfectly, we'd be smashed to kindling.

"WHY am I singing?"

"You'll wake the Old Man."

"I thought that was a BAD thing?"

"There's always the chance you'll amuse him. So sing already!"

"Nobody can hear me! I'm shouting and I can barely hear me!"

"He'll hear you. SING!" Teraeth held up his entire fist. "FIVE!"

I'd sung in strange situations back at the Shattered Veil, but usually it was a distraction from more prurient goings-on, not from imminent threat of death. And the stone around my neck was hot, scalding hot.

I picked out the first song that came to mind, because it was one of the last I'd performed in public. It felt strange to sing it without the harp Valathea to accompany me.

Let me tell you a tale of
Four brothers strong,
Red, yellow, violet, and indigo,
To whom all the land and
Sea once did belong
Red, yellow, violet, and indigo . . .

"Perfect!" Teraeth shouted. "Keep singing! Six! NOW!"

As if it was following Teraeth's instructions, the Maw flung *The Misery* far from the opening. I've never traveled so fast, so dizzyingly, sickeningly fast, in my entire life. We blasted out of the Maw with nauseating speed. As soon as we'd cleared the vortex, I heard the screams of sailors as the kraken moved.

One day they saw the veils
Of the same lady fair
Red, yellow, violet, and indigo
And each one did claim

Her hand would be theirs
Red, yellow, violet, and indigo . . .

We shot toward the rocks of the Desolation, missing being torn apart by the slimmest of margins. Unfortunately, we headed toward a small rocky island that would be large and hard enough to do the job anyway.

The island opened its eyes.

The air trapped in my throat as I saw it. Teraeth whispered in a furious voice, "Keep singing!"

I swallowed my fear and continued the song.

Let go of your claim!
They yelled at their brothers,
Red, yellow, violet, and indigo
And each screamed back,
She will never be another's!
Red, yellow, violet, and indigo . . .

"Gods," I heard Juval say as he pulled himself on deck. "What have you—? That—we've got to turn back."

"There's no turning back," Teraeth said. "We run and the Old Man will chase. He likes it when his prey runs."

As I sang, the island uncurled itself and shook off the accumulated dirt and dust of years asleep. The head was a long and sinuous shape, twisting and joining with a mass of muscle, sinew, and dull mottled scales. The wings, when spread, seemed like they might black out all the sky.

"I'll take my chances with the kraken!" Juval screamed. "That we can fight. That's a gods-be-damned DRAGON you're running us into!"

And so it was.

The dragon was sooty black, the color of thick coal ash. The cracks under its scales pulsed and glowed as if those scaly plates barely contained an inferno.

No forge glowed hotter than its eyes.

No story I'd heard of a dragon—of how big they are, how fierce, how deadly, how terrifying—did justice to the reality. This creature would decimate armies. No lone idiot riding a horse and carrying a spear ever stood a chance.

So they raised up their flags
And they readied for war
Red, yellow, violet, and indigo

The battle was grim and
The fields filled with gore
Red, yellow, violet, and indigo
And when it was done
Every mother was in tears
Red, yellow, violet, and indigo . . .

"Stand back, Captain, or you won't live to see if we survive this." Teraeth's voice was calm, smooth, and threatening.

I didn't look at them. What could I do? I sang. I heard them arguing behind me, and behind that, the noise of crew members screaming as they fought the kraken. It was cacophony on a grand scale, and I couldn't believe the dragon could distinguish the sources of all that noise.

The dragon opened its mouth. At first, I heard nothing, but then the rumbling roar hit me. Ripples spread out over the water, rocks shattered and split from the islands, the very wood of *The Misery* throbbed in sympathy. Clouds scuttled across the sky as if trying to escape the creature. Wispy vapors fell away from its mouth: yellow, sulfurous, heavier than smoke. The creature stared at *The Misery,* still speeding toward it, and I couldn't fight off the ugly certainty that the dragon stared directly at me.

A crescendo of screaming sounded behind me, and someone shouted, "My god! It's on top of the ship!" You can give credit to the dragon that I didn't look. The dragon had me. You cannot turn away from such a creature. It will either vanish or it will destroy you.

Teraeth must've looked away though, and Juval must've thought he had an opening. I really don't know what the Captain was thinking.

I guess he was acting from blind panic.

I heard a scuffle, a grunting noise, the slick scrape of metal. A second later, I heard the unmistakable, unforgettable sound of blood gurgling from a ripped throat.

"Idiot," Teraeth muttered.

Then the lady fair walked over
The carnage of bloody fears
Red, yellow, violet, and indigo
She said, None of you I'll have!
My love you do betray
Red, yellow, violet, and indigo . . .

The dragon's keening changed in pitch. I felt the dragon's song against the surface of my skin, the echo in my eardrums, the vibration in my bones. It was a physical shock, a tangible ecstasy.

He was singing.

The dragon was singing with me.

Then she flew up to the sky
And she's there to this day
Red, yellow, violet, and indigo . . .

Behind me, more shouts, more screams. The kraken scattered men on the deck as she tried to rip open the hold. There was a loud cracking sound, like a giant snapping trees for firewood.

And on a clear night you can
Still see her veils wave—

"Thaena!" Teraeth screamed. He tackled me as the mast fell right across where I'd been standing.

And, since I've never mastered the trick of singing with the wind knocked out of me, I stopped.

The dragon didn't like that at all.

He launched himself into the air, screaming with ear-shattering rage, gigantic wings spread wide against the glaring sun. That titanic creature crossed the distance to the ship in less than three seconds. I'd underestimated his size. He might've fit in the Great Arena in the Capital City, but only if he tucked himself up and rolled into a ball like a house cat.

The Old Man glided over us, his shadow a silken cloak sweeping over the ship. He smelled of sulfur and ash, the hot stench of the furnace and melting iron. As he passed, he idly reached out with a talon and plucked up the kraken still clinging to the deck. Great chunks of wood went with her. The dragon tossed the Daughter of Laaka into the air like a ball of string and breathed glowing hot ash at her.*

I'm sure you've heard stories of dragons breathing fire, but believe me when I say what this one did was worse. That was not fire as you find in a kitchen or forge, not the sort of fire that happens when you rub two sticks together, or even the magic flame sorcerers conjure. This was all the ashes of a furnace, of a thousand furnaces, heated to iron-melting, white-hot strength, and blasted out at typhoon velocity. The heat melted, the ash scoured, and the glowing cloud left no air to breathe.

She never stood a chance.

---

*According to eyewitness reports of the eruption of Mount Daynis in the southernmost edge of Khorvesh, the main cause of death was not the lava or giant boulders that blew upward from the volcano, but a surge of hot gases and smaller debris that behaved like water, flowing downhill and engulfing entire towns and cities in its path.

The dragon gulped down the charred mass of twisted flesh before it could fall back into the sea.

Then he banked and came back around to deal with us.

Teraeth stood up. So did I. The ship started to list, and worse still, Khaemezra and Tyentso came up on deck. I didn't think the two magi would show themselves unless the situation was truly grim, and dealing with the dragon had become more important than keeping the ship afloat.

"Oh god. Relos Var," I whispered. "Relos Var will come now."

"We're close to the island. If we can reach it, we'll be safe. It's consecrated to Thaena; he won't dare show himself at one of the seats of her power."

"Will singing again help?"

"Probably not. Let's just hope you put him in a good mood."

"What happens if he's in a good mood?"

"He flies away."

"And if he's in a bad mood?"

"He turns us all to cinders for daring to wake him from his nap."

I looked around. "If he's going to destroy us, he'd better hurry. The ship's sinking." Ripping away the kraken had opened gaps in the hull. The ship was taking on water.

Teraeth dragged his eyes away from the approaching dragon and looked at where *The Misery* was beginning to go down. "Oh hell."

"I want him."

The dragon's voice was loud and echoing, yet not an animal sound. The dragon didn't speak with the reptilian hiss I expected, but a grinding elemental noise that mimicked speech.

"Give him to me and I will save your craft."

"Yeah, but will you promise to feed me every day and give me lots of care and attention?" I muttered.

"He likes you. That's good," Teraeth said.

"Yeah, I feel really loved." I looked toward the back of the ship. "Taja, I hope those people can swim." I leaned backward to keep my balance.

Juval's body slid slowly across the planks. Tyentso also began to slip. Teraeth reached across and grabbed her by the arm, pulling her tight against him for balance. She gave him an odd look, but didn't protest.

"You may not have him. He is important to me," Khaemezra said. I stared at her, then back at the dragon. Her voice—

"I won't hurt him, Mother."

"I said no."

I looked at Teraeth and mouthed, "Mother?"

The assassin's mouth twitched. "Everyone calls her that," he said.

I shook my head. It wasn't just a figure of speech. Not with that voice. I'd never heard a voice like Khaemezra's—until I'd heard a dragon speak.

"Give him to me or I will–"

But their haggling had taken too long. *The Misery* had suffered too much in our flight. A second crack, much louder, sounded as the center of the ship splintered and broke in half. The bottom half slid into the ocean. The top half fell backward to smack against the water. I felt a moment's sensation of weightlessness as the deck dropped from under me.

The water rushed over my head. Sound vanished, then returned as a dull roar. As the ship sank the vast pull of current sucked me down, trapping me in spite of my efforts to swim free. No matter how hard I tried to swim up, the light faded, a dim glow drawing distant.

The water felt warmer than I expected, but perhaps that was just glowing heat from the stone around my neck.

My body wrenched upward as a gigantic claw plowed through the sea. Enormous talons formed a cage around my body. The last moments I remember were the sharp scent of lightning and ocean water, and the colossal eye of a gigantic black dragon, scales dripping with kelp, gazing at me. What I remember most vividly was that the eye was not the yellow glow of the Old Man's, but blue. Or maybe green.

Or maybe no color at all, except by reflection.

18: What Jarith Found

(Talon's story)

An ornate sword worked in red metal decorated the sturdy wrought iron gates of the Milligreest estate. The wide, perfect lawn of green grass lapped up against dueling yards, stables, and a horse-riding ring. Any flowers were confined to low decorative strips that could neither trip a guard nor hide an intruder. Palm trees lined the main strip of road like soldiers at attention. The main house was surprisingly undecorated: a plain, three-story building of red-orange plasterwork, with a crenelated top and towers at the four corners. It seemed more fortress than palace: there were no proper windows, and only a single, massive front door. The damn thing even had arrow slits.

His escort left him in the care of another group of soldiers, who brought him to the main gate and the custody of yet another group of soldiers. They led him through the front door and into a courtyard filled with fountains and flowering orange trees.

Kihrin was told to wait and left there, alone.

The courtyard ran through the heart of the building. All three stories looked out onto it, with railings on the second and third stories, and wide archways on the first. Braided reed chairs and tables in the center of the courtyard created an area for informal gatherings. The wall closest to the front door was flat and devoid of windows, but someone had, long ago, painted an elaborate mural over the plaster surface.

Kihrin rubbed his sweaty hands on his multicolored trousers and looked at the mural while he waited. The epic painting featured armored Quuros soldiers fighting the Manol vané, who fought back with bows and magic. Kihrin blinked as he realized the Quuros were losing. Losing might have been too mild a term.

It was more like the Quuros were being slaughtered.

"Kandor's Bane," a young woman said. "Painted by the great master Felicia Nacinte* on request of Laris Milligreest the Fourth. Isn't it beautiful?"

---

*Felicia Nacinte's masterpiece *The Rape of Thoris* has regrettably since been destroyed, but

Kihrin looked around, and then up. A girl his own age stood on the second-story balcony, looking down at him.

She was dressed in a stable-boy outfit of dirty ochre kef pants and a short, cropped, and tightly laced vest that might have been fine white linen before she rolled around in the mud. Her long black hair hung in twin braids wrapped in matching dark gold ribbons a little lighter in color than her liquid-brown eyes. Her face was smudged and, despite the blooming bruise on one cheek, lovely. In Kihrin's semiprofessional opinion, she would grow only more so as she grew older. Given a few more years, she would be able to make a man fetch or roll over as easily as he suspected she could draw the curved sword that hung from her belt.

"Very impressive," Kihrin agreed, "if you like battle scenes."

"They're the best kind. Anyway, that's not just a battle scene. That's the most important single event in my family's history. Did you know we're descended from Emperor Atrin Kandor?"

He looked at the painting again. Kandor was there, or at least there was someone wearing a lot of armor with a crown on his head. He'd been shot straight through his chest by a black arrow and was in the middle of dropping a great glowing sword from his hand. Urthaenriel, the Ruin of Kings.

"I didn't know that, no." He turned back to her. "Didn't he get most of the Khorvesh dominion killed?"

"That was a long time ago." She leaned out over the railing. "Does your father know you're dressed up like a street performer?"

"Yes, he does. Does your mother know she shouldn't put your hair in braids like that? People might think you're a girl."

She laughed outright. "You're bolder than I expected. I thought you'd be more of a fainting maid, but you meet me in the practice yards and I'll show you how much of a girl I can be. I bet I beat the pants off you."

Kihrin was hardly in the mood for flirting, but he couldn't let the line pass without comment. "Careful there. I might enjoy that."

She blushed then, although it wasn't with any real shame, and the laughter didn't leave her pretty eyes. "If you didn't enjoy it, I'd say we were doing it wrong," she finally said, a little hesitantly, as if she were just learning this flirting business and hadn't quite finished memorizing all her lines. Then the girl sighed. "Damn it all. Father wouldn't approve. It wouldn't be proper."

"I somehow doubt you only do what's proper. Not wearing that outfit."

---

some of her other paintings, particularly *The Morgage Rout, The Courtship of the Duke's Daughter,* and *A Rose for Thaena,* are on display at the Duke's palace in Khorvesh. I highly recommend their viewing if you ever have the opportunity.

"Eledore, aren't you supposed to be practicing?" Captain Jarith asked as he entered the courtyard through a side door.

The young woman grimaced and sighed the quiet complaint of the born martyr. "I was just—"

"Now, Dory."

"Yes, Jarith," she muttered, and retreated into one of the side passages. She did, however, stop to wink at Kihrin before leaving.

Jarith shook his head. "It's a good thing I rescued you. If I'd come in fifteen minutes later, she'd have you down by the practice yards, betting sword hits against your clothes."

Kihrin smirked. "Most men would fight to lose in a situation like that."

"Yes, but I doubt the High General would be happy to find a minstrel's son from the Lower Circle playing sword games with his pride and joy. That would be unhealthier for you than an encounter with a demon prince."

Kihrin's mouth felt dry as the Wastelands. "That was the High General's daughter?"

"Yes, it was, so don't get any ideas. It hasn't quite gotten so bad that I'm literally fighting off marriage offers, but I can see the day coming. I think when I marry it will be a commoner, just so I can hear the screams of rage from all the royal mothers who have been angling for me like fishermen with poles."

Kihrin felt stupid. "You're a Milligreest too?"

"Do you really think I'd have made Captain so young otherwise? Nepotism is alive and well in the Capital City of our great nation," Captain Jarith said with surprising bitterness.

"Crap." Kihrin grimaced. "I really stuck my foot in it, didn't I?"

"So deep I should fetch you a shovel." Despite his words, Jarith smiled. "I must admit she was dressed like a stable boy. I should take it as a compliment that you could see past the grime enough to think her pretty. Better than the men who only want her because of her father's connections." Captain Jarith gestured, the sweep of his hand taking in the manor. "My family is in a strange situation. We are not royalty, but so many of our family have held high office, as Voices of the Council, generals, or the like, that we might as well be. Those who want power court us, even though we have our distressing Khorveshan ways."

Kihrin shifted awkwardly.

"Yes?" Jarith asked him.

"Why are you telling me this?"

Jarith chewed on his lip for a minute. "You did a brave thing with that demon, and another brave thing asking me to look for that slave girl. I suppose I don't want you to think too ill of us."

"Why would I?" Kihrin paused. "Morea's sister? Talea? You've found out something?"

"I'm very sorry."

Kihrin ground his teeth and looked away. "She's dead?"

"She might as well be. She was sold to a man who counts torture as one of his favorite sports. His slaves don't meet happy ends."

"I could buy her."

"You don't have enough money."

"You don't know that." Kihrin crossed his arms over his chest and bit down hard on the urge to explain how he spent his evenings.

Jarith sighed. "Yes, I do. Because it doesn't matter how much money you have. You don't have enough. You could be a prince of a Royal House and it wouldn't matter. Darzin D'Mon is the kind of man who would invite you over with an offer to return her to you, and then torture her to death right there just to see the look on your face. He loves breaking spirits. It's my shame to think that the same blood flows through his veins as mine."

"What do you mean?"

"He is my cousin." Jarith Milligreest shook his head. "We're a proud family, and our history—" He gestured at the same mural. "We have lived and died in service to the Empire. He is a blight on my family's honor, but at least he doesn't wear the Milligreest name. Unfortunately, I can't make him free a slave he owns by law. If he wishes to kill her, the law says he may."

"It's not right. He can just murder her, and you'll do nothing?"

"She's not legally a person and thus it is not legally murder." Jarith shook his head. "I am sorry. If there were anyone else who had bought her, I could use my father's name to apply some pressure. However, if I ask after her, it would mean her death. My cousin loves me as much as I love him. He'd do it out of spite."

Kihrin shut his eyes and clenched his fists, tried to force down the taste of bile and hate. He looked up at the mural, at the fallen, twisted bodies of Quuros soldiers, dying as pawns in a game they did not understand and probably had wanted no part in. That hadn't spared them.

Jarith clapped a hand on his shoulder. "Come. We have a pleasant library, and good strong ginger brandy, and after the day you've had I think you could use the latter. I will leave you there to wait until my father is ready to speak with you."

Kihrin nodded, and allowed Jarith to lead him inside.

19: DREAM OF A GODDESS

(Kihrin's story)

I woke, alone, lying on a reed mat in a cave full of the wet sound of water dripping off rock . . .

Wait, no.

I'm getting ahead of myself. I should tell you about the dream. Although I suppose it wasn't a dream. Technically speaking, I don't dream anymore. I haven't dreamed since I was gaeshed. My nights are black, filled with nothing from the moment I close my eyes until I open them again in the morning.

So, this couldn't be a dream. Not really.

But in between almost drowning and waking up again, I experienced something like a dream.

It wasn't a hallucination, that's for certain.

My ears roared, a rhythmic sound, advancing and receding to the fury of my heartbeat. For a moment, I thought the noise was my heart. I smiled, because it meant my heart was beating. I was still alive.

Believe me, realizing you're still alive when you should by all rights be dead is a pleasure that never grows stale.

Then I remembered the dragon. I opened my eyes, spat out sandy grit from my mouth, and looked around. I lay on a beach, facedown, with the deafening crash of waves hitting the rocks and shore behind me. The sand underneath my fingertips was an odd, fine black, glittering, as if someone had pulverized onyx. In the distance, I saw rocks offshore, thick white mist, and the bright green of jungle forest on the other side of the beach. The jungle rose in the distance, climbing the sides of a mountain, its top obscured by thick clouds.

The beach was empty, save for me. Then I reassessed my opinion: a girl waded through the white foam of the waves.

The child looked no older than six. Her gathered Marakori shift trailed into the water as she bent over and examined rocks. Her tight mass of bright silver cloud curls glinted in the sunlight.

"Hello?" I tried standing, discovering to my pleasure I could.

I didn't remember seeing anyone like her on the ship. She looked human. Well, she mostly looked human. Her metallic hair hinted at other origins.

As I walked toward her, I noticed something. The tide water was rushing out, but where it should have stopped and came back in again, it continued its retreat. The entire ocean had decided it wanted to be as far from the island as possible. The little girl squealed as the retreating tide revealed pools, seashells, and flopping, confused fish.

"No, that's wrong," I muttered. *What's wrong about that?*

Stories of the ocean. Tales from Surdyeh's knee, tales of lethal waves . . . "Get away from there!"

"Fishies!" The little girl pointed down.

"NO! Get away from the water!" I ran toward her. We were too close to the ocean, far too close.

As I scooped her up, the water began to build into a wall. That wall grew higher and higher while I could only stare, knowing I was too late. There was nowhere I could run to safety before the tidal wave came crashing down.

The wave was gigantic and black, formed from the darkest, deepest waters of the ocean abyss. The wave's shadow swept over the beach, as it rose so high it blocked the light. I shut my eyes and turned away.

And stood there, notably not being washed away and not dying.

Don't think I wasn't grateful or anything: I was just surprised.

I looked back at the wave. The water hung suspended, perfectly still and motionless. Neither growing nor shrinking, the wave hunched over the land like a doom that had changed its mind at the last minute and hadn't quite decided who to destroy instead.

The little girl stuck her tongue out at the tidal wave and made a rude noise.

"Are you okay?" I looked at the kid, then back at the wave. "Why isn't it falling?"

She threw her arms around me and kissed me wetly on the cheek. She smelled sweet, like vanilla cakes floating in whipped cream. "It is! Silly. Too slow for you to see it. It's been falling for a looong time." The little girl wiggled, the way a cat will when it wants to be put down. I let her go and she jumped back down to the wet sand to oooh and aaah over confused starfish.

"I don't—" I shook my head. "I don't understand."

"That's okay. It's been a long time for you, and you don't remember anymore. It's hard to see something that big or old. Most people can't see it at all, won't see it until the final crash. And that will happen fast. Really fast. And then—" She tossed around sand. "Everything is swept away."

"When will that happen?"

"Not too long now." She bent down and picked up a seashell. "A sea spiral. Pretty. No two are ever the same. Chance shapes them. The waves, the sand, the sun, the wind."

"Who are you again?"

The little girl grinned. "You already know."

I swallowed and looked around. The day was beautiful and crisp, kept from being too hot by the marine layer of fog hovering just offshore. The air had a fresh salty sweetness that always eluded major port cities like the Capital or Kishna-Farriga. Overhead, seagulls cried out, hyperventilating in excitement over the uncovered fish. Everything around me seemed real if I ignored the hovering tidal wave hanging over my head.

I set my teeth against each other and looked back at the girl. "Why?" If she was who I thought, then I didn't need to be more specific. I needed no qualifiers with my goddess.

"Isn't it funny how short questions have long answers?"

"Give me the short version anyway."

"There's a war. It's a very old war, it's a very bad one, and it's one that we must win at all costs."

"A war? Against who?" I'd have heard if Quur was involved in an old, long war. "You don't mean the vané, do you?"

"No, I mean the demons."

"Demons? But . . ." I blinked. "The gods won that war. *We* won that war. That's the whole reason that demons have to follow our commands when we summon them." It felt odd, too, to treat this like something that happened a few years ago, maybe a generation at most. If there had ever been a war with demons, it was so old and distant that it had become the stuff of myths.

But I thought of Xaltorath. I thought of an Emperor who primarily existed to banish demons or show up when a demon managed to summon up enough of its ilk to create a rampaging Hellmarch. The people of Marakor and Jorat likely didn't have any trouble believing we were still at war with demons.

She gave me a pitying look. "No, we didn't win. Everyone lost. It wasn't an end to the war, just a pause, an armistice, while both sides retreated to their shelters and recovered from wounds so dire it's taken us millennia to catch our breath." She sighed. "And now we're ready to start the whole thing all over again, except this time we have nowhere to retreat."

I crossed my arms over my chest and stared out at the sea. "How am I involved in this?"

"Big waves start from small ripples. Avalanches begin with a single pebble."

My breath hitched. "I'm—I'm your pebble?"

"Yes. Also, you volunteered."

I stood there trying to remember if, somehow, I might have. Had I? Finally, I said, "I don't remember volunteering."

"Of course you don't. You hadn't been born yet."

"Hadn't been born—" I stopped myself from raising my voice. "And if I don't want to be your 'pebble'? You're the Goddess of Luck. Don't you have servants to fetch your dinner or kill your enemies? I don't want to be your hero. Those stories never end well. The peasant boy done good slays the monster, wins the princess, and only then finds out he's married to a stuck-up spoiled brat who thinks she's better than him. Or he gets so wrapped up in his own majesty that he raises taxes to put up gold statues of himself while his people starve. The chosen ones—like Emperor Kandor—end up rotting and dead on the Manol Jungle floor, stuck full of vané arrows. No thanks."

The little girl tossed the seashell over her shoulder. It shattered against the rocks. "So walk away." Her voice did not sound particularly child-like, but then it hadn't for some time.

I twirled around and spread out my arms to take in the beach, the island, the sea. "Is that really an option?"

"It is. They'll bring in a ship. You could sneak out." The little girl smiled, her eyes sad. "Do you think I wouldn't give you a choice?"

"You haven't so far."

"So I control your own decisions? I forced you to free those slaves on *The Misery*? How interesting. I had no idea I had so much power over you." She bent down to pick up another shell. "Choose to disbelieve me if you wish, but you can walk away. If you want. Go buy that inn, drink ale, play with bar wenches. Leave all those people behind you. Maybe you can hide from your enemies if you abandon your friends."

I angrily kicked a few rocks. "Damn it. That's playing dirty."

"The truth usually does." The little girl walked over and looked up at me with wide violet-colored eyes. "I picked you because of sentimentality, because of nostalgia, but not because you are indispensable. I could choose another. Walk away, if you want. Surdyeh's stories would say that I'm giving you a gift. You say it's a curse. I'll tell you something not one in a thousand would-be-heroes ever realize: it's both, and always will be. Good luck and bad luck. Joy and pain. They will always be there. It won't be better if you follow me. A hero who has never had a bad thing happen to him isn't a hero—he's just spoiled."

"So, this is what? A character-building exercise?"

"What do you think life is? Everyone gets their share of pain, whether they follow me or not."

"Oh, really? It wasn't until I turned away from you that my life went to shit."

"No." She shook her head. "Your attitude did. Look around. Are you the gaeshed sex slave of some slobbering merchant? The castrated musician of a Kishna-Farrigan lord? Owned, however briefly, by dear old Relos Var? Becoming a slave saved your life. You were convinced you were cursed, and so that is all you saw. You turned your back on the good fortune, on the lucky breaks that came your way."

"What about Miya?"

"She doesn't need rescuing." She put her hand in mine. It was small and warm. "No matter what happens, no matter what chains you wear, you decide if you are free. No one else."

"Excuse me while I allow my gaesh to argue otherwise."

She rolled her eyes. "Your gaesh is nothing. You will always be free to decide how you react to the world. If you are always free to act, even if it's to decide on your own death by defying a gaesh, then you are free. You may not have a lot of options, but you still have the freedom to choose."

"What are you saying? I should stop being so whiny?"

She grinned. "Yes."

"Ah, well then." I crouched down, looked at the seashells, then up at the dark wave. "Can I really leave all this behind? Make a new life for myself?"

She squeezed my fingers. "No."

"But you just said—"

"You can walk away. I didn't lie. You have that choice. But choices are rarely clean creatures without entanglements and complications. Just because you decide to run, don't expect your enemies won't chase, or that they will believe you have no interest in hindering them."

"Why do I even have enemies?" I pressed. "I'm *sixteen*. Faris is the only enemy I've earned. What right do these other people have to want me dead?"

She almost smiled. Almost. "Do you realize you're on the verge of telling me how unfair this all is?"

"It IS!"

"Okay. I'll tell Relos Var and all the others to stop picking on you. I'm sure he'll listen to me, since we're such good friends."

"You're a goddess."

"And he's the high priest of the one being in the universe who makes me wake up screaming from night terrors, so it all evens out."

I wanted her to be joking. I wanted her to smile and tilt her head and stare at me with a merry twinkle in her violet eyes as she said she was teasing, but she didn't. Her eyes emptied, spilling all that impish delight into darkness. What was left was haunted. It was not an expression I ever wanted to see in a woman I cared for; to see that horror reflected in the eyes of my goddess was like a bludgeon to my gut.

My goddess.

Well, hell.

I guess she'd forgiven me. I guess I'd forgiven her.

I picked up seashells and turned them over in my hands. Neither of us spoke for a time.

"I don't want to be a pawn," I said.

"Good. This is a war, not chess."

"What do you want from me?"

She exhaled slowly, almost shuddering. "This world is dying, Kihrin."

"Dying? What do you—"

"The sun should be yellow and it isn't. The sky should be blue and it isn't. I am old enough to remember when our sun was not bloated and orange. I am old enough to remember when we did not need Tya's Veil to keep out the radiation.* This world is dying, and we've been doing what we can to save it, but we are running out of sacrifices. Soon will come a day when we have nothing left to give, and when that day comes, the end will follow close behind it, and it will not be a conflagration, but numbing cold and darkness that never ends." She stood up and looked at the looming wave. "If we follow the path we're on, what we have always done, we lose. We only prolong the inevitable. Everyone loses the war. Everyone."

"And you want me to do something about that?" My voice absolutely cracked that time.

"You're my wild card, Kihrin. My ace up my sleeve. I'm going to trust you to do what you do best—find a path that no one else has thought of, break in through the door that no one thought to bar. Find another way."

I sat down on the wet sand. "I don't know how."

She hugged me. "I have faith that you'll figure it out."

I laughed bitterly. "That's playing dirty, Taj. How am I supposed to tell you no when you say a thing like that?"

"I don't play fair," she admitted as she wrapped a silver curl around her finger. "But then, neither do you."

"Not on my good days." I gestured up at the wave. "What do we do about that?"

"Here? Nothing. This is just a dream, and that is just a metaphor."

---

*Radiation of what? I would give much to be able to ask Taja for elaboration on these points. Assuming that this dream was really an encounter with the goddess herself (for the record, yes, I am assuming exactly that). However, in substantiation of these claims, I've been able to find no mention of any celestial phenomena resembling Tya's Veil prior to the God-King Era. And prior to the God-King Era, poetry involving the sun and sky did indeed use "yellow" and "blue" as central color motifs.

She looked up with big eyes. "Sooner or later, everything falls: waves, empires, races, even gods."

The wave shifted, moved.

"Taja!" I whimpered.

The little girl held me tight. "Don't worry, Kihrin. I won't leave you."

The dark wave fell, and brought night with it.

20: Valathea

(Talon's story)

A raging fire burned in the fireplace at the end of the Milligreest library. The night wasn't cool, and so the interior air seemed more suited to baking bread than breathing. Jarith left Kihrin with a dual promise to find the High General and to send a servant to bank the fire.

Different colors of woods forming intricate patterns paneled the walls and ceiling of the large library. None of the books matched, but had the worn and well-thumbed air of regular use. Kihrin felt a bit of grudging respect: he had stolen into too many houses where the "library" was a room whose only purpose was providing the maids with something to dust.

Before he poured a drink or checked to see if the High General had a fascination with smutty morgage romances, Kihrin decided the fire had to go. He circled around an overstuffed leather chair that faced the blaze. Even he found it too hot for comfort and he possessed a tolerance for heat bordering on the magical.

As he grabbed a poker, he heard a throat clear behind him. He flushed, embarrassed as he realized someone was already in the library, sitting in the chair where he couldn't be seen from the entrance.

"I'm sorry, my lord, I didn't see–" Kihrin turned and stopped. It wasn't the General, or any member of the Milligreest family.

Pretty Boy sat there, reading a book.

"Shit!" Kihrin dropped the iron poker and ran.

The door opened as he reached it. The hulking silhouette of the High General blocked Kihrin's only escape.

"Please, I–" Kihrin tried to get around the man.

"What's going on here?" the High General demanded.

Pretty Boy's all-too-familiar voice answered dryly from the other end of the room. "I have no idea. Normally people require at least five minutes in my presence before they run screaming. I believe I've set a new record."

The High General frowned at Kihrin. "Calm down, boy. No one's going to hurt you here. Jarith said you were waiting. What *are* you doing here, Lord Heir?" The question was addressed to Pretty Boy.

Kihrin hid his shudder and tried to pull himself together. "I'm sorry, sir. He startled me. I thought the room was empty. I'm sorry. I'm really sorry. I'll just—go."

The General chuckled. "I can't blame you for being skittish after that demon, but the Lord Heir D'Mon is quite human, no matter what his family name sounds like."

"What was that?" Pretty Boy asked.

Kihrin swallowed and threw a wary glare at Pretty Boy, who stood up and walked toward the pair. The man's hair formed a perfect series of dark chestnut waves breaking over his shoulders. Just as he had been at the Kazivar House, Pretty Boy dressed as royalty, and wore an embroidered blue silk misha over blue velvet kef. These were tucked into tall, black, leather riding boots. Sapphires and lapis lazuli beadwork sparkled from the embroidery of a hawk in midflight, laying on a golden sunburst field embroidered on his agolé.

No, Kihrin corrected himself. Pretty Boy wasn't dressed as royalty. Pretty Boy *was* royalty. House D'Mon.

Kihrin's heart skipped a beat from shock.

General Milligreest pursed his lips in disappointment. "I invited High Lord Therin to attend me at dinner tonight, not you, Darzin."

Pretty Boy bowed. "My sincerest apologies, High General, but my father sends his regrets. I believe he's meeting with a fellow who's put his hands on a vané tsali stone, and you know how obsessed he is about his collection." His gaze flitted idly over to Kihrin as he spoke.

Kihrin clenched his fists and tried to slow the rattle drum of his heartbeat. Oh hell. Butterbelly's buyer. Butterbelly said he had a man who collected the gems. If Butterbelly told them anything, they'd know who'd broken into that villa. They'd know where to find him. *I must leave. I must leave now. Oh shit. I'm as good as dead . . .* He calmed himself.

"Hmm. Yes, I remember."

"What was that about a demon?" Pretty Boy asked as if unfamiliar.

"You must have heard," the High General said with a pronounced growl.

"Oh no. I'm woefully ignorant of the important happenings of the Empire."

Kihrin found himself wishing he could carve away Pretty Boy's smug expression with a shiv.

General Milligreest narrowed his eyes. "This young man, Kihrin, was attacked by the demon prince Xaltorath earlier today. I lost a good man before the Emperor could arrive to banish it. We're still trying to locate the summoner."

"What? Why would a demon prince go after a boy?" Darzin looked at Kihrin with undisguised confusion.

Kihrin was startled: Darzin D'Mon's bemusement seemed genuine, and not some faux emotion worn only for the General's benefit.

Darzin hadn't sent the demon to attack him?

"We're still investigating. Xaltorath may have acted on a whim. He can be capricious in his cruelties. We're still trying to locate the party responsible for summoning the demon."

"I imagine the summoner was eaten. Isn't that kind of summoning terribly hard to control?"

"I wouldn't know." General Milligreest threw the nobleman a look of ill-concealed disgust.

Kihrin edged toward the door. If he could leave quietly, maybe they'd forget about him. He hadn't expected this. He wanted to tell the General that he'd witnessed Darzin D'Mon and Dead Man kill that vané and summon a demon, but the General *knew* Darzin. He knew him well enough to invite him over to dinner. Milligreest wasn't going to believe Kihrin's accusations.

There was no help for it. Kihrin would leave. Kihrin could go back and buy a harp, any harp, claim it was a present and give it to Surdyeh. Ola was right. He'd slip a note to Jarith, tell the Captain what had happened once Kihrin was long gone. Silently he started his chant: *No sight, no sound, no presence. I am not here . . .*

"What good fortune the Emperor showed up, or it would have been a real mess, wouldn't it?"

"It is Sandus's duty to protect the Empire, Darzin. He would never ignore the threat of an unbound demon prince."

"I'll have to remember that. My son will be so relieved."

The General looked around the room in obvious disgust. "Argas's forge! It's like an oven in here."

Darzin shrugged. "I like it that way. So why bring the boy back here? Jarith finally proved a disappointment, so you've decided to adopt?"

"Of course not! He—?" The General looked around, and then stepped out in the hall. "Kihrin? Where are you going?"

Kihrin stopped his casual stroll and turned around, hiding his sigh. "Oh, I'm sorry, Your Lordship. I thought you might wish to speak with the prince in private."

"Don't be ridiculous. Get back here. The faster we do this, the faster we can send you on your way."

"Yes, sir." Kihrin shuffled back to the General.

"That was amazing," Pretty Boy said. "I didn't even notice you leave."

Kihrin kept his eyes on the floor. "Yes, my lord."

"A boy like you could make quite a career with such skills of stealth."

"I have no idea what you mean, my lord."

"Yes . . . of course you don't. Kihrin, you said your name is?"

"Yes, my lord." He contemplated lying, but the High General already knew his name.

"Darzin, leave off shopping for people with a talent for law-breaking until you're outside these walls. Young man, follow me and I'll give you that reward." Qoran walked down the hall with the attitude of someone who expected to be obeyed without question.

Kihrin hesitated before following, realizing Darzin was doing so as well. Every step was like walking on fire, as Kihrin forced himself forward against his body's overwhelming desire to bolt and run. He would collect the harp and go. Darzin didn't know Kihrin was the thief who had witnessed Xaltorath's summoning.

Kihrin reminded himself everything was fine. He reminded himself several times.

Darzin whistled a jaunty tune as they walked, until the General gave him an annoyed look.

At last Milligreest arrived at a set of carved doors, which he unlocked with a heavy brass key. The General swung open the doors.

Against the far wall of the room rested several harps, some floor-length and others of smaller size. Kihrin frowned as he saw that the General kept them uncovered, but at least the room had no window to let in the sunlight, which might have warped the wood of a harp and soured the tone.

Milligreest nodded in the direction of the harps. "Pick one out you like, then I want you to play something for me."

Kihrin turned back to him. "Excuse me, sir?"

Milligreest frowned. "What didn't you understand? I want to hear you play something. That demon broke your harp and you deserve a replacement, but I'm not giving up one of my harps to someone who can't use one, understand?"

Darzin snickered.

Kihrin started to protest the harp had been his father's, not his. Then it occurred to him that the General was his only protection against Pretty Boy, or "Darzin," or whatever his name was. He couldn't afford to upset him. The young man nodded and crossed the room. He would pick something quickly. He would pick something that the High General wouldn't care if he lost—the least valuable harp in the collection—and he would run back to Surdyeh as fast as he could.

Each musical instrument was a work of art, lovely in form, but most of them were too fancy, inlaid with rare woods and metals, set with precious gems. They were harps as art objects, not as musical instruments. If he sold one of these, he'd be arrested as its thief.

One harp looked like it might cost less than the yearly total income of the Shattered Veil: a small double-strung lap harp tucked into a corner. He turned to Qoran Milligreest for permission.

The High General nodded to him.

Kihrin sat down on a stool and pulled the harp onto his lap. The style of the harp was old-fashioned; he groaned as he realized the strings were silver instead of silk. He wasn't sure he could play this: he wore his nails clipped short, since silk-strung harps were played with the fingertips, not the nails. He plucked a single string to test if he needed to ask for picks. To his surprise, a pure clean note rang.

He plucked an arpeggio, and couldn't help but smile at the harp's laughter. The notes were so clear, so perfect! Who wouldn't sound like a master using a harp like this?

"Play it, don't sit there and drool on it," the General admonished, not unkindly. "Figures you'd find the prize of my collection."

Kihrin looked up, shocked. "This?"

"She's an antique. I more than half-suspect this is what Sandus had in mind."

"The Emperor?" Lord Heir Darzin asked. "The *Emperor* ordered you to give that boy one of your harps?"

"The Emperor was impressed. Kihrin was very brave."

Kihrin's fingers paused on the strings, his look one of confusion.

"Yes, young man?"

"General, I don't remember meeting the Emperor." He frowned. He had smacked his head hard when the demon had thrown him. Just because he didn't remember meeting the Emperor did not mean it hadn't happened.

The General's smile was kind. "Remember the man in the patchwork *sallí*?"

"*That* was Emperor Sandus?"

Darzin scoffed. "He might wear the crown, but he's still a peasant. I wonder if he's paid up on his magic license fees?"

"That's enough," the General growled. "Your father may be one of my oldest friends but that doesn't mean I will tolerate insolence from you."

Darzin stared at the General. The bone of his jaw turned white and clenched and his nostrils flared. He tilted his head in the General's direction. "My sincerest apologies, High General." Nothing in his tone of voice sounded sincere or apologetic.

"But that—that's not possible," Kihrin protested. "That man said he was a friend of my father's. My father doesn't know the Emperor."*

Darzin blinked and straightened. His eyes widened as he turned and stared at Kihrin, stared long and hard. Despite Surdyeh's lectures, Kihrin met the Lord Heir's stare.

---

*I rather suspect that statement is wrong on all possible counts.

Why was he surprised Darzin had blue eyes? It was so obvious, in hindsight.

You look like him, Morea had said. *You even wear his colors . . .*

How many noblemen had god-marked blue eyes? How many noblemen who delighted in murder and dealt with demons?

Kihrin stared too long. As he did, Darzin frowned in confusion.

"You have blue eyes . . ." Darzin whispered softly, staring at Kihrin as if to memorize him. A look of dawning comprehension stole over him. Darzin smiled then, cruelly, and ran his tongue over his lips. "And here I didn't think Taja liked me."

Kihrin's hands tightened on the harp.

Darzin chuckled.

The sound of Xaltorath's screaming had not filled Kihrin with more dread.

"Are we amusing you, Darzin?"

The Lord Heir stifled his laughter, giving General Milligreest an embarrassed glance. "Oh, not at all. My apologies. I just remembered the punch line to a funny joke. The young man was going to play us a song, yes?"

The General stared at him a moment longer, then turned back to Kihrin. "Go on, play something."

Kihrin wanted to vomit. He realized with sick dread both Ola and Surdyeh had been right. He shouldn't have come. *Pretty Boy had blue eyes.*

Kihrin bent his head over the harp and fiddled with the tuning while he tried to keep himself from shaking, while he tried to remember something, anything, to play.

Surdyeh had often said Kihrin was a hopeless musician. Kihrin was hurt every time his father said it, but only because he knew it was true. He had no motivation. When he was a child, Kihrin always found more important things to do than sit in darkened rooms practicing his fingering. And now that he was growing up, plenty of new diversions, especially female diversions, attracted him away from lessons. He was a passable harpist, but he wasn't in love with music. When Kihrin's voice broke, he discovered it was good enough for entertainment, and that had been sufficient.

He sat still, trying to remember the old songs that his father had made him memorize. He froze, thinking he had forgotten them, but after a few hesitant strokes, Kihrin began to play with more confidence.

It wouldn't have mattered if he plucked the strings at random. The harp wouldn't allow him to play poorly. The room ceased to be, his worries about demons and royalty ceased to be, and all he felt were silver chords of music floating around him, dancing on the air. For the span of a song, he forgot every concern.

The music died. Kihrin fought the need to keep playing, even though the tips of his fingers ached from plucking silver instead of silk. He looked up and saw Milligreest examining a far wall, his eyes unreadable except for pain and an almost-forgotten wistfulness. Darzin's eyes were closed and his mouth open; the prince shook himself as from a dream.

"Huh. You'll do well by her I think. She likes you," the General commented. "Her name is Valathea."

"Valathea?" The response came out like a question.

"Very special harps, like special swords, are named. She is a vané harp. In their language her name means 'sorrow.'* She has never left the possession of the Milligreest family until now, so you will take care of her." The last sentence had the weight of a command.

"I will, High General." Kihrin covered her. For a moment, he forgot the danger he was in. She was beautiful, the most beautiful harp he had ever heard. Surdyeh would be so happy. How could he stay angry with Kihrin after this? If he sounded this good playing her, how much better would Surdyeh sound?† "May I go?"

"Of course. Go show your father your reward."

Kihrin left as quickly as the burden of the harp allowed.

After he left, the room was quiet. Then Darzin broke the silence. "Well. If you'll excuse me as well . . ."

"Nonsense, Darzin. You wanted to dine with me, did you not? I wouldn't dream of disappointing you."

"Of course, and I'm honored, but . . . umm . . . pressing business. You understand."

"I do not understand. You said you were here to take your father's place. What business draws you away from that?"

Darzin frowned. "I assumed you invited my father here because of the boy. Which I appreciate: he's clearly one of ours. I know you'd rather not share my company; why don't I go inform my father you've found one of our house's lost scions?"

"Think of this as your best chance to impress me. Which you will need to do, if you are ever to convince me that your son and my daughter are not so closely related that marriage is out of the question."

---

*The closest translation of Valathea is "the exquisite sorrow that comes from understanding great truths." It is a female Kirpis vané given name, currently out of vogue.

†Not better at all, I suspect. *"Notrin Milligreest allowed me to examine the Valathea harp, which by family legend traces back to Elana Kandor, widow of famous Quuros Emperor Atrin Kandor. It was said that the harp only plays notes in a minor key, no matter what the skill or intention of the musician. I wished to see this for myself, and Notrin humored me. The harp is in excellent condition, and has been well maintained, and yet, as predicted, I could not coax any music from the harp not best fit for a dirge. When I asked how this had been accomplished, Notrin shrugged and informed me that there was no great skill to it: Valathea only played brightly for those she loved."*–A Study of Enchantment, by Darvok Hin Lora

The Lord Heir ground his teeth in defeat. "Of course." He waved a hand at the harps. "The boy was raised as a street rat, you realize. He's just going to sell your precious harp the first chance he has, maybe even tonight."

"No, he won't. I saw the look on his face. He would die first." The High General shrugged. "Besides, it's not my decision. The Emperor is interested in that boy. I wouldn't want to be the person who allowed him to come to harm."

Darzin D'Mon looked as if he'd swallowed bile. "No. No, neither would I."

21: The Island of Ynisthana

(Kihrin's story)

I woke, alone, lying on a reed mat in a cave full of the wet sound of water dripping off rock. I remembered the dream with unusual clarity, probably because it was the first dream I'd had since Tyentso's summoned demon had torn out part of my soul.

Had it been a hallucination, the product of a near-drowning, or had I really just experienced a heart-to-heart chat with the Goddess of Luck herself? The dream had been surreal, but no more so than any events of the last week. Had I really survived a passage through the Maw, and a Daughter of Laaka, and sung a duet with a dragon?

A real dragon. I felt immortal.

Sure, I thought to myself, *and now you're the gaeshed slave of a vané hag who might also be a dragon, trapped with her rabid son on an island somewhere in the Desolation. If they've saved you for something, you won't like it.*

Taja said I just needed a better attitude.

I laughed out loud.

I lay there and listened to the surrounding sounds: the drip, drip, drip of water and the distant cries of seagulls. Nothing sounded like people or the heavy breathing of a large dragon, so I sat up and looked around the cave.

A few pieces of incongruous furniture decorated the place: the reed mat I had been lying on; a large chest; a table, two chairs. Small lanterns fixed high into the walls provided light. The cave was large, though not large enough to fit the dragon I had seen. The glossy, smooth black stone walls looked like they had melted and solidified many times in rapid succession.

The air was warm and humid against my unclothed skin: the rough Black Brotherhood robe was gone. I panicked for a moment, reached up for the Stone of Shackles, and sighed in relief as I realized it was still there.

I searched through the chest and found a pair of loose-fitting trousers (I'll give you one guess what color), a set of sandals woven from reeds, and a small silver hairbrush and clasp. There was nothing to wear for a shirt, but the kef and sandals fit well enough. I spent several minutes forcing the brush through the mess of my hair before pulling it away from my face with the clasp.

The cave ended in folds of ropy, coiled rock, which let in a bit of light. I walked to the edge, and even with my love of heights I felt a moment's dizziness.

The cave opened out onto the side of a cliff, near the top. The opening was so high I could see above the treetops of the jungle stretched out below me. A thin fog obscured the foliage below, thickening into a wall of white in the distance: the mists of the Desolation. The calls of birds and monkeys, and other sounds I couldn't pretend to identify, echoed in the distance. There was no sign of anyone: human, vané, or otherwise.

I leaned out. A net of interwoven vines grew up the sides of the cliff. The vines spidered, leading not only to this cave, but to hundreds of others. Narrow ramps woven from wood planks and dried vines formed awkward stairs and walkways tracing the route from heights to ground. This cave possessed no such advantage, but if their intention had been to trap me, they'd miscalculated. Many of the vines looked sturdy, and as good as any ladder to a thief such as myself. There was nothing to keep me from escaping.

Except the gaesh.

Except . . . I stopped. Could I escape? They must have boats, or Teraeth wouldn't have needed to memorize the safe route through the rocks. Taja had said they would bring another. I could sneak down to whatever harbor they used, steal on board a ship . . .

I waited for the pain of the gaesh to overtake me.

Nothing.

Khaemezra's words echoed, almost an audible whisper: *I've removed the previous prohibitions.*

Then Taja's words: *You can walk away. If you want.*

I bit my lip to keep from jumping up and down and whooping out loud.

I climbed down the cliff. When I reached the bottom, the jungle seemed claustrophobic. Thick fog blocked most of my vision. I wasn't blind, however: I saw a path formed by the passage of many feet, a smoothed line of rock snaking around the base of the cliff, where it faded into the mist. There was no one around, and no sounds but those the jungle gave me.

I was on an island. The jungle was no shelter for a city dweller like myself. Whoever had me captive, Black Brotherhood or black dragon, was obviously aware of this, which was why they'd made no effort to put me under any kind of guard. The clothes and furniture made me think the Black Brotherhood still had me. Good enough. Once I had the lay of the land, I would organize my escape.

Whistling a tune, I headed down the path.

22: A GOLDEN HAWK

(Talon's story)

Morea stumbled out of bed as Kihrin ran through the door. He carried a large triangular package slung over his shoulder as he panted, out of breath.

"Are you hurt?" Morea rushed to him. "Ola didn't see you, did she?"

Kihrin lowered the package to the ground. "Morea, I need you to hide this."

"What's going on? What happened?" She grabbed for her agolé to cover herself, but he paid no attention to her nudity.

"I have to go. I don't have time to explain."

"What—" She reached for him, realized her mistake, and instead placed a hand on the cloth-wrapped triangle. "The harp? You met with the General?"

Kihrin shook his head. "Yes, I mean, no. He was there. Your noble-man was there."

"MY nobleman? But I—"

"The one with blue eyes. Darzin D'Mon. I saw him." A desperate look haunted Kihrin's eyes. "He saw me. *Shit.* He saw me. He must have sent the demon. I know he sent the demon to attack me, but why did he seem so surprised to find out it had? Was he acting? They were looking for something—" He rubbed the sides of his temples.

She gasped. "Wait—*Darzin* is the one who sent the demon? Oh no!"

"I want you to find my father and Ola and get them out of here. We need to leave the City. We need to leave tonight. Surdyeh should be up-stairs. Find him."

"What do I tell them?"

"You tell Ola I saw a golden hawk. Understand? It's a code phrase that means—" Kihrin stopped midsentence.

"That means what?"

Kihrin ignored her. He looked like he had been stabbed.

"Kihrin, what *does* it mean?" Morea asked again.

He blinked and looked at her. "It means we're in danger. Danger so bad we have to go into hiding."

"Oh." She paused. "Isn't that odd? That Ola would use that as a code phrase? Do you realize that the symbol of House D'Mon is a golden hawk?"

He closed his eyes.

"Ola, how could you?" he muttered. "Somebody set me up. Whoever fed Butterbelly the Kazivar House job must have known . . . Taja, what are you getting me into?"

Morea bit her lip. "What are you going to do?"

"I'm going to find out if we still have time to cover our tracks."

Kihrin ran out the door.

Butterbelly's shop was too quiet.

Kihrin eased himself through the back-alley entrance, fighting down bile. Butterbelly's door hadn't been locked, but that wasn't so unusual. Who did a Shadowdancer fence have to fear? No one in the Lower Circle would be so stupid as to attack someone in the 'dancers.

The nobles might not play by those rules though. Kihrin was damn sure Pretty Boy and Dead Man wouldn't.

He pulled out his daggers as he crept through the cluttered room. A few steps inside, he caught the metallic scent of blood. The kill was too fresh to have decayed yet in the warm night air. The young thief ground his teeth. He continued forward, although Kihrin dreaded what he would find.

Too late.

Butterbelly's killer had left his body sprawled across the wooden table he used for business transactions. Flies hovered over the bloody corpse. A dozen wounds from daggers covered the body; slow, painful slashes across his throat, down his stomach. A few lacerations covered his arms from trying to fight off his attacker, but it must have been over quickly. The killer had left the murder weapons behind: twin daggers buried to their hilts in Butterbelly's chest.

Butterbelly's crossbow still rested in its cradle under the table.

It was never used.

Kihrin had seen dead bodies before, but it took all his strength not to throw up. This was someone he knew.

Kihrin tossed the room as best he could. He even looked in the secret wall safe Butterbelly hadn't thought he knew about. The stolen emerald tsali stone was missing.

Butterbelly had known where Kihrin lived. He had known where to find Kihrin, where to find Ola and Surdyeh. Kihrin could hope that

Pretty Boy and Dead Man now had the emerald necklace they wanted, but if they also desired no living witnesses—and didn't care who they hurt when hunting for one . . .

"Pappa . . ."

The young thief ran.

23: Morning Service

(Kihrin's story)

I stared at the vista rearing up before me as I came around the bend.

The winding trail left behind fog and jungle, switchbacking up the sides of the mountain at the center of the island. The path became cobblestone, although the stone was warped and twisted in sections. No one could approach within five hundred feet of that thin, snaking trail without being seen. There was no cover, no shelter—just barren, black rock. The path ended at a temple.

At least, I assumed it was a temple.

It's not like there was a sign, but generally, if I come around a bend and see a gigantic monolithic cobra carved from black basalt—tail spilling down ancient steps and double doors leading into darkness—I assume it must be a temple.

To what, or rather, to whom though? I had no idea. Even if only eight true gods exist, Quur is the land of a thousand gods.* There had to be a snake god, but I didn't know who that might be, just as I didn't know what gods the Manol vané worshipped. Was Thaena associated with snakes? Not in Quur, but who knows how her worship was practiced outside its borders?

As I stood there, I heard drums, coming from the temple.

I shrugged. What the hell? If the cultists were distracted with religious services, it might be the opportunity I needed. I didn't see any guards, but why would they have guards when there was no way for anyone to invade? Everyone was probably in the temple.

Yeah, all right. Fine. If you insist: *I was curious.*

Walking up to the same temple was a peculiar exercise in vulnerability. I saw no shelter to hide behind, no way to stick to shadows for a stealthy approach. The sound of my borrowed sandals slapped against the hard stone despite my efforts to muffle the noise. I resorted to slipping off the sandals and carrying them by the straps.

---

*An exaggeration. There are, at most, several hundred deities. Maybe twice that many counting dead god-kings.

As I drew closer, the immense age of the temple became evident. The stonework crumbled at the edges. The blocks were cracked as if heated and cooled swiftly. The building was far larger than I'd initially imagined. I couldn't shake the feeling that the building hovered on the edge of collapse, that at any moment those immense tons of stone would crumble forward . . .

I shuddered. Vané wouldn't build something like this, would they? All this stone and heavy oppressive earth was nothing like Lady Miya's ephemeral loveliness, or even Teraeth's razor-quick shadows. This seemed . . . older.

Was that even possible?*

I slipped inside the broad doors without seeing another soul. The air inside was musky and dank, and despite the distance from the beach, it smelled of the ocean. There was an undercurrent of something sweet and rotting. The drums sounded louder now. I felt the vibration in the soles of my feet. After a few moments, my eyes adjusted enough to let me see in the darkness.

The snake theme continued inside the building. Stone serpents twined up pillars and formed the arches over doorways, carved in bas-relief. Even the cobbles underfoot were shaped like scales. The rock shone slick and oily with the watery dampness of the temple. There were statues too: stone women with asps for hair; hugely muscled, scaled men with hooded cobra heads; coiling pythons with human faces. They reminded me of stories Surdyeh used to tell when I was a child, and I suppressed a shiver. Monsters, every one of them.

At least these were just stone.

I followed the sound of the drums, more careful now, more certain I would soon run into the rest of the Black Brotherhood and not sure what would happen when I did. What do you say to the group of cultist assassins who rescued you from certain death? *Hey, thanks, any of you mind telling me how to get back to the mainland?*

The damp tunnel leading deeper into the temple opened, and I found myself standing in the back of a great hall. People filled the enormous room, their features hidden behind the same voluminous black robes Teraeth and Khaemezra had worn in Kishna-Farriga. I slid in quietly, letting years of training and my own inclinations muffle the sound of my steps.

The warm air seemed unnatural when compared to the coolness of the island outside. Vents in the floor released a steady flow of steam into

---

*No. But the architecture might appear older by virtue of being more primitive. Many relics come from eras technically younger than the vané.

the room, to mingle with the incense and the blood on the altar. That altar . . . I had to press my lips together to keep from gasping out loud.

Behind the altar stood a statue different in style from the surrounding architecture. The statue was almost as tall as the height of the room itself, so even from the back, she looked like she might stretch out a hand and touch me. Like everything else, she was carved in black stone, but here and only here could I see the delicate touches of vané craftsmanship. In each hand she held a snake, which reared back to adore or strike at her. I honestly couldn't tell if she was caressing the snakes or strangling them. Gold leaf covered every inch of her stone gown. The goddess wore a pectoral and belt fashioned from skulls around her neck and hips. Roses crafted from iron decorated her hair and dress. The salt air had rusted them to the color of blood.

I swallowed nervously. I knew her. Who does not? She is Thaena.* She is the Pale Lady. She is the Queen of the Underworld. She is the Goddess of Death. Teraeth had said the Black Brotherhood served the Death Goddess, and here was the confirmation.

I scowled as I looked at her. I didn't know what her part in all this was, but I suspected it was every bit as active as Taja's. Then I shivered. Maybe I had called to her, and not the other way around. Maybe when I was on board *The Misery,* the first time—before Tyentso's gaesh. Or maybe back in the Capital City when I'd invoked Thaena . . .

I ground my teeth together and refused to think about it.

The altar dias was not empty. Two men crouched over massive drums, pounding out the beat vibrating through every stone. Two familiar figures stood before the altar. Khaemezra wore a small mountain of embroidered black velvet, as if the heat were someone else's problem. Teraeth stood beside his mother, the only person in the entire hall who wore a different hue. His breeches were dark green, shimmering with silvery highlights. Long strips of silk, greens and golds, shifted and flowed over his torso and trailed down his arms. I was too far away to see the details of the outfit, but even from that distance there was something wild and feral about it.

Khaemezra opened her arms wide, a mirror of Thaena's gesture. The drumming stopped.

She paused for a dramatic moment, opened her mouth, and said . . .

Actually, I have no idea what she said.

I'd never even heard anything like it, let alone understood it. It wasn't vané. The words flowed and hissed, with sibilants and throaty growls.

---

*Although most popular in Khorvesh, Thaena is worshipped in every dominion in the Empire and outside its borders, usually in the form of propitiatory offerings meant to turn her attention elsewhere.

Combined with a voice that sounded less like it came from a mortal creature than some elemental thing—say, a dragon—and it was guaranteed to impress.

I also realized something else: the acoustics in this place were fantastic. The old woman sounded like she was right next to me, the grinding whispers carrying perfectly to the farthest corners of the temple. It was better than any music hall I'd ever visited back at the Capital. The ceremony, ritual, lecture, or whatever, lasted for a few minutes. I found her speech unsettling and disquieting, even if I couldn't understand a word of what she said.

When she finished, she lowered her arms. Teraeth reached under the altar and brought up a chalice with a shallow, wide bowl. He filled the cup from a basin of cloudy water near the altar and added a long splash of something from a red decanter. Teraeth then produced a black dagger with a wavy blade. He sliced the blade against his own arm, and let the blood trickle into the cup.

His mother said something else, and one by one, people approached the altar. Each said a few words, often in whispers. Most spoke that strange hissing language, but sometimes I caught a hint of a familiar tongue.

Then they drank from Teraeth's chalice, which was a bit disgusting considering one of the contents was his own blood. Each time, they paused. When nothing happened, Teraeth motioned them away. The tension amongst those waiting to drink was palpable, as was the relief of those same people when they walked back into the audience.

When everyone returned to their places, Khaemezra spread her arms wide and said an impressive piece of gibberish. Silence followed. No one moved for a moment.

Teraeth stepped forward and put his hand on the knife. Someone in the audience gasped.

"Not you," Khaemezra said, sounding surprised.

Teraeth shook his head. "Me."

"It's not your turn—"

"He almost died because of me. I have to do this."

They stared at each other until Khaemezra took the knife from her son's hand. She flipped the blade over and gave it back to him, hilt first.

"So be it." She walked to the side, as if excusing herself from what would follow.

Teraeth thrust the blade into the air above his head and screamed something in that strange foreign tongue. The drummers started up a furious beat and the people in the audience stomped their feet in time. Teraeth, standing underneath the statue, began to move his arms and his legs. The movements were so rhythmic and strange it took me a moment to realize he was dancing. His dance was not provocative, did not arouse: it was powerful, wild, and angry. The tempo of the drums increased and my heart rate sped up in time and he was whirling and flashing the dagger so fast around his body I was amazed he didn't land in pieces.

Then he stopped.

He faced the audience, head tilted back to gaze up at his goddess. The drumming ceased.

He lifted his arm and with one smooth, graceful motion he brought the blade down into his own heart.

"Shit!" I gasped.

Even though the acoustics dampened the sound of my voice, everyone heard me.

Several things happened at once. First, Teraeth collapsed, his chest soaked in red. Second, several hundred people in hooded black robes looked back in my direction. Third, the two drummers raised their heads, which, because of the nature of their anatomy, meant the hoods fell away to reveal their faces.

Their serpent faces, I should clarify.

They looked just like the statues I'd seen out in the hall, except these were not inanimate. They stood.

I panicked and ran.

It seemed to be the sensible thing to do, under the circumstances.

24: The Hawk's Talon

(Talon's story)

As Kihrin ran into the courtyard of the Shattered Veil Club, Ola opened the door to her apartment. She carried a crossbow in her hands and a worried look on her face.

"Ola, where's Morea?"

"Oh! You just about gave me a heart attack. I was gonna ask you that, sweet cheeks. I heard a scream, and not the right kind. Where's your girl? And what are you doing up and about?" She glued a hand to her hip and looked at him indignantly.

"We don't have time to talk about that. She wasn't inside?"

"Not that I saw. Now what's going on?"

"Give me your crossbow." He looked up the stairs to his room and wondered with sick dread if Morea had even made it that far.

"You give me an explanation, Bright-Eyes."

"Does the name Darzin D'Mon mean anything to you?"

Ola turned gray. She clutched the crossbow to her bosom as if it were a doll.

"Damn it, Ola. You should have told me."

"It's not what you think!"

"He's killed Butterbelly," Kihrin whispered. "He's coming here. Do you understand? His people may already be here."

"Oh goddess," she cursed under her breath.

"Take Roarin and Lesver, then run. Don't stop to take anything. Just leave. You know the safe house."

"What are you going to do?"

Kihrin inhaled, steeling himself. "I'm going to grab your spare crossbow and make sure the others are okay."

He ducked past her into her apartment before she could stop him.

The front parlor was just as he remembered, exotic and sparkling. The masks looked menacing in the dim light. The harp sat by the door, exactly where he'd left it, still covered by its cloth case. There was no sign of Morea.

He crossed over to a cabinet and pulled down the spare crossbow and a quiver of bolts.

He was good with a crossbow, a handy skill for a burglar. Crossbows were useful for grappling hooks and rappelling gear, and sometimes, for guard dogs. He'd never fired one at a person before, but he was pretty sure the technique was the same.

He cranked back the winch on the crossbow. As he loaded a bolt, he heard a noise. It wasn't much. A scuff of leather against tile. Maybe it was Morea in the bedroom, still pretending to be asleep. Maybe.

But Kihrin didn't think so.

He made his way over to the jade bead curtain, parted the strings, and slipped inside.

This room, too, looked normal. Tya's Veil shone in through the windows, limning shafts of teal, pink, and lilac light over the bed linens. He frowned. There were two human-shaped lumps under the sheets.

His stomach twisted. Ola couldn't have missed this. No way she wouldn't have checked.

Kihrin's throat felt thick and gummy as he inched his way to the bed and threw back the covers.

Morea and Surdyeh both lay there.

They had been meticulously posed, hands crossed over their hearts, eyes closed as if sleeping. It only made their slit throats more obvious: deep slashes on each neck, exactly like the wounds that had killed Butterbelly. Blood stained the bedding under their bodies black.

They were dead.

He stared. *No. No, it can't be.* He couldn't be seeing what he was seeing. She'd been alive. They'd both been alive. His father was alive. It had only been a trip to Butterbelly's and back. *They'd been alive!*

Kihrin put his hand to his throat. The stone around his neck was ice.

Unlike Butterbelly, neither Surdyeh nor Morea had been tortured. There was no need. Their killers had only to wait to find their prey—and they were still waiting.

Kihrin didn't have to see beyond the First Veil to reveal the men lurking in ambush; he could feel them.

A man stepped out of the shadows and swung forward with a thick mace. Kihrin ducked back and narrowly avoided the skull-crushing blow. He found himself strangely calm as he calculated his chances: four enemies. They wore armor, weapons at ready. One stepped behind him to close off his exit.

Kihrin aimed his crossbow at the thug by the beaded curtain. He had one shot.

The man by the curtain took the bolt in the chest, a lethal hit. That would have been enough if he'd been alone, but the assassin had brought three friends. Those friends didn't look stupid enough to let Kihrin re-load. The remaining killers moved in, confident in an inevitable result.

If Kihrin had been in a worse situation in his entire life . . . well, it had been just that afternoon, in the hands of the demon prince Xaltorath.

But no High General was coming to save him this time.

He flipped one of his daggers and threw it at the rope holding up the canopy of beaded fabric Ola hung over her bed. The dagger hit true, sheared rope and binding.

Several dozen yards of sateen came crashing down like a net.

The men were armed with maces and clubs. They held nothing they could use to slice themselves free. Maybe they had tucked daggers into their boots but were too startled to unsheathe them in time. The men yelled as they tried to extricate themselves.

Kihrin jumped out of the way and reloaded. He shot two of the men while they were entangled. Then Kihrin pulled himself up on top of a rafter. He reloaded again. His heart was numb. There was no expression in the young man's eyes as he looked the last assailant in the face, saw the now free man's eyes widen in fear. The guard ran for the doorway. Kihrin fired a crossbow bolt through the assassin's back.

Quiet settled over the room.

Kihrin sat there, perched up on the rafter with his back hunched over. It had been easy to kill those men, easier than he thought killing should be. That seemed wrong. A detached, emotionless part of his mind suggested he was too numb to feel anything. If his encounter with Xaltorath hadn't been enough to freeze his soul, finding his father's murdered corpse had finished the job.

Had it been so few hours since that meeting in the street? Years had gone by since then. He had aged decades.

Kihrin reloaded the crossbow. He looked at one of the men, at the weapons scattered on the floor, then looked over at the covered bed. The soldiers hadn't carried edged weapons. *They didn't do this,* he thought. He had to leave, fast. Ola—he didn't want to think about the implications. He climbed down, pausing only to kick a still-struggling form and pick up a mace as he walked through the curtain to the front parlor.

And stopped cold.

All of Ola's candles were lit.

A woman lay on top of Ola's glass table, breasts and hips pressed against the glass. Her arms draped over the side in a way that reminded Kihrin of the brothel cat, Princess, just after she'd caught a mouse and was feeling smug about herself. The woman had pulled down Ola's stuffed raven and was looking at it, nose to beak.

The woman's skin was honey-gold and her brown hair was long and silky. Candlelight gleamed pink over her lithe body. Her clothing consisted of black leather belts, worn crisscrossed over her breasts, her stomach, her hips. The straps didn't serve as either protection or modesty. She wore no weapons he could see, and he could see nearly all of her.

She might have been stunning if not for the madness in her dark eyes.

He almost told her this was the wrong brothel and she should go down the street to the Red Marks if she was looking for rough trade, but the sass died in his throat. She wasn't there for sex.

She was there for him.

"How right you are, my pretty angel," her sugar-sweet voice purred. "I'm here for you. You are my sweet little coconut, and I'm going to crack you open to get at the meat."

She smiled as she leapt to her feet with such light grace she didn't even tip the glass. Standing, the belts hid even less of her. She tossed the raven aside.

He swallowed hard. "Did I say that out loud?"

"No, Bright-Eyes." She grinned. "You didn't."

"That's what I thought." His heart pounded fast inside him. *Another demon. Oh Taja, not another demon.*

"Oh, I'm not a demon, love. Demons don't have real bodies. I do."

"Stop reading my mind!"

She smiled at him fondly. "Now you're being silly. Well done in there, by the way." She nodded back to the jade curtain. "Most people lose it when they see their loved ones murdered. Freeze or run screaming, and either one would have had you clubbed like a veal calf. Of course, you should've finished your kills. One of those men is still alive."

"How sloppy of me. I'll just go back and fix that."

"I don't think so, ducky." She licked her lips as she stared at Kihrin, still smiling, tapping the nails of one hand against her hip. Those nails were long and sharp, painted dark red or black. They looked wet.

Kihrin looked around. "More toughs on the way?"

"Just me," she said.

"Just you. Who are you again?"

"So sweet of you to ask. I'm Talon. I'll be your murderer tonight. You should feel honored, really. I'm only sent after the important ones."

"I'll pass, thanks." Kihrin raised his crossbow and fired, praying she wasn't reading his mind enough to dodge.

She didn't. The bolt hit her in the chest. She staggered.

There was no blood. She smiled at him like a lover as she pulled the bolt from her body. The wound closed at once, leaving no sign of any injury.

Kihrin stared at her in disbelief. "I just want you to know this has been a really bad day." He tossed the crossbow aside as he readied the mace.

She nodded, still smiling. "Don't fret too much, beautiful boy. It'll all be over soon." She tossed the bolt behind her and advanced on Kihrin. "That can't be your real hair color, but you're pretty. I wonder why you're so important."

"Promise not to kill me and I'll explain it to you. Over dinner perhaps?"

She looked at him like an eagle examining a squirrel. "So sorry. I'm planning on having a blind musician and a dancing girl for dinner. Don't worry, I've saved you for dessert. You look tasty."

All the blood flowed out of his face. "You're a mimic."*

She clapped her hands together, a happy child delighted at the compliment. "Someone's been paying attention to his children's stories." Her body shifted then, flickered, and for one brief second, he saw her as a mirrored reflection of his own form before she was a beautiful woman again. "Of course, that was an improvisation. True mastery of your form will come *after* snack time."

"Oh goddess."

"Gods can't save you, sweet." She was calm as she walked toward him and he backed up. "Believe me, I know. I used to be quite devout in my day, and when I really needed my goddess, where was she? Nowhere in the City, let me assure you."

"What have you done with Ola?"

"She's up in one of the cribs banging some cute whore." The mimic lowered her voice to a stage whisper. "Doesn't know this is happening."

"But I saw Ola—" His eyes widened. "That was you? You let me walk in here, knowing what I'd find?"

"What can I say, darling? I like to play with my food. I wanted to see how you'd take the news. Rather deliciously, in fact. Now instead of three brains to eat, I have seven to add to my collection. It's a good thing I can't overeat."

"I can pay you."

"Oh, that's sweet—but I don't do this for money." She grinned. "I can't wait to see the look on Ola's face when she walks in here and sees what I've done with you. It will be worth so many years of aggravation. I think I'm going to torture her to death. Slowly. Oh, truly, this will be an evening to savor through the centuries."

*For my own reasons, I admit to a fascination with mimics. Little is known about them, largely because they're difficult to find: understandable when dealing with a race that changes their shape and coloring. Most scholars dismiss them as the remnants of some mad god-king's experiments, which may be the case, since mimics neither age nor reproduce in any traditional sense. As mimics have no interest in illuminating matters, we may never know their true origins.

Kihrin frowned. "You—wait—this is because of Ola? I thought—Darzin D'Mon—"

Talon paused. A petite frown crossed her features. "You did mention him earlier. What did you say your name was again?"

"I didn't."

"Kihrin?" She cocked her head.

"Stay out of my mind!" He backed up.

"Kihrin." She said his name again, pronouncing it wrong.* "Different color hair—" Her eyes widened. "She *kept* you? Ola kept you *here*?"

Her eyes wound their way up and down his body as if he were a rare work of art. "I can't believe—why that crafty little cunt." When her eyes reached his face, she gave him a warm smile. Her expression was joyful. "You have a necklace. The Stone of Shackles. Oh, never mind the name. You probably don't have any clue what its real name is. To you, it's just a blue stone wrapped in gold. It would have been with you when Ola found you in Arena Park."†

"Ola *didn't* find me in Arena Park."

She laughed. "Oh yes, she did. Oh yes. *She did.* I was there. I was there with my hands wrapped around that little bitch's stinking throat—" She reached out to the air, as if she could still see the memories in front of her. Her whole body shifted again to the form of a man he didn't recognize, before returning to the original form once more. She closed her eyes for a second and shuddered. "Sorry. Sometimes he slips out. Jerk thinks that just because he killed me that gives him special rights or something."

He would never get past her. His fingers tightened their grip on the mace.

Talon lifted a hand toward him. "And I was about to *kill* you." She started laughing hysterically. "Ohhh, well! That would have been—oh. That was close." She grinned and fanned herself with a hand. "That was very close. To think I almost made the same mistake my murderer did. Trust me: *never* kill the person who is wearing the Stone of Shackles. Disaster, every time." She made a swiping motion with both hands.

Kihrin paused. "Wait—are you saying you don't want to kill me?"

"Kill you? Oh darling! That would be terrible. Trust me, that's the last thing you want me to do."

Kihrin looked nonplussed. "Uh . . . yeah, you're right. My position on

---

*This gives the strong implication that his real name is some variation, or rather, that Kihrin is but a mispronunciation of his proper name.

†Although most people are used to calling the strip of land that circles the Imperial Arena "Arena Park," it's never been officially named such. Other nicknames in common usage include "Blood Grounds," and of course the ever-popular "Culling Fields."

you killing me hasn't changed in the last five minutes." He shook his head. "Great. Not just a mimic. A crazy mimic. Isn't that nice?"

"Oh, my darling, I have so much to tell you. I have found you *at last*." She glanced past Kihrin then, and her face distorted into a screaming mask of hate. "NO. YOU FOOL!"

Kihrin glanced behind him in time to see one of the assassins standing in the jade-bead doorway. He was desperately injured, but making one last heroic attempt at completing his mission.

The man had a crossbow of his own aimed straight at Kihrin.

Kihrin jumped out of the way, diving to the floor. Initially, he thought he was successful, but that was shock. He felt a dull blow to his chest, like being hit with a reed pillow. Kihrin staggered back, and the world swung forward to greet him at a tilt. He couldn't breathe. *Gods, he couldn't breathe.* As he tried to draw in air, the pain hit. Kihrin realized he wasn't nearly as lucky as he liked to pretend. The stone at his neck felt bitterly cold, so cold it felt burning hot.

As he fell, not understanding there was a crossbow bolt in the middle of his chest, Kihrin saw something strange. Even though Kihrin was the one who'd been shot, his attacker was the one screaming. The man screamed for good reason: a mass of tentacles, covered in sharp claws, was busy tearing the assassin in half. Bloody gore sprayed all over Ola's fine tapestries.

As Kihrin saw this, he heard a commotion, a door banging open, more voices. But he wasn't really interested anymore. Everything began to darken.

A face filled his vision—a familiar, unwelcome face. Pretty Boy—Darzin D'Mon—looked down at him with undisguised worry. "I arrived just in time."

Talon said, "I had no idea—"

"It's not your fault, Talon. I won't blame you if he dies."

"He won't die," Kihrin heard her answer before he passed out from the pain. "I'm not finished with him yet."

25: Into the Jungle

(Kihrin's story)

I heard shouts behind me as I ran. Someone called my name. I ignored that too. I sprinted down the steps and ran into the jungle. Under the canopy, the light dimmed as the jungle air filled with mist and the fetid smell of earth and orchids. I kept running, jumping over vines and roots and moist green ferns. I ran until I was out of breath and my sides ached.

I didn't think they were following me. I listened and heard nothing but jungle noises.

Something rustled in the underbrush.

I stopped. There was another rustle. I slowly reached down to grab a rotten piece of wood from the jungle floor.

A low throaty noise came from my right, almost a slowed cat purr. A moment later, the head of a lizard poked its way into view. It was a golden-green color, and more like the head of one of the crocodiles living in the Senlay River than a small garden lizard. The head was too high off the ground. As the creature stepped closer, I realized that was because the head belonged to a reptile standing on its hind legs. The reptile opened its mouth in a grin, showing rows of sharp teeth. It purred at me and regarded me with intelligent dark eyes that reminded me of a parrot. It also stood three feet tall at the shoulder.

Another purr answered it, from behind me.

There were two of them.

I raised my arms and waved the stick, yelling, "Hyah!"

The reptile in front of me lowered its head and hissed before making a clicking sound. The reptile circled around me.

I put my hand to my tsali stone. It was neither hot nor cold.

Great. What did that mean?

I looked at the reptile, then at a tree. The lizard looked stable enough on the ground, but I bet it wasn't much of a climber. The reptile saw the motion and crept closer, putting itself between me and the large old tree.

I broke and ran. With a staccato cry, it chased. As it closed the distance, I grabbed an overhanging vine, flipped myself up and over, and actually landed on part of the beast's tail as I ran back the other way. As it tried to turn, and I ran for the tree, five more monsters darted from the underbrush and rushed me. I jumped up, grabbed another vine, and pulled myself up enough to hook my foot over a branch. One beast jumped and snapped at me, but missed grabbing a mouthful of my hair. I swung up and clutched at the branch, pulling myself out of the reach of the pack of lizards. They looked up at me and made that clicking sound, which was starting to seem like their equivalent to a growl. One of them tried to climb the tree, but its fore-claws weren't strong enough and it slid impotently back down.

I heard a whirring noise.

One of the snake men stood in a gap in the jungle foliage. He held a long black metal chain with a weighted end in his hand and he was whirling that chain above his head faster and faster and faster.

"Damn," I growled, and reached for a vine.

I swear the bastard grinned as he let go of the chain.

I swung to the side. The chain missed, but my sense of victory was short-lived. He hadn't been aiming for me, but the branch I perched upon. The wood splintered with a cracking sound as the metal sheared it. I put my full weight on the vine I held. The vine snapped.

Thanks, Taja.

I fell to the ground. Before I could do anything, one of the lizard-hounds had put a foot on my chest, lowered its head until it was almost touching mine, and made its clicking growl of disapproval. Several more snake men with spears appeared, all leveled at me. Fortunately, they seemed content to point and hiss.

I exhaled slowly.

The first snake man, the one who had thrown the chain, said something sharp and hissing in the same language Khaemezra had used. All but one of the giant hunting lizards backed away. Then the snake man said something else, and there were hissing responses and laughter. Human laughter joined it. I craned my neck and the lizard hissed again.

"Szzarus says he'll order his drake off you if you promise not to act like a monkey," a female voice said. The ranks of the lizard men parted, and a woman walked into view.

She was not a vané, but human, with a skin color somewhere in between the olive brown of a Quuros and the ebony of a Zheriaso. Her black hair was matted in long locks, the knots fitted with copper rings, skulls, and roses. She wore a patchwork of leather pieces cut into a tight-laced vest, a loincloth, and tall boots, over a brown and green chemise net that likely made for excellent camouflage in the jungle. Under the netting I saw a lacy outline of black tattoos. She wore two daggers in her belt, a curved sword, and the little sister of the long chain the lizard man used.

She also wore a hell of an attitude.

"Now are you going to play nice?" She cocked her head and looked at me in a way that reminded me of the hunting lizards.

"Do I have a choice?"

"Of course. I could bring you back to Mother in chains." She patted her belt. "Some men prefer it that way."

"I'm not one of them." I glared at her. Something about her seemed familiar.

"I imagine not, although you're fetching in nothing but irons."

My eyes widened. "You were with Khaemezra and Teraeth in Kishna-Farriga."

"I was." She smiled. "I'm Kalindra. Mother asked me to keep an eye on you. She thought you might do something foolish when you saw the Maevanos."

"The Maev—" I stopped. "The Maevanos is a nude dance, not a human sacrifice."*

She snorted and motioned. Two of the lizard men dragged me to my feet.

"Only Quuros would take one of Thaena's most sacred rituals and turn it into velvet-hall entertainment." She glared. "It is the most profound, most holy show of trust we can give our Lady: to ask for her forgiveness and blessing in her own realm, where her power is absolute and no dissemblance is possible. If a petitioner is truly sorry, she Returns them. They are purified and made free of sin."

"And if they're not really sorry?"

"Then they're dead."

"What a shame. I was just starting to like Teraeth."

"Really?"

"No, of course not. He's an ass."

Kalindra smiled. "Shall I tell him you said that when he Returns?"

"If it makes you happy."

The snake men seemed to think the situation was basically handled. Most of them retreated to the jungle with their lizard pets. The largest said something hissing to Kalindra before he joined them. I suspected he lurked a short distance away, just in case.

"What did he say?" I asked her.

"He said, 'Be careful. He looks harmless, but the monkey moves fast when he wants to.' I think Szzarus likes you."

---

*I must admit, I too thought it was a nude dance. Now I understand why that priest of Thaena stormed out of the room when we saw it performed at the Winter Festival, two years previous. Someone really should tell the Revelers Guild.

"Everyone likes me. Just ask Relos Var." I rubbed my hands over my arms as I looked around. "Am I a prisoner here?"

She cocked her head and looked at me. "You're on a tropical island a thousand miles from the nearest village. How well can you swim?"

"A prisoner then."

Kalindra shrugged. "If you like. I can't change the local geography just to make you feel better. I can't easily leave either. Sometimes the things that protect us are the same things that limit our freedoms."

"I don't like it."

"Oh well. That changes everything." She rolled her eyes. "Oh wait. No, it changes nothing."

"So, I should stop complaining?"

"Your words." There was laughter in her eyes, and I'll admit I found it hard to keep up my indignation. "Let's go for a walk. We've time for explanations before Teraeth Returns from the dead."

26: Unhappy Reunion

(Talon's story)

Someone pounded on the door.

"Damn it all. Go away!" Ola shouted.

"Ola! Ola! Come quick." Morea's voice rang clear and loud from the other side.

"Curse it." Ola rolled out of bed and threw on a robe, ignoring the protests of the woman she dislodged. She stomped over to the door and tossed it open. "What is it, girl? This best be important . . ."

Morea stood in the hallway, barely dressed. Tears streaked her face. "They . . . he . . . oh goddess . . . he . . ."

"Calm down, child. Calm down. What happened?"

"Kihrin!" Morea pointed down to Ola's apartments with a shaking hand. "He's gone!"

"Kihrin? Where'd that boy get off to . . . ?" Ola's brows drew together in confusion. "Oh hells. The General. If he—" Without another word, Ola grabbed Morea's arm and half-pushed, half-dragged the slave girl back to Ola's apartment.

Ola marched inside and stopped as she saw the candles, the over-turned furniture, and the gooey mass of something wet and bloody that might once have been a person. Blood covered the back wall and the curtain of jade beads. Someone had been murdered here. Recently murdered in a particularly messy fashion. She fought down bile. It wasn't Kihrin. It couldn't be Kihrin. Who then?

"Morea, what happened—" She turned just in time to catch a punch to her jaw that flung her against a cabinet.

Morea examined her knuckles. "Late again. You're always late, Ola. I haven't quite ever been able to forgive you for that. Don't think I didn't try."

"Morea?" Ola wiped the blood from her face and stared at the danc-ing girl, aghast.

"Not exactly." Morea's shape flowed in front of Ola's eyes, until she looked like a beautiful woman with honey-gold skin and lovely, long brown hair.

"Lily?" Ola shook her head. "Lyrilyn? No, you can't be! I saw you—"

"Die?" Talon smiled. "Oh, I died all right. And yet . . . here we are. Let me explain. Oh, better yet: let me show you."

Ola tried to run, but Talon was on her in seconds. She forced Ola against the wall, hands trapping her own. Even though her attacker was shorter than Ola and looked weaker, Ola couldn't free herself. Talon clamped her mouth over Ola's—a terrible kiss that drew all the strength from Ola's body.

Ola looked at her attacker and flinched. The face kissing her changed. It wasn't Lyrilyn's heart-shaped flower, but a black-skinned Zheriaso, wild and untamed. It was *her* face; the face Ola had worn twenty years ago before age and easy living had stolen her appeal. It was the face that in some part of her mind she remembered still, whenever she looked back at her reflection in a mirror or reminisced about the "good old days."

Ola tried to break away, but the hands holding her in place were strong as iron. Ola tried to scream, but this monster's kiss was a metal vise, crushing her.

A flowing, rushing torrent of memories, thoughts, feelings, and sins overtook her and left Ola drowning. She felt a terrible sense of violation and shame, as if every secret in her soul had been plucked from the darkest corners of her mind and tossed onto the sidewalk outside. She felt this monster who wore her face dig inside her mind.

Then the sensation stopped. Ola was released, lifted into the air, and thrown. She landed like an overstuffed pillow on a throw rug. Ola moaned and tried to crawl away, but strong hands grabbed her by her hair and threw her onto her back. The figure standing above her was once again Lyrilyn.

Her attacker smiled. "You see?"

"You're a mimic?" Ola whispered. She had heard of them, dark rumors told in darker dens of iniquity. Creatures who stole the forms of loved ones to stalk their victims. Demons of flesh who sold their services to the highest bidder as spies and assassins.

Talon winked at her. "It's not what we call ourselves, but close enough."

"This isn't happening. Lyrilyn was human—"

"Yes, that's true, lover. I was once. But you were LATE," Talon snarled. She crouched over Ola, grabbed her by the hair, and yanked her onto her feet. She pulled Ola over to one of the chairs in the room and forced her to sit in it. "Now I am what the Stone of Shackles made me, something you helped create. But you're right. This isn't happening. This is just a dreadful nightmare where Lyrilyn shows up to remind you of your past sins. You know. The part where you did nothing; where you just stood there and watched as that monster murdered your precious Lyrilyn."

Fear choked Ola. This was worse than a nightmare, worse than she could imagine. "Please! I'm sorry. I'm *so* sorry."

"I forgive you," Talon said.

Ola blinked. "You do?"

"Yup. Fortunately, since I was wearing the Stone of Shackles—and how lucky was that? Taja loves me, doesn't she? So when the mimic murdered me, I swapped bodies with my killer, which makes me . . ." She put a hand to her chest. ". . . the mimic. I'll admit, it took a little while to get used to it. Mimics are disgusting. You have no idea."

The fear in Ola's eyes deepened to terror. "What could I do?" she whispered. "It all happened so fast. I didn't know—" Ola screamed as Talon hit her in the face several times.

Talon's expression was sedate, even calm, as she showed Ola the blood staining her knuckles. She wiped her hand off on Ola's face. Then, holding the weaker woman down so she couldn't move, Talon licked the blood off Ola's skin. Ola tried to shake her head, squirm, do anything, but she couldn't move.

Talon said in a conversational tone of voice, "You knew, Ola. You've always known, but you've always been too busy protecting yourself to protect anyone else, least of all me. Remember what we promised each other, late at night in our beds? True love forever? Yet when you had the means to buy your freedom did you even think of me? No. You let me rot."

Ola shook her head. "Therin didn't own you, or I might have had a chance. *Pedron* did, degenerate Pedron. There was no chance of getting you free from him."

Talon's expression turned sympathetic and understanding. "Is that what you tell yourself so you can sleep at night, love? I was so naïve. I didn't just trust you once, I trusted you *twice*. I loved you. And where were you when I needed you?"

Ola licked her lips nervously. "I didn't—"

"I am very disappointed in you, ducky. Very disappointed."

Ola whimpered. "You're insane."

Talon looked at the older woman as if she had just said something profound. "You know, lover, I've often wondered that myself. Am I crazy? It's possible the experience drove me quite out of my mind."

She smiled and shrugged as if she accepted the question was beyond her ability to answer. "Of course, suddenly absorbing 5,372 separate and distinct lifetimes in a matter of minutes is bound to put a little fuzz around the edges of any person's mental faculties." Talon smiled.

"You—" Ola started again. "You've killed that many people?"

"Me?" Talon laughed. "No, of course not. I can only account for 738 personally. Ooo, 741. I completely forgot to add tonight's tally." She made little circling motions in the air as if she were adding figures on a chalkboard. "The mimic who murdered me on the other hand . . . well, he was very old." She turned back to Ola and squatted next to her chair. "Do you know I used to be vané?" She caressed a hand over her hip. "Not me personally. I was born over in the Copper Quarter. This body, I mean, started out life as vané. I would never have thought that. I always assumed mimics were some kind of demon, but it turns out they're some kind of vané. Do you think Miya would laugh at the joke?"

"Please," Ola whispered. "Kihrin? Where is he? What have you done with him?"

"He's safe. The very finest healers in the Empire are seeing to that."

"Oh no. Not them."

"Oh yes. *Them*. It's all arranged. Darzin's taking care of it." Talon laughed at Ola's expression. "I work for Darzin now. Isn't that funny?" She put her hands on either side of her mouth and stage-whispered, "He has no idea I used to be Lyrilyn."

Ola tried to explain, tried to reason with her. Lyrilyn . . . after all these years. "*Please.* His father—"

"Oh, don't worry so; Kihrin will be fine. Surdyeh and that new dancing girl of yours? Not so fine."

"Oh goddess . . ."

Talon nodded and tapped Ola's cheek affectionately. "Yes, exactly. That's what I always used to say. The goddess wouldn't give us more than we can handle." She tilted her head in a position of contemplation. "Of course, that must mean I really am sane. Hmmm?" Again, she shrugged. "Good, bad, crazy, sane. Doesn't matter. I'll let you in on a great secret, Ola. For ol' times sake." Talon winked at Ola.

"Yes?" Ola asked hesitantly. She knew a trap when she saw one.

Talon leaned in close. She leaned in until her mouth rested right next to Ola's ear and whispered, "You all taste just like mutton."

Ola closed her eyes, shivering.

Talon leaned back again, laughing.

"I never meant to hurt you, Lily. You have to believe that." Reasoning with Lyrilyn was her only chance. If she could convince Lily to let her go . . .

Talon nodded amiably. "As much as I have dreamt of squeezing the life from your throat, my dear dark beauty, I see that's true. You didn't mean to hurt me. But you did. And that's nothing compared to what you were going to do to that little baby boy."

Ola felt her stomach lodge in her throat. "No," she protested. "That's not true. I raised him like he was my own child."

Talon's eyes narrowed. In that same instant, Ola threw herself past the mimic to reach the door. Talon grabbed Ola by the throat and lifted her into the air. Ola made grating, gasping sounds as she tried to draw breath. Finally, Talon released her. She fell to the floor in a sobbing pile.

"Ola, Ola, Ola." Talon walked around her, standing one foot on the matron's back to push her down flat. "Don't lie to someone who is reading your mind, sweet. Do you know why I didn't look for you, afterward?"

"No," Ola sobbed, her voice all but lost under the sound of her crying.

Talon bent down and said, "I didn't look for you because I–*knew*–you wouldn't be stupid enough to stay in the Capital. You had one job to do. *One.* It never even occurred to me that you would actually LEAVE Kihrin in this *shithole*." Talon punctuated her last sentence with an angry kick to Ola's side.

Ola held her stomach, gasping as she rolled into a fetal ball. In between sobbing breaths, she gathered enough strength to pull herself up. "If you can read minds, you know I'm not lying. How safe would Kihrin have been, back with his mother's family? With an uncle who'd tried to kill his mother and you could be damn sure would do the same to him? Surdyeh said the stone wouldn't allow anyone to find him. He was *safe* here. Safer than he would have been anywhere else."

"Surdyeh? Surdyeh said that, did he?" Talon glanced over her shoulder, toward the bedroom. "I don't believe I had the pleasure before I killed him. You meet this 'Surdyeh' down here in the Lower Circle?"

Ola closed her eyes as sorrow threatened to overwhelm her. The casual way Lyrilyn spoke of his death left her with no doubt she'd really done it. Surdyeh was dead. "Yes, he–he worked for me."

A small frown crossed Talon's face. "And you trusted him? You trusted him enough to tell him about the Stone of Shackles? Since when have you been that *stupid*?"

Talon's words were a slap across the face, a bracing reminder of Ola's own well-honed paranoia. "He–" Ola inhaled with a sob, and a new expression crossed her face: confusion. Why had she trusted Surdyeh? It seemed ridiculous now. Her brow furrowed. She frowned in concentration as she tried to remember when and where she'd first met the man.

"We were friends–he would never betray me–" Her speech faltered, and she again halted in bafflement. Never betray her? When had she ever in her life thought a person immune to betrayal from another?

"Huh," Talon said. "I *know* you weren't lovers. And you couldn't have known him for longer than you've owned the Club. Yet you trusted him. Doesn't that seem odd? You, who have never trusted anyone in your whole life?"

Ola swallowed, half turning. She rubbed her upper lip. How had they met? "He made so much sense—keep Kihrin here, it would be the last place anyone would look—it was so easy to talk to Surdyeh—"

"He was right, but the fact that you believed him—why that's interesting, don't you think?" Talon grinned and chucked Ola under the chin. "Sweet cheeks, don't you see? Someone cast a spell on you!"

Ola felt her blood chill in her veins. She looked up at Talon with wide eyes. "I didn't know—"

"Oh, I know, sweetheart." Talon put her arms around Ola and helped the shaking woman to her feet, her hands clamped like manacles to keep Ola from running or collapsing. "I know. You feel violated. Used. Believe me, I know *exactly* how you feel. But you should be grateful. Honestly you should light a candle to Surdyeh's memory every chance you have: because of that enchantment, I'm not going to kill you quite yet. Isn't that nice of me?"

Ola's lips trembled. "I didn't know he was a wizard."

Talon patted Ola on the head, and Ola felt her skin crawl as she realized that Talon still had both arms wrapped around her. "Oh sweetmeat, it's not like you had any way to tell. And blind people have a real incentive to learn to see beyond the First Veil. So, isn't that interesting? Surdyeh made very sure you weren't going anywhere, but why? What was his game? And who was holding his leash? I'm dying to know who."

"Gendal." The name came to her lips before she was even aware what she was saying. "I met him the same night I met Gendal." She shuddered.

Talon's eyes widened. "The old Emperor? *That* Gendal? Just so we're clear . . ."

"That Emperor. But Lily, it was years before you fled with that baby." Pure shock drove Ola back to her seat again, and this time Talon didn't try to stop her. "If it was a setup, how could the Emperor have possibly known so far in advance?"

"Oh, I don't know, but I plan to find out. The boy doesn't know, does he? You never told him about his precious family."

Ola shook her head.

Talon shrugged. "His own fault for trusting you." She looked at her nails. "Trust is for the weak. Anyway, you're not going to see Kihrin again, you understand?"

Ola had no problem understanding. She didn't even disagree. If Talon took her back to the Blue Palace, her most likely fate was an extended stay with one of their best torturers before she was finally allowed the luxury of death. "Yes—"

Talon tsked. "Yes . . . what?" Ola saw Talon's hands change into something like claws, and she shuddered in terror.

Ola looked at the mimic who had once been her dearest love, the woman she had once dreamed of running away with to freedom. None of her dreams had ever gone like this. "Yes . . . Mistress." She sobbed in shame.

"Good doggie." Talon pulled Ola up from the chair. "And remember, bitch: if you don't do exactly what I say, I won't bother knocking you unconscious before I eat you alive."

27: Sister Kalindra

(Kihrin's story)

"I know the ceremonies can be a little dramatic, but we're a nice group of people once you get to know us." Kalindra had picked a native island flower and was idly shredding it to bits with her fingernails as we walked.

"A little dramatic? That's what you call a human sacrifice to the Goddess of Death? Not creepy or terrifying? Just . . . 'a little dramatic'?"

"Teraeth isn't human."

I rolled my eyes. "Semantics." I paid no attention to where we were going. Somewhere in the jungle.

She smiled and looked away. "You must have questions."

"A thousand. I just don't know if you're going to be able to answer them."

She tossed the flower she'd been destroying off the edge of the path. "Try me."

I ticked off the questions on my fingers. "Where are we? Who has my gaesh? Does Thaena really wander around the island personally, or do I still need to worry about Relos Var showing up to pay me a visit? What's with the snake people? What's going to happen to the rest of the crew of *The Misery*? Is Khaemezra a dragon too, and if she is, what does that make Teraeth?"

Kalindra cleared her throat. "When you said you had a thousand questions, I assumed you weren't being literal."

"This? This is just a warm-up. Wait until I really get going."

She laughed and continued walking. "I don't know who has your gaesh—probably Mother. You should ask her. 'Here' is the island of Ynisthana, Thaena's personal sanctum of power, which means Relos Var won't show up here if he knows what's good for him. The snake people are called the Thriss, and they have lived here for centuries. Did I miss anything?"

"The crew of *The Misery*," I offered. "And 'Mother' being a dragon."

She paused for a moment, pursed her lips, looked off into the mist. "The crew will be offered a chance to join us or they may return to Zherias when the next ship arrives. They won't be harmed; the only sacrifices we practice are voluntary. Khaemezra is not a dragon—but isn't magic wonderful? She is the most powerful wizard I've ever known. Powerful enough to change into a dragon." Kalindra grinned. "Which makes Teraeth exactly what you think he is: insufferably pretty."

She winked at me and continued walking, now turning off the main trail to a narrow but well-used, winding path.

I let that last bit slide without commentary save a roll of my eyes and then ran after her to keep up. I didn't think Teraeth was pretty. Insufferable? Yes. Pretty? No.

Definitely not.

"Go back to the part about this being Thaena's personal sanctuary. If I stay, am I going to run into the Goddess of Death herself? How does that work? Is it polite to avert my eyes? Would I be expected to bow if we run into each other on one of the trails?"

Kalindra stopped and stared at me as if I were either a difficult puzzle or just being rude, and then continued walking.

"Hey, you said you'd answer my questions." I chased after her. "Don't stop just because they're stupid questions."

She moved aside the wide green leaves of a jungle plant, and beyond I saw a small clearing. The smell of ash and sulfur, as well as something dark and musky, hung thick in the air. The scent rose from steaming pools of water bubbling up from the ground. The pools sunk deep into the black rock in wide overlapping ovals. I suspected they had been widened and deepened by hand.

She moved over to the edge of a pool and waited for me.

"So how does this work?"

She raised an eyebrow. "The bath? It's for cleaning."

"No, I meant the part with a goddess walking around out in the open. The idea that a god has some sacred space where they can manifest . . ." I shook my head. "I've never heard of that, and I'm a minstrel's son. Knowing those sorts of stories is of professional interest to me."

"Or maybe you just don't know everything. Try not to go into shock at the idea." Kalindra picked up a stick and drew three lines in the ground. "So the world is divided into three states of being—life, magic, and death."

"And two Veils that separate them. I know this."

She tilted her head and acknowledged what I said. "And most people believe that the living stay here"—she pointed to the first line—"while the dead stay here," she said as she pointed to the third line. "This area in between, the realm of magic, therefore is the home of the gods, right?"

I narrowed my eyes. "Is this a trick question?"

"In a way. Because it's rubbish. It's wrong. Yes, the gods can see into all the realms at once—that's one of the things that makes them gods—

but divinities still have physical bodies. Those physical bodies still exist in the land of the living. Avatars who walk and talk and do all the things that living beings do. Most people will never meet the avatar of a god, or if they do, they'll remain blissfully ignorant of that fact."* She pointed back to the first line, underscoring it deeply. "Before it was claimed by Thaena, this island was the sanctuary of the god-king Ynis, who loved snakes and reptiles so much he took his human followers and changed them into the Thriss. Ynis thought he was safe here, that no one could touch him or interfere with what he was doing."

She broke the stick and tossed the pieces away, smeared the dirt to obscure the markings she had created. "That's the danger of a sanctuary, and why smart gods don't advertise where their sanctuaries are located. A god's avatar can manifest in their own sanctuary, but that very strength makes them vulnerable. The only way to kill a god is to kill their avatar. Ynis died when Emperor Simillion came calling with the sword Urthaenriel.† Thaena is different, though." Kalindra held out her hands toward the jungle. "She is always here, but yet you'll never meet her, not unless you decide to join our order and dance the Maevanos yourself."

I narrowed my eyes until comprehension settled in. I drew in a breath. "Because she's the opposite, isn't she? Her body, her avatar, isn't in the land of the living at all, is it? She 'lives' in the third realm—in the Afterlife." I blinked. "Can she die?"

"No." She answered without hesitation or doubt. Kalindra was a believer, although that didn't make her wrong. She saw the expression on my face and added, "But don't worry. If Relos Var dared try anything here, Thaena would show up personally to deal with him. Just because she normally lives in the Land of Peace doesn't mean she can't manifest here."

I felt a chill. "So if Thaena is the only thing protecting me from Relos Var . . . I really can't leave, can I?" I felt sick. Taja's assurance that I could leave if I wanted to now tasted like ash.

Kalindra was sympathetic. "I'm sure Relos Var will forget about you eventually."

"I don't even know what this has to do with me."

---

*I have met the witch-goddess Suless while visiting Duke Kaen in Yor. She's a deeply unpleasant woman. Also, don't ever eat anything she bakes. Trust me.

†Urthaenriel, otherwise known as the Ruin of Kings, Eclipser, the Emperor's Sword, Godslayer, Map Burner, Saetya, Tyasaeth, Vishabas, War's Heart, Sun's Shadow, the Severer, Zinkarox. These are all names given by one group or another to the sword of the Quuros Emperor, one of the great artifacts of the world. At school, they teach that the sword was manufactured by Grizzst the Mad for Emperor Simillion at the request of Khored the Destroyer, but I am skeptical.

Kalindra's brown eyes stared at me. "There's a prophecy." She paused. "No really, stop laughing."

I laughed some more.

Kalindra looked annoyed, but waited for me to stop.

"A prophecy? Right. Khaemezra said . . . I thought she was jesting. You've got to be joking! I'm here because of a prophecy? More of Caerowan's Devoran paranoia? That's why Relos Var wanted me? Because some crackpot mad hermit declared I'm going to save the world or something?"

Her smile turned cruel. "It's not that kind of prophecy." She unbuckled her scabbard and laid her sword, chain, and a brace of daggers in a neat pile next to several folded white cloths: towels, from the look of them. Apparently, the Black Brotherhood did indeed use this place as a public bath.

"So, what kind of prophecy is it?"

She unlaced her bodice. "The mineral springs here are good for sore muscles and healing injuries. Your wounds are healing nicely, but a soak wouldn't hurt you."

"You didn't answer my question." I eyed her as she tossed her bodice aside. She made no effort to shield herself from my stare as she disrobed. There didn't seem to be any separation of bathing areas for men and women.

My anger ebbed. I was distracted for some reason.

"I'm sorry. Did you ask a question?" Slit skirt followed bodice, then bracers and open-mesh chemise. Her body was taut and well muscled. As she bent over to pull off her boots, her back revealed a crisscross of old scar tissue—the hallmark of the disobedient slave. My eyes traced the lines of hardship: the scarring around her wrists and ankles, the brand on the back of her thigh. Old wounds, faded scars. If she was anyone's slave, it wasn't recently.

"I forget." I stared at her. She wasn't beautiful. Her face was too long and her nose too crooked. She wasn't soft enough, fresh enough, for Quuros standards, but Kalindra was hard and fierce and wild. She had her own beauty.

She caught me staring and laughed, a soft throaty chuckle. "Aren't the baths public where you come from? You must have seen a naked woman before."

"Not like you."

She started to reply, some whip-quick remark, but it died in her throat as she looked at me. We stared at each other too long. You know what that's like, don't you? You look at someone, and maybe the situation is appropriate and maybe it isn't, but you make eye contact, and all the little protections, all the walls we put up to keep each other out, unexpectedly fail. You look too long and you see too much, and there's this sudden sharp thrill as you realize just how badly you want this other person, and that it's entirely mutual. She stepped toward me, raised her hand to my face.

I knew what would come next. I wanted what would come next, but a dozen ugly images flashed through my mind. Xaltorath's "gift."

I turned away.

I wanted her. I really did, but I didn't trust myself at all.

My hands shook as I pushed the drawstring pants off my hips, kicking them aside. I dove into the pool like a rabbit hiding from a wolf, not caring that the mineral water was scorching hot or how it might hurt.

Maybe I wanted it to hurt.

"Do you know what I like best about staying here on Ynisthana?" Water splashed as Kalindra stepped into a pool.

She sounded farther away than I expected. I opened my eyes. Kalindra had lowered herself into one of the other pools, physically separate from my own. Unlike me, she'd taken the time to grab towels, soap, and sponges.

"What?" I asked.

"You're allowed to say no."

If words were daggers, hers left deep, slow cuts. I felt a release of tension I hadn't even realized was there, a wave of disorientation. How powerful was that idea?

Here was a place where I could say no.

I exhaled and grabbed the edge of the stone pool as if I would drown without the support. I pushed myself up enough to rest my arms against the black slate rock, crossed my hands under my chin. I thought about the ways Kalindra's words might be lies: Khaemezra still had my gaesh, after all. I also thought about Taja's opinion on the freedom inherent in a gaesh. I could still say no. Even to a gaesh command I could say no.

I reached out and touched the back of Kalindra's hand as she reached for a washcloth. "I don't really want to say no," I confessed. "I just don't know how to say yes."

She had a glorious smile. Kalindra picked up my hand. "Then go with the first one, for now, until you figure out how to do the second. And when you do . . ." She kissed my fingertips, slow and sweet as if my hand was fragile and precious. ". . . come find me."

I shuddered again, but it was the good kind of shudder. Something about the slow, gentle way Kalindra moved defied Xaltorath's tainted memories.

Then she put a sponge in my hand. "Now wash up, Monkey. We're going to be late to a party."

28: The Finest Healers

(Talon's story)

Heavy weights forced his eyelids closed, and someone was sitting on his chest. Kihrin tried to breathe, but it was an effort. He was pinned. He couldn't move. He couldn't–

Kihrin gulped air as he opened his eyes. He was lying down, softness wrapped around his body, a pillow under his head. He stared up at a gathered canopy of blue silk, watermarked and shimmering from the reflected light of the morning sun. The air smelled sweet with jasmine and lilac.

The weight on his chest wasn't a man, a woman, or a water buffalo: he was being held down by a single silk sheet.

Kihrin sat up in bed. He was so weak it reminded him of when he was a child with red fever, so drained by illness the very act of movement was a mark of accomplishment. A large white bandage wrapped around his chest. He reached up and felt for the smooth surface of the wire-wrapped gem around his neck. It was still there.

"Oh, he's awake! Master Lorgrin, he's awake!" a woman said. A young woman came into view behind the silk drapes of the four-poster bed. She wore a blue shift that resembled lingerie more than any proper clothing and left about as much to the imagination.

"I–" His tongue stuck in his throat. He was thirsty, and hungry, and, at the same time, nauseated.

Another voice. Male. "Hold him up. He needs to drink this."

Kihrin looked up to see an old man, dressed in the blue colors of a physicker. Kihrin didn't have the strength to push him away as the man pressed a goblet against Kihrin's lips.

"Come, child. You need to drink," the old man told him. "I know you're thirsty. I promise, you'll keep this down. You must trust me."

It wasn't water or any alcohol Kihrin knew, but it was delicious and after his first sip, he drank gratefully. When he finished, the woman lowered him back onto the pillows.

Kihrin slept.

* * *

Later, during those brief moments when he gained consciousness and it was light enough to see, he examined his surroundings. He lay in an enormous bed, canopied with blue textured silk, just as the sheets were also made from silk. Silk was too expensive to be used for anything but clothing for the wealthiest nobles. It was such a valuable commodity in Quur that it was held as equivalent to gold by weight. Using silk as bedding was like sprinkling gold dust in a stable.

The large room was grander and more ostentatious than any room Kihrin had ever seen before. Gilded statuettes and fine porcelain vases filled with fresh exotic blue flowers covered every space that could carry them. A gold chandelier with sapphire crystals hung from the center of the room. Dark blue tiles covered the walls, etched with gold. A week ago, he might have enjoyed his stay, or at least sized up the security for a later nighttime burglary.

Now the room filled him with dread.

There was only one nobleman obsessed with blue who had any interest in him. In his moments of lucidity Kihrin wondered why he wasn't in chains, why he wasn't dead, why his only guards were physickers and pretty slave girls instead of men with swords. It made no sense, and he had no answers.

The next morning, the physicker woke him.

"Remember me?" the healer asked. "I'm Master Lorgrin. Why don't you see if you can sit up on your own today?"

Kihrin did so, grimacing at the way his chest ached. "I thought you bloodletters were supposed to be able to fix someone's injuries with a snap of your fingers. Or do you charge by the hour?"

"Strong enough for sarcasm, I see. That's a good sign." The old man pulled the bandages down over Kihrin's chest and put a hand on his left breast. "You took a crossbow bolt straight through the heart. Tore your right atrium and aorta to bits. I had to use magic to keep your blood circulating while I fixed the damage." He gave Kihrin a sharp look. "You do not want me to rush a procedure like that, or you'll end up dropping dead of a heart seizure by the time you're eighteen."

Kihrin looked at the skin over his heart. There wasn't even a scar. "Uh . . . thank you?"

"Just doing my job," the old man said with gruff tenderness. "As much as it galls me to admit it, the man you really should be thanking is Darzin. The gods must love you a lot, kid, because I would have bet metal that boy never paid any attention to my lessons on cardiac stabilization spells. Yet here you are."

"Darzin–" Kihrin flinched. "Where am I?"

The physicker smiled. "The D'Mon palace. I assume you won't be too surprised if I tell you it's in the Sapphire District of the Upper Circle, will you?"

"Why—why am I here?"

"Probably because your father liked your mother in a special sort of way." He raised the bandages up again. "The heart is almost back to normal function. I suspect you'll be up and around in no time, but I strongly advise you to avoid any strenuous activity for at least another week. Rest, and lots of it. That's an order."

"No, I mean—" Kihrin started to take a deep breath, felt his chest twinge, and thought better of it. "Why am I here, in this room, not in a cell? And did Pretty—I mean, did the Lord Heir bring in anyone else for healing? An old man? A beautiful woman with braided hair?"

"No, I'm sorry, but if he brought anyone back besides you, he didn't tell me—and he would have if they were injured." The physicker looked at him curiously. "But a cell? Why in Galava's name would you think Darzin D'Mon would put you in a cell, my lord?"

Kihrin's throat clenched. "What did you just call me?"

The old man looked apologetic. "Ah, I know. I'm bad with the titles. Don't use them enough. Therin's always dogging me for it. Probably going to get me killed when Darzin takes over. Honestly though, when you've overseen the births of as many D'Mon babies as I have, it's sometimes hard to remember that they're all grown up and toilet-trained too."

Kihrin felt his heart start to rattle. "I'm not a lord."

"I'm sorry, kid. I don't know what Darzin told you, and it's not my place to say. He's waiting to talk to you: I'm sure he'll explain everything."

Kihrin pulled his knees up to his chest, put his arms around his legs. "I don't want to talk to him. His assassins killed my father."

The old healer took a deep breath and grimaced. "Kihrin—it's Kihrin, right?"

Kihrin nodded.

"I'm sorry about the man who raised you. You were obviously close to him and I know that's got to hurt. I'm about to say something to you that will also hurt, so if you don't want me to, just tell me and I'll shut up and go away."

"You can say whatever you want. It doesn't mean I'll believe you."

"Sounds fair," the healer admitted. "So, you need to think about this: that man may have raised you, but he wasn't your father. Your father, your real father, is here, and he's alive. If you were told you were abandoned or adopted, or I don't know, found under a cabbage leaf, it's a lie: you were *stolen*. Kidnapping a royal babe? That, Kihrin, is an executable offense. What Darzin did may seem horrible to you, but it was completely within his rights as a D'Mon to put your kidnappers to death. No one will question his actions. It was just unlucky that you were caught up in that raid, but fortunately you've pulled through and everything will be okay."

"Taja! No . . . It wasn't like that. It wasn't *anything* like that. His soldiers didn't care who I was. He didn't give them orders to save me. He was going to kill all of us." Inside his chest, Kihrin's newly repaired heart felt like it was about to burst open. He squeezed his eyes shut and put his head on his knees. *No! It can't be . . . I can't be Ogenra. I can't. I can't find out I really am Ogenra only after Morea is already dead.*

He remembered all the things Surdyeh never let him do, all the ways the old harper kept him out of the public eye or discouraged him from seeking sponsorship with the Revelers. He felt the dreadful worm of doubt sink into him. Surdyeh had known. He had *known.*

Ola had known too. They had both tried to warn him, in their own ways, about the consequences of seeing the High General. Now they were both dead. Talon had said she was going to kill Ola, and knowing what she was, Kihrin knew there was nothing Ola could do to save herself. She was already dead—had probably been dead for days.

He began to shake.

Kihrin flinched as he felt Lorgrin's hand on his shoulder. "That's enough excitement for one day. I'll let the Lord Heir know you won't be ready to join him for breakfast until tomorrow." He paused, frowning. "You should rest. You're going to need your strength."

Kihrin tried to sleep through that entire day and the next, but Lorgrin was wise to his tricks. At dawn, the old healer pulled back the drapes on the windows. "My next feat will be to summon up a gallon of water right over your head. Don't think I don't know how—being able to create clean water on command is one of the most useful spells I ever learned at the Academy."

Kihrin stumbled out of bed. He stared balefully at Lorgrin. "Now what?"

The healer clapped his hands. On cue a dozen men and women in loincloths and shifts walked into the room, carrying piles of cloth, brushes, mirrors, bowls, bottles, clasps, and shoes.

"You have two options, my lord," Lorgrin told him. "You can prove you're only six months from your majority and go with these good people down to the baths, where they will wash you and clothe you and make you presentable for meeting your peers. Or you can whine and protest and throw a temper tantrum like a child. In that case I will be forced to pinch off a nerve cluster that not only controls pain but your ability to move independently. Then I'll have the guards carry you down, and you'll end up washed and presentable anyway, if a lot more embarrassed. I leave the choice up to you."

"Some choice." Kihrin scowled and crossed his arms over his chest. "You don't have to threaten me. I've behaved."

"Yes, you have, my lord. But I haven't lived this long by being a fool, not where the D'Mons are concerned. There's not one of you without Khored's own temper." Lorgrin moved to the window. "Come stand over here, Kihrin. I want to show you something."

Grudgingly, swinging his glare from the servants to the physicker, Kihrin went over to the window. He stared sullenly at first, but when he realized what he was seeing, Kihrin's jaw dropped open.

Spread out before him was a palace of blue tile roofs and lapis lazuli walls, towers, and spires that ran into each other and formed verandas, pavilions, and courtyards. His gaze found no surface to rest on that was not some shade of blue, or where blue was not the predominant color. Each building, each section of building, was a fantastic delight of delicate archways, leaded glass windows, and intricate stone-carving. He had known the royal palaces were large, but this was almost more than he could believe. All of Velvet Town fit within those walls. *This isn't a palace; it's a city.*

Then his Shadowdancer instincts kicked in, and he started counting guards. The palace architecture looked random. It wasn't; he could find no spot not under the watchful eye of a guard on a rampart or walkway. The walls looked like an easy climb, but lacked blind spots.

"This is the Private Court," Lorgrin explained. "Only for family and the closest servants and slaves. It has three hundred rooms, five hundred or so guards, its own hospital, theater, and gardens. And since this is where the D'Mon family lives, no one leaves or enters without being seen, inspected, and cataloged. If by chance you did manage to leave, you'd have at least two more courts of the palace to cross just to be on the public streets. Then you'd have to deal with the Watchmen who guard the paths down to the Lower Circle."

"So, don't be stupid?"

"Aha! The boy has potential. Keep thinking like that, and you might just survive."

Kihrin looked out over the palace. "I don't want to be here."

"You're a strange kid. Most boys your age would give their left nut to be here."

Kihrin faced the physicker. "I turn sixteen this New Year's."

"I know."

"They can't force me to stay here after that. I'll be an adult."

The old man sighed. "A lot can change in six months. In the mean-

THE RUIN OF KINGS 189

time, Darzin is anxious to speak with you, and the Lord Heir isn't known for his patience. So why don't you let these nice people earn the money they're paid. That way Darzin won't have an excuse to order them whipped."

Kihrin started, shocked, and turned to stare at the servants. Every one of them fixed their eyes firmly to the tile floor. It would be easy to dismiss them as statues.

"I don't need a dozen people to give me a bath. I just had one."

The doctor snorted. "No one downwind would agree with you." He turned to the servants. "Lady Miya told me she ordered the Bath of Petals closed for his use today. Do something about his hair, would you? The kid looks like a witch's apprentice. Let Valrazi know when you're done and he'll send an escort for the boy."

The servant bowed. "Yes, Master Lorgrin. Right away." The man turned and snapped his fingers. A serving girl slid forward holding out a blue linen robe for Kihrin.

Lorgrin turned one last time to the teenager. "You need anything, I'll be at the hospital. Ask someone to show you. I gave up on trying to give directions around the time High Lord Therin was learning to walk. And Kihrin, if you start feeling chest pains? You make someone find me and drag me to you. Don't let anyone convince you it's a false alarm. Understand?"

Kihrin nodded, not trusting himself to speak.

29: TERAETH'S RETURN

(Kihrin's story)

The Black Brotherhood was indeed celebrating when Kalindra and I came back from the baths. Food and drink were in plentiful abundance. I recognized refugees from *The Misery,* but most of the now-freed slaves were recovering from their ordeal. I didn't see Tyentso, and I worried for her. If the Brotherhood hated slavery so much, she wasn't going to be on their welcome list. What were they going to do with her?

The reptilian members of the Brotherhood lounged near large open pit fires for warmth against the chill night air. The vané did too, but in their case, it seemed more celebratory than necessary. Most of the vané were Manol—all midnight blues, forest greens, blood rubies, and black amethysts—but a few Kirpis vané stood out in pastel contrast. They passed around fluted glasses of sparkling fruit liqueurs and golden wines, laughing and talking. Everyone sat or lay on silk floor cushions or low padded couches.

They were a sensual crowd; few talked when they could talk and touch, and if they could touch, why not kiss? I'd grown up in a brothel, but I felt out of my league.

I watched two Manol vané women kiss for several minutes before I realized neither one was a woman.

Maybe it was because they were so beautiful. Maybe it was because Quur has a certain public prudishness about same-gender sexuality that clearly wasn't shared by the Black Brotherhood. Sure, some men prefer men even in Quur, but it's all very discreet. Velvet boys kept politely inside the seraglio or brothel so a patron can maintain the facade that he came for the women. No Quuros male ever publicly admitted he preferred men. No one seemed to care about that here, or, hell, even notice.

I was blushing.

Kalindra found my reaction amusing. "We're usually in a festive frame of mind after a Maevanos. Most of us find looking Death in the eye rather intoxicating, not to mention arousing." She handed me a glass of mulled wine.

"They weren't in any danger during the ritual, were they?"

"You saw the Cup?" I heard the capital letter in her voice.

I nodded.

"Teraeth fills it with poison for the ritual."

The drink paused against my lip. I thought of Darzin and his parties and other poisoned cups. I stared at her.

"If the supplicant is pure, the poison is nullified. If not . . ." She shrugged.

"You people seem fond of that theme."

"It allows little room for argument," Kalindra agreed. "We are brothers and sisters, bound in life and death to each other, each chosen and re-chosen by our goddess. We trust each other because we know, as others can only hold on faith, that we are loved. We hold no fear of Death because we know her caress. Freed from that fear, we find joy in life and all it holds."

"Then why do people view the Black Brotherhood with such dread?"

"Because," Teraeth said as he walked up behind us, "nothing is more terrifying than a man who has no fear of Death, and is happy to die if it means killing you."

"In other words, we're paid murderers," Kalindra said.

I glared at him. He had changed clothes, and now wore a pair of sea-green silk drawstring pants and a green wraparound shirt spattered with golden seashells. He wore a chipped, carved black arrowhead between rows of black shark teeth around his neck.* The shirt opened at the chest, and though the lighting was erratic, the flesh above his heart looked tender and new.

He was so pretty I wanted to hit him, just so there would be something about him that wasn't perfect.

"How long did you have to wait before I gave you a good line for that entrance?"

He grinned white teeth at me. "Not long at all."

"It's rude to eavesdrop."

"Add it to my list of sins." He turned to Kalindra. "How was he?"

I blinked.

Kalindra laughed. "Ah, Teraeth. Don't be crass."

A flush of anger came over me. Had this been some sort of jest? A friendly wager made at the expense of the new kid? Probably it had all been just one more way to try to get their hooks into me, to find out where I was vulnerable.

Which I'd certainly shown them. I felt like an idiot.

---

*The Manol vané as a race are well known for their skill with archery, but most particularly for their use of poisoned ebony arrowheads. Arrowheads that have slain important enemies of the vané are often taken as souvenirs by the archer who fired the arrow.

"How am I being crass?" Teraeth laughed. "Maybe I wanted a recommendation before I made a pass at him myself." He winked at me to show he was joking.

Then he saw the look on my face.

I didn't think it was funny. Worse, as he moved, I caught the flash of silver from my gaesh, hanging around his wrist. He must have taken back the tarnished silver hawk from Khaemezra.

If he decided he wanted me, there was nothing, *nothing,* I could do to stop him.

So much for being allowed to say no.

"Excuse me, Kalindra, but would you mind? I'd like to talk to Kihrin privately."

"Of course. I should finish my rounds anyway. I'll see you later, Kihrin. Behave." She smiled at me before walking back into the jungle.

"Come," Teraeth said. "Sit with me by the fire."

I did, although I wasn't happy about it. I sat as far away from him as I possibly could while still technically sitting "with" him.

At least it was warm.

I pointed at the piece of jewelry containing my gaesh. "That belongs to me."

He unwrapped the silver chain from his wrist and handed it to me, hawk medallion swinging between his fingers. "So it does. Mother wanted me to give it back to you."

I swallowed, staring at the necklace as if I couldn't quite believe it was real. Finally, I took it from him. My fingers shook as I fastened it around my neck. I felt the warm throb of energy from the metal. I inhaled, feeling like I could breathe again for the first time in weeks.

I didn't say "thank you."

We didn't say anything for several minutes. The silence dragged out for long enough that I looked over at Teraeth to see that he was studying the flames. He looked for all the world like a man caught in the middle of an epic bout of brooding.

Except he was smiling. Just an upturn at the corners of his mouth, but enough to turn his expression from harsh to glad. His eyes were far away.

"What's her name?"

Teraeth's attention snapped back to me. "What did you just say?"

"What's her name? You look like a lovestruck puppy." I raised an eyebrow. "Is it Tyentso? It's Tyentso, isn't it? She's a little old for you, but I'm not one to judge. Although I should warn you that she really only seems to get romantically excited about books. If you can disguise yourself as a collection of first-edition *Grizzst's Encyclopedia,* you're all set."

He laughed. "It's no one you know. I was thinking of my wife."

"Wait, what? You're *married*?"

"Not now. I was married in my last life." He waved a hand, preempting the flood of questions I was about to ask. "Yes, I know. No one's supposed to remember their previous life after they're reborn. I just got lucky that way. What about you? Why the hell didn't you sleep with Kalindra?"

I crossed my arms over my chest. "You're changing the subject."

"Damn right."

"It's none of your business whether I did or didn't. And how do you know what happened? Were you spying on us?"

He pointed a finger at me. "That answer is how I know. And I wasn't spying, I just know Kalindra."

"It's still none of your business."

"It's a little bit my business. Kalindra and I are lovers."

I narrowed my eyes. If he'd meant that Kalindra was this "wife" he'd been pining over, he'd have said that. "Well, nothing happened. Anyway, she doesn't belong to you."

"She doesn't belong to anyone. It's part of her charm." Teraeth glanced sideways at me. "I encourage you to remember that when she leaves you one day—which she will."

I rolled my eyes. "Nothing. Happened."

"So you tell me. You weren't worried sleeping with Kalindra was going to get you into trouble, were you? Believe me, that's the last thing we care about here."

He was not taking the hint, so I changed tactics. "Kalindra says that Relos Var is interested in me because of a prophecy. Is that true?"

"You're changing the subject."

"Damn right."

He leaned back on an elbow. "So what am I supposed to say? Yes, it's true. There's a prophecy. Actually no, it's more like a thousand prophecies. It's the collected rantings of a thousand people, the demons possessing them, and whole orders of scholars have spent centuries trying to pull any kind of coherent meaning from them. Relos Var and his lord, Duke Kaen of Yor, believe the prophecies refer to an end time, a great cataclysm, when a single man of vast evil will rise up. The 'Hellwarrior' will conquer the Manol, strip the vané of our immortality, kill the Emperor, destroy the Empire of Quur, and free the demons. In his right hand he will hold Urthaenriel, and with his left, he will crush the world and remake it as he desires." Teraeth sipped at his cup. "Presumably by wiping away the old gods and replacing them with himself, as is tradition."

"Sounds like a sweetheart." My mouth suddenly felt dry. "So it's that kind of prophecy." I thought back to my dream of Taja, and the dark wave she had shown me. *Everything falls.*

"Indeed."

"So, who is this prophesied creep? Relos Var?"

"Duke Kaen seems to think that he is, as you put it, 'this prophesied creep.' Since Relos Var is his most trusted servant, Var's working very hard to make Kaen's grand vision a reality. Which mainly involves finding Urthaenriel. After all, if your goal is to be the prophesied tyrant who will kill all the gods, you probably need the only weapon that's ever successfully pulled that off."

"So where do I come in? I don't know where Urthaenriel is. Shouldn't Relos Var be asking Emperor Sandus?"

Teraeth grinned. "It's all about you, isn't it? Did you ever stop to wonder if it's all about me?" He put a hand to his chest. "I prefer to believe it's all about me."

I flicked a thumb and forefinger against Teraeth's shoulder. "Fine. It's all about you. Jerk. Where's Urthaenriel, since you know so much?"

"Last time I saw it?" He shrugged in a lopsided way. "Falling to the floor of the Manol Jungle, but I assume some Quuros emperor has collected it since then, which means that it's probably locked away in one of the vaults in the middle of the Culling Fields Arena, safely out of reach of Kaen, Relos Var, or anyone else who might want it. Thank the gods."

"Good," I said. The idea honestly did make me feel better. "Still, I wish I knew why Relos Var hated me so much."

"I wouldn't make such a wish if I were you. Someone might decide to grant it."

I drained the rest of my mulled wine and set the cup aside. "There's no curse worse than a granted wish, huh? Doesn't mean I don't want to know." I started to stand.

Teraeth touched the back of my hand. "Hey. Stay with me tonight. I know you've had a hard time of it, and this can't be easy for you. I owe you an apology. Let me make it up to you. I promise I can be very considerate."

I froze. Absolutely froze in exactly the way I had with Kalindra. The flashbacks from Xaltorath hit me so hard I clenched my jaw to fight back bile. I jerked my hand from his.

Teraeth blinked, and then the bastard looked hurt. "I meant no offense."

I rubbed my wrist as I looked at anyone but Teraeth. I wasn't the only person in the area who was being propositioned for a bit of fun, but unlike me, it didn't seem like anyone else was refusing. This was minutes, if not seconds, from turning into something I'd be embarrassed about. I was still not ready. Not with Teraeth. Especially not with Teraeth.

"It's not you. It's—" I couldn't reconcile what I was feeling. Shame? Dread?

Teraeth studied my face. "I killed Juval too quickly."

"No, it's not . . ." I inhaled. I didn't want to explain. I didn't want to stop and explain while all this was going on around us. I didn't want to ever explain Xaltorath. Would Teraeth feel sorry for me? Have pity? Teraeth would want to fix it, and there was no fixing this.

I stepped back. "Do you know where Tyentso is? Can I see her?"

"I don't see why not. She turned down my invitation too." He pointed down one of the jungle paths. "You'll find her on the beach."

I fled as quickly as my feet would take me.

30: Family Reunion

(Talon's story)

The Bath of Petals was the largest bathhouse Kihrin had ever seen. He'd been forced to yell to keep the bath attendants—clearly used to performing all manner of services not directly related to cleanliness—from putting their hands all over him. Finally, the woman in charge snorted and shooed the others away. She proceeded to handle him with the same brisk, matter-of-fact care fishwives give laundry being pounded on a rock. Her attention wasn't the slightest bit provocative—the massage was more like a mauling—so he found her touch tolerable. Afterward, the servants poured something into his scalp that took the dye out of his hair. They trimmed and braided it, and pulled it off his face with expensive gold pins shaped like hawks with sapphire eyes. He was clipped, combed, perfumed, and dressed in the finest clothes, until he was shaking from the idea that Darzin might have saved him for a darker purpose than he'd originally imagined.

Valrazi, the Captain of the House Guard, showed up soon after with a dozen armed soldiers. Valrazi was one of those men who, although in reality very short, was in attitude very tall. He seemed quite competent, and Kihrin thought it was probably inadvisable to make trouble with him purely for its own sake. He went with them without fuss.

He was escorted down long avenues and past graceful colonnades—still inside the Private Court, he reminded himself—until they reached a sculpted garden of tall trees and beautiful flowering hedges, surrounding a long bathing pool. Over a dozen naked women, all young and beautiful (if as varied in color as the flowers in the garden), sported with each other in the water. In an alcove to one side, musicians played a soft air on a double-strung harp and sarod.

Kihrin wondered if they were with the Revelers Guild.

The paving of the garden path led to a crossroads in front of the pool, where a table sat covered with blue linen and a gold breakfast setting. A servant, dressed in bright blue, hovered to the side with a serving cart. There were two chairs: Darzin sat in the one with the best view of the women.

Kihrin stared malevolently. Finally, he shrugged, squared his shoulders, and marched over to the prince. Darzin glanced up and smiled to Kihrin's right. "Thank you for bringing him, Captain. You may go."

"Yes, Your Highness. You're welcome."

Kihrin heard footsteps as the Captain turned on his heels and left.

"Kihrin, so nice to see you up and about. Sit with me. Eat your breakfast and enjoy the view. You must be hungry."

Kihrin ignored the invitation. "What do you want with me?"

"Right now, I want you to have breakfast." Darzin gestured toward the other chair. "I'm glad you're feeling better. I'd thought we'd lost you back there."

"Maybe you shouldn't have sent assassins."

Darzin laughed and popped a cherry tomato into his mouth.

"What did you do with Ola?"

The prince sighed and leaned back farther. His gaze was contemplative. "We must catch up on years of training. One of the first lessons you will have to learn is to avoid asking questions like that. It lets other people know who you care about. And caring about people gives power to anyone willing to use your loved ones against you."

"Is that why you killed my father?"

"He wasn't your father," Darzin corrected.

"He was the only father I ever knew, and you had him murdered."

"A mistake," Darzin said with a shrug, as if he were discussing an accounting problem.

"A mistake? Your crazy assassin slit his throat. That's a mistake?"

"Absolutely. A terrible mistake. Had I realized who you were, I'd have left him alive in our dungeons as insurance on your good behavior. He would have been useful. I even tried to persuade the priests of Thaena to Return him, but he must have been running on the last sands in his hourglass: they said it was his time."

"What about the girl?" Kihrin asked.

Darzin looked bemused. "The girl?"

"You said the priests of Thaena wouldn't Return him because it was his time, but what about the girl killed with him? Did they say it was her time too?"

"Yes, I'm afraid so." Darzin's voice was smooth.

Kihrin knew he was lying. Darzin hadn't cared what happened to a dead slave girl. He hadn't asked for her Return. He hadn't bothered to even check.

While Kihrin fumed, Darzin helped himself to a cup of coffee, added coconut milk, and stirred. "A pity about both. I find I have many questions, just as I will have many questions for Ola Nathera when we track her down."

"But–" Kihrin looked around. He realized none of the servants were within hearing. "Your assassin said she was going to kill her."

Darzin shook his head. "I'm afraid all the commotion over you probably alerted Ola to what had happened. She's fled." Darzin smiled. "Just as well, as some of my servants can be overzealous, and I want answers. I want to know how Surdyeh fits into all this and who was paying him. Someone must have been. I think I know Ola's involvement well enough: she was one of my father's favorite slaves for years, and she was very close to your mother before Ola bought her own freedom. I can well imagine that when Lily ran away with you, Ola would have been the first person she would have gone to for shelter. Foolishly, it seems."

"Lily?"

"Hmm, yes. Lily. Your mother, Lyrilyn. She was quite a woman. I loved her very much."

All the air froze in Kihrin's lungs. He blinked and shook his head. "No. Absolutely not. No fucking way. Not you! Anyone but you."

"Watch your language, son."

"You're *not* my father."

"On the contrary," Darzin said, "I very much *am* your father. I don't take your reaction personally, you know. I don't really like my father either, and I understand Therin's hatred for his father could only be described as epic. Why, your enmity is practically upholding a family tradition."

"This is insane!"

"It all must be a bit of a shock, I admit. You should sit down and eat something. Aren't you hungry?"

Kihrin glared at him. As he did, a wave of weakness washed over him, and he realized despite Lorgrin's healing and whatever else they'd done to him while he was unconscious, he possessed a ravenous hunger. He looked at the food on the table for the first time. Marinated steak, first of all. Then cherry tomatoes in a broth of herbs and spices, and a flaky pastry containing bits of meat and white cheese. Sag flatbread smeared with a thick paste he didn't recognize. He stared at the food and tried to ignore the way his mouth watered.

"Go on," Darzin urged. "Eat." He sighed, exasperated. "If I wanted you dead, I had five days while you were recovering to do the deed. Here." Darzin tore off some sag and ate a little of each dish with a showy wave of his hand. He drank a gulp of water from each crystal goblet and washed it all down with the coffee. "There. If it's poisoned, we both die. Eat."

Kihrin sat and ate quickly, without manners. It all tasted wonderful. Kihrin watched Darzin while he ate, as if the noble were a snake who might bite if the young man turned away from him for even a second.

When Kihrin couldn't eat any more, he shoved the tray away and leaned forward in his chair, his arms resting on the table, his finger brushing up against a sharp steak knife. Kihrin glared at Darzin a little more.

"Let me tell you a story, Kihrin," the Heir of House D'Mon began. The young man scowled.

Darzin stared at Kihrin, then sighed. When he realized the young man's expression wasn't going to soften, Darzin continued anyway. "When I was little more than a boy, I fell in love with one of my great-uncle Pedron's slaves, Lyrilyn. She was extraordinarily beautiful. Dallying with the slaves is far from forbidden, but she wasn't my slave. I took it too far. It was a time of great chaos. I didn't think anyone would notice or care—after all, it's not like my father was in any danger of inheriting. But Therin inconveniently managed to do exactly that and became High Lord, and suddenly I was Lord Heir. My father decided Lyrilyn was an embarrassment. The easiest way to deal with the embarrassment was to eliminate its source. Lyrilyn, being a little sharper than I in such matters, realized her life was in danger."

Darzin paused while he refreshed his coffee, added more coconut milk.

"What happened?" Kihrin finally asked, not able to override the sinking feeling in his stomach.

"She ran away," Darzin explained. "Only afterward did she realize she was pregnant. Lyrilyn sent word to me, but by the time I reached her it was too late. She was strangled in Arena Park during the ascension of Emperor Sandus. The baby was never found. That was fifteen years ago. You're fifteen years old, aren't you?"

"There's no way—"

"Kihrin," Darzin said, "I believed Lyrilyn had lost her baby. But she had a token of my love, a particular kind of vané necklace. This one was prized because it's in our House colors: a blue stone wrapped in gold. I wasn't sure when we met at Qoran's house. It was possible that you were a velvet boy who had paid the Temple of Caless to change the color of your eyes. However, when I found you at that brothel and saw the necklace, I knew you were Lyrilyn's missing son. *My* missing son."

"Why didn't you just take the damn stone? Why didn't you just take it and kill me?"

"The necklace is but a symbol of my love, boy. You are my son. You are the one who matters to me."

"I don't believe you."

"I think a part of you does, Kihrin. Why didn't you tell General Milligreest I was the one who summoned Xaltorath?"

Kihrin stared at him, the blood draining from his face. He *knew*.

Darzin smiled at his son. "Oh yes, I'm quite aware that you're the one who burgled the house of a certain merchant down in the Copper

Quarter, and therefore know I summoned that demon. By the way, who told you that house would be empty?"

Kihrin swallowed bile. "Butterbelly. I don't know who told him. He wouldn't say."

"Hmm." Darzin frowned. "This little adventure has been full of sloppy mistakes, hasn't it? Pity someone killed him too quickly."

"You're the one who killed him—"

"Seems like quite the coincidence, don't you think? That you'd be given a lead on the same house that we were using for our little question-and-answer session?"

Kihrin couldn't stop himself from snorting.

Darzin grinned. "My thoughts exactly. Someone set us up, you and I. I wonder if it was an enemy or a friend?"

"Who knew you were going to—do that?"

The Lord Heir scowled. "That's what I'd like to know. I'm grateful for the nudge in the right direction of course—honestly we may never have found you otherwise—but I'd like to know more about my mysterious benefactor before I start pledging him my vote for the New Year's Ball."*

Kihrin stared down into his coffee cup. It was beautifully made, not solid gold, but paper-thin porcelain with the finest gilding on top. The coffee was rich and black and he was completely numb. He was sitting here chatting—*chatting*—with the man who ordered the deaths of Surdyeh, Morea, and Butterbelly. The man who had summoned the demon who had raped his mind. Darzin was talking to him with that pleasant voice and that pretty face and those fancy clothes, like Kihrin was some kind of old friend, like Kihrin was . . . *family*.

Kihrin set down the cup rather than shatter it in his fist. "You're not my father," he mumbled.

"Son, we've been through this—"

"No. FUCK NO. YOU'RE NOT MY FATHER!" he screamed. The music stopped. The girls in the pool paused from their games.

Darzin's eyes turned flat. It was as if they no longer reflected any light at all, or held any expression. They looked dead.

"Watch your language," Darzin said.

Kihrin didn't respond. His lip curled and his nostrils flared.

"I tried to be reasonable," Darzin whispered. "I tried to be nice. I want you to remember I tried to do this the right way. But you seem to want the wrong way, so I'm happy to oblige you." Darzin turned to the side and snapped his fingers to catch someone's eye. He turned back to Kihrin. "It doesn't matter if you believe me or not. There is a simple magical test

---

*As if the Lord Heir had any right to cast nominating votes for Voices of the Council. Darzin was getting ahead of himself here.

that determines if you have the blood of House D'Mon in your veins. We are one of the god-touched Houses, after all, one of the genuine, original eight Royal Houses. While you slept, a Voice of the Council was here—and my father, the High Lord, stood as witness. The results of that test are irrefutable and legally binding."

"Great. Give my regards to the Council, but I'm not staying." Kihrin rose to leave.

"On the contrary, my son, this is exactly where you're staying for the rest of your life." He waved his hand, and guards rushed into Kihrin's field of view.

This time, they weren't alone. They brought forward a woman dressed in rags and dumped her on the floor. Kihrin didn't know her, but he saw her pain. She was a slave in shackles and she could barely move. She pleaded with the guards, begged them for mercy. They ignored her.

"Since your introduction to the House should be memorable, *son,* I think you should see what is done with new slave acquisitions, much like yourself but for a small quirk of fate." Darzin motioned toward the back, and a large man with a whip stepped forward. "You see, when a slave is first brought in 'from the rough' so to speak, it is usually necessary to break them in. To 'season' them. Watch."

One of the guards ripped away the remnants of fabric from the woman's back. The others cleared a space and the man with the whip swung hard. Kihrin didn't see the strike, but he heard a loud crack and saw a line of blood appear down the woman's back.

She screamed. He flinched.

"The trick," Darzin explained with detached interest, "is to whip them enough so that they understand their place in the household and to break their will completely, but not so much that they bleed to death. Normally—"

"Stop it!"

Darzin continued as if he hadn't heard Kihrin's interruption. "—that balance between injury and death is a fine line. Since we control the College of Physickers, we have an advantage. Being able to ensure someone won't die from their injuries isn't a favor to them, when you're causing the injuries in the first place."

The whip came down several times during Darzin's explanation. Each time the woman's scream and Kihrin's flinch were simultaneous. D'Mon noticed the young man's reaction and smiled.

"You understand that failure to cooperate on your part could have dangerous repercussions? Not for you, of course. I would never hurt you— you are all I have to remind me of my dear Lyrilyn. But I do have to take my anger out on someone, don't I?" He motioned for the slave trainer to quicken the pace of the lashings. The woman's back was a river of bloody cuts, and her screams were fading in volume. Kihrin looked to the side and saw one of the D'Mon healers standing there, his face a careful blank. He understood: when she had suffered enough, the healer would fix her—and they would begin all over again.

"Taja," Kihrin whispered. "Please stop this."

"Say 'please stop it, Father,' and I might." Darzin leaned forward as he watched the woman's bloody back. His expression was hungry.

Kihrin grabbed the gold coffeepot and threw its contents at Darzin. When the older man ducked, he grabbed the steak knife and leapt at the trainer with the whip. The trainer looked up, surprised, but not fast enough to dodge Kihrin's kick to the groin or the follow-up succession of stabs. The whip fell to the ground, followed a half second later by the guard's body.

Darzin was on Kihrin before the dead man finished falling. The teenager felt a grip like a python wrap around his wrist, painfully forcing his hand to release the knife. Caught as he was, there was no way for Kihrin to escape Darzin's knee crashing into his side hard enough to make the world spin. He jabbed out with an elbow, but Darzin dodged that.

"Idiot boy," Darzin said as he punched Kihrin's jaw. "I see you need breaking in too."

When Kihrin staggered from the punch, Darzin grabbed the boy by the hair and shoved his face against the tabletop.

"Grab him," Darzin ordered the other guards.

Rough hands held Kihrin down. He struggled to slip out of their grip and failed. "Fuck you!" he screamed.

"What did I just tell you about watching your language?" Darzin said. "You're a prince. You must learn to talk like something other than a sewer rat."

"Go to hell. You killed *my father.*"

Kihrin heard the fabric of his misha rip and realized Darzin was exposing his back.

"No, I didn't," Darzin said as he picked up the whip from the ground, "but you're making me wish I had. I wonder how much you'll bleed before you learn your place?"

The whip cracked. For a second, Kihrin felt nothing, then a searing pain flared across his back. He ground his teeth to keep from screaming.

Darzin laughed at his reaction. "So where did we leave off? Oh yes, you were going to say 'please stop it, Father.' Shall we begin?" The crack of the whip came down again and this time Kihrin screamed out loud.

"What are you doing, Lord Heir D'Mon?" A woman's voice burned through the gardens.

The nobleman paused. "Miya. I didn't expect you."

Kihrin lifted his head up toward the voice and inhaled sharply.

A Kirpis vané* stood at the entrance to the garden.

Unlike the other vané he'd seen back at the Kazivar House, this vané wasn't in pain, wasn't being tortured. She was extraordinary: light brown skin dusted with gold, with eyes like blue sapphires. Her hair started out the color of blue Kirpis pottery glaze but darkened along its length. By the time it reached her calves it was the same dark blue as her eyes. She gleamed. Her brightness made the gardens seem dark and the sky overcast.

She's in the House colors, Kihrin realized, and then wondered if the coloring could possibly be natural.†

"I have arrived to escort your rediscovered son to his chambers, but I see perhaps you've decided he will not be in need of such compartments. Shall I order the guards to prepare a dungeon cell instead?" Her voice cracked with sarcasm sharper than any whip.

Darzin cleared his throat. "The boy has a temper."

"The blood of House D'Mon runs through his veins, does it not?" The vané's gaze slid over the garden with displeasure before coming to rest on the cowering slave girl and the body of the trainer. She frowned at the physicker stooping over the body. "How badly is that man injured?"

Darzin look confused for a moment, then snorted. "Oh, he was injured very well–fatally, in fact. The boy has a talent for killing." He motioned the guards away from Kihrin, who hauled himself to his feet with murder still hot in his eyes.

"As the father, so the son," the vané woman said.

Darzin laughed. "Good one. And here I didn't think you vané had a sense of humor."

"We do not, Lord Heir. May I escort the young man to his rooms?"

"In a minute." Darzin turned and punched Kihrin in the face, sending him to the ground. "That was for splashing coffee on my shirt."

"I wish I'd done more. Fuck!" Kihrin touched the side of his jaw.

"Watch your language." Darzin grinned. "I do like you, boy. You have a proper D'Mon fire in your heart."

"You have a strange way of showing your affection."

"I've been told that before. And one more thing . . ." Darzin unsheathed the gold sword at his side and crossed over to the slave, still crouched on the floor and sobbing.

"No!" Kihrin leapt after him, but the guards were ready that time.

---

*One does hear rumors, on occasion, to the effect that there are still Kirpis vané inside the Kirpis dominion, despite their diaspora and exile from their homeland after the Quuros conquest, but I have never found any conclusive evidence.

†Technically, no vané's coloring is "natural," but it's a fair question if one is unaware of the mercurial nature of vané appearance.

The crying slave never realized what happened. Darzin's sword entered her back and exited through her front. She gave a single short scream and collapsed near the body of the dead trainer.

Darzin turned back to Kihrin with a cruel smile. "The penalty for killing a House guard is death. And since I can't kill you, I have to make someone pay for your crimes, don't I?"

"You son of a bitch!" Kihrin screamed.

"No, that would be you, my son," Darzin laughed. "Just remember every time you throw a tantrum I'll make sure an innocent person dies. I think you'll run out of sanity long before I run out of slaves."

Kihrin seethed without a word, his eyes never leaving Darzin's.

"He's all yours, Miya. Perhaps you can teach my baby boy some manners."

"Such was exactly your father's intention, Lord Heir."

A flicker of annoyance crossed Darzin's face. "Of course it was."

Miya turned to Kihrin. "Shall we walk? Or do I need the guards to carry you?"

Kihrin jerked himself away from the guards. "I'll walk. Anything to get away from this monster."

"As you wish. Follow me."

31: Tyentso at the Beach

(Kihrin's story)

I found Tyentso sitting on a cliff overlooking the ocean, her hair a sandy curtain whipped in front of her face by the wind. She'd summoned up a trail of glowing mage-lights to illuminate the way from the camp to the beach, but otherwise sat alone and in the dark, staring out at the sea, unsmiling.

I'm pretty sure *she* was not thinking fondly about past lives.

She saw me climb the switchback steps and raised an eyebrow at the bottle of wine under my arm and the two ceramic cups in my other hand.

"Now how did you manage to rate clothing of a nonblack hue? Who do I have to bribe?"

Tyentso looked at her white chemise. "Initiates aren't allowed to wear black."

I blinked. "You're joining them?"

"I'm thinking about it. I don't have many other prospects. However, if anyone shows up claiming that I'm their long-lost queen, you let me know." She patted the grass next to her, offering me a seat.

"Maybe I should join—I'll just have to make sure to flunk all my classes." I poured us both a cup of wine and handed her one. "Feel like entertaining company?"

Tyentso looked perplexed. "Why aren't you down there in a tangle of limbs? That seems like very much the sort of thing you would enjoy."

"Don't be so quick to assume. Why aren't *you* down there in a tangle of limbs? Wouldn't you like the change of pace after all those years of dirty, unwashed sailors?"

She snorted. "Please. There wasn't a single man on *The Misery* I'd have touched except to shove away, and the feeling was mutual." She considered the wine in her cup. "Honesty compels me to admit I'm intimidated by our new vané friends. They are all so . . ."

"Pretty."

"Exactly. Far too pretty." Tyentso sniffed the air as if smelling something off. "I would feel, I don't know, like they felt sorry for the poor ugly witch. I doubt I'll ever find myself in the mood for a pity fuck, but if I am, please do me the favor of slipping some arsenic into my tea."

"You're not–" I stopped when she glared at me. Tyentso's glare could slice a man to ribbons at twenty paces and turn him into a toad besides.

"Don't go all soft on me, Scamp. As it happens, I grew up in a house with mirrors."

I looked back over my shoulder, thinking of the Thriss back at the party. "Okay, but I don't think they care."

"Horse shit. Everyone cares."

"I don't know. When Teraeth had his arms around you back there when the ship was sinking, did you get the feeling he thought you were too awful to touch? Or did I just imagine the way you two were looking at each other?"

Tyentso drained her cup and refilled it from the bottle. "Gods, you saw that? Damn vané held me like he was rescuing his one true love. I thought maybe he was just hard up for a woman, but that was before we arrived on the island and I saw all these little *nymphs*."

I thought about Kalindra. Hell, I thought about me. "He has different standards, I think."

"The one nice thing about looking the way I do is that when a cute bit of something wants into your pants, you don't have to guess whether they have an ulterior motive. The answer is yes." She tucked her legs under her chemise and leaned on one arm. "But they would like you down there. You're not hard on the eyes. You should play."

"I'll have you know I am repressed. Shy and repressed. Also, I'm not ready for that kind of commitment. I mean, if I sleep with the entire Black Brotherhood, I just know I'll feel awkward waking up next to them the next morning. Will they still respect me? What if they want me to meet their mother?" I paused. "Oh hell. I've already met their Mother."

Tyentso chuckled. "Bet they dump you the next morning and never write."

"I should be so lucky." I grinned. "Personally, I kind of think they'd get obsessive and clingy when I tell them I want to see other cults too."

Tyentso couldn't stop herself from laughing that time.

"Come back with me to Quur," I said.

She nearly choked on her wine. "What?"

I leaned toward her. "I want to go back to Quur. I have family there, friends, people who are relying on me. I'm House D'Mon, Ty. I can protect you from the people who had you exiled. The catch is that there's some dangerous people that I need to deal with once I return. Specifically, there's this sorcerer. I don't know his name. I've always just called him Dead Man. He's powerful. I've seen him melt the flesh off a person with a gesture."

"Charming. He sounds just like my late husband."

It was my turn to do a double take. "Please tell me you're not talking about Teraeth in a past life."

She gave me an odd look. "That's a horrifying thought. I prefer to think Thaena tossed my late husband's soul into a bottomless pit and walked away."

"Good. Had to ask."

"Anyway, it's sweet of you to offer to clear my name, Scamp, but I can't go back to Quur. I'm wanted for treason, witchcraft, and every crime the High Council could invent, dig up, or exaggerate. House D'Mon can't protect me from that. If I go back to Quur, I better be pretty comfortable with my own mortality because I will be counting the minutes until my demise."

"Treason? Really?"

She shrugged. "Never happened. Just the opposite. I saved their damned asses, and that was the thanks I got. Not saying I've lived a sin-free life, but as far as I can tell, my real mistake in their eyes was doing all this magic without owning a dick between my legs."

I coughed. "Never really understood the big deal about women knowing magic, anyway."

"Stop flirting with me, Scamp. I'm too much woman for you."

"I'm not flirting. I mean it. I never understood it. If the Royal Houses trained the women, they'd double the number of wizards they have in just a few years. More wizards mean more profit. How is this not obvious?"[*]

"Oh, but heavens, Kihrin, if we womenfolk were running around casting spells—why, it would be the end of civilization . . . Next, we'd want to inherit, own property, have a say in who we married. Who would stay at home and have the babies? Or put up with our men beating us or having a dozen mistresses on the side? Talk sense. Next you'll be telling me that we Quuros shouldn't own slaves."

I shifted uncomfortably. "Ah. Right. How silly of me. Clearly I've been on this island for too long."

"Besides, everyone knows women lack the mental faculties and strength of will to make good magi. We're too much slaves to our baser lusts, chained by our carnal natures.[†] Certainly no woman could ever become a true wizard . . ."

---

[*] One could argue that the Royal Houses benefit from monopolies of scarce resources, but since demand far outstrips supply, Kihrin's argument has merit from a purely economic viewpoint.

[†] The definition of "witch" is one of the most hotly contested words in the Guarem language.

I threw her an annoyed look. "I get it, Tyentso."

She shrugged. "It's something of a sore spot."

"Yeah. At least you're not bitter about it." I pretended to duck as she aimed a rock at my head.

"Quur didn't used to be this way." Tyentso tossed the rock away, a sour expression gracing her sour face. "Four of the Eight Immortals are male, and four are female, their genders balanced with each other. Tya herself is a *goddess*. All the old stories are filled with queens, heroines . . . It took the god-king Ghauras and his bitch Caless to turn women into nothing but whores. Personally, I think Ghauras was overcompensating for something." She held up a pinkie finger and wiggled it suggestively.

"You should teach a class at the Academy," I said, snickering.

"Oh yes. Because they'd really want to see me again, I'm sure."

I raised an eyebrow at her. "They've seen you before? What did you do, disguise yourself as a boy?"

"No. My adopted father was one of the deans," she said.

"You're joking."

She looked surprised. "Oh no. I grew up at the Academy. Used to sneak into the library at night and read until dawn." Her expression turned wistful. "Oh, I loved that library. Honestly, the hardest part about living on board a ship was not having enough room for a proper library."

"Ouch. No wonder the High Council is so unhappy with you. You've read *books*."*

"And paid attention to the student lectures, gods help us all." She gave me a critical look over the rim of her cup of wine. "So, you're not going to stay?"

"They're a friendly bunch, but assassin was never high on my list of career choices," I said.

"I don't think that's what they are."

"But it is." I pointed back over my shoulder. "They told me. Well, 'paid murderers,' but it means the same thing."

"I think it's a cover. Was a cover, I suppose, now that it's blown. A guild of assassins. That's a mildly intimidating thought; it's all part of the game, right? Just another charming aspect of Quuros culture, hiring themselves out to the highest bidder to kill whomever is too annoying this week. That they're mostly vané? Window dressing. A fun bit of ex-

---

According to the Academy at Alavel, a "witch" is "an uneducated magical adept who operates without official license from the Royal Houses." But since women are never given licenses and are forbidden to attend the Academy, the gender-neutral term is almost exclusively applied to women.
*And technically only qualifies as a witch because of a lack of formal licensing. Must be infuriating.

THE RUIN OF KINGS

otic flair. Makes them sexy and dangerous. No Quuros Royal Family would see that as a threat as long as they're the ones doing the hiring."

"If they're not assassins, what are they?"

"I don't know, but they're working directly for Thaena herself in a way her normal priests don't. If that doesn't scare you just a little bit, you're not paying attention. Thaena has always been the strictest adherent to playing by the rules of how gods and mortals interact. That means that either these people are lying about being followers of Thaena—and Teraeth's Return argues against that—or she's suddenly decided that it's necessary to break those rules. Be terrified."

"My momma always used to say that if you're going to lie, save it up for something big."

"Exactly. I'd like to know what rainy day these little bastards have been saving up for."

I sighed and drank a mouthful of wine. "Apparently there's a prophecy."

"Which one? Devoran Prophecies? The Scrolls of Fate?* The Sayings of Sephis?"

"You're familiar with the Prophecies?" I perked up. Unlike Khaemezra, Tyentso had no reason not to give me a straight answer.

"Magister Tyrinthal used to teach a six-month course for advanced students.† He didn't know I was auditing the class, but well, you know how it is." She shrugged. "My late husband was more than a bit obsessed with the topic. If a children's nursery rhyme could be twisted to sound like it referred to that prophecy, he had a copy." She paused. "More than one copy if there were regional idioms or linguistic variations."

She looked off into the distance, her gaze far away. "Hell of a thing to be involved with, Scamp. Those prophecies are nasty stuff; you don't want to know the people involved in that business. You sure as damnation don't want them to know you."

I scowled. "Too late."

Tyentso looked surprised for a beat, and then she snorted and rolled her eyes. "For a second, Scamp, I actually forgot how I ended up on this island. Yeah, you're right. Way too late." She leaned back and drank deep from her cup. "Aw, it's a mess, but right now you've got bigger problems."

"Sure, Relos Var. But I can sneak off the island before he realizes I'm gone. I am good at sneaking."

---

*I'm not convinced the Scrolls of Fate aren't a clever hoax perpetrated by someone trying to muddy the water—or simply profit off the fascination so many hold for prophecies.

†He still does. And it's still profoundly boring. On the plus side, mentally replaying one of his lectures is the best insomnia cure I've ever discovered.

"I wasn't thinking of Relos Var," Tyentso said. Her voice sounded odd. "Run back to camp, Kihrin. Right now."

"What? Why would I–"

A wind picked up and tossed the grass on the cliff face, bringing with it the scent of molten metal and burning rock.

The Old Man landed in front of us.

32: LADY MIYA

(Talon's story)

The vané took Kihrin to a four-story building nestled amongst other tall buildings. Nothing identified it as a Blue House except the number of men in physicker's robes who came and went through its doors. All seemed to know Miya, gave her plenty of room and deferential bows, and addressed her as "Lady." No one asked about Kihrin or how he'd come by his injuries until they chanced to cross paths with Master Lorgrin.

The healer grimaced. "I see the happy reunion went about as well as could be expected."

Lady Miya's look was disapproving. "Indeed."

"I assume you'll want to handle this yourself. The apothecary's all yours." He hooked a thumb toward a door behind him.

She nodded. "Thank you, Master Lorgrin."

"Uh-huh." He shook his head at Kihrin as they passed.

Inside, small drawers recessed into the walls filled the room from floor to ceiling. The air had a funny, herbal smell. Several tables took up the center, covered with scales, mortars, pestles, and large thick books opened to drawings of plants.

"Sit down," she told him with a stern voice.

Kihrin did, feeling sullen and sorry for himself while the vané woman opened drawers and pulled out bottles, flasks, and bundles of herbs.

She slammed the ingredients down on the table, making everything jump.

"What did I do to you?" Kihrin said. "Upset I killed that guard? Or because I spilled coffee all over your precious Lord Heir?"

She picked up a heavy stone mortar and pestle and slammed it down on the table in front of him. "These are for you: mugwort, goldensheaf, blood of varius, carella, and white lotus."

"No thanks, I just ate."

Her upper lip started to curl. "You would not want the wounds to become infected and you do not know what diseases that woman may have sheltered in her body. Your wounds are most assuredly contaminated with her blood, lingering on the lash. Do you not wish to make a salve for your back?"

"Very funny. I don't know how to do that."

"Oh? You do not?" Her voice dripped sarcasm. "But you must want to heal. So heal yourself."

"I already told you I don't know how." He stood.

"Ah." She crossed her arms as if she'd won the argument.

Kihrin blinked. "Ah? What do you mean 'ah'?"

"Wanting something is not enough. Talent and desire is meaningless without skill and training."

Kihrin glared. "Is that a riddle?"

"This is not a game, young man. I am making a point. Are you understanding it?"

"Since I'm apparently an idiot, why don't you just explain it to me?"

Her nostrils flared white as she grabbed back the mortar. "My meaning is that you do not have the training to deal with a man like Darzin D'Mon, so provoking him is much the same as walking into a tiger's den after smearing yourself with fresh blood. You may wish to kill Darzin, but desire is not enough."

"He killed my father! He killed Morea."

"So? Does that make you more capable of besting him? Do you think fortune will favor you because your cause is just and your heart is full of vengeance? As you said yourself, he is a monster. One does not slay a monster with good intentions."

"He has to sleep sometime."

Lady Miya sighed. "My, and are you so young and yet already a professional assassin? A member of the Black Brotherhood? Or perhaps you have come to us much disguised, and are in truth Nikali Milligreest, famous throughout the Empire as the most skilled of swordsmen?"

Kihrin swallowed and looked away. The fear and hate of the earlier encounter began to ebb, leaving him weak and trembling.

"He makes me so angry," Kihrin whispered.

"He makes me angry too," Miya said. "But you must learn to control yourself. You will not live long in this House if you continue with this foolish behavior." She added the ingredients to the bowl, measuring out portions by quick handfuls. "Darzin has enough choleric in him for both of you. You push him and he will respond in the nastiest, most vicious way he can imagine—and he's made himself something of an expert in this area. This House has enough problems without you provoking him to do something the rest of us will all regret."

"Provoking him? I didn't—"

"Protest your innocence to someone who did not hear the entire conversation," she said matter-of-factly. "I have known Darzin twenty years longer than you, and I tell you now he spoke true: he was on his best behavior this morning. That he treated you with kindness was an insult beyond your forbearance, and so, you lost your temper. As a result, he lost his. And because of that, two people died."

"Don't blame this on me. If you were listening the whole time you could have stepped in sooner. That woman would still be alive."

She raised an eyebrow. "And what possible reason could I give for interfering with a D'Mon ordering one of his own slaves whipped? With you, I could intercede. I could do nothing to save that girl."

"All you vané are supposed to know magic. You could have–"

"I may not allow harm to come to a D'Mon if it is in my power to stop it without the loss of my own life." She picked up the pestle and began mashing the herbs and flowers.

Kihrin's eyes widened. "You're gaeshed."

"Of course, I am gaeshed. I certainly would not be here of my own free will. I am the High Lord's seneschal, and highest ranked of the serving staff of the palace. I am also the High Lord's gaeshed slave. Darzin was hurting you, so I could intervene."

"You could intervene? But you–?" He sat down again. "But I'm not a D'Mon. At best, I'm Ogenra."

She looked oddly at him. "Who said you are Ogenra?"

"Well I–" He blinked. "I have to be. He said my mother was a slave. What else could I be?"

"Darzin claims he married Lyrilyn. He has even produced documents to that effect–and witnesses. You are not Ogenra. You are legally Darzin D'Mon's firstborn son, second in line to the D'Mon seat."

He stared at her while all the blood drained from his face. "He–what?" The information refused to sink in. He didn't understand. He'd always dreamed of being Ogenra, as had every orphan in the Lower Circle, but that was as far as the dream had ever gone. He never dared imagine he might be an actual member of royalty. And here he was, being told he was a prince? In line to one day become High Lord himself?

The whole world tilted on its axis.

Miya didn't notice his shock. "Truthfully, it would not have mattered. I know it is common perception that Ogenra are illegitimate House bastards, but the reality is more complicated. Any child, even a bastard, can be part of a House if they are formally recognized–as you have been."

"He really is my father?" He spoke in a whisper.

She looked away. "I can't say.* Regardless, it is his claim. And High

---

*Note the wording here. I am inclined to interpret this literally: not that Miya didn't know, but that she had been ordered to keep silent. Questioning someone who is gaeshed is a bit like talking to a demon–and for the same reasons.

Lord Therin was quick to publicly substantiate those claims—he's been less than pleased that Darzin's son Galen might one day inherit."

"Gods, why?"

"Ruling a Royal House requires a certain ruthlessness of character. Galen is a sweet boy. I do not think High Lord Therin believes the house fortunes will prosper under the care of a 'sweet boy.'"

"But I'm street trash. A throw away from Velvet Town!"

She set down the mortar and pestle and turned to Kihrin, staring at him with angry blue eyes. "You are *never* to refer to yourself that way again. I will not stand for it. You are Kihrin D'Mon, Royal Prince and second-ranked heir to House D'Mon. You are descended from a hundred generations of magi, including three Emperors. You are royalty, and you are *born* to rule.* You are not, and you will NEVER be, street trash."

"But I just—can't be. This is some kind of game. He's evil."

"Truth and evil are not opposed concepts. Let me demonstrate: this will sting." He felt wetness on his back that flared into vivid red pain he recognized as alcohol on an open wound.

Kihrin gasped. "OW! Thaena's teats."

"Watch your tongue."

"The whipping didn't hurt this bad."

"Oh? Darzin must be losing his touch. But better a little pain now than an infection later." She smoothed the mash of herbs over the whip marks. The herbs were soothing and cold and, after the astringent, rather nice.

He felt her fingertips on his back, and heard her say something he couldn't understand in a light, rolling tongue. A pleasant warmth spread out over his skin.

"Couldn't you have just used magic to heal all of it?"

"I could," she admitted, "but it runs the risk of complications." She walked in front of Kihrin, pulled out a chair, and sat down. "What do you know of magic? Can you see past the First Veil yet?"

He nodded. "As long as I can remember. How did you know I could?"

"I didn't. That's why I asked. But you are a D'Mon: it seemed a safe assumption. What of talismans? Have you learned what they are? How to construct them?"

He swallowed and shook his head. "Mages use them. I know how to check if someone's wearing them—mostly to stay away from that person."

"I'm sure that was wise when you lived in Velvet Town, but now you're going to have to learn to make them yourself." She began putting away

---

*Lady Miya just made a slip of the tongue here, since, technically speaking, Quuros royalty are forbidden from "ruling."

the herbs. "So consider this your first lesson. Do you understand the material requirements for magic?"

"Yes." He nodded. "No object can be affected by magic, unless the wizard casting the spell understands the true nature of the materials that make up the object."

"Very good. You've had formal training?" She seemed surprised.

"I was learning from someone but, uh . . . she died."

"I feel sorrow for your loss."

"Thanks." He didn't really know what else to say.

After a moment's pause, she asked: "And what else?"

Kihrin blinked at her. "What else?"

"Yes, what else can you tell me about material requirements and magic?"

"I–" He frowned. "Uh, if you do understand the true nature of an object, you can affect it?"

"Rewording your original response does not make it a different answer."

"Uh . . ." He fought the urge to throw up his arms in frustration. "I don't know. Different objects have different auras. So do different people. If you put two people right next to each other, their auras won't look the same. Iron has a different aura than copper, which is different than a wooden coin that's just painted copper."

"So taking that observation into consideration, what is a talisman?"

Kihrin floundered as he tried to come up with a suitable response. How would he have any idea what that made a talisman? All he really knew about talismans was that they echoed the aura of the person who wore them, so it was like seeing a stamp slapped down multiple times, each time a shade off from its correct position. Then he blinked.

"Wait, a talisman has to have an aura that's different than its intrinsic nature, doesn't it? If it's a coin or a piece of jewelry or whatever it is, the aura isn't metal or whatever it should normally be–the aura is the same as the person wearing it. How is that even possible?"

"One may change the aura of an object into something it should not be," Miya explained. Her tone was gentle and proud. Her smile suggested she was pleased at his response. "And if one does it just a little, the object might still look like a coin or a piece of jewelry, the way a mirror can show your image but not be you."

He stared at her and then narrowed his eyes. "Why? Why would someone want that?"

"Because if I presented myself and attempted to change your aura in order to harm you, and you wore four talismans, then in effect I have to change your aura five times rather than once. So it is a protection, you see, from other wizards." Miya held up a finger then. "But there's always a price. For every talisman you wear, your own magic and ability to affect the auras of others is weakened. A witchhunter is nothing more than a wizard who wears as many talismans as they can maintain. In doing so, they make themselves almost completely immune to magic—but they may never cast a single spell."

"So, it's a balancing act?"

She nodded. "Exactly so. And the talisman rule applies to healing as much as harm—if you cannot change someone's aura, that also means you cannot cure them."

"I wouldn't mind," he said, with a somewhat wistful expression. "Learning how to heal people, I mean. That seems like it would be a fine thing to know."

She studied his face for a moment, then nodded. "All right." She crossed to the far side of the table, returning a moment later with a large book. She handed it to the young man.

He opened the book. It contained page after page of neat, perfectly drawn pictures of the human body, in separate pieces and the whole together.* "You want me to read this?"

"I want you to memorize it."

"Memorize?" His voice went a little squeaky.

"I'm willing to train you at your own pace, but you must have a foundation of knowledge to build upon. One cannot fix a thing if you do not understand how it is broken, and you will not be able to recognize how it is broken if you do not know how it should normally function. So yes, memorize. When you are done, we'll move on to body chemistry and cellular composition."

"Move on to what?"

She smiled. "You'll see." Miya picked up the mortar of crushed herbs and scooped the rest of the mixture into a small glass jar. "Put this on any other bruised areas, such as your jaw. When you run out, return to me or any of the House physickers and we'll replenish your supply."

"Thanks, I appreciate—" He paused. "Why am I going to need a steady supply?"

Her expression turned grim. "Darzin's son Galen does. And *he* is a sweet boy."

Kihrin gave her a startled look. "Great," he murmured. "That's just great. Does he beat his wife too? I assume Galen's mother wasn't a slave girl."

"I do not believe you need me to provide you that answer."

He sighed. For just a moment, talking to Miya about learning

---

*At a guess, probably Sarin D'Mon's *Anatomy of the Human Body,* which I understand is still used as the basic primer for entry-level study.

magic, he'd forgotten where he was. "No. No, I guess I don't. Of course he beats his wife, and then he sends her here to be patched up good as new when he's done. Isn't it great when all the healers work for you? You can get away with almost anything."

She started to say something, then stopped and shook her head. "Come along, Your Highness. It is time I showed you to your rooms."

33: The Dragon's Due

(Kihrin's story)

Every time I've seen the Old Man I am reminded how enormous dragons are. Artists never get it right. I think it's because they have this overwhelming need to paint in an opposing knight or wizard or the like—and making the human large enough to be noticed messes with the scale. Take the largest creature you can imagine . . . the Old Man was larger.

It's hard not to freeze in place, trapped by one's own awe.

He landed on a red-hot volcanic island of molten stone offshore from Ynisthana itself. Yet he was so large I was positive he could reach out with a claw and rip both of us in two without effort. He was less a living creature than a monument to the uncontrollable. As he landed on the island, an upwelling of lava fountained into the air, as if the very ground reacted to his presence with fire.

"I have come for what I am due," the Old Man said.

Tyentso uttered a curse to make Madam Ola blush, and shoved me behind her.

"Hey—" I started to protest.

"Do not hide the golden voice. He is mine," the Old Man growled.

"Nobody said you could have him. Just the opposite."

"I don't care," said the Old Man.

"Kihrin, run."

I remembered Teraeth's caution: running just gave the Old Man something to chase. "I don't think—"

The dragon lunged.

I ran.

Tyentso moved her arm, and a wall of fire-hardened glass thrust skyward from the beach, twenty feet thick and tall enough to block my view of the horizon. The glass turned red immediately, then white-hot as it slagged. The temperature soared to oven-like heat as scouring winds picked up. The wall shuddered as the dragon slammed into it from the other side. Then it exploded toward us.

I ducked to the side as an enormous glob of molten glass hit the ground near me.

Everything fell silent.

I turned back.

The dragon floated in midair, frozen. It blotted out the sky. Lava dripped from the dragon's claws and fell, sizzling, into the ocean waves.

Tyentso picked herself up. Part of her chemise had burned, scorch marks marred one of her arms, but she was miraculously still alive.

Khaemezra walked out onto the cliff.

I don't know if Khaemezra had been spying on us or the dragon, but she must have been nearby. The old woman was a bit less hunched and frail than she had been on the trip over, as if this island had rejuvenated her. She was taller, straighter, and younger.

"I made myself clear, Sharanakal. You may not have him." Her craggy voice carried with perfect clarity over the waves and sand.

"Release me! Release me this instant, Mother."

She pointed an old, thin arm toward the sea. "Go then, and do not return."

The dragon shuddered. He shook off his paralysis like a dog shaking water from its fur, then flapped his wings, raising himself high in the air.

He looked at me. At least, I think he was looking at me.

The Old Man flew off into the sky.

We watched him go. No one said anything for several long, tense moments. Finally I couldn't stand it anymore. "How do you kill something like that?"

"You don't," Khaemezra said. "You might as well kill a mountain."

Tyentso moved one hand over her arm, wincing as she probed the edges of the burn. "You called him Sharanakal. Is that his true name?"

"Yes," Khaemezra said. She gathered her robes and turned back toward me. "Are you hurt?"

"No, I'm fine." I looked at Tyentso. "Sharanakal? Why do I feel like I should know that name?"

"Because you're a minstrel's son, I imagine. Sharanakal may not be as famous as Baelosh or Morios, but there's only eight dragons in the damn world," Tyentso said. "You've managed to gain the obsessive attention of one of them. Aren't you the lucky bastard?"

My heart beat drumroll fast. I felt faint from more than just too many cups of wine. I felt powerless, helpless, and trapped.

What I didn't feel was lucky.

Once I'd woken up on the island and the Old Man wasn't using me as his favorite toothpick, I'd decided the danger was past. The Old Man had let me go. I was safe. From Relos Var? Maybe not. But at least safe from the dragon. A whole cult of people lived on this island without being bothered by giant dragons, so I was safe, right?

Wrong.

Khaemezra didn't seem sympathetic. "Child, whatever possessed you to think waking Sharanakal was a smart thing to do?"

I clenched my jaw. "It was Teraeth's idea."

Khaemezra's nostrils flared. "Yes, that does sound like something my son would suggest."

"Let's stop throwing around blame. That little ditty saved all our lives on the ship," Tyentso snapped. She waved at Khaemezra. "Except you, of course, who was never in any real danger. So you don't get to complain, Mother I-can't-get-involved."

"Is he going to leave?" I asked. In the still night, with the crashing of the waves behind us and even the jungle insects not daring to make a noise, my voice sounded small.

Khaemezra stared at me. "Eventually. When he grows bored."

"How long will that take?"

Khaemezra didn't answer.

Finally, Tyentso waved a hand. "A decade or two. Maybe longer. And you can't out-sneak a dragon, Scamp. He'll *find* you."*

I don't remember choosing to sit. I just found myself sitting, as though my legs had decided they were tired of waiting for me to do the right thing and had acted of their own accord.

I only looked up when I heard Tyentso speak. "I've made up my mind. I'd like to join the Brotherhood."

Khaemezra regarded her. "You were unsure just a short while ago."

"Ah, but someone really needs to teach Scamp here some magic. If nothing else, some fireproofing spells wouldn't go amiss. Something tells me he's going to need them."

I leaned forward. "Wait, magic? You're going to teach me magic?"

"Someone damn well better," Tyentso said. "If Mother will let me." Tyentso raised an eyebrow. "Will you?"

Khaemezra scoffed, although the sound managed to be more affectionate than dismissive. "Yes, I believe I will."

"I'm trapped here," I whispered.

"For now," Khaemezra agreed. "If I have learned one lesson in all my years, it is that no situation lasts forever. In the meantime, what do you want to do?"

"I want to leave," I said, my voice rising.

"I know you do, but problems are opportunities with thorns attached," she explained again. "Let's use your stay here to better prepare you to tackle those problems successfully. What do you *want*?"

---

*There is a story concerning the dragon Baelosh where he promised Emperor Simillion he would hunt him down and kill him after "a short nap." The short nap lasted twenty-five years, and when Baelosh woke, Simillion was dead.

I had a hard time thinking past the "I'm trapped here" part of our conversation. All I could think about were the invisible bars to my island cage, my jailer a giant fire-breathing dragon. Taja had said I could leave, but she hadn't mentioned the cost. I was trapped.

Tyentso put a hand on my shoulder and squeezed. "Perhaps you'd like to send a message to your family?"

I blinked and focused on the two women. "Can you? Can you tell Lady Miya I'm alive?"

"Yes. Anything else?"

I breathed deep, still trying to calm down. "Do you have anyone on the island who's good with swords? I was learning swordplay, and I'd like to continue."

"A sword isn't much use against a dragon," Khaemezra pointed out, although I was alert enough by that point to notice she hadn't refused.

"I know that. The sword is for killing Darzin."

Khaemezra smiled. "Then I believe I know just the man."

34: Promises

(Talon's story)

The door handle jiggled.

"Go away!" Kihrin shouted at the door.

The door opened an inch before it caught on the chair Kihrin had wedged under the handle.

Lady Miya said, "Please, Kihrin. This is unseemly and does not serve your cause. Why are you hiding in your room?"

"I don't want to see any of you!" he shouted back. Kihrin lay on his rumpled bed, which was in the same state as his clothes. He hadn't changed, or done much in the way of hygiene, since Miya had shown him these rooms.

He'd been impressed at first. Rather than the room where he'd originally woken, Lady Miya had taken him to the family's private wing—the Hall of Princes where the High Lord, his sons, and direct heirs kept their quarters. Kihrin's new suite of rooms was a palace in and of itself, an amazing confection of jeweled walls and plants that made the place resemble a garden as much as a living area. The centerpiece was a lavish bed crafted from the interlaced boughs of four living trees.

Then Kihrin saw the trap.

The ornate lattices covering the balcony openings were gilt-covered iron. The flowering vines hid nasty thorns. The main door locked from the outside as did the side door connecting his suite to whoever lived next door.

Whoever had used these rooms before him had also been a prisoner.

That's when the enormity of Kihrin's situation rolled down on him. Darzin could do anything. Darzin could kill him, maim him, sell him as a slave; all of it would be legal. Parents had absolute power over their children. Legally, Kihrin was Darzin's child. Surdyeh couldn't do anything about it because Surdyeh was dead. Ola? Ola was probably dead too.

He couldn't close his eyes without seeing Morea's slashed throat, without hearing the sound of a demon's laughter. He couldn't sleep for the nightmares.

A taste of pain to prepare him for the feast of suffering.

Kihrin had jury-rigged a chair barricade and lain back on his bed to sulk. He had been there, still sulking, for several days.

Yes, you were sulking. Don't interrupt, Kihrin.

As I was saying, when Lady Miya asked Kihrin to open the door for her, he refused, yelled at her, and assumed she would go away.

A scraping noise made him look up. The chair unhooked itself from under the door handle and slid to the side, all without being touched. That same door then swung open, revealing Lady Miya, arms crossed over her chest, eyes full of fury. Kihrin sat up in bed, startled.

"I should have realized when you healed me," Kihrin said. "You're a witch, aren't you?"

Lady Miya walked into the room and the door slammed shut behind her, again, without her touching it. "Do you know what a witch is?"

Kihrin ground his teeth. "Of course I do. A witch is someone who isn't licensed by one of the precious Royal Houses."

"And do you think I am not licensed by one of the Royal Houses?"

Kihrin's gaze hardened into something icy and unfriendly. He shrugged and laid his head back against a tree trunk, crossing an ankle over a knee. "I guess that makes you the one who taught him how to summon demons?"

Lady Miya paused. "Excuse me? Taught who?"

"Darzin." Then Kihrin sniggered. "Humph. Darzin D'Mon dabbles with dastardly demons. There's a dirty ditty in there somewhere."

The vané crossed over to him, her step angry. Miya frowned as she took in the dirty linens, the unchanged clothes. Kihrin hadn't even bothered to replace the shirt that Darzin had ripped open to whip him over breakfast several days before.

"Why do you believe he summoned a demon?"

He tilted his head and stared at her. "Because I saw him do it. Well, okay, I didn't see him do it, but I'm sure he did. He admitted as much. I wouldn't be here if I hadn't broken into the place where he'd summoned it." Kihrin massaged his temples. "Taja! If I'd just gone away. It wasn't any of my business anyway, and now . . ." He shook his head. "They're dead. I can't believe they're dead."

Kihrin slid out of bed, angry and fast, launching himself away from her. "What do you care anyway? You don't know me and you don't give a *damn* about me. I'm just another D'Mon and you don't serve this family by choice. Did my 'father' tell you to look in on me? My 'grandfather'?"

"No," she said, her voice quiet. "Lyrilyn was my handmaiden."

Startled, Kihrin turned back.

"Not originally," Miya clarified. "Lyrilyn was one of the harem slaves of High Lord Pedron, a maniac who nearly destroyed this House. After Therin killed Pedron and became the new High Lord, he allowed me to pick whoever I wished to be my assistant. I chose Lyrilyn."

His throat felt like it was closing in on itself, but he choked out a question. "You knew my mother?"

She sat down on the edge of the bed and motioned for him to join her. "There is so much . . ." She took a deep breath. "There is much I may not say. So much the gaesh will not allow me to communicate. I can tell you this: in all the time I knew Lyrilyn, she was never pregnant."

"What? Wait, but I thought—" Kihrin swallowed. He felt uneven, unsteady. It occurred to him it had been a long time since he'd eaten.

"Darzin claims Lyrilyn was your mother, but you must not forget that Darzin will lie as suits his vast ambitions. He is not to be trusted."

"You don't need to tell me." Kihrin scowled. "You're saying she wasn't my mother? Then who was?"

Miya started to say something and then shook her head. "I cannot say. And while I know such an answer is not one you wish to hear, it is also not a pressing worry. This demon-summoning matter is. Please, tell me of this fiend."

He wanted to shout. He wanted to demand answers. Instead he rubbed his arms and tried not to think about his rumbling stomach. That made him aware that he was wearing a shirt in rags. Fighting to keep from blushing, he walked over to the closet. "He said his name was Xaltorath."

"Ompher guide me," Miya breathed. "That is no minor demon."

"It took Emperor Sandus to banish him," Kihrin told her. He pulled out a shirt so ornately embroidered that it would have cost him all his profits from a year of burglaries. He put it back and pulled out another one, even worse. He suspected all the clothes would be the same, so he picked one at random and dressed himself. "But it was Darzin who summoned him. He was looking for something called the Stone of Shackles."

Silence.

Kihrin turned back to face her. She sat there on the bed, staring at a wall, her expression unreadable.

"Did I say something wrong?" he asked her.

Miya looked at him with eyes the same blue as his, the same blue as Darzin's, but she was vané and they were both human. Some magic must have made them that color, but he supposed that was true for the D'Mon family. God-touched eyes.

"What is it?" Kihrin asked.

"You wear the Stone of Shackles," Miya said in a flat voice. "The gem you wear around your throat *is* the Stone of Shackles."

His hand went to the tsali stone around his neck. "What? How?"

She looked down at her hands. "It's my doing. I gave the necklace to

Lyrilyn. She must have had enough presence of mind to give it to you."
She smiled sadly. "My sweet dove. Loyal to the end."

"I don't understand," he said. "If I'm wearing this stone that Darzin wants so badly, why didn't he take it? I was stuck in bed for a week while Master Lorgrin healed my heart."

"The Stone of Shackles cannot be removed by anyone but its wearer. Darzin cannot steal it from you. By free will alone may it be given away. As I did to Lyrilyn, and, I must assume, Lyrilyn did to you. So she kept me that promise at least. She did protect you, even if she could not smuggle you to the Manol." She closed her eyes and held her breath for a moment, as if expecting pain, then opened her eyes and exhaled.

Kihrin felt like he was a child again, full of questions. "Why would she take me to the Manol Jungle? I'm not vané—" His voice died in his throat.

Miya's motherly attention wasn't what gave her away, for Kihrin had grown up around Ola. He was used to that look from a woman who wasn't his birth mother. Rather, it was Kihrin's years spent in the Lower Circle, his years with the Shadowdancers, spent in the company of people who cared nothing for each other—unless there was profit in it for them. Even if Lyrilyn had been Miya's closest friend, Kihrin didn't believe the vané would give up so great a treasure on her handmaiden's behalf. Butterbelly had offered fifteen thousand thrones for the necklace. Butterbelly, who wouldn't have offered a fair price to Tavris himself if the god had wanted to fence a dragon's hoard.

No, he couldn't believe Miya would do that for Lyrilyn's newborn child.

But for her own baby?

She was so beautiful, so wild. So other from everything mundane and human. Yet if she were his mother, he would have inherited more than the blue eyes. That ombre blue hair seemed like a truer flag of allegiance. Blue eyes proved nothing. Everyone in House D'Mon had blue eyes, just like everyone in House D'Aramarin had green eyes.

He couldn't bring himself to ask: *Are you my mother?*

Miya reached over and took his hand. "You are not full vané, but you have vané blood in your veins through your D'Mon lineage. You could claim sanctuary with our people." She squeezed his hand. "Kihrin, what happened at the Shattered Veil Club was not your fault."

He opened his mouth to protest, but she continued. "If Darzin summoned Xaltorath, it was but for one purpose: *to divine your location.* A demon of such power is strong enough to find someone hidden by magic, even someone hidden by a magic as strong as the Stone of Shackles. Whether you had stumbled upon Darzin by chance or fate, the result would have been the same; Xaltorath would track down what he was sent to hunt. I do not think Darzin would have had any desire or patience to keep your father alive so he might protest your removal. Darzin and Darzin alone shoulders this responsibility, not you."

"Darzin wasn't looking for *me* though," Kihrin said. "I surprised him. He hadn't expected Xaltorath to attack me."

Miya smiled, a quirking at the corners of her mouth. "How refreshing. He is not yet omniscient. So the demon was ordered to find the stone itself. I wonder for what purpose Darzin could desire its possession."

"I don't know. For nothing good." So Darzin had been lying about everything. He hadn't gone to the priests of Thaena to have Surdyeh Returned, he hadn't given the Stone of Shackles to Lyrilyn, and Darzin probably hadn't loved or even married Kihrin's so-called "mother" at all.

Miya leaned over and kissed him on top of his head. "Eat something, bathe, and come out of your room. The High Lord has assigned you tutors, and there are matters of etiquette you must learn."

Kihrin pulled his legs back under him. "I can't."

"Why not?"

"Because it—" He shuddered. "It would feel like letting that bastard win."

"Darzin?"

"Yeah." For a moment, he thought about telling Lady Miya about Dead Man too, but he decided it was best if he kept that secret a while longer. If he was right, and Dead Man was the High Lord, then he was her master anyway.

"Listen," Lady Miya told him. "Mourn for those you have lost. Hold them in your heart and never forget them. Trust none of us in this house of pain. But if you wish their deaths to have meaning, if you wish to one day have your revenge against Darzin, you must not sit here. You must take everything you have learned in the Lower Circle, in Velvet Town, and you must apply that skill to dealing with those around you and staying alive. Please. Believe me when I say neither your mother nor your father would wish you to throw your life away in grief."

"My father—" He looked away.

"The musician who raised you. What other father matters?" She smiled. "What would he want you to do?"

Kihrin scowled, but the scowl didn't stay on his face. A moment later he wiped his eyes and smiled back at the vané woman. "You're right, Lady Miya. I should do what Surdyeh would want."

"Shall I have the servants bring you dinner?" Lady Miya asked.

"Absolutely," he said, his expression determined.

He would do what Surdyeh had wanted from the beginning: he would run and hide, the first chance he had.

35: RED FLAGS

(Kihrin's story)

Six months passed. The teacher Khaemezra had promised—
What?
Are you kidding? All the Black Brotherhood secrets I know and that's what
you pester me about?
Fine. Yes, Kalindra and I became lovers. No, I won't go into detail. You're the
one who's absorbed a thousand minds, Talon. You should know how this works.

As I was saying, after six months, the teacher Khaemezra had promised
me still hadn't materialized. I learned general weapons with Szzarus, and
magic from Tyentso whenever she had free time. Her classes were short,
not because she didn't want to teach me but because I found myself incapable of learning. Despite my talent for invisibility or my ability to see past
the First Veil, I proved inept at any other form of magic.* Tyentso blamed
the Shadowdancers for leaving off my training after Mouse's death, and
cursed them enthusiastically at the end of every failed lesson.

The molten mound of volcanic rock off the coast of Ynisthana became
a cone-shaped island, growing a few feet every time the Old Man stopped
by—which was often.

I stayed away from the beach.

Unable to excel at the magic I needed to escape, I threw myself into
physical training. I worked myself to exhaustion during the day—and to
a different sort of exhaustion with Kalindra during the night. Slowly, we
unraveled the lingering effects of Xaltorath's assault while the months
chased after each other in rapid succession.

Teraeth was right about one thing though: eventually, Kalindra left me.

I remember the morning well. I was halfway up the side of Ynisthana's volcano, a perfect cone of black basalt rising through the mists
until it ended in a bowl-shaped caldera. We hadn't yet left the tree line
for the narrow trails up the side of the mount.

---

*It's not uncommon. The vast majority of guildsmen only know one spell, not because they
have no desire to learn more but because they have no ability.

There I was, sneaking up on Teraeth, feeling for the first time in months like I might get the drop on the man. He was good at stealth, but I was better. As I watched him prepare a trap for his fellow assassins using nothing but a few branches and jungle vines, I felt satisfied. I had a blackjack in one hand and I mentally chanted my spell of invisibility as I approached. He had no idea he was about to lose the contest.

The Black Brotherhood often trained through contests and challenges, tasks set by Khaemezra or other leaders. Even though I never wasted an opportunity to remind them I wasn't one of their initiates, they always invited me to take part. Our task that day was simplicity itself: reach the top of the volcano, steal the flag Kalindra had planted there, and bring it back to the temple.

No other rules applied. If I liked, I could've waited for a student to reach the top first, ambushed them, and stolen the flag. Or, were I to reach the flag first, I might replace it with a duplicate. The intrigues were legion. Nearly anything was permitted.

Thus, I snuck up on Teraeth, who I was sure would be my major competition. When I was so close to the man I smelled the scent of his skin, I swung up and around, letting the blackjack fall–

Where it swung straight through the empty air of an illusion.

"Hell."

But it was too late.

While I had been ambushing Teraeth, he had been ambushing me.

I turned my body to the side just as Teraeth's foot swung through the space where my head had been a moment before. I felt indignant. Then the Stone of Shackles turned cold.

Okay, so we weren't playing.

In theory, the Brotherhood wasn't supposed to use lethal force on me. I wore the Stone of Shackles, which would cause unpleasant, if unclear, complications should anyone kill me. Easier said than done: Teraeth had a bad habit of forgetting to pull his punches.

What can I say? I don't think it was anything personal, just that Brotherhood members are trained to kill. Once you get that instinct into your system, it's a hard thing to get back out again.

I tried to grab his leg as it passed to throw him off balance, but he was too fast. He kept spinning and I barely understood what was happening before his other foot hit me across the face.

I went down.

I wasn't out though. When he approached, I grabbed him by the shirt, pulled him to the side, and punched his jaw.

He tapped the side of my neck with the cold edge of his dagger.

"Slow yourself," he hissed, "and yield."

I looked down at the knife. It seemed sharp. I could take the poisoned edge as granted.

I said, "If you're going to slit my throat, get it over with."

Teraeth scoffed, but the way the stone's temperature turned back to normal told me I'd reminded him that he was about to do something rash. He backed away from me, returning the knife to his belt. "Fine. We'll do it your way." He picked up a length of vine. "Would you rather be tied up or unconscious—"

I was already running up the mountain trail.

Behind me, I heard Teraeth's laughter, then his footsteps, fast and close.

The volcano itself was stark. I'd never learned its name, assuming it wasn't called Ynisthana. There was a kind of beauty to that bleak rock, home to nothing but patches of moss and lichen, silhouetted against the teal sky. The scent of sulfur hung thick from wisps of smoke escaping the caldera. The rock underneath my feet shimmered with the suppressed heat of the fires below. The temperature grew warmer as I climbed until I was gasping for breath from more than exertion.

I wished Tyentso had been able to teach me how to protect myself from fire.

When I reached the summit, the red flag sat there in the open, pinned under a rock.

Teraeth was right behind me. As soon as I reached the lip of the caldera, I jumped up onto the largest boulder in the area and slipped my invisibility back over me.

"Damn it!" Teraeth's hand slashed through the space where I had been a moment before. Then he stopped, casting his head to the side as he examined the ground.

He was looking for any dislodged scree that would betray my position.

I grinned. There was something so feral about Teraeth when he hunted. He reminded me of one of the island drakes, completely focused on his prey.

Then I saw the ship.

The volcano rose thousands of feet into the air, which meant that when standing on the summit it was possible to see a great distance on a clear day. That day was beautiful and balmy, making it easy to see the many islands that formed the chain of which Ynisthana was just one link.

"Teraeth, there's a ship out there."

He spun toward the sound of my voice. "You're not going to distract me that—"

I turned visible and hopped down off the rock, pointing. "Look!"

Teraeth followed the line of my arm, although his gaze was still wary. He probably thought it was a trick.

There really was a ship though, a ship with black sails making its way around the island toward the main harbor, coming from the opposite direction to the Maw.

"So?" Teraeth bent over and picked up the red flag. "It's a supply ship. Nothing interesting there. Leave it. We still have a challenge to finish."

I gave him a look that suggested he might very well have lost his mind. There were plenty of people on the island who had been waiting for that supply ship for months now. Had she not joined the Brotherhood, Tyentso could have left on that ship, headed back to Zherias to find more work. Most of the survivors of *The Misery* would probably leave on that ship.

If not for the Old Man, I would have left on that ship.

I ran back down the mountain, although to be fair, it was more like calculated sliding.

Others had noticed the ship already, or had been warned to expect its arrival. As I started down the path toward the harbor, I recognized one figure ahead of me in the distance as Kalindra.

She too was heading toward the harbor. Unlike me though, she had a bag slung over her shoulder. She wasn't dressed in the black robes of the Brotherhood, but in simple traveler's garb, including the patterned veil of a Zheriaso native, worn like a shawl. It hadn't occurred to me that she was of mixed blood that included some Zherias stock. Kalindra was lighter skinned than Ola, but not by much. The knots in her hair should have been a clue.

But she was leaving.

"Kalindra!" I shouted.

She glanced back at me, put a hand to her forehead in the manner of someone trying to keep the glare out of their eyes, and turned away again. She kept walking toward the bay.

"Let her go," Teraeth said. "You knew this day would come."

I startled. Teraeth had followed me after all.

"What's going on?" I asked. "She's leaving?"

"A lot of people are leaving," Teraeth said. "Others are arriving. It's the way of things."

"Okay, but why wouldn't she say goodbye? When's she coming back?"

"She's not."

I stood there and stared at him, my mouth dry, my hands working at my sides making silent fists—releasing them, starting over. I couldn't process what he was saying. I didn't like being on this island. I didn't like being imprisoned here, and frankly, I hadn't quite given up on the idea that Khaemezra controlled the Old Man; that the dragon was her way of making sure I stayed and did what I was told. I know a thing or two about cons, after all.

Kalindra made all that tolerable. Kalindra was the reason I could stay sane. With Kalindra I didn't have to be controlled by what Xaltorath had done to me. With Kalindra I could feel normal.

She couldn't leave. She just couldn't.

"What?" I finally said.

He didn't look at me. "She won't be back. Her new assignment is long-term."

I knew what the Black Brotherhood did for a living. "Who's she being sent to kill?"

"It's not that kind of assignment. Anyway, it's none of your concern."

I took a step toward him. "Excuse me? Not my concern?"

Teraeth's upper lip pulled into a sneer. "What part of that was too simple for you, Your Highness? This is Brotherhood business. You had your chance to join, and you refused. It's a courtesy I'm even telling you this much."

"I don't recall your mother saying I had to join. Anyway, aren't you forgetting that Kalindra was one of my teachers?"

Teraeth's stare turned hateful. "It seems she was taking too many liberties with the curriculum."

My stomach tightened. "What?"

Teraeth paused. "It's . . . never mind. I spoke rashly."

"No. Explain yourself. Too many liberties? What did you mean by that?"

He looked abashed. "Never mind my words. I'm not happy that she's leaving. Your new teacher is arriving by the same ship. He'll take over your training, just as Mother promised." He turned away to leave.

I ran ahead of him until I blocked his path. "No. You're not walking away from me, Teraeth. She was taking too many liberties? Are you saying she was sent away because we're lovers? Everyone on this island is bedding everyone else, usually in groups. I pick one woman and stay faithful to her and she's punished for it?" I pointed a finger at him. "Is this your doing?"

That stopped him. "My doing?"

"I'm just curious if you're sending her away because you're jealous of me or because you're jealous of her?"

His nostrils flared out as he stared at me, disbelief and fury naked in his eyes. "You arrogant little bastard."

"Tell me I'm wrong."

Teraeth scowled as he stepped toward me. "You already know you're wrong. Kalindra is my friend and I care about her, but I'm not in love with her, nor she with me. Neither of us expected monogamy from the other. And as for you—" His eyes narrowed. "Don't insult me by suggesting that the only way I would be welcome in your bed is by removing all rivals. You may be too shamed by your precious Quuros masculinity to admit you want me, but that's your problem, not mine."

Teraeth finished by lashing his hand through the empty air in front of him. "Anyway, Kalindra's assignment has nothing to do with *me*. Mother thought Kalindra was in danger of falling in love with you, so it would be best she left—before the relationship progressed beyond all recovery."

"Kalindra . . ." I ran down the hillside, toward the harbor.

Footsteps behind me, then something heavy crashed into my back. I rolled to find that Teraeth had tackled me. He followed that up by punching me in the face, which was like being hit with a maul. I twisted aside to grab one of his arms, hoping to throw him off-balance enough so I could gain my own. He pulled his arm out of reach, twisted around, and grabbed my wrist in such a way that if he wrenched hard, my arm would break or dislocate. His legs pinned mine and all he had to do was bring a knee up to leave me too incapacitated to do more than vomit.

"She's not for you," Teraeth told me, his face inches from my own. "You like her, she's safe, but you don't love her. You will never love her. Letting her become emotionally attached to you is nothing more than cruelty."

"You don't know that." I tried to break free, but Teraeth knew tricks that my teachers had only just suggested might exist.

"I know she's not a blood-haired Jorat girl with eyes like fire."

I stopped struggling. "What did you say?"

"A Jorat girl," Teraeth repeated in a thick voice. "With hair the color of midnight or sunset, worn in the old center-cut style of Jorat's god-touched. Perfect chestnut-red skin and coal-black socks on her hands and feet. Her eyes are like rubies reflecting flame, glittering with all the colors of a bonfire. Lips like berries, ripe and so sweet—"

I couldn't hide my shock or horror. How did he know? How could he know about her? The only two individuals who had known about her were the demon who had placed the image in my mind and Morea. It was conceivable that the mimic who had murdered and eaten Morea also knew, but that meant . . .

"Get off me!" I pushed again, and this time he didn't resist.

He rolled off and tumbled onto the grass, landing with a leg crossed over the other and his head supported on one arm.

I stood, drawing shaky, gasping breaths. "I didn't tell Kalindra about her. I didn't tell anyone on this island about her. You tell me how you know about her, and you tell me right now."

Teraeth ignored me and continued the description. "She smells like apples and dark, smoky musk and when she smiles at you it's like looking at a small piece of the sun . . ."

I growled, "Tell me, damn it . . ."

"And you'd think she'd have a fiery humor, but instead all that flame has tempered her . . ."

I grabbed Teraeth by the shirt, pulled him into a half-sitting position, and pushed him back against the nearest tree. "You've seen her. You know who she is. Tell me. Tell me right now!"

Teraeth smiled. "But I thought you wanted to spend the rest of your life with Kalindra?"

I stared at him.

Simultaneously, I became aware of him. Aware of his sweat, aware of how I was pressed up against him, aware of how very little space existed between our bodies. I'd meant to threaten him, meant to intimidate him, but his hands rested lightly on my hips.

The look in those green eyes was not fear.

I let go of his shirt and stepped away. Embarrassment brought all the blood to my face. I felt torn to pieces by my emotions, shame and lust and my anger at Teraeth for being, once again, right. As soon as he'd described the Jorat girl, I'd stopped even thinking about Kalindra, and damn it, I knew Kalindra. She was real; she made me happy. I didn't want her to leave. I definitely didn't want Kalindra to leave—but I didn't want to let go of Xaltorath's fantasy girl either.

Teraeth straightened his tunic. "I didn't think so."

"How did you know? How did you find out about the Jorat girl, Teraeth?"

The briefest sympathy flashed over his features. I don't know, maybe I imagined it. "The ship's leaving soon. Head down to the harbor to meet your new teacher."

I wasn't about to be distracted so easily. "I swear by all the gods I will never trust you again if you don't answer me."

The snake statues lining the temple entryway showed more emotion than he did in that moment. Almost imperceptibly, he shook himself. "That's also your choice, but I wouldn't be so free with that sort of vow if I were you."

"To hell with you! There are only two creatures in the whole world who knew about that girl: one's a demon and the other's a mimic. How am I supposed to trust you?"

Teraeth looked angrier than I can ever remember seeing him. Not just angry, but hurt. He tilted his head, stared at me like he was contemplating exactly which of several hundred different options would be best used for my immediate execution.

Teraeth said, "I'm an assassin. Only a fool would trust me."

He stood up and walked back to the training ground, red flag in his hand.

36: Testing the Lock

(Talon's story)

All Kihrin's hopes of escape drowned the first time he tried.

He planned his escape for a full day after the revelation of his new status. If he stayed with the D'Mons, he would be a danger to everyone around him. If he fled, Darzin would have no reason to hurt anyone else. The best way out of the situation was to vanish.

Kihrin's plan was simple: walk out the front door. The servants of the D'Mon family suffered from the ancient habit of obeying anyone giving orders. Combined with his own ability to pass unnoticed, he was confident he could stroll right out of the palace grounds.

That morning he asked the servants to dress him in the nicest clothing in his wardrobe, pocketed a few valuable items, and walked down to the stables of the Private Court.

He cleared his throat at a groom to catch his attention. Kihrin nodded to the man, his expression light. "I'll need a coach." He explained nothing more.

"Right away, my lord." The groom nodded at a runner, who took off toward the stables.

Kihrin breathed a sigh of relief. The man hadn't known his name. No instructions to keep "the yellow-haired boy" inside. From here, all Kihrin had to do was go down to the waterfront, ditch the coach, and contact the Shadowdancers. Once he was safe, he would find Ola and they would both vanish.

Darzin would never have a chance to summon another demon.

Kihrin waited while the stable hands readied the horse and carriage for him. During those agonizing seconds, the huge iron gates of the Private Court opened, and another coach entered the courtyard.

Taja! Just act like I belong. I'm not doing anything I shouldn't be doing. He hid his shaking hands behind his back. *And please let that be anyone but Darzin.*

The coach stopped in front of the steps. The doorman rushed forward to relieve the carriage of its passenger—a woman of middle age. She wore an elaborate teal bodice and an agolé satin wrap covered with diamonds.

The diamonds did a fine job of making her the sparkling center of attention wherever she traveled. They didn't do such a good job of concealing the fact she no longer possessed a maiden's figure. The color of her gown drew attention to her bright vermilion hair. The hair drew attention to her face, covered with enough makeup to plaster the walls of the Upper Circle. Her countenance creased with distaste for everything her eyes fell upon.

Finally, those eyes fell upon Kihrin.

"What is he doing here?" She lashed out at the groom, ignoring the young man.

"His lordship was waiting for a coach to be made ready, my lady. Welcome back home, Your Ladyship." The man bowed.

"His Lordship?" An ivory fan whipped against the doorman's face and just as quickly vanished back into the cavernous recesses of the woman's purse. "Idiot!"

She stared at Kihrin with unconcealed hostility. "Waiting for a coach? Where were you going, boy?"

Kihrin bowed, swallowing his anxiety. "My lady, I was going to retrieve a present given to me. Lord Darzin thought it might be a good idea."

"Lord Darzin thought so? Fetch a present?" The lady snorted in disgust. "Did someone give you a new ribbon for that pretty yellow hair?" She grabbed his hair and yanked him down until they were eye to eye.

"Ouch! Damn it. Stop that." He tried to extricate himself, but found he couldn't without resorting to outright violence.

"I'll put you in ribbons, you stupid fool! Come on." Still pulling on his hair, she walked inside, saying to the groom, "Fetch my packages out of the carriage and deliver them in my room. Not a scratch on them, or you'll pay for them with your teeth."

A few yards inside the door, Kihrin dug in his heels, grabbed his hair, and pulled. "Gods damn it. Let go of me, you hag."

She dropped his hair and glared at him. "I shouldn't, but you're lucky enough to be doing something stupid when I'm in a good mood." She tugged off her gloves and dropped them on the floor in the middle of the hallway. "Come with me quietly and there'll be no need to have the guards drag you with me in chains."

Kihrin glowered. "I was just going to go fetch—"

"You were running away," she corrected. "I have lived in this house for fifteen years. Believe me, I know the signs." Just then remembering something, she held out the back of her hand to him. "How rude of me not to introduce myself. I am Alshena D'Mon. That is, I am your stepmother."

"My condolences," he whispered under his breath as he kissed her hand. To his complete surprise, she giggled.

Her face turned serious again. She removed the ivory fan from her purse and spread it wide, waving it to cool herself. She presented her right arm to Kihrin and said, "Come now, child. Walk with me. We will talk about why what you did was so stupid and how it might easily have resulted in your death. Then we'll discuss how you can avoid being stupid in the future. If such a thing is even possible."

She smiled. "You should try to pay attention, young man. It might well save your life."

37: The New Tutor

(Kihrin's story)

I sat on a grouping of volcanic rocks and watched the schooner anchored in the small narrow bay. We were on the opposite side of the island from where the Old Man was building his new mountain bed, which was probably a vast comfort for everyone present.

A small gathering of Brotherhood members assembled on the black beaches to welcome the ship and ready those who would sail away on her. Kalindra stood in that crowd. I'm sure she knew I was watching, but she never turned her head.

The crew of the ship lowered a small boat over the side, whose passengers rowed it to the beach. A tall human man climbed out of the boat, holding several packages and a displeased scowl I saw from a hundred feet away. More boats followed the first one. Kalindra and her associates assigned to foreign destinations rowed out to the ship. Within half an hour, the beach was empty except for the few Brotherhood still unloading supplies and the single new arrival.

The man dressed simply, though his boots looked expensive—the thigh-high Quuros style popular among duelists and horsemen. He was bald and taller than most Quuros, the height of a vané. He looked familiar.

The newcomer stood there and scanned the beach, the island, his expression a study in reluctance and distaste. His gaze rolled over me and stopped dead.

I didn't feel like moving, so I sat there and waited as the new arrival marched up the beach toward me. I returned the man's stare with cool hostility. My mouth was full of the bitter taste of Kalindra's departure and the skin on my cheek throbbed from Teraeth's punch.

Seriously, that man has a right hook like a morgage gladiator.

"So, you're the one who's caused all this fuss," the newcomer said as he crested the rocks.

I scowled as I remembered where I'd seen him before. "I know you. You're that bartender from the Culling Fields with the cute daughter."

He raised an eyebrow. "I don't know you. Aren't you that velvet boy from the Shattered Veil Club?"

I flushed with anger. Not just because of the slam, but because this man was supposed to be my teacher; I felt a double dose of betrayal. He was no swordmaster. How could he be? He looked like he spent more time cleaning the bar, chatting up customers, and sampling his own wares than he ever spent practicing fencing forms.

Darzin would pick this man apart.

"No. I'm not."

"Then maybe I'm not here to teach you the proper way to serve ginger wine." He offered me a hand up. "Call me Doc."

I ignored the hand and stood on my own, brushing myself off. "Let me guess. People come to your bar and you cure what 'ales' them."

"Oh, that's a good one. I should have someone make a sign for the bar."

"You picked a hell of a place to take a vacation. The view's nice, but the women here will kill you."

Doc laughed, not pleasantly. "So nothing's changed." As he looked up the side of the mountain, Doc's expression turned grim. "Where is she?"

He couldn't be referring to Tyentso. "Khaemezra?"

"Yes."

"Don't know. Really don't care right now either, except . . ." I ground my teeth and started walking. "I guess I need to give her a piece of my mind about a few things. Anyway, follow me. I'll take you to Teraeth. He usually knows."

I was a few steps up the path before I realized Doc wasn't following. I glanced back to see the man still standing there, looking toward me with an expression of paralyzed shock.

"What did I say?"

"Who's Teraeth?" Doc asked.

I blinked. "You're one of the Black Brotherhood, right?"

Doc raised his chin. "I never said that."

"You know enough about them to know who Khaemezra is. How could you have avoided meeting her son?"

Doc flinched as if slapped. He closed his eyes for a second while he clenched his fists. Then he remembered to exhale, released his hands, opened his eyes. "You must be mistaken. Everyone calls her Mother."

"Except in this case she's his mother. Why are you acting like she killed your favorite cat?"

"I'm just surprised." He swallowed several times. "How old is he?"

"Khaemezra said he was around my age, so somewhere between fifteen and twenty. He acts like he thinks he's old as Ompher and twice as wise."

"Take me to him."

I blinked at him. He looked like a nobody, you understand. Nothing special about him except his height. He even had a bit of a potbelly. He didn't look like a great leader, a hero. He looked, completely and fully, like a bartender.

But High Lord Therin couldn't have ordered executions with more command. Whoever Doc was, he was a man who expected to be obeyed. His voice snapped orders with more skill than a razor-lined whip.

To be honest, he reminded me of Teraeth. He didn't look like Teraeth, but then again, neither had Teraeth for the entire sea voyage from Kishna-Farriga.

Manol vané are *very* good with illusions.

I was tempted to look beyond the First Veil, but I didn't have the time.

He fell in step behind me as we climbed back toward the cliffs. Normally you'd expect the person walking in back to seem subservient, but he acted like I was an honor escort. His movements were easy and graceful, a dancer who had spent so long practicing his steps they had become a permanent accent on every motion. I supposed the middle-aged man was a better spy than most: he looked ordinary.

Relos Var looked ordinary too.

When I crested the ledge of Teraeth's rooms, I saw him sitting crosslegged on the floor, reading a small, well-worn book. I wasn't too surprised to see Teraeth had broken out a bottle of vané wine and helped himself to several glasses. He didn't look happy to see me. The feeling was mutual.

Teraeth raised an eyebrow at Doc. "You must be the Quuros we're expecting."

Doc didn't respond, but he spent a long moment studying Teraeth. From the frown on his face, he didn't like what he saw.

"Hey Teraeth, where's Khaemezra? I need to speak with her."

"As do I," Doc said. "Go fetch your mother." He made the order dismissive and condescending.

Teraeth set down his glass. "I don't take orders from you."

Without asking permission, Doc sat down in one of the reed chairs. "She's probably in the temple, and as I recall, the temple is insufferably hot and damp even by Manol vané standards. So your mother may join us here."

I glanced sideways at the man. "You've been to the temple? I thought you weren't a member of the Black Brotherhood."

"By that I take it you've been to the temple. Are *you* a member of the Black Brotherhood?"

"I am not your servant," Teraeth said, his voice as close to growling as I'd yet heard from the man, "and the High Priestess is not someone who obeys anyone's beck and call. She does not–"

"Let her decide that," Doc interrupted. "In the meantime, I am not asking your opinion. I am giving you an order."

"You don't order me around!"

"I just did."

"She's killed people for such insolence," Teraeth snapped.

"Yet here I am," Doc said with a cold smile.

"Do you have any idea–?"

"Who you are? You're Teraeth. Your father was an idiot and a fool, and the fact you took his name instead of your mother's means you're an idiot and a fool as well." Doc paused. "Or did you mean who you *really* are? Because I know that too. Still an idiot. Still a fool."

Teraeth's expression didn't change. Not so much as a muscle tic or flaring of nostrils. Yet I knew I was looking at a man who had just put Doc down on a short list of names Teraeth made a point of crossing off one by one.

Teraeth spun on his heel and dove out the cave entrance.

Doc sighed, leaned back in his chair, and inhaled. I think he'd been expecting Teraeth to attack him. I'm not sure if he was relieved or disappointed that Teraeth hadn't.

"Cute kid," Doc said.

"Just curious: has anyone ever told you that you're an asshole?"

His eyes widened in mock surprise, and then he laughed. "Every time I cut someone off. I need a drink." He reached for Teraeth's bottle.

"I wouldn't touch that if I were you."

Doc grinned. "Your warning is noted." He uncorked the bottle and pulled a drought that would have made an elephant pass out. He stood still, eyes closed, body tense, not even breathing. Then he inhaled deeply and faced me. "You have that look on your face. Go ahead and ask."

I shrugged. "On the way over you said you had no idea who Teraeth is. That exchange I just saw makes me think you were being less than entirely honest."

"I've never met him before. That doesn't mean I don't know his type. He's young," Doc said while setting aside the bottle and leaning back in the chair. The collar of his shirt flipped open, revealing that he was wearing a tsali stone around his neck–a green stone wrapped in gold. "And since he's a vané that makes him arrogant, egotistical, and insufferable. Given a few hundred years, he'll mellow into something resembling a real person, but since we don't have that long, I guess he just rubs me the wrong way."

"Oh, come on. The look on your face when I said his name—"

"The vané have peculiar rules for the naming of their children," Doc said. "That's all."

"What do you mean?" I leaned forward. Relos Var had also reacted strongly to Teraeth's name, had mentioned something about Teraeth's father, but I had never gotten a good explanation. Doc's view of Teraeth's father seemed even less flattering.

"Nosy, aren't you?" Doc retorted.

"It's my defining characteristic. Speaking of which, what are you doing here? You can't tell me you came all the way here from the Capital just to speak with Khaemezra."

Doc looked surprised. "She didn't tell you? I'm here because—" He stopped and chuckled. "It's a long story, kid."

"I've got time."

"Nobody's got that much time. Let's just say that back in the day, me and a nephew of mine used to run around the Capital with this low-ranked priest of Thaena and a fresh-off-the-farm kid from Marakor, who only barely just qualified as being a wizard." He smiled, looking off into the distance. "Those were some days."

"Is that—is that supposed to mean something to me?"

Doc shrugged. "Only as much as that low-ranked priest of Thaena ended up becoming High Lord Therin of House D'Mon, the fresh-faced farm kid became Emperor Sandus, and my nephew Qoran clawed his way into the High General's chair. Me? I opened a bar."

"So you're the underachiever."

"I didn't have anything to prove."

"Doc, it's so good to see you again," Khaemezra said from the cave entrance.

I hadn't heard the rattle of anyone climbing up the ladder. Khaemezra and her son were simply there.

"What did you do, fly?" I whispered to Teraeth. The vané only glared at me in response, as if to remind me we were still in the middle of an argument.

Believe me, I hadn't forgotten.

"How have you been?" Khaemezra crossed the distance between them, bending over to kiss Doc on the cheek.

She seemed genuinely pleased to see the man, smiling warmly.

"I've been keeping out of trouble, Khae," Doc told her as he stood.

"Really? After all these years, you've finally figured out how to do that?" Khaemezra's eyes sparkled with merriment.

"Yes," Doc agreed. "The trick of it is to stay far, far away from you."

Khaemezra's smile froze into ice and cracked. With a single sentence

Doc opened wounds, and they sat visible and fresh on her face. When she recovered herself, she gestured toward Teraeth with a forcefully light flick of her wrist. "This is my son, Teraeth."

"So I've heard."

"I see you've already met your new pupil Kihrin," she continued.

"Mother Khaemezra," I said, "we need to talk about this. You're breaking our deal. You promised me a swordmaster, not a barkeep." I glanced over at Doc. "No offense."

They both ignored me. They reminded me of two cats locked into a staring contest. Doc broke eye contact first, as he glanced at Teraeth. "Is he everything you wanted?"

"At least he follows orders," Khaemezra snapped.

"Enjoy it while it lasts."

Teraeth cleared his throat. Surprisingly, he didn't seem pleased to see his prediction about Khaemezra's anger coming to pass. He put his hand on my arm. "Kihrin, we're needed downstairs."

I jerked my arm away from him. "I need to talk to Khaemezra."

"No," Khaemezra said. "Follow my son outside."

"Yes," Doc agreed. "Khae and I have a lot to discuss. Kihrin, I'll see you at the training yard at dawn. Consider yourself excused from your other weapons classes from now on."

I lingered a moment, but neither Khaemezra nor Doc had anything further to say to me. I scowled and began the climb down.

38: THE HIGH LORD

(Talon's story)

"I can't blame Miya for not telling you," Alshena D'Mon said as they walked through the palace. "She's sweet in her own way, but sheltered as a veal calf. I'm not sure it would even occur to her there might be any danger outside the estate."

"I am aware of the dangers of the City," Kihrin snapped.

"Of course you are. Darzin tells me he found you in a whorehouse." She sniffed at such an indelicate idea.

He sighed. Kihrin was tired of explaining that he hadn't actually whored himself at the Shattered Veil Club.

"I'll make this simple. We are House D'Mon, one of the twelve families who once ruled the Empire. But such ruling is no longer allowed, and it is forbidden for any direct member of a Royal Family to make laws. Now, instead of ruling the Empire's politics, we rule its economy, which is better. We have all the money and none of the irritating responsibility. Each House controls a section of industry, a chosen monopoly we license and regulate. As you may have already discerned, House D'Mon controls medicine and healing. Every midwife, herbalist, and physicker in the land pays us dues.* And that's good—sooner or later, everyone needs a doctor, so our House provides essential services. Unfortunately, *every* House provides essential services, so there's quite a cat's game going on at all times to see who is ranked ahead of whom. Each of our twelve Houses is ranked in order, and that ranking is very important. So important that people have been killed and will kill for it."

"For ranking."

She rolled her eyes. "We are fourth ranked of the twelve Royal Families. The means there are three Houses above us we would love to destroy, and eight Houses below who feel the same way about us. It would not be inaccurate to say the Royal Houses live in a constant state of undeclared war."

---

*Not technically true. There is quite a trade in illegal practice, primarily in Yor, Marakor, and Jorat.

Kihrin blinked. "For ranking?"

Alshena sighed. "Yes, for ranking. Ranking is everything, you silly child. The Houses don't rule, but we elect the people who do, and how many votes we are allowed to cast is based on our rank. Thus, ranking determines who will become a Voice, and it's from the pool of Voices that Council members are chosen. The number of Voices we appoint determines what sort of deals other Houses are willing to make with us for our support. Ranking is the difference between living in a palace like this, or dying at the end of an assassin's dart."

She pinched an imaginary piece of lint off her agolé while they walked. "Now, given that fact, why were you being extremely stupid just now?"

Kihrin grimaced. "It would have embarrassed the House?"

Alshena pursed her lips. "Oh, that is good answer. Just what Darzin or Therin would have wanted to hear you say." Her ivory fan lashed out and rapped him on the knuckles.

"Ow!" He winced and shook his hand.

"No, you fool, that answer is rubbish. You were being stupid, because all the Houses employ spies. We spy on each other constantly. The spies spy on the spies. It's an enormous cottage industry." She smirked at her witticism.

"Some of those spies also do work as assassins. Off the record, of course. No House wants a priest of Thaena informing the Council that the latest dead son of House D'Talus was killed on orders from a member of such-and-such House. It's very important that you remember the dead can talk in this town. While they never lie, they also can't reveal information they never knew in the first place. In any event, if a person were to lower their guard and present a lovely 'opportunity,' then of course the advantage would be taken. Some members of a House are so peripheral to the health of the House that they are unimportant and might be ignored. The firstborn son of the Lord Heir would not be considered one of those."

She leaned over and pinched his cheek hard. "You were being stupid because you were walking in the House colors shouting 'please kill me' to anyone listening."

They turned down the corridor of the South Tower, heading in the direction of Kihrin's rooms. For a length of hallway, neither spoke.

"I see," Kihrin finally said.

He turned to face the noblewoman. "May I ask a question, Lady Alshena?"

"You may try. I have no control over your success." She smirked again.

"Well," he said, "the mother of the previous heir would have a great deal to gain by *not* saying anything, and letting me throw myself in front of the knives. Why didn't you?"

She stopped in front of the set of doors before his, paused for a moment, and then laughed. "If I thought I'd live to see the day Galen inherited a single coin of the House D'Mon fortune, I'd call the coach for you myself. This is just staying on the High Lord's good side." She looked at the tall wooden door behind her. "Well, here we are."

Kihrin frowned. "This isn't the door to my room."

Alshena stared up the length of her nose at him. "A fact of which I am well aware, I assure you." She knocked.

A moment later a muted "come in" came from inside the chamber, and Alshena opened the door.

Inside was a small room by palace standards. None of the trademark D'Mon decoration or ornamentation graced the interior. A mahogany desk covered with books and papers sat offset from the center of the room. A map of the Empire tiled the floor. A small bookcase in the corner contained a collection of well-used tomes while a door set in the same wall led to further rooms. The wall opposite from the desk held a medium-sized portrait of a dark-haired woman wearing deep blue.

A man sat in the chair behind the desk. He didn't look up when the door opened. Kihrin's first impression was that Alshena had delivered him into the hands of the family wizard. He had that sort of look to him—chestnut-brown hair, golden when the light hit it, clipped short and practical. The sleeves of his linen shirt had been used to blot his pages too often. He was slender with a handsome face—saved from being too pretty by a neatly groomed mustache and beard. Kihrin would have placed him in his midthirties because of a slight silvering at his temples. He would have guessed that the man was Darzin's older brother, except Darzin wouldn't be Lord Heir if he had one.

Alshena curtsied. "I found him trying to leave the estate, Lord Therin. I thought you might wish to speak with him."

The High Lord? Kihrin looked around the room to see if he'd missed an old man hiding behind the drapes. Kihrin was supposed to believe this was the High Lord? Did he use magic to make himself look so young?

Kihrin glared at his stepmother, but she didn't seem inclined to explain.

The man behind the desk looked up and examined them both. Kihrin felt a shock as the man's gaze passed over him: High Lord Therin's eyes were sharp, calculating, and a distinctive, bright blue. Despite his slender build and his youthful appearance, his presence made him seem larger. Kihrin found himself reminded of General Milligreest.

Most importantly, he looked nothing like Dead Man. Kihrin frowned. When Darzin had said his father was meeting with Butterbelly, Kihrin assumed that meant Darzin's father was the other person who had been present for the demon summoning. If Dead Man wasn't Pretty Boy's father, who was he?

Therin D'Mon put down his pen.

"Thank you, Alshena. That will be all."

Alshena curtsied again, then left, shutting the door behind her.

Therin looked at Kihrin for several heartbeats, his face holding the faintest suggestion of a sneer.

"One guard dead and an escape attempt in a week. I must say I'm surprised it took you so long to try to run away."

Kihrin clenched and unclenched his fists. "I was in mourning."

"Yes, of course. Please sit down, Kihrin."

Kihrin sat down, thinking, *At least he used my name instead of "boy."*

Silence loomed. Therin picked up his pen and continued writing. When he finished, Therin blotted the paper, put away the pen and ink, and tucked the sheet in a drawer. Finally, he stood up and looked out the window.

"It would be a mistake," Therin said as he gazed out over the Blue Palace, "to think of House D'Mon as a family. We are not. Never mind that the men and women at the top are related through blood or marriage. This is a company, a corporation of skills and talents, with the singular function of providing a service for as cheaply as possible, while being paid as much as possible. It is a business. Every Royal House is, and anything else is just so many god-king tales for the common folk. I do not care who your parents really were, and I do not care whether or not Darzin's story is true. You are god-touched and you have talent and you are therefore a useful commodity, an investment. As long as I believe you are a sound investment, your stay here may even be enjoyable. Do I make myself clear?"

"Yes, my lord—but Darzin's lying. I'm not god-touched."

Therin almost smiled. "You misunderstand, son. You *are* god-touched. That is not under dispute. No matter if Darzin is your father or isn't, at some point within four generations, one of your ancestors was a member of this House. There is a mark it leaves on our members, a mark that can be detected. I double-checked the accuracy myself. It is the singular part of Darzin's claim that I have no doubt is absolute truth: our blood runs through your veins."

"So I could still be Ogenra?"

The High Lord scoffed. "Do you know what an Ogenra even is?"

"I thought I did, but Miya said—"

"Lady Miya."

Kihrin faltered. "Excuse me?"

"You will always call her Lady Miya."

Kihrin flushed with embarrassment. He fought the urge to stand straighter, tug down his clothing, act like he was being reprimanded by Surdyeh. "Yes, sir," he said instead. "Lady Miya said that illegitimacy had nothing to do with it."

Therin nodded. "Indeed. All my grandfather's children were illegitimate—he was fond of raping his slaves. An Ogenra is nothing more than a blood relative of a House who has not been formally presented to the gods. They can never inherit, never wear the name, never even wear the colors or live on our land until that pact is formalized—but since they are not members of the House, they can be elected as Voices; they can serve on the Council. They can do something we cannot: rule."

"Alshena mentioned something about that, but I don't understand. I thought you do rule."

"We have power. It's not quite the same thing."

"So technically I'm Ogenra until you present me?"

"You were presented while you were unconscious," Therin corrected. "It is formal and irrevocable and done. Darzin has made public claims that will be difficult to avoid fulfilling, particularly since he's seen fit to provide the documentation that proves you aren't even a House bastard. Necessary, that—his wife, Alshena, belongs to House D'Aramarin, and they would have used any excuse to protest a bastard being taken as heir over their daughter's legitimate son."

There was nothing much that Kihrin could say to that. He studied the wood of the desk and wondered if he could get away with slipping his sight past the Veil. He could take it for granted that Therin would be a wizard too. The most expensive physickers healed using magic.

"You don't think he's your father, do you?" Therin asked.

Kihrin was quiet for a few moments. Finally, he said, "No."

"Why?" Therin asked, with a surprising amount of sympathy in his voice. "Is this just instinct talking? You can't bear the idea that he might be your sire? A lot of people find that they cannot tolerate their parents, young man. It's not that uncommon. I hated my father with every breath in me, and I know Darzin holds no love for me, a feeling which is quite mutual."

Kihrin shook his head. "No, there's just no gain in it."

"No gain in it?"

"No, Lord. What does he gain by claiming me as his son? He didn't have to recognize me when we met at the High General's house. He could have ignored me. Instead he sent assassins to kill me, and for some reason—for some reason he changed his mind and decided to save me. I should be dead. He wanted me dead. Instead, I'm his long-lost son." Kihrin shook his head. "From all I've been told, including by you, people up here don't do anything unless there's something to gain. Even if I really am his son, what does he gain by admitting it? He already has an heir. He pisses off House D'Aramarin by pushing Galen aside. He's clearly not sentimental. That means he has another motive."

Kihrin debated mentioning the Stone of Shackles, but dismissed the thought. He had no idea how much he could trust this man, and while he might be new to royalty, he was not new to the idea that it was unwise to show his hand too soon.

Therin returned to his chair. "I too don't know what Darzin wants, which isn't a situation I enjoy. He could have claimed you as Ogenra and no one would have questioned it. Instead, he puts you under him as next in line for the House Seat. The cynic might argue the only thing keeping certain individuals from having Darzin killed is the thought of who would inherit after he was dead."

Therin leaned forward. "But sometimes we must make the best of the cards we are dealt."

"I'm sorry?" Kihrin was startled by Therin's analogy, so close to his own thoughts.

Therin said, "Even if you could prove Darzin faked the evidence, I have already accepted you into the House—so it does little good to try to find proof of Darzin's lies except to embarrass us. And you can't go back to the Lower Circle. You know how the Shadowdancers deal with those who murder their own."

Kihrin nearly stood from his chair. "What!? But I didn't kill anyone—"

"A Collectors Guild pawnshop owner with the adorable and no doubt accurate nickname of 'Butterbelly' was found dead, with two knives stuck in him. Your knives. A cutthroat named Faris is swearing to anyone who will listen he witnessed a fight between the two of you over a necklace you stole. The Shadowdancers will likely stab first and never bother to ask questions at all if they find you. Fortunately it's unlikely the Shadowdancers will ever come looking for Rook in the Upper Circle."

"*What* did you say?" Kihrin stood, only the most extreme self-control keeping him from fleeing the room.

Therin smiled. "Your 'on-the-job' name, your street name. Publicly you were a singer, the assistant of a blind musician named Surdyeh, now deceased. Your parentage was unknown but everyone assumed, quite laughably, that you were from south of the Manol, from Doltar. I suppose that proves vané are so rare people have forgotten what they look like. You were recruited into the Shadowdancers by Ola Nathera, called Raven, who originally used you as bait in a number of successful con schemes. Eventually someone realized that you'd figured out how to perceive magic and had learned your first spell—"

"I don't know any spells," Kihrin protested. "I can see past the Veil, but that's it—"

Therin waved the argument away with his fingers. "The trick you do to pass unseen. It's not just wishful thinking that the guards never notice you. We call self-taught students of magic 'witches,' but it's a dirty little secret that almost all of us figure out at least one spell before we've had formal training. Everyone who learns magic has a witch gift–the first spell, the first map–that unlocks all the others.* For most wild talents, it never goes beyond that first spell, but had Mouse lived longer she would have handled more advanced training. You were too good to leave wild. The spells that Keys learn are all focused, of course–ways to open different kinds of locks, how to recognize the tenyé signatures of materials commonly used for gates and lockboxes, how to remove wards put up by the Watchmen. That sort of thing."

Kihrin blinked and looked away. The world tilted crazily. The room suffocated. His mouth was a dusty, white, Capital street in the middle of summertime. Seconds ago, escape had been possible.

Now it was not.

He closed his eyes for a moment, fighting his sense of despair. "I thought the Junk Boys controlled the Shadowdancers."

"Everyone does, including, amusingly enough, the Junk Boys–although you should cultivate the habit of referring to them by their proper name: House D'Evelin." He smiled. "I took control of the Shadowdancers over twenty years ago. An indiscretion of youth."

"So that's how he knew," Kihrin muttered.

"Excuse me?"

"Your son. That's how he found me so easily. He's a Shadowdancer. You're all Shadowdancers."† He cursed. "Taja! All these years I've been working for you."

"No one is more embarrassed than I am. All these years I've been looking for you, and you were hidden right in front of me, right out in the open. I owned Ola Nathera. She was freed years before your birth, so it never occurred to me that she would know anything about what had happened to you." He sighed.

"Where is she?" Kihrin asked, his stomach still crawling on the floor.

"No one seems to know. Ola disappeared the same night Surdyeh was killed. I think she ran. She's always had a healthy sense of self-preservation. She was smart enough to realize we would have hard questions for her

---

*Not true. A witch gift depends on talent arriving before skill, so that a child stumbles onto a power before they've learned the rules of how that power works, including what might otherwise be self-imposed limitations. Sometimes, particularly when a child is part of a Royal Family, it's entirely likely that they will receive formal training to use magic before they stumble onto such a gift themselves.

†House D'Mon's control of the Shadowdancers is not technically illegal, except in as much as the Shadowdancers regularly break the law, but it would certainly be an extraordinary scandal if this were ever made public.

as soon as we found out she'd been hiding you. There would be no way she could have claimed ignorance."

"You've been looking for me for years?"

Therin's expression was unreadable. "Yes."

Kihrin felt sick. Now he understood why Ola had been so set against him meeting the General, why she had been willing to go so far as to drug him. What he didn't understand is why she had lied in the first place. Had she planned on using him as a piece of blackmail?

He wished he believed her only motive had been to protect him from a family she had apparently known all too well.

"Was it just personal between you and Faris? A friendship soured?"

Kihrin looked away. "No."

"What was it then?"

He ground his teeth. "He and his friends murdered Mouse, but I couldn't pin him for it. It would have been my word against all of theirs."

"I understood she was killed while committing a burglary." Therin raised an eyebrow.

"You call it what you like."

Therin chewed on that piece of news. "Then I'll assume the little accident that Faris ran into a few years back, the one where the Watchmen ended up taking a hand, was not an accident."

"I was hoping he'd end up in the mines," Kihrin said, as close as he'd ever come to admitting he'd framed another Shadowdancer.

The corner of Therin's mouth twitched. "Something tells me you're going to fit in very well here."

The room settled into an awkward silence.

"You didn't have to kill him," Kihrin finally accused in a heated whisper. If Therin D'Mon was Master of the Shadowdancers, he could have ordered Butterbelly to tell him what he needed to know. That death, at least, had been unnecessary.

The High Lord looked up, surprised. "Kill who? Surdyeh? I didn't."

"Butterbelly. You didn't have to have Butterbelly killed." Kihrin turned back to the High Lord. "You had a meeting with Butterbelly to buy the tsali stone he was selling. Later that same evening, he's dead and the tsali stone's gone. You're telling me you didn't do that?"

The High Lord stared. "If I had known he had a tsali stone for sale, yes, I'd have met with him. But I wouldn't have killed him afterward." Therin sighed. "He was a *really* good fence."

"Then who did?"

"One of Darzin's agents." Therin tapped his fingers on the edge of the desk. "I believe my son ordered it to cover up a murder he committed. What bothers me is that I don't know why he committed the murder in the first place."

"Does Darzin need a reason?"

Therin shrugged with one shoulder. "Everyone has reasons for their actions, even if they do not make any immediate sense. As you so eloquently put it, we don't do anything unless there's something to gain."

"So what do you want me to do about it? I can't even beat Darzin when he's unarmed."

"You seem to be intrinsic to his plans, so I want you to find out what he's up to. If I am right, it will be something that may well require his removal. I do not expect you to handle that. When the time comes, I will deal with my son. If the risks seem great, understand that if you find me the proof I desire it will leave you as Lord Heir. And I can make quite certain that neither Faris nor any other Shadowdancer ever bothers you again."

Kihrin stared at him with skeptical eyes. *Sure,* he thought to himself. *You'll handle him. But he can summon up a demon prince. How will you handle that?* He didn't say anything though. He only trusted Therin slightly more than he trusted Darzin, which wasn't saying much.

Therin pulled a new sheet of paper from his desk, and reached for a fresh crow quill. He said, "Darzin tells me the High General gave you Valathea. That's a rare privilege."

"You know about Valathea?"

"Of course. I have even heard her played. I was disturbed to discover she's no longer in your possession."

"It's safe," Kihrin said with a sullen voice.

"Of course she's safe. She's in your room. I suggest you not be so careless with her in the future. Now go—and try not to be too exuberant with your rehearsals. Your bedroom is adjacent to mine."

39: In Search of Music

(Kihrin's story)

Instead of going to my room, I headed to the Thriss village, looking for Szzarus.

"Monkey!" Szzarus greeted in Thriss. I couldn't understand most of his language, but I'd picked up that word.

"Szzarus," I said. "I know your people have drums. I was wondering if you have anything else? I've seen oboes a few times. Do you have anything with strings?"

He flicked out his tongue and tasted the air before saying something that sounded like a question.

"You know . . . strings?" I pantomimed strumming. It was too much to hope for a harp, but maybe someone in the village owned something that passed for a lute.

He made an acknowledging sound and motioned for me to follow.

The village was small and tidy, and filled with Thriss who lived on the island because of their dedication to Thaena. I'd gathered it was considered something of a monastic retreat among Szzarus's people, so there were no children. Once a Thriss decided they'd stayed long enough, they went back to their homes on other islands or the jungles of Zherias. Some, like Szzarus, never left at all.

He showed me inside one of the cob houses. Neatly tucked into a corner were several drums, nearly as large as the ones used at the temple: cymbals, a tambourine, an amazing array of rattles, and a long-necked instrument with a deep squat bowl and a spike at the base. He motioned to the last one.

I picked it up gently. It only had three strings, and as I plucked them, Szzarus handed me a wooden bow strung with silk. The silk was too loose to be any good for bowing across the strings with tension. I had no idea if it was broken or if there was some trick to holding it that I didn't understand. Szzarus gestured toward the long-necked instrument.

I sighed and handed it back to him. "Sorry, big guy, but I don't think I can use this. At least not without a tutor."

Szzarus shrugged and hung the bow from one of its tuning pegs.

"What kind of instrument are you looking for?" Teraeth asked.

I resisted the urge to leap a foot into the air. He must have used magic to sneak up on me.

"What are you doing here?" I lifted my head and glared at Teraeth. "We've nothing to say to each other."

He leaned an arm against the hut door. "I'm just trying to help."

"No, you aren't," I snapped. "What is this? Because I didn't leave with you the way Khaemezra ordered, you followed me back here? I don't need the company, so why don't you fuck off."

Teraeth just grinned, and said something to Szzarus. I didn't catch most of it, although he did use the word "monkey." Szzarus responded, laughed, and left the room.

"What did you tell him?"

"The truth: you don't need his help." Teraeth straightened. "Shorissa owns a lute, and Lonorin keeps a zither. As it happens, Lonorin thinks you're adorable, so if you ask, I'm sure she'd be willing to lend it to you. See? I'm helping."

"You're an asshole."

"I don't believe being one disqualifies me from doing the other. Either is better than what you're doing right now, which is being a *child*."

"I'm being–" I sucked in a deep breath, held it to the count of three, and then released it in a hiss that any Thriss would have applauded. "I was being adult and mature and dealing with the reality of my situation. And then what happens? First, your mother sends Kalindra away. Then, instead of the sword trainer Khaemezra promised, she brings in 'Doc.' I think we can both agree that he possesses the sort of natural charm I wouldn't cross the Senlay to save from crocodiles."

Teraeth didn't laugh, but he made that almost-smile I'd come to interpret as the next best thing. "He knocked me down a few rungs, didn't he? I would've thought you'd like him for that."

I scoffed. "Maybe I don't want the competition."

"So, let me help you."

"Help me?" My laugh was unfriendly and bitter. "I don't trust you or Khaemezra. Tyentso's the only person around here who's played straight with me. What does that say, considering she's the witch who gaeshed me in the first place?" I looked back at the instruments. I couldn't play any of those without a lot of practice. "Maybe Szzarus can give me lessons." I moved to go past Teraeth.

He blocked me.

"Teraeth, get out of my way."

"I met her in the Afterlife," Teraeth said.

His answer so startled me that I couldn't put his response into any context.

Then I realized he was talking about the Jorat girl.

His eyes had a faraway look as he lowered his arm and walked into the hut. I was free to leave at that point—if I wanted to. "It was during a Maevanos. I was in the Afterlife, and . . . well . . . so was she."

"Then she's dead. You're saying she's dead." Dread clenched around my throat. I shuddered and let out a long stream of air. It didn't make any sense. I knew it didn't make any sense. Here I was hung up on some woman whom I'd never met and had no idea if I'd even like if I did meet her. I knew it was stupid.

But it didn't change how I felt.

Teraeth raised his hands in a gesture of surrender. "Technically speaking, so was I at the time. Not everyone who wanders through the Afterlife is on their way to the Land of Peace." Teraeth seemed to be choosing his words carefully. "But no, as it happens, I don't think she was dead. Some beings can survive and travel through those lands at will. Were I the sort to place wagers, I would say she's one of those."

"You mean demons? But she can't be . . ." I tasted bile. Yes, yes she could be. Xaltorath had been the one who had shown her to me, after all. Still, I rejected the idea. Xaltorath—indeed any demon I'd ever heard of—were all horrific and awful. They were not beautiful.*

"Demons can freely travel in the Afterlife, but so can gods," Teraeth said.

"She's not a god," I answered automatically.

"Oh, because you would know. Aren't you the expert now?"

"Anyway, that might explain how you met her, but it doesn't explain how you knew she was important to *me*."

He made a scoffing sound and looked away for a moment. "That's one of those questions you probably don't want to ask. You won't like the answer."

"Teraeth—"

"I could wax poetic about reincarnation and destiny and how some souls are tied together through lifetimes. Alternately, I could remind you that you've been spending your nights in bed with my ex-girlfriend and you talk in your sleep." Teraeth held out his hands. "Pick the answer that makes you more comfortable."

My gut twisted. "Kalindra told you."

"Kalindra told me," he agreed. "I recognized the description. Look, I understand that we haven't given you a great deal of reason to trust us . . ."

"Yeah, that part where you told me only a fool would, didn't help."

---

*Only because demons seem to prefer our fear to our desire. There's no reason a demon couldn't be beautiful if it wished.

He smiled. "My mother–" Teraeth paused and looked down at his hands. "Khaemezra has never been very good about just explaining matters. You see her as a priestess, but in her heart, she's a soldier, a general. Her instinct is to only give out information if it's strictly necessary. I know how frustrating that can be. I used to rail against her reticence, demand answers. I was so eager to rebel against her that I–" Teraeth broke off and gave the far wall that same distant stare.

"You what? Finish the sentence. I want to know what you did."

"I nearly doomed all of us," Teraeth finally said, bringing himself back to the present. "Don't be the idiot I was. We are here to help you. Please accept that help."

"Even if that help is from a *bartender*?"

The thing about anger–especially the thing about righteous anger–is how addictive it is. I didn't want to let go of it. I didn't want to calm down. I wanted to be furious, and here Teraeth was being sympathetic and reasonable. He made me irrationally angrier.

Teraeth shook his head. "Whoever he is, I'm quite sure that he is more than a bartender or he'd never have gotten away with speaking to Khaemezra like that."

I paused. "Or speaking to you like that. What's the deal with your father?"

"It's none of your business." The answer was habit, instinct, and as soon as he said it, Teraeth's expression closed off, but he didn't amend the statement or correct himself.

I pressed my lips together into a tight line. If we hadn't just gone through this, maybe he could have said that and I wouldn't have cared. Was it any of my business? But I'd been kept too long in the dark about too much, been the last person to know. They knew everything about me, and I knew nothing about them. That had become intolerable.

"You're right," I said. "It's none of my business. But you're going to tell me anyway. You'll tell me because you want to be my friend and you want me to feel like I can turn to you for help. Don't act like your mother."

We stared at each other.

Teraeth threw up his arms and walked away, but only a few steps before he turned back. "Fine. You know how your family name is D'Mon because your father's family name is D'Mon?"

"Just answer the damn–"

"I am. Let me finish."

I stopped myself. "Okay. Go on."

"Well . . ." Teraeth held up his hands. "We vané do the same thing. Only we choose a parent and that parent's family name becomes the first syllable of our name. There aren't that many vané, so for us lineage isn't something separate that we skip in casual conversation. My name starts with 'Ter' just as my father's name starts with 'Ter' and his grandmother's name started with 'Ter' and . . . you get the idea. It's nothing mysterious. When you hear a vané's name, you have a pretty good idea who their family must be too."

"Wait. Wait. You're telling me your name isn't Teraeth at all? It's . . . 'Aeth'? 'Raeth'? How does that even work?"

"This is why I didn't want to talk about it." He pinched the bridge of his nose. "My name is Teraeth. Family name and personal name. They're never separated. Before I knew who my father was, I took my mother's signifier, Khae. After I found out who he was, I changed it. I took his name, not to honor him, but to remind myself of his sins."

Now that was interesting, and I couldn't stop myself from looking intrigued. "Sins? Is that why Doc reacted like I'd just set fire to his tavern?"

"Did he?"

"Oh yeah."

"Who's the most famous vané you've ever heard of whose name starts with 'Ter'?"

"I don't know a lot of vané . . ."

"I promise you've heard of this one."

It took me a minute. Then I remembered my stories, told on Surdyeh's knee. "Wait . . . Prince Terindel? Terindel the Black? The guy who was demanding human sacrifices from the locals in Kirpis? There's a song about him. Hell, I think there's a play . . ."

Teraeth laughed ruefully. "Terindel wasn't demanding human sacrifices. That was just a story I—never mind. The Kirpis is home to the largest ariala and drussian deposits on the continent. The Kirpis vané owned them; Quur needed those mines to fuel their war against the god-kings. Atrin Kandor made up an excuse to justify taking the land. Easy as that. And now . . . now Terindel's my father."

"And you took *his* family name over Khaemezra's?"

"Like I said, I wanted to remind myself." He shook his head. "And people think Thaena doesn't have a sense of humor." He cleared his throat and walked over to the musical instruments. "What did you used to play?"

"A harp," I said, frowning at his heavy-handed change of subject, "which for some reason the slavers didn't feel fit to let me keep."

Teraeth blocked my path again. "If you need a harp, we can always have one brought over from Zherias."

"Thanks, but I don't really feel like waiting six months for another ship to return."

He smiled. "It wouldn't be six months. Maybe an hour or two."

I stopped and narrowed my eyes. "What?"

"Ynisthana is at the heart of an old magical gate system, not too dissimilar to the one that runs through Quur, although ours is a lot smaller. One of the routes goes from here to Zherias. It's not something we advertise or use often for security reasons. For you though?" He shrugged. "I'm sure Khaemezra would make an exception."

I crossed my hands over my chest. "Are you seriously suggesting that Khaemezra's had a way to get me off this island *the whole time*?"

Teraeth tensed, likely because he sensed I was back on the cusp of losing my temper. "Yes, but at a high cost. It might take the Old Man a few days to realize you aren't here, but when he finally does, he would probably blow up in a literal way. If we were lucky, he'd just erupt the volcano at the center of the island, but he'd probably start attacking cities in Zherias and the nearby coast. Maybe even go as far south as Kishna-Farriga. Thousands would die. And then he'd start searching for you. He knows your aura, and he can fly."

My mouth dried. "Someone should do something about him."

"If you'd like to step up to the job, be my guest."

I ignored that, for obvious reasons. "So you can leave whenever you want. Anyone else can leave whenever they want. *I'm* the prisoner."

He cocked his head. "Hmm. Good point. I guess it is all about you."

I closed my eyes and breathed deep and tried my hardest not to punch him. He'd punch back and my face still hurt from the last time.

I walked past Teraeth to the door opening.

"What do you want with a harp anyway?" Teraeth asked.

"It's none of your business," I snapped, and left in search of someone willing to fetch me one from Zherias.

40: Interlude in an Abattoir

(Talon's story)

Alshena D'Mon descended the long flight of stairs from the Court of Princes down the hall to the east wing of the palace. She tapped her fan on the wall as she walked, tapped it against the tapestries and the carved wood paneling, tapped it with a fierce staccato beat of excitement.

Servants and slaves scattered when they saw her coming.

Alshena rushed down a different set of stairs: seldom visited, quiet, and dusty. At the end of the stairs she found a blank wall, unpainted, and pressed the mortar in a certain way. Pressing in the wrong way would have been fatal, but that didn't concern the noblewoman. She knew the sequence so well she could repeat it in her sleep—if she ever slept.

The red-haired matron of House D'Mon hummed a dirty sailor's tune as she walked down the revealed dark passageway. It led down shadowy twisted stretches of tunnel that Therin D'Mon himself hadn't used in well over a decade. Finally, the tunnel ended in a dim room.

As Alshena entered the chamber, a man to her left screamed. His shackled body arched up from the low wooden table as he vomited black blood, splashing his body and the floor. A slow stain of sickly smelling bile spread in a pool as the man stopped twitching and lay in obscene rictus.

Alshena lifted the edge of her agolé and stepped over the liquid.

"Ducky, you used too much," she said.

At that statement, the shadow resting against the wall moved forward, and revealed himself to be Darzin D'Mon. He sighed. "I'm aware, love. I just can't seem to balance this formula." He looked disappointed, before his head snapped back up again and he scowled at Alshena. "Gods, do you have to look like her? You know I can't stand the bitch."

"Perhaps you shouldn't have married her then," she replied. "Do you realize she looked like this just to annoy you? She's really quite pretty."

"She's really quite dead," Darzin said.

She bent over and touched the black fluid oozing from the dead man's body. She sniffed it once, wrinkled her face in disgust, and wiped the liquid off on the dead man's clothes. "Ugh. Must you poison them? It ruins the flavor."

Darzin sighed. "I didn't kill him to satisfy your appetites, Talon. And the whole reason I ordered you to murder my wife was so I wouldn't have to look at her anymore." He waved his hand at her form in annoyance.

"Oh, very well. I brought you a new flavor to sample, anyway." At that sly pronouncement her figure wavered, then shifted and flowed. When she lowered her arms, Alshena D'Mon was gone. In her place was a stunning teenage girl, with dusky skin and waist-length hair fashioned into tiny braids. Both the girl's hair and fingertips were henna dipped.

Darzin smiled. "Very nice, sweet. A recent snack?" He ignored the dead man lying in the middle of the torture room. He crossed the floor and ran his fingers down the woman's arms, around to the small of her back. He nuzzled his mouth against her neck with all the tenderness of an illicit lover.

Talon nodded, looking up at him through thick eyelashes. "She was so sweet. I should give your new 'son' a thank-you gift for leading me to her."

Darzin looked her in the eyes and then laughed. "Well, yes, I suppose there must be some advantages to working in a brothel." He continued chuckling as he removed his arms from around her. "He has good taste, at least."

Talon leaned over the table and rubbed her reddened fingers down Darzin's arm. "I bet he'd taste good too. Oh, he's so pretty. I just want to eat him up. Can I have him, dearest? Please?"

Darzin shook his head and snickered. "Don't be ridiculous, Talon. He's my son."

The room grew quiet.

Talon scraped a sharpened nail against the edge of the blood-soaked table, carving a deep channel in the wood. "If that boy is your son I am the Virgin Duchess of Eamithon," she growled.

Darzin threw up his arms. "Fine, love. You're right. He's not my son, but since his real father will never have the stones to admit the truth, claiming him lets me control the brat. So, no, you can't kill him." He paced the room several times.

Talon sat down on the edge of the table and drew up her legs. "He is so sweet, Darzin. Fifteen years old and jaded as a ripe peach. His brain would taste just like ginger jelly."*

---

*Mimics eat brains, apparently absorbing their victim's memories and skills. Although I suppose that was obvious enough from Talon's side of these transcripts. It should be emphasized that she clearly doesn't need to eat a person to access at least some memories.

"You can't have him."

Talon thought about it for a moment. "You know—"

Darzin frowned at her, half-amused and half-worried by her over-whelming appetites. "This isn't negotiable, my dear. You want a new slave? I'll buy you anyone you want, but not him."

Talon snapped at him, "Don't interrupt me. That's not what I was going to say!"

"My apologies, sweet," he said with mock seriousness.

Talon pretended to busy herself with counting her toes. She said, "This girl he liked so much. The one I ate, Morea. She has a sister. Dear Kihrin was looking for said sister. I think he wanted to play hero and rescue her from her bad, nasty slave master."

"How sweet," Darzin said. "A real-life reenactment of the Maevanos."

"Shhhh . . . don't interrupt while Nana is explaining the rules of the game," Talon said. "With Morea dead, little Kihrin might still want to play hero. Since this sister is as beautiful as Morea was, why, she might even make the poor boy fall in love with her—especially if she was tragic, if she needed to be rescued. She'd be able to get the young boy to do almost anything for her . . ."

Darzin smirked. "Yes, I see where you're going with this."

"Why, he might even take off the Stone of Shackles for her." The look of sweet delight she gave him, angelic under any other circumstance, could only be described as the purest evil.

"The Stone—?" Darzin raised his eyebrows in surprise.

Talon snarled, and her voice took on a demonic quality as she hissed, "Don't play games, human. Despite how I appear, I am thousands of years older than you and it is just possible I am not an idiot."

"I didn't mean to imply—"

She traced a design with her littlest finger in the silk of Darzin's shirt. "Haven't I served you for all these years now? Done whatever you asked? Seduced whoever you wanted? Slept with whoever you wanted? Torn to little itty-bitty pieces whoever you wanted?"*

"Always," he agreed, eyeing her.

Talon leaned forward until her face was right next to his. She whispered, "To my kind, that stone he wears around his neck is as obvious as a lightning strike on a clear night would be to you. It hums to my body of its power. It vibrates with magic. It sings."†

---

*Mimics make such good spies and assassins that it's almost a cliché to find their services sold in this regard, although most of their employers never realize they are not hiring humans.

†Not an ability that I associate with mimics. I'm left to wonder if this is a talent unique to Talon, a facet of mimic physiology of which I had been previously unaware, or if Talon was simply lying. I lean toward the last one.

Darzin gazed at the shape-shifter in amazement. "I had no idea you had this ability."

Talon blushed and looked away, a perfect imitation of a cloistered virgin. When she looked back, her expression was more serious. "I take it this is why you took so long to find him? Because the stone shields him?"

Darzin scoffed. "It was pure luck I stumbled upon him at all. I can only assume that when Lyrilyn ran with him, she gave the baby to that whorehouse bitch my father used to own."

"Poor Therin. He frees Ola and she repays him by stealing the son he won't admit is his anyway." She paused. "Are we sure Therin didn't put her up to it? It would be a canny move for him, if Therin wanted to keep an eye on his son without admitting who daddy is."

He frowned and studied the far walls of the dungeon before shaking his head. "No. If he knew where Kihrin was the whole time, he'd have damn well shown up when the High General said he'd found one of our Ogenra in the Lower Circle. But you ate the brat's keeper, that Reveler musician. Didn't he know anything?"

She feigned disappointment. "Ola was the mastermind behind this. There were rumors she was a Zheriaso witch—there might be truth to that."*

"This whole thing has been a disaster. Somehow, she paid for her bond price, and Therin let her buy back her freedom. Who does that? He should have taken the metal and whipped her until she learned her place. Instead she took the brat and raised him right under our noses, and none of us noticed. Downright embarrassing. We've had no luck finding her either, not with all our people out looking. Maybe, as you say, she is a witch. I'll see if the Academy can send a witchhunter out to help."

"When you do, tell them to check all the bakeries and sweet shops."

Darzin smirked. "If I had my way, we'd just kill the brat and give him to you. However, from what little we've researched on the Stone of Shackles, the necklace lends its wearer a kind of immortality, so we don't dare. And like most of those damned rocks, it can only be removed by the owner willingly."†

"Well, that shouldn't be hard. Who do we have to torture?"

Darzin scowled. "A dead musician or a whorehouse madam. Unfortunately, Thaena wouldn't Return the musician, and I can't find Ola anywhere."

She looked disappointed, giving no hint of her own culpability in

---

*Obviously, it was the reverse. I take some consolation in knowing that Talon lied to absolutely *everyone.*

†Thank the secrecy of the vané. None of us really understood how the Stone of Shackles worked.

Surdyeh's death or Ola's disappearance. "Someone could cast an enchantment on his mind, perhaps?"

"Not likely to work, even assuming you could locate an enchanter. Ironic and unfortunate if Ola turns out to be one—but that would explain a few things." Darzin snaked an arm around the girl's waist and drew her closer. "I'm surprised you're even able to read Kihrin's mind."

She shrugged. "I don't use magic for that. I can read anyone's mind. It's like reading a book over someone's shoulder. Although it's faster if I gobble down the whole book all at once."

He pulled away from her. "Anyone's mind?"

"Oh, anyone weak-willed. Don't think I haven't noticed that you've learned to shut me out."* She pretended to chide him.

He settled back beside her. "Nothing personal."

"Of course. I still have plans for the boy. Mentally, he's quite a mess, you know. I'll have fun with that." She paused. "'If I had my way' and then 'we,' you said. Are you working with someone I don't know about?"

"Just a group of like-minded men who share the same goals. Nothing to worry about."

"The others want him alive, then?"

Darzin ran his hands along her shoulders while nodding. "At least until we've convinced him to give up the Stone of Shackles." His eyes never left Talon's body, heedless of the fact they were just inches from a fresh cadaver. "Afterward, I don't think they'll care what happens to him." He stopped moving his hands. "This slave girl's sister . . . what's her name? I'll send my men to buy her. She might be useful leverage."

At that, Talon threw her arms up and sank back down on the table next to the dead man, pulling Darzin on top of her almost-naked body. She laughed at the delightful joke. With leisure, she unbuckled, unbuttoned, and unfastened the Lord Heir's clothes, oblivious to the blood and gore around them.

"That's the best part, darling," she whispered. "You already own her."

---

*I suspect there are very few members of the D'Mon household who haven't been subjected to Talon's close mental scrutiny over the years. Darzin was clearly not immune, despite Talon's false reassurance that he was too strong-willed.

41: REFUSAL

(Kihrin's story)

Words cannot express how much I loathe you.

Do you honestly expect this charade to continue?

Why should it, Talon? For your amusement? Do you think that after you have tormented me, betrayed me, haunted me at every turn, murdered my friends, orchestrated all of this, that I would want to play story time with you?

Take back your damn rock.

I've had enough.

42: THE YOUNGER SON

(Talon's story)

My dear Kihrin, don't be like that. We are having "story time," as you put it, as a sign of my respect.

Your cooperation is unnecessary. You think I don't realize the necklace around your throat holds your gaesh? I can force you to tell me. Or I can steal the information from your mind as easily as ordering a drink at the Culling Fields. You can't stop me.

Do you think I do this only for my amusement?

Now look here. This rock we've been passing between us may look like a normal stone, worn smooth by the river, but your father Surdyeh was quite an enchanter. He taught me a few tricks. Any words spoken by the person holding this stone are stored inside to be heard again later.* Think of your story, told in your own words, being heard by Emperor Sandus or General Milligreest; a revenge that carries beyond the grave. I'll turn this stone over to whoever you like. I will make sure this reaches them, and they'll hear what it contains.

Your enemies believe you're no longer a threat to them, but you could be their worst nightmare—a voice they can't silence.

So. Whether you wish to continue is your choice.

Why don't you think about it? We'll skip your turn for now. I can continue easily enough. Let's see . . .

Now I'm going to tell you about another young man, only a year younger than our poor, ill-fated hero, but worlds apart in every other respect . . .

Galen D'Mon was fourteen years old when Kihrin joined House D'Mon. And while Galen couldn't remember every year of his existence, he also couldn't remember a time when he wasn't afraid. Fear was his constant accessory, never unfashionable, never forgotten. He lived his life much as soldiers on the front do, always expecting the ambush, always fearing

---

*You're reading the resulting transcription of the recording she made. So, at least for this singular occasion, she was good for her word. I wouldn't count on it ever happening again.

the next attack. No street urchin from the Lower Circle was as skittish as Galen D'Mon.

He was a handsome lad, but he didn't know it. He was talented and intelligent, but didn't know that either. Instead, he knew he was a failure. He knew his mother, Alshena, spoiled him, and therefore he was soft, weak, and womanly. He knew he would never be clever enough, strong enough, cruel enough, or brave enough to please his father. He knew he was not the sort of scion his father Darzin wanted, and he knew first-hand that his father met disappointments with violence. Being his son did not spare Galen. Far from it; being Darzin's son meant he was subject to his father's cruelty more than any other. The irony of being a D'Mon, after all, was that one was never far from a healer. There was no need for a man like Darzin to hold back.

Anything could set his father off. If Galen did not obey an instruction he would be beaten, but if he obeyed too timidly he would be struck for being meek. His father mocked him if Galen dressed too fashionably (never mind that his father always wore the latest trends), but slapped him and sent him back to change if he caught Galen "dressing like a commoner." He was beaten for being impertinent and beaten for being shy. Galen always did well in his studies, but his father cared little for his scholastic achievements and forbade sending "his heir" away to the Royal Academy in Kirpis to study magic.* Galen excelled at horsemanship and fencing, but he could never do well enough to earn a single word of praise: only the admonishment that the heir to the D'Mon name should do better and Darzin himself had been much superior at the same age.

So, when Galen was informed he was no longer heir, that he had been replaced by a previously unknown son of Darzin's, his reaction was not anger, bitterness, or despair at fate's fickle cruelty.

Instead, he felt relief.

Finally, the duty and responsibility of living up to the D'Mon name might fall to someone else—anyone else. If Galen was a failure as an heir, surely, he was good enough to be a second son. No one expected much from second sons.

The next morning, Darzin invited him to breakfast in the Conservatory and disabused Galen of his naïveté.

"Try to become his friend. Earn his confidence," Galen's father said as he attacked a piece of fried pork belly with a knife and fork. "But you must never forget this boy is your enemy."

---

*I find this astonishing. I can see no sense to this at all, except perhaps some dark part of Darzin's mind feared his son possessed a talent for magic greater than his own. It is, after all, unwise to abuse a child who may one day learn the ability to summon demons.

"I thought he was my brother," Galen said. He was sweating from the heat in the Conservatory. It was always blistering hot there. The association had become so intense over the years that Galen couldn't step one foot into the room, not even during the cool of evening, without feeling nauseated.

"What does that have to do with anything?" his father snapped, and cuffed Galen's head for emphasis. "He's a whore's son and a bastard, a thief and a murderer. Don't for one minute think he'll look at you with any sort of sibling affection. Do you see that stain right there?" He pointed to the floor with his knife.

Galen looked. A single dot of dark red marred the otherwise spotless floor. He didn't think it was tomato sauce. "Yes, Father."

"He killed a man right there," Darzin told him. "Killed him clean. Didn't hesitate." Darzin made a succession of quick stabbing motions with the knife. "He'd have done the same to me if given a chance. He'd do the same to you."

"You must be proud of him." The words slipped from Galen's mouth before he could stop them.

Darzin paused with a cup of coffee halfway to his lips. "Don't give me that tone, boy."

"Yes, sir," Galen said. He frowned and picked at his food: baked wheat cakes with imported apples cooked with cinnamon and fried strips of seasoned pork belly. The sight made his stomach turn. He didn't think the cakes would be so bad normally, but the temperature in the room was so hot and the pork was so greasy. He would have rather had some nice bland sag bread with fresh fruit and mint, maybe a nice glass of yogurt and rice milk. He was pretty sure he could keep something like that down, but it was commoner's fare and his father would not allow him to eat street food.

"He's a wild one, I'll give him that," Darzin continued. "If he wasn't—" Darzin paused as he speared a slice of apple. "A wild one, without a doubt. You'd think a boy raised in a velvet house would be more effeminate, but not that one, no. Killed that guard smooth as buttering a piece of bread. He'd make a hell of a killer with a little training." Darzin looked thoughtful for a moment as he chewed. He gave Galen a hard stare. "My father never gave a damn about any of his children and he still doesn't. I made myself a promise I would never be like that. You know that's why I'm so hard on you, don't you? Because I care. I want you to be the best."

"Yes, Father." With great effort, Galen didn't sigh or act like he had heard this speech before. He would have preferred his grandfather's indifference to his father's loving attention.

"The boy's in a murdering frame of mind right now. I understand why, but he needs to calm down. What happened with that blind old man was a mistake, nothing more. It wasn't personal. You can help. Your sisters and your cousins are all too young. You're the only person in the family close to his age. Put him at ease. Be nice to him. Show him some kindness. He could use a friendly face."

"A friendly face that tells you everything he says?" Galen asked.

Darzin smiled. It was one of the first genuine smiles Galen ever remembered his father directing at him. "That's my boy."

43: THE DRAGON'S DEAL

(Kihrin's story)

This rock? I won't deny the tenyé pattern has been changed. Something's been done to it.

Seems like a sucker's bet though. First you threaten my parents and now you say you've been on my side the whole time? How stupid do you think I am?

Don't answer that question.

All right, Talon. I'll continue. But only because I'm gambling that the small part of you that's Surdyeh is still on my side.

It may be a sucker's bet, but it's all I've got. Where did I leave off?

Have I talked about my deal with the Old Man? No? Okay.

We'll pick it up there.

So, because I've never believed in being stupid in halves, I walked down to the beach to see the Old Man.

The new sub-island he had created formed a craggy mess of black rock and fresh flowing lava. The rock solidified and cracked open again and again as the Old Man repositioned himself or sank his talons into the ground for a good stretch. My mouth dried as I saw how large the island had grown. It was no longer a minor protuberance of rock, what one might dismiss as a simple outcropping pulled up by the waves only to be torn down again later. The Old Man was growing himself a new bed, sized to match his proportions.

On the edge of the island, the Old Man had built a bizarre rock garden of lava pillars, grouped together in odd clusters. I didn't understand what purpose they might serve. They weren't shelter or furniture, and their shapes seemed too irregular and uneven to be decorative.

As I walked forward, carrying the harp a helpful Black Brotherhood adept had brought me from Zherias, a dark shadow fell over the beach. I hadn't needed to introduce myself: the Old Man must have heard me long before I was visible. The great dragon rose, eyes glowing with molten fire, head turned in my direction.

It occurred to me this might be the last stupid thing I ever did.

"Do you prefer to be called the Old Man?" I called out. I set the harp down next to me.

"I have worn many names," the dragon responded with that voice that seemed far more fitting coming from his throat than it did when Khaemezra spoke. **"Earth Terror and Ground Shaker, World Ripper and Night's Fire. I am the Betrayal of Foundations, the Toppler of Cities. I was there when Kharolaen burned and its people choked on boiling ash, I laughed as Ynalra drowned in lava."** The dragon chuckled. **"Yes, call me Old Man."**

I took a deep breath. "I'd like to make you a deal."

The dragon shifted. His neck moved forward and his head pointed at me. **"Do you want me to teach you magic? Destroy your enemies? Show you how to become a god?"**

I paused in surprise. "You can do that?"

"Oh yes," the dragon purred, **"in the old days you little mortals would come by the score. You would ask for my favor, my knowledge, my genius to solve all your problems for you. You would beg and supplicate yourselves, seeking my counsel and wisdom. Is that what you want?"** His eyes thinned down to slits while slow thick clouds of sulfurous smoke trickled down from his nostrils.

The worst cons are the ones so over-the-top, so desirable, that they are too good to be trusted. Being a god and destroying all my enemies did sound like the solution to many of my problems, but at what cost? I wasn't so naïve as to think the Old Man would do such a thing for free, if he could do so at all.

"With all respect, what I'd like is for you to let me leave the island unharmed. So here's my offer: I'll play for you tonight. A special concert just for you. I'll play anything you want. In the morning, you let me leave. What do you say?"

The dragon settled back on its haunches. **"Play."**

Later, Teraeth's hand fell on my shoulder. "Kihrin, what are you doing? You're not supposed to be here right now."

I looked up, blinking. The sound of morning seagulls hunting for breakfast echoed in the distance, playing a counterpoint to the crashing waves coming down on shore. The sky was a shroud of dull violet gray, tinged magenta to the west where the sun was rising. The air smelled of seawater, rotting kelp, and burning rock.

"I–" I cleared my throat. "What–?" The last thing I remembered, the Old Man had agreed to free me if I played him a few songs,* but that had been last night.

---

*Kihrin needs to pay more attention to what people are actually promising, rather than what he wants them to have said.

It was dawn.

"Play," the Old Man's voice ordered, and I felt my fingers jerk toward the strings. This differed from a gaesh command. The specter of unbearable agony and certain death enforced a gaesh's orders, but I *could* refuse. Not this time though.

Teraeth cursed as the dragon spoke. I don't think he'd realized that the mountainous pile of black rock offshore was the Old Man until the dragon moved.

Most people see something that enormous and assume it must be a hill. It's too large for us to process as a living creature when it isn't moving.

I bit back a scream as I touched the strings. There was blood on my fingertips, blood from playing so long and hard on the harp I'd torn skin and nails.

Yet still I played.

"Teraeth," I said as I bit back on whimpering, "help me. I can't stop."

"He has you under his thrall," Teraeth said. "I'm not strong enough to break it. Let me get Mother."

"Run," I said.

But as he did that, the sand of the beach rose, much as it had when Tyentso had been fighting off the Old Man. A wall of thick molten glass blocked Teraeth's escape. We looked at each other, but I couldn't stop playing, and Teraeth had no retreat. Teraeth cast his gaze around him for something, anything, but what weapon did he have against a monster such as that?

"Play," the dragon crooned, **"sing, and play for me. Sing me songs of ancient Kharolaen and sing of the ocean cities of Sillythia. Sing of Cinaval the Beautiful, and tell me the ballad of Tirrin Woodkeeper's Ride."**

I felt a panic well up in me I fought back down. "I don't know those songs. Can you hum a few bars for me first?"

"SING."

I ground my teeth together. Whatever spell he was casting, he wasn't a gaesh. I tried to find strength in that, strength enough to resist. "This wasn't our deal!"

"Deal? DEAL?" The dragon rose on his haunches, spread his wings to blot out the sky. **"You're nothing but a pathetic mortal. An idiot soldier who follows orders, accepts the world around you without criticism or curiosity. An uneducated fool whose only worth is to keep me entertained. I don't make deals with ants."**

I could only stare. As insults went, that was oddly specific. Also not true, given my lack of military service. I found myself reminded of Relos Var and the way he'd hated me so much, for someone I'd considered a stranger.

The dragon lunged.

His massive head snapped toward Teraeth, who dove to the side. The dragon's mouth closed on air. The Old Man lifted his mouth up to the sky, shook his head, and gulped down . . .

Nothing?

I raised a hand to shield my eyes. Teraeth lay across the sand, his expression one of repressed pain as he cradled one arm. He was alive though. So was I. Hell, even the borrowed harp seemed undamaged, still resting against my knee.

What had the Old Man eaten?

A moment later, the Old Man finished his phantom meal and let out an angry roar. He flew off, circling around in a wide spiral before flying out to one of the other islands.

We watched him go, neither of us saying a word, barely daring to breathe lest he hear and circle back.

"I *really* shouldn't have suggested you sing," Teraeth finally said.

I started laughing, weakly, as I leaned forward and rested my head against the harp. My fingertips ached and I felt like I had been awake for the last twenty-four hours—which was probably true.

"Not one of your better ideas," I agreed. "But then coming down here to play for him wasn't one of mine."

Behind us, the molten glass wall that the dragon had erected darkened to black, then disintegrated back into particles of sand.

Teraeth and I scrambled to our feet, not sure what we were about to face next.

As the wall collapsed, Doc stood on the other side. His expression was pure anger.

"You're late," he told me.

44: Fencing Lessons

(Talon's story)

Galen met Kihrin for the first time later that same day. When he arrived in the training room, his father, Darzin, was there with his new brother. Both wore the padded jackets used in practice, although the new boy's jacket fit too tightly across the shoulders. As Galen watched, Darzin kicked at Kihrin's legs and moved his arms, explaining again the proper start position. The young man looked like he had never held a sword before.

Probably, he hadn't.

"Galen. Good." His father nodded at him. "I started early. Kihrin, this is your younger brother, Galen."

The young man raised his hand to Galen, his eyes clouded and his expression unhappy. Darzin's initial introduction gave Galen a chance to examine his new brother. He was riding on the cusp of majority, with fine features and golden-brown skin. His hair was pale—when he stepped under the light of a window it flared bright gold—and tied back away from his face. Galen thought his new brother had the sort of features women and men both would obsess over. The sort of face that could only be worn by a man who was too pretty, knew he was too pretty, and so could only be an ass about it. This was Darzin's troublemaker, his wild son, the one to whom Galen would now be compared in all things.

Any relief that Galen had felt, that he now had a brother to divert attention from him, was drowned by the malicious certainty that Kihrin would never be treated as he had been. That he was, literally and figuratively, golden. Galen felt hate seep into him.

He smiled and waved back.

"We will start again with the basic footwork and handwork forms. Once you've learned these to my satisfaction, we may move on to bouts." Galen watched his father tug Kihrin's shoulders into alignment, until the young man looked over his right shoulder. "Not today, of course. It will be months before I'm satisfied with your advancement. Understand you're starting quite late, Kihrin. It takes years to make a good swordsman, a lifetime to make a master. You may never make it, but you are my child and you will try, even if it kills you."

"At least I have your love." The young man's voice was bitter and sarcastic. There was no tenderness in the expression he turned on their father.

Galen was surprised when Darzin punched Kihrin. Galen would have expected to be hit if he dared respond to their father that way, but he had assumed Kihrin would be given more leniency. He was even more surprised by the violence and anger behind Darzin's strike, much worse than anything his father ever directed at him personally. Darzin hit Kihrin with the pommel of his sword, straight to the jaw, throwing the boy's head back and splitting his lip.

Galen expected the boy to fall, run, cry, but again, he was surprised. Kihrin staggered to the side, put his hand to his face, and wiped away the blood. The look Kihrin threw at their father might have withered plants and curdled milk. Then he stood up straight and returned to start as if nothing had happened.

"Your first lesson, son," Darzin hissed, "is that you do not ever talk back to me. Understand?"

The young man stared at Darzin.

"Well?"

"Am I supposed to answer or would that be talking back?"

Galen flinched when his father hit Kihrin again, this time knocking the teenager to the floor. The boy flipped over on his back and lay resting on his elbows, while blood dripped from his nose and stained the white jacket. Galen pretended to study the tiled ceiling. It seemed safest.

"Ah, a trick question," Kihrin said. "Thanks for the clarification."

"You're too stupid to know when to quit, boy," Darzin growled.

"Yeah, I've been told that before . . ." Kihrin answered and then added, ". . . Father." He sounded cheerful.

Even though this was normally the answer Darzin expected from Galen, something in the way Kihrin said it set Darzin on edge. He raised his hand, still holding the practice sword, as if to strike at the boy. Kihrin returned the lethal, hard stare and didn't move.

Galen honestly wondered if he was about to watch his new brother's death—just hours after he discovered he existed. Darzin didn't kill Kihrin though, or even beat him.

Darzin tossed the practice sword to the ground. "I'll be lenient because you aren't used to this house, but do not try my patience. I have little of it to spare." Darzin turned and glared at Galen. "Do something useful for once in your life. Talk some sense into your brother." He turned on his heel and stalked out of the room.

For a moment, neither of them said anything. Kihrin picked himself up off the floor and wiped his bleeding nose on his sleeve. "I call that a win for me."

"You should know—I mean, about Father—" Galen was uncertain where to start.

"Forget it," the older boy replied. "I expect it goes with the territory."

"Father's not so bad once you get to—"

His brother's reaction was an immediate sneer. "Really? So how often do you end up at the apothecaries for bruises and cuts? Just curious."

Galen tried to meet Kihrin's stare. He felt himself cringing. "It's . . . fencing. Accidents happen sometimes."

"I'd believe you, except I've seen your father's demonstrations of warmth."

Galen bit his lip. "He's your father too."

"That's what he says." Kihrin crossed his arms over each other. "He's already shown he likes to hit me. How long has he been hitting you?"

The silence was thick and wooden.

"It is a father's right to discipline his child," Galen finally answered.

"Or kill them or sell them as slaves. But a bully is still a bully, even if the law gives them the right." Kihrin stalked around the room, scuffing his boots against the inlaid wooden flooring. "It's the same garbage up here as down below, except in the Upper Circle no one would dare say a word to someone like your father. Too rich. Too powerful." He turned his head and spat blood. Galen stepped back. It was shocking from pure contrast: such an uncouth gesture from someone born of royal blood.

"He *is* your father," Galen repeated. "I can prove it."

Kihrin's eyes were irate as he looked back at Galen. "Can you?"

"Follow me. I'll show you."

45: RISCORIA TEA

(Kihrin's story)

I stepped forward, clutching the harp with bleeding fingers. "It wasn't—I didn't—"

"Not your fault," Doc said. "I saw. We should consider ourselves lucky the Old Man wasn't in the mood to breathe fire." He turned his head to Teraeth. "How badly are you injured?"

Teraeth inspected his arm and winced. The skin was bubbled and crisped. "Badly, if we didn't have healers on the island who could cure worse."

"Then you should go see them."

Teraeth started to protest. He looked at me, back to Doc, and then did something I never imagined Teraeth doing in a thousand years: he behaved. "As you say."

He withdrew.

That left me on the beach with my new "teacher."

Doc beckoned. "Come on. Let's not stay here. At some point the Old Man will figure out he was tricked, and it would be best for all of us if we're not out in the open when he returns."

"Tricked . . ." I hefted the harp. "You're the reason he acted so weird?"

"Yes. Now follow me. It's time for your first lesson."

"I'm injured. I haven't slept."

Doc gave me a hard look. "And it will be a while before you do. Your enemies won't wait for you to be well rested before they strike. Why should I do differently before we train?"

"You've got to be joking."

He didn't smile. He wasn't joking.

Doc walked back toward the caves. I watched him go before turning back to the ocean, and the draconic volcano the Old Man was still building. Doc was right: the Old Man would come back. He wouldn't be happy when he did. Then there was the matter of what Doc had done to make the dragon attack thin air. How had he pulled that off? How had he disintegrated that wall? Was he a wizard?

There was only one way I was going to find out.

I followed him.

Doc led me past the caves, to the far side of the mountain, where he stopped before some recently cleared vines and an old stone door. I hadn't seen this place before. Hell, this might have been the first door I'd seen yet on the island. I didn't think they used doors there.

For someone who claimed he wasn't a member of the Black Brotherhood, Doc seemed to know all their secrets.

Doc pushed against the door. It swung openly easily, even though it was carved from a ton of solid basalt. I expected darkness beyond, but I guess Doc really had been waiting for me, because lamps were lit. The room looked more like something associated with the temple than the natural caves the Brotherhood using for sleeping quarters. The floor was satin smooth and the walls looked like scales carved straight from the rock itself. The accoutrements of weapons training—a rack of blunted swords, wooden mannequins, a training ring with positions—lined the walls and marked the floor.

A loaf of crusty bread and a pot of tea sat on a table. Smelling them, I was reminded I hadn't eaten since the day before.

I set the harp down by the door and pointed to the food. "May I?"

Doc nodded. "Help yourself."

I did. The tea was plain and the bread was a rough, dark grain, but both were at that moment the most delicious things I had ever eaten.

I looked up from the food. "You're not human, are you?"

He raised an eyebrow. "Well, I *have* been accused of being hard on my students."

"No, I meant . . ." I paused, exhaled, tried again. Everything was a bit fuzzy, kind of like feeling drunk. "You're too tall, you're wearing that tsali stone, there's that thing between you and Khaemezra, and the way you act like you've hated Teraeth's father for a thousand years. Which I'm thinking might be literally true. I figure that makes you some kind of vané, just disguising yourself as human. You get bored in the Manol or something?"

"Color me surprised. You're not as stupid as you look. Although your guess is based on a few fallacies. For example: Khaemezra isn't vané."

I blinked at him. "What?"

He shrugged. "She's not vané. There are other races in the world besides vané and human. Originally there were four, all immortal, but gradually the races fell, lost their immortality. The vané are the only immortal race left. The others? The voras became human. The vordredd and the voramer retreated and hid. Khaemezra is *voramer.*"

I exhaled. "Not immortal. So *that's* why she looks old."

"Khaemezra looks old because she wants to look old."

"Wait. What does that make Teraeth?"

"Complicated." He laughed. "Never let it be said the goddess Thaena doesn't have a sense of humor. Or should I be thanking Galava for that practical joke?"

"I don't understand what you're talking about." Eating wasn't helping my dizziness. I still felt weak.

"I'd be surprised if you did."

I tried to focus my eyes, my thoughts, but they kept slipping away. "Why . . . why are the vané the only race that's still immortal?"

"Ah." He sighed and looked down at his hands. "That's my fault."

"What? You're personally responsible?"

"Yes. Me personally. The vané were supposed to have been the ones to sacrifice their immortality, *not* the voramer. It was, as they say, our turn." Doc slapped the table and stood. "Ancient history. What's important now is that you have a great deal to learn," Doc said, "and as you've seen, your enemies will not go easy on you because you're young and inexperienced. For that reason, neither can I."

The edges of my vision blurred. I looked at the cup of tea. Neatly camouflaged among the rest of the tea leaves floated small slivers of riscoria weed.

Wine was the best way to hide the taste, but strong tea was almost as good.

"I take back what I said about you being smarter than you look. A *smart* man would have been much more paranoid about eating or drinking something handed to you by a stranger," Doc said.

"You—" But my intention to call him bad names and hurt his feelings was short lived. Dizziness overwhelmed me.

My blurring sight became a soft blackness that wrapped around me and gently pulled me down to the stone floor.

46: THE CRYPT

(Talon's story)

"We're not supposed to be here," Galen cautioned as they crouched together in a five-foot-high servant's access at the far side of the palace. He held up a blackened iron key with sober dignity. Galen regretted showing the hidden room to his new brother so soon, but he relished the opportunity to share such a juicy secret. He didn't see any way his new brother could fail to be impressed.

Kihrin grinned at Galen. "Aw, but that's when it's the most fun."

Galen couldn't help himself. "Yes! It is, isn't it? Uncle Bavrin showed me this room, and I think he learned about it from one of his older brothers, Sedric or Doniran, before they died. I come here when I don't want anyone to be able to find me."

He unlocked the door and pushed against it. It didn't open smoothly, even though Galen always oiled the hinges. The edges of the rough flagstone floor caught at the base of the door. Galen kicked at the bottom until the edge cleared the worst of the obstruction and the gap widened enough to allow them both to enter. Slipping inside had been easier when he was ten.

Inside, the room opened again, and they could both stand. Even before Galen lit the lantern he kept by the doorway, Kihrin let out an appreciative whistle. Galen felt immensely consoled. He would have been upset if his new brother had shown no admiration for the safe haven of Galen's childhood.

Under the lantern's flame, the contents of the storeroom became clear. In the center of the room loomed a golden statue of a woman, her head crowned by delicate metal roses, her neck and hips encircled by a belt of skulls. In her hands she held blades: dozens of knives, daggers, shivs, keris, and thin stilettos. They looked like fatal blooms. The flickering torchlight gave her life so she loomed over them in deadly benediction.

"Wow."

Galen nodded. "Thaena herself! I don't know what that statue's doing here, of course, but–" He shrugged. "A lot of stuff was just thrown in this room to be forgotten."

"That's real gold." Kihrin walked over to examine the statue.

"Yes, yes, it is. The Black Gate itself doesn't have a statue that's solid gold."

Kihrin raised an eyebrow. "Neither do we. That's gold leaf. It would collapse under its own weight otherwise."

Galen deflated. "Well." He pointed. "That's dried blood on the skulls!"

"Okay, so that part's creepy." Kihrin looked sideways at him, then added, "You should charge admission."

"Nobody knows it's here. Okay, nobody but you, me, and Uncle Bavrin." Galen smiled at Kihrin and set off searching through the amassed clutter.

"Nobody but you, me, Uncle Bavrin, and whoever put this here in the first place, you mean."

"They've probably been dead for years," Galen said, waving his brother over to the side. "What I want to show you is over here."

"How did they even move it into this room?" Galen's brother mused. "There's no way it would have fit through that narrow little passage."

"Kihrin, over here," Galen insisted.

"Aren't you even curious?" Kihrin didn't look at him. His stare traced out the contours of the statue, judging the size against the tiny doorway they had crouched to enter. He held up his hands to help measure and compare. "No way. Not unless that statue can be broken up into pieces."

"I told you, they threw a lot of junk into this room."

Kihrin bit his lip. "But why—all right, all right. What is it you need to show me?"

Galen held up the painting and pulled off the velvet cloth covering.

Kihrin's face grew pale. "Taja . . ."

"Well?" Galen balanced the painting up against the stack of others behind it, and took a few steps back. "You see the resemblance, right? He looks just like you."

Galen didn't know when the portrait had been painted, but it showed a High Lord in the height of his power. He was handsome, impossibly pretty, with golden hair and sapphire eyes—the distinctive blue of the D'Mon god-marked royals. Galen had always seen the resemblance to Darzin in the picture, but that was nothing compared to how closely the portrait resembled his new brother. It was as if someone had reached forward in time to draw Kihrin as an older man; there could be no question he was related.

Kihrin didn't speak, but Galen thought his expression was answer enough. Galen found himself feeling guilty. He'd only meant to show Kihrin he was part of the family, to show Kihrin he shouldn't insult the D'Mon name. Kihrin's expression wasn't shocked or embarrassed. He looked heartbroken. For the first time, Galen realized Kihrin hadn't been waiting on proof nor seeking it. The revelation Kihrin truly was a D'Mon was not a rescue, but a sentence.

Kihrin walked over to the painting and knelt in front of it. He traced the writing on the gold nameplate at the bottom with his finger. "Pedron D'Mon," the young man whispered.

"He was our great-great-uncle. His mother was this vané slave with golden hair who was murdered by one of the family after she gave birth to Pedron's sister, Tishar. A lot of people think that's why he turned out so bad. Because he hated House D'Mon for killing his mother and wanted to destroy us."

"He looks like me. That's . . . that's creepy." Kihrin frowned. "So this vané slave had three children, right? Pedron, Tishar, and Therin's father?"

"Uh, no. Therin's father was Pedron's half-brother. Therin's mother was noble born."

"That doesn't make sense."

"It gets better though. My mother says that Pedron owned your mother. That is, Lyrilyn. You know, before she married our father."

"Lady Miya mentioned that, but she forgot to mention how much I look like Pedron."

"It was ages ago. And your mother, you know, betrayed Pedron, sided with his nephew Therin to help him kill her master." Galen rested his hip against one of the crates as he spoke. "Nobody ever talks about what happened, you know. They all just whisper about it with these big capital-letter voices like everyone's supposed to know what happened, and of course I don't. It's all so frustrating."

"Pedron . . ." Kihrin whispered and touched the side of the painting again. It wasn't reverence exactly. More like dread. "What's this written underneath?"

"What?" Galen blinked. "It's his name."

"No, there's writing underneath. Bring that light over here."

Galen did, and saw that someone had carved words into the frame underneath the name plaque.

"*Wizard, thief, knight, and king. The children will not know the names of their fathers, who quiet the voices of their sting.*" Kihrin read the words and then raised an eyebrow at Galen. "Not what I'd choose to have engraved on my portrait, but who am I to question a dead evil High Lord?"

"I never noticed that before. What does it mean?"

"Uh, he has terrible taste in poetry?" At Galen's glare, Kihrin raised his hands. "How would I know what it means? I still can't figure out how they got the statue in here."

"It sounds like a prophecy," Galen said as he bent over to look at the frame again.

"A prophecy meaning what? Really bad family life? A rash of Ogenra?

Wait." Kihrin stared at the portrait a moment longer and then he laughed. "Wow. Oh, I get it. Pedron really got around, didn't he?"

"What do you mean?" Galen blinked at him.

Kihrin started to answer and then stopped. "I mean the children won't know the names of their fathers. It's not prophecy: he's *bragging*. Think about it. You brought me here to convince me Darzin's my father, because I look like this High Lord Pedron. What you've really done is proven that High Lord Pedron *wasn't* our great-whatever-uncle."

"Wait, I don't understand—"

Kihrin brandished a strand of his hair. "Don't you get it? I wouldn't have this hair unless I was related to Pedron's vané *mother,* the one with the distinctive golden hair. What was her name again?"

"Uh . . . I don't remember. Val-something?"

"Okay, well, she's the key. Therin is our grandfather, right? And I have D'Mon blue eyes and *her* hair. I wouldn't have both if Therin wasn't related to Pedron's mother, so no matter what you've been told, Pedron's not some great-uncle. We've got to be descended from him."

"But that would mean—" Galen's eyes widened. "That would mean Pedron was actually Therin's father . . . Kihrin, Therin *killed* Pedron."

"And Therin was actually telling me the truth when he said he despised his father. Apparently hating your dad really *is* a family tradition around here. I get it. I'm one of the club." Kihrin began picking up trinkets, thumbing through neglected, forgotten books. There were boxes and chests, wardrobes and bookcases, jars of esoteric ingredients and statuary of a decidedly lewder nature than the goddess in the center of the room. "There's a part of me that wants to feel all sorry for myself, but honestly I'm just glad I didn't grow up here. I don't think I would have liked it much."

Kihrin picked up a small leather book from a desk and Galen's tongue froze in his mouth. He couldn't say anything without showing Kihrin it was important. Galen knew better than to make that mistake.

Kihrin flipped through the pages with increasing eagerness, reading while Galen struggled to breathe.

"Huh," Kihrin said.

"What is it?" Galen said, trying not to sound nervous.

Kihrin held up the book. "More poems. Guess Pedron really was a fan of the art." He tucked the book under his arm.

"You can't take that!"

"Why? Grampa Pedron's not going to miss it," Kihrin replied. "I could use a good set of poems like this. A few of these will make great song lyrics."

Galen stared. "Song lyrics? You really think so?"

"Absolutely. Whoever penned these knew what they were doing, and this is a handwritten journal, so I bet it's unpublished material. This is a great find and—" Kihrin stopped.

"What?" Galen asked. He was at once pleased and uneasy.

Galen watched his brother open the book again. Kihrin pursed his lips. "The paper is new. The ink isn't faded."

"Maybe Uncle Bavrin left the book here?" The lie sounded weak even to Galen's ears.

Kihrin stared at him. "You wrote these, didn't you?"

"No! Uh—" Galen stammered.

"Sure," Kihrin said. "Daddy doesn't approve of poetry?"

"Not writing it, no. D'Jorax are the entertainers, and he thinks they're gauche. You won't tell him, will you?" Galen cursed himself for a fool. Now Kihrin had something to use against Galen, and he wasn't so naïve as to think his brother wouldn't seize that advantage.

"Tell Darzin D'Mon? I wouldn't tell him to wipe shit off his face. He can rot and die for all I care." Kihrin handed the book to him. "Have you shown these to anybody?"

Galen shook his head.

"You should have them published. Under an assumed name, of course. Wouldn't want to embarrass the old man with how talented his kid is."

"Oh, I'm not that good."

Kihrin raised an eyebrow. "Yeah, you are. Hell of a lot better than I could ever do, that's for sure. Surdyeh always said—" He stopped and looked away, grimacing.

Galen stepped forward. "Surdyeh?"

Kihrin shook his head, as if trying to throw off whatever gloom had seized him. "My father. The man who raised me. He was a musician. You know: gauche. Always told me there was no sense in trying my hand at poetry because I hadn't seen anything worth writing about."

"What happened to him?" Galen asked.

"'Daddy' didn't tell you?"

Galen shook his head.

"Darzin had him murdered. One of your father's assassins slit his throat." Kihrin's voice was harsh, angry, dagger-sharp in its accusation.

"Do you know that?" Galen asked. "Or are you just—"

"Darzin doesn't even deny it. He killed Surdyeh and Morea and Butterbelly—and if someone were to make me a wager, I'd lay more than even odds he killed Lyrilyn too, no matter what he says really happened."

Galen looked down at his feet. "I'm sorry."

"It's not your fault," Kihrin said.

"I'm still sorry." Galen paused. "You know, if you want to use some of my poems for songs, I think I'd like that. You're a musician, right? Like your father?"

His brother nodded. Kihrin's face looked wet in the lantern-light. Galen realized his brother was crying, silent tears running down his cheeks. Like earlier when Galen watched Kihrin spit, he found it shocking.

"Don't let Father see you cry," Galen said in a rush. "He hates it. He says it makes you weak."

Kihrin scoffed and rubbed his eyes, and wiped at his mouth where the wound from fencing class was bleeding again. "Darzin's a real asshole, you know that? Somebody should tell him beating up his children and sending assassins to kill old men and girls—*that* makes him weak." He walked over to the statue of Thaena and traced the edge of a stiletto with a bloody fingertip. "If I ever have the chance, I swear by all that's holy I'll put a sword through him—ow!" Kihrin quickly drew his finger back. A thin line of fresh blood marked the cut. "Shit, those are still sharp!"

Galen said: "Oh gods, are you okay?"

"Yeah, unless embarrassment counts. It's only a nick."

Galen chewed on his lip. He'd never grown up with much in the way of religion, not of any kind, but it seemed a dire omen. The room was darker and more frightening than before.

Kihrin leaned in to examine the blades. "I don't see anything that looks like a poison. I think I'll stop by Lady Miya's anyway, just to be on the safe side." He laughed. "And here I thought the biggest danger was going to be you sticking a knife in me."

"Me? But I'd never do that!"

"Yeah, I know that now. I just didn't know then. You invite me to go to some secret location alone, just the two of us? Maybe you're looking for the chance to be number-one son again, you know?" Kihrin shrugged. "I couldn't be sure."

"Oh bother," Galen said, feeling ill. It hadn't occurred to him his actions might have been interpreted that way. And if Kihrin had decided to preemptively defend himself, who was there to say otherwise, or even witness what had happened? He felt monumentally stupid. He hoped his father never found out about this.

"Don't worry about it," Kihrin said. "I think you're okay, even for a D'Mon. Anybody who can write poems like that can't be all bad."

"I didn't . . . I mean . . . thank you."

Kihrin grinned. "Let's go find Lady Miya before I drop dead of ancient poison, okay?"

Galen found himself returning the smile. "Okay."

47: THE MOTHER OF TREES

(Kihrin's story)

"Your Majesty?"

I blinked awake from where I'd dozed off. Then I blinked again and looked around with growing dismay.

I wasn't in the practice room where Doc had drugged my tea.

Doc wasn't around for me to kick either. Instead, the man who addressed me was a Kirpis vané, with milk-white skin that managed to look elegant rather than sickly. His soft pink cloud-curled hair was almost hidden by a glimmering battle helm. His eyes were pink too. He would have reminded me of a rabbit if not for the fact most rabbits aren't so heavily armed—or have a look in their eyes that suggests they'd be happiest drenched in the blood of their enemies.

Okay, he still reminded me of a rabbit, but I was too upset by my circumstances to find it hilarious at that moment.

"Your Majesty," he repeated, and stepped forward to unroll a sheet of vellum across the table. The vellum was an intricate map, although I didn't recognize the location and couldn't read any of the writing. "This day will be glorious. Our soldiers have confirmed Queen Khaevatz is inside the fortress, and the last barrier rose is catching fire. The day we end her reign over the Manol vané has arrived."

He looked at me expectantly. And waited.

I had no idea what to say.

I had no idea where I was. Some sort of tent, although not the simple tent of a commoner or even the practical tent of a soldier. No, this was an elaborate confection crafted from silk and rare woods, with jeweled lamps hanging from threads of purest platinum. Fine carpets covered the floors and a brazier of sweet-smelling herbs burned in a corner. A wooden mannequin stood to the side of the room, the sort one might expect to use as an armor stand. Next to it was a weapons rack filled with swords, spears, and bows so elaborately carved that most Quuros soldiers would never use the damn things; they'd just put them up on a wall to be admired.

And Sir Rabbit still waited on my answer.

"Good," I said. My voice didn't sound like my own. "That's . . . good."

He noticed my hesitation but misunderstood its cause. "I've dispatched a messenger, as you ordered. Should this day go wrong, Valathea and Valrashar will both be escorted to safety."

I blinked. "Wait. Valathea?" He couldn't mean my harp, could he?

"Your wife, the Queen?" He looked confused.

I cleared my throat, waved a hand, and pretended I wasn't even more confused myself. "Of course. Thank you. It's not that." I thought about saying something more. "I have every confidence in you" perhaps, but the more I said, the more likely I'd reveal myself as an impostor.

Was this another god-inspired vision? Or just a regular vision brought on by being drugged by Doc? It seemed too coherent to be a hallucination, and too literal to be another of Taja's allegories. Was this going to happen every time I fell unconscious?

My reverie was interrupted by Sir Rabbit, who leaned over the desk and gave me a good, hard stare. "I know it's not my place, Your Majesty, but you can't be having second thoughts. Queen Khaevatz is tainted with voramer blood and no right to claim a vané throne. She has no respect for her vané ancestry. No matter what your feelings for Khaevatz, she's conspired with the Quuros, conspired with their bastard Emperor Kandor. You are doing the right thing for the Kirpis people."

Wait. I knew this story. Kandor. Atrin Kandor was the Emperor of Quur who'd conquered the Kirpis and pushed out its vané natives, before turning his attention to the Manol in the south.

Invading the Manol hadn't gone so well. He'd been slaughtered, leaving behind the sword Urthaenriel as the world's most expensive apology for crashing a party uninvited.

The Manol vané queen, Khaevatz, was usually given credit for Kandor's death.

But King Kelindel of the refugee Kirpis vané had fled Quur's invasion to join forces with Queen Khaevatz. He'd helped her, uniting the previously warring Kirpis and Manol groups. He hadn't tried to kill her. Hell, he'd married her, uniting the Royal Families into a single bloodline. I'd never heard any rumor that she wasn't full-blooded vané.

It seemed wisest to play along until I could understand what was happening. I nodded. "I'm fine. Let's do this."

He stared at me a moment longer, probably because I'd used five words where most vané would have used ten. He nodded and walked outside. I was expected to follow.

I stopped and looked around the room for a mirror and came up empty. King Kelindel evidently didn't waste time on such frivolities. However, a shiny shield hung from one of the racks, which worked as well as the real thing. I stared at "myself."

I wasn't surprised to see I was Kirpis vané. I'd expected that with the clothes and the silk and the fluffy pink Kirpis vané general. However, my overall appearance hadn't really changed.

I looked older, sharper around the edges, paler in skin tone, and I wore armor I'd never seen before in my life. But I still had the same gold hair. I still had the same blue eyes.

And I still had the Stone of Shackles around my neck.

Why change my appearance, if whatever or whoever was doing this left so many of the details exactly the same?

"Your Majesty?" Sir Rabbit peeked his head inside when I didn't follow him right away.

"Lead on," I said.

We exited the tent into darkness. It took a few seconds to adjust to the dim light. I started to walk forward and stopped as my senses reoriented. We weren't on the ground. The darkness wasn't caused by the time of day, but by a canopy of tree cover so thick it blocked out the light. Woven into this thick jungle foliage were wonders: birds with plumage brilliant enough to shine even in darkness, luminescent butterflies, and flowers like jewels. Perfumes floated on the air so thick and heady it was like breathing wine.

The Manol Jungle. Home to Teraeth's people—and the refuge claimed by the Kirpis vané.

Apparently, they had claimed that refuge by force.

Contrasting with the natural beauty was an unnatural state of conflict. Many of the bridges linking tree to tree were on fire. Whole buildings, palaces, were burning or crumbling, the stress of the battle too much for their delicate construction. Lights twisted in the distance like a thousand fireflies locked in battle. I heard the ongoing conflict, a dull roar of orders shouted, screaming men wounded, and arrow volleys launched into the dark.

"Shields up!"

I startled at the screamed order as a group of men and women I hadn't noticed raised shields up over our heads. Some of those shields were metal, some wood, but a great many of them had a ghostly patina of energy. The energy fields locked fingers with neighboring fields to form a glowing phantasmal wall. The incoming arrow fire bounced harmlessly against this barrier and fell into the vast unending dark between the trees.

A black Manol vané arrow hit the wooden bridge and made a hissing sound as the liquid on the head came into contact with the wood.

"Ready your bows!" A tall woman with daffodil-yellow, cloud-curled hair and skin the color of celery shouted the order.

No one expected me to do anything. No one waited on me to give orders, which was a vast relief, since I had not a clue what such orders should be. Another Kirpis vané woman rushed forward, pottery-blue dress fluttering like butterfly wings over gleaming sharantha armor. She gestured into the gap between this giant tree and the one across the way. As she did, shining silver plates of metal appeared out of nowhere, interlocking into a tile mosaic stretching forward in a straight line. The bridge she formed might have seemed ancient, a glorious work of art, but there were no supports, no joists, no mortar. The only explanation for why it didn't all tumble into the darkness was the correct one: magic.

"Nock!" The next order sounded.

Everyone had light-colored skin and hair—a pastel rainbow of flower shades, in combinations wholly unnatural on a human. In this murky jungle, they nearly glowed in the dark, and often literally glowed as spells triggered for protection or attack. Nowhere did I see the enemy we faced; Manol vané arrows fell from nowhere. Spells materialized with no clue as to their origin.

One group of Kirpis vané with shields stayed behind to protect the archers and the sorceress maintaining the bridge. The second group marched forward with Sir Rabbit and myself. I was meant to follow: we marched forward.

"Mark!"

Sir Rabbit put a hand against my chest, a silent plea for me to bide for a moment.

"Draw!"

The whole world held its breath.

"Loose!" A wall of light sailed up into the air. The Manol vané's arrows had been poisoned.

Ours were on fire.

Sir Rabbit and my guards began running.

They used the arrow fire as cover, hoping to make more distance in the moment the other side was forced to raise their own shields. There was a long way to go, and we had an enemy that was still in the fight.

I didn't realize it at the time, but I hesitated too long. Presumably this was a practiced maneuver, but I hadn't practiced. I lagged.

A black-hafted Manol vané arrow took me in the shoulder, cutting right through my mail. The pain was extraordinary, a burning fire spreading out through my arm as the poison coursed through me. I dropped to the ground as my heart seized, like being kicked in the chest by a horse.

A bright flash of light followed.

I was back at the start of the bridge. Sir Rabbit put his hand out to make sure I didn't start the run too soon.

What had just happened?

"Draw!"

I looked around. No one acted like anything was odd or unusual.

"Loose!" The Kirpis vané arrows flew into the night.

They started running.

This time I was ready. I started the run in time with the others, careful to keep myself under the shields. The Manol vané didn't have the Kirpis vané's organized, regimented groups of archers who made orchestrated volleys of attacks. They had free agents roaming the trees, archers who could be silent and attack when and if the right opportunity presented itself.

Assassins, I thought. *Naturally.*

Another group of Kirpis soldiers waited for us on the next tree support, although more of them were dead than alive. The bridge had been cut, even as they had won the day, leaving them to hold the position on their own until reinforcements arrived. They had fought valiantly, and very nearly to the last man or woman.

All of them, no matter how injured, went down on one knee as I passed.

I wanted them to stop. If the Manol vané archers hadn't realized I was someone important before, they sure as hell knew now.

A mass of twisted plant matter burned in front of us, hacked at with some weapon. Sir Rabbit nodded at it in a way I think was supposed to be meaningful.

That's when the Manol vané attacked.

It took a while to realize the things moving in the shadows were not forest animals. Their dark colors blended, helped by clothing that was not a single color but slices of green and gray and bitter violet. Teraeth once told me the Kirpis vané want to be seen, but the Manol vané don't want to be seen until it's too late. I wondered how the Kirpis—with their rigid formations and their bright colors and their *visibility*—could possibly win enough to make a final push into the heart of their enemy's defenses.*

Then I saw how.

If the Manol vané attacked with silent precision, each nick of their weapons a deadly touch of poison, they rarely drew close enough to deliver that threat. Every Kirpis vané on the platform was a sorcerer. As the Manol vané attacked, our side summoned dancing blades crafted from violet fire, or called lightning. A figure ran toward me, coming to within a few yards before he dissolved into bright yellow pollen and scattered on the winds.

But I didn't see the figure behind me. A cry alerted me and I turned, but I didn't even have my sword out. I was wearing one. It had banged against my leg as we ran across the bridge. I fumbled to free the damn thing before one of the Manol attackers closed with me.

---

*Really, that's a question the Kirpis vané should have been asking too.

I failed.

I looked up in time to meet a pair of wine-colored eyes and feel the icy coolness of a sword slicing across my throat.

Light flashed.

I was back at the start of the platform, the Manol vané seconds from revealing themselves.

"Ambush!" I called out as I drew my sword.

This time I batted my attacker's sword out of the way so she missed the deadly strike. While she was out of alignment, I made a clumsy swipe across her middle that made her scream. It did not, however, stop her from lashing back at me with a dagger that pierced glove and flesh. Fire screamed up my arm before darkness and that bright flash of light started everything over.

I died three times getting past that Manol vané assassin, and another five making it out of the ambush. Every fatal misstep was followed by a bright flash as I restarted far enough back to figure out where I'd gone wrong. A swing of the sword this way, a step to the side, the realization that being too timid in the wrong circumstances was as bad as rushing forward in others.

I learned by dying, and every death carried me further forward.

Then we were moving, running, driving our enemies back with spell, bow, and sword. We crested a platform strung between two giant branches.

Before us lay the Mother of Trees.

I didn't understand what I was seeing. I couldn't comprehend. It just seemed like a humongous wall at first, one that had been built up with palaces and verandas, graceful pavilions, and stained-glass windows glittering like jewels. Only when I looked up could I perceive the sweep of branches, the distant velvet of green leaves. This was a tree to hold up the whole world, the sort of place where Galava must live, if any place were consecrated to her. It seemed ageless and immortal, a tree that had always and would always exist.

Naturally, we were setting it on fire.

I swallowed bile as I saw the fires scarring its bark, the signs of violence burning those beautiful forms. The metal bridge formed in front of us, making up for the one that had been cut away in a last-ditch effort to defend this bastion.

But we could not be stopped.

I wanted to ask questions. I wanted to say something. Could I order them to turn around? Who was right here? Was anyone right? I felt my sympathy sliding toward the Manol vané purely because I found myself flinching at the destruction of their homeland. I didn't know what the Manol vané's Khaevatz had done to so upset the Kirpis vané's king. She had never, as far as Surdyeh had taught me, sided with Quur or aided Kandor. She had slain the Quuros Emperor, not helped him.

This was all wrong.

My companions shared none of my reservations. They plowed through all opposition. There were a few more bright flashes, a few more restarted narrations, as I failed to stop attacks. I was certain these would have been no problem at all for the Kirpis vané king I pretended to be. Never had I been so aware of how little Darzin had taught me of fighting techniques. Six months of training with Kalindra and Szzarus was not enough to make up for a lifetime where I had never touched the hilt of a sword, except to steal it.

My guards pushed open massive doors carved with jungle animals and hunting birds, all surrounding an enormous carved tree whose inspiration needed no explanation. The halls were empty, but any vané who might have guarded them had already thrown themselves into defense of the palace elsewhere. We walked through unimpeded.

Finally, we reached a hall deep inside the tree itself. At the far end of the hall, branches from the main tree had been sculpted and trained until they formed a chair. A woman sat in the chair, composed and calm.

Her skin was black, so dark it looked blue at the highlights, and her hair was a dark green fall of silk that reminded me of the underside of a fern. Her eyes were green and brown and all the colors of the hallway they reflected. She wore a gown of green silk and feathers that looked like it had been woven from dreams.

"Khaevatz," I said, the word escaping my lips so thoroughly without my intention that for a moment I thought someone else had said her name. She was a figure out of legend, a name whispered even in Quur with reverence, fear, and awe. She was as old as the world itself, alive to see the rise of every nation, god-king, and monster.

Surdyeh used to say that when Queen Khaevatz finally died, the whole world wept at her loss.*

She tilted her head, regal and almost painfully gorgeous. "Terindel. Shall we finish this at last?"

I nearly choked. Teraeth's father, Terindel? That was the wrong name . . .

Sir Rabbit made a gurgling sound as a Manol vané revealed himself and sliced open the white-skinned vané's throat.

They had one last ambush prepared for us.

I shouted and swung at the assassin, but he was obscenely fast. Clos-

---

*In a sense. There was a freak weather phenomenon that year that covered much of the continent with a giant and rather spectacular storm. The argument can indeed be made that the storm was not natural, and thus "the world wept."

ing in on him was suicide, but I managed to distract him with the hilt of a thrown dagger while one of my men took care of him with a spell. More Manol vané appeared, more defenders giving their lives for their queen. Which they did, but the Manol vané took everyone they could with them.

I wouldn't have survived. A dozen times over I wouldn't have survived. Although each time I died I began again, free from injury, my body felt like I had swung every blow and dodged every arrow. I was tired. No, that was too light a word. I was exhausted.

At last I was alone in the throne room with Khaevatz, who had not moved a hair's breadth from her seat the entire time.

"Surrender!" I called out. Surrender was the proper thing to ask, right? She didn't die here. I *knew* Khaevatz didn't die here. It would be centuries yet before she breathed her last.

"Poor little king," a man's voice mocked. "How bitter the gall must taste, to have traveled so far, conquered so much, and yet still lose."

I blinked. The image of Khaevatz wavered, then broke like a stone tossed into the reflection on a pond. The stone in question was a Manol vané man, stepping through the illusion of the queen and walking down the steps toward me.

It was Teraeth.

"Ter–" The word died on my lips. No, this was not Teraeth. They looked enough alike to be brothers, yes, but the voice was different, the posture, the manner. This was a man with the green-gray eyes of a hurricane-tossed sky and hair as black as the ocean depths. He held a single sword in his hand, and his open shirt gave me a glimpse of the emerald-green tsali stone around his neck, the very same stone Doc wore.

"Queen Khaevatz sends her apologies, but she can't be in attendance. She's meeting with your brother, Prince Kelindel–soon to be King Kelindel, I believe–over what should be done about the whole Emperor Kandor business. He's quite willing to put the entire vané race to the torch to make up for your crimes." The man strode down the steps toward me. His smile was malice. "I've been honored with the privilege of ensuring that Prince Kelindel's path to the throne is clear. Congratulations. You've united our peoples after all, if not in the way you had in mind."

I had no more chances to protest or ask questions. Whatever my role in this weird reenactment of ancient vané history, this man was coming at me with a weapon.

He meant business.

He swung at me. I ducked while I tried to bring up my sword. I felt a razor-hot burn against my arm, his sword sliding down to nick at a weak spot in my armor. Normally that would be enough to start the scene over, since the Manol vané seemed so fond of poisoned weapons.

It didn't.

I rushed forward, hoping I might throw him off by attacking. He took a step to the side, swung at me, and I saw my opening.

I stabbed for it, seeing the feint too late. His look was contemptuous as his sword ran me through.

My vision went black.

There was no flash of light that time.

48: Family Dinner

(Talon's story)

Aunt Tishar (technically Kihrin's great-great-aunt) peered at him from across the table. "Darzin mentioned you're a musician."

She looked younger than Therin—in her midtwenties, surely—and Kihrin reminded himself that she was old enough to be Surdyeh's grandmother. The vané traits were pronounced on her; it wasn't difficult to believe her mother had been pure-blooded. Her hair sparkled golden and her eyes were so pure a blue they seemed unnatural.

She looked a lot like Kihrin.

The resemblance wasn't as close as that painting of her brother Pedron, but it was there. In her appearance, Kihrin traced the origins of his own blue eyes, his own yellow hair. She was, like her long-dead brother Pedron, proof that claiming Kihrin as a D'Mon wasn't a mistake.

Dinner was the only meal that brought the whole family together, eaten in a grand dining room large enough to swallow armies. Kihrin had been dismayed to realize how large his new family was. There were easily a hundred people present with some right to the D'Mon name, spread out over a dozen tables whose position indicated their proximity to the heights of favor and power.

Kihrin would have rather sat at one of the back tables, shielded from Darzin's glare, but Taja's luck was not with him. Kihrin was expected to sit at the table with his father, Darzin, his grandfather the High Lord Therin, and their immediate family. Even so, he doubted he could name half the people at the table, uncles and aunts he had rarely, if ever, seen.

Kihrin nodded as he ate. "Yes, my lady. I'm better at singing than playing though." He picked at the food on his gold-rimmed plate. He still wasn't used to the way the nobility ate their meals: the current course, one of a half dozen, was a small piece of rare salmon in a delicate cream sauce. Kihrin didn't think it was bad, but it was very bland to his taste, and he wished the dish had come with a selection of pepper relishes or voracress sauce.

"How droll." Alshena D'Mon snickered as she finished her third glass of wine. "Though I suppose it's better than the skills you might have picked up in those slums, with that pretty face of yours."

Kihrin gritted his teeth and glared.

Darzin's wife giggled as if she scored a point.

"Mother, please . . ." Galen whispered from next to her.

"Awww, my son thinks I'm being scandalous," Alshena teased Galen with a grin, but the boy frowned and looked down at his lap.

"And how is that new, Alshena?" Uncle Bavrin commented.

She laughed and fanned herself.

"You'll play at the New Year's Festival masquerade, of course?" Tishar continued, ignoring the tipsy matron.

"Absolutely not!" Darzin said. "A D'Mon playing at entertainment like he was common help? Will not happen."

"I'm not that good anyway, Aunt Tishar," Kihrin agreed.

"Qoran wrote me a letter in which he said you were the best he's ever heard," Therin said. Up until that point in the conversation, Kihrin would have sworn the High Lord was paying no attention at all to their chattering. "The High General has already agreed to attend our masquerade. You'll play a song for him from that harp he's presented you."

"Father—" Darzin was furious.

"He'll play, Darzin. That's final."

Kihrin watched the two share a murderous look across the table. Darzin was the first to back down. "Yes, sir."

"That gives you three months to practice." Tishar leaned over and whispered to Kihrin. "I bet we'll have all the royal daughters drooling over themselves."

Darzin, who was close enough to hear her whisper, stopped and guffawed loudly. "Now I see what your game is, Tish. You want to find him a wife. Give it a rest, the boy's fifteen!"

"You and Alshena weren't much older when you married," Tishar replied.

"Look how well that turned out," Uncle Devyeh muttered under his breath.

Darzin either had the good grace to ignore him, or, more likely, simply hadn't heard. Alshena did though, and stared daggers at her brother-in-law.

"I'd give it a little time," Darzin said. "Give people a chance to forget that his mother was a common whore."

"Don't you mean common slut, sir?" Kihrin corrected.

All conversation stopped at the table.

Darzin stared at him. "What did you just say?"

"I said she was a common slut, Father. Lyrilyn was a slave, right? So she couldn't really sell her body. It wasn't hers to sell. Thus, she couldn't be a whore. But she could be, and frankly, was probably required to be, sexually willing. And she was almost certainly a commoner. Thus, my mother was a common slut." He stopped. "But you had to free her before you could marry her, didn't you?"

Darzin glared. "Yes . . ."

"Then I apologize, Father. You were right. She was a common whore."

There was silence. Family at the table stared at Kihrin, mouths open. Alshena was frozen in perfect shock and Darzin's face had turned an unflattering shade of purple.

Lady Miya started laughing.

Her laughter was magical, a building ring of crystalline bells. Any retort, threat, or violent outburst Darzin might have planned was overturned by the sound; everyone at the table looked at her before they began to chuckle themselves. Therin gazed at his seneschal with astonishment, allowing himself the rare honor of a smile.

Only Darzin continued to murder Kihrin with his eyes.

Bavrin grinned, looked over at Uncle Devyeh, and said, "I guess that settles it."

Devyeh nodded. "Quite."

"Settles what?" Alshena asked, her voice dangerous.

Bavrin jerked a thumb in Kihrin's direction. "He's one of us, all right."

Tishar raised an eyebrow. "Was there ever any doubt? The boy is the mirror twin of Pedron."

Lord Therin snorted. "Let's hope he's less depraved."

Darzin dropped his knife and fork with a loud clatter on his plate, and even the High Lord paused. "Son," Darzin began. "You're done tonight. Go to your room."

The newest member of the D'Mon family stared back in obvious amazement. "What? But what did I–?"

"NOW! To your room."

"You're the one who called her a whore," Kihrin protested.

Darzin stood then, his face still red and his nostrils flared with rage.

"Fine!" Kihrin stood up from his seat and ran out of the room. No one tried to stop him, or indeed said anything at all, to him or to each other.

Kihrin was halfway down the main hall when he heard footsteps behind him–hard, fast, angry clacks against the marble tiles. He turned just as Darzin, face contorted in anger, punched Kihrin in the jaw.

"Don't you–ever–" Darzin hit Kihrin again, this time in the arm as Kihrin raised a hand to defend himself. "Mouth off to me in front of family. I will *kill* you. You understand me, boy? I will fucking kill you."

He drew back to hit the young man again, but this time Darzin hit the tall brass vase Kihrin brought between them. Darzin howled while his son backed away.

Kihrin's lip was bleeding and his jaw swollen, but he sneered as he looked as his father. "What have you told me about watching your language, Father?"

Darzin stopped and stared at the boy, his expression one of fury and incredulity. "Are you actually baiting me, boy? Are you that fucking stupid?"

Kihrin laughed with mocking delight. His eyes were glazed, the gleam of someone pushed so far they passed beyond all caring of consequence. "I must be; I hear it runs in the family."

For a moment, Darzin simply glared at the young man with flat, dead eyes. "Then let's do something stupid together. It'll be a bonding moment. I wonder how well you'll play the harp for that stinking fat general without any thumbs?" Darzin unsheathed a dagger from his belt.

Any humor, sarcastic or otherwise, left Kihrin as he considered his father's insane eyes and realized that Darzin truly intended to do it. He backed away, slowly, while his father advanced.

Kihrin swallowed bile, and tried to reason with the man. "The High Lord expects me to play . . ."

"My father," Darzin said, "should be used to not getting what he wants by now. I very much doubt he'll even attend."

"You do this," Kihrin said, "and you better kill me. Because if you leave me alive you won't live long to regret it."

"Promises, promises," Darzin replied. He reached out and grabbed for the young man, but Kihrin ducked under the hand. Darzin pushed out his leg for Kihrin to trip over, and as the boy stumbled he grabbed the back of Kihrin's shirt, and when that ripped, the back of Kihrin's hair.

Kihrin screamed, and flailed back an elbow, but didn't hit anything important. He was all too aware that his father held an unsheathed dagger in his free hand and was contemplating where best to use it.

"Let's cut that face a little," Darzin said. "It'll give the healers something to practice on."

Kihrin threw himself forward. He felt the hair on his scalp start to rip, but it gave him the leverage to kick back with one leg and catch his father in the groin. Darzin's hold on him let go, for just a second. Kihrin ran through a side door, every bit as afraid for his life as if he were still a Key running from the Watchmen.

Darzin was through the same door a few seconds later, but he stopped and frowned. The parlor was empty and dark, with only the moonlight from the Sisters shining in from the window to give any real illumination. He paced around the room several times before looking out an open window. Darzin D'Mon noted the long drop to the ground as well as the climbing trellis that would have made descent safe and easy for someone trained in a life of crime. He cursed.

"You can't treat him like Galen," a stern voice called from the doorway.

"He's mine to do with as I wish," Darzin said as High Lord Therin stepped into the room.

"Just as you are mine, my son, and what you are doing is unacceptable. If you want someone to abuse, buy a slave for the task. Since you have decided to bring that boy into this house as your heir, you will treat him appropriately."

Darzin stopped and looked at his father. "Did I imagine the 'or else' at the end of that sentence?"

"You have excellent hearing."

"Or else what?" Darzin's expression was spiteful. "Perhaps you have forgotten—it is this family's good name and rank that I am protecting here."

"Oh, you're protecting something," Therin said, "but I have my doubts that it is the honor of House D'Mon."

Darzin's eyes narrowed. "Don't threaten me. I know secrets you would rather leave buried."

Therin smiled. "Go ahead. Tell the world. I'll be the talk of a few social clubs—a bit of salacious gossip to fire the cold blood stirring in harpy veins. My secrets are merely embarrassing—they are not treasonous."

"Pedron was your father," Darzin snapped. "Where was your loyalty?"

"Pedron was nothing but a villain who cuckolded the man who raised me," Therin corrected. "I showed that dastard as much loyalty as he deserved."

"You don't know—"

"You may have been just a child during the Affair of the Voices, and so your role was not suspected, but don't think for a moment that I didn't realize where you were spending your nights. My own son. I willingly and gladly handed over Pedron, but not my own child, something which you have given me cause to regret on numerous occasions since."

"You would be just as culpable," Darzin said, after a long and shocked pause, "for hiding me."

"Perhaps so," Therin admitted. "The difference is that I can quite easily be pushed to the point where I no longer care. You, on the other hand, will always be the most important thing in your world. If we must play a game of bluff, I will win, for the simple reason that I am never bluffing."

Darzin clenched his teeth together. "I should have killed that slut myself when I realized she was pregnant."

Therin slapped his son across the face. "Be gone from my sight,"

Therin whispered, harsh and furious. His anger was trademark D'Mon: lethal, deadly menace.

Even Darzin was taken aback. He stared at his father for a moment, before turning on his heel and walking out the door.

The High Lord watched him go, then walked over to a side table. He poured himself a glass of sasabim and stared at the glass for a dozen or so seconds. Then he sat down by the fireplace. He didn't drink at first, staring at the unlit woodpile.

After a moment he said, "You can come out now. I know you're here."

Kihrin stood up from where he had sat motionless, his shadow blending with the curtains behind him. He pressed a handkerchief against the side of his face, which was swollen and bleeding.

"How did you know?" the young man asked.

The High Lord shrugged. "When I was younger I befriended a man who had a similar magical talent. I've learned to recognize the way the mind slides away from a corner of the room. Also, the dogs."

"The dogs?"

"Yes," Therin said as he gestured toward the open window with his drink. "Dogs. They patrol the open court, and you are too new for them to be used to your scent. Had you left by the window, I would have heard them barking."

"What was the Affair of the Voices?" Kihrin asked.

Therin sighed. "Something that happened before you were born."

"I think I need to know."

Therin stared at the boy for a moment, before nodding. "The various Royal Families are known as the Court of Gems. Or rather we like to call ourselves royalty, but we are not true rulers and have not been since the founding of the Empire. We did something. No one is sure what anymore. It's a secret lost to the ages.* All anyone knows is that it was terrible, so terrible that the Eight Immortals spat down a curse on us, and a fate. They decreed that no member of a Royal Family would ever rule in the Quuros Empire, save those few who could win the right to be Emperor. If so much as a single member of a family breaks this taboo, the gods have promised to come down and wipe out that family down to the last babe. So the Court of Gems rules by proxy, through the Ogenra we push into power with granted lands and titles, and through the representatives we elect to be Voices. We are merchant princes, our strengths economic and our politics republican. It is enough for most of us, but some pine for old days so long ago when we made the laws—and we decided who lived and who died ourselves. Twenty-some years ago, a secret

---

*Not that lost. The Royal Families murdered Emperor Simillion, and the gods were annoyed because he had been in the middle of doing something for them.

cabal formed to change this status quo. They believed they were the cul-
mination of a prophecy, fated to destroy the Empire." Therin's mouth
twisted. "Presumably to make it over, gloriously renewed. People are always so willing to plow under fertile crops and murder nations if they can
convince themselves they'll be planting the seeds of something better."

"Wizard, thief, knight, and king, the children will not know the names
of their fathers who quiet the Voices' sting. That prophecy?"

Therin frowned, and leaned forward toward Kihrin. "Where did you
hear that?"

"It was a rich man's idea of graffiti. Which one was Pedron? The wizard?"

Therin narrowed his eyes. "No. Thief. Pedron didn't grow up in the
Upper Circle. His mother smuggled him out of the palace before her
death, and he grew up in the Lower Circle. When he was reclaimed by
House D'Mon he'd already formed the Shadowdancers." He waved a few
fingers dismissively. "Gadrith D'Lorus had believed that the prophecy
referenced Ogenra children of various noble houses who were later
claimed and made legitimate. Children who would overthrow the Voices
and 'quiet their sting.'"

Kihrin whistled. "Gadrith D'Lorus? Gadrith the Twisted was part of
this?"

"Oh yes. He was the 'wizard.' There were a few others, all dead now.
I never thought Gadrith did a particularly good job of shoehorning people
into the prophecy roles he wanted, but there's no reasoning with someone who thinks they're the Chosen One." He sighed. "It makes me sick
to think that Darzin was helping that disgusting little cabal." As he stared
into the fireplace, Therin's eyes were haunted with an emotion that Kihrin
had never seen in a D'Mon's stare: shame.

But shame was not the feeling that rose within him. He turned on his
grandfather and said, "So how long do you intend to keep covering up
for Darzin?"

Therin's eyes flicked back over to Kihrin. "I have been liberal with
you. Do not push your luck."

"Someone has to," Kihrin retorted. He wiped more blood off his face
with the handkerchief. "I'm curious: what's it going to take before you
do something about him? Hard proof that he's broken the gods' own laws?
How many people will he have to kill or torture? I'm starting to get the
idea that when people talk about a fate worse than death, what they mean
is someone unlucky enough to end up as one of your son's slaves. Do
you have any idea what he does to them?"

"He owns them. He can legally do what he likes."

"Sure, and he 'owns' his children too, and obviously the fact that he
beats his own children whenever the whim takes him doesn't seem to

bother you. There's plenty of Lower Circle thugs with no more education than the gods gave fish who would be embarrassed to treat their
own blood that way. So what's the line that Darzin has to cross? I really
want to know. Torture? Murder? Rape?"

"Enough!" Therin shouted, throwing his glass to the ground where it
shattered in punctuation to his rage. "Don't you dare speak to me in this
way."

Kihrin sneered. "What are you gonna do, old man? Hit me too?"

Therin's jaw worked noiselessly, as he stared at Kihrin.

The young man shook his head. "I guess I take after you more than
Darzin, because just like you, I can be pushed to the point where I don't
care anymore. That bastard took everything I loved from me. Everything. But don't go patting yourself on the back because you protected
me, because you let him do it–"

"I never–"

"You did!" Kihrin screamed. "He summons demons and he murders
people and he commits treason and you cover it up . . . What is that possibly going to teach a man like Darzin–except that he can do whatever
he feels like and you'll always be there to clean up his shit? And you can
sit here and feel sorry for yourself, at your great nobility and restraint in
dealing with your rabid dog of a son. Well, you know what? You made
that rabid dog the way he is, so there's nothing noble about your refusal
to put him down."

Therin did not reply, but he looked mortally wounded. Slowly, he
slumped down in the chair, his gaze on the floor. Kihrin found himself
growing angrier, and his desire to lash out grew more intense.

"I hope you're proud of your boy," Kihrin spat. "As far as I'm concerned, you deserve each other."

After Kihrin left, Therin sat there and stared at the unlit fireplace for
several hours, only leaving to fetch a new glass and bottle of liquor. He
was still there when Lady Miya finally came looking for him, and put
him to bed.

49: CRITICAL LESSONS

(Kihrin's story)

When I woke, I lay facedown—drooling onto the black rock floor of the training room. I ached all over. My arms, my neck, my shoulders, my thighs, and my calves. Every part of me felt like I was back in the rowing galley of *The Misery*.

I groaned and raised my head. Doc sat a small distance away. He'd thrown out the tea and replaced it with a bottle of wine, and he had poured a cup for himself. He was staring at my borrowed harp, although given the unfocused gaze on his face, he wasn't seeing the harp at all.

When I made a sound, Doc looked over, saw me, and stood up. He didn't look happy.

"That was pathetic," Doc said as he walked over. He didn't offer me a hand up. "How many times did you die? Three dozen? Four? What was Darzin teaching you? The most efficient way to impale yourself on your enemy's sword?"

I almost defended Darzin, but I stopped myself in time. My so-called father had only trained me in fighting so he'd have an excuse to punish my lack of progress. "You drugged me. Let's talk about the fact that you drugged me!"

"I told you I wouldn't go easy on you."

I took a deep breath and bit back on the impulse to start shouting. The drugging wasn't the important part, anyway. "I'm familiar with riscoria weed. It doesn't cause visions like that. How did you *do* that?"

He seemed pleased I'd noticed, and he tapped the green tsali stone around his neck. It was the same stone the Manol vané had been wearing, the one who'd taunted and killed me in the vision.

The exact same stone.

"Chainbreaker," he said.

I blinked. "I'm sorry. What?"

Doc chuckled at my confusion. "You wear the Stone of Shackles. I wear its brother, Chainbreaker. You and I are part of a very small and exclusive club with only eight members in the whole world."

I traced the stone around my neck. "Eight? There are eight of these?"

"Yes. Each with its own powers, gifts, and curses." He pursed his lips. "So let's talk about your training."

"No. I want to talk about the Stone of Shackles and Chainbreaker. I want to talk about that illusion you put in my mind."

Doc sighed and rolled his eyes toward the ceiling. Suddenly, he wasn't there anymore.

The tip of his sword pricked the skin of my neck so quickly I'm not sure I saw him move as more than a faint blur. "You want real? This is real, young man." A small drop of red welled up on my collarbone, just above the Stone of Shackles, which burned ice-cold in case there was any doubt of my teacher's earnestness. "What is *real* is that you have entered a world that hates you and is only too glad to leave your decaying corpse slapped across the garbage heaps of life. What is real is that you have neither the training nor the skill you require to survive until your next birthday. What is real is that hiding in a cave from monsters like Relos Var is no way to have a life at all."

"I can't leave," I spat back, although I didn't lean forward the way I might have otherwise, in consideration of that sword. "You can't have missed the dragon out there. He'll kill me if I try to leave."

Doc laughed in an unfriendly way. "The Old Man isn't going to kill you. You wear the Stone of Shackles."

"I know that! But that's not going to stop–" I paused.

"You don't even know what that means, do you?"

I stared at him. "It would kill him. I know that much."

Truthfully, I'd assumed the damn thing wouldn't work on a dragon. That he would be immune to whatever magic this rock possessed. I stared down at the stone. I thought I might scream if it turned out I'd had the power to leave the island this whole time, but there was only one way to find out. Ask.

"What does it do?"

"If I killed you right now while you wore that chunk of rock, your body would still die, but the Stone of Shackles would switch our souls. My soul, and not yours, would be the one to go stand before Thaena, while you would find yourself enjoying a new body. Specifically, you'd find yourself enjoying *my* body. Not necessarily a situation to your liking unless you're impatient to become middle-aged and soft around the center." He chuckled, seeming to find that idea more amusing than I did.

I felt like the stone floor had just shifted. A hundred little pieces fell into place. Why Talon had refused to kill me. Why Miya had given Lyrilyn the Stone of Shackles. Why it had seemed like that same stone had failed to protect Lyrilyn from being murdered.

That wasn't how the Stone of Shackles worked. Lyrilyn died, but Lyrilyn's soul lived on–in the body of the mimic who had slain her.

A few other things fell into place too.

I raised my hand, wrapped my fingers around the edge of his sword, and slowly pushed the blade away. I pulled a chair away from the table and sat down.

Not much time had passed while I was unconscious, though it seemed like lifetimes for me. The lamps were still lit, although the oil level had gone down. The tea was cold, but the bread was not yet stale. An hour at most.

"In the vision," I said, "I was wearing the Stone of Shackles. I was Terindel–I was *King* Terindel. I was wearing the Stone of Shackles when I was killed by a Manol vané who just happens to resemble Teraeth more than a little . . ."

Doc raised an eyebrow and motioned for me to continue.

"You"–I pointed at him–"said Teraeth's father was a fool and an idiot."

"Doc" Terindel chuckled and drank the cup of wine. "Yes, well. I would know, would I? I've had almost five hundred years to contemplate how my hubris lost me the Kirpis crown. I was a fool and an idiot, and it cost me everything." He flicked thumb and forefinger against Chainbreaker; a bell tone rang. "I've gotten so good at using this hunk of gem I forget I'm wearing an illusion sometimes."

And the illusion fell.

He looked exactly the same as the Manol vané man I'd seen in the vision, the one who'd struck that final blow for his queen. The clothes were different, but that was all. He certainly didn't look like Terindel the Kirpis vané, the man who'd led his forces against the Manol vané.

But I knew it was him.

Terindel had been killed by a black-skinned Manol vané, and since he'd been wearing the Stone of Shackles at the time, he'd survived–in the body of the man who'd slain him.

"When that trinket around your neck was first given to me," Terindel explained, "I never wanted to use it. It would save my life but at the cost of my throne. That's the problem with 'royalty,' you know. It rests on the laughable idea that your body, your bloodline, is worthier of virtue than your skills, your intellect, your soul. And the Stone of Shackles doesn't care about bloodlines. I became, literally, the thing I hated: one of those impure Manol vané."

"Wow. Uh, so . . . do you still think . . . uh, I mean . . ." I cleared my throat.

"Am I still screamingly racist? No, I like to think I've gained a bit of perspective." He set down the cup, sheathed his sword. "You are never more vulnerable than in the moments after your soul switches with your killer's. The stone doesn't come with you, and many of the skills that we

rely on for survival, from swordplay to spellcasting, are tied to the training and talent of our bodies. As soon as I realized what had happened,
I ran. I didn't have time to pick up the Stone of Shackles, but my new
body was already wearing Chainbreaker. Important lesson there: you're
not immune to the effects of a Cornerstone just because you're wearing
one of the others."

I nodded. That too made sense. Lyrilyn hadn't taken the time to pick
up the Stone of Shackles either. Or if she had, she'd only had time to
tuck it into my swaddling clothes. "What about Valathea?"

He glanced over at the borrowed harp. "I don't know what you mean."

"Your queen. Your wife. She was supposed to be taken to safety."

Terindel's jaw tightened. "She was betrayed. They sentenced her to the
Traitor's Walk." He paused. "I think we're done here. You should rest."

"I think I'm going to go have another chat with the Old Man."

Doc stared at me. "That's not wise."

I stood up from my chair, intent on running back to the beach.

"You can't leave," he told me.

"Watch me," I snapped. Then my body betrayed me. The whole universe tilted on its axis, flipped, and spilled me down against that smooth
rock floor.

50: THE LORD HEIR'S WIFE

(Talon's story)

Kihrin arrived back in his rooms in a rage. All the simmering frustrations and anger that had boiled inside of him for months overflowed in a torrent. How could any man be so unfeeling? Therin didn't care. Therin was an emotionless monster with no regard for his so-called family. Therin had told him the D'Mons weren't a real family, but until that moment Kihrin had thought it was just hyperbole for the new kid. Now he believed. As long as Therin had Darzin around to tyrannize the lives around them, the old man never needed to dirty his own hands.

Kihrin felt a homicidal urge to destroy, but his rooms had been secured against petty vandalism. There were few chairs, and the cloth draperies made unsatisfying victims. The supply of pottery broke nicely, but was soon exhausted.

Then Kihrin saw the harp.

It sat just where Therin's servants had left it, right where he'd ignored it ever since its arrival. It squatted like a malignant vulture, overseeing death and pain and hate. The High General had said its name meant sorrow. Well named, since it was the cause of the greatest sorrows of his life. He advanced on the harp, picked the thing up in his hands, raised his arms high–

"If you destroy that, darling, whatever will you play for the High General?" Alshena D'Mon's voice called from the doorway. She walked inside, fanning her face. She was always fanning her face to keep her plaster-thick makeup from running. "Not that I particularly care, ducky, but I do think you'll regret this in the morning."

Kihrin caught his breath and lowered the harp. Her sharp voice cut right through his soaring anger. He felt weak. "I didn't hear you knock, Lady." He looked away. Kihrin was in no mood to deal with his father's tipsy wife and her barbed jokes.

Alshena smiled. "I didn't. I'm a terribly rude creature, but I do believe I heard the sound of breaking pottery."

Kihrin looked over at the heaps of damp soil and broken porcelain.

"Yeah. Uh—I was just—redecorating. I'm fine. I don't really want company right now, if it's all the same."

Alshena raised a well-lacquered eyebrow. "Of course," she agreed. "I only came by to thank you."

"Thank me?" Kihrin leaned against one of the four-poster tree trunks of his bed, his equilibrium gone.

Alshena nodded. "Yes, I might have been concerned when I saw Darzin follow you out after dinner—" To his complete surprise, she looked embarrassed. "I admit your conversations with both my husband and father-in-law were rather loud, and could be heard quite clearly from down the hall. I hope Darzin didn't hurt you too badly."

Kihrin looked at his feet. "Oh. No. Just a split lip. I have a salve for it."

"Thank you." She said the sentence as if its utterance hurt. "It's not easy to stand up to my husband. You're either very brave or very stupid, and though I haven't quite decided which yet, I have decided I like you." Her eyes were glassy bright from all the wine at dinner.

Kihrin sat down on the bed. His tongue felt thick and immobile. He couldn't think of anything to say that wouldn't sound trite.

Alshena nodded, and turned to leave. At the door, she paused to face him once more. "I didn't believe you were Darzin's son until tonight."

Kihrin looked up at her with a stricken expression. "But now you do?"

Alshena looked around the room. "May I come in? I know you didn't want company, but I find I really do."

"Well, someone seems to have, uh . . . dropped some dishes. It's kind of a mess." He looked around for a chair, but the room wasn't designed for entertaining.

He was about to suggest they go to the patio when she pointed. "I'll sit on the bed."

"What would people say?"

"Nothing, unless you tell them," Alshena replied. "And you don't strike me as the gossipy type." She sat on the green linens and arranged her agolé around her legs. Kihrin fought the urge to tell her it was proper for a lady to pull her agolé down when she sat, not up, but the flash of leg had given him an uncomfortably strong mental image of the rest of her—he was still fighting off demon flashbacks.

"Do you have anything to drink?" Alshena asked once she was positioned to her satisfaction. "I could use a drink in the worst way."

Kihrin paused. He shrugged, embarrassed. "I'm sorry—I don't know. I'm sure there's a wine cabinet hidden around here somewhere . . ."

"Go look. I'll wait, ducky."

He stared at her for a moment, but Alshena showed no inclination to leave, and seemed oblivious to his feelings on the matter. She picked at the bark of one of the corner posts with a long red-lacquered fingernail.

Kihrin sighed, and looked for something he could give her so she'd go away. After a few moments, the young man returned with a wine bottle and two glasses. "I found this." He poured one glass, but as he began to pour the second Alshena stopped him, leaving the second glass with only a small amount of sparkling gold liquid.

"I am old enough to drink," Kihrin reproached her.

Alshena smiled sagaciously. "I'm sure, but why don't you read the label of this excellent bottle of wine you've found?"

Kihrin studied the bottle. The writing on it was unfamiliar to him, a strange spidery script. "I can't read this."

Alshena nodded. "It's vané." She took the smaller second glass and stared at its contents critically. "There's more than enough here to–how would your friends say it in the Lower Circle?–'knock me on my ass,' I believe."

Kihrin stared at the glass like it held snake venom. Finally, noticing the faint mocking grin on his stepmother's face, he shrugged and took a sip.

It was fire, then a shivering rush of euphoria. A wave of excitement raced through him, lighting every inch of his body's nerves to the experience of being. He smelled the soil from the pots and the rose hips and lemon peel of Alshena's perfume. Then the feeling faded as the sip ended.

"Damn."

Alshena beamed. "Strong stuff. I suppose I should thank Lady Miya for this next time I see her."

Kihrin looked up from the wineglass. "Lady Miya? Did she put this here?"

Alshena shrugged. "I have to assume. These rooms were hers once, after all."

He frowned and shook his head. "These rooms belonged to the High Lord's late wife."

"Lady Norá? Yes, they did." Alshena coughed. "And Miya was Norá's handmaiden. Then Norá died and Miya took over these rooms, and your mother Lyrilyn was *her* handmaiden. Look at this bed and tell me that a vané didn't sleep here." She gave him a look suggesting he was being very naïve indeed.

"So why did she give it up? Why aren't these still her rooms?"

"That, my young stepson, is one of the other great scandals of House D'Mon." She sipped the wine just a little, expressing an obvious shiver of delight at the effects. "You see, when Lady Norá died, Darzin must have been, oh, ten years old? It's been well over twenty-five years. Anyway, Lady Norá died giving birth to his brother, Devyeh, and the priests of Thaena wouldn't Return her."

"That's not unusual," Kihrin said. "They refuse people all the time."

"Yes, but Therin had been a priest of Thaena—before he'd looked around one day and found eight people in line ahead of him had all mysteriously died.* That was what made him High Lord. Did you know that? Anyway, and here he is, High Lord of the Physickers, and his wife dies in childbirth? And his goddess won't bring back the only woman he'd ever loved? He severed all ties with the priests that day, and crawled into a bottle to nurse his wounds."

"This was the Affair of the Voices?"

"Just after," Alshena said, "and the House just about fell apart. We came very close to not having a House D'Mon."

He snickered. "Oh, the tragedy. What saved the House?"

"Who. Miya. She moved into these apartments next to Therin and started issuing orders, claiming they had come from the High Lord himself. Most of the healers knew it was a lie, but everyone was so desperate they went along with it." Alshena paused in the middle of her tale and added, "Now think about that piece of information, my sweet. Lady Miya comes off as an angel made flesh, but she ran this house like a general for two years and we moved up in rank during her tenure. I will never underestimate that woman; saints do not prosper in this town."

"You told me she was a sheltered veal calf."

"I lie a lot. It's part of my charm." She winked at the young man.

He laughed and shook his head. "She had the suite decorated like this?"

"I'm not really sure. It was before I married Darzin. It could be that she did, or it's possible that Therin ordered it as a sort of thank-you for her assistance. But by the time I came onto the scene, this suite was already vacant."

"Do you know why?" Kihrin tucked his legs up under himself as he sat on the bed across from her.

"Darzin likes to say Therin came to his senses and realized he was letting the house be run by a slave and a female too, so he took back his power and put her in her place. Personally, I don't think she would be seneschal if Therin had just wanted to punish her for daring to save this House from extermination."†

Kihrin narrowed his eyes. "But that's not what you think happened."

Alshena stopped fanning herself. She clicked together the ivory blades of the fan and set it down on the bed next to her. "I think they fought over your mother."

*It really wasn't that mysterious. The family members that Pedron didn't sacrifice in order to summon demons died during the Affair of the Voices. It was a violent time.

†Additionally, not only did Therin D'Mon marry a Khorveshan woman, but all his daughters received private training and served in the army. Clearly Therin does not possess Darzin's overdeveloped sense of misogyny.

Kihrin started back, surprised by the unexpected answer. "Lyrilyn?"

Alshena nodded. "Yes. They were friends. Miya didn't like the attention that Darzin was giving Lyrilyn and told Therin to put a stop to it, and Therin refused."*

Kihrin looked away. "Of course."

"After that, Lyrilyn ran away. It caused a huge rift between Miya and Therin. Lady Miya moved out of this suite, which was then boarded up. The next year I married Darzin in an arrangement made between House D'Mon and House D'Aramarin. Today she runs the household and Therin–"

"Therin runs House D'Mon?"

"I was going to say hides in his rooms from the rest of the world, but sure, that works too."

"How old were you?" Kihrin asked. "You know, when you married my–when you married Darzin?"

Alshena pursed her lips. "Sixteen." Then she laughed. "Darzin was different then. He was handsome, charming, devastating. He–he was a stubborn young rake who didn't care who you were or what your position was. He told people what he thought of them, and be damned the consequences." She turned her stare to him. "A lot like you, dear."

Kihrin scowled as he drank more of the wine. "I don't want to believe I'm related to either of those bastards. I don't know who I hate more: Darzin or his father."

Alshena stood up from the bed and began to pace. She moved until she stood behind Kihrin. She smoothed down his hair, gathered it in her hands, and placed the gold locks over his right shoulder. Then she knelt over his left shoulder and whispered, very softly, "Do you know why Darzin beats Galen?"

Kihrin turned his head and stopped, realizing the gesture put his face provocatively close to hers. "He's a bully?"

"No," she said, still caressing his hair with her hand. "It's because he wants a son who's like him. Ruthless. Smart. Hard. Things Galen will never be. I love my son but I know his faults. He will never be what his father wants. How could he be? He's had it beaten out of him." Then Kihrin heard her intake of breath, and a ragged, gasping sigh.

He realized Alshena was crying.

His reaction was immediate and instinctive. Kihrin turned and put his arms around her. Although her proximity still produced troubling and uncomfortable flashbacks, he tried his best to ignore them. After a second's hesitation Alshena hugged him, and openly cried against his shirt. He let her sob, patting her hair with one hand while his other fist

*I don't believe any of this is true, although I do think Lyrilyn and Miya were close.

tightened into a ball around the bedsheets. Kihrin's whole world was filled with the rose and citrus scent of her skin, the pressure of her body through the suddenly thin fabric of her dress.

He reminded himself, repeatedly, that she was Galen's mother, twice his age, and he didn't like her. Unfortunately, she was soft and warm and clung to him in all the right ways, and Kihrin was more than a little drunk himself.

Finally, Alshena drew back. "Oh, I'm sorry. I'm so sorry, I just—it's so difficult sometimes."

"I can't even imagine what it's like to be married to that monster," Kihrin said.

"It's not like I had a choice. Oh dear, look how you're trembling!" She sniffled and wiped away her tears using the hem of her agolé, which pulled it far enough off her to reveal jeweled undergarments and little else.

Kihrin used the brief reprieve to stand up and walk away from his stepmother. He crossed his arms over his chest and inhaled deeply. "It's not because of you," he said.

Alshena wiped her face. Strangely, the makeup had the effect of aging her, and with less of it she did not seem nearly so old as before. Kihrin found it shocking: he was used to thinking of her as an unattractive, horrible clown creature. She was younger and prettier than several of the more successful whores who had worked at the Shattered Veil.

"Hmmph," she said. "A word of advice, dear boy: when a woman sees a man go to pieces like that in her presence, the last thing she wants to hear is, 'It's not because of you.'"

"There was a demon prince," Kihrin tried to explain. "He did things . . . put things in my mind . . . I can't . . ."

She blinked at him. "You're joking. You must be joking."

"It's—" He looked away, embarrassed.

"I wondered why you weren't sleeping with any of the slave girls," she commented.

Kihrin's head snapped back up. "You've been tracking that?"

She sniffed. "Of course we have. The first step to hooking you up with some appropriate and politically well-connected young lady is establishing whether you do, in fact, prefer young ladies." She paused. "Tishar and I were starting to wonder."

"Yeah, well . . ." He rubbed his arms. "You and Tishar can rest easy. I prefer girls. Usually. I mean—" He shivered. "Oh damn."

"Quite so, from the sounds of it." Alshena wiped the last of her makeup off her face. "What a lovely change of pace. Now we can go from awkward and uncomfortable silences discussing my husband and what a monster he is, to awkward and uncomfortable silences talking about your problems with sex." She raised an eyebrow. "I assume you can perform—I mean—you're not—"

He glared at her. "That is not the problem."

"Oh good. Excellent." Alshena smiled. "Then I know exactly what you should do."

"You do?" Kihrin asked.

"Oh yes." Alshena D'Mon examined the bottle of vané wine, then filled both of their glasses.

She said, "You should have another drink."

51: THE ROCK GARDEN

No. Stop right there, Talon. My turn again. And I warn you right now: if you try to describe the rest of that evening, I'm not playing anymore, no matter what kind of threats you make.

Are we clear?

Good.

Anyway, I woke to the sound of Khaemezra and Doc arguing.

"How many times are you going to make this same mistake, Khae?" Doc snapped. "You've got to stop treating people like enlisted soldiers. People aren't going to blindly follow your orders."

"I'm not asking him to blindly follow my orders," Khaemezra corrected. "Nor you. All I want from both of you is that you make sure he's ready."

"He didn't ask for this."

"Actually, he did."

Doc sighed. "I hope you appreciate how difficult this is. He's the spitting image of Pedron—and you know my feelings about Pedron."

So. That answered whether they were talking about Teraeth or me.

"Don't you mean he's the spitting image of King Terindel?" The venom in her voice could have melted stone.

Silence ruled. Khaemezra had struck too close with that comment. Doc needed time to recover from the attack. "Teraeth should have named himself after you," he finally said.

"Teraeth feels the lineage can be redeemed." There was a brief pause. "Don't call him a fool, just because you don't agree." Sounds of swishing fabric, growing soft. She was leaving, walking to the door.

"Just be careful, Khae. Don't make the same mistake with this one that you made last time."

She laughed. "As if I've only made that mistake once."

I held my breath as silence once more filled the room, interrupted only by the soft scuffs of the tiny voramer woman retreating.

A booted toe nudged my shoulder. "How much of that did you hear?"

I rolled over as I looked at my hands. Any injuries on them were long gone. I assumed I had Khaemezra to thank for that. "So Valathea was sentenced to the Traitor's Walk. What happened to her?"

"So, you heard most of our conversation, if not all of it." He scowled. "Get up. It's time to continue your lessons."

"Answer my questions first."

"I'm not here to answer your questions. I'm here to teach you how to fight."

I pretended I hadn't heard him. "You're not here as a favor to Therin or Khaemezra. You're here because I'm descended from Terindel. Not from you, technically, as you aren't in Terindel's original body anymore. But I'm guessing–" I made a moue. "What was your daughter's name? Valrashar? I'm guessing she ended up being sold as a slave. She was supposed to be executed along with your wife, Valathea, but someone decided to make a little metal on the side and she ended up being owned by the D'Mons, where she gave birth to Pedron and Tishar. Am I close?"

I thought he was going to ignore me. He picked up the loaf of dark bread and dropped it down on the ground next to me. Then he sat down on the stone floor, pulling his feet up into his lap.

"They told me Valrashar had died fighting," he said. "I never looked for her. My wife . . ." He grimaced. "I traveled deep into the Korthaen Blight, all the way to Kharas Gulgoth. I was too late to save her."

My throat tightened at the grief in Terindel's voice, still raw after centuries. "I'm sorry."

"I didn't have anywhere to go after that. Word had spread about who I really was. No vané would have anything to do with me. I met a woman–" He stopped and laughed at some secret humor. "I met a woman in Kharas Gulgoth. She'd been traveling with Valathea, been kind to her, so even though she was Quuros and human, I stayed my hand. I helped her. She was widowed herself, pregnant with her late husband's child, and I guess it seemed fitting that I protect her. Maybe I was just looking to do something right for once in my life."

"What . . . what happened?" I took the opportunity to finish off the rest of the bread.

"When Elana Milligreest went back to Khorvesh, I went with her. Nothing came of it for years; we were both in mourning. But I helped her raise her son and I came to view them as a new family. Sadly, they were a mortal family. Elana died and went to the Land of Peace and I looked after her children, and then *their* children. I became that odd cousin or uncle who's always popping in for holidays with gifts from his travels. I was going by the name Nikali when Qoran's mother asked if I might keep an eye on her troublemaking son, when he went to the Capital."

I blinked. "Nikali Milligreest? *You're* Nikali Milligreest, the swordsman? My father Surdyeh used to tell stories about you. The one where

you fought off those men behind the Temple of Khored and how you defeated–" I cleared my throat. "–how you defeated Gadrith the Twisted."

He snickered. "I love how awestruck you sounded right there. Several-
thousand-year-old vané king? Whatever. Khorveshan ne'er-do-well who
killed a few idiots in drunken duels? Set up the altar, boys, it's prayer
time."

"Well, I . . . I mean . . . there's some pretty cool stories about you, that's
all. What happened? You get tired of it all and change your name to Doc,
open a bar?"

"One gets tired of the hero worship. I also adopted a daughter."

"Tauna. I've met her. Khorveshan, right?"

"Naturally. She's a Milligreest actually, a second cousin of Qoran's.
Truth is, I had a lot of fun tagging around with Qoran. Got into some
trouble, did a good deed or two. And then . . ." He shook his head. "I
never realized my Valrashar had been a slave in the Capital the whole
time. Then I met Therin. The moment I saw him–I knew what must have
happened. Too late by then. She'd been dead at least a decade. Onto her
next life and rebirth, I suppose."

"Does Therin know?"

"Gods no. Hey buddy of mine, did you know that I was once your
great-grandfather? Though not anymore, because I've switched bodies
since then. Oh, also, your aunt Tishar is technically the long-lost heir to
the Kirpis vané throne, and if anything happens to her, you're next. Best
not to tell anyone; it would be awkward all around, but most especially
for the Kirpis vané."

"Yes, I suppose the fellow currently on the vané throne might take
objection to having competition."

"What competition? Tishar's welcome to lay claim to the Kirpis. I'm
sure Quur won't mind at all." He rolled his eyes.

I stood, trying to ignore the way my body protested. I couldn't believe
how sore I was. "If you don't mind, I have something else I need to do."

Doc crossed his arms over his chest. "I do mind. I played story time
with you. Now comes practice."

"Sorry for giving the wrong impression, but I wasn't asking permission." I grinned at him as I backpedaled toward the door.

He gave me a flat stare. "When you're done trying to goad the Old
Man into swallowing you whole, get your ass back here. We have a lot
of ground to cover."

I tipped my head in his direction and ran.

I was a little surprised when he let me go like that. I'd assumed he'd try
to stop me, and I hadn't been sure what I could do about it. I had a lot
of questions, and nothing at all like answers.

But at least I had a plan. Well, it was kind of a plan.

If you didn't look too closely.

My heart slammed inside my chest as I raced back down to the beach. Smart? No, not smart, but I wanted off the island, and from what Doc had just said, I had the means. The Old Man wasn't going to kill me. He didn't dare unless his fervent desire was that he die and I become an incredibly destructive dragon. So, I could call his bluff, and if I did that, well . . . I would be free to leave the island whenever I wanted.

When I made it back to the beach, everything was still except for the sound of crashing waves. No bird call interrupted; the seagulls had gone elsewhere to hunt. The jungle noises and the warbles of hunting drakes didn't carry this far down to the black sand.

I felt weak and shaky, near to collapse even after my rest. I must have slept for some time; it was evening now and the stars overhead twinkled behind the rainbow colors of Tya's Veil.

And yes, the Old Man had returned to his perch.

The dragon shifted. My pulse sped up.

"You didn't bring the harp," the dragon whispered. **"No matter. Sing for me."**

I felt the tug of the dragon's will, the incredible force of command pushing those sentences into my mind.

"No," I said. "I want to talk to you."

"Sing for me!" the dragon bellowed, and I nearly tripped and fell backward.

"Talk," I insisted.

The dragon curled his tail around his body and beat his wings, sending waves crashing countercurrent against their shore-facing kin. **"Talk?"** He cocked his head in a way that reminded me of parrots or the hunting drakes the Thriss used. **"The Malkath vordredd talk using a method of tapping that carries for great distances over coated copper wires. The vorfelané clan Esiné talk using precise finger movements. The voramer sing in low-pitched notes that carry for hundreds of miles underwater. The vorarras enchant crystals to carry images of the gazers to each other. What sort of 'talk' did you mean?"**

I cleared my throat. "I want to talk about the Stone of Shackles."

The dragon twisted on the rocks, the giant loops of his body drawing up under him like a cobra coiling. **"Rolumar's Gem, the Stone of Shackles, Soulbinder, the Crown of Kirpis. Its first power is to warn its owner of physical danger and its second power is to swap souls and its third power makes the taking of gaeshes possible. None of which is of any interest to me, little man."**

I pulled myself up. "But I'm wearing it. And that means you're not just going to kill me."

The dragon leaned its long neck forward. **"I was never going to kill you, tiny fool. Now sing."**

I shook my head. "You can't . . . you can't control me. That worked once, but it won't work again."

The dragon settled down again, resting its head against a clawed hand in a human gesture. **"Sing me the Ride of Tirrin Woodkeeper. Oh, or I know, why not sing to me of Sirellea's beauty, and the tragedy of Kinorath's ambitions? Do you know 'The Fall of Dimea'? It's a newer song . . ."**

I shook my head. "I'm leaving, Old Man, and you can't stop me."

A terrible rumbling shook the whole island, shook the water and the waves and caused sand to thrum in ripples. Rocks tumbled down the scree-laden sides of hills.

The Old Man was laughing.

"Ah," he purred. **"Do you not know those songs? Has so much time passed? Very well. My garden, sing for your newest companion. Sing for him so he can learn."**

And then to my horror, the pillars began to sing.

I suppose it would have been fine if they had just been enchanted rocks, but they weren't. From the center of each pillar, a figure pulled away as if trying to escape mud. They were still covered in rock, but it was a thinner layer, enough to keep them trapped but not to hide their shape. The rock only retreated fully from their faces, letting them open their eyes, open their mouths. They did not scream, even though the horror in their eyes made it clear it was all they wanted in the whole world.

Each of those pillars was a person.

I saw the way their eyes rolled in mad terror—the panic and despair as they were allowed to see freedom, if just for a moment—while they sang for the Old Man's pleasure. The worst thing was how glorious they sounded: they were a perfect sunrise, a walk through a well-tended garden in spring, the laughter of someone you love. I could have listened to them for hours in rapt wonder if I didn't understand the atrocity that had been committed to capture that sound.

And I knew at that moment what the Old Man intended to do with me.

"Never," I whispered in horror. Underneath that initial revulsion dwelt a deep well of dread. I felt an instinctive and infinite terror, akin to the blind panic of those afraid of tight spaces. The worst part was how familiar this feeling was. I knew what it was like to be trapped and unable to move, conscious and yet kept prisoner inside my own body.

I had been through this before. I didn't know where. I didn't know when. I didn't even know how. But somehow, I had been through it before.

And I would rather die a thousand times than go through it again.

Then I wasn't on the beach anymore. At some point I had started running, and jungle leaves lashed against me as I passed by without pausing. I ran and ran and ran.

It was hours, though, before the sound of the Old Man's laughter faded from my ears.

52: Dark Streaks

(Talon's story)

Fine, we can skip ahead. I enjoyed the next morning more anyway.

Darzin D'Mon was in a wonderful mood as he walked up the stairs of the southern tower of the Blue Palace. He whistled to himself and contemplated something he identified only through its absence: boredom.

Darzin D'Mon was never the most introspective of men. He was, even he admitted, poorly gifted in the arts of self-examination. In most cases, he found this to be more benefit than hindrance. For he was not the sort to whine about his situation or be moved into bouts of self-pity, reactions that weighed down his father with guilt and doubt. If he didn't like his situation, he changed it, and if he couldn't change it, he didn't let it gnaw at him. But there were enemies even he found himself hard-pressed to challenge. Enemies who snuck up on him not by stealth or means of magic, but through success and wealth and prosperity.

Winning was fun, but after the winning . . . then what? So often too easy, too often so boring: the victories had tasted stale of late. Darzin found himself venturing further and further afield to find distractions capable of keeping his interest. His forays into his father's underworld Shadowdancer cartel had stemmed from such a desire. He longed to fill his nights with something other than the same old pleasures and entertainments.

But this—ah, this was different. Darzin warmed at the thought of his young adopted "son." A challenge indeed. Tricky. It would be easy enough to break the boy. Few had the fortitude to resist the malice and torture that Darzin could unleash if he chose to do so. No, Darzin didn't doubt for a moment he could grind Kihrin's will underfoot as thoroughly as a cut flower on hot cobblestones, leaving nothing but a faintly perfumed smear. But destroying the boy's mind wasn't the goal. It would, in fact, make the true goal impossible to obtain. If the boy could only give the necklace of his own free will, then he had to possess enough will, enough spirit, to make such a foolish choice.

So then, subtlety was the necessary ingredient, something to which

Darzin was unaccustomed and therefore found unexpectedly, delightfully challenging. He needed to make Kihrin miserable, but not too miserable, desperate, but not so despairing that he wanted to end it all. Once Darzin had shown with painstaking clarity that there would be no shelter or happiness for Kihrin within House D'Mon; then and only then could Darzin offer the path of escape—

For the reasonable price of one sapphire necklace.

And after the boy gave up his only protection?

Darzin smiled to himself. It would be nice to kill the boy in front of his father. He'd enjoy the look on Therin's face—just before Therin too saw the bloody end of Darzin's sword.

He was still smiling when he turned the key in the lock and walked into Kihrin's room, unannounced.

Then he stopped smiling.

For a moment, he forgot where he was. He forgot who he was. Most importantly though, he forgot who *she* was. For the span of a few seconds, not more than a few hammered, pounding heartbeats, Darzin looked at the scene with the eyes of any man who had just discovered his wife in the arms of another.

Those few seconds were nearly enough to ruin everything.

Darzin had entered the room quietly from force of habit. He found his "son" still asleep in that preposterous bed, but the boy wasn't alone. Alshena lay next to him, the sheet partly covering her naked body. Her red hair spread out in ripples over the boy's chest. One arm draped possessively over his abdomen.

A discarded bottle of wine lay next to the bed, along with clothes—Alshena's agolé and undergarments, the boy's boots, kef, and shirt. The boy's necklace, that damned sapphire, rested uncovered in the hollow of his throat. There was no doubt, could be no doubt, of what had happened here.

The brat had bedded *his wife*.

Only when he redoubled the pressure of his clenched fist did he realize he had, unknowingly, drawn his sword. Darzin stepped forward, and raised his arm to strike down the appalling little bastard who would dare do something like this to him.

Then he saw the bruises on Alshena.

Her body was marked by the signs of a violent infidelity: scratch marks down her back, bruises on her thighs, even bite marks. These two had not made love, but battled, and Kihrin had proved a merciless opponent. Perhaps that explained why a ripped piece of embroidered blue silk had been used to tie one of the boy's hands to a tree trunk, where it was still trapped, even in sleep.

But Talon can't bruise . . .

And it was only then the Lord Heir remembered that it was not his wife in bed with the boy, and never had been. The real Alshena D'Mon had been dead for weeks now, her body and brain devoured by the ever-hungry mimic who had taken her place, her soul sacrificed to summon Xaltorath. The very same Xaltorath Darzin had used to track down the Stone of Shackles—and also its bearer.

Darzin knew Talon was skilled at improvisation. If she had seen an opportunity, she wouldn't have waited for permission to take it. All the anger drained away as Darzin understood her intention: *Talon was giving him a gift*.

The mimic raised her head to look up at him. She smiled, those green eyes shining, large and luminous in the soft morning light. She nodded: *Do it*.

Darzin didn't think he'd ever seen Talon look so beautiful.

He steeled himself and took a deep breath. Then he grabbed a fistful of her lovely red hair, and dragged her, screaming, out of the bed.

"HOW DARE YOU? YOU WHORE!" Darzin raged as he back-handed her across the face and sent her stumbling away from him. "You would cuckold me with my OWN SON?" He hit her again, hard enough to split her lip and splatter red blood across delicate skin.

Kihrin woke. "Leave her alone!" his "son" shouted.

"Please, darling, please, I can explain—" his "wife" sobbed.

Darzin hit her a third time, a punch to the face that bloodied his own knuckles and would have likely broken her jaw if she had been any mortal woman. Alshena fell to the floor, sobbing and gasping for breath. She pleaded, cried, begged for forgiveness.

Her performance was flawless.

"Stop it!" Kihrin screamed. "You want to hurt someone, hurt me. You like that well enough!" The boy twisted at the silk holding his wrist, but his anger and struggling bound the silk into a tighter, stronger twisted vine. The more he pulled, the harder the knot resisted.

"Time for your next lesson, son," Darzin hissed. "No one takes what is mine. I'll kill her before I see her in the arms of another man." He raised his sword and hoped Kihrin would call his bluff. He could pretend to kill Talon easily enough, but he wasn't ready.

"NO!" Kihrin screamed. "*Please Father*. It's not her fault. It's mine. I did this! I raped her."

Darzin paused.

Kihrin repeated, "I raped her. I was drunk and I . . . got carried away."

There was a long silence as both men focused on Kihrin's wrist, still tied to the trunk of one of the trees. The Lord Heir raised an eyebrow and pointedly stared at Kihrin.

The room was quiet, even the sound of Alshena's crying muffled by her hands.

Kihrin stared at his wrist and sighed. "That, uh . . . that would have gone better if I wasn't still tied up, wouldn't it?"

Darzin smiled. "Yes. Yes, probably."

"Yeah. That's what I thought too."

"As bloodied as she is, there's a good chance I would have believed you," Darzin pointed out.

"Ah. Well, good to know if I ever feel like framing myself for rape." The young man's eyes were filled with self-loathing and pleading desperation. "Please don't kill her, Father. I'll do anything you want."

Darzin stared at his so-called son. He contemplated asking for the necklace right there. It's possible the boy might agree, just to save Alshena's life. An even more delicious irony, since the boy was only here because of the real Alshena's sacrifice to Xaltorath. But what was a one-night affair to a youth who had drunk deep from the cup of decadence? The boy had been so rough on her. His tastes were not those of a novice, but of the hardened libertine.

Kihrin was, like Darzin himself, hard on his toys.

He could not take the chance. When Darzin made his move, there could be no doubt and no options for Kihrin—no way out.

Darzin knelt over Alshena, who cringed away from him. "Get back to our rooms, bitch. If I ever catch you doing this again, or if anyone ever finds out about this, I'll have my men sew shut that greedy cunt of yours for good." He slapped her one more time to make sure she understood.

Alshena nodded her blood-smeared face and crawled to the door like an injured animal, whimpering and leaving bloody tracks in her wake. Darzin watched her for a moment, a slight smile on his lips, before he turned back to Kihrin. The boy was trying to untie the taut silk knot around his wrist.

"I used to know a nobleman who had the legs of his wife amputated. Said it was like clipping the wings from a parrot—it kept her from flying away." Darzin walked over to the table and poured himself a glass of water. "Said she didn't need to walk for what he wanted her for anyway."

"That's sick," Kihrin hissed.

"No, it was stupid," Darzin corrected. "He bled to death in bed one night when she bit off his testicles. Everyone has their limits. Break a slave, yes. Make sure they know their place, absolutely. But only a fool pushes a slave so far they have nothing to lose by killing their master—and then gives them opportunity to do just that."

"I thought we were talking about wives."

"Just between you and me, there's not much difference." Darzin sheathed his sword. He slid a dagger out of his boot and threw it. The blade sank into the wood of the tree, severing the silk scarf holding Kihrin tight.

The boy rubbed the skin of his wrist, scraped raw in the struggle to free himself. He looked at Darzin with suspicion in his eyes. "Why aren't you angry with me?"

Darzin feigned surprise. "Angry at you? Gods above, boy, I'm *proud* of you."

His "son" stared at him in horror.

Darzin bit down on the urge to laugh and continued with an expansive wave of his hand. "Why, this was very well done. Sleeping with another man's wife is a mark of pride and distinction—for everyone but the other man, of course. You are finally starting to act like a royal. Any other woman and I would have been patting you on the back and complimenting your technique. You bypassed many of the common blunders—for instance, you weren't in her rooms, thus greatly lessening the chance, under normal circumstances, that her husband would walk in. And those little love marks you left on her—even if her husband never found out who did it, he would know she had been raped or seduced. Either way it's a black mark on his honor." He paused. "The bondage was an odd choice. Was that my wife's suggestion?"

Kihrin shook his head. "Mine."

"Why?"

The boy shrugged. "I like it that way sometimes."

"Huh. Everyone has their tastes, I suppose, but I recommend you stamp down on that fetish. It's never a good idea to leave yourself vulnerable. Tie your partner up. Don't let them do it to you." Darzin sipped his water for a moment while his son picked himself out of bed. "Speaking of which, I see we run to similar tastes in our women. Not so surprising, but you should take some basic precautions."

Kihrin's eyes narrowed. "I'm not an idiot. I have a ring from a Blue House . . ."

Darzin rolled his eyes. "I meant about not killing them."

The horror returned to the young man's eyes. "Killing—!"

"I saw what you did to Alshena. Now, her tastes run rough herself, and I'm sure she was goading you on every inch of the way. But don't try to deny you have a dark streak in you, that you don't enjoy the pain as much as the pleasure."

Kihrin turned away. "No! I—" But the denial seemed to stick in the boy's throat.

"You can find yourself in trouble if you go too far," Darzin told his son kindly. "I know. I've been there myself. It can be a real dilemma. Be gentle with other men's wives and save your true passions for the slave girls. Nobody cares what happens to them. You know—I will even do you a favor. I have a batch of slaves I'm sending off to the Octagon for resale this afternoon. Most of them are a bit threadbare, but only by my standards—the girls are lovely and well trained. I'll give you a couple. You can take your pick."

The boy looked up at him with eyes so full of equal parts hope and despair Darzin almost laughed out loud. Really, the lad made it too easy.

Then those blue eyes hardened to ice, and Kihrin said: "Other men's castoffs don't interest me, Father. Only other men's wives."

Darzin was torn between the desire to laugh and the desire to hit him. Kihrin was such a little—

Such a D'Mon. So much like Darzin himself that he sometimes thought he was looking in a mirror. *No,* he corrected himself. *Not like me. Like Pedron. Like Pedron reborn.* For a moment, Darzin found himself chilled. He almost shuddered, and instead pushed dark memories from his mind.

Darzin smiled. "Suit yourself. You seem to prefer learning things the hard way." Darzin walked to the door, sidestepping the small puddle of blood.* "Oh," he said as he paused at the door. "It should go without saying, but I'll do so anyway: touch Alshena again and I won't kill you, I'll kill her." He grinned. "It's about time I traded in for a younger wife anyway, so I'd love the excuse."

He left his son like that, looking after him with eyes as flat and cold as the still surface of a distant lake.

Just like Pedron. He would have to be careful with that boy.

Dark streak indeed.

---

*I've always wondered how mimics manage that, since they don't seem to bleed most of the time.

53: SPEED TRAINING

(Kihrin's story)

I returned to training with Doc. Seasons followed each other in quick succession while I lived and died a thousand times in illusions crafted by Chainbreaker. All the while I tried and failed to find a way past the Old Man. I understood now that he didn't have to kill me, but offered a threat worse than death. No matter how much progress I made under Doc's tutelage, no sword would free me from the dragon.*

"If only I was better at magic," I whined to Tyentso one day as we both ate lunch. I rarely saw her outside of meals anymore: my lessons with her had faded even as Doc's had increased. "I have no damn talent at all."

Tyentso snorted. "If that were true, you'd never have seen past the First Veil, Scamp. Most poor fools never do."

A year on Ynisthana had been kind to Tyentso. Her skin had lost the leathery texture it possessed from years at sea. Her hair, no longer cracked and dry from the salt spray, hung lustrous and shiny. She'd put on weight from an island routine that encouraged her to eat regular meals, and muscle from the heavy exercise. Her face had a blush of color that had been missing when she served on *The Misery*.

True, her nose was still sharp enough to cut a man and her chin was a spear point, but the creases on her forehead were mostly gone. I think no one had been as surprised by the transformation as Tyentso herself. She was bemused to find her company sought out by members of the Brotherhood for something other than study.

"I know one spell. One! And it doesn't work on the Old Man. I've tried. He can still see me."

Tyentso swirled her spoon in her bowl, frowning. "Magic isn't just a matter of memorization, Scamp. You have to change how you see, change how you think. You are forcing your will on the universe. Not one in a thousand people can cast the simplest spell." She let her spoon fall into the bowl. "Anyway, dragons aren't creatures who know magic, they *are*

---

*Not true, but I suppose it is still accurate to say that no sword Kihrin had access to would be capable of such a feat.

magic. Worse, they are magical chaos vortexes. It would be difficult to use magic to fool one."

"Doc did it."

"Doc is using an artifact. Yours would work on him too, you just wouldn't like the result."

"If you're trying to cheer me up, Ty, you're doing a lousy job of it." I pushed my bowl away. "How did you learn? Did it take you years of staring at a candle or trying to make a leaf move?"

To my surprise, Tyentso blanched, took a deep breath, and looked away. "No."

"Well? What then?"

She stood up. "It wouldn't work for you, Scamp. I don't recommend it."

I cocked my head in surprise. In all the time I'd known Tyentso, she'd never dismissed a question with no explanation. She never shut me down without an involved lecture on why I was being stupid.

I grabbed the edge of her chemise. "Ty, what did I *say*?"

She snatched the fabric away from me and opened her mouth to snap a reply. She closed it again. "Leave it be," she said, her voice sounding tired.

Tyentso picked up her dish and carried it to the kitchen for cleaning.

A week later, Tyentso showed up at my room after dark. It wasn't like that. In point of fact, I had a vané woman named Lonorin with me, whom Tyentso shoved out with a firm and impolite hand.

"So, you decided you like those pretty vané flowers sprinkled on your bed after all, have you?"

I sighed and threw a bedspread around me. "I thought we'd established I'm not your type, Tyentso."

"Not only are you not my type but you're young enough to be my son, which is a terrifying prospect. These vané immortals may not have any standards, but I sure as hell do." Tyentso lifted a basket covered with a black cloth. "Anyway, I brought tea. I promise it's not drugged."

"If you wanted to kill me, you had plenty more opportunities before this." I motioned her over to the small reed table and chairs beside the mattress. "To what do I owe the visit then? It's a little late and I'm a little naked."

"I know a way to break past your magical block."

I tilted my head. "Okay . . . I'm listening."

She pulled the teapot and several cups out of the basket. "The problem is that it's dangerous. Not to mention gods-awful unpleasant. And I wouldn't have offered at all, but . . ." She winced as she poured the tea. "I won't lie, Scamp, I feel bad about your gaesh."

I chuckled and reached for the tea. "You must have gaeshed a thousand people in your life, Ty."

"But I didn't know it couldn't be reversed. And I sure as hell didn't know that when you finally die and travel past the Second Veil, the gaesh will pull you toward Hell."

I froze, felt a shudder run over my body. "What?"

She scowled. "When you finally die, you're not going to the Land of Peace. No one who's gaeshed does, apparently. I finally understand what the demons get out of it and why they ever agreed to allow us to summon them."

I stared at her until her cheeks turned red, she cursed, and turned away. "Damn it all, I didn't know! I knew damage to the upper soul could interfere with passage to Thaena's realm, but I didn't think a gaesh caused that kind of harm. You think the demons stop to give mortals a full lecture on what happens to the souls of those they gaesh for us? That every soul taken is a chance for them to add to their power? Not a chance. I found out here—it's not taught at the Academy."*

I fought to swallow back my nausea. I hadn't put the pieces together, hadn't realized what a gaesh could mean. This would make it easier for Xaltorath to claim me, later. Not even death would free me. I felt the same sense of claustrophobia, the same itchy, ugly feeling of being cornered and caged, that I'd felt when the Old Man had shown me the poor souls kept in his "garden."

"So . . ." I drained my cup of tea, set it back down in front of Tyentso. "Why do you think you can teach me magic now, when you haven't been able to before this?"

She examined her fingers for several long, tense seconds before she looked up. "The dirtiest, nastiest part about learning sorcery is that words aren't enough. Learning to cast a spell isn't a matter of memorizing charts, reciting formula, or drawing little glyphs on the floor. Magic is about teaching someone the right way to *think*. No language, not even the old voras tongues, can describe the precise patterns of thought, the mappings of consciousness, necessary to cast the simplest spell."

I swallowed and leaned back. "Okay. So . . . I'm back to my original question. How are you going to teach me?"

Tyentso's eyes brightened as she lifted her chin. "By making you learn the same way I did: mind to mind. You're going to have a ghost possess you, and then I will—"

"Hold on there." I straightened. "I'm going to what?"

---

*Gaeshes are considered a variant of a wizard's magical talismans, dangerous only because an enemy who puts their hands on one may use it against the gaeshed subject. It's not taught that a gaesh causes this kind of spiritual damage. Unsettling news to me as well.

Tyentso cleared her throat. "A ghost. A ghost will possess you, and while doing so, the two of you will be in close mental contact. It should be enough so you can intuitively grasp the spellcasting process. It worked for me. I see no reason why it wouldn't work for you."

I swallowed hard. "Let me get this straight. You want me to let a ghost take possession of my body and teach me magic. Assuming that would even work, and assuming I'm crazy enough and desperate enough to agree, where are we going to find a ghost sorcerer?"

Tyentso raised her hand. "Me. I'm going to be the ghost."

54: The Carriage Ride

(Talon's story)

"I'm not running away! I just need a carriage. Go ask the High Lord—" Kihrin D'Mon's angry tone echoed clearly through the stable court-yard. He was red-faced, and looked like he might jump up and down in frustration at any moment.

"Is there a problem?" Tishar D'Mon asked as she walked down the steps. She motioned to one of the grooms. "My carriage, please."

The Lord Heir's newest son paused in the middle of his argument with the stable master, who stepped around Kihrin and bowed to Tishar. "My lady, I am under strict orders not to allow the young man to leave the grounds without an escort."

"Ah," Tishar said. "Well that's not a problem at all then, but thank you for watching out for him." She held out her hand to Kihrin. "I'm so sorry I'm late. Shall we?"

The young man caught on quickly. He bowed over her hand before releasing it to her again. "It's my fault, Aunt Tishar. I should have mentioned I was waiting for you."

"See Hosun?" Tishar smiled at the stable master. She'd known Hosun since he was a small boy with a fascination for horses, apprenticed to the old stable master. She'd fooled him not at all, but Hosun would play along anyway.

"Of course, my lady," Hosun said with a dry smile and a bow. He turned back to the stable. "My lady's coach!"

Kihrin exhaled as the stable master walked away. "Thank you," he whispered to her.

"You're welcome," she whispered back. "And where are we going today?"

"The Octagon?"

The answer surprised her. "It's nothing worth seeing, my dear. Just a lot of miserable souls and the vultures circling their misfortune."

"Please." There was so much emotion trapped in that single word she half-expected the boy to fall to his knees.

She gave him a thoughtful look. He was clean and properly dressed, but little details gave away his hurry: the way his hair had been pulled back into a gold clasp, the bruising on his wrist that someone had neglected to treat by salve or healer.

Her examination was interrupted by Hosun returning with the carriage.

"Where did you get *that*?" Kihrin's jaw dropped open. He stared at the transport with undisguised wonder.

Tishar smiled. Her own reaction had been much the same when she had first seen her carriage, over a quarter-century earlier. The carriage was as much jewelry as transport, an artisan crafting of rare dark woods and jeweled accents that left no question of the royal nature of its passengers. The enchantments that magically created a smooth ride over any surface were far costlier than all the gold and precious stones decorating it. Many had offered to buy it over the years, and as many had tried to claim it through machinations.

But it was hers alone.

Hosun had hitched four matching golden horses to the front of the carriage, and sent along not just her usual driver, Sironno, but also a half dozen guards in the House colors to sit on top.

He was feeling protective today. Perhaps he had cause.

"My brother, Pedron, gave it to me," Tishar said as Sironno held the door open for them both. "Just before he sent me away to marry the Lord Heir D'Evelin." She nodded to the driver. "Take us to the Octagon. Use the northern route."

"Yes, my lady." He bowed to her, and waited until they both sat inside before closing the door.

"Thank you," Kihrin said, although he was fighting his own distraction as his fingertips lingered over the soft velvet cushions.

"I am curious why you are so eager to go to the slave market. Don't tell me you want to own one of your own." She didn't even try to tone down the disapproval in her voice.

He winced and looked away. The brooding expression on the young man's face reminded her more than a little of Pedron.

Also of Therin.

"If you're wondering if you can trust me with whatever secret has you looking so grim," Tishar said, as Sironno cracked his whip and set the horses out onto the city streets, "the answer is no."

Kihrin threw her a shocked look.

She continued, "You have no way of knowing who I'll tell or how I'll use the information. I can't provide you with any guarantee worth the breath I'd use to speak it." She leaned forward. "Nothing is gained without risk, young man. Sooner or later, you're going to have to take a chance on someone."

He scowled and stared at his hands. "Maybe none of you are a good choice."

"Oh, we are a house of serpents, true enough." Tishar smiled at him. She pulled down the blinds over the windows, habit more than need driving her motions, and activated a lantern of mage-light. "If it's any consolation, I was married to Pharoes D'Evelin for almost twenty-five years. I outlived him. I outlived our sons. Despite how young I look, I am old and jaded and so very done with games of Empire. It's not that I can be trusted, as much as it's unlikely you have anything I *want*."

He smiled, although she wasn't blind to the fact that smile didn't reach his eyes. "I need to buy a slave Darzin just sent to the Octagon. Her name is Talea."

"Ah, excellent. Now we have something." She held up her hands. "Further considerations: you are not legally an adult, my young nephew. Not yet. Not until the New Year's and your birthday. If we enter the Octagon and you buy this Talea, Darzin may simply claim her again, as he may claim anything you own, for you remain your father's property."

His eyes went very wide. Then he closed them and tilted his head back until it hit the back of the carriage. "I'm an idiot."

"Don't confuse ignorance with stupidity, young man. You just aren't used to having a father who doesn't actually care for your welfare." She gestured. "My recommendation: don't try to buy her yourself. Buy her on your grandfather Therin's behalf. He may be a little irritated to have you making purchases against his credit, but he'll be willing to work out a repayment plan."

"That could work." He chewed on his lower lip. "I have the metal to buy her. That's not the problem."

"You must really like this girl."

Kihrin shook his head. "I've never met her."

Tishar raised her eyebrows and waited for an explanation.

"I knew her sister. Back at the Shattered Veil Club. She was murdered because of me." He swallowed, looking like he'd just eaten something foul. "I saw Talea as they led her away. He'd just offered me my pick of any of his slaves. I could have chosen her then. But I refused him." He let out a dark laugh. "He'd have killed her if he'd realized she was important to me."*

"I applaud your swift adjustment to D'Mon family politics," Tishar said. "I don't doubt for one second you're right." She made a motion as if saluting him with a phantom wineglass. "I believe that only leaves the matter I came looking for you to discuss in the first place."

---

*No, but only because she made such excellent bait. Although, who knows? Darzin might well have been stupid enough to kill her.

Kihrin blinked. "Wait. You were looking for me?"

"Yes. You see, I wanted to share my secret with you. Do you know how I've managed to survive so many years in this city?" She didn't wait for an answer before pressing on. "It's because I've never forgotten my mother was a slave. If not for my brother's efforts, I probably would have ended up as one myself."

He frowned. "Slavery isn't inherited."

"No, but why would a slave owner spend money raising a free citizen? Technically only a parent can sell their children, but when the parent is themselves a slave, a great deal of . . . *pressure* . . . can be applied to force their cooperation. A loophole I saw exploited all the time when I shared a roof with House D'Evelin."

She paused enough to note Kihrin looked sick to his stomach. *Not quite as jaded as you thought, are you, young man?* "Never forget we've built this Empire on the backs of slaves and servants and they are—all of them—*disposable*. People hate my brother, Pedron, because he tried to overthrow this way of doing things, but I ask you: would that have been so terrible?"

Kihrin swallowed. "He, uh . . . the wrath of the gods though. The risk of triggering the curse . . ."

She waved a hand. "He thought he could prevent that. He didn't think he was an evil man. He thought he was doing what was right—what needed to happen for the good of the Empire. He wanted to fix those things. The tragedy is that he fell in with people who were only too willing to exploit that idealism to obtain the goals they wanted, and then set him up to take the fall should their plans be discovered."

"You mean he was just a victim in the Affair of the Voices?"

She sighed. "No, probably not. I hold no malice against Therin for doing what he did. If he hadn't, the gods' curse would have killed all of us. Sometimes though I cannot help but wonder how it might have gone if Pedron had succeeded. There was so much that he wanted to change, so much that he was powerless to change because of who he was. Who knows how different the world would be now?"

"Different isn't always better, milady."

"Hmm." She pursed her lips and then shook her head. "I learned from him. From his mistakes as well as his successes. I have tried to be a benefactor as much as my position and gender have allowed. In a house with the likes of Darzin D'Mon stalking its halls, the servants are *grateful* to have any shelter from his particular sort of storm. And so they tell me things. For example, that Alshena left your apartments this morning on her hands and knees, blood everywhere, but she never managed to make it to one of the healers."

It was a low blow, a surprise attack, and the stunned look Kihrin gave her was very nearly heartbreaking. Shame and desperation mixed in equal measure with dread and loathing.

"It wasn't—it wasn't like that—"

"I know. You're not the one who hurt her. Darzin left your apartments not long after. I suspect he treated the injuries that he himself caused, to stop any idle gossip from the healers. As to what happened that made him beat his wife, in a manner that's frankly excessive even for Darzin, the maids who cleaned your bed seemed to think that was obvious enough."

All the color that had reddened his cheeks just a moment before drained away entirely. "What do you want?" he finally asked, sounding resigned.

The boy was a fast learner. Of course, he expected blackmail.

Tishar sighed. "I want you to answer a question." She held up a hand. "Listen first. You see, I suspect I've been in your position, but perhaps I'm wrong. I have my own memories of such evenings. It starts with drinks and some reason to do the drinking. Someone you trust who smiles while they keep your glass full. And then the night goes on and everything becomes a blur. Not an unpleasant blur, truth be told. Except later. Later, when they're not paying attention to you saying no and the clothes are gone and hands are places they shouldn't be." She raised a single finger, tapped the side of it against the tip of her nose. "My single question, dear boy: did you *want* it to happen?"

Kihrin looked away. "It was all just a terrible mistake. One thing led to another. If I could erase it I would. He found us the next morning. I thought he was going to kill her. He still might."

"Kihrin," Tishar said. She leaned over in the carriage and started to pick up his hand, didn't follow through on the motion when he flinched and pulled away from her. "Kihrin," she repeated. "I know how tempting it must be to blame yourself for what happened, or even to say it was no one's fault, but I want you to remember that only one of the people in your bedroom last night was legally of age."

He scoffed and rolled his eyes. "I'm almost sixteen."

"Surviving a date on a calendar will not miraculously give you the wisdom to deal with this. You're *almost* sixteen. She's twice that. Consider that if there is one skill we royals universally practice with dutiful persistence, it's *drinking*. Alshena could drink a morgage to the ground, so if last night was a case of 'one thing leading to another,' it only happened because Alshena wanted it to. My question is: did you want it to? Because if you did, say the word and we never need speak of this again."

He couldn't meet her eyes. He looked at his hands, at the hem of her agolé, at the bejeweled, quilted walls of the carriage.

Tishar waited.

". . . no," he whispered. "No, I didn't want it." He cleared his throat, raised his voice. "I think she was trying to help me."

"And did she help?"

He made a face. "No. Gods no."

"Then I think I'm going to pay her a visit. She's been acting oddly for months now. It's long past time I called her on it."

"I don't want any trouble," Kihrin protested. "She's been through enough."

Tishar snorted as they turned down the road toward the Octagon. "Wait until I'm finished with her."

55: The Pale Lady's Judgment

(Kihrin's story)

I'm impressed you had the guts to tell the truth about that, Talon.

Then again, what do you care? You've done a lot worse than take advantage of a teenage boy, haven't you?

Anyway, Tyentso's plan . . . well, it didn't go as well as we had hoped.

To start with, because Khaemezra refused to help us.

We found Khaemezra the next morning, and I admit I'd assumed she'd agree. After all, why not? She was High Priestess of the Goddess of Death, and what we were asking her to do seemed normal for the weirdness that was a regular part of her religion. Tyentso would die. I'd have a magic lesson. Khaemezra would bring Tyentso back to life again. Easy.

Except apparently it wasn't.

Tyentso cleared her throat, gave me an apologetic look, and turned back to the Holy Mother of the Black Brotherhood. "It's a small departure from the Maevanos ritual. All I'm asking is we take a few hours out before my Return, that's all."

"Ty thinks this would work," I added.

The old woman looked furious we would even make the suggestion. She stared down Tyentso. "This is about Phaellen, isn't it?"

I had no idea who that was, but Tyentso turned white.

"Who's Phaellen?" I asked.

Tyentso crossed her arms over her chest. "Phaellen D'Erinwa. He is . . . he was the ghost who taught me." She took a deep breath. "It's not important." Tyentso returned her gaze to Khaemezra. "I didn't think you knew about him."

Khaemezra glared. "I know *everyone* who dies."

"And that's not creepy at all," I said. "I'm not thrilled about the idea of being possessed, but I'm even less happy about being trapped here by the Old Man. So, if there's some reason why Tyentso can't do this—besides flouting the normal rules of the Maevanos—please tell me so I can start working on my next harebrained scheme to get off this island." I snapped my fingers. "I've got it. Any idea where I can buy five crates of hedgehogs?"

"You shouldn't be trying to leave at all. You are still in training."

I inhaled and fought back the impulse to say something nasty. "I don't like cages. I especially don't like what the Old Man wants to do to me."

Khaemezra's nostrils flared. "A ghost is not simply a dead spirit. Souls are not meant to stay on this side of the Veil, removed from the body that nurtured them. When you die, you travel past the Second Veil, into the Afterlife. Everyone does. That includes people who experience the Maevanos. To become a ghost, someone who lingers on this side of the Veil, requires you to be dead, yet too weak, angry, or tied to this world to successfully make the transition. That is dangerous. The lower soul drains away, and if you spend long enough trapped in that state, you—or rather, Tyensto—would be left unable to be Returned or to move on to the Land of Peace to one day be reborn." Her eyes were hard as she gestured toward Tyensto. "And let's not forget: you have yet to undergo a Maevanos. There is no guarantee that you would be allowed to Return."

"I haven't gone through it because . . ." Tyentso licked her lips.

"Because you suspect you might be found unworthy," Khaemezra finished for her. "And what if you're right? You have not led a pure life, my child."

"I know what I've done." Tyentso's eyes met mine. "But this is important."

I winced. I knew she was doing this as an apology, doing this because she felt guilty about the gaesh. And I hadn't exactly absolved her of that guilt, had I? Did I really want to have Tyentso's true death on my hands if this didn't work? "Ty, I don't want to get you killed."

"Getting me killed is the whole point, Scamp. Anyway, lecturing you on magical theory until your eyes roll back in your head isn't working, so let's try something new. Learning this way was good enough for me. It damn well better be good enough for you, because I don't intend on doing this twice."

"Are you certain you want to do this?" Khaemezra said to Tyentso again. "You will keep no secrets while dead. Who you are, what you are, will be laid bare." Her quicksilver stare turned to me. "That includes to him."

"Stop trying to scare me, old woman. I'm doing this."

A smile quirked the corner of Khaemezra's mouth. "It seems you are." Khaemezra picked up a knife. She offered it to Tyentso.

"Hey now. Wait a minute. When you say we're doing this, you don't mean right now, do you?" I looked around, wondering if two Thriss with drums were about to appear.

Even Tyentso seemed taken aback.

"Yes. I mean right now. Your request is untoward enough that I don't want this to be a part of our normal services. This way I can give you my full attention should anything go wrong." She said it like something going wrong was less a possibility than a certainty.

My mouth went dry.

Tyentso took the knife. "Doesn't this need a bit more ceremony?"

"No," Khaemezra said. "All you need is the will to face Thaena."

I raised a hand. "Okay, so wait a minute, why don't we all take a breath and—"

Tyentso stabbed herself.

Her blood spread out in a slow stain of pure red across her white linen chemise. Tyentso gave Khaemezra a look of dull accusation before she collapsed on the floor. She seemed small and frail and inanimate.

Khaemezra stood still and silent.

"What next?" I asked her.

"We wait."

"That's it? We wait?"

The High Priestess tilted her head. "She must find her way back through the wild lands of the Afterlife. That is not an easy thing to do."

"And if she can't?"

"Then today will not be the day you learn magic from a ghost."

"Right. Right." I started to pace, not knowing what else to do.

I stopped. "Isn't there anything I can do to help?"

Khaemezra stared straight ahead and ignored me.

I sighed and paced some more. Finally, I sat cross-legged next to Tyentso's body and put my hand on her shoulder. I tried to shift my vision past the First Veil.

The First Veil was magic, and the Second Veil was death. It made sense then that I shouldn't, as a mortal, be able to see past the Second Veil. But if Tyentso was trying to work her way forward, then I probably didn't need to. If I could see past the First Veil, and perhaps see *almost* to the Second Veil, maybe I could act as a beacon for her to find her way back.

I admit the logic was suspect, but what did I have to lose?

I shifted my vision past the First Veil easily enough. I'd been able to do that since I was a child. Now I strained for more, focused with sight and something beyond sight. I struggled without moving, trying to push my vision past the normal auras. It was like staring at a mosaic so hard your eyes crossed, the intensity of the stare making the accuracy of the sight worse.

I reached out. I reached inward. I despaired.

A hand came down on my shoulder. Without looking, I knew it was

Khaemezra, her gold-dusted bone fingers tightening on my flesh like iron claws.

My view of the universe shifted.

My previous experiences with seeing magic now seemed as effective as the vision of a newborn kitten. For one thing, I still saw the normal universe with perfect clarity, but simultaneously I also "saw" energy everywhere. There was something like sound too, as if every visible object made an audible sound. Each thing—living or not—existed with its own musical accompaniment, each with a beat, a vibration, a chord. Music and light were, well, everywhere, and it all vibrated against everything else, sending out ripples interacting and magnifying and canceling each other.

I looked up at Khaemezra, only to realize I had been wrong.

This was someone else.

The woman with her hand on my shoulder was a stranger. Her skin was supple and smooth and darker than the floor of the Manol Jungle. The highlights that limned her cheekbones and danced across her forehead glistened blue. Her hair, or her equivalent to hair, reminded me of butterfly wings, delicate and transparent with highlights that shimmered opalescent with greens and blues and violets. Her mouth was small but her lips full, and her nose was flat with nostrils that seemed peculiarly shallow. Her eyes were large and tilted and had no visible iris or pupil. They reflected the golden scales of her dress in mercurial shimmers with no color of their own.

Only then did I notice the belt of roses worn around her hips, clasped with a tiny skull, the matching roses worn as a diadem on her head. I realized that I had indeed seen her before.

Or, at least, I had seen statues of her, made of onyx and gold leaf.

I wondered, absently, why we called her the Pale Lady.

Thaena met my eyes.

Dread spiked through my soul. What I felt was not a sense of my own mortality or the dark void of a final end, but the most profound sense of nudity. Thaena didn't look at me, she looked *inside* me, to every corner of my soul. Thaena knew me better than I would ever know myself. She had always known me, known me before I was born and was now simply waiting for me to return to her.

I looked away.

Thaena's grip tightened on my shoulder. The Goddess of Death turned back to the other woman in the room.

A woman, I noted, who didn't look like Tyentso.

She was young. Older than me, but not old enough to be my mother. This was a stick-thin woman, a sharp-featured Quuros. Her hair was a mass of lavender-gray cloud-curls that swirled around her head like a building storm. Her most striking features were her tilted eyes: large and black, with the endless labyrinthine depths of a god-touched member of House D'Lorus.

She had the same crimson stain spilling down the front of her chemise as Tyentso. She looked real and solid and I would never have thought her a ghost.

But I knew better.

"Tyentso," said the Goddess of Death, "once named Raverí, daughter of Rava.* I have seen your soul. You have been judged."

Tyentso straightened, looking shocked. "Wasn't there supposed to be a test?"

"The test was your life," Thaena replied. "And you have failed it. You are a murderer and a demonologist, an arrogant liar who betrayed people who trusted you and sent the souls of hundreds to Hell. What sacrifice were you unwilling to burn on the altar of revenge? You never had a life worth living. What have you done with yourself but spread misery? What do you leave to the world that made it even the tiniest bit better than it would have been without you? Spend as long as you like teaching Kihrin, assuming he will have anything to do with you. I will not be Returning you."

And with that, the Goddess of Death left the room.

---

*This follows vané naming conventions. I wonder if that was intentional or just coincidence? There's always been rumors of Kirpis vané persisting in the Empire, inside the Kirpis forest, even after the diaspora. Never proven, of course. The Quuros citizens of the Kirpis and Kazivar dominions do keep showing up with Kirpis vané traits like cloud-curled hair though, often in pastel hues.

56: THE OCTAGON

(Talon's story)

When the carriage arrived, Sironno held the door open for Tishar and her nephew, while her guards formed an honor line behind them.

She'd worried that after their conversation in the carriage, Kihrin would be too distraught to deal with the rest of the outing. She'd worried for nothing: as soon as Sironno opened the door, Kihrin sauntered out of the carriage, a perfect picture of bored insouciance.

He held out his arm to her. "Shall we?"

"Of course. This won't take long."

"Everyone's wearing orange," Kihrin whispered to her.

"It's House D'Erinwa's color," she explained. "I never wanted for anything while I was married into their House, but I hate that color. I've always looked hideous in orange."

The public areas of the Octagon were not rank brick and wrought iron, but marble and shaped raenan stone, more appropriate for an Upper Circle salon than a slave house. The most exclusive areas of the Octagon were indeed a little different from salons. Where one might otherwise see fine art, the Octagon presented the finest in flesh to a jaded royal audience.

The main gallery, lush with hanging plants, artwork, and fountains, contained a simple black slate board that visitors examined before continuing on their way.

Tishar made her way to it.

"Normally, you would use this to direct your inquiries," she told Kihrin. "They change it daily, depending on seasonal variation. Room 1: menial labor. Room 3: entertainers. Room 4: services. Room 7: pleasure. Room 8: exotics. The list goes on. Our tasks, however, require more personal service. Fortunately, I know exactly who to see."

With a brilliant smile, she turned on her heels and marched with practiced, fear-inspiring intensity up to a man who was obviously the majordomo, and held out her hand for him to kiss. He smiled up at her as if she were his favorite person in the entire world. She leaned down and whispered her needs into his ear. Moments later, a side door opened for their benefit.

"Guards, you may stay out here," Tishar informed them.

The lead nodded, used to the routine, and fell into position.

Taking Kihrin's arm, Tishar walked him into a small side passage, barely large enough for two people, and cramped compared to the opulence of the main hall. The corridor continued for a long time.

"Is this a servant's tunnel?" Kihrin asked.

She indulged him with a smile. "Something like that."

When the tunnel ended, Tishar and Kihrin stood in a small round room. There were two doors, a staircase leading up, another staircase leading down, and eight tunnels exiting from the room like spokes on a wheel. Twelve guards were stationed around the room, surrounding a small, wrinkled little man seated behind a desk.

"Humthra!" Tishar called out to the small, wizened man.

He didn't look up.

Tishar marched up to the paper-stacked desk of the hunched-over gnome. "Humthra!"

"Humph," the old man said, and continued to write in his ledger.

"Humthra, I must ask you a question," Tishar said.

"What?" The old slave master looked up. He glanced at Kihrin. "Huh. Middle-teens, excellent physical condition. Yellow hair and blue eyes, very rare. Vané stock, second generation. I'd place the opening bid at . . ."

"Humthra!" Tishar screamed.

"What?" the old man squealed.

"I need to look at today's registry, Humthra." She pointed back to her nephew. "HE is not for sale."

The old man snorted. "Why not, you silly woman? You'd make a fortune . . ." Then he blinked and looked back and forth between Tishar and Kihrin. "Oh, is he your son? For you, Tish, I'll double the opening bid . . ."

Tishar looked back at an uncomfortable, embarrassed Kihrin and smiled apologetically. "So sorry. Humthra can be a little . . . focused." She turned back to Humthra. "The registry, Humthra."

"Oh yes, of course. Here." He turned around the large, heavy volume he had been looking through.

"No . . ." She turned to the front, then flipped through pages. "This is this morning's registry, Humthra dear. I need this afternoon's."

"Oh, right here."

Kihrin sounded stunned. "Those are just the slave sales for this afternoon?"

"Yes," Tishar replied as she moved on to the afternoon's figure. "Here we are . . . one lot bought from Darzin D'Mon. . . . oh, you turned these around fast, Humthra."

"They were in good condition," the old man explained. "Didn't need any cleaning up."

"Lucky you." She moved an elegant gloved finger over the vellum until it stopped. She involuntarily made a low growling noise. "Throne, chance, and chalice," she muttered. "He's back already? I thought he was still at the Academy. Did he wash out?"

Humthra looked up. "Who?"

She pointed to the ledger entry.

"Oh!" Humthra shook his head "Oh no. He graduated early and top of his class. Proved everyone wrong who doubted he was really his father's son. High Lord Cedric sent him down to buy whatever caught his eye."

Tishar found herself chewing the inside of her lip. "And no doubt to make sure that what catches his eye is female and still breathing."

"Aunt Tishar?" Kihrin asked. "Is there a problem?"

Tishar threw a sympathetic glance at her nephew. "Oh darling. I'm so sorry, but . . . I'm afraid there's a problem buying Talea."

"What do you mean? Someone's already bought her?"

"Not bought. Buying," Humthra corrected. "He's still here."

"Can we outbid him? Who is it? Can't we still buy her?" Kihrin directed the rapid questions at both of them. The poor boy looked like his heart was breaking.

Tishar sighed. She dreaded explaining this. "It's not so simple. The auction house offers an option of outright sale for interested parties who don't mind paying a premium—in this case, twice the estimated auction appraisal. According to the registry, he intends to buy at least one of the slave girls Darzin sold to the house, but he hasn't left yet. It's possible that we'll be lucky and he won't buy any of them, or won't buy the one you want. It's also possible he may buy all of them."

"Is there anything we can do?"

Tishar turned back to Humthra. "Darling, can we stay for a while on the south balcony? You know how I miss that wonderful tea the Octagon serves."

Humthra had already turned his attention back to the registry. He mumbled something that sounded like, "Whatever you like," and waved them away.

The two started to walk back up the narrow corridor. "What we do is go to my favorite balcony and drink some truly wonderful Zheriaso tea. It would be criminal to miss the opportunity."

Kihrin raised an eyebrow at her. "But Aunt Tishar—"

"I know the perfect spot, dear nephew. It overlooks the main hall, so you can't help but see any slave buyer who enters . . . or leaves . . ." She winked at him.

His eyes widened as he took in her meaning, and then he nodded. "A cup of tea sounds perfect."

She patted his hand. "Smart boy."

Kihrin straightened next to Tishar, and hissed, "That's her!"

Tishar glanced through the intricate wooden screen concealing the balcony, and saw a young woman being led away by collar. Tishar was forced to admit she was exceptionally lovely. She wasn't sure who had decided to put the girl's hair in braids like that,* but Tishar suspected it wouldn't take much to make it the newest fad, considering how fetching the hairstyle was on the slave girl.

Then her attention focused on the man who led her. He dressed in heavy, high-collared robes of black, trimmed with thread of silver. And if he wasn't using magic to keep from collapsing in the heat, Tishar was half-morgage. The symbol of House D'Lorus was embroidered above his heart. She frowned down at him from behind the screen. He wasn't what she had expected.

He was a large man, tall and broad of shoulder, with the perfectly smooth pate of one bald by nature rather than art. Only his head and his elegant, long-fingered hands showed under his dark clothing, and both were a warm olive brown that looked slightly gray against all the black and silver. He wore no jewelry except a carved moonstone puzzle brooch against the cradle of his throat. His face was strong featured, with high cheekbones, a straight nose, a long upper lip, and a mouth capable of great depth of expression. She knew he was young, only twenty years old at most, and never married. There was a chiseled hardness to his features that made her wonder if he was older.[†]

I might have considered him a handsome bed partner, she thought to herself, *under other circumstances.* He glanced up at the balcony screen then, and the corner of that expressive mouth twitched in a sardonic smile. Although she knew it was impossible, it seemed that for a fraction of a second, their eyes met. Something about him did indeed bear the classic stamp of House D'Lorus–for his eyes were solid black, both iris and cornea,

---

*I do. Talea had previously worn her hair straight and unbound, but Talon wanted to make sure Kihrin would recognize Morea's sister, so had the woman change Talea's hair to match. Since the style is Zheriaso, I assume Ola is the ultimate source.

[†]It's very odd to read a description of oneself written by other hands, although I must admit Tishar's description flatters. She had a keen eye for detail, or more likely, Talon gave her one in retelling her story. I find it curious that Talon would paint any part of me in a pleasant light: we were not exactly friends.

turning them into endless voids. Then he and his entourage passed into the main hallway underneath the balcony, out of her sight.

Tishar sat back, stunned.

He couldn't possibly have known she was there. He couldn't possibly have known anyone was there. Her imagination . . . Surely her imagination . . .

"That was the man who bought her, wasn't it?"

"Yes," she said. "And she was the only one he bought." Tishar leaned back against her chair and sipped the excellent tea.

"What do we do now?" Kihrin asked. "Maybe I could offer to buy her from him . . . although Taja! Did you see that outfit? Only a wizard takes themselves that seriously . . ."

"My advice is to forget her."

Kihrin turned back to look at her. "What do you mean?"

"That was the Lord Heir D'Lorus. If you are wise, you will stay far away from him. There are men who like to be considered dangerous, and then there are men who simply are dangerous, and care not what your opinion of them might be. He is of the latter stock."*

He narrowed his blue eyes, and his expression turned ugly. "House D'Lorus? He's related to Gadrith the Twisted?"

"Related? You could say that. Thurvishar D'Lorus is Gadrith's only son."†

---

*Again, flattering. Also untrue. I care a great deal what people think of me. For example, those who think I am dangerous are less inclined to interrupt me while I'm reading.

†There were always rumors this wasn't true, but I think everyone assumed I was an Ogenra plucked up by High Lord Cedric D'Lorus after the Affair of the Voices. No one questioned too closely: truth in the Upper Circle is whatever a High Lord says it is.

57: Ghost Walk

(Kihrin's story)

I stared at the doorway Thaena exited, as if staring might make her return. I heard an inarticulate noise next to me, and when I looked, I saw Tyentso's ghost standing there. Tears streamed down her face, the same look of dull shock there as when she had taken her life.

"Tyentso–" I reached out a hand, and was surprised when my fingers passed right through her arm, leaving a glowing trail where the two images intersected.

I'd forgotten she didn't exist in the same world as me. Well, not as a living person.

She flinched regardless, shook her head, and wiped her eyes with the back of her hand. "So let's begin then."

I blinked. She couldn't mean to go through with the lesson on magic, could she? "Ty, this is exactly what I didn't want to happen. You know, your body hasn't been dead for long. Is there some way we can fix it? Restore you to life? Could I heal you if you guided me?"

She laughed, bitter and hard. "You could heal the body but then what? Return my soul without Thaena's permission? It wouldn't be life, Scamp. I'd be some horrible parody of it, while my lower soul drained away to nothing.* What's done is done. I damn well knew the risks."

I swallowed. "What she said about you . . . ?"

Tyentso raised an eyebrow. "Are you asking me if I'm innocent?"

"Just tell me you had a good reason."

"I can't do that, Scamp. Every fucking thing she said about me was true. I'm a *terrible* person. I've done all those things and more. But you know what? I knew this was going to be a one-way trip from the start. I'm just so angry at myself for thinking that she might forgive me." She shook her head. "That's never been my luck."

"I can't–" I struggled to find the words. "You can't be that bad."

She scoffed. "You're so adorably naïve. I was younger than you when I orchestrated my first murder. I was never caught."

---

*This is, incidentally, exactly what Gadrith the Twisted is.

"So? I tried to get someone killed a couple years ago. Unlike you, I just sucked at it. And I would have gleefully killed Darzin if I thought I could get away with it. And I've done worse. People I love are dead because of me." I closed my eyes and choked back on a full confession.

"Oh goddess. Shut up."

I opened my eyes again.

Tyentso glared at me. "This isn't a fucking contest, you ass. I'm not going to drag out my sins to see who's graded higher on the awful-person test. It doesn't matter anyway. You think Mother Death is going to leave one of her special prophecy brats to rot in the Afterlife? Not likely. Me? I'm disposable. You aren't." She didn't make it sound like a compliment, but were I in her shoes I wouldn't be happy about the situation either.

I opened my mouth to protest, but paused. I could have tried to explain to Tyentso what the Goddess of Luck had said to me about that very fact. However, I didn't think Tyentso would graciously accept me having visions sent from one of the Eight Immortals as proof that I wasn't special. Tyentso had sacrificed a lot for me–far more than anyone should give–and she had every right to be more than a little upset about the outcome.

"If you want me to leave," I said, "I understand."

She was in the middle of a sigh when some idea occurred to her, and her eyes narrowed. "You can see me."

"Uh, yes?"

"Is that your doing or Thaena's?" Tyentso's tone was full of fierce curiosity.

"I was trying to see beyond the Second Veil–"

"Mortals can't do that," she snapped.

"Then I guess it was Thaena's doing."

She pursed her lips, nodding, and then held out her arm. "Take my hand."

"I can't–"

"Take my hand!" she insisted.

I reached for her, knowing as I did my fingers would slide right through hers.

Instead, her fingers vanished when they touched mine, as if dissolving into acid.

Then the world went dark.

Literally dark, and not because I was blinded or unconscious. Tyentso was gone, and I was instead in a dark cave that looked like Khaemezra's room but with all the furnishings removed. The basalt walls had been replaced by something softer. Roots grew through the ceiling and up through the floor, and the air was thick with the smell of humus and rot.

A more ambiguous quality coated everything, a sense of decay and disintegration reminding me of tombs and corpses left long undisturbed.

I tried to move forward to look outside, but found I couldn't move at all.

"Easy now, Scamp." I heard Tyentso's voice even though I didn't see her. "What are you seeing?"

"Where are you?" I asked her. "What are you doing? Stop it."

My hand moved without my orders then, fingers turning back and forth in front of my eyes. It was as if I'd never seen my own hand before and wanted a better look. I hadn't thought to move my hand, hadn't wanted to move my hand.

I realized where Tyentso was: she was inside me, controlling me.

"Everything's going to be fine. Don't worry."

"No. I need you to stop this. Stop it please. Stop."

Everything that I had feared would happen if the Old Man dug his claws into me was happening now. Right now. It didn't matter that Tyentso was a friend, and that I had asked for her help. I had known she was going to do this, but somehow just hadn't realized what possession would mean or how it would feel to be thoroughly under someone else's control. Unable to physically protest, my very soul rebelled hard against the idea. I couldn't run. There was no way to move, no way to hide from this. I was trapped.

I panicked.

You wouldn't have known it to look at me, of course. I couldn't even widen my eyes, but inside, I was screaming. A giant sense of revulsion and denial welled up inside me, even as I drowned, each metaphoric flail dragging me under a little bit more. The whole universe pressed down, and something inside me pressed back. There was a terrifying moment when I could feel not just myself but the sense of something other. Something far away and yet so close I felt its presence in the room, in my heart, under my skin, trapped and angry. Terrible. Hateful. Hungry.

Something inside me snapped.

And that quickly, I was no longer on Ynisthana.

58: The Price of Freedom

Once Tishar established they wouldn't be able to buy Talea, she left Kihrin in the great hall with two of her guards and withdrew to the private salons a second time.

The great hall was the main auction arena of the Octagon. Vendors wandered up and down the aisles, selling sweetmeat-stuffed sag or cooled teas for the patrons. Watching the cleaners, who didn't wait for guests to leave before sweeping the aisles, Kihrin deduced this hall never closed; there was always someone up on the block for sale. Kihrin also realized right away that royalty seldom came to this hall. While it was the closest to entertainment of all the auction blocks, it was also the equivalent of slumming. The slave masters of this hall didn't hold themselves with the same sober professionalism of the salons, perhaps because they sold to merchants and commoners.

One such smarmy salesman took note of Kihrin and his guards and attached himself to the young man as an unwanted tour guide.

"Would Your Highness care to see the inspection pens? A rare chance to see the slaves before they go up on the block, yes?"

"I'm not looking for anything," Kihrin said.

"Oh no? But Your Highness, we have everything! Need a pillow girl? Servant boy? Exotic tastes are our specialty . . . Zheriaso, Doltari, old, young, fire-hairs from Marakor and piebalds from Lake Jorat. I have a half-morgage virgin from Khorvesh who is delightfully alien and yet quite beautiful . . ."

Kihrin stopped and looked at the slave master. "What about trouble-makers?"

"Troublemakers?"

"Sure. Troublemakers. Thieves and the like. Ones sentenced here in court to slavery as punishment for crimes."

The slave master raised an eyebrow, and his gaze on Kihrin changed its regard. "Oh. You want *gladiators*?"

"I want cheap and expendable," Kihrin corrected.

The slave master snapped his fingers. "This I can provide. Please follow me, my lord."

Merit sighed and changed the position of his legs, at least as far as the chains let him.

There wasn't much else to do, although he spared a minute to curse the fates that brought him here and the people specifically involved. He elaborated on what he'd begged the gods to do to their genitalia, in detail, then spat to the side.

Across from him, his cellmate spared him an affectionate chuckle, which of late had become Merit's way of judging his creativity in the cursing arts. If he came up with something clever, Star might even laugh.

Merit had never learned his cellmate's proper name, but he'd taken to calling him "Star." A diamond-shaped patch of white marked his forehead, like he was a horse or something. His skin was patterned in a way that looked more like animal coloration than tattoos. The name seemed to amuse Star, and Merit's street sense told him that his fellow prisoner was best kept smiling. Merit didn't think he would want to be on the receiving end of Star's unhappiness. It didn't take high-born schooling to figure out Star was bound for the gladiator's arena, and that he'd do well there.

For a while, anyway.

Merit had little such faith in his own chances. It was enough to make him wish they'd taken a hand instead.

The door at the end of the row clanged open. There was noise up and down the aisles as prisoners and soon-to-be slaves leaned over to take a look at who was coming in for an inspection. It could only be an inspection: it was the wrong time of day for food. Merit craned his neck to see Venaragi was leading a nobleman down the rows. He growled to himself and leaned back into the shadows. Nothing good ever came from the royal lot looking down here—they didn't want gladiators and they weren't about to trust any of the folk sentenced to these blocks with weapons or guard duty. Merit slouched down to avoid notice, although he saw out of his peripheral vision that Star hadn't made any sign of either recognizing or responding to Venaragi's entrance or his high-born guest. His loss, Merit supposed.

If this was a jail, there would have been whistling, or catcalls, but no one was so foolish here. To draw that kind of attention was tantamount to asking for Thaena's hand in marriage: an early, unpleasant grave. The footsteps stopped near his cell, and he all but held his breath.

"Hey Merit," a familiar voice said. "How's the arm healing?"

Merit looked up, surprised. The man who stood on the other side of the gates dressed in blue silks, with enough embroidery and jewel work to make Merit drool. For a moment, the sophistication of the nobleman's garb was so distracting Merit forgot to look at the man's face, but finally he did.

"Rook?" Merit stood up and made it two feet toward the bars before the chains pulled him back. "Thaena's teats! It's you."

Rook pulled up one side of his mouth in something like a smile. "I was hoping to spot a friendly face down here. Instead, I get you."

"Shit," Merit said. "You're looking friendly enough to me. Faris said you'd sold yourself to some noble fop as a play toy, but I didn't believe it! But look at you . . ."

Rook turned his head. "Hey Barus." He motioned to one of the blue-dressed guards near him. "Am I a noble fop's play toy?"

The guard shook his head. "No, my lord. You are Kihrin D'Mon, eldest son of the Lord Heir D'Mon."

Kihrin looked back at Merit and shrugged. "Who knew?"

Merit blinked. "You lucky son of a bitch."

Kihrin's laughter was mocking. "I guess it must seem that way." Then he scowled. "You still running with Faris's gang?"

Merit turned his head and spat. "That weasel's the reason I'm in here. Bastard let me fall for him—said I still had two hands left to lose."

"Hm." Kihrin looked him up and down, then turned and snapped, "Slave master, how much for this one?"

Venaragi, who had been pretending not to listen to their conversation, scurried over. "Oh that one, milord? He's heading for the Arena . . . probably have him fight leopards. He'll fetch at least five thousand thrones at market."

"Five thousand thrones for this worthless piece of garbage? He doesn't look like he even knows how to hold a sword!"

"Oh, he's a clever one though. I'm sure they'll teach—"

Kihrin sighed, exasperated. "What about the other one? I'm dipping into my personal allowance, you understand. I'm not trying to buy a virgin pillow girl."

"Him, I will sell you for five hundred thrones," Venaragi offered.

Both Merit and Kihrin blinked simultaneously.

Merit looked over at Star. The man was chewing on a small sliver of wood, paying no attention to the conversation at hand, even though it involved his own sale.

"Why so cheap?" Kihrin asked.

"Milord wanted cheap, did he not?" Venaragi replied. "We haven't been able to sell him, and so the price drops lower. Soon we will be paying someone else to take him off our hands."

Kihrin looked at Star. "What's your story?"

Star looked up, his dark eyes glittering in the torchlight. He rolled the splinter of wood back and forth across his lip for a second, then clenched it in his teeth. "Story?"

"Yeah, your story. How'd you end up here?"

"Milord, there is no need—"

Kihrin raised two fingers of his hand. The slave master stopped talking.

Merit's eyes widened. *My, my, how quickly he's gone native,* the street thief thought to himself.

Kihrin turned back to Star. "So? Let's hear it."

The splinter of wood bobbed up and down against Star's lip. "Horse thief."

"That's it? Your price down to five hundred thrones and the Octagon all but giving you away because you're a horse thief? Why haven't they sold you as a gladiator?"

"They have." A coarse chuckle escaped Star's lips. "Twice."

Kihrin tilted his head and stared. When Star didn't elaborate, he looked at Venaragi for an explanation.

The slave master scowled. "He runs away. He's very good at it. You said you wanted troublemakers . . ."

"You were going to sell me a slave who has successfully escaped from the Pits? Twice?" An echo of warning crept into Kihrin's voice. Merit leaned back against the slimy, mossy wall and watched, keeping a bland expression.

Sometimes it was just nice to watch a pro work.

"No, no, I was going to warn you—"

"Hell you were. You were going to let me buy this man and never say one word about his history and be done with him. When my Aunt Tishar hears about this, she'll tell Humthra and—"

"No, no!" Venaragi exclaimed, eyes suddenly wide. "I find you other men, yes? Strong, well trained . . . I have troglodytes. You have never seen the like . . ."

"No," Kihrin said. "I'll take this one." He pointed at Star. "For double his price. And you throw in the other one for free as an apology for what you tried to pull. He's a runaway in the making too, and you know it. I'm doing you a favor by taking him off your hands now."

Venaragi looked over Merit and his cellmate for a moment, then nodded. "Very well, my lord. You have a deal."

The slave masters of the Octagon were only too happy to be rid of them all, and they couldn't get Merit and Star out of their cell fast enough. As they left by the slave gate, Merit grinned and turned toward Kihrin. "Son of a bitch! I can't believe you did that! Rook—"

Kihrin grabbed him by the arm, precisely where Butterbelly had hit him with a crossbow bolt months before, and pushed him into an alcove. The spot was still tender; Merit bit the inside of his mouth.

"Understand something," Kihrin hissed at him. "The only reason I didn't buy you and feed you to the crocodiles in the river is because you only started running with Faris last year. Thank Taja for that, because if you were one of the old guard, I'd have bought you just to watch my guards disembowel you."

"If I was one of the old guard," Merit said through clenched teeth, "Faris wouldn't have given me up to the Watchmen."

Kihrin's grip on his arm loosened. Kihrin looked behind them at the two D'Mon guardsmen, then back at Merit.

"I need you to do me a favor."

"I was wondering what the price for all this love would be."

Kihrin snickered. "Nothing's free, huh? I want you to go to the Shattered Veil Club in Velvet Town. You know where that is?"

"Yeah, but they shut it down. Nobody's real sure why—"

"Never mind that. You go to the building in the back. You take the stairway up to the second floor, and there's a small room. I want you to bring me back anything you find there. Anything. Take the place apart. I'll pay you for what you find. Better prices than you'd make with one of our fences."

"Hey, Rook," Merit whispered. "The word is you killed Butterbelly. If people find out I'm helping you . . ."

"That's my insurance you won't talk. You go mouthing off where I am and I'll make damn sure that people know who bought your freedom. Scabbard won't understand. He won't understand at all."

Merit swallowed. He saw just how bad it could go. "All right. I'll play it your way. If I do find anything, where do I bring it? I don't think I can just come calling on your palace with a note or something."

"No, I—" Kihrin chewed on his lip for a moment.

"What about the Culling Fields?" Merit said. "We can both make it there, and I can leave any packages with a bouncer there who owes me a favor."

Kihrin thought about it, then nodded. "Okay. What's the name of this bouncer?"

"Tauna. She's cute."

Kihrin blinked. "The bouncer's a woman?"

Merit grinned. "Yeah. I really love that bar. This will take me a couple of days . . . I'll leave it for you at the end of the week?"

Kihrin helped Merit out of the alcove. "Deal. Here's a hundred thrones for new clothes and the like, and Merit . . ."

Merit smiled. "Yeah?"

"Don't make me come find you. There isn't any place in the City where you can hide. I know all the safe houses. Nobody wants me to come gate-crashing with soldiers."

Merit started to open his mouth to dress down Kihrin for suggesting anything so stupid, but the cold look in the Key's eyes stopped him. Kihrin didn't care anymore for Shadowdancer rules or Shadowdancer propriety. He thought he was better than that now, more powerful than that. He'd let this whole royal birth craziness go straight to his head.

Or maybe, a small voice inside Merit whispered, he'd simply cased the situation the same way he once would have cased a house, and figured out which way the dice would fall . . . the Royal Families play a different game, by different rules.

So instead, Merit pursed his lips and said, "Whatever you say, boss."

Kihrin watched Merit run off and hoped he wasn't making a mistake. He'd never known the man, except that he'd been picked by Faris as one of his bully boys. He had no idea if he was trustworthy or not.

It was a fishing trip, in any case. He didn't know if his father Surdyeh had left anything worth finding. If he had, logically it would have been taken by Darzin's people, or Therin's.

He turned his attention to the last slave. "Do you have a name?"

The man grinned with teeth that needed brushing. "Sure."

Kihrin waited, then rolled his eyes. "What is it?"

The man paused, flicked the toothpick from one side of his mouth to the other. "Star."

"Star?"

The slave shrugged. "Sure, why not?"

Kihrin looked at him. Star was clearly an easterner, taller than any locals save the few oddities such as himself. His coloring was politely described as bizarre. Still, his appearance sparked a memory.

"You're Joratese, aren't you? From the plains?"

Star ducked his head in a gesture probably meant to signal agreement.

Star lazily looked at Kihrin, then at his two guards, then back at Kihrin.

He was, Kihrin realized, sizing up his chances to make a break for it. He remembered Morea's advice on the basic stupidity of trying to turn a Joratese into a slave.

Then Star scowled at the gates of the Octagon and said, "You didn't want me. You wanted the thief. So now what?"

"I don't know. What can you do?"

"Well," Star said slowly, "I can steal a horse for you."

59: Kharas Gulgoth

(Kihrin's story)

You killed Merit? Merit's part of your collection?
When did that—yeah, right, never mind.
I'll continue.

We stood outside. Bruised clouds circled in a spiral over our heads like the sky-dwelling cousin of the Maw. The air stank, humid and sulfurous, lashed with a whisper of acid that scratched the back of my throat with each breath.

No, this was not Ynisthana.

"What in the hell did you just do, Scamp? I've never felt anything like that."

"Me? It wasn't *me.*"

"It damn well wasn't me! I was never any good at gates. Who else could it have been?" Tyentso floated in the air, her feet just above the ground, right next to me. I hadn't felt her leave my body.

We were outside, but also standing in the remains of a ruined city. Blocks of stone and metal showed their age, slouched under the weight of years and pitted from the scabbing air. A thin silvery grid of light traced the edges of buildings, outlining where the walls should have continued but had since collapsed. It was as if the whole city had been protected by a magical ward—and the ward had survived long after the structures themselves collapsed into decay.

I think the city must have been beautiful once. So many of those shapes suggested wide balconies and delicate plazas, tall pillars, and graceful fountains. Now? It was a skeleton grown corrupt but not yet rotted away enough to collapse entirely.

"Where are we?" Tyentso's voice was quieter now. I didn't have the sense she expected me to answer the question. "This is the Korthaen Blight."

"What? No!"

"Pretty sure, Scamp." She crossed her arms over her chest. "Of all the places you had to choose, good job picking the morgage homeland. At least I'm already dead."

"I didn't *do* it." I swallowed as I examined the area, half-expecting bands of morgage to be hiding behind every stone. At least I could stay invisible.

Directly ahead of us was a building that wasn't falling away to nothing. Its stones were whole. No pits or cracks marred the surface of its perfect walls. I couldn't tell what purpose the building had originally served. It might have been a temple or a palace, a great university or some hall of government.

It probably wasn't the stables.

Eight beams of light, each a different color, streamed to the topmost point of the building from the different compass points of the sky, the light traveling so far that I couldn't see the origin of any single beam. That light smashed together, lighting a crystal rod with a faint glow, before the whole was lost to whatever lay inside the building. The view was beautiful, or would have been if it hadn't filled me with so much dread.

"I've been here before," I whispered.

Tyentso stared at me. "When?"

I shook my head as I walked toward the building. "I don't remember."

I wrestled with my fear. Tyentso wasn't possessing me anymore, so it was all a bonus from here on out. Plus, I wasn't trapped on the island anymore, so that was even more a plus. Yes, if we were in the middle of the morgage-ruled Blight, that was a problem. Yet I still knew how to turn myself invisible, and they couldn't do anything to Tyentso. So that wasn't nearly the challenge that it appeared at first. All a matter of perspective.

Everything was going to be fine.

I walked inside the building and stopped in my tracks.

Like the rest of the city, this was probably beautiful once too. Inlaid stonework and graceful statues, all of it in a style very different from normal Quuros ornamentation.

In the center of that vast space, someone had carved a sphere out of the palace or temple or hall of government. Walls, ceiling, floor, and columns sheared away, as if everything within a fifty-foot distance of the center of the great, echoing hall had simply been annihilated.

A man floated in that negative space.

I shuddered even as I stepped forward. I found myself moving to get a better look, ignoring Tyentso's hissing warning to be cautious. I had to know. I had to see him.

I couldn't make out details. He was a silhouette, the blackest thing I have ever seen. He had no features, no clothing, no reflection at all that might give one a sense of depth and shape. That silhouette wasn't large—shorter than myself—nor was he a big or heavily muscled man. And yet

I knew that silhouette, knew that body. It was as if I was looking at something so familiar to me, that if I could just concentrate I'd remember how I knew and why he'd called me there.

He opened his eyes and looked at me.

Now, I know what you're going to say. He was darkness incarnate. Utterly black. He was the opposite of the light that pulsed down from the roof and kept him trapped in floating suspension. How could I even tell he had eyes, let alone that he had opened them? All I can say is that I could tell. His hate washed over me with an intensity keener than the Old Man's fire. He knew me. I knew him. The pure fear I felt under his gaze was fear such as I have never felt before. I had never been as afraid of anyone or anything before or since.

And then I felt his will against mine, pulling me to him. I felt the overwhelming desire to go to him, to join with him, to be part of him.

We would be whole. We would be free.

Nothing would ever chain us again. Nothing.

"Ty . . . I need your help."

"My goddess," Tyentso whispered. "I think I know who that is. I know . . ." She stared for a moment, shocked into absolute stillness. Then she shook it off. "Kihrin, we need to leave."

"Possess me," I said, grinding my teeth as I stepped forward. "Do it right now."

To her defense, Tyentso didn't demand to know what had changed from just a few minutes earlier. She simply took control of me.

The next few seconds were shaky. I think I was screaming, or trying to. I might have cried. I know I struggled to run back to where that silhouette waited for me.

None of that mattered, thankfully.

Tyentso sprinted me right back out of the prison and kept running until we reached the edge of the city. I felt her loosen her control, just enough that I could talk and move on my own but not so much that she couldn't reassert herself if I proved to still be under that monstrosity's power.

I bent over and was sick all over the stone walkway.

"Scamp," Tyentso said, "I think that was Vol Karoth." She sounded numb. "You brought us to Kharas Gulgoth itself."

I shuddered and was sick again, sick until I dry heaved. Logically, I had no idea who Vol Karoth or Kharas Gulgoth were. Although as the son of a minstrel, you'd think I'd be slightly more familiar with stories concerning the destruction of an entire race. Yet it didn't matter: I knew this place. I knew that creature. I knew him in my soul. She was right.

"Gadrith used to talk about this place all the time," she continued. "Kharas Gulgoth is where the King of the Demons, Vol Karoth, is imprisoned, trapped by the gods themselves. Gadrith wanted to use him. Evil bastard dreamed of coming here, but never had the guts."

Images formed along my peripheral vision, phantoms that had been summoned, not from the living world, but from Tyentso's memories. One of her phantoms, a tall man in black robes, strode down the avenues, his face hidden in shadows.

Then the full meaning of what she said sank in. "*Gadrith?* How do you know Gadrith the Twisted?"

I felt her surprise. The phantom wizard of House D'Lorus seemed to echo that surprise, turning his head to stare at me.

I recognized him: it was Dead Man.

"How do I know–?" Tyentso laughed. "I thought you realized, Scamp. He was my husband."

"Dead Man–" I'd have thrown up again if I had anything left. And it all came crashing back. Thaena had said Tyentso's true name was Raverí, which meant that she was Raverí D'Lorus, Thurvishar's publicly acknowledged *mother,* apparently never executed after all for her role in the Affair of the Voices. She still probably knew more about Gadrith's methods and motives than any other living being, save his gaeshed adopted son.

What were the odds that I'd run into her on board *The Misery* by accident?

I knew enough by this point to recognize Taja's meddling touch when I felt it. Just this once though, I didn't feel upset by that fact.

"He's not dead?" She'd been following the train of logic as if it were her own. I felt her dismay, her disgust, her shock. Tyentso hated Gadrith, hated him with a pure emotion I couldn't hope to match for the man. I think she was ready to open some sort of magical portal to take me back to him right that instant, and rid the world of him once and for all. The only thing stopping her was the small and inconvenient matter of still being dead herself.

Besides, she was never any good at opening gates.

"We have to return to Khaemezra." I stood and leaned against a wall for strength. I felt drained, as if just being in the same room as Vol Karoth had pulled away some of my life. Then my fingers felt an odd shape in the rock, and I realized that it was a bas-relief.

Someone had carved away at the rock with a chisel, smooth, beautiful work that didn't match the style of the city. Curious, I looked at the rest of the scene. A long story had been carved down the street, filled with figures engaged in combat. Eight people, four men and four women, gathered around a glowing crystal that threw off rays of light. Another eight figures, the same figures, followed, but each one was holding a symbol:

a skull, a coin, a sword, cloth, an orb, a wheel, a stream, a leaf, and a star. I stepped farther down the street and traced out more patterns: the eight figures fighting monsters with the heads of bulls or hands like talons, creatures with serpent tails instead of legs and tentacles instead of arms. Then another scene, where just one of the eight, the one with the star symbol, left the battle escorted by a ninth person. Another ring of eight people followed, each one carrying a crystal, this time with the star-symbol man at their center. The ninth man was there too, only he held a sword. The next image showed the ninth man plunging that sword through the man with the star symbol.

The next scene . . . I swallowed as I traced it. The man with the star symbol was gone, nothing left of him but a silhouette carved into the stone, a negative outline with angry chiseled lines radiating out. No sign of the nine men and women who had been there, just nine undulating shapes, each crawling away in a different direction. There were eight shattered pieces of crystal, and a single, twisted sword. After that, images of people dying, demons everywhere, fire raining down from the skies.

This wasn't a story with a happy ending.

"Who carved these?" I asked, touching the images. I looked around. It wasn't chance I'd found these scenes, because they were replayed on every stone surface along the thoroughfare. Again and again, as if generations had spent their energy recording a single, horrible event.

The boom of drums echoed through the city.

"I've heard the morgage who live in the Blight view this city as sacred," Tyentso said. "You need to hide, and you need to do it right now."

I heard footsteps, approaching fast.

I flattened myself against the wall and began repeating my invocation of invisibility. A second later, a dozen male morgage warriors jogged down the avenue. They were giant men, easily the largest I had ever seen, and their inhuman nature was evident. Their skin was a mottle of yellow, brown, and black, and their noses ended in tendrils above each nostril. These fell down the sides of their mouths in a way that—from a distance— might be mistaken for mustaches. Their eyes were quicksilver without iris or sclera. And, of course, they had the famous spikes on their lower arms. Poisonous spikes, as Roarin back at the Shattered Veil had taken great joy in demonstrating back in the day. Not all half-breeds had them. He'd been so proud.

These weren't half-breeds though. They were full-blooded morgage, the same warriors who had terrorized the dominion of Khorvesh. Quur only became the military power the world fears today due to the urgent need to put them down.

The morgage are the only force who still regularly invades Quur.

They trotted down the street, heads swinging from side to side as they looked around.

They were hunting.

I was confident they wouldn't be able to see me, but then those nose tentacles twitched. They stopped. The tentacles twitched again.

One of them bent over near the spot where I had vomited up my breakfast.

"Run," Tyentso whispered to me.

I swallowed and stayed where I was. "If I run," I thought back, "they'll find me for sure."

There was commotion, talking. None of it was in a language I understood, but the quality of their voices sounded like something Khaemezra might call family.

"Then I suggest prayer, Scamp," Tyentso said.

I'd heard worse ideas. Taja might even answer. I kept my spell playing in the back of my mind but I didn't know if I had to pray out loud for it to work. Would Taja hear my thoughts? I wasn't sure. I thought about her, and rescue, as hard as I could without breaking the spell.

Nothing happened.

Another figure strode down the main street. The warriors scattered to make room. This figure was smaller, dressed in a yellow robe decorated with tiger stripes. One of the warriors called out and pointed to the mess I'd left on the streets.

"Laaka," Tyentso whispered. "That's a woman."

"Yeah?" I didn't understand. Yes, it was a woman. I couldn't see what she looked like under the robe, but from the scale I could assume either a woman or a child. "So?"

I felt her exasperation. "Have you ever seen a morgage female before? Ever? I knew a professor back at the Academy who was convinced the morgage have no women and reproduced through some sort of asexual budding. Given how the morgage seem to hate our women, I thought they must keep their own prisoners, locked away somewhere."

"She's not a prisoner. She's giving orders."

Indeed, while Tyentso spoke, the newcomer flipped back the hood of her robe. Underneath was a morgage woman, probably of middle years. She had the same eyes, the same tentacle nose as her brethren, but her skin was black. That is, except for a stripe of silver scales that ran down one side of her face. It began at hair that wasn't the iridescent ribbons I'd seen on the goddess Thaena, but sharp spikes. The men bowed their heads to her in respect, while one of them gestured, clearly indicating they wanted her help finding the trespasser.

I slipped my vision past the First Veil. "Ty, she's a sorceress."

"Oh, of course she is. We need a distraction," she said.

As if on cue, a dragon flew overhead.

The morgage reaction was immediate. They were not happy to have that sort of visitor, for which I couldn't blame them: I wasn't thrilled myself. My first thought was disbelief that the Old Man had followed us so quickly. Then I realized that this dragon was the wrong color—a rainbow of metallic shimmer overlaying white, as if someone had spilled oil on top of marble.

Not the Old Man.

The morgage shouted, pointed, and began running, clearly intending to organize a defense.

"Now!" Tyentso yelled in my head.

I ran.

I heard shouts behind me immediately. I didn't think they could see me, but sound or smell or some other quality gave me away. I pulled a dagger out of my belt as I dashed, slashing back behind me as I heard footsteps slamming down in chase. I dodged to the side as one of the morgage came crashing through the space where I'd been a second before. I slashed across again, this time making contact along his back as he passed. He roared. Unfortunately, I don't think I'd done much more than confirm my presence and make him mad. I certainly hadn't slowed him down.

"If you feel like helping, be my guest!"

Tyentso snapped, "Are you going to freak out on me this time?"

"No!" *I hope not . . .*

Easily five more morgage were in pursuit. I shuddered as Tyentso took over my body again. In some ways, she made the situation worse. In any event, I stopped being invisible. The morgage screamed in triumph as they saw a target. The Stone of Shackles around my neck turned to ice.

Tyentso chanted something long and unpronounceable, but I felt my mind shift as she cast her spell, felt what she did. It was a more effective magic lesson in under two seconds than I'd ever had before in my entire life.

The closest morgage fell back with his hand to his neck, eyes bulging, and gasping for air. Tyentso had pulled all the moisture from his lungs, and without that lubricant, his air passages were sticking to each other, closing—effectively giving him an asthma attack. One of his fellows stopped to help him while the others advanced toward us, if more cautiously.

Then I felt an agony of fire pierce through my leg. One of the morgage had thrown a spear right through my right thigh, pinning me to the ground. My own momentum pulled against the wound before I could stop myself, making it worse. There was blood everywhere, all of it mine.

"Tyentso!" I screamed

"I'm working on it!" The next spear impacted and shattered against an invisible wall of air. I felt myself (under Tyentso's direction) putting up a wall of fire to keep our pursuers back.

But even through the flame I could see that morgage sorceress making her way toward us, and I didn't think that fire would keep her at bay for very long.

"Concentrate on what's happening right now," Tyentso admonished. She was right of course. I had more pressing problems.

"First, the spear," Tyentso said. She put my hand on the shaft and I felt her changing the tenyé of the wood until it was brittle and weak, easily broken.

"Ty, if that's nicked the artery and you pull it out . . ."

"Think I've never seen a wound before, Scamp? This is going to hurt."

I bit back on a scream as the edges of the wound started to sear. She was burning the wound, cauterizing it. My vision blacked around the edges as I threatened to pass out.

"Stay with me, Scamp! We're not out of this yet."

I blinked away the darkness. I must have been out for at least a few seconds though, because I'd already pulled out the spear. I'm pretty sure the damn thing had chipped bone. It sure as hell had done a lot of muscle and blood-vessel damage. I needed to splint and bandage it. I needed to clean out the wound. I needed to treat it for the poison or toxins almost certain to be used to coat a morgage spearhead.

I didn't have time for any of that.

"You don't know how to fly, do you?" I asked as I limped in retreat.

"You wouldn't enjoy the landing . . ."

"Pretty soon I'll be willing to take the chance." I laced the invisibility back around me, although it wouldn't do too much good to stop anyone from following since I was leaving a trail of my own blood as a marker.

I heard the morgage behind us, the low chanting as that sorceress did her job, the shouting of the warriors. I started looking around for ruins that might make reasonable hiding spots.

Then the glowing lattice of energy that had covered every wall and floor of the ruins leaped upward and formed a cage around me. I slammed into the web of energy as I tried to escape, and arcs of pain slashed through my body.

A ball of smoke flew toward me, coming not from the center of the city where the morgage were, but from the outskirts. That ball lengthened and grew darker, swirling up into a man-sized shape.

A voice from inside the smoke said, "You're a long way from home, little brother."

A spike of panic welled inside me, and I thought for a terrifying moment that it was somehow Darzin. *Darzin had somehow managed to track me down.*

But it wasn't.

The man who stepped out of the smoke was Relos Var.

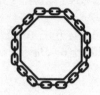

60: The Invitation

(Talon's story)

The two half-brothers sat cross-legged on a makeshift blanket, spread out on the stone floor in Galen's secret hiding spot. A single tallow candle wedged near the base of the statue of Thaena illuminated their meal.

"The Culling Fields?" Galen exclaimed. "Why would you want to go there?"

Kihrin had stolen a basket of fresh-baked sag, fruit relishes, and peppered meats meant for the serving staff. He'd suggested they come here so their father wouldn't catch them eating "common food." Galen had leapt at the idea for many reasons, not least of which was that their father was in an even more foul temper than normal. Galen thought the harder his sons were to find, the better.

Although cramped, the small storeroom never grew hot, no matter what the temperature outside. Galen suspected a great deal of fitted stone sat over their heads, acting as insulation against the scorching sun. The storeroom possessed no windows; he had only the vaguest idea what their true location might be. The tunnel that reached this place contained twists and turns that Galen had never mapped. He liked to fancy they weren't on the D'Mon grounds anymore.

His brother smeared a piece of sag bread with mango relish. "Why shouldn't we go to the Culling Fields? The place is a legend. I've never had the metal to go. I want to watch a duel."

"But we're too young. Father will never agree to it."

Kihrin grinned. "He already has."

Galen's jaw dropped. "He—no! How did you do it?"

"I gave him a gift."

"What?"

"You know that Jorat fireblood mare he's been trying to mate with his own stallions?"

Galen nodded. He did indeed know, and suspected she was the reason for their father's bad mood. Darzin had shipped the horse all the way from Jorat, bought for a bargain from some ancient horse farm fallen on hard times. Then Darzin discovered the mare was so large, wild, and nightmarish she mauled anyone who came too close. The mare had only been on the grounds a week, and had killed five groomsmen and escaped from her stall twice. Darzin himself didn't dare go near her. Galen thought it was only a matter of days before his father took the whole thing as a loss and had the horse put down.

"Well, I found a Jorat horseman. Bought him at the Octagon. If he can't make that mare behave herself, I don't think anything will." Kihrin bit into bread with happy enthusiasm. "Darzin was so grateful he agreed to let us go."

"Wow." Galen blinked in surprise, and then his expression grew serious. "But you know if that slave of yours fails, Darzin will have him killed."

"No slave of mine. I gave him to the High Lord. If Darzin wants to kill one of the High Lord's slaves . . ." Kihrin shrugged as if it were none of his concern.

"Ho ho! That's clever." Galen grinned. "I'll have to tell Mother about that one."

Kihrin's expression soured when Galen mentioned his mother. "Sure. Right." Then he asked, "Is she . . . uh, well? I haven't seen her at dinner for a few days."

"What? She's fine. She's had a fever," Galen said, giving no indication such an excuse was thin at best—for the Royal Family who specialized in magical medicines.

"Ah." After an awkward pause, Kihrin continued, "So do you want to go?"

Galen rolled his eyes. "Of course, I want to go! Father never lets me go out."

This statement made his brother pause. "Never?"

Galen shook his head. "He says I'd shame him."

"But," Kihrin said, "you must have friends . . ."

Galen found himself flushing with embarrassment. "I do have friends. I see them several times a year at social events. There's Kavik D'Laakar and my cousin Dorman D'Aramarin.* I'm going to see them at the New Year's Festival parties. And I have teachers and sometimes I speak with the children of some of the serving staff, as long as Father doesn't find out."

His older brother jumped up and offered Galen his hand. "Come on then. Let's go see this tavern my father always used to go on about."

---

*Growing up as royalty can be an excruciatingly lonely existence, especially for a child in line to inherit. Every child from a rival family is assumed to be some sort of saboteur or spy, and every child from inside the family is a potential rival. Some families purchase companion slaves for their children, but such a relationship can hardly be a healthy one.

"Right now?"

Kihrin nodded. "Absolutely right now. Before Darzin changes his mind—"

A loud clanging noise echoed in the room and both boys froze. Kihrin frantically gestured to the tallow candle, and Galen snuffed it, plunging the room into complete darkness.

It was like that for several minutes. Galen found the darkness uncomfortable and disquieting and, although he would never admit it, even frightening.

Then he felt a hand clap over his mouth, and he almost screamed before he realized Kihrin had found him. The older brother tugged on Galen's shirt and whispered, "Look at the light!"

Galen was about to turn on him and chide him for talking nonsense when he realized that no, Kihrin was right, there was a light.

The light formed a fine thread, almost hidden behind rows of stacked boxes and old broken chairs. The light crossed behind them, near the floor, then up from floor to ceiling, then across the ceiling and back down again. Galen, tracing that tiny path of light with his eyes, realized what he was looking at was a doorway. He'd never noticed it from this side, but it was big enough to take Thaena's statue and all the other larger objects.

Then he heard the voices.

"It could stand a good dusting," said one voice. Something about the tone made Galen's skin prickle. Kihrin's hand on his shoulder tightened, either from warning or fear.

"I can't very well call in one of the serving staff, now can I?" Galen knew that voice: it was his father, Darzin. Galen put his own hand on top of his brother's and squeezed back.

There was a third voice then—a rich, velvety baritone. "Of course you can. You'd simply run yourself out of serving staff." Then the same voice asked, "What was this place?"

"Originally a mausoleum," the first man explained in his dry, dead voice. "The tomb was built for Saric D'Mon the Eighth and the four dozen concubines he had ordered to be killed upon the occasion of his death.* It was converted into a demon-summoning chamber by High Lord Pedron twenty-five years ago. The doors in the various alcoves and down

---

*The fad of killing an entourage to guard one's tomb fell out of popularity when people realized that such murdered innocents tended to make poor guards to the tomb, even if Thaena did allow the souls to linger as undead. The story goes that the four dozen concubines of Saric D'Mon VIII all animated, broke out of their tomb, and went on a killing spree that began with the High Lord successor who had authorized their deaths. When twenty-some soldiers and five members of the family had died, the concubines fell to the ground, dead once more.

those hallways lead to the burial chambers for Saric's wives—Pedron used them to hold prisoners awaiting sacrifice. For a brief time after that, this was a chapel to Thaena under the direction of Therin, but abandoned after he turned away from the church."

"And I've been using the place to test poison recipes," Galen's father added.

"Yes," the third man agreed, "that fits your reputation." He didn't make it sound like a compliment.

There was a moment of quiet, and then Darzin said, "You should watch your student. He seems intent on getting himself killed before you're ready to slay him yourself."

The first, horrible voice answered with a cold laugh. "He's capable of taking care of himself."

"D'Mon," the third voice said in an unfriendly way, "I understand why you're necessary, but don't make the mistake of thinking that means I have to be nice to you. You're a small-minded, petty bully who has no understanding at all of the real nature of power. If my master didn't need you, I would take great delight in turning your bones back into the mother's milk from which they were born, and consider myself to have done a service for the public good."

Again, a long pause.

"Thank you for letting me know where we stand with each other," Darzin finally said.

"My pleasure" was the response. "Although I'd hoped you'd be stupid enough to attack me."

"Enough games," the dead voice snapped. "Do you know your parents met on this very spot, boy?" he said, addressing the third voice again. "Pedron was holding your mother in preparation for a virgin sacrifice, in that cell right over there, before your father Sandus rescued her."

"This cell here?" It was all Galen could do not to gasp when the light from the edges of the doorway dimmed. There could be only one explanation: the third man was now standing directly in front of the door, perhaps only a score of feet away from them. If Galen could hear every word that these men said, the reverse was true as well.

"If my memory serves me correctly, yes."

"So, this is the place where Pedron was claimed by his demon? No wonder you wanted me to see it."

Darzin snapped, "Yes, yes, it's just dripping with sticky-sweet sentiment. The point is: will it work for the ritual?"

"Of course," the third voice agreed. "It's perfect. The vibrations are almost impossible to ignore. This place is so close to Hell you probably wouldn't even need the sacrifice to catch Xaltorath's attention."

"You'll have your sacrifice," Darzin said. "I insist."

"Oh, we're agreed on that much. I said you wouldn't need it to catch his attention. I said nothing about what it would take to keep him on his leash. This one isn't for amateurs. Our little pet would rip this city apart given half a chance, and he'd start with us."

"So we've seen," the first voice said. "The last sacrifice was entirely unsuitable. He almost escaped from us. This time it must be blood."

"I have no shortage of that," Darzin replied.

"Very well. I leave it in your hands," the grim voice answered. Galen heard footsteps, pacing. "And either clean the place up yourself or have someone else do it and dispose of them afterward. This dungeon reeks of sweat and fear."

"Yes, my lord," said Darzin, in the most deferential tone Galen could ever remember hearing from him.

There were more footsteps as the men walked away, and the light snuffed out. Galen started to move, leather boot scuffing against the stone as he tried to stand, but Kihrin's hand on his shoulder prevented it. Too late, Galen realized they were not yet out of danger, and he nearly screamed when he heard that third voice again.

"Don't come back. Next time he'll find you." The rich timbered voice was so soft and quiet that Galen almost thought it spoke directly into his mind. The man must have had his mouth pressed against the door. Kihrin's hand tightened on his shoulder hard enough that Galen bit his lip to keep from yelling out.

"Are you coming?" Galen heard his father say loudly, but from an echoing distance. "Or do you enjoy playing with yourself in the dark?"

"Only dark to someone such as yourself," the baritone voice corrected. This time Galen heard the man's shoes scuff against the slate floor as he walked away. There was also a swish of fabric: robes of some kind or a heavy cloak. After a moment, a clanging sound echoed that Galen could now identify: the sound of a heavy iron bar being moved against a door.

Fabric moved as Kihrin somehow managed to shove all their food items back onto the blanket, sweeping it all up into a ball in the dark.

"Quick, take my hand," Kihrin whispered.

Galen started at every noise as they rushed back out along the tunnel. He was so terrified he was close to tears. When they reached the servants' hall, Kihrin stopped Galen from running. He dropped the blanket filled with spilled jars onto a servant's cart. Still holding Galen's hand, he strode briskly to the front of the First Court and called for an escort of guards and carriage.

At least he looked calm to most. Only Galen could tell by the weight of his intertwined fingers that Kihrin was shaking.

Then again, so was he.

61: GUARDIANS OF THE CAGE

(Kihrin's story)

Relos Var looked the same as when I'd seen him last. Time had left no mark on him, even though years had passed since our last unfriendly meeting. He still dressed in plain garb, and looked like no one of any importance if you couldn't see his aura.

Wait . . . little brother?

I was definitely not that. Maybe he meant it the way Darzin liked to call me "boy."*

"Raverí?" Relos Var looked at me curiously. "What are you doing in there?"

"Oh fuck. He can see—"

Relos Var waved two fingers. "Come out of there."

I felt a ripping sensation and Tyentso stood by my side. She stared at her hands, then at the glittering strands of energy surrounding us, before muttering a curse that somehow didn't melt the very stones, although it made a good attempt.

Relos Var's smile was delighted. "I am so pleased you survived that unpleasantness in the Capital, Raverí. I hope you're not still working with your father. The only thing worse than a power-hungry fool is a power-hungry fool who thinks he's smarter than everyone else."†

Tyentso's stare was ice. "I guess that confirms he really is still alive."

"Oh, I wouldn't call it 'life,'" Relos Var replied.

"Tyentso, who are you talking about?" I'd have thought they meant Gadrith, except for the "father" bit.

"Gadrith," Tyentso said. "He means Gadrith."

"Uh . . . no? Gadrith's your husband," I said.

"Yeah, he was that too." She scowled. "Don't look at me like that, Scamp. I wouldn't have married him if he had any interest in sleeping with me. Or anyone, really."

"Don't kid yourself, Raverí. Yes, you would have," Relos Var said. "Now

---

*A bad habit Darzin almost certainly picked up from Gadrith.

†One might say this about Relos Var too, of course.

I admire a woman who's willing to make any sacrifice to get what she wants. Perhaps you and I can come to some arrangement? Your life for service to me?"

"You can't do that," Tyentso said, shaking her head. "You can't Return me back to life."

Relos Var took her denial in stride. "You will find that there is little I cannot do."

I looked to the side at Tyentso's ghost. "Can you get us out of here?"

"Only by possessing you," Tyentso said, "and I can't do that right now. Look at your hands."

I did. Both hands were covered in the same tracery patterns as the cage, and the ruins. It didn't stop me from moving, but I assumed it would stop Tyentso from possessing me.

"If you're going to kill me," I spat at Relos Var, "get it over with."

He chuckled. "Kill you? Why in all the heavens would I do that? You're going to save us all. What have they been teaching you?"

I couldn't tell if he was joking.

"I lament that while you are in the right place," he said, "this is the wrong time, and my plans are not ready for you yet. Now why don't we get you out of here and see about healing that wound, before those pesky morgage come back and make our lives difficult—"

A spear impacted the wall of energy and shattered. Another landed next to Relos Var's feet.

"Too late," he said. He waved a hand, and shards of wood flew backward toward their point of origin.

The morgage were ready. They raised shields and (in the case of the singular woman) a magical field of energy to stop the reversal of their attack.

"I hope you realize this can only end one way," Relos Var called out. He clenched a fist, and one of the morgage warriors erupted in flames, screaming. "Let us go so you may return to your important duties."

The woman spoke, and to my surprise she spoke Guarem. "No deal, traitor. You are not welcome here in the lands you destroyed, nor will you be allowed to take what belongs to us."

I had a feeling that when she said "what belongs to us" she meant me.

I'll be honest: I was growing a bit tired of being passed around like a favorite dish at dinner.

"Oh, rip the Veil," Relos Var said. "One experiment goes awry, and people never let you hear the end of it." He raised his fist again, squeezed, and another morgage went up in flames.

They didn't retreat. Even if two of their members were almost certainly dead with more to follow, the morgage didn't take a single step backward.

I cast about for something, anything, I could do. My leg hurt with a desperate pain and the stone around my neck chilled my flesh: I was a long way from being safe. Even though Relos Var was rapidly escalating a wizard duel with the morgage sorceress, the magical prison he'd crafted around me hadn't lessened in strength. Tyentso couldn't return to my body, where she might talk me through casting a spell.

If I was going to do something, I'd better do it fast.

"Dear Taja," I whispered, hoping my words would go unnoticed in the commotion. "Hear my prayer. I'm in a lot of trouble right now and I need your help. Relos Var is here and—"

I lost my voice.

"Stop that," Relos Var snapped. He gestured again, and my arms locked at my sides. "I am trying to help, but this is no place for such a discussion."

"No, it is not," a woman said. My heart leapt as I heard her voice, although I had only ever heard it before in a dream. "And the idea that you are trying to help is every bit as laughable."

Taja appeared in the middle of the street.

I guess she'd been listening after all.

She didn't look like a child this time, but her silver hair, her eyes, and her white skin remained the same. I knew her immediately.

Taja gestured; the prison surrounding me faded. Her attention, however, focused on the sorcerer. "Leave now, or I will force the issue."

Relos Var tilted his head and regarded the goddess. "Here? In my sanctum? There is no place on this planet where I am stronger or you are weaker. You don't dare have a true fight with me here."

I blinked.

The plan had rather counted on the fact that a goddess—not just any goddess but one of the Three Sisters—would be someone no sorcerer would be so foolish as to fight. He'd backed down against Khaemezra, so it followed he'd back down when faced by a genuine goddess.

He would have to. Right?

Except he didn't seem to be playing along. In fact, everything about Relos Var's manner suggested that he didn't think he was outmatched. He was prepared for a violent confrontation, even though he couldn't be that powerful. And yet . . .

"You might beat one of us here, but not all of us," said another woman's voice, more familiar than Taja's in many respects because I heard it so often.

Thaena appeared in the center of the street, but the Goddess of Death was not alone. With her was a third woman, whose appearance almost made me cry out—because I didn't expect to recognize her. Yet I did.

The third goddess had chestnut-red skin and hair the color of flame, full lips, and high cheekbones: one of the most perfect faces I had ever seen. She wasn't Joratese—she had the wrong kind of hair and no horse markings—but she still resembled the Jorat girl that Xaltorath had once shown me. The resemblance was too strong to be a coincidence. She wore a shifting shawl around her shoulders woven of red, green, and violet light.

So, this was Tya, Goddess of Magic.

All the morgage who weren't busy putting out their kin fell prostrate to the ground. I suspected their reverence was saved for Thaena, but who knows? Maybe being a god, any god, was enough, as one could argue it should be. And these weren't just any gods, after all: the appearance of the Three Sisters was the sort of omen capable of dooming emperors and cursing whole countries. It had happened before.

"All of you? Perhaps." Relos Var shook his head. "But all of you are not here. Whereas all nine of us are."

The three women exchanged looks.

"You're bluffing," Taja said.

"Maybe. Possibly. But even if I am, what are the odds that a fight with the four of us—here, in this place—wouldn't wake *him*?" Relos Var sighed, long and suffering. "I made all of you. Do you think I cannot destroy you if I wish it?"

Thaena scoffed. "You've been trying for millennia. If we're so easy to dispense with, what's stopping you?"

Which, I noticed right away, was not a denial. Relos Var had made the gods? That was a ridiculous notion. How could that be possible? How would that even work?

My eyes fell back to one of the bas-reliefs covering the walls. Eight figures. Eight symbols. Thaena's symbol was a skull. Taja's symbol was a coin. Tya's symbol was her rainbow veil . . . I knew I'd match each symbol to one of the Eight Immortals, the true gods who only tolerated all others. And that ninth figure . . .

I looked back at Relos Var.

Tya nodded in my direction. I knew, even without speaking, that the spell constricting my voice had been lifted as well. The pain in my leg faded.

"You're not taking him," Taja said. "We will not allow it."

"You shouldn't have brought him back," Relos Var said. "It was cruel."

"Far less so than what you did," Thaena said.

"I'm not your enemy," Relos Var replied.

"But you are," said the Goddess of Magic, "and our sin is how long it took all of us to realize."

They locked stares then, Tya and Relos Var, and something passed between them. Tya looked at him the way one might look at a person once loved, someone who had hurt them deeply: with regret and sadness and no small measure of hate. They were not friends, but maybe they had been once. Maybe even more than that.

So, because I've always been a bit of a fool, I interrupted. "All I want to know is who you're keeping prisoner in the center of the city."

Taja walked over to me, put her hand on my shoulder. "That's not important. Let's get you out of here."

"I think it is important," I said. "He opened his eyes."

Everything stopped.

Everyone stopped. Even Relos Var stared, blank faced. Some of the morgage warriors didn't seem to speak Guarem, and they were too busy prostrating themselves before the divine to listen. But Relos Var, Tya, Taja, and Thaena all looked at me with the same expression.

Dread.

"He speaks true," the morgage priestess said, rising to her feet. "The hungry one stirs, restless. It will not be long before he wakes once more."

"The hungry one? Is that what you call it? What is that thing?" I repeated.

Relos Var tilted his head and regarded me. "They haven't told you?"

"Haven't told me what?"

He smirked. "I bet she thinks you don't need to know." He straightened his misha and tilted his head toward the three women in a way that was akin to a salute, before turning back to me. "When you grow tired of their evasions and their cleverly twisting truths that counterfeit better than lies, come find me. I will not deceive you."

Taja snorted.

He glanced at her, his look both scolding and condescending.

I almost stabbed him then. I had the knife in my hand, the weight of the hilt resting lightly against my palm. In that moment of distraction, I almost went for him. I'd learned, you see, that talismans alone didn't protect a sorcerer from steel. Catch a wizard in the right moment and he's as vulnerable as anyone else.

But I didn't. His words had been baited well; I couldn't help but nibble. And I wasn't so stupid that I couldn't see the Three Sisters weren't telling me even a fraction of the whole story.

I stayed my hand.

He turned back to me, and his eyes flickered down to the steel in my hand. "Until next time," he said.

Without any further fanfare, Relos Var vanished.

Thaena turned to the morgage, speaking to them in their native tongue. Orders, from the sound of things, which they were quick to follow. Tya pulled the veil over her face and started walking slowly through the street, holding out her hands. The silvery strands outlining the memory of walls strengthened as she crossed over them.

"Who are you, Scamp?"

I turned back to Tyentso. "Come on, Ty. You know who I am."

She shook her head. "No, I don't. And I don't think you know either." She waved a hand around her. "This shit doesn't happen to the runaway children of fourth-ranked Houses."

Taja cleared her throat, and we both startled as we realized we had been standing there ignoring a goddess. "I think it would be best if I take you both out of here. It's not safe."

She glanced toward the center of the city, and I myself wondered just who exactly it wasn't safe for.

"Taja, how did Relos Var find me? How did he know I was here? Why did he call me his little brother? And what did Relos Var mean about making you? He was going to fight you . . . how could he think he could fight a goddess–"

She set a finger against my lips. "Now is not the time."

"Oh, you might want to make the time. Real soon." Tyentso held out her hands as the goddess gave her a dirty look. "What are you going to do to me? I'm already dead."

"No. You're just catching your breath," Taja replied as she moved her hand to my shoulder, and rested her other hand on one of Tyentso's phantom arms. Despite her incorporeal nature, the Goddess of Luck touched her without difficulty.

The universe shifted.

62: THE GRYPHON RING

(Talon's story)

"I just don't know who I can trust," Kihrin confided in Galen as they rode in the carriage to Arena Park. "Therin's going to want proof about Darzin, and what do I tell him? I overheard him speaking to someone who I *think* summoned up a demon? I don't know who Darzin's partner is, but now there's a third person. And I don't who that person is either, except he knew we were spying on him and didn't rat us out, which makes no sense." Kihrin stopped to chew on a thumbnail. "I don't get it. Whoever he is, he's clearly part of their plot. Why wouldn't he tell them we were listening?"

"Maybe he only wants them to think he's helping," Galen suggested. "Maybe he's a double agent. Or maybe—oh, he didn't seem to like Father very much, did he? Maybe he's hoping we'll get Father into trouble." Galen's eyes went wide as he worked himself up over the idea.

"Maybe. But it's a hell of a risk if his master figures out what he's up to. I certainly wouldn't want Dead Man mad at me."

"Dead Man?"

"Yeah. That's my nickname for the fellow with the spooky voice. Believe me, he looks even worse than he sounds. He's a wizard, and I don't mean like the way Darzin's picked up just enough tricks to get by. Dead Man is one of the scary wizards. I saw him kill a man by pulling his soul out of his body and then stripping the skin and muscle off his bones."

"You've met this man?"

"Not met exactly," Kihrin admitted. "More like spied on. But you don't want to mess with someone like that. I know you don't think it's possible, but trust me: he's scarier than Darzin."

"Oh dear. We've got to tell *somebody* though."

"Who?"

"You could tell Miya. She'd believe you. She likes you." Galen's tone was wistful. He thought the seneschal of the house was elegant and lovely, but she never had time for him the way she made time for Kihrin.

"Great!" Kihrin replied. "And what's a gaeshed slave going to do about it again?"

"Oh." Galen chewed on his lip. "I see your point."

"I could tell General Milligreest, but then he'd want to know why I didn't say anything months ago when I was over at his estate. He'd probably think I was making the story up because I didn't want to stay with the D'Mons. He'd throw the whole thing back in the High Lord's lap, and we know Therin is as likely to cover it up as do anything about it."

"What about Aunt Tishar?"

Kihrin looked excited for a moment and then his expression fell. "I don't think so. I mean, I think she'd believe us, I'm just not sure what she could do about it besides put her own life in danger. She starts asking the wrong questions and Darzin will just kill her. And even if he doesn't, will people believe her? I mean, she's still Pedron's sister."

"Mother says she was rather more than that . . ."

Kihrin stared at Galen, incredulous. "You're joking."

"I am not! It's what Mother says. That they were . . . you know . . . and that he was always giving her gifts and the like so she wouldn't say anything about it. Mother says Master Lorgrin had to cast a special working to ensure she was a virgin for her wedding night."*

Kihrin looked ill. "No wonder she—" He shook his head. "If that did happen, I'm sure it wasn't her choice."

Galen shrugged. "I don't know. What if it was? It must have been very hard for them, both half-vané and always being stung for it, their mother killed because of it. Why wouldn't they turn to each other? I think it's kind of romantic."

"So you'd put your little sister, Saerá, to the mat for a thrust? You'd be all right with that?"

"NO. Gods no. That's completely different."

Kihrin laughed. "Uh-huh. Sure it is." For a minute, all was quiet inside the coach, then Kihrin thumped the seat next to him in pure frustration. "*Oh.* If only I had a way to contact Emperor Sandus. He'd take this seriously."

"The Emperor? Are you out of your mind?"

"No." Kihrin looked at Galen. "Remember what Dead Man said? About the third person being Sandus's *son*? I'm pretty sure I could get Sandus to take this seriously. And, Sandus is the one who banished that demon the first time and healed me. He's real big on stopping demons. He'd want to know about this, and he'd believe me too. But I'm pretty

---

*Given that the vané have no special prohibitions against incest, this is possible, but I think it more likely that this is just malicious gossip.

sure I can't just walk up to the palace and ask for an audience, you know?"

"Oh no," Galen agreed. "That's just the place where they throw the parties. I know that. He doesn't live there. I've heard that he really lives in a giant palace made of diamond in the middle of Rainbow Lake, on an island guarded by two gigantic dragons."

"Galen," Kihrin admonished. "Everyone knows there isn't an island at the center of Rainbow Lake."

"I know that," Galen said. He gave his brother a wise, knowing wink and said, "It's invisible."

Kihrin raised an eyebrow. "I'll believe it when I see it."

They were still laughing as the coach rolled to a stop in front of the Culling Fields.

Kihrin had been raised on stories of the Culling Fields tavern, although he had never been there himself. Surdyeh refused to take him, saying the crowd there was too rough and there were too many opportunities for Kihrin to get himself into trouble. Kihrin now realized "trouble" meant "being recognized as a D'Mon." Kihrin had, naturally enough, placed a visit high on his to-do list, but he'd never found the time for two reasons: one, because visiting required a trip to the Upper Circle; and two, because the tavern sat in the very shadow of the Citadel. The Watchmen spent time there when not on their rounds. The tavern was guaranteed to be swarming with off-duty militia at any and all hours. Most Shadow-dancers, Kihrin included, avoided the Culling Fields as if they were handing out free samples of the clap with each ale. Kihrin had no trouble understanding why Merit would suggest the place. There was hardly any other location in the whole Capital less likely to have a Shadowdancer present to witness their exchange.

Kihrin saw, as he helped his brother down from the carriage, that the Culling Fields was less a tavern than a full inn. Three stories tall, it was so large that the upper floors were available for let. It was probably twice the size of the Shattered Veil Club, which made it a very large building indeed. Unlike the Shattered Veil, or indeed unlike any other building in Velvet Town, the Culling Fields stood alone on the boundary of a large green area of fields and woods. Cobblestone walkways led to and from the building, and branched off to form a circle around that area of the park.

Kihrin knew the park had to be the famed Arena itself, where would-be emperors fought for the right to rule. It wasn't precisely what he expected. It was not a coliseum, but merely a circular open space divided between forested woods, briar, and a bit of meadow. It was lined with a few small, ruined buildings that looked in imminent danger of collapse from age. Still, Kihrin saw where the tree branches abruptly cut off, forming a kind of dome shape over the area. Many of the trees inside had a blasted, wild look to them; there was something perverted and strange to their shape and color. A litter of debris—weapons and armor and old skulls—peeked out from under a cloak of grass and leaves.

The Emperor had been crowned here, through trial by combat, since the founding of the Empire itself. It was where Kihrin's mother (if she was his mother) Lyrilyn had met her fate, and where Ola had found him as a newborn babe. He no longer doubted which of Ola or Surdyeh's stories had been the true one. Why both of them had been willing to lie about that truth and pass it off as fiction—ah, now that was where the mystery lay.

Kihrin turned back as Galen tugged on his sleeve. "Come on. The door is this way. There aren't any duels going right now, or there'd be a crowd."

Kihrin said, "I thought you said you'd never been here before."

"I haven't," Galen replied, "but Father tells stories. He fights a lot of duels here."

"Yeah, that doesn't surprise me."

The front doors were open, and a large man who might as well have been wearing a sign that said "bouncer" nodded to them as they entered. Kihrin could tell right away that this wasn't like other taverns—the large glass windows that looked out from the tavern to the dueling area of the Arena wouldn't have lasted fifteen minutes in a regular bar. Also, no bar Kihrin had ever seen could afford to use the sheer quantity and variety of mage-light he saw.

The tavern was also sublimely crowded. People of all ages, sexes, races, and stations bumped shoulders together with seeming disregard for the fact that their neighbors were of all ages, sexes, races, and stations. Except Kihrin assumed that they occasionally remembered and then it all devolved into one of the Arena's famous duels.

"We're looking for a female bouncer named Tauna," Kihrin whispered to Galen.

"We are?" Galen asked, surprised.

"Just follow my lead." Kihrin walked inside the taproom as if he'd been there before and knew exactly where the choice spots were located. There was a bland-looking bartender serving drinks: bald, tall, thin, and a bit potbellied. He raised an eyebrow at the pair as they walked by.

"Do you realize we're the youngest people in this place?" Galen said.

"Our metal is old enough."

Kihrin found them seats at a table, ordered a pepper beer for each of them from the wench, and took the time to give the room a thorough examination. There were a number of women present, although most of them looked like the help or sparkling drinking accessories. Not one of them looked like anyone he would describe as a bouncer.

"Kihrin." Galen tugged urgently on his sleeve. "What is that?"

"Hmmm? What? Who?" Kihrin looked around.

"Over in the corner. Look at him! He's not human."

Kihrin glanced around the room. The focus of Galen's attention wasn't easy to see, since he blended with the wall behind him. He had no hair at all, but wicked porcupine-like spikes coming off his head, and a nose that might not have been a nose at all. It didn't end so much as turn into tentacle-like protrusions, which twitched and moved on their own. There were more spikes coming off his arms, and talons instead of nails, but worse than any of this were his eyes—which practically glowed with re-flective firelight. He was huge and covered in muscle.

"Oh, they have a morgage. It's really rare to see a pure-blood."

"That's one of the morgage?" Galen was practically whispering. "No wonder they're such a problem."

"You usually only see the half-breeds left over from whenever the mor-gage go on a rampage. The only work they can find is bone breaking or the like. I'm sure he's one of the bouncers here."

"Indeed. Who'd want to mess with *that*?"

"You'd be surprised. They probably have wizards on staff as well." Even as he said the words, Kihrin noticed a lively game of cards at a nearby table. One of the gamblers was a woman, dressed in kef trousers and a man's misha tunic, her feet wrapped in tall boots she raised up to rest on a stool. A sly grin crossed her face as she presented a winning hand to her groaning opponents.

"That'll be her," Kihrin told his brother, gesturing at the woman with his chin. He quickly signaled a waitress and put a silver chance on her tray. "A drink for the woman at the table over there. Tell her it's from her old friend Merit."

The woman took the money, nodded at Kihrin, and left in the direc-tion of the game.

"Who is this woman?" Galen asked. "What are we doing here?"

"I'm trying to find out some information." Kihrin flashed a brilliant smile at his younger brother. "Trust me."

Galen blushed and looked away. "I thought we were here to have some fun."

"Did you *see* her? Trust me, this is fun."

Kihrin leaned back in his seat and tried to act nonchalant as he saw the waitress drop off the ale and message. A moment later the woman dressed in men's clothing pardoned herself from the group of gamblers and made her way through the crowd, avoiding their table entirely as she walked to the back stairs and out of sight.

"Hey! Wait, she was supposed to—"

"Your drink, my lord," the waitress said as she set the glass down on the table.

"We haven't finished our pepper beers yet—" Galen started to protest.

Kihrin threw him a dirty look and shook his head.

"Thank you," Kihrin said as he tipped the waitress.

The moment she turned away, he fished a key out of the drink and grinned.

"Did you bring me here just so you could meet a girl?" Galen didn't hide his indignation.

Kihrin gave his brother an odd look. "Why, jealous?"

"What? No. That's stupid." Galen was even redder now. "Why would I be jealous of some tavern wench I've never met before?"

Kihrin leaned over. "We're here because what I'm doing may or may not be legal. And I certainly don't want Darzin to know about it. You still in? Because if you're not, you can stay here while I finish my business."

Galen swallowed. "I'm in. Of course I'm in."

"Okay." Kihrin waved the key. "Then let's go meet a girl."

The door was locked, but then, that's what the key was for. Kihrin ushered Galen inside and then shut the door behind them.

"If you're expecting something out of Velvet Town, you're going to be very disappointed," Tauna told them both. The woman sat in a chair in a corner of the inn room, looking out toward the Arena Park through a window. "I don't do kids for any price."

Galen crossed his arms over his chest and looked thoroughly annoyed at being called a "kid."

Kihrin just nodded and pulled up a chair for himself. "Merit said he'd leave his present for me with you."

The woman raised an eyebrow. "Present? Is that what you call it?"

"Sure, why not?" Kihrin paused. "Unless he hasn't found anything . . . ?"

She reached behind the mattress and pulled out a smallish satchel before tossing it on the bed. "I didn't say that."

As Kihrin started to reach for the satchel, Tauna tsked and shook a finger. "Ah, ah, ah. Payment first, my lord. Merit said this isn't a freebie."

"How much?" Kihrin asked.

"One thousand thrones," she said, as if she were listing the price of a glass of brandy.

"What?" Even Galen seemed shocked.

She smiled at that. "Just between you, me, and sweet pea over here, your friend doesn't know what he's found, or he'd be asking ten times that. One thousand's a bargain price."

Kihrin tilted his head and looked at her critically. She was confident and calm and doing a good job of suggesting she didn't care how the bargaining came out, one way or the other. "How about I give you two thousand thrones and you tell me what you didn't tell Merit?"

"Make it fifteen hundred so I don't feel so guilty about robbing the cradle." Tauna reached for the satchel herself and pulled it into her lap. As Kihrin handed her the wad of promissory notes from the Temple of Tavris, she opened the bag and pulled out a roll of vellum, several wads of silk string for a harp, a bundle of old clothes, and a gold ring set with an intaglio ruby.

Kihrin's breath caught as he saw the ring.

She saw and grinned. "Oh, you've seen one of these before?"

Kihrin reached for the stone. "Yes, I have."

Galen leaned forward and also examined the ring, but his expression was less intrigued. "It's just a gem."

"No, it's not. Give me a second." Kihrin grabbed the ring away from Tauna and spent a few minutes staring at it. "This isn't the same ring I saw before. It's just the same design. My father had this?"

Tauna's eyes widened. "Oh sweetheart, I don't know the details. Merit said you paid him to do a job. This is the job. That's all I know." She leaned forward. "But I've seen the rings before, worn on the least likely of fingers. All of them carved with that same crown and gryphon. It's a kind of club, I figure, a very secret club that pays no attention to race, sex, or class.* I've seen that ring on Council Lords and I've seen that ring worn hidden around the necks of slaves—or least on people pretending to be slaves."

Kihrin sat there frowning, moving the ring back and forth in his hands. Galen hated how unhappy he looked. "This is . . . this is about your father? Surdyeh?"

---

*The Gryphon's Men. At least, such is what I call them—I have no idea what they call themselves. There are many groups who are interested in the prophecies, for many reasons, but I begin to think that I have underestimated this cabal in particular. What their goals are is still unknown to me, but looking at the evidence, we can clearly count Kihrin's adopted father, Surdyeh, among their ranks. And at least one Emperor, as well.

Kihrin nodded. He turned back to Tauna. "Would you be willing to find out more information on them for me?"

She stood up. "Not in a thousand years. I'm sorry, but I know enough about staying alive in this town to not meddle in some things. Tell you what though. I'll pass the request on to my father. Maybe he can help you."

"Who's your father?" Galen asked.

"Doc,"* Tauna said. "He owns the bar." She started walking to the door. "Now if you don't mind, I have a room full of suckers to finish fleecing."

---

*She's adopted. I checked.

63: Tea with Death

(Kihrin's story)

Things blurred for a bit. I was aware of events, but disconnected from them. The sound of coughing as Tyentso gasped for air and was Returned to life. Voices as people talked about her and probably about me. One of those voices was Doc's and another was Teraeth's. Eventually, Tyentso's voice joined in. Shouting. Everyone seemed excited, which I suppose was to be expected.

Then quiet. Everyone left.

A hand came down on my shoulder. A moment later, Khaemezra sat down across from me. "What happened, Kihrin? How did you end up in Kharas Gulgoth?"

I stared at her. Her appearance was a lie, just as much an illusion as the one she had woven when we first met in Kishna-Farriga. Her name was a lie. Everything about her was a lie. She wasn't Khaemezra, High Priestess of Thaena.

She *was* Thaena. I saw the truth now.

I wondered if Kalindra had known when she had claimed Thaena only lived in the Afterlife. Had Kalindra lied to me, or had Khaemezra lied to her?

"Kihrin?"

I clenched my jaw and looked away.

After a beat, I turned back, met her gaze, even though it was stupid, even though she terrified me. "How could Relos Var have created the Eight Immortals? The Eight created the world. You–" My voice cracked. "–created the world. Yet when he said he *made* you, you didn't protest."

Khaemezra sighed. "Were my parents still alive, they would object to both the idea that Relos Var made me and equally to the notion I helped make the world. The Eight did not create the universe. We were *empowered*."

"By Relos Var?" My voice cracked again.

Her reluctance to talk about this was palpable, but I was long past caring. "That wasn't his name back then, but yes, by Relos Var."

I found myself standing. "I've worshipped the Eight since I was a child!

Worshipped Taja! You—" I pointed a finger at her. "—you lectured me on *faith*. And you were never gods at all?"

"Sit down, Kihrin."

"*No.* The whole reason the Eight went after the god-kings is because they were all false gods. And you're sitting here telling me that you're no better than the god-kings who enslaved—"

"Not one more word!" The second time, her voice was Thaena's, and not just that of an old woman. In her anger, the illusion dropped, and she was Death once more—ebony-skinned and waterborne. "Sit. Down."

I sat.

"If you were *anyone* else, you brash little bastard, I would strike you down for daring to say such a thing." She stood, effectively trading places with me. "If we had our way, there would be no temples, no altars, we would *not* be called gods. We never wanted to *be* gods. And we have no interest in enslaving the people we sacrificed everything to save."

"Sacrificed? What sacrifice? He made you GODS."

She held up a finger. I swallowed and shut up.

"Imagine that you are a soldier, Kihrin," Thaena said. "Imagine that you are locked in an endless war against an enemy whom you literally cannot see. That was us, fighting the demons. Trying to fight them. Failing. Now imagine someone comes along—a clever, *clever* man—and tells you that he can give you the keys you need to fight these demons invading your home. He can give you the keys to drive them back so millions of your people will live. All you must do is let yourself be tied to a cosmic force. You will have power beyond imagination. But you will be removed from your race, from your family, from your friends, from everyone you care for. That's not the worst part. The worst part is that the job will *never end.* You will be a soldier standing on the wall *forever,* guarding those who cannot protect themselves. You cannot die and you will serve until the end of the universe. You will never be able to put aside your burden, hand it off to someone else, and go back to a civilian life. Would you volunteer for *that*?"

Something made me take the question seriously. I had the weird, itchy feeling that she wasn't really asking me hypothetically. I bit my lip. "I think I might. I . . . yes. If I knew what I was getting into. If it was my choice."

Thaena nodded and looked away. She mumbled something.

"What was that?"

She turned back to me. "I said: that's what you said the last time, too."

I stared at her. My mouth went quite dry. I didn't really know how to respond to that. I certainly didn't want to jump to the conclusion that she seemed to be suggesting. "You—" I cleared my throat. "Are you suggesting that—"

"Yes?" A flicker of amusement, brief and bitter, returned to her eyes.

"Okay, so if anyone accuses me of hubris, uh, I guess they'll have a point, but are you implying that I have held that job? I used to be one of the Eight?" I laughed nervously. "I mean, that would be impossible. Because, for one, you don't have a missing member of your group. All eight of the Eight Immortals are accounted for. And for two, surely, I would remember if I was a god! That whole problem with Darzin and Dead Man would have been easier, although I guess Relos Var would still have been a thorn. And also, because, uh, you just said the Eight can't be killed. I mean, unless you were being hypothetical there too."

"None of the Eight has ever been killed," Thaena said. "We're tied to elemental forces. You'd have to destroy the force—luck or death, magic or nature—to destroy us."

I exhaled. "Okay then."

"However," Thaena continued, "lest Relos Var claim I'm being *deceptive*–" Her voice dripped with bitter venom. "–you should know that we have not been eight in number for many years."

"What?"

"In the Capital, if you ask someone who the eighth member of the Eight is, they will say Grizzst. In Eamithon, they will think you a fool for not knowing the eighth member is Dina. In Jorat, he is called the Nameless, his statue blank and covered by a shroud. The Vishai worship him as Selanol, the sun god, and claim that he is dead. None of these is right, but the Vishai are perhaps closest to the truth, even if the name they worship has drifted over the years. What they don't understand is that S'arric never technically died."

"So where is he?"

"You met him tonight, locked away in the center of Kharas Gulgoth. He opened his eyes as you approached."

I drew a shaky breath to restart the beating of my heart. I felt my gorge rise. "So that was a god?" I must admit a part of me was relieved, consoled. You see if that figure was the eighth, well, then it meant that Thaena had been speaking hypothetically after all.

I'm not sure why I thought that was better, really.

"Yes," Thaena said. She looked haunted. "The demons renamed him Vol Karoth."

I tried not to think about how the very name sent shudders through me. "But why did *I* go there? I had no idea that place even existed."

"Do you really want to know?" Her glance was scathing.

"I just asked. I'm tired of being lied to."

Thaena's nostrils flared. "I have never lied to you."

"But you sure as hell aren't telling me everything. What about the prophecies? Are those even real—or are they just a propaganda game played by one side against the other?"

She walked behind me and gathered my hair, pulling it over one of my shoulders. "For a very long time we assumed they were a long-term mind game being played by the demons. Then more and more of the prophecies began to be fulfilled, in very specific ways. Now we are mostly trying to discover if they are a prediction of unavoidable events given by a race that does not perceive time the same way we do, or if they are instructions on how to derive a specific outcome. Are they colorful future histories or recipes couched in symbolism?"

"Which way are you leaning?"

"Toward the recipes," Thaena admitted. "Plus, Relos Var seems to be interpreting it that way, so we can't afford not to as well."

"So, you're trying to stack the deck. Just like they are. You'll have all the trumps in your hand when you figure it out." I tried looking back at her, but she was standing directly behind me, so close I could feel the glittery coldness of her dress against my skin.

"Yes. And since it is difficult to repeat certain variables, it may be that we will never have this chance again. Even now, we do not control certain important cards. Before Xaltorath found you, he did worse damage elsewhere, and you have seen for yourself what Gadrith has twisted his adoped 'son' Thurvishar into. He may well be beyond our aid."*

I remembered the Lord Heir of House D'Lorus and shivered, in spite of myself.

"He's part of this too?"

She nodded. "Sadly."

"And here I was hoping he could be someone else's problem."

"No, I'm afraid he is yours. Someday."

I flinched as I felt her fingers on the back of my neck, her nails picking at the chain of my gaesh. "I still feel like you're not telling me everything."

"That's because I'm not," she agreed as she untied the necklace clasp. "You're young and what you are not yet ready to know would fill the Great Library back in Quur. I have my reasons. I think they're good reasons. Obviously, you're in no position to judge, but knowing you, you'll keep pushing until you find out. Maybe Relos Var will attempt to make it a wedge between us, which I will not tolerate. So, remember that you asked for this." She sighed. "I don't know for certain why you appeared in Kharas Gulgoth tonight, but I don't think any outside force was responsible. You did it, and you did it as a primal response to being possessed by Tyentso."

---

*Let's just comment that I'm glad I wasn't written off as unsavable. I found that "may" to be very reassuring.

I could hear her voice but couldn't see her, and it made me all kinds of nervous. "Yes. I guess that's possible. I just . . . kind of panicked."

"That is on me. It didn't occur to me that given your past, it would be perfectly understandable for you to have a response to that sort of stimulation. I should have also expected the sympathetic response that transported you to the middle of the Korthaen Blight."

I frowned. I didn't know of anything in my past that qualified as justification for my reaction. And I knew enough about magic to know that a "sympathetic response" was flowery language for a common magical technique: like calls to like. I really didn't know of any reason I'd have any sort of sympathy with a fallen, imprisoned god.

I closed my eyes. I did know. I could lie to myself for a thousand years, but on some level, I knew. I just couldn't say it. I couldn't make that leap, admit that truth out loud.

"I have a cousin named Saric," I mused. Then I shook my head. "So S'arric was the one in the drawings I saw on the walls of Kharas Gulgoth. A man—I'm assuming Relos Var—led one of the Eight away from the others, and performed some sort of ritual. And afterward, everything was a mess and S'arric was just a dark outline. So that must be the morgage telling the story of how S'arric became Vol Karoth, yes?"

"Yes."

"Okay, so why S'arric? I assumed Relos Var lied about what would happen back then. You all acted like he betrayed you and killed your favorite puppy. I'm guessing S'arric was that puppy: brave, loyal, not too bright. I saw the looks Tya and Relos Var were giving each other too. You all knew Relos Var. He could have lured any of you into that ritual. Why did he pick S'arric?"

"Kihrin . . ." Her tone was placating, faintly scolding.

"No," I said. "I have to know."

"Isn't it obvious? When Relos Var invented the ritual to create the Eight Gods, he assumed he would be one of the recipients. When he was not, the rest of us assumed that he would be content with the judgment of our government. And we were, all of us, wrong." She paused. "He picked S'arric for the purest of petty emotions. Jealousy. S'arric was his younger brother."

You're a long way from home, little brother, *Relos Var had said.*

You shouldn't have brought him back. It was cruel.

She must have felt it when my whole body went tense. "He called you brother, didn't he?"

"And you weren't going to say anything, were you?" I pulled away from her, thumped the reed mattress with my fist as I turned around. "See? This is why we have trust issues. Are you serious? He hates me because in another life I was the brother he murdered?"

As I leaned back, the gaesh necklace stayed with her. Not just the gaesh necklace, though: I saw she was also holding a necklace I hadn't seen in years. The necklace of star tears.

My mouth suddenly felt dry.

She piled the necklaces into one hand. "Haven't you been listening? He did not murder you. I could have fixed it if he'd only *killed* you. He did something much worse."

Thaena shook her head. "Var likes to claim that he didn't mean for things to happen the way they did, but I never believed him. He was as jealous of you as streams are jealous of the sea. At first we thought he had slain you. It was only after Vol Karoth tracked us down one by one, like a shark stalks fish, that we realized the truth."

"Which was?" I whispered.

"Relos Var hadn't destroyed your former body, he'd changed it. And the monster he created using your flesh, Vol Karoth, didn't have to kill us. He could feed. Feed forever on our energy, and through that, on the very concepts that powered us. He will eventually destroy the world, of course, but . . . he'd started with S'arric, and S'arric's power was over the sun. The sun has a lot of energy. When he's free, Vol Karoth feeds. He's already turned our sun bloated and red, aged it far beyond what it should be, but it will be a while before he's done with it. The sun and stars still exist and that meant you couldn't be truly dead. Instead, your soul was still there, still trapped and imprisoned inside your own usurped body. And none of us dared face Vol Karoth to free you."

What killed me, no pun intended, was that every word felt true, the pieces of the puzzle fit so well. I had to fight not to think too hard about what it would be like to be trapped in such a manner, locked away in a body that was completely and utterly under another's control. To be locked that way for centuries, millennia, the dull numb passage of time grinding down one's mind until there was only a gibbering lump of identity. How could anyone stay sane?

"Well, someone must have," I said, "or I wouldn't be here."

She smiled. "When Emperor Atrin Kandor threw himself at the Manol vané and dragged most of the men of Khorvesh to their deaths, his wife, Elana, took it upon herself to journey into the Blight. Her aim was to try and negotiate with the Dry Mothers. She was only partially successful at brokering peace with the morgage, but she did free your soul, which was a feat no one had been expecting."

"Wait. Elana Milligreest? Doc's Elana?"

Her smile was wry. "The same."

"I hope you thanked her."

"Of course," Thaena said, "then I did what any good general does when fighting an endless war against an impossible enemy: I sent her back to the front."

I thought about that. "Is that what you did to me?"

"Yes. If it's any consolation, you volunteered," she said.

I sighed. "Yeah. I suppose I probably did." I tugged a lock of my hair in her direction. "I have to ask though . . ."

"Yes?" The slant of her eyebrows suggested that she was very nearly at the limit of her patience for answering questions that night.

"Would you have Returned Tyentso if this whole mess hadn't happened? Were you lying when you said that she'd failed your test?"

She hadn't expected that question. A bit of the old humor returned in the crinkle of her eyes. "The true test was seeing how she'd react to the idea of being judged and found wanting. Even when her hour was darkest, she never lost focus on the reason she was there in the first place."

"So you lied."

"Yes." She waved the hand holding the necklaces. "I lied. I do that. I lie, and sometimes I send unprepared children out to fight demons. The world is an imperfect place."

The movement reminded me of what she had in her hand. I couldn't take my eyes from my gaesh, from the star tears. She saw the look, and her smile grew gentle. Then she—

You know what? Fine. I'll tell you. But only because I know there's no hiding it from you anyway. There's no point in trying to keep it secret.

Anyway, she took one necklace in her left hand, and kept the other in her right. The hawk necklace began to glow. It was a subtle thing at first, but the luminescence grew stronger and more vibrant. The glow dripped off Thaena's fingers and pooled in her left hand like the light of a hundred captured fireflies. As I watched, the glowing ball fell away from the silver necklace entirely, drifting from her left hand to the star tear necklace held in her right. Finally, the nimbus sank into the diamonds, making the starlight shimmer even more brightly. Then she reached up and refastened the necklace around my neck and kissed me on the cheek. I felt a chill, the kind I associated with crypts and stale, old graves.*

"Why—?" I could barely articulate the question.

"Slavers' gaeshe are crude things, and easily recognized by those who know their signs. It is best that your gaesh be in something whose value

---

*I certainly couldn't have done what Thaena just demonstrated. Even Gadrith, who has an affinity with tsali stones and their creation, had never given the slightest hint that he could move spiritual energy from one vessel to another beyond their initial creation.

cannot be questioned. No one will wonder why you keep these so close, and greed will prevent their casual destruction. This necklace is worth a kingdom. You're a good match."

"But if you–" I inhaled. "You could reverse it. If you have that kind of power–"

"Oh Kihrin." She patted my hand like she was my grandmother. "I have moved a cut flower from one vase to another. That does not mean I can rejoin it to the rosebush. This heals when you die and not before. I would slay you and Return you whole, but I feel certain Xaltorath is waiting for that to claim you, and it is not worth the risk."

"Why would he? He's not the one who gaeshed me."

She snorted. "Oh, but he *is* the one who gaeshed you. I would know his psychic stench anywhere. He is a wild card, and I do not yet understand his part in this, but until I do, I would not risk playing into his hands. So, I will not kill you."

I shook my head. "I never thought I'd hear someone apologize for why they're not taking my life."

"I do not make the rules, sadly. I never have. Long before I was born, people have died, gone to the other side, and eventually been reborn. It is the cycle. I am simply one of the soldiers standing watch at the walls, and nothing more." Thaena reached over and tapped the necklace of star tears around my neck. *"And the prince of swords shall keep his soul in the stars."* She shrugged. "I have no idea if this is what the prophecies meant, but it's just as easy not to take the chance."

Thaena waved a hand toward the exit. "Now go. I have much to do, as do you."

64: THE D'LORUS FETE

(Talon's story)

Darzin tightened his grip on Kihrin's arm as they exited the carriage into the guest court of the D'Lorus palace. "Do not embarrass me," he whispered.

Kihrin tried to jerk his arm away, but failed. "If you think I'm going to embarrass you, why bring me?"

Darzin's lip curled, but he didn't respond.

The guards fell in behind them both, but the blue-garbed men of House D'Mon seemed out of place against the grandeur of the Dark Hall.

Kihrin was surprised to see the D'Lorus palace was not a single color (that color being black). Black was present, from the dark marble steps in front of the great hall to the ebony trim on the windows. However, someone had decided that if black were the only color available, madness would be the sure and certain result—so virtually every available surface of the Dark Hall was decorated with artwork. Sketches and murals and intricate paintings, of virtually every subject and mood, covered the walls to the point of concealing their base color entirely.

As Darzin tugged him along, he reminded himself of his lessons. House D'Lorus controlled the Binders, whose color was black and whose symbol was a flower. D'Lorus, a House with few members, whose Lord was Cedric and Lord Heir was his grandson, Thurvishar. D'Lorus, who controlled the magic Academy at Alavel, and to whom all wizards owed at least some scholastic fealty. D'Lorus, small and fading, but dismissed only by fools.

Inside the Dark Hall, a swirl of color from paintings, lights, and the rainbow hues of other guests pulled the eye in a hundred directions. Kihrin might have lost himself gaping in wonder if a violent yank on his arm had not brought him back to the task at hand.

"What did I *just* say?" Darzin snapped.

An unfortunate response was curtailed as a cultured, resonant baritone voice greeted them. "Lord Heir D'Mon, I presume? I'm so glad you could make it to my gathering."

Kihrin recognized the voice: it was the third man. The one who had been with Dead Man and Pretty Boy in the crypts, the one who had caught Galen and him spying but let them go. Kihrin fought the desire to swallow, to look nervous, to shuffle his feet.

The same man he had seen at the Octagon.

Thurvishar D'Lorus walked down the shallow steps leading from the second floor to the great hall where guests mingled. He dressed much as he had been when Kihrin had spied upon him, while having tea with his aunt Tishar. This time the Lord Heir of D'Lorus was wiping his hands on a white rag, as if he'd just come from the privacy or a meal. He finished and tossed the cloth to a servant as he closed the gap between himself and Darzin.

The rag was stained with blood.

"Problems?" Darzin asked. He hadn't missed the blood on the man's hands either.

"No, no problems," Thurvishar replied. He stopped and looked at his hands. "Oh, yes." The wizard shrugged. "One of my grandfather's men tried to steal something that belongs to me. I'll have his body strung up later as an example, after the party dies down."* He gave the pair a self-deprecating smile. "You'll pardon me, of course, if I don't offer to shake hands."

Darzin's expression held a look of grudging respect. "Not at all. I always appreciate the need for an appropriate level of discipline, especially in the form of object lessons. May I introduce you to my firstborn son? This is Kihrin D'Mon. Kihrin, I'd like you to meet Thurvishar, Lord Heir of House D'Lorus. He's just returned from the Academy."

Kihrin bowed as he'd been taught. "I'm honored, Lord Heir."

"Tall, aren't you?" Thurvishar said in lieu of more formal greeting. "Call me Thurvishar. Lord Heir's my father's name." He smiled as if daring either of the D'Mons to commit the faux pas of mentioning his treasonous father, Gadrith the Twisted.

Except Kihrin knew it was a lie. Gadrith wasn't Thurvishar's father at all.

So, he smiled back. "Don't you mean 'was your father's name'?"

Darzin coughed to cover his laugh, although the way his hand tightened on Kihrin's arm suggested mixed signals and a warning not to do that again.

The Lord Heir D'Lorus only smiled. "Yes, exactly so. Well, I hope you enjoy yourselves. I believe my grandfather is wandering the crowds, fielding the curious questions of our peers as they attempt to discern just how evil I really am." He waggled his eyebrows at Kihrin. "Now, with your pardon . . . ah, High Lord Kallin. So glad you could make it . . ."

---

*Yes, that really happened. I had my reasons.

He disappeared in a swirl of black velvet as he left to meet the red-cloaked leader of House D'Talus.

Darzin squeezed Kihrin's arm again. "Don't get into any trouble."

"You're leaving me?" The young man didn't hide his surprise.

"I have people to meet," Darzin said. "The wine table is over there." He pointed to a crowded area where young men and women in elegant black robes poured wine into fluted crystal glasses. With that invitation given, the Lord Heir of D'Mon turned and walked into the crowd, smiling as he greeted a favorite.

Kihrin wasn't heartbroken to see him go. Enough interesting activity swirled around the Dark Hall to keep the young man occupied. The young women were captivating, which was unsurprising. The Royal Houses were rich and powerful enough that he imagined no ugliness was allowed to show its head amongst their carefully manicured gardens.

Still, it was one thing to think of such things objectively, and quite another to see a shapely brunette walk by—wearing clothing that would have made a Shattered Veil Club velvet girl blush. She caught his gaze, smiled, and gave him a frank appraisal.

Maybe being royalty wasn't so bad.

"Kihrin? Kihrin, is that you?" He heard a familiar voice and turned.

Jarith Milligreest stood in front of him, holding a glass of wine. He wasn't dressed in formal military attire that evening, but wore a white misha with a red embroidered vest over black kef tucked into boots. He might have passed as a noble himself, if he'd stayed with a single color.

The man grinned and clapped Kihrin on the shoulder. "My father told me you're a D'Mon and I admit, I didn't believe it could be true . . . but to see you here!" He lowered his voice and said, "My condolences on your father. Surdyeh's death was a tragedy."

Kihrin nearly lost control of himself right then. It was the first time anyone had given condolences on Surdyeh's death without some manner of caveat—how he must have deserved it, how Surdyeh had been a criminal. It was the only time when Kihrin knew the person understood. Jarith had met the man. Jarith had seen the worry on his father's face, Kihrin's concern in turn on the streets in the aftermath of that demon attack. His throat tightened and he felt the threat of tears hovering at the corners of his eyes. Kihrin shook his head and managed to stammer out, "Thank you."

"Come then, I have to parade around and make a good impression, and I will not be so gauche as to drag you with me. Later, some friends of mine are going to gather in a room upstairs and have a card game. Look for the door with a vase of peacock feathers outside. You're welcome to join."

The young man ducked his head. "Thank you. That's kind of you."

Jarith laughed and clasped his hand to Kihrin's before he let the younger man go. "Kind? I'm just looking for anyone who's not depraved beyond reason. We outsiders need to stick together. There's safety in numbers, you know." He gave Kihrin a friendly wink before he, too, headed into the crowd to continue mingling.

Kihrin looked around. He couldn't see the violet-eyed brunette anymore, but probably for the best. The last thing he wanted to do was start an incident.

Most of the guests were past their majority by a decade or more. He spotted a group of teenage boys over in one corner, but he knew a closed gang when he saw one. They'd let him know how they felt about him on their own terms, assuming they didn't just dismiss him out of hand for his scandalous upbringing.

Key training kicked in. Everyone was here in the great room, near the food, wine, and entertainment. A few were leaving for private assignations and meetings in upper rooms. Yet there were exits from the room that didn't seem to lead to the kitchens or the servants' areas.

Kihrin made sure no one was paying attention, most of all Darzin, and quietly headed into the back rooms of the Dark Hall.

Kihrin didn't know why he was surprised to discover House D'Lorus owned a magnificent library. The room hadn't been locked and the passage of feet and the wear on the carved mahogany doors suggested regular, steady use. Once inside, Kihrin had taken a few minutes to admire a room nearly as large as the great dining hall at the Blue Palace—but given over entirely to books, scrolls, tablets, and maps.

The room itself was three stories tall, but open in the center, so the higher stories were reached by catwalks and ladders. Every inch of wall space and every section of shelf was lined with books. Kihrin wasn't in love with books—he'd grown to loathe the giant medical textbook Lady Miya was forcing him to memorize—but the quantity of volumes present couldn't help but elicit admiration. Some books sat under glass, and some lay on special pedestals, and some were chained to desks to prevent their removal. There were maps too, on tables and under great gilt frames hanging from walls.

A painting rested on one of the lone walls not covered in bookcases, a painting of an elegant woman with long shining hair and hot black eyes. She wasn't as pretty as many of the women he'd seen in his short stay in the Upper City, but she was handsome and defiant. The subtle slant of a hand on her hip, the tilt of her chin, managed to convey that she was a woman who would never do as she was told. Kihrin liked her immediately.

"My mother, Raverí," Thurvishar D'Lorus said. "She was sentenced to Continuance for her role in the Affair of the Voices."

Kihrin only jumped a foot off the ground, and didn't yelp, although it was a close thing. He turned around and tried to pretend he'd known the Lord Heir was there the whole time. "Sentenced to Continuance? What does that mean?" He hadn't heard Thurvishar approach, hadn't had the least inkling that he wasn't alone in the room. He found himself disconcerted.*

"Oh, you wouldn't have run across it in the Lower Circle, would you? When a female member of royalty, who is expected to provide an heir, is condemned of capital crimes—she's kept in prison until the baby is delivered, and *then* executed. That way the House continues."†

Kihrin felt a shudder. "That's, uh. . . ."

"I believe the word you're looking for is 'vile,'" Thurvishar said. "Anyway, I'm surprised to find you here. Most people would rather be looking for the wine cellar."

Kihrin paused. It hadn't occurred to him that he might be trespassing. He took a step toward the door. "Oh, uh. I didn't realize it was off-limits. I was—" He waved a finger in a circle. "I didn't touch anything."

"Interested in books?" Thurvishar asked. His voice was a purr Kihrin couldn't help but find menacing.

"Sure. Why wouldn't I be?" Kihrin crossed his arms over his chest as he continued maneuvering toward the exit. "I can read."

"Much to your new family's surprise, I'm sure," Thurvishar agreed. "Were you looking for anything?"

"No. I didn't mean to intrude. I should get back to the party." As Kihrin reached for the door handle, it opened on its own.

Morea stepped into the room.

Kihrin felt a moment's dizziness. He knew it wasn't, couldn't, be Morea. This was Talea, the twin sister Thurvishar had purchased. Still, the resemblance was palpable, a dagger pressed against Kihrin's throat. A dagger pressed against his heart when she flinched from him, pulling away with a widening of eyes and a look bordering on panic.

Thurvishar held out his hand to her. "It's all right, Talea. I'm here."

The young woman edged past Kihrin like a feral cat avoiding a hound and rushed to Thurvishar D'Lorus's side. Thurvishar put an arm around her waist and pulled the young woman to him, stopping to kiss the top

---

*I used magic. I'm not by nature good at the arts of stealth.

†I believe High Lord Cedric D'Lorus paid a veritable fortune in bribes to maintain the fiction Raverí died in captivity after giving birth. We all knew it wasn't true, but better an executed Lord Heir's wife than admit the witch-hunters were never able to complete their mission.

of her head. "Please forgive my slave. Her last owner treated her poorly, and she's still recovering."

Kihrin swallowed. "Of course."

Talea looked up at Thurvishar. "My lord, you asked—" She glanced at Kihrin then, quick and uncertain, as if she didn't know if she should speak while he was in the room.

"It's all right, my dear," Thurvishar reassured her.

"You said I should come fetch you before the card game began," she reminded him.

"Ah, yes! So I did." Thurvishar snapped his fingers and smiled before turning to Kihrin. "I would never neglect the passions of a fellow bibliophile. Stay and read if such is your fancy. Alas, my presence is required elsewhere."

Kihrin bit his lip. "Is this Jarith Milligreest's card game?"

Thurvishar paused, his eyebrows drawn together. He gave a single nod.

"I was invited to that," Kihrin admitted. "The door with the peacock feather vase, right?"

"Indeed," Thurvishar said. "Follow me then. I'll show you the way."

65: HANGOVER CURES

(Kihrin's story)

"Wait! Gadrith!" I said as I sat up quickly.

Too quickly. My head swam, and I fought back the urge to throw up.

"Don't shout," Tyentso mumbled from a few feet away. "That's not a name I want to hear when I'm this hungover. Or ever. Ever would be best."

Teraeth groaned and smashed a pillow over his head.

We'd ended up on the brick-lined patio, next to the fire pits. I'd only meant to check on Tyentso and make sure she was all right after the ritual, but when I found her, Teraeth was already there. He'd broken out several bottles of vané wine because "a successful Return from a Maevanos should be celebrated." Then Doc found us, and he'd brought a whole tun of the potent coconut rum the Thriss distill.

It all got a bit fuzzy after that.

"Oh, my head." I rubbed my thumbs into my temples. "No, I meant . . . with everything that happened . . . ow. My eyeballs ache." What had I been going on about? I was pretty sure it had been something important.

Someone dropped an entire rack of cymbals near my head, or at least it felt like it when the tray clattered to the ground. I swear I felt the vibrations in my bones. Given the noises Tyentso and Teraeth made in protest, I wasn't alone in that opinion.

"Pathetic," Doc said, although the smile on his face betrayed his amusement. "I would expect a D'Mon to be better at handling their liquor. Don't they have a spell for this?"

"Six months," I protested. "I was only at the Blue Palace for six months. Miya didn't have a chance to teach me how to cure hangovers. Is that tea?"

"I have rice porridge too," Doc said. "Wake up, lovebirds. Come eat breakfast. You'll feel better."

I blinked and looked around. We'd all passed out in various states around the fire pit, dragging over the large pillows that the Brotherhood kept for just that purpose. The important thing of note, however, was that we were fully dressed in the same clothing each of us had worn the night before. That made it unlikely that any sexual shenanigans had occurred.

Good.

"Ha ha," I said, taking his offered hand. "How much did we drink?"

"All of it," Doc said. "It was amazing to watch."

"Would you please shut up," Tyentso groaned. "I hate you so much."

I started to stumble over to her, then found myself sitting down on a bit of brick edging. I exhaled and tried to stop the world from spinning.

"Yeah, you think it's bad," Tyentso mumbled. "Just wait until you're my age. My body can't handle liquor like it used to." She paused to glare at Doc. "Why are you sober? You matched us drink for drink, you old bastard."

"I've owned a bar for over twenty years. I know when to cut myself off."

"Gadrith," I repeated.

Teraeth sighed and removed the pillow. "What *about* him?"

"So much happened . . ." I grimaced. Everything was loud and bright and horrible. "Note to self: don't mix vané wine and rum."

"Note to self: don't mix vané wine and *life*." Teraeth stood, slowly and with a care suggesting he too was having trouble with his balance. "Try to focus," he said. "What were you saying about Gadrith?"

"He's not dead."

"Yes, he is," Doc said. "You're still drunk. Now come on. Let's get some tea into you, and maybe some food if you can keep it down. You'll be better for it."

"No, the kid's right," Tyentso said. "Gadrith tricked everyone, Nikali."

So she *had* known Doc back when he was Nikali Milligreest. I tucked that information away.

Doc/Terindel/Nikali raised an eyebrow. "I've put that name behind me, along with a long list of others. It's Doc now." He frowned at Tyentso. "What are you talking about? I killed Gadrith myself. He's dead and his soul is safely in Thaena's hands."

"No, he's not," she said. "That damn rat tricked us. That rice porridge sounds fantastic."

"I want an explanation."

"You'll get your damn explanation," she said, "after I get my fucking breakfast."

He laughed. "Yes, Your Majesty." Doc helped Tyentso to her feet and guided her to the table where he'd set out bowls.

One for each of us, I noticed, including Teraeth, although I wasn't so naïve as to think Doc had changed his opinion about his "arrogant" son.

Did Teraeth *know* he was Doc's son? I wracked my memory to see if the subject had come up during our drinking. I couldn't be sure. We'd talked about a lot of things. I dimly remembered Teraeth going on for several hours about how Atrin Kandor had dammed the Zaibur River to create Lake Jorat—and why that had been such strategic genius.

Teraeth picked up one of the bowls and stared at it.

"Yes," Doc said. "Every bowl is poisoned with my very own hangover cure. At least you won't have to worry about the headache." He grabbed one of the bowls and filled it with a porridge mixed with ginger, chopped turtle eggs, shredded pieces of island duck, and wild mushrooms. I had to admit it smelled delicious. More ginger, in the form of tea, sat on the tray in a large Kirpis blue-glazed teapot.

"I wouldn't put it past you," Teraeth muttered, but he too began adding toppings to his breakfast.

I dragged myself to a seat. For a while none of us concentrated on anything except eating, not throwing up what we'd just eaten, and a mutual agreement to be as quiet as possible while fighting the good fight.

Teraeth stirred a spoon through his porridge. "Did you add something to this?"

"I told you: I added a hangover cure. Feeling better?"

"Surprisingly." Teraeth took a healthy draught from his cup of tea and returned to eating the rice porridge with greater enthusiasm.

I concentrated on eating. It really wouldn't have mattered what breakfast tasted like, but the fact that Doc had managed to make this delicious was a nice bonus.

Finally, when Doc resumed giving Tyentso and me dirty looks, I said, "Okay, back in the Capital, there is this sorcerer working with Darzin to locate the Stone of Shackles. He was probably the one who taught Darzin how to summon Xaltorath. And because I didn't know his name, and because he was *extremely* creepy, I've always called him 'Dead Man.' Thanks to Tyentso, I now know who he is: Gadrith D'Lorus."

"Gadrith D'Lorus is dead," Doc still insisted.

"Well, you're not entirely wrong," Tyentso said. She saw the look on Doc's face and waved a hand. "Okay, look. Nobody knows more about Gadrith than I do."*

"Yeah, about that—" I started to say.

She pointed a finger at me. "Do not judge me, young man. None of us have lived a perfect life."

"Oh? I didn't marry *my father.*"

"Yeah, well, I did it for the oldest reason there is."

"Greed?" Teraeth had an eyebrow raised and an incredulous look on his face.

"No." Tyentso scowled. "Revenge." Then she chuckled. "Funny thing

---

*Respectfully, I beg to differ.

is, it wasn't even my revenge. I'd found this ghost who was willing to teach me magic. I wanted vengeance against the Academy dean who'd ordered my mother executed as a witch, and *he* wanted justice for his murder by Gadrith D'Lorus. We struck a bargain. Call it a trade of revenges. Anyway, my plan went off without a flaw, but then I found I was stuck with this ghost until I'd fulfilled my end of the deal and punished his murderer too."

I made a sympathetic noise. I knew firsthand that being possessed by a ghost was not what I considered a good time. Being stuck with one for *years?*

"Still, Ty—marriage?" Doc seemed amused. "You humans frown on that sort of thing, last I checked."

"Oh please. I tell you I've murdered someone and you don't care, but incest? Oh no! What will the children think?" She rolled her eyes. "You have to understand: I couldn't get close enough to Gadrith to kill him. He never left his library except to go to the summoning chambers. Most of his servants were animated corpses. I thought his father the High Lord might welcome me in as an Ogenra, and that would give me a way past the guards and the wards." She exhaled. "I never expected the bastard Cedric to order me to marry his son, and saying no would have—" She coughed. "—let's just say refusal wasn't an option."

Tyentso waved a hand. "The point is: I have studied Gadrith. His witch gift—the very first spell he ever figured out—was how to rip someone's entire upper and lower soul out of their body and turn it into a tsali stone."

Teraeth whistled.

My eyes widened. "Wait. I've seen him do that!"

"I can't imagine it would be a huge leap," Tyentso continued, "from rock collecting using people, to stealing just the lower soul and absorbing it. When he murdered Emperor Gendal, he didn't just kill the poor bastard. Gadrith stole the man's magical power and added it to his own. He made a habit of that, and I can remember—" She paused to wet her throat. "—I can remember Gadrith boasting that the same ability would let him live forever, fool Thaena herself. I thought he was just bragging, but what if he was right?"

"Impossible," Doc said.

"No," Tyentso disagreed. "He was good at manipulating souls. What if he'd prepared for his own death? What if he planned it all out, so when you killed him, he'd already tucked most of his upper soul away somewhere safe? He could have sent a sliver of his soul—something like a gaesh—and all his lower soul to the Afterlife. Thaena might well think— at least for a little while—that he'd died. If Thaena thought it, it stands to reason Therin would too."

I raised a hand. "Wouldn't he have actually died? You can't live without your lower soul—" I stopped myself.

I was reasonably certain a healthy chunk of MY lower soul was currently living inside an imprisoned demon king in the middle of Kharas Gulgoth.

"You can if you know a way to keep stealing and feeding on the lower soul of others," Tyentso said. "And if you've been paying attention, you'll note Gadrith *does*."

"Damn," Teraeth said. "That . . . would work."

"What about his corpse?" Doc snapped.

Tyentso shrugged. "What about it? He's Lord Heir to House D'Lorus. Thrones to diamonds his body was neatly preserved and handed over to his father, High Lord Cedric, for a proper burial in the family crypts. All Gadrith had to do was possess his own body, and he was back in business. Miserable, sure, because if we're right he's trapped in a halfway state between living and dead, but the point is, he still *exists*."

"Taja!" I set down my cup and grabbed at the blue stone around my neck. "Don't you see? That's it! That's why he's been chasing after the Stone of Shackles. If he gets his hands on this, he can just goad some fool into killing him and wham . . . he'll have their body, just as if it had always been his own. No more existing inside an animated corpse. That's *why* he wants it."

I was elated. Not even the remnants of that hangover could dampen my mood. To finally have some answers, to finally feel that just maybe I understood what the hell was going on, felt amazing. I beamed at the others.

Naturally, Teraeth had to ruin that.

"No good," he said. "If that were true, Gadrith would have known how to steal the necklace from you. The fact that you're still here, alive and in the body you were born in, means he doesn't understand how the necklace really works."

"Not necessarily," Doc said. "Gadrith could easily know the necklace makes its wearer switch bodies with their murderer, but I'd be very surprised if he understood that the Stone of Shackles *stays with the original body* when the switch happens. After all, when Therin showed up with Khaeriel, she still wore the necklace, even though she was now trapped inside the body of the woman who had murdered her, Miya. Gadrith must think the necklace transfers along with the soul."

My throat tightened. "What did you just say?"

"Khaeriel?" Tyentso raised an eyebrow. "Queen Khaeriel? The vané queen? She's been dead for decades."

"Well, you're not *entirely* wrong," Doc said, grinning as he tossed her phrase back to her. "Khaeriel's body died, sure, but her soul never made it to the Afterlife."

I kept staring at Doc. "My mother—" I inhaled. "Are you certain?"

"As Death. Don't tell me you never suspected."

"I just didn't want to believe—" Like so many things, I'd known, but hadn't wanted to take that final step of admitting the truth to myself. Of course, Miya was my mother. However— "Wait. Khaeriel? You're saying that Miya is Queen Khaeriel?"

Doc sighed. "Use that brain. I know it hurts, but try."

Teraeth snickered.

I scowled. "I hate you both. Just give me a straight answer."

"You know Miya owned the Stone of Shackles—and gave it to you when she tried to have you smuggled out of Quur. How do you think *she* got it?"

I leaned back against the chair. A long time ago, when I had first run into Gadrith and Darzin, Dead Man and Pretty Boy, they had been asking those very same questions, hadn't they? About the Stone of Shackles. *Her serving girl ran off with it,* Gadrith had said.

No one's seen Miyathreall in years.

Miya.

"Miya was Queen Khaeriel's handmaiden," I said. "Except not what she really was, was she? She was Queen Khaeriel's assassin."

Doc beamed. "Exactly. But, since Khaeriel was wearing the Stone of Shackles, Khaeriel was transferred into Miya's body. Same thing that happened to me, history repeating itself."

Teraeth set his elbows on the table, cup in hand. "She would have been extremely vulnerable just after the transfer. Magic is physical as much as spiritual. A new body means you have to learn spells all over again."

Doc gave him a nasty grin. "You would know."

Teraeth stared at him with narrowed eyes. "That's good, coming from you."

"I get why Doc has experience with this," I said, "but why do you, Teraeth? You've never owned the Stone of Shackles, have you?"

Teraeth didn't answer.

"Ask him who he was in his last life," Doc said cheerfully. "Go on. Ask him."

"I don't *care*," Tyentso said. "Let's try to focus."

I cleared my throat and raised a hand. "But Tyentso cast magic when she possessed my body yesterday. She didn't have any trouble."

"Oh, I just made it look easy," Tyentso said. When she saw our raised eyebrows, she elaborated, "It's not as easy as milking a bull elephant, but if you know how to compensate, if you've taken a lot of time to learn how the other person thinks, you can make adjustments. I've been studying Kihrin since we both arrived here, to try to figure out what his particular triggers are for magic."

Doc gestured in Tyentso's direction. "Most people don't have the opportunity to study their murderer for years before the soul swap takes place. In Khaeriel's case, that meant that she would have wound up as Miya—with no ability to defend herself from being gaeshed and sold into slavery. Of course, it's been twenty-five years, so she's probably had time to figure it out."

"My mother is the vané queen?" I was a little stuck on that part.

"No, your mother is a vané handmaiden possessed by the soul of a vané queen," Doc corrected. "Or, Miya was a traitor and an assassin—as she attempted to kill the queen—and you are *her* son. Although since King Kelanis is probably the one who ordered Miya to assassinate his sister, Queen Khaeriel, I guess that makes you the son of a patriot too. Vané politics gets complicated. You might want to draw up a chart."

"Damn, Doc," Tyentso said. "Do you enjoy stealing sweets from little kids too? Back off. He's gone through a lot in the last day."

I raised a hand. "I'm fine, Ty."

"Scamp, you're not fine. Nobody gets blackout drunk like that because they're fine. I should know. I drank more than you did because I am not fine." She finished her tea and flipped her cup upside down on the table. "So, what are we going to do about Gadrith?"

"Nothing?" Teraeth responded. "Kihrin can't leave the island and as long as we keep the Stone of Shackles away from Gadrith, he's doomed to a miserable, cursed existence. Let him stew. It's what he deserves."

"Except he has to kill people to survive," I said. "He has to devour the lower souls of innocent people to sustain his existence." I scowled at the look Teraeth gave me. "You do remember what 'innocent person' means, don't you?"

"Innocent . . . that's a synonym for naïve, yes? It's not your problem. Let the Court of Gems deal with their wayward necromancer. They've earned him."

I shook my head. "It's just a matter of time before they summon up Xaltorath again and send that monster after me." I shuddered. "I don't know what I'll do if that happens."

"It won't happen. They've already tried it," Teraeth said.

"What?" I felt the whole world tilt. "They've already what now?"

Teraeth made a circle with his finger. "Gadrith and Darzin summoned up Xaltorath to track down the Stone of Shackles about a year ago. Mother told me. You have, or rather had, an Ogenra second cousin who vanished without a trace so they could have their sacrifice. Didn't work. Xaltorath can't get near this island. They don't know where the stone is and therefore don't know where you are either."

"And in the meantime, I'm just . . . trapped." I nodded to them. "Trapped on this island, trapped with all of you. No offense."

"None taken," said Teraeth.

"I can't do anything," I muttered. I tapped my foot against the ground and felt an anger burn in my gut. I hated feeling trapped. I hated Gadrith for being able to do whatever he wanted to whomever he wanted and get away with it, even to the point of tricking the Goddess of Death herself. I hated him because of the damage his stupid obsession with this stupid rock had done to my life. I hated Darzin for being Darzin, for murdering so many people, including my father Surdyeh, often for no other reason than just because he could. I hated what he'd done to everyone around him, what he'd done to Galen, what he'd done to me. I hated that people were going to die to feed Gadrith's hunger, and I hated Teraeth's insistence that none of this was my problem.

. . . wait.

I looked up and realized Teraeth was staring at me, had been staring at me for some time now, his face an unfathomable mask. Or not so unfathomable. I was starting to know his quirky little moods. When he was pressing a point just to see if I would press back. How often he supported a position not because it was what he believed, but just to see if I could defend mine.

"What does Gadrith want?" I asked out loud.

"I thought we established this," Doc said. "The Stone of Shackles—"

Teraeth smiled to himself and looked away.

"No," I said. "I mean yes. He wants the Stone of Shackles. Sure. Of course. Who wants to exist as an animated corpse? But he was plotting bullshit long before he faked his own death. The Affair of the Voices. He killed Emperor Gendal, but he didn't try to replace him. He let Sandus take the crown—"

"'Let' might be the wrong word," Doc interrupted.

"What does he *want*?" I pressed. "Chasing the Stone of Shackles is nothing but a detour before he returns to his real goals. What are those?"

"The prophecies," Tyentso said. "He wants to fulfill the prophecies. He wants to pull down the gods and put himself in charge. Make a universe that works the way he thinks it should. Remake the world. Make it better, whatever 'better' is to him."

"Okay, so what do the prophecies say will happen next?"

Silence.

I looked at the three of them. "Come on . . ."

Tyentso sighed. *"And ash will fall from the sky as the Great City burns, and the howls of sinners will echo with the screams of the righteous, for the Thief of Souls has come. When the demons are freed, no man shall wear the crown but has first known death."* She cleared her throat. "From the Sayings of

Sephis. I could quote you some of the Devoran Prophecies, but it's pretty much more of the same."

"Cheerful," Doc said, "but that could mean anything."

Teraeth scoffed. "Sure, as long as 'anything' is violent and horrible and burns the Capital to the ground."

I stood up, ignored the way my head gave a warning protest, kicked the chair I'd been sitting in, and walked way.

"Kihrin—" Tyentso started to say.

"Before I was kidnapped," I said, whirling back to them, "I never lived anywhere but the Capital. And I hated it. I hated everything about it. I wanted to leave more than I had ever wanted anything else in my life. I wanted to be free from my father Surdyeh, free from Ola, free from that life. I wanted to run away to somewhere else. Anywhere else. Except now that I *am* anywhere else—" My throat closed up. I thought of Miya and Galen, Tishar and Lorgrin, Star and Scandal. Maybe, on a good day, Therin. People I loved still lived in the City. People I loved who could still be put in harm's way. "Does that prophecy mean what I think? Gadrith's going to destroy the City?"

"He'll probably start a Hellmarch," Tyentso said. "The Capital has never seen one inside its walls. That 'frees the demons'—and since he's labeled himself the Thief of Souls, it all goes downhill from there. But—" She wagged a finger. "If you're right, he's not going to do any of that until he's put his hands on the Stone of Shackles."

"Nothing in what you just quoted says that he has to wait," Teraeth pointed out.

"Except he does," I said. "He's *been* waiting. This all started, what, over eighteen years ago? For what has he been waiting if not the stone? He could have done whatever he was planning years ago. We know what he wants. Let's use that."

Teraeth leaned forward. "Are you suggesting making yourself bait?"

"Why not? I'm the one person Gadrith will be absolutely focused on and the one person Gadrith can't just kill outright. The Stone of Shackles won't let its wearer die if they're killed by someone without a viable body, and Gadrith *is a corpse.* He can't steal my soul, he can't strip the flesh from my bones. He literally cannot kill me."

"Oh Scamp, there's a lot he can do to you that wouldn't be fatal." Tyentso made a face. "Believe me, nobody wants Gadrith to see justice more than I do, but you're still in training—"

"Actually, his training's nearly complete," Doc said. "I wouldn't say no to a few more centuries with him, but he's made great progress."

"And I'm just the distraction, anyway," I said. "The point isn't that I kill Gadrith, the point is that we lure Gadrith out in the open so *Emperor*

Sandus can kill Gadrith. I'm sure he'd love to help us out just as soon as we explain the situation to him."

"You're all forgetting Kihrin's still trapped on this island," Teraeth said, "and none of the rest of it matters until we figure that part out."

Doc snickered. "If you have any ideas, we'd love to hear them."

I stretched, put my hands behind my head, and looked around. Ynisthana was beautiful. I couldn't argue that the island wasn't just eye-bleedingly beautiful. Thanks to Thriss farms, abundant fishing, and shipments from Zherias, food was never an issue. The women were gorgeous, and the sexual taboos absent. A lot of people would never want to leave a place like this, and I couldn't blame them for that.

But I couldn't stay.

I turned back to the others. "When does a prison guard stop looking for an escaped inmate?"

Doc gave the matter some consideration. "When the inmate's been found?"

"Or when he's dead," Tyentso said. "That's what Gadrith did."

"Right. Guards don't chase after a prisoner they've already killed."

"What are you suggesting, Scamp?"

I grinned. "The Old Man won't keep looking for me if he thinks he already knows why I'm not around. Especially if he thinks it was his fault." I turned to Teraeth. "So how do you think your mother would feel about destroying the island?"

66: The Game

(Talon's story)

"The full dark path," Morvos D'Erinwa said as he laid down the Pale Lady, Black Gate, the Hunter, and the Blood Chalice. "Read them and weep for your children, now left destitute to beg on the streets."

"Not so fast," Kihrin said. He turned over his cards, revealing the Crown of Quur, the Scepter of Quur, the Arena, and the Emperor. "I do believe I've beaten that hand." There were groans from around the table as the young man grinned.

Jarith Milligreest rubbed his forehead as he regarded Kihrin. It wasn't so long ago that Jarith had known him as a minstrel's son, and to see him here like this as a member of House D'Mon—as his own second cousin—was jarring. He was happy to see Kihrin, just shocked at how much the boy's status had changed, and how quickly. He nearly hadn't recognized him, and he was still bemused at the idea that Kihrin was Darzin's son. "Is that the second imperial flush you've drawn tonight?"

Kihrin nodded as he pulled the money from the center of the table. "Something like that, yes."

Thurvishar pushed his cards away in disgust. "No one is this lucky." The Lord Heir of House D'Lorus nursed a glass of wine while Talea rubbed his shoulders.

He'd lost a lot of money.

"Now, nobody likes a sore loser," Kihrin said. "You'll win yours back later, I'm sure."

Jarith shook his head. "It is a little uncanny, Kihrin. Maybe you should quit while you're ahead." He didn't like the look on Thurvishar's face, and he didn't like the hungry glint in Kihrin's eyes.

Jarith was not a fool. He'd recognized Talea when she entered the room, knew she could only be the very slave girl he had traced to Darzin D'Mon's custody, now owned by Thurvishar. She didn't want to have much to do with the younger D'Mon though. She avoided him the whole evening, as if she had developed a natural but unavoidable aversion to the color blue. She only had eyes for Thurvishar, and Kihrin only had eyes for her. And every risky winner-takes-all bet Kihrin made seemed aimed at one goal: putting Thurvishar in a position where he would be forced to bet her.

This, Jarith was certain, could only end in disaster.

The Captain sighed inwardly as Kihrin ignored his good advice. "And deny these kind lords the chance to win their money back? What kind of friend would I be?"*

"I have an idea," Thurvishar said. His voice was a dangerous, unfriendly purr. He picked up the cards from the nobleman who was dealing and shuffled them. He offered the deck to Jarith. "Pick a card."

Jarith shrugged and pulled Bertok, God of War. "Shall I show it?"

"Please."

Jarith turned the card over.

Thurvishar then offered a card to Kihrin. "Now you."

"What's this supposed to prove?" Kihrin frowned.

"Humor me," Thurvishar said.

Kihrin picked a card and turned it over. It was Khored, God of Destruction, a higher card than Bertok.

"Again," Thurvishar said.

Jarith pulled a Two of Coins and Kihrin drew Godslayer. Everyone was frowning now.

Thurvishar began flicking cards from the deck in front of the players at the table. "One for you, and one for you, and you, and you and you, and Kihrin—" He paused. "Kihrin's card wins." He began again. "You, and you, and you, and you, and you and Kihrin—has high card. One more time . . ." He dealt the cards again. "And Kihrin's hand wins." Thurvishar turned his stare to the adolescent. "You're cheating."

Jarith stood up. "Let's not get carried away here. I'll admit he's lucky, but that doesn't mean he's cheating."

Kihrin was sputtering. "You shuffled and turned over the cards! How could I possibly have cheated?"

The cards whirled up in a spiral from the table, sailing into Thurvishar's outstretched hand. He pushed them toward Jarith. "There are ways to cheat luck. There are ways to warp the odds. Maybe House D'Mon's little blond whippet has found his witch gift and can unwittingly turn the odds to his favor? But I know this: even a lucky streak has its losses."

"So, what do you propose?" Jarith asked, trying to be a peacemaker.

"I propose he gives the money back he's taken and leaves," Thurvishar said.

Kihrin shook his head. "I will do no such thing. Thurvishar, you have my word. I *didn't cheat.*"

---

*In all seriousness, never bet against Kihrin D'Mon at cards. Or hazards. Or any game of chance. He has Taja's own damn luck. Literally.

Thurvishar shrugged, scowling, rubbing a thumb along his temple as if fighting off a headache. "And what is the word of a whore's son worth, anyway?"*

Silence.

Jarith looked around the room at a sea of shocked and blinking faces, although a few were already beginning to smirk. They were happy to see the new and too lucky scion of House D'Mon picked to pieces by D'Lorus's prodigal son.

Jarith shook his head. "The usual terms, I assume?"

Thurvishar stared at Jarith. "Excuse me?"

"My apologies. Please allow me to explain my position more clearly." Jarith slapped Thurvishar's face. "You just called my cousin a whore's son, and he's too young to duel you."

Thurvishar seemed taken completely by surprise. He could only stare, lifting a hand to his cheek.

Kihrin reached for Jarith's arm. "What are you *doing*? You don't need to do this. I've been called a lot worse."

Jarith frowned. "Honor is at stake. I'm sorry. One day you'll understand."

"What the hell is going on here?" Darzin's voice called out from the entrance. Jarith wasn't too surprised to see him, but he was a bit taken aback by how quickly he'd arrived. It was possible that someone had gone for Kihrin's father as soon as Thurvishar began making allegations about the boy's luck.

"Well," Thurvishar said, sounding bemused. "It seems I've just been challenged to a duel by the High General's son."†

The next day, Galen stood next to Kihrin on the cobblestone path surrounding the Arena, with their father, Darzin, their mother (or stepmother) Alshena, and a shocking number of immediate family. This included Uncle Bavrin, Great-Aunt Tishar, and their grandfather, the High Lord Therin. Even Lady Miya, who normally never left the Blue Palace, stood at the High Lord's side.

"I didn't think we'd be back here so soon," Galen confided.

Of course, the reason they were back at the Culling Fields was made painfully clear by who else was present: High General Qoran Milligreest, his son Jarith, Thurvishar D'Lorus, High Lord Cedric D'Lorus, and a host of spectators. Everyone wanted to be here to see *this* duel.

Kihrin didn't look so pleased. "This should never have happened."

"For once," Darzin D'Mon said, "we're in agreement." He gave Kihrin

---

*Yes, I really did say that, but with all apologies, being an ass was the whole point.
†No, that wasn't part of the plan at all.

an unfriendly look, then said to Galen, "Remember this: the honor of the House should be defended by the House, not by some outsider, even if he is a distant relation. No matter how this ends, we won't come out of it looking as we ought." He looked like he might box Kihrin around the ears, but the motion was brought under heel as he remembered the watching crowds.

"Who's that?" Kihrin asked. He pointed to a small man dressed in plain tan misha and kef, unusual by his lack of decoration. His head was shaved save for a lock above his right temple, braided in a long rope that hung down past his shoulders.

"That's Caerowan," Darzin explained. "He's a Voice of the Council, here to officiate and witness the duel."

"Isn't there any way to stop this?" Kihrin complained.

"No," Darzin said.

Galen watched his brother inhale in frustration before he let the matter drop, at least for the moment. Galen tugged on Kihrin's sleeve. "I'm sure Jarith will be fine. He must be a very good swordsman, right? Whereas, I'd be surprised if the D'Lorus Lord Heir has ever spent much time practicing with a blade."

Their father snorted and the two young men looked back at him. "As much as I find myself torn on whom I'd like to survive this little duel, I'm afraid the advantage is in favor of Thurvishar D'Lorus. Don't forget that sword craft is less than nothing against a skilled wizard."

Kihrin frowned. "But they're fighting a duel. They won't be using magic."

Darzin chewed on a thumb as he watched the two men take up position in front of the Voice and begin the traditional description of disputes, slights, and remedies. He snorted again. "There is no law inside the Arena. No rules. No consequences. They can promise anything they want *outside* the Arena. It means less than nothing once they pass through its gates."

Galen saw Kihrin startle and stand straighter, watching the impending duel with ill-concealed concern. He wondered how Kihrin had become so close to the Milligreest scion when in theory he had only met the older man the other night. Jarith seemed nice enough though, and he was a cousin. Galen was well aware that if Darzin had his way, Galen would find himself married to Jarith's younger sister.

Most of the customers at the Culling Fields turned out of doors to watch the spectacle, with bar wenches shuttling from tavern to field to serve drinks and take orders, while the rich sat at small outside tables and chatted. The inside of the Arena looked like a park, albeit a park with grass that looked odd with small copses of twisted and warped trees. There were buildings too, ruins of ancient structures with black yawning mouths for doors and windows. These were said to be enchanted to kill whoever entered them. The grass was an illusion of sorts, an idyllic deception that concealed skulls and bones: the bodies of generations of dead wizards, warriors, and sorcerers, their weapons, and their secrets. One could still pick out faded remains, a skull here, a thigh bone there, a rusted ancient sword sticking up from the grass like a warning to all who would try their hand inside the Arena's boundaries.

Kihrin turned to Darzin. "What do you mean? There's no law inside the Arena? How does that work?"

Darzin shrugged. "Dueling is illegal. So are certain kinds of magic and murdering your fellows so you can be the man to grab the Crown and Scepter and name yourself Emperor. This land was once the Imperial Palace—they say it's where the god-king Ghauras met his demise—and ever since it has been held to be a place outside the rule of law. No crime can be committed within its boundaries because no action committed within its boundaries is considered criminal. All things—no matter how repugnant—are allowed." He smiled. "So, technically speaking, a man might promise any restriction on dueling outside the Arena—say, oh, it's only to first blood—and change his mind as soon as he is inside."

Kihrin was horrified. "And no one can do anything?"

"There are consequences," Therin said, who had been listening to the entire conversation. "Give yourself a reputation as a man who breaks his word in duels and no one will believe your word regarding anything. And you will find people working against you."

"Yes," Darzin agreed. "Quite. Even I stick with dueling agreements." He paused. "Usually." He fetched a glass of wine from a waitress's tray and pointed. "But look, the duel for your honor is beginning."

Galen watched as the two combatants finished their talk, and the Voice of the Council waved a medallion. In response, a line of golden energy etched the outlines of a door hanging in empty space, then golden light filled in the rest of the door. Jarith and Thurvishar walked through the light, which collapsed behind them.

Galen tugged on his brother's sleeve. "Do you see? Thurvishar doesn't have a sword."

Kihrin looked at him, frowned, and narrowed his eyes at the two men inside the Arena. Jarith did have a sword—a long, curving Khorveshan scimitar. Thurvishar seemed to have no weapons at all.

"Jarith couldn't have agreed to let him use magic. He couldn't have been that stupid . . ." Kihrin worried at his lower lip.

Galen had to wonder.

As soon as both men were through the gate the duel had technically begun. Thurvishar didn't seem to notice this, however, and stood there, looking tall, proud, and vaguely bored.

"You said you'd summon a weapon!" Jarith shouted. "Do so, wizard, or pick up that rusted blade sticking out of the ground behind you. I will not attack an unarmed man."

Thurvishar smiled. "I have already done so. It can hardly be helped if you do not recognize it."

"You're starting to grate on my nerves. I'm not–" As Jarith advanced on Thurvishar, he tripped, and pitched headfirst into the grass. His sword stuck blade-down in the soft earth like many of the weapons scattered around the clearing.

"For my weapon today, I choose . . . *you*." Thurvishar gave that damning, maddening slow smile.

Next to Galen, Darzin let out a low whistle, more appreciation than shock.

"Why you–" Jarith's foot slipped on the wet grass and he pitched backward this time, crying out as something sharp hidden in the lawn sliced across his shoulder. There was a general gasp from the crowd.

"Luck is not solely the province of Taja," Thurvishar said. "Luck can be manipulated. Luck can be twisted. Luck can be used as a weapon."

Jarith was careful not to move. "I didn't challenge you because you said the boy was lucky, or even that he cheated. I said he–" His voice went silent.

Galen leaned forward. "What happened? Why can't we hear them anymore?"

Darzin frowned. "The wizard's blocked the sound. . . . Interesting."

Kihrin pushed himself through the crowd, ignoring Darzin's attempt to grab him. Galen, smaller and quicker, followed easily, ducking under arms and around distracted spectators. As they reached the area where the Voice stood, Galen realized the High General was also present, a volcano in the process of continual, simmering eruption.

The General gave both the D'Mon sons a nod of recognition as he saw them approach. The High General's focus, however, was elsewhere. It rested on the small white-robed man, Caerowan, the D'Lorus Lord Heir, and most of all, on his only son.

They waited as the two duelists finished their conversation and the black-robed man offered Jarith a hand up. Jarith took it, and the two of them walked, together, to the edge of the Arena. They did not require a gate to exit–simply crossing the perimeter seemed to be sufficient.

Jarith's expression wasn't that of a man humiliated and defeated. He bowed to the Voice, Caerowan, and said, "By your leave, the duel is complete and all parties are satisfied."

"All parties are *not* satisfied," said the High General.

Jarith looked up, surprised.

Thurvishar's expression did not change at all.

"This duel," Qoran Milligreest explained, "was inappropriate and ill-advised. You are not royalty. It is not becoming to our family that you purport yourself as such."

Jarith blinked. "Father—"

"General," Milligreest corrected.

The young man flushed red and stood straight as a rod. "Yes, General."

"Your assignment has been changed. You will report to Stonegate Pass for further orders, effectively immediately. You are dismissed." The General's anger bubbled at the surface, ire burning like a great heat. He turned to Thurvishar, gave him a short, angry bow, and said, "My apologies for this unpleasantness, Lord Heir. I hope the duel was finished to your satisfaction."

"Oh yes," Thurvishar said. "Now if you'll excuse me . . ." He returned the bow and walked into the crowd, presumably to bask in congratulations and perhaps even order a drink.

The High General turned to Kihrin and for a split second it seemed he would unleash a similar anger to that reserved for his son. "Kihrin."

Kihrin swallowed. "High General."

"I would say it's good to see you again, but I don't want to lie. May I instead say that I would take it as a kindness if you would avoid involving my family with your politics? Or better still, learn to fight your own duels."

Kihrin nodded, and looked in Thurvishar's general direction. "I didn't—yes, High General. Thank you. I'll do that." He turned back to Milligreest. "He was only trying to help me, you know."

"You may leave," the High General said, stony once more.

Galen saw their father and grandfather making their way over to them through the crowd. "Come on, Kihrin," he started to say. "Kihrin? Where—?" Galen D'Mon looked around.

Kihrin was gone.

67: The Destruction of Ynisthana

(Kihrin's story)

We didn't do anything immediately. In fact, implementing my plan took another two years. That may seem like a long time, but despite Khae-mezra's worry that I would leave the island too soon, I did see the wisdom of finishing my training. I had a lot of magic to learn from Tyentso, more sword work from Doc, and then I had to learn how to play the saymisso* from one of the local Thriss musicians.

I needed a string instrument, you see, that was more portable than a lap harp.

Once I was running through Doc's lessons without any "resets," and once Tyentso had grudgingly agreed that I had learned as much as I was probably going to learn from her given my own natural inclinations, only then did I go to Khaemezra for permission.

To my surprise, she agreed, announcing the whole thing "inevitable."

So that just left the fun part.

We picked a bright sunny morning just after a Maevanos, when it would seem normal that most of the residents of Ynisthana were out of sight, presumably sleeping off the drinking and bedding of the night before. No drakes hunted in the jungle and no fishermen were out cast-ing their nets, but those details were easy to overlook if you happened to be a giant, self-absorbed, narcissistic dragon.

I dressed myself in a pair of black kef and sandals, hair pulled back and tied with a length of white cloth I'd salvaged from an initiate robe. My gaesh was secured in a pocket. I wore the Stone of Shackles around my neck, shining like a piece of long-dead sky.

I wanted there to be no question that I was wearing the damn thing.

I left behind weapons. They would be useless anyway. The star tears of my gaesh made easy and effective talismans, sharpening my tenyé with protections from magic and fire—the latter a special spell Tyentso

---

*A Thriss musical instrument consisting of three silk strings strung over a short sounding chamber with a long neck played with a variable-tension bow. The Khorveshan spiked violin probably evolved from this earlier version.

and I had worked out together. I was pretty sure they wouldn't truly ward off the Old Man's fury—I wasn't that powerful—but I hoped the spells would buy me a few precious seconds just in case I found myself in the wrong position. The only objects I carried were my saymisso and bow, tucked under an arm.

I walked down to the beach, which was empty of all life. I couldn't see the Old Man, but his island was there off the coast, along with his "rock garden" of trapped singers. I counted thirty-six of them, and felt my throat constrict.

"I'm sorry," I whispered as I sat cross-legged on the beach and rested the spike of the saymisso in the sand. "I'm so sorry."

I drew the bow across the strings.

I heard a roar. Seconds later, that monstrous shape flew in from a nearby island and spread his wings to blot out the sky. Sitting there and playing that instrument instead of fleeing was one of the hardest things I have ever done. Every instinct pushed me to run screaming. I played a lullaby, keeping the bow strings stiff with my hand while I pulled a long plaintive note and let it echo in the air. Hot winds scoured passed me, but I ignored that.

The dragon landed on his island and growled with a sound like an earthquake. He was still magnificent, terrifying, and profoundly wrong—a perversion of the natural order on a scale that was in its own way tran-scendent.

"Have you decided to die? To give yourself to me? To surrender?"

"No," I told the dragon. "Not this time. I am curious about something. What was your price for betraying your mother? Was it jealousy? Your mother was chosen to be one of the Eight and you weren't. Did you think you could manage things better than she did, or was your betrayal a mis-guided attempt to make her proud of her little boy?"

The Old Man spread his wings and hissed, **"You are a fool."**

"I've been told. It's probably even true. But a while back I snuck out while you weren't looking and stopped by Kharas Gulgoth. Maybe you remember the place. Big city, kind of run-down, lots of magic, and a giant demon god sleeping in the center. Sound familiar?"

"So, you do remember." He had that lethal menace in his voice, worse than his periods of insanity.

"No," I admitted, "but I can read a book if I stare at it long enough. There were these drawings all over the place telling the same story again and again and again. It took me a little while, but I realized that the squig-gly lines at the end weren't rays of energy or a depiction of chaos—they were dragons.* Eight men and women who thought they could become

---

*These concepts aren't mutually exclusive.

gods became monsters instead." I pointed a finger. "You were one of them, Sharanakal. You were human."

"We only wanted to balance the inequity of power, knowing it was only a matter of time before the Eight Guardians became corrupted. Those idiots had chosen warriors, soldiers, healers—the carrion crows of the battlefield. People who blindly followed orders, people they could control, to give unto them power unrivaled." The dragon stood, far too large for the island on which he perched. He rose upon his haunches and roared to the heavens, the thunder in his voice trembling the ocean and the rocks and bringing every bit of animal noise on the island to a complete halt. The dragon's black serpentine head whipped back to stare at me with volcanic eyes.

"Sounds like you had good intentions. Sounds like it wasn't really your fault."

"No. It was your fault. YOU!" His head snapped forward, lunging toward me. **"*You*. You were a naïve trusting FOOL. How could you believe his lies?"**

I had expected this response, anticipating it. That didn't mean it was an easy thing to endure. "It was Relos Var's fault," I corrected, taking a deep breath to keep myself from running as that head dove for me.

He stopped very close—close enough that he had broken Khaemezra's commands and trespassed onto the island proper, close enough that I felt my fire protections kick in to keep me from being scorched. I couldn't look him in both eyes, but had to stare in one only, where I watched as the heart of a thousand fires raged.

"We, who were pure, thought our purity would bring resistance to evil. But this is foolishness, for the soldier understands that purity is impossible, that evil cannot be destroyed, only tempered and channeled. The soldier knows he is a tool, and will not suffer to be wielded by his enemies. We, in our arrogance, thought we were above such usage. Hubris!"

"Relos Var created the ritual," I said. "Relos Var was the one who convinced you that they'd made a mistake when they chose eight other people to fight the demons instead of you. It should have been you from the start, right? You thought you'd become a god, but Relos Var turned you into a monster. You blame me, but he lied to me too. He used us both. You and I are alike. We're both victims."

That eye widened. **"We're not alike. You are far worse than my own cursed existence. You are Vol Karoth's Cornerstone,* the shell**

---

*How would that even be possible? To take a soul and turn it into a tsali stone is one thing. A tsali stone may in turn be transformed into one of the artifacts we call Cornerstones, like the Stone of Shackles and Chainbreaker. But Kihrin's soul is clearly *not* one of the eight known left behind from that rivening, a great unending hunger that can never be filled, that will devour and devour as a star that collapses under its own weight eats without ever being sated. You are the only piece of his soul left, and when he wakes, he will reclaim you. Let me save you. In my garden, you will be spared that fate."

I shuddered. I didn't dare take too long to contemplate what he was saying. I might start screaming. "That's kind of you, but I'm going to have to refuse your generous offer. But don't think I'm not appreciative. In fact, I wrote a song for you. Would you like to hear me play it?"

The Old Man folded back his wings and regarded me for a long, slow, silent moment. I actually worried he might say no or fly away.

"Yes."

I exhaled with relief. "That's what I hoped you'd say."

I bent my head down and drew the bow over the strings. The song itself was a wordless overtone, low and droning, and the musical accompaniment wove its way around it in high arches and long, flowing sustained notes. It didn't take very long before the Old Man ordered his garden to begin singing accompaniment.

It was beautiful. I can't deny it was beautiful.

I lengthened the notes, let them build. What I didn't think the Old Man could tell was that it wasn't purely musical talent. I wasn't just playing music.

I was casting a spell.

It had taken months of work to figure out how. Tyentso didn't think a spell like this had ever existed before. We had practiced by using the temple gate to sneak off the island, never for more than an hour at a time, while I practiced against every kind of rock I could find—until I had found a type of onyx that was the perfect match.

The garden statues sang so melodically I think they could tell what was about to happen and welcomed it. Underneath the intertwined notes, a deeper resonance began to vibrate. Sand danced in circles away from me. Ocean waves lost their rhythm and collapsed. I built up the sound, note by note, and the dragon's aura of cacophony wasn't enough to stop the relentless vibration, a pattern that I built and stacked higher with every note—

The harmony cut off sharply as the garden statues cracked and crumbled to chunks of rock no bigger than my fist.

Thirty-six trapped men and women died in an instant, free at last to return to the Afterlife. I felt guilt—even at that moment I felt guilt. It was impossible to truly know for sure if it was the fate they would have wanted.

Cornerstones. However, even if we assume the dragon was speaking metaphorically, it still implies a strong connection between Kihrin and Vol Karoth, which is terrifying.

If they would have chosen death and later rebirth over an endless immortal prison trapped in stone.

All I knew for certain was that it's what I would have wanted. I wondered if Elana Milligreest, who had freed me from my prison inside Vol Karoth in another lifetime, had questioned if she was doing the right thing too.

I wished I could meet her just once, to tell her that she had.

In that same moment, the Old Man became a statue himself, temporarily frozen by his own outrage.

I was already running.

The roar that rose on the air behind me made the ground shake so hard I was thrown off my feet. A great rumbling echoed, and over my head, the mountain at the center of Ynisthana erupted in a giant cloud of smoke, ash, and lava bombs.

"How dare you!" the Old Man screamed. **"The mountain will bury you in lava, the molten rocks will be your tomb. You will spend eternity screaming in despair and pain. You will never know peace."**

Now that's a standing ovation, I thought as I picked myself up and kept running.

I was halfway up the slope when a large crack opened in the ground in front of me. Lava fountained into the air, a wall of fire threatening to burn me to ash.

"Kihrin!" Teraeth tackled me and pushed me to the ground as one of the lava bombs came uncomfortably close to finalizing our plans in an unexpected way. The threat was real; the Stone of Shackles felt like fire at my throat, as it prepared to keep me alive at any cost. There was no one, after all, who was directly responsible for my impending demise.

That's not what the Old Man saw, however.

"NO!" the Old Man screamed.

What the dragon saw was Teraeth tackling me to avoid the lava bomb. Because of that tackle, the Old Man saw me trip and fall, stumbling toward the just-opened crack. I tried to grab the edge, but screamed as my hand met volcanic rock hot enough to sear flesh from bone. I fell. Likely I'd have impacted on the surface of the lava and burned to death, but the eruption was still in progress. My screams were cut short as my body was churned under in the lava fountain.

Teraeth, for his part, staggered—exactly as you might expect for someone who had just been possessed by the soul of the man he had accidentally killed. He put his hand to his chest, but found only that black arrowhead necklace, and no sign of the Stone of Shackles. Teraeth stared horrified at his hands, looked at his body, disbelief evident on his expression.

"I am not that dramatic," I protested.

"Shhh," Teraeth told me. "And yes, you are."

We needed to keep low. The air was growing hard to breathe, and gods help us if a mudslide or ash flow decided to make its way down the mountain.

We watched as the illusionary Teraeth turned to run just as an equally illusionary river of burning cinders came streaming down the mountain. He was engulfed in but an instant, and this time, without air to breathe or the Stone of Shackles to keep him alive, the result seemed sadly all too predictable. Kihrin, now Teraeth, would burn to cinder, choke on ash, and die quickly and painfully.

"Damn you, fool." The dragon's voice was so loud I could still hear it over the eruption. **"Come back here and let me save you."**

"That's our cue," I said, grabbing Teraeth's hand. "Come on."

The dragon started ripping into the mountainside not far from us, no doubt trying to recover and save a nonexistent illusion of Teraeth. Since the mountain really was erupting, it wasn't long before he was tearing huge gouges of molten rock out with his claws, scattering them all around. Tears of lava ran down his face, making it seem like the Old Man was crying.

Perhaps he was.

We were forced to dodge to the side as a giant slab of basalt landed right where we had been hiding. The rock elongated and distorted, flowing to the sides of us. I looked around.

Tyentso stood farther up the beach, gesturing. "Come on then. What are you waiting for? The whole mountain is about to come down around our ears."

"Too late," Teraeth said while staring toward the center.

I followed his gaze and inhaled sharply. A real ash flow surged down from the volcano, looking graceful as a slow-moving cloud if one didn't know better.

"Run!" Tyentso screamed, which seemed like solid advice: the gate that was to be our escape route lay in the center of the old Temple of Ynis, now rededicated to Thaena.

That meant we were going to have to run *toward* the death cloud if we wanted to escape.

"We can't," Teraeth said. "We'll never make it in time."

I knew what he was talking about. I'd paid attention all those times the Old Man had created similar clouds. There was zero chance we would run faster than that air would move. I wasn't worried about Doc. Khaemezra was with him, and she was more than capable of protecting them both.

Us? I wasn't so sure about us. Even if the burning cloud didn't kill us, the mountain was spitting out molten rocks that slammed into the ground. Just one hit would be enough.

Tyentso started running anyway, and she had a determined gleam in her eye that told me she was going to try something insane. Probably, she meant to try holding back that cloud through force of will alone, and much as I thought of her skill as a magus, I didn't think she was that powerful.

I'm not sure Relos Var was that powerful.

"Stop Ty!" I yelled at Teraeth, although I was running too. "I need her help!"

Teraeth didn't run faster than me, but he could use one of his illusions to catch her attention.

"Scamp, we need to *go!*" she shouted.

"We can't outrun it," I said, "but maybe we can redirect it." I pulled out the saymisso and ran the bow over the strings. "The mountain's mostly basalt, right?" I looked at Teraeth for confirmation, but he just shrugged. Evidently, he hadn't paid attention.

"Basalt and obsidian," Tyentso volunteered. "The cloud itself will be pumice."

"I don't need to match the composition perfectly, just enough to cause a landslide." I frantically thought back over my knowledge of Ynisthana geography. The best place to divert the flow would be at the caves, which had the advantage of having already been hollowed out (assuming they weren't filling up with fresh magma). The trick was keeping all of us alive for long enough to make sure I could cast the spell.

As if to emphasize that point, the Stone of Shackles went hot around my neck. I looked up in time see a giant glowing orb of rock batted to the side by Tyentso.

"What can I do?" Teraeth asked, looking as nervous and uncertain as I'd ever seen him, but then his illusions were useless against the foe we fought, and he likewise faced nothing he could poison or stab.

"Guide us," I said. "I'll be playing. Ty will be keeping us both alive. Neither of us will be watching our step. We need to be just close enough to see the caves and not an inch closer."

That cloud seemed like it was just seconds from swallowing all of us, but I knew it wasn't a short trek up that mountain, and the scale of the damn thing made judging distance difficult.

I muttered a prayer out loud to Taja, because I needed all the luck she could give me.

Three times on the way, Teraeth either pulled us to the side or Tyentso used her magic to save us from lava fountains or fast, lethal projectiles. I didn't have a target yet. This wasn't what I'd spent years practicing, but the theory seemed sound. If I could collapse the cliff edge away from the temple, the cloud would follow that easier path, and we would reach safety.

If I miscalculated, I would either damn us to an earlier death or bury the temple in burning ash, making escape impossible.

Finally, Teraeth pulled us to a halt. Ahead of us was the mountain and the giant cliff face that housed both the caves used as shelter by the Black Brotherhood and, farther to the side, the large temple built into the mountain. The volcanic avalanche would reach that temple, and just after would reach us, in a matter of seconds.

The spell I cast at that moment was considerably less subtle than the first. I had no time to waste on a stealthy ritual that would go unnoticed until it was too late. While I played I hoped Doc was still using Chainbreaker to cloud the Old Man's mind, because if the dragon felt me cast this same spell a second time from somewhere else on the island, the whole con would be for nothing. He'd know I was still alive.

I bowed the strings violently, seeking the necessary disharmony and vibration so they could be amplified. All I was doing, you understand, was encouraging rock to do what it wants to do anyway. Rock wants to crumble. Stone wants to turn back into sand. You might think the ground would fight this, but you'd be wrong.

Everything falls.

"Damn," Teraeth said next to me, while Tyentso said nothing as she concentrated on keeping dangerous gases out of our breathing air and boiling rocks away from our skin.

The sound of the volcanic eruption was so loud we couldn't hear the avalanche, but a giant section of the cliff face detached, sheared away, and collapsed to the ground, rolling downward into the jungle. The glowing cloud acted like a river that had just found a new course made available; it jogged to the right, following the new bed as it wreaked its path of destruction.

We ran for the temple.

68: The Lion's Den

(Talon's story)

Thurvishar D'Lorus raised an eyebrow as Kihrin D'Mon entered his private curtained booth at the Culling Fields.

"You didn't have to humiliate him, you know," Kihrin said as he sat at the table. "I'm glad you didn't kill him, but you didn't have to make him look like a fool."

The corner of Thurvishar's mouth quirked as he regarded Kihrin with affection. "But he is a fool. He is absolutely a fool. He seems like a nice man, don't mistake me. He seems loyal and brave and true to his friends. However, only a fool challenges someone like me to duel in the Arena and doesn't come prepared for the possibility that I will melt his spine." He picked up the bottle of Raenena wine he'd had waiting for him on ice and poured himself a glass of pale blue liquid. "Be grateful I'm a nice man myself, and only delivered an object lesson."

"That's right. You like object lessons, don't you?" Kihrin remembered the blood on the man's hands from the night before.

Thurvishar swirled the blue liquid in its glass. Then he focused his attention on Kihrin again. "I do. Had circumstances been different, I like to think I'd have made a fine teacher. Now why are you here?"

"You wanted everyone watching to think you twisted chance, but if you had, if you could really do that, then you shouldn't have lost last night." Kihrin paused. "Unless losing was the whole point. I've worshipped Taja for a long time, but I never had a run of luck like that. Never. I didn't win last night because I cheated. I won last night because *you* cheated. You wanted to spark a duel—just not with Jarith."

Thurvishar smiled. "You're smarter than you look, kid."

"Who did you expect you'd be fighting anyway? Darzin?"

"If I had fought Darzin," Thurvishar admitted, "our duel would have ended very differently. Darzin is many things, but not a fool." He gave a small half-smile and shook his head as he stood.

"Why do you hate my father so much?"

Thurvishar paused, one hand on the curtains. "I don't hate your father at all. I hold him in high regard. He was, after all, one of my father's closest friends."

"But you just said—" Kihrin frowned. He knew that Thurvishar hated Darzin. He remembered the threats exchanged between the two men, the unequivocal anger. How could he look Kihrin in the eyes and claim—

"My father," Kihrin repeated. There was a catch there. A play on words. Thurvishar's father wasn't Gadrith; his father was Sandus. *His father.* "Wait. Do you hate Darzin D'Mon?"

"Passionately," Thurvishar answered. "I'll leave you with this thought, young D'Mon: an interesting quirk of the Arena is that it is beyond all divination, all clairvoyance. If a wizard can prevent sound from escaping—a simple trick I assure you—there is no force in all the universe that can discern the dialog of a conversation held within its borders. It really is a shame I couldn't provoke you into a duel, or that you are too young to be considered a fair opponent. What an interesting talk we might have had."

The wizard set down his glass, left enough coin on the table to pay for several nights with his pick of bedmates at the Shattered Veil Club, and walked out of the alcove. Kihrin could only stare, mouth open.

Kihrin hid in the stables.

Now one might think the stables a poor place to hide from Darzin's attention, since the Lord Heir was famously fond of horses, but Darzin seldom ventured into the stables themselves. Instead, the grooms did all the mucking and feeding of the horses while he rode them or presented them to guests at his leisure. And when Darzin did come to claim a horse, Kihrin could count on him not being at the stables for at least a few hours. The location was therefore free of interruption, provided he didn't draw attention to himself.

Like play Valathea—which was exactly what he was doing.

To be fair, he didn't have a good place to practice. If he tried in his room, the High Lord complained of the noise, although Kihrin thought the room soundproof enough so no one could hear him. If he practiced elsewhere, Darzin always found him, and Darzin hated the idea of Kihrin playing at the upcoming New Year's Ball. After the duel between Thurvishar and Jarith, Darzin wanted Kihrin to keep a low profile until the High General forgot Kihrin existed.

Kihrin didn't know what Lord Therin thought, only that if he never reminded Therin about the harp or his promise, Therin would never change his mind about Kihrin playing. Indeed, it was really Therin from whom the young man hid.

He'd built himself a fortress of straw bales to keep the sound from echoing into the main stable. Behind that wall, he practiced notes, biting down on the way each played refrain reminded him of the people he had lost. He wished Morea were still alive. He wished Surdyeh were still alive. He had so many questions, and no answers but a strange intaglio-carved ruby ring.

Kihrin's reverie was interrupted by the sound of a horse's whinny. He paused with his nails on the strings. This was a stable, after all: there were horses. And yet this wasn't coming from one of the stalls, and was much too close. He peeked around one of the hay bales, looking over the side of the loft to the stable beneath.

"Ah," he said, smiling. "It's you, Scandal. Escaped from your cell again?"

The Jorat fireblood, Darzin's prized but never-ridden possession, was below looking up at Kihrin. She was an enormous horse, blue-gray throughout her body but with white stockings and a white mane and tail. He had been told her size was normal for the breed, but she seemed too large for a human being to actually ride. Not that she would let anyone ride her anyway; the horse's typical response to anyone who tried was murder. She was also quite the escape artist, although her attempts had been half-hearted since Star's arrival.

She tossed her mane and blew air in a way that seemed like agreement, then stamped her front hoof repeatedly against the ground and lowered her head. Kihrin smiled. He liked to think that she was applauding his performance.

"She likes it when you play. Can't keep her in her stall if she hears you," Star said as he came around the corner.

Galen had been surprised when Darzin hadn't had the horse killed, but Kihrin understood well enough. As long as Darzin owned her, he could boast of her lethality, her size, her divine breeding. (Was she not the equine equivalent of a god-touched royal, after all?) He could laugh if anyone suggested she should be ridden or bred, while keeping his private frustrations hidden. If he killed her though—he could only admit his attempts a failure. The deaths had stopped since Star's arrival; but she remained a magnificent specimen worthy of envy and admiration. Darzin had decided she was worth the effort in exchange for bragging rights.

Kihrin fished in his satchel, pulled out an apple, and tossed the fruit down to the mare. He'd learned she liked apples. They were an expensive, exotic treat—not native to the areas around the Capital—but what did he care about spending D'Mon metal? "For you, my lady," he told her, giving her a bow. "Shall I continue playing?"

The mare expertly caught the apple from midair, and nodded vigorously.

He pulled the harp up from behind the hay bales, sat down on the edge of one, and began to play once more. It was risky—Darzin would certainly hear him if he came into the stable area proper—but Darzin never let the fireblood horse anywhere near him, so he hoped it would balance. He played a vané song, the one he had been practicing for the New Year's Ball, and once again let the silver chords of music wrap themselves around him.

Star leaned against the wooden frame of the barn entrance, a piece of straw having replaced the sliver of wood as his favorite toothpick. He listened with half-closed eyes. The fireblood horse moved her head the way a human might move their hands in time with the music.

"What are firebloods?" Kihrin asked when he finished the song.

"Horses," Star answered.

Kihrin sighed. "They're not like other horses."*

"No," Star agreed with a shrug. "Not like other horses. Come on, Scandal. We're finished here, you think? We should get you back before the little men panic and run." He chuckled at the thought, a sound mirrored by the gray horse.

"Why do you call her Scandal?" Kihrin asked as he watched the giant horse turn and trot out of the room.

Star shifted the piece of hay from one side of his mouth to the other. "Because you call her Scandal."

"It's not her name," Kihrin said, laughing.

Star shrugged. "She likes it." He gave the adolescent a wink and ducked back around the side of the door, following his charge back to her stall.

Kihrin smiled and put Valathea away in her case.

"There you are," Lady Miya said.

Kihrin looked down to see the seneschal of the house standing in the same doorway Star had just vacated.

"Lady Miya? Is something wrong?"

The elegant woman raised her chin. "The High Lord wishes to speak with you."

"You've been avoiding me," Therin D'Mon said to Kihrin after Lady Miya left them alone.

Kihrin crossed his arms over his chest. "What gave me away, my lord?"

Therin raised both eyebrows, and Kihrin fought the temptation to

---

*As much like a normal horse as a Thriss is like a normal human. Firebloods, crafted by the god-king who once ruled Jorat, are so far removed from normal horses that they must be considered a separate species at this point. They are intelligent and perfectly capable of understanding Guarem, even if they cannot speak it themselves.

fidget or worse, to apologize. Instead he looked around the High Lord's office, noting nothing much had changed since he was there last, save perhaps a different set of papers now occupied his grandfather's attention.

If "grandfather" was the right word now.

"We are allowed the privilege of being friends with the High General and his family," Therin said as he dipped his quill in ink and signed the next piece of paper, "because we do not abuse that privilege, because we do not rub it in the faces of our peers that we receive special favors. Having his son fight your duels for you . . . how do you think that makes us look?"

The room grew silent save for the sound of the quill tip scratching against paper. Therin looked up. "Well?"

"Like we're well connected and it would be dangerous to cross us?" Kihrin suggested.

"Jarith Milligreest was left looking like an idiot because of that association. Why would anyone presume Milligreest would jump to our aid after that kind of embarrassment?"

Kihrin took a deep breath. "That wasn't my fault. I didn't ask him to fight that duel for me."

Therin leaned back in his chair and regarded the young man. "I think you have me confused with someone who cares if it was your fault. I really don't. This isn't a matter of who is at fault. This is a matter of how it affects appearances and how it stains the reputation of our family. Understand?"

Kihrin fought not to roll his eyes. "Yes, my lord."

Therin tilted his head. "You don't agree."

"What gave me away, my lord?"

"So what is it? What do I not understand about the situation?"

"That it involves Darzin. He's doing something."

"I'm aware Darzin is 'doing something.' I asked you to find out specifics, not use him as a free license to embarrass the House. You'll need to come up with a better excuse." He waved a hand. "Consider yourself confined to your suite until the end of Festival."

Kihrin's eyes widened. "You can't do that."

"It's done. If I can't count on you to behave yourself, I won't give you the opportunity to disappoint me a second time."

Kihrin worried at his lip for a moment before he sighed heavily and spoke. "Darzin and Thurvishar are working together. I overheard them talking. They were with a third, someone I call Dead Man. I don't know his real name. They're planning something. Another summoning, although I don't know why. They were scouting an underground chamber. Pedron used to torture people there and I heard one of them say that you had turned it into a Temple of Thaena. I also heard them say that Thurvishar's mother had been held as a prisoner there, to be sacrificed."

Therin stared at him. There was disbelief in those eyes.

Kihrin fought down his anger. "I saw it. Well, I heard it. But it was Thurvishar D'Lorus. I know it was. I recognized his voice."

Therin slammed his quill into the ink bottle, splattering blue ink across the paper in front of him. "You must never lie to me, nor think your upbringing as a minstrel's son gives you some license for creative invention."

"I am not lying!" the young man protested.

Therin stood and walked to the single window, gazing out over the roofs of the Blue Palace. "Part of what you say is true," Therin said as he looked back at Kihrin. "There was a young lady found in a chamber used by my uncle Pedron. A friend of mine married her afterwards–"

"Sandus. The friend was Emperor Sandus, right?"

"–before she was murdered, as was their son. I don't think Sandus would appreciate the suggestion that the Lord Heir of House D'Lorus is his long-dead child."

"But Thurvishar said–"

"How old is Thurvishar D'Lorus? Twenty? Cimillion would be younger than you, if he had lived. Thurvishar is far too old, never mind that he looks nothing like Sandus." Therin shrugged. "To be fair, he doesn't resemble Gadrith either. We've all long suspected Cedric D'Lorus plucked some anonymous Ogenra from obscurity and claimed the child as his grandson. Thurvishar is a D'Lorus. One only has to look at his eyes to see that."

"That can be faked. If the four Houses that were added to the Royal Families can use magic to change their eye color, why not use magic to make someone look like a D'Lorus?"

"They found the bodies, Kihrin."

Kihrin was taken aback for a minute, but only for a minute. "Did you test to make sure they were the right ones? Did you ask Thaena?"

Therin drew back. "No." He deflected. "Yet what possible reason would Gadrith have had for keeping Sandus's child alive? And if he had, why would High Lord Cedric lie about it after his son Gadrith died?"*

Kihrin's face twisted into defiant anger. "I don't know. Fine. Thurvishar still met with Darzin. They are still planning something together. You wanted me to find out what Darzin was plotting, remember?"

---

*Oh, that would be because Cedric D'Lorus was terrified of Gadrith. Yes, Cedric was perfectly aware of his son's continued existence. I think the High Lord hoped that if he ignored the situation, it would all just go away.

"So find out," Therin commanded. "Something other than speculation and innuendo."

"Make up your mind. I can't do that from my room."

Therin frowned and mulled the matter over before waving a hand. "Fine. Consider your confinement rescinded. For now."

"Just tell Emperor Sandus so he can do something about it . . . before they call up that demon." Kihrin couldn't believe that this was all going to fall apart because Therin didn't want to dredge up some old, bad memory of Pedron's dungeons.

"Perhaps I will, if you come to me with something more persuasive," Therin said. "Do you think that's too much for you?"

"No," Kihrin said. Then he added, "But I'm going to need more metal . . ."

69: THE WAYWARD SON

(Kihrin's story)

A heavy rain of ash fell over the harbor, piling up along the crates and coating the pier like a blanket of dirty snow. The sky to the east was red from the ongoing eruption of Ynisthana's volcano. The air cracked with lightning through towering black clouds that strangled the night sky.

The other side of the gate on Ynisthana led to a harbor town in Zherias, an odd shanty sort of place that existed as a stop for fishermen, traders, and pirates looking to unload their merchandise. Only a few people permanently lived there, with everyone else a migrant population who sailed in for a few weeks at a time before continuing on to other ports of call.

This made it wonderfully easy for the Black Brotherhood to slip in without anyone noticing. Most of the Brotherhood members had holed up in safe houses in town before dispersing for wherever Khaemezra set up the new training camp.

I sat on a crate, watching people load up a familiar, black-sailed ship, the same one that I'd seen come to the island a half dozen or more times. However, this was different and more beautiful in all the ways that mattered.

This time, the ship would be taking me back to Quur.

"You do realize that you're being an idiot, don't you?"

I looked over my shoulder and glared at Teraeth. "You do realize no one asked your opinion, don't you?"

He ignored me and sat down on a crate opposite mine. "Why have you appointed yourself the only person who can stop Gadrith and Darzin? Do you think men like that are rare? Believe me, they're not. The only thing exceptional about those two is the fact you know their names. The Court of Gems is filled with men and women just as vile, every bit as evil. The whole system is set up, rigged, to support them. Are you going to stop *all* of them? Overthrow the Royal Courts, the High Council?"

"Of course not—"

"Why not? It would be the right thing to do."

I found myself taken aback. He'd ambushed me; my mouth worked for a moment without making a sound.

He leaned closer, resting his elbows on his knees. "Your problem isn't that you're stupid. You're not stupid. But you think that evil is like the Old Man, like Relos Var, like that thing sleeping in the middle of Kharas Gulgoth. You think evil is something you can just slay."

I scoffed. "Should I point out that none of those are 'something I can just slay'?"

"Oh, but you would try, wouldn't you? Except real evil isn't a demon or a rogue wizard. Real evil is an empire like Quur, a society that feeds on its poor and its oppressed like a mother eating her own children. Demons and monsters are obvious; we'll always band together to fight them off. But real evil, insidious evil, is what lets us just walk away from another person's pain and say, well, that's none of my business."

I flashed back to years earlier, breaking into the Kazivar House, telling myself the torture I witnessed there wasn't my problem. I shook it off. "What the hell is wrong with you, Teraeth? Do you want me to go to Quur or not? One minute you're suggesting I'm an idiot for returning to the Capital and the next you're telling me I should start a revolution to overthrow the government. Make up your mind."

"It's your mind that I'm worried about. I want to make sure you're not just doing this because you feel guilty about being away from your family for four years. Between slavery and the Old Man, you had an excuse, but now you get to choose. Gadrith really isn't your problem—"

"Yes, he is—"

"No," Teraeth corrected. "He's not. Yes, he is evil and yes, people will suffer and die if he continues to roam about free, but he has no reason to go after the D'Mons. Is it about Darzin? Because if Darzin's the issue, I'll arrange for him to be taken out of the picture. Easily. They'll never find the body and we can concentrate on the real enemy: Relos Var."

"We can't kill Darzin," I muttered. "I'd love to, but we need him to lead us to where Gadrith's hiding."

"Thurvishar—"

"Isn't stupid enough to be that sloppy." I glared. "And I've paid attention to the spy reports. After that last assassination attempt, do you even know where Thurvishar is spending his nights these days?"

Teraeth put his hand to his chest. "That wasn't us. The D'Lorus family have their own enemies. It can't be too surprising that someone else thought it was worth the risk of removing the D'Lorus Lord Heir. And you're trying to change the subject."

"Why do I have to be the one who takes down Gadrith?" I stood up. "Haven't you been paying attention? I won't be. All I'm going to be is bait. You're going to be the one who follows Darzin back to wherever Gadrith is hiding so you can tell Tyentso. She is going to be the one who contacts Emperor Sandus and lets him know where to bring the wrath of the Empire. And *Sandus* is going to be the one who puts that bastard permanently in the ground. See? Team effort."

"That's not what I meant." He stood up too, scowling.

"I know what you meant. Why am I doing this? Because someone damn well should. Because four years ago when I saw Gadrith and Darzin torturing that vané, I could have put a stop to this whole thing if I'd just known who to talk to. Now I do know, and I'll be damned if I'm going to let those bastards ruin any more lives when I can stop them. This isn't about Relos Var or Vol Karoth or any demon prophecies. This is about Galen. This is about Talea. This is about Thurvishar." There were other names, of course. Miya, most of all. I knew in that moment that regardless of what happened with the others, Therin and I were going to have a *talk* about my mother's freedom.

Teraeth raised an eyebrow in surprise at the last name I'd spoken aloud. "Thurvishar? I don't think he should be counted–"

I flicked my thumb and forefinger at the gaesh around my neck. "I know how someone acts when they've been gaeshed. I would bet you whatever price you named Gadrith has a trinket somewhere on him that contains a sliver of Thurvishar's soul. That's why Gadrith never bothered to lie to Thurvishar about his real parentage; he knew Thurvishar would never be able to tell anyone. Thurvishar may be the D'Lorus Lord Heir and he may be an amazing wizard, but he's still a slave. Just as much as any of the other people I named." I shook my head. "Killing Gadrith and Darzin may not save thousands. It may not even save hundreds, but it will absolutely free those people. So why am I doing this? *Because I can.*"

Teraeth blinked at my vehemence, and then began to laugh.

I took a deep breath, feeling the anger wash over me. *To hell with him.*

As I turned around to leave, Teraeth grabbed my hand. "Wait, wait. Please, I'm sorry. I promise I wasn't laughing at you." He let go of my hand and sat back down on the edge of the crates, still grinning but looking more embarrassed. "Did Khaemezra or Doc ever tell you who I used to be? In my past life?"

I paused, sensing a rare opportunity had just presented itself. I turned around. "No."

He nodded. "I started to remember right around puberty. All of it. Not just my last past life either. I also remember being in the Land of Peace." Teraeth gave me a sideways glance. "It's nice."

"What does this have to do with–"

He ignored my interruption. "So naturally, I remember when the Eight Immortals showed up and asked for volunteers: four souls willing to help fulfill the prophecies. But there was a price. They had to be willing to leave paradise, to be reborn to all the pain, hardship, and suffering of the living world. And do you know who the first volunteer was? Without a second's hesitation?"

"You?"

He chuckled. "No. *You.*"

My stomach rolled over. "Teraeth—"

"You showed up in the Land of Peace not too long after I did. And for five hundred years, give or take, you never spoke. Not a single word. Not to anyone. You just stared off into nothing, like for you the Land of Peace was anything but. And the gods didn't expect *you* to volunteer. I remember the shock on their faces when you did. One of them asked you why you wanted to go back and you said—" He gestured toward me, inviting me to finish the sentence.

My throat tried to close on me, but I still managed the words. "Because I can."

"Because you can. And that was the moment I knew—" He stopped himself.

"Yeah? Knew what?"

He didn't answer for a long beat. The silence started to loom when he finally spoke. "Knew I couldn't let you get one up on me, obviously," Teraeth said, looking away. "You were going to make me look bad."

"Please tell me you didn't volunteer to be reborn because of your ego?"

"Oh yeah," he agreed. "That's me. Nothing but conceit. Plus, my wife raised her hand as soon as she saw you do it, and there was no way I was leaving the two of you alone with each other for an entire lifetime."

I stared at him. "I swear to the gods, Teraeth, I can't tell whether or not you're joking."

He grinned at me and brushed ash from his nose.

"You boys ready to be on our way?" Tyentso walked up behind us. "I've prepped all the weather spells we'll need to make sure we arrive back in the Capital exactly on time."

I sighed inwardly as I saw that opportunity to get a little more information from Teraeth stand up, dust off its shirt, and mentally gag itself.

So much for that.

"I'm good," I told her as I stood. "We're still on schedule?"

"The pieces are all on the board." She motioned to the black-sailed ship. "Last one to claim a bunk buys the first round at the Culling Fields."

70: The Raven Returns

(Talon's story)

Faris watched the crowd mill through the streets of the Lower Circle. Most of the crowds in the Capital vanished during the monsoon months. They drained from the City to return to farms and fields, where they made extra metal helping with planting or simply escaped the floods of the rainy season. The New Year marked the official end of the monsoons, and the City's population exploded to nearly a million people as its migrant workers returned. Everyone took to the streets for the weeklong New Year's celebrations of thanks to the gods. Nobles expressed their humility and success with gifts and gestures of generosity. Tradesmen timed their return to the City to show off new wares. The whole event was overcrowded and frantic, filled with too many people all trying to fit in too small a space.

For a thug like Faris, it was heaven, a mugger's market where he could leisurely pick off the juiciest targets and make every Shadowdancer quota. He watched the roaming crowds like a barn owl looking at a field of mice, a situation of such plenty that he could afford to take the time to pick the perfect target.

A flash of gold caught his eye. Faris bent forward from the rooftop where he was perched with the rest of his boys.

"Hey," he muttered to himself, then turned his head and smacked Dovis in the arm. "Hey!"

"What?" The younger boy rubbed his forearm.

"Look at the boy in the blue," Faris said. "The one with the guards and that other kid walking next to him."

"Yeah? Looks like a royal." The kid shrugged, although the embroidery on their chosen mark's clothing earned an appreciative glance.

"That's Rook," Faris said. "That's gods-damned Rook. I can't believe it. That's Rook!"

"What? No!" The group responded with skepticism and disbelief.

"This is our chance. Let's get him."

Dovis put his hand on Faris's arm. "Are you sure, boss? Those are armed soldiers down there. That doesn't make for a good mark."

Faris slammed his good hand across Dovis's face. "Shut up, rat. This is my team. We do what I say." He pointed down to the crowd. "We follow him. We follow him and wait for an opening. There'll be one. Always is."

Kihrin held up a piece of elaborate jewelry decorated with hematite and silver. "Can you make this larger?" he asked the vendor.

"But of course, my lord. How much larger would you like?" The merchant leaned over with great courtesy. He could smell the sale.

"About, oh–" Kihrin held up his hands about two feet apart. "It's for a horse," he explained to the bemused and now wide-eyed man.

Galen blinked next to Kihrin. "What?"

The gold-haired boy nodded. "I'm sure she likes jewelry." He kept a completely straight face, although his blue eyes danced with mirth. Kihrin turned back to the jewelry. "Let me know when you have something. Deliver it ahead. The Blue Palace, yes?"

"Yes, my lord. Uh, for a horse?" The merchant hadn't quite gotten over his shock.

"She's a very special horse." Kihrin winked at the man.

Kihrin was laughing inside, thinking of how that would probably be misinterpreted.* Somehow that made it even better.

Kihrin made a show of continuing to look at the jewelry, placing brooches against his agolé or Galen's, looking at belt clasps and jeweled shawls. He watched as the guards gradually moved to stand outside the tent, which wasn't very roomy to begin with.

He tapped Galen on the shoulder and crooked a finger for the younger man to follow him toward the back of the tent. When they reached the very back, he tipped the shopkeeper several thrones plus the price of two dark brown sallí cloaks meant for rich merchants and then ducked through the back entrance. Kihrin gave one cloak to his brother and spread the other one around his own shoulders, covering the distinctive D'Mon House blue.

"Run," Kihrin whispered to his brother.

Galen hesitated, but then Kihrin had grabbed his agolé and was pulling him through the crowds and the boys were both laughing as they sprinted away from their minders, losing themselves amongst the street fair. They paused, grinning and holding their sides, to catch their breath.

"Think we lost them?" Galen asked.

Kihrin nodded. "For a little while, anyway. Long enough, I think, for us to have a little–" He paused, his gaze swinging upward.

---

*It would hardly be the first time that rumor's been spread about a noble, although in Kihrin's case it would be exceptional for having no core of truth to the tale.

The crowd had parted to form a small empty circle around them, as if the mass of people had an innate survival instinct suggesting Kihrin and Galen weren't safe. Into that gap stepped a familiar face, and Kihrin groaned.

"Hey, lookie here," Faris said. "If it isn't old Rook, all prettied up. Taking your girlfriend to see the street fair?"

"You know, even for you, this may be the worst mistake you've ever made, Faris."*

Faris didn't seem to agree. "Oh no. I'm so going to enjoy this."

Kihrin looked around. No sign of guards who might be catching up to their location, no sign of other Houses' guards who might be inclined to interfere, and no Watchmen who could be called in as protection. Faris smiled unpleasantly, and Kihrin saw that he had his whole gang with him. They had knives and saps and small little clubs that could be tucked under cloaks.

"What do we do?" Galen asked. His hand rested on his sword.

"Same thing we did last time," Kihrin admitted. "Run!" He pulled a knife from his belt, flipped it up, and tossed it. The handle smacked against one of the adolescent's hands, but several of them had ducked to avoid the possible blow and it bought them a small opening.

Kihrin ran to the side of a market stall, where boxes led to a cart that could be climbed to reach a trellis, which in turn reached the roofs. He paused when he realized that Galen was not behind him.

"Galen. Come on!"

The young man had his newly purchased brown sallí cloak in one hand and his sword drawn in the other. As the gang continued to chase Kihrin, Galen threw the cloak over several of their heads and ran one man through with his sword. Galen stepped to the side, then sliced the sword across another boy's groin. There was a stunned gap of silence as the street thieves realized that they had picked on a real swordsman and several of their number had already paid the price.

"Forget him," Faris yelled. "I want Rook."

"You should be used to disappointment by now!" Kihrin yelled. He only had a few knives left, but with those few he could make the street gang below second-guess the wisdom of their goals. He tossed one of the knives at a second thug, followed quickly by a throw at another target that hit true.

Faris looked around to realize that he was rapidly running out of gang members, and Galen was heading his way.

"This isn't over, Rook!" Faris shouted, and then he ran into the crowd.

---

*I think the worst mistake he ever made was what he did to Kihrin's teacher, Mouse. His sands flowed downhill from there.

As Kihrin climbed back down from the roof, Galen cleaned off his sword on the discarded cloak. "We should wait for the guards," Galen told him.

"Oh, hell no," Kihrin said. "We're out of here, right now. Come on. Have you ever been to a brothel? Because believe me when I say this is the time to get us off the street."

"But we don't have time to go all the way to Velvet Town . . ."

Kihrin smiled and tried to act like he hadn't been rattled by Faris's appearance. Truthfully, he'd almost managed to forget that there were members of the Shadowdancers who would gleefully shiv him at the first available opportunity. And there were others who, like Faris, didn't need the excuse of Butterbelly's murder. He didn't like that he'd put Galen in jeopardy, although if he were being honest with himself, Galen had saved the day.

He spotted the painted board of a massage house and ducked into the tent, hand around Galen's wrist. His brother seemed a little panicked, so Kihrin whispered, "Relax. It's just a massage. Nobody's going to do anything you don't want."

"Right." Some of the stress seemed to go out of him.

A short, fat man took one look at them, immediately decided that their coin was made from the right metal, and ushered them into separate rooms—just separations in the tent made by hanging more panels of cloth. Kihrin wasn't planning on getting a massage or any of the other no-doubt stellar services the mobile massage service offered, just in case Faris managed to track him down and came back with more people. He just wanted the additional distraction.

He was about to tell the cloaked woman who entered the room this fact—that he was going to pay her metal and she'd have to do absolutely nothing for it—when she flipped back her hood.

"Ola!" He started to rush forward and then paused. "Ola?"

She'd lost weight. She'd lost so much weight she was almost unrecognizable, although her coloring was the same as before. Her skin was loose from the quick slimming and hung in folds. Her eyes looked haunted.

"Yes," Ola said. "It's me."

But Kihrin didn't close the gap between them. "There's a mimic . . ."

The woman nodded. "I know the one. I managed to escape her, although it wasn't easy. Oh, Bright-Eyes. My boy." She held out her hands to Kihrin and moved forward.

He didn't let her get too close. "How did you find me?"

"I've been waiting for you to leave the palace. I know you well enough to know you'd duck out the back of that merchant's tent. Then it was mostly a matter of following the shouts and screams. You still do love trouble, don't you?"

He scowled. All that was possible. Ditching the guards would have been easier than ditching a fellow Shadowdancer.

"Ola . . . Ola, what's happened to you?"

Ola grimaced. "Well, ain't it clear enough? On the run from the Shadowdancers. On the run from everyone. It don't exactly give a girl much chance to eat, now do it? And it weren't easy to find you, either . . ."

Kihrin looked down at himself, which reminded him that his kef was beautifully embroidered and made from the finest materials, that his clothes were bejeweled and worth a fortune. He looked back up at the woman he had once considered his mother. "Why didn't you tell me? When were you going to? If I had known my family . . ."

The Zheriaso woman shook her head. "I was doing what I thought best for you, child—"

"That's never been your style."

Ola closed her mouth, exhaling through her nostrils, and then nodded. "Maybe there's some truth to that, child. But that don't change our situation now, do it? I need to get out of the Capital." She pointed a now bony finger at Kihrin. "You could stand to come with me. You and I both know that there ain't nothing but pain for you in this City."

Kihrin looked to the side, looked to where he imagined Galen was being treated to some hopefully appreciated affection. "I can't just—"

"You want to bring him with you?" Ola said. "It doesn't bother me none, but you best make sure he's real serious about wanting to leave all the riches and wealth behind, because once we're all gone, there's no changing his mind later."

"Where were you thinking?" Kihrin asked.

"Doltar," Ola said. "So far south that Quur would never find us. We can settle down, live our lives, not be looking over our shoulders forever."

"When?" Kihrin raised an eyebrow. "Now?"

"No, not until the end of the Festival," Ola said. "No ships will be leaving the harbor before then. You'll come with me, yes?"

Kihrin thought about Galen, and he thought about someone else besides. "You'll take two. Will you take three?"

Ola clasped him on his shoulder. "Yes."

71: THE TRIP HOME

(Kihrin's story)

Nothing of import or significance happened on our ship voyage to the Capital. We had good weather thanks to Tyentso. Nothing attacked us.

I had all the time I could want to worry over the future.

For the first few days, we made plans we agreed would mean little or nothing, because of the possibility of changing political climates. We weren't going in blind, mind you. Thanks to the Brotherhood's information network, we knew that Therin was still alive, as was my mother Miya, and my great-aunt Tishar. House D'Mon had fallen two ranks and was now ranked sixth. Jarith Milligreest was back in the City from his tour at Stonegate Pass, but only for long enough to take care of minor chores before rejoining his father, the High General, who was in Khorvesh visiting their family along with Jarith's new wife and baby son. Both Thurvishar and Darzin were lamentably still around.

We didn't know what Gadrith and Darzin might have planned or prepared for in the four years I had been gone, but we knew they were still looking for me. The Brotherhood had sent several agents over the years—and once Teraeth himself—disguised to fit my general description, just to see if anyone was paying attention.

The answer? Someone was very much paying attention. If the Black Brotherhood agents hadn't been arrested on spurious charges by the Watchmen, waterfront spies (probably loyal to the Shadowdancers) pointed them out. In all cases, it had never taken more than an hour for Darzin to personally show up and check whether I'd returned to the Capital.

So, I was going back in disguise.

We all were. Tyentso had even more motive to make sure no one realized Raverí D'Lorus, convicted traitor and witch, had returned to the Capital, and Teraeth—

Well. It probably wasn't good for a Manol vané to be seen in the Capital just on general principle.

I had time on the trip to think about my situation, what I was leaving behind and what I was heading toward. I had time to think about my mother and my father, and who they might be. Thanks to Doc/Terindel, Miya's role was not in question, but the father's role? My father?

Oh, but there was only one person it could be. Not Darzin, no . . . Someone so ashamed of and yet chained to his relationship with Miya he demanded all call her "Lady" as if she were his titled wife. It would explain too why I looked so much like Pedron D'Mon, who was not in fact my great-great-uncle, or even my great-grandfather, but just my grandfather. Kihrin, son of Therin, son of Pedron. The golden hair had skipped a generation, helped along by a pure-blooded vané mother. The blue eyes had been there all along.

As Therin himself had once promised me, my status as a D'Mon was never in question.

My chest felt tight as the ship entered the natural inlet leading to the Capital City. The cause eluded me at first, danced in front of me. Then I recognized it as delayed sentimentality. Before I had been kidnapped and sold into slavery, I had never left the City's confines.

I was surprised to discover I missed the Capital.

I missed the white spiraling towers that made the City look like something from a children's god-king tale in the distance, the crush of people and the way the noonday sun reflected off the Senlay River to create a blinding brightness. I missed the stifling heat bouncing off the white stone streets with homicidal fury. I missed the scent of the khilins firing bread and roasting meat and I missed the sound of vendors hawking their wares through the streets.

I had been homesick for four years, but I hadn't realized it until I returned.

The artificial stone-wrought harbor of the Capital formed a half-circle as the sculpted breakwaters reached out toward the bay like a greedy demon's claw. It was early summer—months to go until the autumn monsoons closed the City. The harbor was busy with frantic activity. Trading ships from Kazivar delivered grains and wines. The large loggers from Kirpis arrived with hardwoods and cedars. The small Khorveshan merchants off-loaded carpets, textiles, herbs, and dyes. Ships from Zherias and Doltar added their own mercantile imports and purchased exports to the overall clamor of background noise. Most of all, I found my gaze drawn to the bloated slave ships hulking by the side of the harbor to unload their grizzly living cargo. I unclenched my hand when I realized it was gripped tightly around the ship's rail.

Security on the docks had changed considerably in the years I had been absent. The large, famous dragon-carved Jade Gate, a wonder of the known world, was closed for the first time I could remember in my entire life. Someone had gone to the trouble of building a large wooden guardhouse and a smaller door next to the Jade Gate, which now constituted the only harbor entrance to the City. There were far more Watchmen on the wharf than I had ever seen before, and more distressingly, these increased numbers seemed to be normal. Most of the guards concentrated on the slave ships and tracking their human cargo. The air hanging over the docks was stifling and tense, filled with the undercurrent of suspicion and resentment.

"When did all this start happening?" I asked the ship's captain, Norrano, as we approached the docks.

Captain Norrano shrugged. "A few years back. Some prince was kidnapped and ever since, the Quuros have been paranoid about foreigners. Revoked the old open city laws."

I suppressed a nervous sigh. "Ah."

Norrano chuckled. "Ah, it'll calm down in a few years, I'm sure. Until then, they're only letting foreigners into the Merchant's Quarter and the adjoining Lower Circle sections."

"Of course," I agreed. "Couldn't keep visitors out of Velvet Town, could they?"

"There would be a riot, young man," the Captain agreed with a tug on the single diamond earring he wore. "Now if you'll excuse me, I have a lot of work to do now that we're docking. Damn customs agents are twice as hard to bribe now given the new merchant laws." He walked away, muttering under his breath.

I found Teraeth as the sailors were throwing ropes over to the dock hands waiting on the pier below to anchor the ship. He didn't look anything like a Manol vané. He'd traded in his normal appearance for an illusion of a Quuros. Specifically, a Khorveshan Quuros, and the way he wore his misha, the sash around his hips, his boots just so, was so perfectly authentic that on more than one occasion during the trip I'd found myself wondering how Jarith Milligreest had snuck on board.

He was looking at the sparkling city's silhouette with thinly disguised anger.

"Why do you hate Quur so much?" In all the years I'd known him, his hatred for my homeland had never wavered, not once. Ola hadn't shared the smallest portion of his animosity, and she had been an actual slave in Quur.

Teraeth scoffed. "Because I'm capable of observation? Ask the Marakori how much they like being under the Quuros thumb. Ask the Yorans. Ask any slave. The corpse looks whole and healthy on the surface, but scratch past that and it's nothing but rot and worms."

"That's a charming visual—" I shook my head. "—but this is personal for you."

He chuckled. "Maybe a little."

"But even you have to admit we have a fantastic sewer system." I leaned forward against the railing. "You ready for this?"

"Not even a little bit," Tyentso said as she passed by.

At Tyentso's own suggestion, she was dressed as a servant. There were no potentially suspicious illusions to disguise her appearance—already altered from the one she'd worn herself when she was Raverí D'Lorus. Wire glasses perched on her nose and she wore her hair pulled back in a severe knot. She looked useful, efficient, and like no one a nobleman would ever expect to serve his bed. Her staff had been left behind, and she wore no talismans. We all agreed it would be best if her aura didn't betray her magical skill.

"We'll be fine," I told them, mostly so I would believe it myself.

Four years, I'd been gone.

A lot can change in four years.

We all turned at the sound of the plank being lowered off the edge of the ship, followed moments later by footsteps. A thin, officious-looking man with a prudish face presented himself, followed by several Quuros Imperial soldiers.

"Captain . . ." The man looked at his parchment critically. "Norrino?" He mouthed the word like a distasteful obscenity.

"Norrano," the Captain automatically corrected.

"That is what I said," the thin man snapped. "I am Master Mivoli with the Harbor Master's office. I will need to see your complete cargo and passenger lists."

"Yeah, yeah," the curly-haired ship's captain passed over several sheets of vellum. "Whatever blows your skirt up."

The inspector scanned down the list of names and called them out, quickly and efficiently marking people off. He passed by Teraeth's and Tyentso's identities without comment, but then something on the list made him blink and turn pale. I had a pretty good idea what that might be.

Master Mivoli raised his head and scanned the crew and passengers until he stopped dead at me. He swallowed.

I smiled, but he couldn't see it, since my face was covered by a mask.

"Witchhunter Piety?"

Honestly, I'm not even sure why he felt he had to ask. Nerves, probably. My identity was not in question. I wore the black colors of House D'Lorus, including a deep hood and, in case there was any doubt, the carved wooden skull mask of the professional witchhunter. A thin gauze cloth covered the eyeholes, making it impossible to see what color my eyes might be. The rest of the outfit fell into the established theme: the coat of talismans, so covered with octagon-shaped coins they took on the look (and role) of scale armor; the belt of daggers made from different metals and alloys.*

"Yes." I stepped forward. He took an unconscious step back.

A witchhunter had one job, after all. Even if Mivoli was legal and licensed and paid his dues to House D'Laakar strictly on time, I was still dressed up as something that nightmares were made from. I watched a determined look come over the man's face as he gathered himself up. Mivoli's eyes unfocused, and I knew he was looking beyond the First Veil.

And . . . my aura looked right. I knew it did. I'd spent weeks enchanting all these damn talismans, so many that I didn't have enough magical power left to see beyond the First Veil myself nor cast the least spell, not even my witch gift of invisibility. Mivoli probably saw a multi-stamped aura so strong and crisp that even Relos Var would have been just a little impressed.

Except for the part where I couldn't cast any spells.

"I'll need your identification," he said, and held out surprisingly steady fingers.

I was ready for this part too, and handed him a specially stamped disk of blended metal alloys that was supposedly impossible to counterfeit.

We hadn't bothered. The real Witchhunter Piety was also a real member of the Black Brotherhood. (He was currently enjoying a well-earned vacation on Zherias.)

Master Mivoli checked the disk against his records, saw it was genuine, and waved a hand toward the docks, indicating I was free to go. He didn't ask me what my business in the Capital was. He didn't ask me where I was going.

The answer was already known: whatever and wherever I wanted. Witchhunters weren't technically above the law, but the distinction was subtle.

When I disembarked, I found a Black Brotherhood carriage was already waiting (truthfully, I was almost disappointed that it wasn't an extravagant black color), which both Teraeth and I used. Tyentso left by herself, although if everything went to plan she would be met by her own ride a block away. We didn't waste any time giving directions that someone might overhear: our driver already knew where to go.

As soon as we were both inside the carriage, I pulled off the mask and hood and tossed both to Teraeth's seat. "Think anyone noticed us?"

---

*Technically, it's not necessary for a witchhunter to keep a variety of different metal weapons on themselves (the normal counter for magical sabotage practiced by the Quuros military). The daggers they use stay close enough to the wielder's body to be covered by the same aura field that protects the rest of their body. Still, I suppose it has become tradition.

Teraeth pulled a silk agolé from one of his bags and handed it to me. One side was gold and the other side was blue. "Probably not. Our people will let us know if they spot anything."

I took one of the daggers from my belt and started cutting the coins off my coat, staring at each one for a moment to pull back the talismanic energy before I tossed the metal out the carriage window. Some urchin was going to have a very good day. Being a witchhunter sounded like fun, but it didn't really make someone immune to magic, just immune to certain kinds of body-affecting magic. If I wore enough talismans, a sorcerer like Gadrith wouldn't be able to melt the flesh off my bones or turn me into a fish, but he could still electrocute me or set the air around me on fire. The witchhunters that House D'Lorus had sent after Tyentso had never lasted long.

All things considered, I'd rather be able to do some magic of my own.

"You know, I still think it would be better if we were explaining things to the High General himself," Teraeth said. His disguise didn't need any modification, but he preferred working with daggers. He made a motion to me to hand them over.

"Maybe." I stopped cutting talismans free for long enough to unbuckle several braces of daggers. "But I can't be sure High General Milligreest wouldn't just drop me off at the Blue Palace like a trussed-up pig. I get the feeling he still thinks of me as Therin's troublesome brat of a son, the one who can't be trusted to tell the truth and shouldn't be left alone with the valuables." I paused. "Well, second-most troublesome brat. As long as Darzin's still around, anyway."

Teraeth traded my daggers for his sword and scabbard. "You think the High General knows that Therin's your real father?"

I rolled my eyes. "They *all* knew. Qoran, Sandus, Doc if I'd gotten to know him when he was still here. Emperor Sandus once told me he considered my father a good friend. He wasn't talking about Surdyeh." I buckled the new belt and draped the gold-side agolé around myself before continuing my work with dismantling the talismans. I'd leave a few, because I was not an idiot.

"I could still come with–" Teraeth started to say.

"No, stick to the plan." I checked out the window as the carriage pulled to a stop. My stop. "Meet up with Tyentso. I'll join you as soon as I'm finished here."

He pulled a long silvery spike out of his belt, flipped it in his hand, and put it back. "Okay. Let's get this started."

72: THE NEW YEAR'S FESTIVAL

(Talon's story)

Galen looked at himself in the mirror and groaned. "What am I supposed to be?"

Kihrin rolled his eyes and reached over to straighten the gilded, jeweled stretched leather mask on his brother's face. "The sun. You see?
You're half the D'Mon crest, and I'm the other half, the hawk." Then it
was Kihrin's turn to scowl at himself in the mirror. "Be honest, I look
like a chicken, don't I?"

"Oh no, not at all," Galen said, putting his hand on the other boy's
shoulder as he looked at their reflections. He kept a straight face for as
long as he could and then muttered under his breath, "Bwawawok!"

Kihrin tried to elbow him, which only highlighted the fact that his
sleeve arms had feathers sewn along them. Galen laughed as he dodged
his brother's swing. "Okay, so maybe a bit like a chicken." He picked up
his brother's mask from a table and tossed it to him. "Fortunately, we'll
be in disguise."

"Aren't you two ready yet?" Darzin's voice called to them just before the man stepped through the door. Darzin wasn't dressed as a
hawk or a sun, but wore a suit of dark colors, green and black, savage
and wild, with a helmet crowned by deer antlers. It looked feral and
wicked.*

Darzin examined his two sons and snapped his fingers. "Come on,
we'll make the entrance together, then attend the greeting line. Once
everyone's seated, you're on your own."

Both young men nodded their heads, knowing better than to disagree.
As they shuffled past their father, Darzin looked at Kihrin and shook his
head. "Remind me to have our tailor whipped," he muttered. "You look
like a chicken."

---

*He attended the D'Mon party dressed as the goddess Thaena's hunter? He really does have an
extraordinary talent for getting under one's skin. I can only imagine how Therin reacted to
that particular heresy.

* * *

Each of the Houses held their own party for New Year's, and since there were twelve Houses, and only six key nights (because no one dared throw their party on the Day of Death, and the Day of Stars was reserved for the Imperial Ball), the appointments for party times were drawn by lots. The losers were relegated to daytime positions with smaller crowds, since most Festival revelers were sleeping off the activities of the night before. Ideally, a House wanted a time either at the beginning of the New Year's Festival—when they might be held as the standard to which all other Houses must aspire—or at the end. Then they might make the best and most lasting impression on drunken and malleable minds, before the casting of lots for council Voices.

The D'Mon party was on the penultimate night, and it was a grand masquerade. Therin had ordered the entire Third Court emptied and the outside walkways strung with blue mage-lights. Open manicured lawns became a hive of activity. Workers spent weeks installing plants imported all the way from the Manol Jungle; specialists employed by the House had grown them into fantastic sizes, shapes, and colors that existed nowhere in nature. The scent of blue orchids and rare, impossibly crested birds-of-paradise mixed with exotic liquors and rare spiced wines. Professional revelers skipped along tightropes and performed feats of acrobatics from high wires.

The greeting line was deadly dull, and it was all Kihrin could do to keep himself awake. There was a lot of shaking of hands and bowing.

And then he saw the girl.

His heart almost stopped beating. He nearly choked from an emotion he could scarcely name. She wore a dress of red metal scales, layered to resemble the skin of a dragon, the tail trailing on the ground while delicate metal bat wings stretched out to either side. Her hair was black, but it had been washed with some sort of dye so it shimmered crimson. And her eyes, underneath that draconic half-mask, were red.

"Who are you?" The words were out of his mouth before he could stop them.

She giggled and turned her head to the side. "Silly! You're not supposed to ask that . . . this is a masquerade."

Kihrin instantly knew he'd made a mistake. Her hair covered her head completely rather than forming a single stripe from front to back. Her skin was too pale and her eyes were a single tone. They didn't glitter with the yellows, oranges, and reds of a roaring fire.

Still, what he saw of her was lovely, from her full lips to the ample cleavage pushed up by her tight raisigi. Kihrin leaned toward her and whispered, "What good is a masquerade if one can't uncover a few secrets?"

Someone cleared their throat, and Kihrin realized he was holding up the line.

"Sheloran," Galen whispered to him. "She wore that dress to the last masquerade too."

"What?"

"Sheloran D'Talus," Galen said. "That's who she is. She's the High Lord D'Talus's youngest daughter."

Kihrin smiled. "Ah. Good to know."

There was a shadow over both, and Kihrin looked up to see that Therin D'Mon stood there, dressed in leather elaborately worked and gilded to appear as metal armor. He looked like a knight or a general, including the eight-span circle and dragon of the Imperial crest. "Come with me," the High Lord ordered. "It's time for your performance."

Kihrin's stomach flipped over. He hadn't been sure Therin would remember, or would want him to go through with it.

"Good luck!" Galen told him.

All he could do was nod at his brother, before Therin's hand took his arm, leading him off to the stage area. His harp, Valathea, waited for him next to a small stool. As Therin walked him over like a prisoner being led to the gallows, he saw the crowd contained a great many of the more important nobility. This included the High General and the Council Voice Caerowan, who'd overseen Thurvishar and Jarith's duel. Lady Miya watched from underneath a shaded jungle tree whose branches had been twisted together with flowering vines to form a bench.

Basically, everyone was watching.

After the Reveler musicians announced they had a special surprise guest, he took the stage. Kihrin told himself he was still a musician, still back with his father: this was nothing more than a new commission.

He put his hands to the strings, wondering if he would freeze or faint or worse still, just play poorly, but no: Valathea would have none of that. He played with all that was in him. Reveler magic made sure every corner of the Third Court heard. Even the Revelers, he noted, gave him a grudging round of applause when he finished, loath to admit anyone might play as well as they. Afterward, he left Valathea for servants to take back to his room while he walked down, mask still present, to join the others.

Propriety and the honor of both House D'Jorax and House D'Mon were appeased by the fact that he had never been directly identified. Everyone knew, of course, but they could pretend his identity was a mystery. Perhaps House D'Jorax would even claim he was one of their own musicians in disguise.

Therin turned and left without saying a word, and Darzin had never been present at all. The young man knew he shouldn't have been surprised, but his gut still clenched and his throat tightened. He had thought that Therin at least might say a kind word . . .

"I believe Lord D'Mon enjoyed your performance," Lady Miya said as she approached. She added in a quieter voice, "But he will never admit it." The vané woman leaned over and kissed Kihrin's cheek, the part showing behind the mask. Then Miya looked behind Kihrin and said, "High General, I approve of your gift. She is in good hands with the skill of these fingers."

To Kihrin's surprise, Qoran Milligreest bowed to the woman. "I'm glad to hear it. Caerowan, what do you think?" He looked to the Voice, the strange, small man dressed like a peasant.

"Very well played," Caerowan agreed. "The harp is particularly interesting. Do you know its history?" This last question was directed at Kihrin.

Kihrin swallowed and wondered how to make a retreat. "Ah, no. It's a Milligreest family heirloom, is it not?" He pointed to the General. "He's the man you should be asking."

"And the hawk costume you wear—" Caerowan turned to Milligreest. "The hawk plays a significant role in prophecies relating to the Hellwarrior."

"That's a hawk?" Kihrin watched the High General make a valiant effort to keep from rolling his eyes. "I don't put a great deal of stock in those stories."

"What's a Hellwarrior?" Kihrin asked, and ignored the dirty look the High General gave him.

This seemed to throw the Voice into confusion for a moment, and he frowned as if he were wondering if Kihrin might be mocking him. Then he gave a tight smile and tilted his head. "Ah, there are a set of prophecies, you see."

"Gods, I really don't think the young man needs to be bothered with such trivialities," Qoran snapped.

"But I'm very interested," Kihrin insisted, not because he was, but because it so clearly annoyed the High General.

"There are a set of prophecies," Lady Miya whispered to Kihrin, "that foretell the end of the world, ushered in by a herald called War Child, or the Hellwarrior, or Demon King, or Godslayer. The End Bringer who will usher in the annihilation of our world."

"Stories," Milligreest growled. "God-king tales. The delusional fancies of superstitious, crazed men and women who hide from the reality of the world. Prophets, seers, and insane monks have been foretelling the end times since the beginning of the Empire, and always the danger is right on our doorstep. Something must be done."

Kihrin turned to the High General. "So it's just a way of selling something?"

The High General let out a bark of laughter. "Just a way of selling something? Oh yes. Oh yes, indeed." He chuckled, clasped the young man on the shoulder enough to stagger the boy, and then looked forlornly into his goblet. "My drink is empty, as was foretold. Something must be done." With that, he stalked into the crowd.

Caerowan hadn't moved, and stared at him intently.

"May we help you, Voice?" Lady Miya asked.

"I still have questions for the young man," Caerowan explained.

"You're not Quuros, are you?" Kihrin asked, starting to feel peevish about the attention he was receiving.

The little man looked at him and blinked, owl-like. "I'm a Devoran priest," he said. "Devors is part of the Empire, although not within any dominion." He paused. "Yes, I am Quuros."

"How can you have a priest of an area? I thought priests were the devotees of gods," Kihrin pressed.

"We are not priests in the same sense," Caerowan explained, his voice calm. "Do you know what a gryphon is?"

The question was unexpected enough to make Kihrin pause, and he looked back at Lady Miya to see her staring at the Voice with angry, narrowed eyes. Kihrin turned back to Caerowan. "Yes," he said. "I've heard stories. It's a monster. Half-eagle and half-lion." He added, "They don't really exist, you know."*

The small man smiled. "Did you know the name Therin means lion?"†

"Do these questions have a point, Voice?" Lady Miya's hand closed on Kihrin's shoulder protectively.

"The High General, although I hold him with the greatest possible respect, sometimes sees only what he wishes to see—and not those truths that may hold the Empire by the throat," Caerowan explained. "We have been watching the signs, Lady. And while it would be pleasant to believe the threat is a storyteller's fancy, the time is upon us."

"Kihrin D'Mon," Miya said firmly, "has no part in any prophecies, nor any association with gryphons or a so-called Hellwarrior. Your precious Thief of Souls died when Nikali slew Gadrith D'Lorus." She spoke with a grandeur and authority that allowed no room for dissension.

---

*They really do exist and live high in the Dragonspire Mountains, but I suspect their inclusion in matters of prophecy is meant to be taken as metaphor.

†"Therin" does comes from a root word that meant lion in the old Guarem, but it's also a common name. My own name is a variation. This is what I hate about prophecy. Any old thing becomes hugely significant.

Thief of Souls . . .

Kihrin remembered that Xaltorath had once called him by that very title. He hid his shudder.

The Voice seemed about to say something else, but instead he put his hand to his chest and bowed. "Yes, of course, Lady. Forgive me."

When the Voice put his hand to his chest, Kihrin noticed the ring on his finger: an intaglio-carved ruby, set in gold. It was all he could do not to give a shout of alarm, but instead he had to smile and duck his head as he watched the Devoran priest take his leave.

"Weird little man," Kihrin said to Lady Miya. "Why would he ask me if I knew what a gryphon is?"

"I do not know," Lady Miya said, as they both watched the man fade into the crowd.

But Kihrin could tell she was lying.

73: Returning to the Red Sword

(Kihrin's story)

Commander Jarith stepped through the door to the Milligreests' estate courtyard, an angry look on his face. The courtyard looked the same as the last time I'd been there at age fifteen, down to the damn mural of Emperor Kandor dying in the Manol, but Jarith looked older. The man would never wield the sheer physical mass of his father, but he was looking like someone comfortable giving orders and having those orders followed.

"Darzin, I am a busy man and I do not have time for your—" He stopped as he realized who was waiting for him. *"Kihrin?"*

I stood up. "Did you miss me?"

The Citadel Commander crossed the space between us and clasped me around the chest, thumping my back. "Kihrin! You devil! Look at you . . . Where have you been? Do you have any idea how many people have searched for you?"

"I saw the changes in the harbor."

Jarith sighed as he let go of me. "Yes. We turned everything upside down. My apologies for the greeting. The guards said a D'Mon was here to see me. I thought it was your father trying to cause trouble." He motioned for me to follow him. "How did you know I was here? I'm usually at the Citadel but I'm preparing to leave for Khorvesh . . ."

"Ah, well aren't I the lucky one then? Good timing."

"Indeed! I was just finishing up some paperwork. Mind coming inside my office? Do you want anything? I only have maridon black but I can go to the kitchen for something stronger if you prefer."

"No, no, that's not necessary," I said. "Tea would be fine." Jarith showed me through hallways that were familiar even though I'd only been inside the house once. His office was a clutter of orders and scrolls, notations marked on maps pinned to walls. A chair serving as a filing cabinet for a stack of reports was cleared away, so I might have a place to sit. Evidently, he was a man who liked to bring his work home with him.

He cast his eyes around the room. "Damn. I thought I had some tea—wait here. I'll be right back." Jarith walked out of the office, leaving me alone.

"Where would I go?" I said to the empty air. I fought the urge to run, the paranoid, itchy feeling that Jarith had invented himself a flimsy excuse so he could go fetch the soldiers with halberds and spears. *Focus,* I told myself. Jarith was not in league with Darzin, and Jarith's father was in Khorvesh. Jarith was happy to see me.

To distract myself from my anxiety, I examined the walls. The map focused predominately on the dominion of Jorat, on the other side of the Dragonspire Mountains. Small pins marked various towns, although I couldn't tell what the pattern behind them might be. More pins held up pieces of vellum and paper, all sketches of the same subject.

It was a dragon.

Not the Old Man, I saw with no small relief, but a dragon all the same. I realized the towns had to be rampage sites and felt a shiver run through me. *Those poor people.*

There was one last piece of paper nestled in the middle of all the dragon sketches: a wanted poster written in curiously precise, neat lettering. The Duke of Yor, Azhen Kaen, was offering a truly obscene amount of metal for the death of someone from Jorat called "the Black Knight," who evidently needed no further qualifier. The sketch of the knight in question looked like something out of nightmares, although I knew a group of assassins who would've approved of his fashion sensibilities.

What this Black Knight had to do with the dragon eluded me, but I knew one thing: anyone who Relos Var's puppet Kaen wanted dead that badly instantly marched to the top of my interesting-people list.

I pulled the wanted poster off the wall and tucked it into my coat.

"Sorry about that," Jarith said as he returned with a pot of tea and two cups on a tray. He poured the tea, which, true to his word, looked like some variation of maridon.

"Well it's not like I gave you any warning," I said as I took my cup and returned to the chair. "This is more hospitality than I deserve."

For himself, Jarith nudged aside a mound of paperwork and leaned a hip on the edge of his desk. "By Khored. What happened to you?"

"Oh, the usual. Kidnapped, sold into slavery, kept prisoner by a dragon. Same old stuff."

Jarith laughed, shaking his head in wonder (and assuming I was joking). "You have no idea how good it is to have you back. We've almost started wars because of our insistence on searching ships for gold-haired prisoners. I've had my agents following up on every lead, no matter how preposterous."

"You have agents now? You really have moved up in rank."

"Ah well, Stonegate Pass is a shit assignment, but it's a fantastic career builder." He picked up his tea and gulped down some as he studied me. "Does your family know you're back?"

"Not yet," I admitted. "Talking to you was the higher priority."

Jarith frowned and set down his teacup. "Than your own family? What's going on?"

I cleared my throat and pulled a set of letters out of my coat. "I thought you would want to be involved in this. It concerns Thurvishar D'Lorus."

The frown didn't leave his face, but only deepened some. "He's not my favorite person, but we've stayed out of each other's way. I don't hold a grudge."

"I do," I admitted. "He was involved with my kidnapping." Which was technically true, even if I was certain Thurvishar hadn't actually been responsible for it. Before Jarith had a chance to respond, I tossed one of the folded pieces of vellum in front of him. "That is a letter from Raverí D'Lorus testifying that she never bore any children. Not to Gadrith D'Lorus, not to anyone. Thurvishar D'Lorus is *not her son.*"

He picked up the letter and opened it. The frown had graduated to a scowl. "I'm sure that was true at one point, but I can't imagine that House D'Lorus let her write letters during her sentence of Continuance . . ."

"Except Continuance never happened."

He blinked at me. "What?"

"She's not dead." I leaned forward. "Between escaping slavers and navigating my way back here, I tracked her down, Jarith. High Lord Cedric D'Lorus lied about having her in custody, and he lied about Continuance, and he lied about executing her after Continuance was finished. Raverí had an inside man over at the Council, and he gave her enough warning to skip town ahead of the witchhunters."

Jarith looked incredulous. "What idiot would have been foolish enough to jeopardize their entire career by helping a convicted traitor escape justice?"

I coughed. "That would be your father. Why do you think I came here first?"

It was rather remarkable, watching all the color drain from his face. Of course, I'd just suggested that Qoran Milligreest was guilty of the sort of crime that got one sentenced to lifetime enslavement *at best.* "Why would my father have—"

"Because your father is a good man and he knew perfectly well she didn't deserve what the Council and House D'Lorus were going to do to her." I gestured toward the back side of the letter. "Also, they were lovers. It's all in there."

He stared at me. What Jarith didn't do was tell me that was impossible or that his father would never do that. He probably knew better. The affair part wasn't even necessarily a great scandal, given how Khorveshans often played fast and loose with polygamy, much to the reproachful delight of the rest of the Empire. Helping a witch escape the witchhunters, though . . .

Jarith sat down. Then he reached over and finished the rest of his tea while he read the entire letter, start to finish. "Okay." He paused. "Okay," he said again.

I snatched the letter out of his hands and magically set the whole thing on fire.

"Wait, what—" He stood up again.

"I'm not trying to blackmail you, Jarith. I figure there's two ways that you can react to this. The royal way would be to kill me, try to figure out where I've hidden Raverí, and do whatever you can to cover this up. But I'm betting you're going to go for option number two."

Jarith paused and cocked his head. "What's option number two?"

"If I'm right, there's a much bigger problem brewing, and once we uncover that? Nobody is going to have any time to waste thinking about who helped a girl leave town without anyone noticing twenty years ago."

"Okay, I'm listening." Jarith didn't sound panicked, which was good. I needed him rational.

"So, High Lord Cedric lying to the Council about Raverí's fate is a problem for him just as much as it would be for your father, but let's be realistic, it happened twenty years ago. I rather suspect the Council would just as soon let that be water down the river. But Thurvishar isn't Ogenra. He isn't god-touched. The eyes are faked, and the test results were too. If you were to test Thurvishar right now, he wouldn't have the tiniest trace of royal blood in him. He would, however, test as half-vordreth with a hell of an aptitude for magic."

"Why—" Jarith blinked. "Where would High Lord Cedric have even found a half-vordreth? The only vordreth I've ever even heard of is—" He stopped looking concerned and began to look horrified. I'm guessing he was mentally going over the stories his father had probably told him about Emperor Sandus and his wife, Dyana—his *vordreth* wife.

"That brings me to my second letter," I said as I laid it, still sealed, on the desk in front of him. "Which, to save you time, I'll simply explain is from the High Priestess of Thaena herself, verifying that she cannot confirm that either Emperor Sandus's wife nor son are actually dead because neither soul crossed beyond the Second Veil. You know who else never made it fully past the Second Veil? Gadrith D'Lorus. A fact which I can confirm, because I've seen him with my own eyes."

"What?"

"Gadrith D'Lorus faked his death. A lot of High Lord Cedric's crazy, inexplicable behavior starts to make a lot more sense once you realize that he's still taking his marching orders from his son Gadrith. But Gadrith isn't perfect, and he's screwed up this time."

"There's no way Gadrith is still—"

I held up a hand. "Hear me out. Thurvishar isn't Gadrith's son.

Thurvishar is Emperor Sandus's son. Why did Gadrith lie? I honestly don't know. It might be because of the prophecies that he and Relos Var seem to be so obsessed with, or it might just be that Gadrith thought Thurvishar was too young to eat at the time.* Fortunately, the truth is easy to confirm: because if I'm right, Thurvishar is both gaeshed and half-vordreth. That is eminently testable."

Jarith narrowed his eyes and studied me. Then he walked over to a cabinet and proved he'd lied earlier by pulling down a bottle of brandy. "And how do you know what Gadrith looks like?"

"Raverí showed me."

He poured himself a shot and didn't offer me any. "And how do you know she's really Raverí D'Lorus?" He wrinkled his nose. "Not that I can imagine anyone volunteering to be hunted as a witch and a traitor."

I grinned and held up a third letter. "This one's from your uncle Nikali." I tossed it over so it slid to a stop next to the second letter on the desk. "He said you'd know it was really from him."

He gulped down the rest of his drink and walked back to the desk. "I'm not going to lie, Kihrin, you're starting to scare me. What the hell have you been up to while you were away?"

"Oh, we so don't have time for that." I gestured toward the paper. "Do you believe me? At least enough to pull Thurvishar in and run those tests? Keep in mind he won't come willingly if he realizes what you're doing. I'm sure he's been ordered to keep Gadrith's secrets hidden by any means necessary."

Jarith didn't answer right away. He broke the wax seal on the letter and read it. I had no idea what wording Doc had used, but it must have been persuasive. He set it down and nodded. "I'll see it done."

---

*He's overthinking this. As far as I've ever been able to tell, Gadrith originally kept me for ritual purposes, and then later decided I would make an excellent host body once he obtained the Stone of Shackles. That's why he made me Lord Heir—so he'd have his old position back once he swapped souls with me.

74: Thefts and Murders

(Talon's story)

"What are we doing?" Sheloran D'Talus asked Kihrin, later.

He pointed down from their vantage in the tower. "This has one of the best views in the whole Blue Palace," he told her as he watched through one of the ship's glasses that the guards kept there. "We're watching a spy."

"A spy?" Her red eyes went wide. "How dangerous! Who is he?"

"He? Maybe it's a she . . ." Kihrin said.

They'd discarded their wings in a corner of the watchtower where they wouldn't interfere with their movements, and Kihrin had removed the heavy feathered shirt. "Is it a she?" Sheloran questioned coyly. "And is she fabulously seductive?"

He shook his head. "No. Sadly, no." He pointed. "The little man in the staid clothes. The one with the shaved head."

Sheloran peered through the spyglass. "Isn't that a Voice of the Council?"

"That makes him especially dangerous," Kihrin agreed.

"Well, he's leaving," the young lady announced, disappointed that there would be no sexy, dangerous, covert shenanigans.

Kihrin reached over and took his turn at the spyglass. Caerowan was talking to various nobles, one after another, and then the Voice of the Council met up with a group of servants and led them away from the party.

He was heading toward the Private Court, off-limits to all but family.

Kihrin closed the spyglass and helped Sheloran to her feet. "I'm afraid our game may have just become serious. Would you do me the favor of finding the guard?"

The woman raised her chin. "What shall I tell them?"

"We have intruders in the Prince's Court."

When Kihrin reached the court, there was no sign of Caerowan or any of the men that Kihrin had seen accompanying him. The young D'Mon prince cloaked himself in shadows and looked for any sign of the intruders. No matter what the Voice's perceived rank, this was a part of the palace in which he was unquestionably trespassing.

He heard a scuffle, a muffled curse, and homed in on that noise. As he came around a corner, he saw one wall of the Hall of Flowers had been magically breached. It was now background to a lattice of glowing green energy, a circle of glyphs and sigils, through which he could see a hallway of rough brick and cobblestone.

Two men carried a wrapped triangular package through the opening while a third man supervised. Green energy leaked from his fingertips as he worked to keep the magical portal open. Caerowan was last in line.

That package. Kihrin's heart skipped as he realized what it was. It was a harp. It was *his* harp.

They were stealing Valathea.

"Hey!" The shout was out of his lips and he was running.

The two men carrying the harp vanished through the opening in an instant.

"Abide," Caerowan told the Gatekeeper.

The Devoran priest lingered as the young man raced up to them.

"You son of a bitch. That doesn't belong to you!" All thoughts of stealth vanished from the young man's mind.

Caerowan reached out with a hand, grabbed the wrist Kihrin was using to hold his sword, and twisted. Kihrin flew over Caerowan's head and landed on the tile floor. Caerowan put a knee to the young man's chest and bent down. "She will be returned to you, Your Majesty.* This I swear."

"You're crazy," Kihrin said as best he could while struggling to draw breath in his lungs.

"Sadly no."

The pressure on Kihrin's chest released, and Caerowan ran through the portal, the mage who had opened it following a second later.

Kihrin rolled to his feet and chased after, but there was no sign of the gate. He turned at the sound of footsteps running fast in his direction. "Guards! Guards, there was a theft—"

The soldiers stopped and looked at him oddly. The lead man bowed. "M'lord, your presence is required immediately. It's your mother."

Kihrin was at a loss. Who did the man mean? Ola? Then he realized they had to mean his stepmother, Alshena D'Mon.

"Show me," he said.

---

*Caerowan would know the correct form of address is "Your Highness." One may surmise Caerowan didn't believe Lady Miya's assurance of Kihrin's non-involvement in matters of prophecy.

* * *

She had been poisoned.

That was everyone's immediate assumption, because the Lord Heir's wife had been drinking some wine of unknown source when the convulsions had taken her. Death had come on swift wings thereafter. Poison left her a corpse with red skin and a rictus grin. Her body was taken by the physickers of the House, who announced her beyond their ability to repair.

Everyone assumed that neither Therin nor Darzin would petition the Black Gate for her Return.

Galen had taken one look at her and had been ordered to his rooms because it wasn't seemly for a noble of the House to cry so in public. Darzin didn't seem joyful—but Kihrin thought his expression was too ambivalent for the murder of his wife. No matter that he hadn't loved her, Alshena's murder should have stung his pride.

Tishar's expression could have been cast from iron.

Galen was still drying his eyes when Kihrin found him. With no words, Kihrin crossed over to his younger brother, put his arms around him, and let the younger boy sob.

"I hate this place, I hate this place, I hate this place," Galen said again and again. "He killed her. He killed my mother!"

"You don't know—"

"Who else would it have been? She wasn't important. Now you're here, I'm no longer heir and there was never any chance she'd be mother of a Lord Heir, let alone a High Lord." He sniffled and wiped his nose on his sleeve. "Who else but Darzin? Who else but my father? I know how he beats her, how he hates her. Hates her because he blames her for my weakness."

"You're not weak," Kihrin told him.

"I *am* weak," Galen corrected, tears still streaming down his cheeks. "I am weak and I am wrong, and I wish I weren't. I don't like the things our father wants me to like, no matter how hard I try."

"You're fantastic with a sword," Kihrin said, trying to find what words of comfort he could.

"Not good enough, it seems." Galen shook his head. "Never good enough, or strong enough, or cruel enough to please him. He'll beat me now, for daring to cry over my mother's corpse."

"Galen, you're fourteen. No matter what he says, I bet Darzin wasn't any better at fourteen." Kihrin reached over, took his brother's hand, and squeezed it.

Galen sat there, eyes a vivid blue from the tears. He met Kihrin's gaze. "I don't like girls," he confessed.

Kihrin bit his lip. "I know."

"You do?" Galen frowned, confusion now showing in his features.

"I'm sure everyone knows," Kihrin admitted. "It's not really too hard to figure out, when you don't even stare at pretty girls when they're wearing almost nothing. Aunt Tishar and–" He floundered, not wanting to mention Alshena's name. But if they had taken such pains to note his own sexual interests, surely they had done so with Galen. "You know, it means nothing. Men worked at the Shattered Veil Club, and they always had plenty of customers. Some men like . . . men."

"It's weak," Galen muttered.

"Dragon shit," Kihrin said. "It's an excuse for gossip and after that, nobody cares."

"That's not true," Galen said. He wiped his eyes. "You know that's not true."

Kihrin sighed. "Yes, you're right. That's not true. It should be though."

An awkward silence settled between the two boys.

"Have you ever–" Galen started to ask. He stopped himself, and turned away, face reddened.

"Yes." Kihrin's voice was quiet.

Galen looked up. "What? You have?"

"I didn't like it," Kihrin confessed. "And I just–" He shrugged. "I just like girls, I suppose."

"Oh." Galen cleared his throat. "I mean, of course. That makes sense." The stifling silence returned.

"I'm running away," Kihrin said. "You could come with me. Where I'm going, no one will care." The idea seemed plausible enough. If they were incognito, no one would care if they took wives or had children or not.

"You're running? You'd never get away–"

"I am. I will. I have a way." Kihrin squeezed Galen's hand. "Come with me?"

Galen stared at him, and then he nodded.

75: Confrontations

From the Ruby District, I made my way to the Culling Fields invisibly, but I wore my hood up, just in case.

When I entered the tavern, the first thing I noticed was that it was as crowded as the last time I'd seen it. The second thing I noticed though was Teraeth leaning against the bar, chatting up Tauna Milligreest. Doc had said that he'd left a way to contact Sandus with Tauna in case of emergencies. We all agreed this qualified.

I knew Teraeth had a weakness for Khorveshan women, but I couldn't help but wonder if Teraeth knew he was hitting on his adopted sister.

I started to wander over in his direction when I saw Tyentso. She had set up shop at one of the larger round tables, cleared it of its normal contents, and had instead covered the entire table with small glass tumblers filled with water. At least, I assumed it was water.

Sitting next to her was a Marakori man wearing a patchwork *sallí*. He had a plain copper circlet on his forehead, and although I couldn't see it currently, I was equally sure he owned a matching wand somewhere on his person. No one in the bar seemed particularly concerned or interested in his presence, but to be fair, he still didn't really look like anyone special. He also looked young, but then unlike his friends Qoran, Therin, or Nikali, he would never age as long as he owned the Crown and Scepter.

Why would anyone think this was the Emperor of Quur?

My mouth felt very dry.

I walked over to their table and pulled up a chair.

Tyentso nodded to me, although her focus remained on the tumblers. "I'd make introductions, but—"

"We've met," Emperor Sandus said. "Although it's been a few years. Tyentso's been explaining the situation to me." He didn't look happy, but then I suppose I couldn't blame him.

If I'd just found out that my mortal enemy had been claiming my son as his for all these years, I probably wouldn't be happy either.

I looked down at the table. If one was paying close attention to the tumblers, or rather to the liquid inside the tumblers, they might notice that the images reflected against their surfaces did not correspond with the interior of the bar. I'm sure most people just thought Ty was playing an insanely intoxicating drinking game. What she was really doing was monitoring the City for the sort of changes that would indicate a Hellmarch starting. She'd sworn she could do it; something about how demons absorbed heat affecting the ambient temperature in a way that could be followed, like changing weather patterns.

"That's good," I said. "I assume that means you'll help?" I saw the look he gave me. "Yes, you're right. That *was* a stupid question. If you'll come with Teraeth and me—"

Emperor Sandus smiled tightly. "Under an illusion or invisibility or some other method, I assume. I have what may be a better idea, if you're amenable."

I held out my hands and tried not to show how nervous he was making me. "Of course."

He set down three rings on the table. "Each of you takes one of these. They're enchanted. Focus on them and you'll be able to communicate with me directly. That way there is no chance that someone will notice me too early and do something rash. I guarantee that both Gadrith and Darzin know exactly what I look like. Sadly, I've never met . . ." His mouth tightened. ". . . Thurvishar."

My hand shook as I picked up one of the rings.

You see, it was set with an intaglio-carved ruby.

I was aware that Tyentso made pleased noises, because communication had, after all, been one of the weak spots in our original plan. In the bar, people still drank and laughed and argued as prelude to duels. They clinked glasses and made toasts and threw insults at each other in varying degrees of venom. It all sounded muted, underwater, unimportant.

I thought about the vané whom Gadrith and Darzin had tortured and murdered, who had owned such a ring. I thought about my father Surdyeh, who owned such a ring. I thought about Caerowan, who had stolen Valathea from me, and owned such a ring.

I met Sandus's eyes. "When we're done here," I said, "you and I are going to have a very long talk, Your Majesty."

He smiled sadly. "Yes. I imagine we will."

I picked up a second ring for Teraeth and left without another word.

So far everything had gone perfectly to plan.

Now came the hard part: going home.

Lady Miya flew down the marble steps and into my arms. "Kihrin!"

She hid her face in the cloth of my agolé, muffling the sound of her crying. I smoothed her hair and touched her cheek.

The crying stopped with a shocked sob and my mother pulled aside the cloth of my misha, to look at the star tear diamond necklace I wore underneath.

"It's a long story," I said. "I promise I'll explain later."

My mother tore her gaze from the necklace to focus on me. "Where have you *been*? We received a message you were safe, but we couldn't be sure of its provenance."

"I know," I agreed. "I hope it was some comfort, and I'm sorry I wasn't able to return sooner. I think we should go inside, don't you?" I looked up the steps of the First Court to see Therin standing there, watching me with an unreadable expression.

"Grandfather," I lied, nodding my head at my father.

"Kihrin." Therin nodded back. His voice sounded tight. "I expected them to bring you back in pieces."

"Me too," I said with a mocking grin. "But it's nice to see your confidence in me hasn't changed since I left." I walked past Therin, my arm still wrapped around my mother.

Therin's face flashed over with suppressed anger. "Were you kidnapped or did you run away?"

"I would have run away," I admitted. "I won't deny I was planning to, but the former happened before I could get around to the latter."

I could tell there were questions my father wanted to ask. I could see it in Therin's scowl and the sharpness of his blue eyes. I also saw that, as angry as Therin was, it was self-directed.

That didn't mean I forgave him.

"Come to my office," the High Lord ordered. "I'll talk to you in private. Once word spreads you're back, it will be nothing but celebrations and parties for the next week."

"Therin," Darzin said, entering the courtyard. "Kalovis said you were waiting for someone and I . . ." His eyes locked onto me like shackles.

"Good evening, Darzin," I said. The smile was genuine enough, if only because I was very much looking forward to how I hoped the rest of the evening would go.

Well enough.

For a full two seconds, Darzin's face was a frozen study in surprise. Then he broke into a full grin. "Why, you son of a bitch!" he said. "I just knew I'd see you again." He actually seemed happy, which made a certain amount of twisted sense. With me back, plans could proceed, couldn't they?

Darzin stepped toward me as if to hug me in sheer exuberance. I stepped back nonchalantly, falling just outside Darzin's reach.

That smile faded in the onslaught of my cold, unreceptive stare.

"Careful there, son. Keep up that expression and I'll think you don't love me anymore."

"Anymore? That would imply I did once. Why would I start now?" I placed my hand on my sword hilt.

Darzin noticed the movement. "I bet you still don't have a clue how to use one."

I locked my eyes with his. "I'll take that bet."

The smug grin on Darzin's face softened. The hatred in his eyes was naked and brutal as we stared at each other. After four years, it hadn't subsided in the slightest. The Stone of Shackles chilled my neck.

I moved first.

Arguably, I moved fastest, but killing Darzin was not the goal.

Also, I'd forgotten about Lady Miya.

Even as I drew my sword and attacked my brother, even as he drew his sword and responded, a great wall of air rose up between us, driving us both back. My sword was snatched from my hands and clattered against the marble floor. His sword flew to the side and embedded itself into a wall.

Lady Miya lowered her hand. "If you are going to fight, you would be best served to do so when I am absent."

I laughed. The gaesh. Of course. All manner of violence might be committed by one D'Mon against another in private, but if she was present, Miya was obligated to intervene.

And here I'd worried I wouldn't be able to drive him off believably.

Darzin paced, sneering. He wiped his mouth with the back of his hand. "I must admit, I didn't think you had the stones to actually attack me. Lucky for you, Miya's here to protect you."

"She wasn't protecting *me*. Why don't we send her away so we can finish this conversation properly?"

"Enough, from both of you," Therin said. "I will not have you dueling in my House."

Darzin never broke his stare with me. "It hasn't been your House for a few years, old man." He walked over to where his sword still quivered, embedded in the wall, and rescued it.

I realized Darzin was leaving. I wanted him to but I also had to make sure that Teraeth was in position. Since I couldn't see Teraeth, I thought buying a little time would always be in good taste.

"Running so soon, big brother?"

That made him pause. "Big brother?" Darzin looked surprised. "Our father actually told you the truth? I'm amazed he had the spine."

"I figured things out." I held out my hand and my own sword sailed back into my grasp. Darzin saw the visible demonstration of spell use and frowned, probably not liking the idea that I'd picked up some magical training. "I figured out that you're nothing but an over-preening fool, who isn't smart enough to be more than a necromancer's lackey. Tell me, what has Gadrith promised you? That you'll be the head of House D'Mon? Head of the Council? Or are you just doing this because you know how much it will upset our father?"

He actually started to answer. Then Darzin smiled. "Better watch your baby boy, Therin. He seems to have lost his mind."

"No. Stop him!" I tried to make it sound good, as much as I could.

Darzin ran back into the palace.

Therin made no move to chase. "What is going on here? Kihrin, you have a lot of explaining to do."

I ignored him.

Now we just had to hope that Darzin was stupid enough to go running straight to Gadrith.

Because as soon as he did that, it was all over.

Darzin's astonished question about Therin telling me the truth hovered in the air between us. My father ignored it. He didn't ask what either Darzin or I had meant. He didn't try to protest that we weren't brothers.

Because he knew that was a lie.

"What exactly is going on?" Therin demanded.

"I don't suppose I could convince you to release Lady Miya from her gaesh?" I saw the look on Therin's face and waved a hand. "Never mind. We don't have much time now. Probably not more than a half hour. Darzin's off to warn Gadrith I'm back. I honestly do not know what Gadrith will do when he finds out, but we're going to be ready for him."

"Gadrith's dead," Miya said, but she didn't say it with much conviction.

"He's not." I pulled back the collar of my misha, revealing both the Stone of Shackles and the necklace of star tear diamonds. Lady Miya already knew about the latter, but my father hadn't yet seen them.

He flinched. "Where—?"

"You remember where these star tears ended up after you bought Miya with them, don't you? With a certain old vané hag who just happens to be a High Priestess of Thaena?" I let the collar of my misha fall forward again. "Take my word for it that I know for a fact that Gadrith didn't travel past the Second Veil. He found a way to fool you and Thaena both."

Therin stared. After a moment, he seemed to shake off the paralysis that had seized him. "I will talk to you in private. Now."

"No," I said. "We don't have time. I just pushed Darzin to do something rash and a mimic has infiltrated this household. I need to find her before he returns."

"A mimic?" Whatever news Therin had expected from me, that wasn't it.

I turned to Lady Miya. "Lyrilyn was murdered by a mimic while she was wearing the Stone of Shackles. Your former handmaiden never left the house, but she did switch allegiance. She works for Darzin now."

I was dumping a lot of information in their laps at once, but I couldn't give my father a chance to demand that I provide proof. I needed them acting first. The proof would come soon enough.

"Oh, that poor girl," Lady Miya said.

Therin looked like he'd been slapped. No matter how good Therin's information networks had been, I'd just told him that Darzin's were much better and why.

"Is there anyone who's been acting oddly? Inconsistent?"

"A mimic isn't going to reveal themselves so easily," Therin said. "The mimic could be anyone." He gave me a thoughtful stare.

"That paranoia's coming just a little late. Please try to remember that I'm the one who just warned *you* about the mimic."

"No, it is not you," Lady Miya said. "And it is not just anyone, either. Ola. It has to be Ola."

I startled. "What? Ola's here?"

"Yes," Therin said. "We captured her. I was so angry when you first disappeared that I would have let Darzin kill her. However, Lady Miya said you would never forgive me—if you ever made your way back to us—if I allowed the woman who'd raised you to be executed. So she's our 'guest.'"

"That's the mimic," I agreed. "Where is she?"

"Your rooms," Lady Miya said.

Therin scowled. "We still can't be sure she's the mimic."

I sighed. "Yes, we can, because Ola's dead. Ola Nathera is in the Land of Peace. I heard that straight from Thaena's mouth. Which means the Ola you know is the counterfeit." I felt under my agolé for yet another letter tucked away. "Lady Miya, please go find Aunt Tishar. This is for her. It explains what's going on and what I need her to do."

She took the letter and left.

"Kihrin, I need to know—"

"You need to do what I say for once," I said, turning on him. "Evacuate the palace. The one thing I have not been able to plan for is exactly what Gadrith will do once he realizes I'm back, and wizard duels are messy. Get everyone out."

"Think, Kihrin. Where could Gadrith D'Lorus have been hiding for all these years?"

I raised an eyebrow at my father. "There's a whole guild of wizards dedicated to the craft of opening gates between distant lands. I don't know why everyone thinks hiding would be so difficult."

I started to walk off.

"Did Khaemezra tell you? I mean, about—" Therin choked on whatever he'd been about to ask.

I stopped. "Which part? About you being my father?"

He stared at me with haunted eyes. "No," he said. "No, absolutely not. Darzin's your father."

I scoffed. "That's not true and you know it."

"It IS true. It is true and you will *not* contest it."

I narrowed my eyes. "Would you like me to tell you how I know you're lying? I mean, the ways are nearly endless, but let's start with the fact that I know you're lying because I know Miya is my mother. And Miya's hatred of Darzin isn't personal. She hates him on principle, she hates what he does to people around him, but she doesn't hate him in the way she would if he'd forced himself upon her. And frankly, if he had done that, you'd have murdered him—son or not. But her feelings about you—" I pointed at him. "—are more complicated. And you have her gaesh, so it's not like she could refuse your smallest whim. So, settle a curiosity for me: it *was* rape, wasn't it?"

Therin hit me.

For a second neither of us moved. I felt the sting where his signet ring cut my lip. Therin wouldn't look at me.

Again, I started to walk away.

"Where are you going?" my father asked.

"The others are doing their parts. Me? I have a mimic to kill."

Honestly, I still don't know where it went wrong.

A thousand times since I've replayed how it went, how it could have gone if I'd been a little wiser or if this had all just been practice under Chainbreaker's spell. If I'd asked a servant to deliver the letter to Tishar while Miya had stayed. If I hadn't argued with Therin and so he'd come with me to confront you. If Tyentso had come with us instead of staying at the Culling Fields to monitor for a possible Hellmarch. If I had insisted on Emperor Sandus coming with me personally instead of waiting for a signal on his damn magic ring.

In any event, none of that happened.

I went to Ola's room alone.

76: Betrayal

(Talon's story)

Bear with me, love. We're almost finished, Kihrin. At least, as finished as my story can be.

Escaping from the Blue Palace proved to be distressingly easy.

Now that Kihrin understood his skill at stealth had a magical source, he used it to shelter Galen and himself as they snuck their way out of the Upper Circle. They wouldn't have been able to escape without it: with Alshena murdered, the High Lord had locked tight the entire palace for mourning.

"Where are we going?" Galen whispered.

"The Standing Keg. It's a pub in the Copper Quarter," Kihrin told him. They had left wearing sallí cloaks and brown kef, and nothing on them anywhere that was blue. They'd left any traceable valuables behind too, stopping only long enough for Kihrin to collect his promissory notes from the Temple of Tavris before heading down to the Copper Quarter.

Kihrin didn't need House D'Mon. He had enough savings for him to live on comfortably for the rest of his life. Enough for Galen and Kihrin both.

The Standing Keg was all but empty as customers instead lingered in the New Year's Festival stalls and wine gardens. And Kihrin gave no sign he recognized the aging Zheriaso woman tending drinks as Ola. He and Galen claimed a table, and he allowed himself to relax just a little. Step one was complete.

"Who are we waiting for?" Galen asked.

"You'll see—" Kihrin's words cut off as the door opened, and Thurvishar stepped through, accompanied by his slave, Talea.

Kihrin waved them over.

Thurvishar's presence was noticed; he wasn't a man easy to overlook. He towered over the two boys before he pulled out a chair to sit.

"This is irregular," Thurvishar told them. "But I admit I am intrigued. My condolences on your mother." He said this last to Galen.

"Thank you," Galen said, his voice wooden.

"It's simple enough," Kihrin said. "I have a business proposition for you." Then he paused as the old dark-skinned Zheriaso waitress approached. Kihrin pretended not to recognize Ola and waved her over. "Oh, uh, I suppose we should order something." He looked at Thurvishar.

The bald man raised an eyebrow. He cast his eyes around the bar as if a place like this couldn't possibly have anything to offer a palate as refined as his. "What is your best then?"

"Kirpis grape wine, my lord, from the vineyard at Rainbow Lake," Ola told him. "It's fresh. This year's stock."

He sighed. "A bottle of that and four glasses."

The waitress looked at the three men. "Four?"

Thurvishar seemed amused. "Look again, woman. There are four of us here." He nodded his head toward Talea.

Ola cleared her throat. "Uh, right. Sorry, m'lord. I'll bring your wine at once." She left.

"Are you enjoying your stay with Thurvishar D'Lorus?" Kihrin asked Talea.

The slave girl eyed Kihrin as if she had not yet decided whether he was a snake. "I am. Very much."

"But wouldn't you rather be free?"

The slave's eyes widened with undisguised shock.

"*Very* inappropriate," Thurvishar murmured.

Kihrin turned back to him. "I know that you're not a fan of Darzin D'Mon. And I know that you, he, and a third man are plotting something together. You're the man who warned us away. You're the one who knew we were listening at the door." He leaned forward. "All I want is for Talea to have her freedom. I promised her sister that much—"

"My sister? What about my sister?" Talea interrupted.

"How unfortunate," Thurvishar said. "Do you wish to explain to her or shall I?"

Kihrin breathed deep and addressed Talea. "I knew your sister before she was murdered. I'm sorry. I'm so sorry."

Talea stared at him, stared at him like a woman stabbed, like a woman in shock from pain.

No one had told her that her sister was dead.

Kihrin said to Thurvishar, "I know my money doesn't mean much to you, but you'd be vexing Darzin if you let her go, and I bet that does."

Ola came back and uncorked the bottle in front of Thurvishar, then poured four tin goblets with the dark red wine. Thurvishar thanked her and did not drink.

Kihrin rolled his eyes. "Aren't you the paranoid one?" He drank deep from his own cup and motioned for Galen to do the same.

"I have enemies who would gladly kill me just for my potential,"

Thurvishar said. "But allow me to understand your meaning. You want me to free Talea and hand her over to you—for what? The possibility it might annoy Darzin?" He chuckled and took a drink of wine, wincing. "Talea, dear, don't drink this. It's not worth touching your lips to it."

The slave girl's grimace suggested the warning had come too late.

"I can pay metal. I know what you paid for her. You'd take no loss." Kihrin ignored the ugly looks that Talea gave him. It didn't matter if Talea liked him, but it mattered he freed her, if only for Morea's sake.

"As you said, metal means little." Thurvishar paused. "What about the harp you played so well last night? One couldn't fail to notice the aura of magic laced around it like silken thread."

Kihrin's heart sank. "She was stolen last night."

Thurvishar shook his head as he drank more of the wine. "How inconvenient for both of us." He studied Talea with those dark, all-black eyes before returning his attention to Kihrin. "I'll take your necklace then."

Kihrin put his hand to his throat. "I can't give you—"

"You can." Thurvishar reached into his robes and pulled out a pair of charms, enameled dragons wrought from silver. "These will protect you both from scrying.* Nothing so powerful as what you wear, but enough to keep your family from tracking you down. You can have Talea, these necklaces, and my silence—but you give me the tsali stone."

Kihrin's expression hardened. "I can't do that—and how did you know—?"

Thurvishar smiled. "Perhaps you mistake my meaning. This has stopped being a deal from which you can walk away. You're not planning on returning to the Blue Palace, sending the young lady on her way in life with a smile and a small stipend while you resume your noble, pampered life. You're planning to run. To do so, you must buy my silence, because even if I cannot scry for you, I can scry for *him*." He pointed to Galen, who turned red and looked like he was on the verge of tears.

"You wouldn't . . ." Kihrin said.

Thurvishar raised an eyebrow. "Truly?"

Kihrin stared at him. "Why do you want it so badly?"

"Because you have no idea what you wear around your neck," Thurvishar said. His voice was sad.[†]

Kihrin reached for the clasp at the back of his neck, a clasp that had never been unfastened in all his life. He didn't know if it still functioned, and as he worked the latch, his fingers felt thick, clumsy, and heavy. It was all he could do to lift his hands behind his shoulders.

---

*They would have worked too, against everyone but me. This means they would have worked against everyone but me and Gadrith.

[†]Of course, I was sad. This was starting to seem like a scheme that might work.

Kihrin stood. "I can't." He listed.

"You mean you won't," Thurvishar corrected.

"No, I mean–"

Galen collapsed at that moment, wine spilling as the young man's tin cup fell from his hand and his head hit the wooden table. Kihrin fell to his knees. He gasped, looking over at Ola. "You–you–"

"I'm so sorry, Bright-Eyes," Ola murmured. "He'd have noticed if I hadn't drugged everyone's wine." Her whispered confession was punctuated by the sound of Talea collapsing in an unconscious heap. "I'm so sorry."

As darkness overtook Kihrin, Thurvishar yelled, *"Trickery!"* Then came a loud cracking noise, blinding light, and ozone.*

It was quiet.

Talea's eyes opened, although to be fair, it would be more correct to say Talon's eyes opened. Part of the inn was on fire. People panicked, screaming, but all that mattered to Talon was the sickly sweet scent of burning flesh.

Talon ran over to where Ola lay on the ground, electrocuted.

Thurvishar hadn't meant to hit Ola, but his blind random strike had done the job all the same. The wizard had held on for far longer than Talon had expected–the drug slower to act with him than any of the others.† Talon had to fight down the urge to murder him, the blood-borne desire to make him pay for killing Ola, but she knew she couldn't.

Instead, Talon wept over Ola's body. "You won't die," she murmured to her former lover. "We'll live together forever, you and I. Surdyeh has missed you. We'll be together. You'll see. I have one thing I need to do first. One little thing."

Talon returned to Kihrin's side, changing as she went. Until when she stood above him, she looked like Kihrin's old enemy Faris, hand missing and scowl attached. It would be better this way. Witnesses would remember Faris, and Faris was the sort it would be easy to claim had fought too hard to bring back alive–assuming he was ever found at all.

He wouldn't be.‡

Talon reached down to touch Kihrin's face. "Ducky, your father Surdyeh and I have been talking," she told him, although she knew he couldn't hear her. "You know, he's the one who started this all. Giving you to Ola. Making sure you learned certain skills. He wasn't behind

---

*Regretfully, I suspect that I am the one responsible for Ola's death.

†Because I'm only half-human, and the vordreth have a considerable immunity to the effects of most alcohols and drugs. I suppose Talon would have known that if she'd ever read my mind, but I am not easy to read, not even by a mimic.

‡There is a bounty for his capture to this day. It's never been claimed.

the job at Kazivar House where you first saw Darzin–if I had to put metal on it, I'd blame the Goddess of Luck for that. But he works for Emperor Sandus, and he's brought me around to his way of thinking. We've decided that this is for the best. I know it won't be pleasant, but sending one's child away to school never is. Trust us: it will hurt us a lot more than it hurts you." She paused. "Although to be fair, it'll hurt you rather a lot."

She patted down Kihrin's body until she came away with an intaglio ruby ring. Talon smiled at it. "The gryphon must fly," she quoted in a fond tone, as she threaded the ring onto a chain and fastened the chain around her neck.*

Then she tossed Kihrin over her shoulder and set out from the bar, heading for the docks, and the slave ships.

---

*It's a measure of how desperate Therin was to recover Kihrin, that he consulted with the church of Thaena afterwards. Unfortunately, given the Goddess of Death's own particular biases in this matter, I can understand why the answers were inconclusive. Darzin used his own methods to find out Kihrin's location too–and those methods involved Talon's ability to gain the memories of those she consumes. Talon apparently failed to find any answers–and what she told Darzin to excuse her failure here was equally misleading. I think I can say with some conviction, however, that the Gryphon's Men now count a mimic amongst their members. I am unsure whether that is a good thing, or horrifying beyond belief.

77: GADRITH'S WAY

(Kihrin's story)

I suppose it's just my turn now, isn't it, Talon?
So be it. Let's end this.

A large iron padlock locked the door to my old room. A padlock to make a Key from the Lower Circle pale, mutter under his breath, and warn any and all to find an easier target. I probably would have needed twenty minutes or more to pick open the damn thing.

Fortunately, I had the key.

The room inside had changed little from what I remembered. It seemed odd to think we were both four years older. I crossed over to the bed on silent feet, not wanting to disturb the occupant, not sure if my magical stealth would be enough to hide me. I held a thin spike of metal in one hand, and my sword in the other.

The bed was empty. Talon was gone. I reached down to touch the sheets and cursed. The fabric was still warm. I'd missed her by minutes.

"Kihrin?"

I turned back to see Galen standing in the doorway, mouth open in astonishment.

I still had the Veil slipped from my eyes. I examined Galen. I hoped that mimics couldn't hide their tenyé.* Under that assumption, I decided that Galen was himself and not a shape-changed Talon, tucked the spike into my belt, and put a finger to my lips. I walked back to the bronze door, closed it behind me, and replaced the lock.

I clasped my hands on my brother's—well, I suppose my nephew's—shoulders. "Galen!"

He looked older now, well past his majority. His hair showed some of his mother's redness, but he also resembled his father a great deal. Galen dressed in what I assumed was the latest fashion—a blue misha dyed to fade to black at sleeves and hem, worn over dark kef that faded back to

---

*He's wrong. Mimics can do this, but I'm less certain that they can hide from the kind of very intense scrutiny Kihrin learned to perform while on Ynisthana.

blue at the boots. He had a sword at his hips and the embroidered hawk and sunburst design of House D'Mon over his breast.

He continued to look at me in stunned amazement, and then he hugged me back. "Kihrin! It really is you . . . I thought you were a ghost for a minute there."

"I've thought the same more times than I care to count and have escaped by thinner margins than I care to remember. But still alive so far," I said, laughing.

The laughter didn't quite echo in Galen's eyes, and his arms fell back. "Sounds like you've had some wonderful adventures." He didn't hide the bitterness in his voice.

"It's not like that," I told him.

"Is it not?" Galen asked. "Isn't it like you promised that we'd leave together and yet you abandoned me? Because that looks like how it is."

I inhaled, sharp and shallow, and it took everything in me to keep from raising my voice. "Would you like to hear how the slave masters whipped me raw? How I wore manacles on my ankles for so long they cut into my flesh? Abandoned you? You know that's not what happened."

The Galen I knew would have flinched, backed up, backed down, but this Galen had grown harder. His nostrils flared and his blue eyes narrowed. "Should I feel sorry for you? Shall we compare injuries?"

"It's not a contest," I snapped at him.

"Everything is a contest," he said. "I learned that lesson late, but I learned."

My chest felt heavy as I regarded him with a lifted chin. "I'm sorry, Galen. I didn't mean to leave you."

"You say you're sorry like it will fix something."

I sighed. "I'm not here to try to—"

And I paused as a scream echoed down the hallway.

We both paused.

Screams weren't out of place in the Blue Palace. Slaves were whipped and sometimes people were tortured, for either information or amusement. And even more mundanely, physickers often treated patients here—any of which might be a rational cause for screams.

But another scream followed that first, and then another. Galen and I both rushed to one window at the far end of the corridor. We looked out on the Court of Princes to see several servants in the blue livery of the House being run down and ripped apart by soldiers. But these were House D'Mon's own soldiers. The men-at-arms ambled, moving with an odd stuttering gait, but their sword swings hit true.

"What—?" Galen's reaction was one of shock.

Hollow dread filled me. "No," I said, "this is too soon. This is way too soon. How did he get here so soon?"

It had only been a matter of minutes since I'd seen Darzin. I had thought—*we'd all thought*—we'd have more time. Gadrith had kept such a low profile the entire time I'd been in the Upper Circle before. He was patient and cautious and always, *always* kept to the shadows.

I focused on the ruby ring.

Nothing happened.

I didn't have time to debate if I was doing it wrong or if Emperor Sandus had somehow given me a ring that was defective. "Galen, you need to run. Run out of here, leave the palace, and go to the Citadel." I shook my head. "I'm an idiot. I never thought he'd make his move this quickly."

"Who? What?" Galen's eyes narrowed. "This is your fault?"

"Galen." I reached over and grabbed his arm. "Those guards are dead. Dead, do you understand? But they're still moving. That's Dead Man's work. You do remember Dead Man?" I'd have used the name Gadrith, but it would have just confused matters.

Galen blinked and nodded. "Thaena . . ."

"If he's moving in the open like this," I told him, "then we don't have time to argue."

Someone clapped, slowly, from the other end of the hallway. My blood chilled. As I turned, I reached up to clasp the Stone of Shackles around my neck: it was lukewarm, because the man I faced had no intention of killing me.

Gadrith D'Lorus stood at the end of the hallway, black robes pooling on the marble floor around him. "Truly spoken, young man. You don't have time to argue. Or time for anything." His smile was terrible. "I don't believe I've yet had the pleasure, Your Highness, but it's long past due you and I met in the flesh."

"Run," I told Galen as I pulled out my sword.

Gadrith cocked his head and stared at me. The sword in my hand turned red hot. The coating of steel covering the drussian core melted and dripped off, making me glad I had my protections from fire. The sword itself was largely intact, because . . . well . . . I'd been expecting him to do this. That's the whole reason I'd taken the time to acquire a sword that only looked like it was made from Quuros steel.

"I—" Galen turned to flee.

Galen's legs froze together as if they were wrapped with rope and he was pulled hard off his feet. He hit the floor with a loud thud.

I remember thinking, *I suppose this settles whether he's Talon,* but the consolation was scant.

"Stay," Gadrith said. "I insist."

Fighting Gadrith alone hadn't been part of my plans at any point. Seen close up, in person, Gadrith's resemblance to his so-called "son"

Thurvishar was the wispiest and most unconvincing of phantasms. His skin was pale and the hollows under his eyes made his face look skeletal. His black hair fell in stringy curls around his face, like dead, withered moss. He looked of the gallows, an impression that had not changed by the smallest degree since I had first laid eyes on him—over four years earlier.

I stared at him and wondered if I could take him. But I was wearing enough talismans to be more witchhunter than mage at that moment, reducing my repertoire of spells to simple cantrips like returning my sword.

Likely not.* It was kind of the whole reason we'd all insisted on giving Emperor Sandus the honor of being the one to take Gadrith down.

Still, I didn't have much choice. At least I was still wearing the Stone of Shackles: Gadrith didn't dare kill me outright.

But as I ran toward him, the ground under my feet melted and flowed, marble turning to liquid and then hardening only after I had sunk to my calves. The entire length of floor rose up, trapping my arms and sword, keeping me pinned. And since the magic hadn't affected me directly, the talismans had been no help at all.

Thurvishar stepped out into the hallway behind his adopted father.

"Bring them both," Gadrith told Thurvishar. "We have many things to discuss."

We were a somber party. Galen was unconscious or faking it, and Gadrith didn't seem inclined to make conversation. Thurvishar pulled small pins out from his robes and began murmuring over them as we walked, then sticking the pins into my misha.

Talismans, I realized. He was making talismans *for me,* far in excess of what my magical aptitude required, thus ensuring I could cast no spells of my own.

"How did you get here so fast?" I asked him. I had to find a way to delay them. Teraeth was out there somewhere. Sandus was out there somewhere. "You can't have had more than five minutes once Darzin found you."

He gave me a sympathetic glance, but didn't answer.

Thurvishar brought both of us to the main ballroom where the rest of the family was being gathered. Many of them had no idea I'd returned before I was dumped on the ground next to them. A piece of shaped rock bound my arms and legs. I couldn't move, run, or fight. I could only struggle against shackles made of solid marble, molded to fit me perfectly.

Undead soldiers, still wearing the livery of the house, stood watch

---

*At least he had a realistic sense of the odds.

along the walls and all their unliving attention focused on their prisoners. I saw my uncles Bavrin and Devyeh—I mean, my brothers Bavrin and Devyeh—plus my great-aunt Tishar. There were also all the cousins who were, I suppose, nieces and nephews. No one who looked like Teraeth though, which meant he was still at large. An unpleasant lump forced its way down my throat as I saw an unmoving Lady Miya, lying on the floor next to a comatose Therin D'Mon.

"You *bastards*. If you—"

"They're asleep," Gadrith said. "I'm not of a mind to deal with sorcerers."

Darzin walked into the ballroom, leading several young women. One of whom, I noted in a distracted way, was Sheloran D'Talus, now dressed in blue.* She ran over to Galen and bent down next to him, her eyes widening as she saw me.

"Is that everyone?" Gadrith asked.

Darzin shrugged. "Pretty much. One groom in the stables is causing some trouble, but nothing that should interfere with what we're doing."

"Darzin, you slime. This is your family!" I screamed at him.

He looked over at me and smiled. "I'll be the head of my own family when we're done here." He tilted his head at Gadrith. "Do you have everything you need?"

"Not quite." Gadrith snapped his fingers at two of the zombies. "Bring that table over here."

I watched as the undead did as ordered. I thought about my options. Teraeth was still out there somewhere. I had to think that if they'd already encountered him and killed him, gloating Darzin would have bragged about it. As soon as either Teraeth or Tyentso realized something was wrong, they'd bring in Emperor Sandus.

Unfortunately, I didn't know how much time that would take, and whatever was about to happen here, it was a sure guarantee I wouldn't like it. The trick remained to discover what I could do about it. My skill with sorcery was currently hampered, and even if I wasn't wearing all these talismans, I was unlikely to best two wizards of D'Lorus caliber. Then there was the fact my entire family was gathered into this room, with huge potential for collateral damage.

I found myself grateful that at least Tyentso and Teraeth hadn't been caught in this. Indeed, it seemed likely my enemies had no idea they existed.

The idea was almost a comfort.

---

*She married Galen when the lad turned sixteen. It was a beautiful wedding, if absent of any qualities of love. That's hardly unusual for royal weddings, however.

"That one looks strong," Gadrith said, pointing to my brother Bavrin. "Bring him."

Bavrin thrashed and fought as the walking corpses pulled him up and pushed him toward the table. He too had decided that whatever was about to happen was nothing he would like. Devyeh stood and rushed to his brother's defense.

Gadrith threw Devyeh an annoyed look and pointed a finger at him. I recognized the gesture and cried out, but it was too late.

My brother's skeleton fell to the ground and his flesh made a messy mound on the other side of the table.

There was cacophony after that; people screamed and sobbed. But Gadrith's voice cut over the tumult. "Quiet!" he said. "Now you understand the price of rebellion. Be. Quiet." The necromancer turned to Thurvishar with an aggrieved expression. "Do something."

The man nodded, squared his shoulders, and bowed his head, concentrating. A lull fell over the group of prisoners.

Thurvishar had not calmed them, I realized. He had stopped any sound from escaping their immediate presence. It was the same trick he'd used during his duel with Jarith years before.

Gadrith returned to his work as I surveyed everyone around me. No one had any visible weapons I could see. I didn't think there would be any exceptions: it was too easy for a wizard to tell if someone wore metal.

A scream cut short returned my attention to Gadrith, who had bent Bavrin over the table. He had one hand clenched like a claw over Bavrin's chest, a gesture I also recognized from the first time I'd spied on Gadrith. I watched as thin filaments of light floated up from Bavrin's chest and coalesced into a ball in Gadrith's outstretched hand. Bavrin began to spasm, then he stilled, and never moved again.

Gadrith pushed Bavrin's body off the table and set a delicate uncut blue crystal on a black velvet cloth: a tsali stone.

"No," I said. "No . . ."

"Bring that one." Gadrith pointed to Master Lorgrin.

I remembered what Tyentso had said about Gadrith's witch gift: he could pull someone's soul out of their body and add its power to his own. "You can't kill everyone here, damn it. You don't think the Emperor won't figure out what you're doing?"

Darzin walked over and kicked me in the face. My vision flashed white as the pain hit, then I turned my head to the side and spat blood. When I looked back, it was to see that Gadrith had already killed Lorgrin, and was placing a yellow stone next to the blue one.

"He's right, you know," Gadrith said in a conversational tone to Thurvishar, who was watching his father with such a careful poker face he might have been listening to a lecture on the best crops to plant come spring. "Not everyone here would make a good tsali stone." He paused and removed the silence spell around Tishar. "Hello, dear Tishar. Have you been enjoying your carriage? I made it for your brother, especially for you."

The vané-blooded woman looked stricken. "Enjoying it less now I know your vile hands touched it."

"Ah, that saddens me to hear." He motioned with a hand. "Her next."

"Gadrith, please, I beg of you!" Tishar pleaded as the undead took her by the arms.

"Alas, such entreaties mean little," he reassured her.

"Gadrith, stop this," I said.

Darzin hit me again. "Shut up."

Tishar spat on Gadrith as the zombies hauled her to the table. She cast around the room for any means of egress, any possible escape. Her eyes met mine. "Please," she mouthed, but I don't know if she was asking Gadrith or asking me.

It hurts to think about it. It hurts to remember. I watched her die. Watched as that bastard pulled Tishar's soul from her body.

She made a beautiful blue stone. Of course she did.

"Stop this!" I shouted, not caring if Darzin hit me or worse. I knew he wasn't trying to kill me: not when I wore the Stone of Shackles. "What do you want?"

Gadrith paused and turned. "Ah? I've been hoping you'd ask, though young man, you shouldn't ask questions when you already know the answer. You know what I want."

I looked down at the outline of the Stone of Shackles through my shirt. "You want this."

"I want that," Gadrith agreed.

"For fuck's sake," Galen cried out. "If that's what he wants, give it to him!"

"Your son is wise," Gadrith complimented Darzin.

Darzin's mouth twisted into the ghost of a smile. "Thank you."

"Him next." Gadrith ordered his undead to take Galen.

Darzin's smile faded. "What? Killing my heir was not part of our agreement."

Gadrith didn't answer except to raise an eyebrow.

"He's my *son*," Darzin reiterated. He crossed over to stand in front of Galen, who seemed more shocked by his father's defense than by the deaths of family.

"Make another," Gadrith suggested. "You said Kihrin cares for him."

"Go ahead," I said. Oh, it hurt to say those words. Hurt because I knew Gadrith wasn't bluffing, but I sure as hell was.

Gadrith cocked his head at me. "What was that?"

I shrugged. "Kill him. Kill all of them if you want. All you're doing is destroying the only bargaining chips you have. You can't kill me. I know you can't kill me. You can disfigure me, torture me, rape me, whatever—we both know it's not permanent. You have one of those zombies do it and the stone won't let me die. I'm not giving you the Stone of Shackles, and there is nothing you can do that will convince me otherwise. How long do you want to play this game? Until the High General shows up? The Emperor? I've already messaged the Emperor, so your chance to catch us by surprise is gone."

"You mean with one of his little toy rings?" Gadrith gestured in the general direction of my bound hands. "I really don't think you did."

"I told him you were still alive before that," I sneered. "He's on his way."

Gadrith smiled. "That's very helpful of you. I didn't need the assistance, but I'm not so proud I'll refuse it."

I fought to keep the sneer on my face, to not look at Galen, to not give them any sign I actually cared what happened to him.

Gadrith turned to Thurvishar. "Is he telling the truth about his loved ones? Is there no one here whose death would touch him?"

Thurvishar flinched, as if that were the one question in all the world he had hoped Gadrith would not ask.* He gave his father an open glare.

"Tell me," Gadrith said. "Now!"

The next flinch I recognized: self-correction from an almost-disobeyed gaesh order.

He sighed and pointed. "Her."

Thurvishar pointed at Lady Miya.†

"I don't care about her," I protested, keeping my voice steady, keeping the disdain clear. "Why would I care about some vané slave? She's nothing."

Darzin sighed and rubbed his jaw. "Kid, even I'm not buying that one."

"Bring her," Gadrith said.

I could barely breathe as I watched them pick her up, still unconscious, and drag her over to the table. "Look, there's really no point—"

Gadrith formed a claw with his hand over her heart.

"Stop!" I screamed. "Stop. Please stop. If I give you the stone, will you let everyone else live?"

I knew. Even then I knew there would be no letting me live.

---

*Pretty much true. I couldn't lie, you see.

†How did I know? The same way I know so many secrets. It's *my* witch gift, and the reason Gadrith kept me around for so long. That's all that needs to be said on that subject for the moment.

Gadrith paused, letting the few strands of light fall between his fingers back to her body. "I'm not interested in them, young man. What you wear is all I desire. Their deaths are only meaningful if they will lead me to that purchase."

I licked my lips. "Release me. Release me so I can give you what you want."

Gadrith studied me, then motioned to Thurvishar. "Do it."

Darzin walked back over and yanked me up to my feet. "Don't try anything stupid," he suggested as I felt Thurvishar's marble binding fall away.

I yanked my arm from Darzin's and slowly played with the fastenings of the necklace. I needed to buy time. I needed to delay things just long enough–

Gadrith formed his hand into a claw again over Miya. "I will count to three."

I pulled the Stone of Shackles off my neck.

It was easy this time. I held it out to Gadrith. "It's yours."

Thurvishar shook his head and turned away as though he could not bear to watch.

Gadrith's fingers trembled as he walked away from my mother and claimed the gemstone. "You're brave," he said. His voice was flat, and I couldn't tell if the emotion he was expressing was sarcasm or sincerity.

He fastened the Stone of Shackles around his neck.

The room was quiet. I couldn't hear the sounds of sobbing although I knew the dead were being mourned. Still, everyone seemed to be holding their breath, as if waiting to see if Gadrith would break his word.

"Well?" Darzin asked.

Gadrith put his hand to his neck and smiled. "It's everything I've always wanted."

Then he waved his hand. "Bring Kihrin. Leave the others." He turned and walked from the room, his undead falling in behind him.

And that's the end of my story.

I lost. You all won.

And we all know what happens next.

78: THE LIGHTHOUSE AT SHADRAG GOR

(Talon's story)

That's it? That's where you're leaving off?

Oh Kihrin, I never protested that you didn't fill in the gaps while you were a slave on board The Misery, *but you can't just leave the story there.*

Very well. I suppose I started all this, it's only fair I finish it.

Kihrin made the barest of token protests as Thurvishar D'Lorus took him by the arm. He moved with the slowness of one drugged or injured, but then he looked at the wizard.

"It would have been better if I'd given you that stone years ago, wouldn't it–before I was kidnapped?" His voice was dull and black.

"Probably," Thurvishar agreed. "I can't claim to know for certain."

"Where are we going? Ol' Pedron's summoning chamber down in the crypts?" Kihrin hadn't forgotten certain conversations overheard in years gone by.

"Not yet," Thurvishar said. The wizard paused and stared at a section of wall that glowed with spiraling runes of rainbow colors. The wall faded, grew misty, and then Kihrin could see beyond into a giant chamber of rough, natural stone with large shuttered windows. The new room was lit by mage-light. It could have been anywhere.

"Hold on," Talon said. She looked like Talea (although more accurately, she looked like Morea). "I'm coming with you."

Thurvishar scowled at the mimic. "Would you mind looking like someone else?"

She shrugged and changed into Lyrilyn's form. "Where is Talea, anyway?"

"Safe and a long way from you," Thurvishar answered. "I'm not inclined to let you collect the whole set. Where have you been?"

"Pretending to be the High Lord in case anyone showed up asking questions. Don't worry, I'll go back to sentry duty once we're finished." She gave Kihrin a wink before returning her attention to Thurvishar. "Shall we?"

He blocked her way. "Your skills aren't needed here."

She smiled. "Ah, ducky, don't be like that. Besides, someone needs to be the dear child's jailer while you and Gadrith are busy preparing your little spells. Would you rather it be Darzin? I don't think that would work out."

Thurvishar studied her. "Fine. Go."

He held open the magical gateway until the others were through.

They arrived inside a thick stone tower, with walls that slanted inward. A strange noise came from outside—a low thrumming hum. Thurvishar banished the gate. He paused, and frowned as he looked around. He kept wards here to tell if the lighthouse defenses had been breached. Those wards had been triggered. Someone had been here and then left again.

He would mention it to Gadrith later, but only if he was asked.

"Something wrong?" Talon asked.

Thurvishar shook his head. "Nothing that concerns you. Bring him upstairs," Thurvishar said, "and be careful. He's thinking of running."

Kihrin threw Thurvishar a shocked glance. "How—?"

Talon raised an eyebrow. "How indeed?"

"Never mind that," Thurvishar said. "Bring him along."

Talon reached for Kihrin; he shook her off. "Don't touch me," he snarled.

"Aw, ducky, you'll hurt my feelings," she told him.

"Good." Kihrin turned back to Thurvishar. "This won't work, you know. I brought friends with me. They'll find us."

Thurvishar motioned for Kihrin to follow up a set of winding stairs around the edge of the tower. "Yes, I know. Teraeth and Tyentso. Actually Teraeth and Raverí D'Lorus, which will be a fascinating reunion when Gadrith finds out." He shrugged. "I'm sorry, but they won't make it here in time."

"You sound awfully certain," Kihrin said.

"I am." Thurvishar unlocked an iron door nestled under the landing between one stairway and the next. He opened it for Kihrin. "You'll stay here until we need you. For what it's worth, I'm sorry it worked out this way."

Kihrin looked inside. It was a jail cell, and not a huge one, although it seemed cleaner than most of its ilk. "Why are you so certain?"

"This is Shadrag Gor," Talon said, wonder and awe in her voice. "This is the Lighthouse at Shadrag Gor. I thought this place was a myth. Is it really outside of time?"

Thurvishar ignored her question. "Don't kill him. Don't hurt him. Don't *eat* him. I don't have to spell out the consequences if you have a lapse in judgment, do I?"

Talon shrugged. "I know why you want him. Gadrith didn't kill *all* Darzin's family. You can always use someone else—"

She made a gurgling sound as a green energy field arched out of Thurvishar's hands and pushed her form to the wall, pushed so hard that her body deformed and pulsed. Talon tried to shift, but the field of energy conformed to her every shape and edge, so she was the one forced to accommodate it.

"I've had time to research dealing with you," Thurvishar said. "I took advantage. Do as you are told or I will destroy you. Understood?"

"I should have killed you in that bar when I had the chance," Talon muttered, "but damn, you're sexy."*

Kihrin sat down on a small stool, the room's only furniture, kicked it onto two legs, and balanced with his back against the wall. "Never mind Talon's flirting. Why are we going to fail? The Emperor's waiting, Thurvishar. He knows. Even if you try to use me as a hostage, he's still going to stop Gadrith."

"You're going to fail for the same reason we were able to respond so quickly. Because time *does* move differently here in Shadrag Gor," Thurvishar explained. "It may not take long for your friends to conclude something is wrong. But by the time they realize that the plan has gone awry, several weeks will have passed here. And you will already be dead."

And then Thurvishar left. Which brings us full circle to now, doesn't it? Several weeks have gone by, we've had a lovely time and . . . oh yes . . . I hear footsteps on the stairs.

Now it's over.

Thanks for the rock, ducky. I'll keep it safe.

---

*I can only beg your pardon: she really did say this. Believe me, my ego is not so fragile that I feel the need to invent compliments.

PART II

THE SUNDERING

(Thurvishar—an aside)

There is a consensus held amongst most living beings that, given a choice between life and death, most of us will choose life. Life, with her bed mistress Hope, is laced with infinitely more possibility than her sister Death. People address her as Queen of the Land of Peace but flinch when her name is uttered out of turn. There is, always, that nagging suspicion that Death is a cheat, that the Land of Peace is anything but. Death offers no solace. Or worse, Death might truly be as the priests commend it: a place of justice where we get what we deserve.

And truly, few among us are willing to stare at that bright mirror and see our reflections. For all of us harbor that secret guilt, we shall be found wanting, shall be judged undeserving. Death is that last and most final of exams–and the majority of us, I suspect, would wish for a few years' more preparation.

Not yet. Dear goddess, not yet.

I found myself thinking of this as I watched a boy of twenty years offer his life to save his family from certain death and oblivion. There were few in that room who would have volunteered to take his place. Darzin thought him a fool, no doubt. And Gadrith admired him as one might admire a strange, alien creature one could only study but never understand. I cannot say what I would do, were I given the same option as Kihrin.

But then, this is not my story.

79: BEGINNING DEMONOLOGY

Kihrin paused after he had finished telling his story to the mimic. He shook his head. "Juval had described my seller as someone who looked like Faris," Kihrin said. "I never doubted it was him. His final revenge. He was always drugging people at the Standing Keg. But it was you, wasn't it? You would never let me escape."

"Never let you escape? Have you spent the last four years under Darzin's thumb? I orchestrated your escape so perfectly even you were fooled." Talon shook her head. "I suppose it is too much to expect a little gratitude from my own son."

"I'm not your son!"

"You were Surdyeh's and Ola's son. And they are me. It's close enough."

Kihrin lunged at her, but the bars blocked his progress. "I was gaeshed because of you . . ."

"Shh," Talon said. "Quiet. Let's leave that as a surprise for the others, shall we?"

They both paused at the sound of footsteps on the stairs above. Someone was whistling a jaunty tune. Kihrin's gut tightened, recognizing who it had to be.

"Hello, Darzin," he said.

The Lord Heir of House D'Mon grinned. "Hello little brother. Ready to die?"

Kihrin shook his head. "I don't know. How long have I been here?"

"Three weeks, give or take." Darzin smiled at Talon, grabbed her hand, and presented her knuckles with a kiss. "Did he give you any trouble?"

"He's been a *very* good boy," Talon said.

"No," Kihrin said. "I've decided. This isn't a good time for me. Why don't you come back never?"

"Bring him," Darzin said, and then wrinkled his nose. "Hm, he's ripe, isn't he?"

"Do you see a bathtub in this cell with me?" Kihrin snapped.

"I offered to clean him with my tongue but he said no," Talon complained. She opened the prison doors and formed a large violet tentacle that reached out to wrap around one of Kihrin's arms.

Darzin grinned. "Yes, well, I can't imagine why." Darzin grabbed Kihrin's other arm and, while Talon still had him confined, bound his hands. "Let's go. We have an appointment with an old friend."

Kihrin gave him a bemused look and Darzin chuckled. "You remember Xaltorath, don't you?" He laughed. "Oh gods, the look on your face, kid. I swear it makes everything worth it."

Talon reached over and tore the necklace of star tears from Kihrin's neck.

"I'm surprised you didn't do that weeks ago," Darzin told her.

"I was hoping you'd let me eat him," she admitted, then shrugged. "But since that's not going to happen now, I'll settle for treasure." She winked at Kihrin and tucked the necklace away before she followed behind Darzin. The three of them then walked down to where Thurvishar waited, next to the open gate.

"Thurvishar?" Talon asked.

The wizard looked toward the mimic, raising an eyebrow. "Yes?"

"Catch." Talon tossed him a small stone, smooth and plain.

Kihrin's eyes widened. He gave Talon a bitter, angry glare, but he didn't explain why he found Talon's "gift" to Thurvishar upsetting.

Thurvishar caught the stone and looked at it. "What's this?"

"Just a keepsake to remember him by." Talon winked at Thurvishar. "I'm sure you'll figure out a good use for it."

"Talon, you bitch," Kihrin said.

"You were right," she replied. "It *was* a sucker's bet."

She was still laughing when everyone walked through the gate, and Thurvishar collapsed the magical portal behind them.

Kihrin had never seen the other side of Galen's hiding spot, the underground tombs built for a D'Mon High Lord. They'd been claimed by Pedron, his son Therin, and later, by Darzin. Still, he recognized the place. He knew it in his bones, prompted by the chill that settled there. The stench of ancient death and fresher poison gave it away. The tenyé of the room vibrated, ugly and evil. Every surface of the stone had been decorated with the tiniest of glyphs, forming whorls and eddies of bloodred paint.

Not paint. Of course, it was real blood.

Thurvishar followed behind, shutting off the gate from Shadrag Gor. Gadrith waited in front of a black stone altar lit by candles. Shackles sat at the corners of the altar. Gadrith himself held a wicked, evil knife, a multipronged, barbed contraption, which looked like its purpose was to drill through flesh and tear out chunks.

Darzin whistled as he dragged Kihrin into the final, prepared ritual area. "This is even more elaborate than last time."

Gadrith seemed amused by Darzin's flattery. "This is more important than last time."

Thurvishar looked at Kihrin. "We painted the glyphs at Shadrag Gor, in a room the same size as this, then used magic to transfer them. Thus, we could take as long as we needed to."

Darzin raised an eyebrow. "He didn't ask."

Thurvishar ignored him, walking to the back of the room to stand behind the altar. "Don't forget your lines, Darzin. Remember, he's your family, so you have to be the one to do the ritual."

"Oh, so that's why they haven't killed you yet. I've been wondering." Kihrin looked back at Darzin. "Good news, Darzin, you're about to out-live your usefulness."

"Shut up," Darzin snapped. He dragged Kihrin over to the altar and pushed him onto it. "Help me," he said to Thurvishar.

They both wrestled Kihrin into position and clamped the manacles around his wrists and ankles. That was followed by a spell to silence him as Kihrin refused to stop cursing.

"I must remember that one about the morgage and the goat," Darzin said. "Inventive."

"Should I remind you time moves at the normal pace here?" Gadrith said. "This is not where I want Sandus to find me."

"No, Master. I'm sorry." Darzin bowed and looked rather uncomfortable. He took up position behind the altar and began to chant.*

At first, nothing happened. However, one archway leading to the various tombs, cells, and antechambers became darker than the mage-lit halls should have allowed. That darkness was less a lack of light than a palpable abyss, an absence so profound it took on a distinct character of its own.

Out of that darkness stepped Xaltorath.

He was smaller than when Kihrin had seen him four years earlier. He also wore an ornate set of curling armor that didn't seem very protective. In fact, it only stressed how little he wore, and how alien he was.

"Xaltorath, I have called you as the old ways require," Darzin told him.

SO I SEE. AND YOU ARE HERE READY TO SACRIFICE YOUR YOUNGER BROTHER, WHOSE DEATH WILL NOT BE MUCH SACRIFICE.

Thurvishar and Gadrith gave each other uneasy looks.

---

*As I do not intend to put so pernicious a summoning as the calling of Xaltorath into public hands, the ritual itself will not be described here. Some knowledge is best lost in the sands of time.

"Nothing in your call says it has to be someone I'll miss," Darzin protested. "The same blood runs through our veins. Isn't that enough?"

PERHAPS. WE SHALL SEE.

Xaltorath's form shifted then, flowed like water, and when it stopped, he was a mocking parody of Tya, Goddess of Magic. He resembled a beautiful woman with red skin that looked hard as bronze and smooth as glass. Her eyes glowed red and her arms and legs no longer looked dipped in red gore but dyed by black ink. Her hair looked like flame. The gold armor covered even less on her, more bedroom jewelry than clothing.

Kihrin struggled. He would have said something, but the spell gagged him.

Xaltorath ripped the magical silence away with a wave of her hand as she slinked to the altar and rested a hip against its edge. ***HEY HANDSOME. MISS ME?***

Kihrin tugged at his restraints. "Get away from me!"

Xaltorath walked her fingers across his stomach. ***MM-HMM. POOR LITTLE BIRD. YOU'VE BEEN IN BETTER SITUATIONS.*** She winked at Kihrin, sharing the joke with him, but ignored the other men in the room. ***WANT TO HAVE SOME FUN?***

"I don't think it'll be much fun," Kihrin snapped.

Xaltorath shook her head. ***OH, BUT IT WILL. YOU AND I COULD SPEND ETERNITY ENJOYING OUR IDYLLS. WE'D HAVE SUCH FUN TOGETHER. I WOULD GIVE YOU EVERYTHING YOU DESIRE.***

Kihrin shook his head. "I don't think so."

Xaltorath changed again, although not by a wide margin. Her skin shifted from bloodred to a cinnamon brown and her body lost some of its ripe curve. Her features shifted so she might not have changed them at all, but her hair went from being flame to a darker hue—a red so deep it was almost black, running in a single stripe across her head from front to back.

TRULY? she asked again, this time her voice a throaty purr.

Kihrin made a noise that might have been a whimper. "No," he said. "Not even for her."

A HERO. SO FULL OF SELF-SACRIFICE. Xaltorath straightened and looked at Darzin. ***YOU'RE RIGHT: HE'S PERFECT. GIVE ME ALL OF HIM, HEART AND SOUL, AND I WILL DO ALL YOU ASK OF ME.***

Darzin smiled. "With pleasure."

He grabbed the knife, and without prelude brought it down hard on Kihrin's chest.

* * *

Kame hated New Year's. The money was good enough—and Kame was never at a loss for customers willing to slink into an alley or return to her crib at the joy house. Yet the whole city felt strung into thin streamers of twisted energy, ready to snap. She made more metal, but she sported more injuries. Some years it seemed like the price she paid to the Blue Houses was more than what she earned.

She loitered at the corner of a warehouse by the docks, watching the sailors load their ships while the good weather prevailed, before they cast off for foreign ports. Kame looked for the stragglers, the lost, the men who had a few hours of free time. Or really, a few minutes would do. Most of the sailors were already ashore, drinking in taverns, or rutting in some other crib. She turned as she heard the sound of water splashing.

A giant parody of a human waded to shore, three times the height of a tall man and no natural color. His skin was white, except for where it was purple or green, and his hands looked like they had been dipped in blood. The monster had a large tail that slapped the ground behind it like a crocodile. The demon grinned as the few people on the docks noticed it. They cried out in terror.

Kame was paralyzed. It was huge, giant, and horrible. It was . . .

The demon saw her, smiled an impossible obscene rictus, and reached for her. She screamed and screamed.

Blood splattered the cobblestones and splashed against the warehouse wall, but Xaltorath didn't pause to enjoy his kill.

He had a schedule to keep.

80: The Blue Palace

Teraeth moved to follow as soon as Darzin retreated into the Blue Palace.

He had to hand it to the Lord Heir; the man moved like he meant it. Darzin openly sprinted as soon as he was out of sight of the First Court, running as though he were being chased.

Well, he *was* being chased, but Teraeth was certain Darzin didn't know that.

The run was, if anything, a reminder of just how large the royal palaces were. Darzin didn't seem intent on the wings of the palace used primarily by royalty, but one of the smaller passages just off the servants' quarters, used for storing food.

Teraeth came around the corner a second after Darzin and stopped.

The corridor was empty.

Teraeth paused. He heard no sound of footsteps, no shuddering whisper of lungs eager to catch their breath after a run. Nothing at all.

He slid his vision past the First Veil in case Darzin was using some sort of illusion or magical concealment. Nothing.

Teraeth focused his concentration on the intaglio ruby ring. "Your Majesty, we have a problem. I could use your–" There was a clapping sound and a rush of air. "–help."

Emperor Sandus stood next to him. "What's the problem?"

Teraeth didn't bother with pleasantries. "Darzin may have used some means of magical transport. I was right behind him, and he's vanished."

Sandus looked thoughtful. "Okay, let's see if that left any traces."

The Emperor moved his hands in a peculiar, twisting fashion. Thin traceries of energy followed the lines on the floor, the walls, every edge, before settling into one particular stretch of wall as a tangled mass of glowing runes and sigils.

"A gate," Teraeth said, recognizing the signs. "A hidden gate."

"A *locked* hidden gate," Emperor Sandus corrected, "but it very likely leads to wherever Gadrith has been hiding."

"Can you unlock it?"

The Emperor smiled grimly. "It would be my pleasure."

* * *

Tyentso sat at her table at the Culling Fields, watched her glasses, and wished that someone else—*anyone else*—had invented a method for detecting demonic incursions. She would rather be with Teraeth and Kihrin, finally bringing some justice to that son of a bitch Gadrith.

Of course, the "fuck you" thrill of performing major divination magic in public almost made up for it.

The detection method was simple enough: demons were energy beings who were drawn to and fed on additional sources of energy. They didn't set fires just because they craved destruction; they also fed on resulting heat. Therefore, any area with freed demons rampaging through it vacillated between hot and cold in highly identifiable ways if you knew what you were looking at.

The glasses on the table in front of her thus formed a sympathetic temperature map of the entire city. Tyentso could tell with a glance which streets had working khilins and which houses were rich enough to afford visits from the Ice Men.

Someone slid a hot cup of green tea onto the vacant seat next to Tyentso, who looked up to see a Khorveshan woman smile at her.

"You said you didn't want beer," Tauna said, "so I thought you might like a different option."

"Thank you," Tyentso murmured. She started to turn to face the young woman when a flash of blue caught her attention. "Wait, what was that—"

She concentrated. A wave of cold had registered in the Upper Circle, but with none of the heat spikes that would have suggested freed demons on a rampage. She studied the map, then her eyes widened as she realized what other sort of magic would draw heat without giving anything in return.

"Necromancy," she whispered.

The disturbance was centered around the Blue Palace.

Tyentso focused on the ring on her finger, activating the connection that would allow her to talk to the Emperor.

Nothing happened.

"Oh fuck."

There were no guards at the front gate to the D'Mon estate, and no one protested when Tyentso used her magic to unbar and open the door.

Something was wrong.

Tyentso looked around the First Court. The signs of violence were obvious, but none more so than the pile of bodies that lay near the entrance to the royal stables. A massive gray-and-white horse stood over the bodies as if it had appointed itself as a soldier to protect the dead.

The horse tossed its head and whinnied at Tyentso as if daring her to approach closer and put herself within the range of its sharp hooves.

"Whoever you are, turn around and leave," a voice said.

High Lord Therin stood at the main set of doors separating the First Court from the palace beyond. He looked as though he'd been in the middle of a battle, and carried an open blade in one hand.

"Therin?" Tyentso said. "What's happened here? Where are your guards?"

"Dead, mostly." He held out the sword in a threatening way. "We've been attacked, but the Emperor is here now. I suggest you find shelter until this is all over." He smiled grimly. "Don't take it as a suggestion."

Tyentso stared at him for a moment. "Yes, of course, High Lord. I'm sure you're right."

They both stood there.

"I can't help but notice you're not moving," Therin said.

"Funny. I can't help but notice you're not Therin," Tyentso responded.

Talon narrowed her eyes. "What gave me away?"

"Truthfully, it was a lucky guess, but thanks for confirming." Tyentso grinned and cocked her head to the side, looking past Therin. "Where have you been?"

Teraeth stepped down into the court. Like Therin, he looked like he'd fought his way to the front. "On the other side of the continent, apparently. I'll take it from here. Look around and see if there are any survivors."

Talon sighed. "It's way too late for survivors, duckies. You two should just turn around while you have the chance."

Tyentso began stepping to the side, circling around Talon (who still looked like a very good impersonation of Therin). "Where's the Emperor?" she asked Teraeth, not taking her eyes off the mimic.

"The harbor. There's some sort of problem down there."

"That would probably be Xaltorath," Talon said. "Don't leave. I've so much to talk to both of you about."

Tyentso raised her hand, and a section of the ground rose up, forming a wall between herself and Talon. The mimic snarled and rushed forward, but the wall prevented her from following.

"Forgetting someone?" Teraeth pulled several daggers from his belt.

Talon turned back around. "Oh yes. Kihrin's pretty little killer. Too bad you didn't have more time with him. You might have won him over."

Teraeth's expression went flat. "Kihrin's not dead."

"Oh, he very much is, I'm afraid, but there's good news: I think Darzin will let me eat the body." Talon grinned. "Hey, you might still have your chance to get into Kihrin's pants, after all."

Teraeth attacked.

As he slashed at her, Talon lashed out with an arm, quicker than eyes could follow. That arm elongated, transformed, until it looked like nothing human. It was now a thin winding tentacle, with wicked sharp blades where an octopus would have suckers.* The deadly lash passed through the spot where the illusion of Teraeth had lingered a moment before.

Talon laughed. "Aha! Oh, this will be a challenge!" As she finished speaking, she felt a sharp blade slice through her back. She formed another tentacle out of muscle and lashed out, rewarded this time with a hiss of pain and a splatter of blood against the cobbles.

Talon turned, eyes forming on the skin of her shoulders, her back, her thighs as she moved to find the assassin. "You should run, little vané."

"And miss my chance to kill a mimic?" Teraeth said. "I'd never forgive myself for letting that opportunity slip by."

"But slip by it will," Talon scoffed. "Not being able to feel your mind is disconcerting, but not so troublesome that I won't feast on your brain, regardless."

"Try me."

Teraeth reappeared, swooped down on her with both blades outstretched. When she lashed out her arms at him, Teraeth sliced at her legs, but those limbs, too, formed serrated edges to slash back.

"What will you do?" she mused. At that moment, she didn't look very much like a she, or a human, or any creature outside of an insane man's worst nightmares. "You cannot sever my arms. You cannot decapitate my head. I have no organs for you to injure. I have no veins for you to bleed. And yet—ah, ducky—all of that I can do to you . . ." She spun around, laughing as she lashed the air at random. "Aw, don't hide, ducky. I so want to know you better. You seem like such fun."

He didn't answer.

Talon waited for a beat, but when Teraeth didn't make a move or give her anything to respond to, she thought it was at least possible he'd snuck off. She formed tentacle after tentacle and spun them through the air, thrashing against space as if to discern his location through blundering chance. One of her arms struck something, there was a gasping sound, blood, and for just a second, Teraeth's illusions dropped—enough for her to tell where he was.

Talon didn't hesitate. She turned all her arms upon him, like some obscene sea creature, tentacles wrapping around the assassin. She lost herself in the joy of slaughter as she ripped the vané apart, cherishing each wound like a lover's caress.

Then she felt a stabbing sensation in what might be considered her back (if only because it was the opposite side to where her attention was focused) and the phantasm she had been embracing crumbled into wisps

---

*One wonders if there could be a connection between mimics and the Daughters of Laaka?

of magical vapor. She fell to the ground, unable to move or twitch or change so much as a single muscle. The tip of a large silver spike impaled her body.

Teraeth became visible. He was uninjured.

The vané walked around the mass of tentacles and flesh that lay still and silent on the ground. "Kihrin knew you were here," Teraeth told her. "He's known for years. It gave him a great deal of time to prepare for how he would deal with you."* He reached down into the crawling mess of flesh and pulled back a necklace of star tear diamonds. He stared at the jewels with dread in his expression.

He turned and raced after Tyentso.†

Tyentso found the remaining living members of the D'Mon family, a huddled mass of nobility silently crying over dead bodies. A young woman with red hair was trying to wake up the High Lord.

As she moved inside the ballroom, the unmoving soldiers guarding the family twitched and came to a semblance of life, shambling in her direction.

Tyentso rolled her eyes. "Oh, I don't think so." She repeated the mnemonics over in her mind and pooled the energy. Then when she stretched out her hands, a wave of violet power ripped from each soldier. They collapsed like puppets with cut strings.

She walked over to the girl, becoming aware as she did that a young man—also dressed in D'Mon colors—stood close beside her. Every eye in the room was upon her, but not one person yet spoke.

"Quieter than I would have expected for D'Mons," she said. "Oh, I see." She undid the spell of silence Thurvishar had cast earlier.

Then everyone babbled at once, but as Tyentso noticed the pile of bodies pulled to one side, she whipped the air with an angry gesture. Everyone fell silent again. "I'd recognize Gadrith's handiwork anywhere."

"Who are you?" Sheloran asked.

She motioned to the girl trying to wake High Lord Therin. "A friend. Step aside. I'll wake him."

"Can you do that without hurting him?" the young man asked. "And really, who *are* you?"

---

*I'm guessing that this spike is the twin of the one that Kihrin was holding, when he thought to surprise Talon in his rooms. It must have been enchanting to deal with her. Neatly done, that.
†Speculation as to what became of the mimic called Talon has been rampant. To my knowledge this is the last time anyone saw the creature. Teraeth later testified he was too concerned over Kihrin's fate to take the considerable time necessary to destroy her. And the magical spike that kept her paralyzed would not have led to a permanent end. Since her body was not found later, we must assume she remains at large.

She raised an eyebrow at him before turning back to the High Lord. "No one who would see the smallest harm come to Therin D'Mon."

"I'm Galen D'Mon, and while I appreciate you destroying those monsters, I must know–"

She ignored him and instead placed her hand on Therin's forehead. "It's not a complicated spell. A deep sleep for all intents and purposes." Her fingers tightened, so they almost took on the shape and quality of outstretched talons.

Therin gasped and opened his eyes, then cast around in a panic as he realized where he was. He saw Tyentso bending over him and sneered, "Get away from me, woman . . . What are you doing here?"

"She wouldn't tell me her name," Galen said.

Tyentso sat back on her heels and smiled. "Allow me to explain."

Tyentso pulled an illusion over her native form, something that might be recognized.

Therin blinked at her. "Raverí? Raverí D'Lorus?"

"I thought–" But then Galen's expression registered confusion. "Wait, I've seen your portrait at the Dark Hall."

"What are you doing here?" Therin asked.

"Plotting to kill my husband–a second time," the sorceress explained. "Now, Lord Therin, if you would be so kind as to stand over here while I wake your seneschal, I want your face to be the first thing she sees."

"Why?" Therin asked as he scrambled to his feet.

Tyentso chuckled. "Because I'll live longer. She is liable to annihilate any D'Lorus she sees right at this moment." She paused. "Do you even realize what a powerful wizard she is?" Tyentso shook her head. "Never mind that. Just stand over there and look pretty. That should come easily enough for you."

Therin stepped in front of Miya.

Galen stood next to him. "What is happening?"

"I would ask you–" Therin said. "What's happened to Kihrin?"

Then the sound of Miya waking distracted Therin, and he didn't see the look of shame come over his grandson's face.

"Therin?" Miya held out her hand for his. "What happened? Was that Gadrith?"

"Apparently," Tyentso said.

Miya turned to look at her and then her brows drew together. "Why do I–? Raverí? Is that you?"

"Isn't it nice to be remembered," the sorceress said. She turned to Galen. "What happened to Kihrin? I saw the look on your face when Therin asked."

Galen swallowed a lump down his throat. "They wanted a necklace he was wearing. A vané stone. And when he wouldn't give it to them,

Gadrith started killing people, ripping out their souls." He looked over to the pile of bodies.

Therin hadn't noticed them before, but as he did, his face turned ashen. "Bavrin. My son . . ." he whispered. "And Lorgrin and Tishar. Where's Devyeh?"

Galen's expression sickened. "The bones are his."

Therin turned to his grandson. "You say he was ripping out souls. Did he make tsali stones? Where are they?"

"He took them," Galen said.

"He'll feed on them," Tyentso said, "but if we can get to Gadrith before he does that, and destroy the gems, their souls will be released. They can be Returned, or at least go to the Land of Peace."

"Never mind that," Miya snapped. "Kihrin. What happened to Kihrin? What happened to the gem he wore?"

Galen's expression tightened. "I don't know why Gadrith wanted that gem so badly, if he could just make more any time he wanted."

Miya stared at Galen as though she might shake the answers from him. "Did he give it to them? Tell me now!"

When Galen didn't answer right away, his wife, Sheloran, did. "Yes," she said. "He did. Gadrith would have killed you, Lady Miya. And Kihrin couldn't stand for it. So, he gave them what they wanted."

The vané flinched.

Therin frowned. "I don't understand. Why is a vané tsali stone so important?" He shook his head. "I used to buy them just to destroy them and release the souls, but that can't be why Gadrith wants one."

Tyentso gave Miya a cold smile. "Do you want to tell him or should I?"

The vané woman seemed defeated and deflated. She had a look of numbed horror on her face. Finally, she seemed to realize that Therin was waiting on her answer. "He wore the Kirpis Stone of Shackles." She shook her head. "It's powerful. I understand better than anyone. But to go through all of this . . ."

"They took Kihrin," Galen said. "They said they'd need him to summon a demon."

The room was quiet although the sound of muffled sobbing continued from the survivors. Galen looked at the High Lord, Lady Miya, and Tyentso: all three wore an expression that said louder than any declaration that he had just told them grim news.

"I see I came late to the party," Teraeth said as he stepped into the room. All his illusions had been dropped. He once more looked like a Manol vané.

Lady Miya looked at him, and turned, hand raised as though to cast some kind of spell.

"Now now," Tyentso said. "This is a friend."

Miya lowered her hand. "My apologies. It's been a rather–" She didn't finish the sentence, but looked over at Therin. "We must find Kihrin."

"Easier said than done," Teraeth commented. He held up the necklace of star tears. "The mimic guarding the front had this on her. I'll take that as a bad sign." He nodded at Tyentso. "Spike worked like a charm."

"At least one thing's gone right," she agreed, but she looked furious as she said, "We have no idea where they might have taken him."

Galen raised a hand, like a child answering questions from a tutor. ". . . I think I know."

Therin led the way into the underground chamber, through a secret door in the palace grounds, which he had thought unused for over a decade. He realized his mistake as he saw the runes painted in blood on every surface and the mage-lights that still lined the ceiling in spinning glyphs.

Miya gasped as she saw Kihrin's body on the altar. They hadn't moved him. They hadn't even removed his shackles. Kihrin had just been left there, abandoned. The blood oozing from his chest, from the gaping hole there, was all the evidence anyone needed about his fate.

He was dead.

"Ah, hell," Tyentso muttered. "Why didn't he join the damn Brotherhood when he had the chance?"

Teraeth looked haunted. "Wouldn't have mattered for a demon sacrifice."

She and Teraeth both rushed over to look at the body, leaving Therin, Miya, Galen, and Sheloran. Therin stood there with a stony expression, his fists clenched into tight balls, his jaw clamped so hard that the skin there was white. Miya breathed fast and shallow, like an injured deer, unable to look away from the sight on the altar.

She turned her head toward Therin and whispered, "This is *your* fault."

The tendons on his neck strained, but Therin didn't respond.

Tyentso took the necklace from Teraeth's hand and looked at the stones with a critical eye. "We could try anyway."

"It's risky," Teraeth said. His voice was flat.

"Might work is better than won't work because we didn't make the attempt."

Tyentso turned to Therin and Miya. "Help us out here. We need to carry his body over to the temple district."

Therin shook his head and snapped out of his stupor. "He was sacrificed to a demon. You can't resurrect someone without their souls."

Teraeth looked ready to slit throats. "He was gaeshed while he was a slave." He pointed to the necklace in Tyentso's hand. "That contains his gaesh."

"He was what—?" Miya stiffened. "What?"

"Gaeshed. You should be familiar with the idea," Teraeth snapped at her.

"Haven't lost your touch for diplomacy, I see," Tyentso muttered. She held aloft the glittering chain of jewels. "This contains a sliver of his soul. Not much of it, but a tiny piece. The rest of his soul is enjoying the company of a demon prince, but if we can send this part to the Land of Peace, there's a chance that Thaena can heal the damage."

Miya rushed over to the body. "I'll help," she said. She concentrated, using magic to break the shackles and lift Kihrin's corpse. Therin nodded as he followed her.

"I don't understand something," Galen said.

"This isn't the time," Therin snapped.

"No." Galen shook his head. "I think this is important. If the demon didn't get his soul—didn't get his whole, entire soul*—that means the ritual failed, right? The demon isn't bound?"

Everyone paused.

Therin looked at Tyentso. "Do any of you know who they were summoning?"

Tyentso examined the runes and glyphs painted into the walls. "Xaltorath." She blinked then. "That mimic was telling the truth. Xaltorath . . . there's no way he would have just grinned and swallowed down a partial soul. That means . . ."

"He's not under their control," Miya and Teraeth said simultaneously.

"Is that good?" Galen asked.

Tyentso shook her head, looking bemused. "I have no idea. I suspect the only person who knows is Xaltorath."

The group formed an odd sight, sprinting through the streets of the Upper Circle. They would probably have drawn more attention from guards (albeit as an escort) if it were not for the plumes of smoke lifting into the night from the west, near the docks. A few tried to interfere with the group or question them, but given the presence of a High Lord, no one thought about it for long.

The Cathedral of Thaena was one of the largest of the temples in the Ivory District, only to be outdone by the Church of Khored. This had been financed almost entirely by the D'Lorus family as an apology for the actions of their wayward Lord Heir. The closer they journeyed, the

---

*It was never going to work anyway, you see. That's the funny thing, isn't it? Neither Gadrith nor Darzin ever really understood just who Kihrin is. If they had, they'd have never attempted this—because Xaltorath had named a price they could *never* pay. Kihrin's soul hasn't, I suspect, been whole for centuries.

heavier Therin's feet felt, until it was all he could do to lift one foot and put it in front of the other.

Others had had the same idea, for by the time the group arrived at the church, it was already crowded with bodies. Priests in white robes wandered the thin space between corpses as they performed last rites. One man, tall and thin with straight, wispy black hair, saw them walk inside and performed a visible double take. He rushed over to them. "Therin, is that you?"

"Kerris," the High Lord said as he clasped the man's hand. "It has been a long time."

"Too long," the priest protested. "What has–" His eyes fell upon the body.

"He is my son," Therin said. He paused, and then added, "He is my only son. Devyeh and Bavrin are both dead."

Galen gave Therin a shocked look when he didn't name Darzin, but he was the only one to do so.

"I understand, I'll see what can be–" The priest stuttered to a stop a second time as he saw the ugly wound in the corpse's chest. "I cannot–"

Teraeth handed him the necklace. "He was gaeshed. This contains all we have left of his soul. Will it be enough?"

The priest shook his head as he examined the necklace. "It would take a miracle."

Tyentso smiled. "Aren't you in luck?"

81: THE BORDERLANDS

The young man ran. He could remember nothing else. There was no memory before the running; no memory of what brought him to this place. No memory of who he was or what he had left behind.

He was a fragment of himself.

His existence drifted only in brief seconds of "now"–in the rabbit-like beat of his heart and his choking, struggling breath. In the tripping gait of his feet as they pulled through tangled nightshade and the sweat that ran down his moist brow. He at least knew why he ran, though that was no consolation.

He ran because there were dogs.

The grim, dark forest gave no shelter or warmth. The woods were freezing cold and murky, covered with a perpetual layer of ice and swampy muck from the unending drizzle of sleet. The ice shattered beneath his steps, sucking him down into the sticky mud, leaving an obvious track for any who would follow him. The winds howled, tearing at the branches of willows and yews that clutched at his clothing and hair with homicidal intent. The roots of trees, tangled poisoned black lotus, and deadly herbs tripped at him–while thorns and bramble formed unassailable walls to block his flight.

He didn't know who he was, but he didn't need to be told he was dead.

He still bore the injury: an ugly gaping hole in his chest where his heart should have been. In its place, he felt a profound sense of loss and isolation. There was a cold, numb realization: although he was in the Land of the Dead, he hadn't the faintest clue where he was supposed to go. Nothing in these woods seemed friendly.

It was not truly a dead wood: there were slugs, worms, snakes, all manner of rats, hyenas, wolves, and worse. Ravens and owls mocked him from tree branches. Still other things he could not identify, and, indeed, prayed he would never be able to identify, slithered and crawled at the edge of his vision. These slipped into nearby streams or into an impenetrable shadow just before he might have seen their forms. Everything looked on the edge of starvation, as if none of the animals in this terrible forest had seen a proper meal in all their lives. They all eyed him as if he might be the natural remedy to their ills.

Still, he was mostly concerned about the dogs.

He could hear the hounds call out to each other behind him. He didn't know why he assumed they hunted him, but the cold sweat that broke out along his spine allowed for no argument. He knew their foul teeth would tear him apart when they caught up with him. When they did; not if.

He tired, his pace growing slower and more desperate. The trees cleared before him and he gasped in despair. The ground ended a few steps beyond, turning from marshland to the thick inky water of a stagnant lake. Those depths lost themselves in endless blackness that seemed more like thin tar than water.

A sick yellow mist snaked across the lake with sentient malice. As he watched, the water rippled and moved as an enormous serpentine shape rolled over in its depths. He looked around in horror, but save for the tiny eyes of feral creatures that watched him from the shadows, he was alone. There was no egress.

He was trapped.

The hounds ran into the clearing with a flash of searing fire and predatory joy.

They were not truly dogs. They looked as if they had once been people, before some fell power had warped their legs and arms, twisted their bodies, and sculpted them like wet clay. For all the sharp teeth and snapping jaws, their faces were human enough to be a recognizable horror. They bayed and growled and sniffed the air for their quarry, running down to the water's edge and then circling in frustration.

One hound, too eager to continue the chase, waded into the black lake, barking and sniffing as if to track over the water itself. The water agitation increased, and the dog was pulled under the waves with a terrified yelp.

After that the dogs didn't stray into the murky blackness, but barked from the shore.

The hunting party descended on the location of their hounds with a thunder of hooves. There were a dozen riders. None were human. Some had their hoods back, revealing the heads of animals, monsters, or sometimes animated skulls. Some hunters had animal horns and the obvious leader of the group was a black shadow with the antlers of some enormous stag. He had the same hideous glowing eyes as his dogs.

Their horses were terrifying too. Some of the equines were little better than animated corpses, the blood still falling from rotting flesh. Others were moving skeletons, with glowing spectral eyes and cold fire surrounding their hooves. There were horses with the hides of snakes and horses made from shadows and darkness; their supernatural origins were all too clear. Frost covered the ground as they passed by, and icicles formed at the ends of tree branches.

The master of the hunt waved his sword in frustration as he saw the tracks lead straight to the water's edge. He screamed strange words that burned and hissed into the air then turned his shadow horse and galloped back into the forest. The others turned and followed him, with the hounds yapping to catch up.

The fugitive, grasping at thin branches in the highest portions of a sickly mangrove tree nearby, breathed his first breath after they had left. He didn't know how long it would be before the hunt master realized he had been deceived and returned. To give weight to his worry, he heard the sound of hoof beats as he lowered himself.

He had no time to move back up the tree; he was trapped on a lower branch, with only the possibility that the shadows would still conceal him.

A straggler demon, wearing ornate metal armor and cloaked in long, flowing black, rode into the clearing. The hood of his cloak covered a more concealing helmet. In his right hand, the hunter held a long spear, and in the left hand he held the reins of his mount. He rode a magnificent creature, a giant stallion warhorse with a coal-black coat and hooves of burnished fire. The horse was elemental, full of burning energy and the inferno's warmth, melting the frozen ground as it moved.

The fugitive could not help but think this rider's horse was far superior to any of the other demon steeds, but that thought brought little comfort. The hunter moved through the glade, with none of the impatient rush of the rest of the pack. He dismounted his horse and bent over to examine the tracks leading to the water. Then, as the young man watched him, not daring to move, the demon raised its head, and saw the fugitive.

He leapt at the demon hunter. He hit the cloaked figure hard, bowling him over and knocking the spear from his hand. The giant horse screamed in rage.

But the young man had mistimed his attack: as the two rolled, both splashed into the lethal black water.

The terrified man lashed out, hitting the hunter in the stomach and jaw. He might as well have hit a tree; though the demon staggered back, the young man was certain he'd caused no real damage. He scrambled up to reach the spear, but he felt an iron-like hand grab him by the throat and drag him underwater. He couldn't stop himself from groaning as the hunter grappled with him. He tried to free his neck from the demon's grip, but immersed in the foul liquid of the lake, he couldn't gain the leverage he needed. He twisted, trusting in the oily water to make his attacker's grip weaken, and elbowed his assailant. He felt the hit strike home, and the grip on him released. He pushed himself up into the air, gasping.

There was movement behind him. He kicked with all his weight, but the hunter grabbed his leg. His opponent was stronger than him–stronger than four of him. The figure pushed his foot away from him, sending the hunted young man sprawling onto the tidal line between water and land. Realizing his opportunity, he scrambled up and grabbed the spear, dodging the demon horse's flashing hooves.

His hand closed on the weapon and a surge of energy rode up his arm. He felt like he was holding a forge, an inferno, the sun itself. It was the first true warmth he could remember experiencing, yet for all that it seemed familiar.

Armed, he turned back to the demon in the water. The dark surface of the lake in front of him broke, and a being rose from the depths. He gasped and took a step back.

A dragon rose from the lake.

The beast was long and sinewy, its body made of snakelike coils that twisted and flowed back into the water. He thought the dragon's color black, or at least a midnight blue. The silhouette of the dragon, its scales and teeth and the depths of its eyes, was outlined in a pale luminescence. The glow made it look otherworldly, ethereal–less like a dragon than the ghost of a dragon. A ghost, in a land of ghosts.

"Run!" the demon yelled to him.

Its voice was female.

The demon only had enough time to turn in the dragon's direction before the monster struck. It snatched up the demon knight and sank razor fangs through black armor with an awful crunch. The dragon shook the demon and tossed her body to the side. She screamed, awful and high, before she was silent.

He had that much time to look at the dragon before it attacked, snapping its long neck forward to swallow him whole. The man barely readied the spear. He knew as he did it would be a gesture of defiance and no real defense. He felt two sensations, simultaneously–the flux of energy cascading over him as the spear pierced the upper roof of the dragon's mouth and pain as the creature's teeth crushed the skin, muscle, and bone of his right leg. The sensation added to the constant pain of his missing heart, and with it came a different pain: the return of memory.

Every memory.

Every memory of *every* lifetime.

He screamed–as primal and brutal as the demon's voice–and felt himself lifted into the air by the dragon as it flipped back its head to finish the act of swallowing.

There was a short pause as the dragon realized something was wrong.

The dragon lifted its clawed hands to clear the obstruction from its mouth, but it was too late. Light, the bright yellow light of a sun that had not been seen in the living world for thousands of years—and in this place, never—glowed hot and brilliant between its teeth. Liquid star fire dissolved the surrounding flesh through gashes that opened in the dragon's skin.

The incredible light, and the sound of the dragon's death-cry, carried for miles in every direction. The dark lake's waters splashed thick and viscous against the shoreline from the force of the body that crashed back down beneath its surface. The force sent out ripples that faded, and grew still.

The woods were silent, as if from shock. Finally, the man dragged himself to shore. He held the spear in one hand and dragged the demon's body with the other, which he let drop once he'd cleared the water.

Walking was an act of will made possible only through the spear's magic. If he had been alive, his twisted, crushed leg would surely have meant his death. The hell-horse kept trying to close with him. He had to threaten the beast with the spear to keep it at bay. He pulled the helmet from the fallen knight's head and stared at her face.

Her skin was red and her hair was a single black red stripe across her head. If her eyes were open, he knew they would be all the colors of the forge. Here in the Afterlife, he could see her soul, see the sticky black corruption of demonic taint. But worst of all, he recognized her. He *knew* her, knew her even if her appearance had changed with her rebirth, even if she no longer looked like the woman who had once saved him from a fate much worse than death.

He knew in that moment what a sick joke Xaltorath had played on him.

"Elana . . ."

He put his head in his hands and wept.

82: A Meeting of Wizards

Xaltorath was having a grand time.

He killed everyone he met, often in spectacular ways, rending limbs apart, eating children whole, and using the skulls of husbands to bash in the heads of their wives. He left a large burning path of destruction behind him, reveling in the carnage as he called his brethren from Hell so they too could play. They raped and destroyed and devoured the souls of those slain.

He loved humans. They had such a delicious heat to them. They felt such pain. He could never hurt them enough to satisfy his appetites.

Ahead of him, standing in the road, was an innocuous-looking man in a tattered patchwork sallí cloak. One might have dismissed him if it were not for the simple band around his head, the long narrow wand held in his grasp.

One would never have recognized Sandus as the Emperor, wielding two of the most powerful artifacts in the entire world, if one hadn't known better.

Xaltorath grinned. ***I HAVE BEEN WAITING FOR YOU!***

Emperor Sandus was not amused. "Go home. Send your people home."

Xaltorath stopped to pick bits of someone's leg out of his teeth. ***NOT THIS TIME.***

Sandus nodded as if accepting the answer and pulled back his arm. A stream of red energy pulsed forth, not fire so much as boiling gas. At the last moment the beam deflected and landed on a series of nearby apartments, which went up in flames.

"He's right," Gadrith said, as Sandus looked around for the source of magical aid. "The demon and I have a bargain. He helps me and in return he burns this city to the ground. You can't say that they don't have it coming. This city deserves to burn."

Sandus inhaled. "So the boy was right. You're still alive."

"Technically? No. I'm not." Gadrith held his hands up, letting the full sleeves of his long black robes fall back against his elbows. "Shall we finish this? Once and for all time?"

Sandus stared at the demon, then at Gadrith. "The last time we fought, you lost. Have you forgotten that now I am Emperor?"

"Oh, I have never forgotten. You are what I made you."

Xaltorath turned away from them and started toward the center of the City. He reached over and tossed a shopkeeper to his death, splattering the back of his skull against a brick wall.

"So, who shall you deal with first, Your Majesty?" Gadrith said. "The demon prince? Or the man who destroyed your family? Would you like to know what I did with the soul of your wife? I'm willing to go into explicit detail."

Sandus's nostrils flared. He chanted in a foreign tongue. Balls of deadly energy formed around his hands. He answered by tossing them straight at Gadrith the Twisted.

He expected it to be the beginning volley of an epic mage duel, the first round of a fight that only he could handle, because Gadrith was so very dangerous.

Instead, Gadrith took the blows to the chest, gritting his teeth together in a horrible smile. He sank to his knees while the energy burned his skin and consumed his body.

Gadrith laughed as he died.

Too late, Emperor Sandus realized his terrible mistake.

"We can't stay here while the City burns," Tyentso said to Teraeth.

The vané chewed on his thumb as the church to his goddess* filled with bodies, living and dead. Refugees poured inside—thinking they could find shelter here from the demons ravaging the City.

But even the Cathedral of Thaena wasn't safe. The demons would come there too.

"I'm not capable of taking on a demon prince," Teraeth admitted. "Even my arrogance has its limits."

"Clear the way," a deep voice bellowed, and the people who stood over Kihrin's corpse looked up to see Qoran Milligreest and a group of soldiers carrying someone on a cloak.

Tyentso's eyes widened. "I thought he was in Khorvesh."

"He's the High General," Teraeth whispered. "Someone must have brought him back through a gate."

Therin tore his gaze away from his son's corpse as he heard Milligreest's voice. His breath caught. "Is that . . . Is that Jarith?"

The soldiers laid Jarith's body down on the floor in what clear space

---

*And mother.

was available. There was no obvious injury on the man, but that did not change that he was dead, his face frozen midscream.

Milligreest said to Therin, "Can he be Returned?" His voice was even and tight, thick as iron bars.

"I'm not sure—" Therin bent down to look at Jarith. It was as if he had never stopped being a priest, the old ways returning to him by instinct.

"If a demon tore his soul out, there's nothing that can be done," Tyentso said. "I'm sorry, Qoran."

The High General's head whipped up at the sound. He looked at her, brows drawn together as he tried to place a voice he hadn't heard in twenty years. Recognition dawned, and the man shook his head. "Raverí, you shouldn't have come back."

"Never knew what was good for me," Tyentso answered. She turned to Teraeth. "Give us a moment?"

Teraeth frowned at her and the High General, then nodded as he returned to Lady Miya's side. Therin followed, either to give Tyentso and the High General their privacy or because he was protective of Miya around males of her own kind.

"How bad is it?" Tyentso asked.

Qoran scowled. "As grim as I've ever seen it. Why have you—"

She laid a hand on his arm. "That can wait. First, I have to deal with Gadrith."

"You won't need to," Qoran said. "Gadrith's the only thing that's gone right so far."

Tyentso's expression tightened. "What?"

Qoran shrugged. "Sandus killed him. At least we only have to worry about Xaltorath."

"Sandus killed . . ." Tyentso exhaled. "That bastard. That slimy morgage-sucking, goat-raping demon's cunt!"*

The High General blinked at her, taken aback by the naked anger of her words.

Tyentso leaned up and kissed Qoran on the cheek. "I've missed you, Qoran. But Sandus is dead, and Gadrith is very much alive. You and the others need to stop Xaltorath. I'll take care of my . . . husband."

She turned away from him and ran outside into the burning night.

---

*Apologies, but I shortened this curse from the full version. Although the original was, uh, creative.

83: Xaltorath's Daughter

The hunting demons came back the second time, quiet save for the occasional soft growl from the dogs. No doubt it was one thing to skirt the edges of the dragon's lake domain, and quite another to come near when the dragon might be injured, angry . . . hungry.

They inspected the edge of the water until they were certain that there was no dragon about to descend on them—and then continued with their search. The demons gave shouts of triumph as they found the body of the unconscious woman.

The hunt master dismounted, motioning to two of his men to grab the woman by the arms and hold her up in the air. He grabbed her chin and turned her head from side to side. She was tall and lean. A single stripe of hair ran from her upper forehead to the base of her neck, black or crimson, depending on how the light struck it. The skin of her face was a red-brown hue, but her hands were black.

The demon laughed and said something. Then he pulled a knife from his belt and moved to slice open the woman's throat.

Kihrin stepped out from his hiding space and whistled to draw their attention. He spun the gold spear in his right hand with practiced ease. "Why are you doing that, buck-head? She's one of yours, isn't she?"

The horned demon turned, surprised and pleased. **So quaint. You think that all our kind are friends? The strong prey on the weak. It is the only law.**

"Really?" Kihrin chuckled. "That's . . . stupid. Impressively stupid. I know demons aren't smart, but no wonder you all lost the last war. Step away from her. I didn't leave her there for you to kill."

The demon licked his knife before he put it back to the unconscious woman's throat. **Drop your weapon and surrender, or I feed on her soul.**

"Again with you being an idiot," Kihrin said. "You really can't help yourself, can you? I'm not saving her from *you*. I'm giving you a chance to leave here and go back to your masters before it's too late. Take it."

The demon laughed. **You'll take on all of us? By yourself?**

Kihrin smiled with the warmth of a man who didn't believe himself outmatched. "You must be young. Tell me, did your masters even bother to tell you just who it was you hunted tonight?"

The demon's expression hid in shadow, but his growl carried through the air well enough. **A boy. A boy not yet past his first quarter-century, no matter the vané blood that runs through dead veins. A boy named Kihrin.**

"This life, sure. Didn't Xaltorath tell who I used to be? He has to know. I'll give you one last chance . . ."

The demon walked away from the woman. **Tear out his lower soul. Bring the spear and the rest to me.** Hounds, demons, and hell-horses advanced.

Kihrin snapped his fingers. Nothing happened. A few demons laughed as they advanced, then pushed their horses to a gallop to ride him down.

The demons ordered to hold their captive up for the master's pleasure had less than a second to register that their victim had woken. Then she kicked one demon away from her. She grabbed the other by the tentacles above its ears and twisted its head in a perfect circle to the sound of snapping bone. The second demon came at her with a glowing sword that radiated a heat-sucking cold fire. She ducked under the weapon, drew her hand into a fist, and punched him.

Her hand went through his armor, and then through his chest, exiting through his back in a spray of gore. She twisted his spine into two pieces, then let the corpse fall away. She moved with beautiful grace, as if violence were a dance she had practiced since childhood.

Her eyes burned with all the colors of a forge.

She tore the sword away from its dead owner's grip before it could dissolve. The color of the weapon turned from blue to red.*

She began her slaughter in earnest.

Meanwhile, Kihrin set the spear to the ground, and readied to take the demonic charge. The demon steed did not impale itself so much as dissolve, reduced back into energy and chaos. The energy flowed up the spear and added itself to his own, which he used to move his attackers back into each other. Just for fun, he put out every bit of cold fire in a two-hundred-foot radius. Torches went out. Cold-fire hooves stopped burning. He stabbed at hounds, with much the same result as the horses. A few of the dogs faced their demise with pleading, shining eyes—obscenely grateful for oblivion.

The master of the hunt decided that it would be best if he rode elsewhere, fast. As he galloped away, the spirit of the rest broke with his exit.

---

*Demons are associated with cold, and the eating of fire and heat. That this woman is just the opposite—exactly the opposite—seems odd, and merits further research.

In a matter of seconds, the clearing was empty save for the man, the woman, and the fading soul-forms of annihilated demons. He summoned up a glowing ball of mage-light.

The two people stared at each other.

The woman reached up to retrieve her cloak from where it hung off the tattered branches of a tree. When she had draped it across her shoulders, she turned back to him.

"That," she said, pointing at the spear, "belongs to me."

Kihrin smiled. "I don't think it would be in my best interests to return Khoreval to you, before you've promised me I won't be her next victim."

The woman stopped, startled. "You know her name?"

"Of course. Who did you think named her?"

The woman blinked at him with those fiery, fierce red eyes. "That's not possible."

"Ah, the skeptical sort. Still, it's the truth."

The woman looked out toward the lake as she rubbed her solar plexus through the doublet. "I thought that dragon had finished me—"

"Xalome." He laughed. "That was Xalome. She's dead. For a while."

"And why am I not?"

He seemed reluctant to answer. "Because I healed you. I healed both of us."

"You attacked me," she continued, frowning. "Then you healed me, and then you left me here for that pack of demons to slaughter, before you rescued me again. Are you always this indecisive?"

Kihrin sighed. "I suppose that depends on who you ask. I didn't think they would hurt you."

"They're demons," she pointed out.

"So are you." His expression was haunted.

She swallowed and looked away, but she did not correct his statement.

Kihrin pointed to the deeper, darker parts of the woods. "We can't stay here. That demon that escaped will report back. And sooner or later, probably sooner, they will send a contingent that knows how to fight."

"I'm not afraid of them," she defended.

"I can see that, but we still shouldn't stay. Do you know how to reach the Chasm?"

She tilted her head as a sad smile crossed her lips. "What a strange man you are. You just denounced me as a demon, and yet, you expect that I'll help you? Would that not be odd behavior for a demon?"

"Usually," Kihrin agreed, "but you were trying to help me back there. I didn't realize it, and I screwed things up because I thought you were with them, but you weren't hunting me. You were hunting the demons."

"Being their enemy does not make me your friend," she said.

He bent down on one knee in front of her. "Then what is your pleasure? If it's in my power to grant it, it's yours. Tell me your heart's desire and I will make it real."

She drew away from him as if his proximity might burn. "Don't make such offers. You sound too much like a demon with such pretty words."

She put two fingers to her lips and whistled; a few moments later the large fire-horse trotted into the clearing and whinnied to her in greeting. She retrieved some of her armor, making a face at the sorry state of it, and tied it to the saddle before hauling herself up onto the massive horse.

As hunting horns sounded in the distance, the woman turned to Kihrin and presented her hand, to help him up behind her. "Very well. I still await a good explanation of why I should help you, but I'm willing to take us to shelter first."

84: The D'Lorus Duel

With the City on fire, no one noticed when the wall of energy surrounding the Arena fell.

"This will work?" Darzin asked for the third time, cursing himself. He knew his fear was showing, but he couldn't stop himself. He'd been in the Arena plenty of times, as a duelist.

This was different.

The trio walked inside the Arena with no one to stop them and none to even notice their passing. They didn't need a Voice of the Council to create a door for them; the man who wore the Crown and wielded the Scepter possessed his own power to take down the barrier of magical energy.

"Keep your eyes open," Gadrith said, for it was Gadrith, even if he looked like a plain Marakori man wearing a patchwork sallí cloak. The Stone of Shackles glittered around his neck, for he had taken the time to reclaim it from his old body, as well as Thurvishar's gaesh. "You and Thurvishar will stand as lookouts while I search the ruins. Neither of you may come inside: you would die." He smiled. "It appears only the Emperor may enter without suffering a horrible demise."

"Is that you, husband? I hardly recognized you without your D'Lorus wardrobe," Tyentso said as she called out from behind them. The agolé draped around her body was a dark cloud whipped by the wind.

Gadrith turned and cocked his head as he regarded the woman. It took him a moment to recognize her, but then his eyes widened. "Raverí. What a surprise, but 'husband' is not the proper word for our relationship."

"Oh, is this where you reveal you're my father?" She tilted her head. "I've known that for years." She put a hand to her chest. "Phaellen told me before we ever met."

"Who's Phaellen?"

Tyentso rolled her eyes. "Really, Gadrith? You *murdered* him."

Gadrith gestured for more information. "And . . . ?"

"House D'Erinwa? Your roommate? You lured him into the woods and botched making a tsali stone out of him, leaving his upper soul to haunt the forest as a damned, twisted shade. Does that sound familiar?"

"Oh!" Gadrith looked offended. "I botched nothing. I made an important breakthrough in separating the upper and lower souls."

"Oh, so you do remember him?"

"Yes," Gadrith said. "He snored."*

Tyentso just stared. "I hate you so much."

"Whereas I've never thought of you much at all," Gadrith admitted. "Except I found it disappointing when you ran off before we could have you sentenced to Continuance. That was inconvenient. Fortunately, Sandus provided me with a substitute." He looked down at his borrowed body, then over at Thurvishar. "You know, it occurs to me you really are my son now. Isn't that interesting?"

Lightning played over Gadrith's body. He spasmed from electrocution, before he shrugged off the surge of power, tossing the electrical arc down into the ground.

"Focus," Tyentso said. "We're talking about me here." She raised her hands in the air, a dueling pose if weapons were words and spells rather than sword and shield. "In case I haven't made it clear, old man: this one's to the death."

"Let me deal with her," Thurvishar said.

Gadrith cut him off. "No. This will be my treat. Keep watch for Milligreest and his coterie of little friends."

Thurvishar gnashed his teeth in frustration, but did as he was commanded and turned away. He motioned for Darzin to follow him as they left the center of the Arena to wait along the perimeter.

Gadrith turned to his daughter and attacked, chanting as he channeled a beam of violet energy at her that should have melted the flesh from her bones.

She caught it, her expression incredulous.

Gadrith smiled. "Did you think I would be powerless? That it would take me months to learn how to use Sandus's body? Sorry to disappoint you, daughter, but I've been preparing for this moment for decades. I know how Sandus casts better than he did."†

Tyentso straightened. "No matter. I've waited thirty years for this. Show me your worst."

---

*I doubt that was the only reason. Phaellen D'Erinwa was also top of his class. After his disappearance, that honor fell to Gadrith.

†It's true. He studied Sandus at every opportunity. He never let me help, even though I would have made the task easier. I suppose he wanted to make sure I couldn't find some loophole that would allow me to betray him. To be fair, I would have.

* * *

Dark clouds raced overhead like dogs coming to heel at the sound of a trumpet. The trees loomed, casting shadows against the red glow of the burning city. It was difficult to guess if those clouds were rain clouds or accumulated ash.

"Really?" Gadrith raised an eyebrow. "Storm magic?"

"You were always such a snob," Tyentso said as a thick zigzag of light raced down from a black cloud to strike at her enemy.

The lightning strike diverted to hit a thick rusted iron spear that Gadrith levitated from the ground. The electricity raced down the metal and exploded into the dirt.

"There's no shame in that," Gadrith said. "But I prefer my violence to be precise." He pointed a finger at her and chanted.

Tyentso staggered as her heart jerked in her chest. She felt the blow through her reclaimed talismans, through all her protections, painful as a kick from a warhorse. She had taken the blow as though she were a novice, and tears sprang to her eyes.

Gadrith smiled, his tone full of patronizing contempt. "And you thought you were a match for me. Don't forget I'm wearing the Stone of Shackles. How were you going to deal with that?"

Tyentso made a fist with her left hand to hide the fact it had numbed. Gadrith's attack had struck too true. "This fight's not done yet."

Gadrith started to say something, but a giant chunk of ice hit him in the shoulder, throwing him forward. More ice fell, less gentle hail than frozen ragged shards, and Gadrith was forced to throw up a wall of energy over himself to halt the onslaught. As he did, an enormous gust of wind hit his undefended, exposed flank and sent him hurtling into the air, to land outside his magical protection. More hail pelted him while several lightning strikes crashed into the area.

The smoke and vapor of melted ice obscured Tyentso's view, and while she stood there, waiting to defend herself, she concentrated on stopping her heart from exploding.

She wasn't naïve enough to think she had won.

"Was that your best, daughter?" Gadrith walked out of the smoke, uninjured. The first glance was wrong. He was singed a little at the edges, his patchwork sallí cloak burning along one side, but he himself wasn't injured enough for it to have much meaning.

Tyentso raised her chin. "The best that's likely to work on–" She paused and studied her father. "So powerful," she murmured.

"It's time to end this," Gadrith said.

Tyentso's eyes widened. She extended a wicked, curved finger toward Gadrith. "You have no protections . . . no talismans. Your old ones don't work on this new body!" She narrowed her eyes and threw the whole of her will behind one last spell.

Gadrith hissed as his hand turned to water, dropping away from his body to fall on the soft grass. "No," Gadrith said. "Why can I still feel my hand . . . ?"* He pointed his other hand, still whole, at her and squeezed. "Enough play. Now die!" He sounded desperate as more of his arm dropped away. The effect was spreading to the rest of his body.

Tyentso stopped her scream with clenched teeth and arched backward, her face ashen from pain. Her chest again felt like her heart was bursting. The blood slowed in her veins even as it pounded in her ears with urgent need. Tyentso was a river piling up against a curve now dammed. She was a road broken, a pathway piled high with debris.

The spell on Gadrith lessened, then ceased, as Tyentso lost the ability to concentrate. Her eyes rolled back into her head and the lightning struck around them with insane pastel hues.

Then the lightning stopped. The storm lost its cohesion.

Tyentso died.

It had been close. A few seconds more and she would have won. Gadrith concentrated as he looked at the stump of his arm and willed it to regrow. The arm did so, but it was misshapen and uneven, covered with shiny skin like that of a scar. He tucked it under the edge of the patchwork sallí.

Gadrith paused and looked at Tyentso's body. Her face looked peaceful for such a painful death, as if this were just a nap after a long, hard day. "Your best was impressive, daughter."

He regretted he didn't have the time to make a tsali of her soul.

Gadrith walked back to the others.

---

*My assumption, inaccurate as it may be, is that this spell would turn Gadrith to water without technically breaking the bonds between body and soul. So, as a kind of living water incapable of thought or act, Gadrith would still be "alive," preventing the Stone of Shackles from activating. Clever.

85: Death's Front

Kihrin saw the Chasm in the distance and despaired.

"Have the borders grown so large?" he said. "It will take us days to reach that."

The young woman turned her head. "Grown so large? There aren't many even aware that the border has changed size . . ." She paused. "You've been here before?"

"Everyone's been here before," Kihrin said. "Most of us just don't remember after we're reborn. I have to find a quicker way to reach the Chasm."

"Then I must too. I don't have days. Soon I'll waken."

The trees cleared around them as they neared a hill, upon which sat a small stone keep that looked to be in a state of disrepair. No soldiers manned its walls and no lights were present through the arrow slits. The only reason Kihrin could tell it was there was the outline it created—against varicolored lightning bolts that cracked the gray sky.

"What do you mean, you'll waken?" Kihrin asked her.

The horse they rode tossed his head and made a snickering sound as she led it up to the keep walls. The woman pulled the spear from Kihrin's grip. "I mean that I'm asleep. When morning comes, I'll cross back through the Second Veil and wake up in the living world once more."

She touched the tip of the spear to the door and, rather than disintegrate the wood, the great iron-clad door swung open. "This is as safe as we can be until we reach the Chasm," she told him. "So, you may make your case to me here."

"Elana—" he said.

She frowned at him, nudged the horse into a walk, and rode him inside the fort.

The place was long abandoned, now a home to spiders, rats, and whatever other creatures of the borderlands sheltered inside its walls. There was dust everywhere but nothing that spoke of large-scale destruction: no demons had breached the walls and looted the contents.

"What was this place?" Kihrin asked as he slid off the side of the massive horse.

"You don't know? You said you were old."

"Older than this," he replied.

She stared at him. "That would be old indeed." She gestured with a black hand. "This was a border fort. Once protecting the bridges across the Chasm, but now left behind as the Chasm shifts." She too swung her leg over the horse and then led the beast over to the side. Kihrin couldn't escape feeling the horse watched him for any signs of mischief.

"If the Chasm is moving, that's—" He shook his head. "That's not good."

"Also, my name is *not* Elana," the woman said as she whirled back to face him. "And I dislike the way you look at me. I want to know the price for this healing of yours and how you have accomplished it." She brushed her hands together and a shower of red flaked off and fell away—demon blood, from those she'd ripped apart.

"I'm sorry," Kihrin said. "Elana was the name I knew you by a long time ago."

"It's never been my name," she insisted.

He chose not to argue. "Okay. So what is your name then?"

"Answer my questions first," she replied. Her hand tightened on the spear, but then she set it aside.

He exhaled and tugged at his shirt, wincing at the large and obvious hole cut into the fabric. "There's no price for your healing. Your healing was *payment*. Your injury was my mistake, one that would never have happened if I'd realized you were not my enemy."

"But how? Such an injury—that was a dragon! I should have been destroyed. You're not a god—if you were you would not be gaeshed, would not be missing your heart." She paused. "Except you're not missing it now. I remember what I saw when we first fought, the wound that gaped in your chest. How is it you are healed as well?"

Kihrin pulled the shirt from his back, wadded it, and tossed it to a chair. It dissolved before it landed, as if to underscore the unsubstantial nature of his current existence. "Since I was missing a heart, I needed a replacement. So I used Xalome's heart." He cleared his throat. "I, uh, actually used it on us both."

"You—what?"*

At her stunned look, he elaborated. "This would never work in the living realm, but here reality is malleable. And no, I don't know what effect it will have. As far as I know, it has never been done before and perhaps could only be done because it was the Dragon of Souls, slain in the realm of Death." He shrugged. "I didn't know what else to do."

---

*My sentiments exactly. Kihrin, you insane idiot. Don't ask me what that will do: I have no idea.

"You split a dragon's heart between us," she repeated. "A dragon. A monster of chaos and evil."

Kihrin crossed his arms over his chest and nodded. "But as a bonus, it seems to have worked."

She blinked several times as if in disbelief and then rubbed her fingers through the stripe of hair on her head. She paced to the far end of the room and turned back. "A dragon's heart?" Her voice was soft.

"Okay, we're past that point. Also, there's no way to reverse it." He grinned. "You're welcome."

"You're welcome?" Her voice cracked. "You arrogant mule." Her nostrils flared with anger. "I only keep an advantage against my enemies because they do not realize my soul is untethered from my body and roams here while I sleep. But you—" She began sputtering. "You have ruined that. There is no way the presence of a *dragon's heart* will not taint my aura, and once they notice, they will ask questions I do not want answered!"

Kihrin held up his hands. "Easy there. Try to remember that you would've died. Discorporated. Whatever happens to demons or baby demons or whatever you are when they die. How did Xaltorath manage that in your case, anyway?"

A second later her hand was around Kihrin's throat, lifting him off the ground as she pressed him into dusty tapestries still hanging from the stone tower wall. **HOW DO YOU KNOW OF XALTORATH?**

Her hand collapsed on empty air as Kihrin vanished. She snarled and whirled around, but the tower was empty.

"Show yourself!" she screamed.

As she looked around the room, her eyes fell on the spear, and she rushed for it. Before her hands could close on Khoreval, it lifted to the far side, and Kihrin turned visible again, this time holding the spear pointed at her. She checked herself, hard, to keep from being impaled.

"Calm down," he ordered, no longer smiling. "Because this spear will work on you, and I would never forgive myself."

She paused, teeth still ground together, eyeing him like a crazed bull wanting to charge.

"In this last life, this one I lived most recently—when I was fifteen years old," Kihrin said, "Xaltorath found me on the streets of the Capital City and raped my mind."

The woman sucked in her breath. On her exhale, her anger ebbed.

"He showed me unpleasant things. Truthfully, I still don't understand what the point was. Maybe there was no point but torture, but he showed me a woman. A woman I could never hurt." He kept one hand on the spear while he pointed with the other. "He showed me you."

Confusion muffled the rest of her rage. "Me? She showed you *me*? Why?"

Kihrin bit his lower lip. "I don't know. So I would trust you? So I would never trust you? I think he's trying to fulfill a prophecy, but I don't know if the point was to bring us together or keep us apart."

She rolled her eyes. "I am sick to death of prophecies."

"Oh, we're agreed on that." He pulled the spear up and walked over to one of the slit windows. "It's a discussion we should save for another day. Right now? My heart was missing when we first met because it was pulled from my chest to summon Xaltorath, and he's rampaging through the streets of the Capital City. If I can't get back to the land of the living . . ."

The girl looked at him. "What if you do? Surely you'll just die a second time? You killed a dragon, so I cannot dismiss your skills, but she is the demon queen of war. Here you've had Khoreval to aid you. You won't have that advantage when you Return."

"Wait. Is Xaltorath male or female?"

"Xaltorath is a demon. She is whatever gender amuses her." She raised her chin. "She has been female when I've met her."

"I see."

"My point is this: what do you propose doing to stop Xaltorath, which would not be done better by the Emperor?"

"What bothers me is Gadrith's admission he wants the Emperor to show up. I think Xaltorath's whole role in this was nothing but a diversion to draw the Emperor's attention. They are up to something, and it will be something terrible."

"Gadrith?" Her eyes narrowed. "Gadrith, minion of Relos Var?"

"Don't tell Gadrith that. I'm sure he doesn't think he's the minion of Relos Var."

She scoffed. "Relos Var excels at pulling the strings on all manner of puppets, even those who hate him."

Kihrin chuckled too. Mostly, he watched the Chasm before them with reddened eyes and a sick heart. "I have to stop Gadrith. This is all my fault."

"I doubt that," she said. "Don't blame yourself unfairly for something you couldn't possibly be responsible for causing."

"I don't think I am," Kihrin said, still looking out at the distance. He turned back to the woman. "Will you help me? Please?"

"Who is Elana?" she asked instead. "A wife? A lover?"

"No, none of those," he answered. "Not for me, anyway. We should hurry."

"Tell me her story," she said. "And I will tell you my name."

He hesitated a moment before answering. "I was . . . imprisoned. It was a lifetime ago. Literally. I was . . . dead. But trapped. And Elana freed me." He laughed. "I guess I never have had good timing for running into you, have I?"

"You didn't—" she protested. "Whoever you think I was. This woman Elana. Whoever you have worked me up to be, you must let that person go. She doesn't exist. I'm not someone who will come scampering to you because you snap your fingers or flash that pretty smile." She paused. "Do you have any idea how insulting the idea is? That Xaltorath would try affecting the prophecies one way or the other by showing my image to you? Never was your image sent to me. As if all that were required for a future romance to fail or succeed would be your endorsement alone? As long as *you* want it . . . well, I, of course, would bow to your whims over my own opinions."

"Hey, I said nothing about romance."

Her expression turned flat. "Don't be coy. I have eyes to see how you look at me."

"And who just said my smile was pretty?" As she turned redder, he said, "Maybe he—sorry, *she*—wanted to make sure the prophecy failed, and she knew you would react this way. Maybe she just wanted to ruin things." Kihrin cleared his throat. "And as much as I'm enjoying this conversation, we need to leave."

She crossed over to the dusty, unused hearth. It was very large, befitting the size of the tower, tall and wide enough to march a column of soldiers through it. She stared at it.

"What are you doing?"

"Lighting a fire."

"Don't you need something to burn?" Even as he asked that question, flames flickered and built in the hearth, blue and purple and with tiny flecks of green, nothing like a natural fire. "Never mind. My bad. Now what?"

The woman pulled herself onto her horse's back and held out a hand for Kihrin. "Now we ride."

As he took her hand, she said, "My name is Janel Theranon."

He settled in behind her, handing the spear back to her. "Thank you. I only wish I would remember."

"Remember?"

"I won't remember when I wake. Neither of us will."*

She started to say something, perhaps a denial, but instead she shook her head.

"So. Why did we light that fire?"

---

*I know: if Kihrin does not remember what happened to him while he was dead, how could I write of it? How could I even begin to speculate what happened to him in the Afterlife? It is, as I have mentioned, a result of my witch gift. Even if the knowledge and memories are not actively accessible, a deep-buried part of Kihrin does remember.

She smiled and tightened her hands on the reins. "I'll show you."

The horse tossed his head with excitement as she urged the great beast forward, and with a fierce, wild cry, she leapt her horse into the flames.

The horse landed on a hillside of bones, leaping clear of the bonfire flames behind it. They were now in another place.

They were, Kihrin realized, at the Chasm.

He was at a loss to hear much over the roar of an avalanche of rock and debris falling in reverse, flying up out of the giant crevasse in the earth to block out the sky. The rock wall created was never-ending, and he didn't know where it went or how it gathered. But the net effect gave him a moment of dizziness as if everything were upside down.

"Duck!" Janel pulled him down, sliding sideways across the horse's saddle as a large ball of lightning sailed through the space where they had been a moment before. The roar of battle surrounded them on three sides as demons galloped and stomped and slithered and danced at humans who fought with spears, swords, maces, and arrows.

Kihrin's every instinct was to slip off the horse and rush into the battle like sliding into a warm bath, but Janel held on to his arm. "No!" she screamed over the din. "Cross the Chasm."

He looked at her and then at the wide, ugly crack in the earth. He could see the crack move, trees toppling on the far side as the Chasm grew wider.

No, not wider, he realized. It was moving. Moving as if the canyon itself was encroaching farther into the Land of Peace.

"I'll never be able to cross that!" he screamed back.

Janel impaled a demon, letting it turn to light on her spear, before she looked back over her shoulder at him. "There's a bridge. Can you not see a bridge?"

"What? What kind of bridge–" He squinted and looked at the Chasm. There was a bridge, a rickety, small, and neglected thing swinging in the high winds like a toy in a hurricane. "That? This is a joke, right?"

"No!" Janel turned in her seat and put her arm around Kihrin's waist, pulling him off the back of the horse. "If you can see it, you can cross, but here we must part ways, for I cannot."

The horse screamed a warning. They looked over to see a large group of demons riding toward them–their focus making it clear they were not here to attack the normal soldiers guarding the Chasm.

"Go!" she said again.

"Come with me," Kihrin said.

"I cannot . . ." Janel protested. "I cannot *see* the bridge. No demon can!"

He put a hand on her ankle in the stirrups. "You're infected, but the transformation isn't complete. Something is keeping it at bay. You're not truly a demon."

She cocked her head and looked at him with a sad expression. "Yes, I am." She kicked her horse into a gallop then, and the beast screamed as it sprang forward to meet the incoming charge.

As Kihrin scrambled back toward the Chasm, the sound of Janel's laughter floated toward him. She impaled a demon on her spear, held forward like a knight's lance, while she casually ripped the arm off another demon and used it as a mace. There was something about the way she reveled in that stark, horrible brutality that reminded him of Xaltorath. He saw the resemblance.

Still, there were so many demons. Far too many for even a demon queen's daughter to fight.

Kihrin looked at her, then back at the bridge.

"What the hell. I'm already dead," he muttered to himself as he ran into the fray.

"You were supposed to cross the bridge!" Janel screamed when she saw him again, sometime later.

"Not without you!" he screamed back.

"I cannot see the bridge. What part was unclear to you?" She pulled her spear out of a dead demon, not paying attention as it disintegrated.

"But I can! I can lead you."

"Why would I want to go to the Land of Peace?" she yelled, clearly exasperated. "I'm not dead." The surrounding dim ebbed as the demons fell back, regrouping for another onslaught.

"Are you sure?" The lull in the fighting made it quiet enough to talk in a normal tone of voice. "Shouldn't you have woken by now?"

Janel paused, and a look of horrible realization came over her. She put her hand to her chest where the dragon's teeth had bit deep.

"I'm pretty sure if you die here, you die in the real world too," Kihrin said. "Just because I could heal you here doesn't mean that what I did affected your living body." He held out his hand to her as a mighty bellow seemed to shake the ground where they stood. "Come on. I'll lead you across."

"It will destroy me . . ." she protested.

"No. No it won't. I'm sure of that!" Kihrin yelled.

She took his hand and slid off the side of her steed. "I would take it as a kindness if you did not kill me any more than I may already be."

"I promise, my lady."

As a gigantic demon crested the rise, the pair took off running for the slender rope bridge.

86: RETURNING

Kihrin sat up and gasped for breath.

Teraeth bent down next to him. "Took you long enough. What did you do, stop and pick flowers?"

Kihrin glared at him. "Some of us haven't died before, thank you very much." He shook his head. "I don't remember what happened to me while I was dead. I remember dying though."

"No one remembers what happens to them in the Afterlife," Teraeth agreed.

"Really? You don't remember?"

"All right," Teraeth allowed. "*Most* people don't remember. Don't blame me. You didn't want to join the Brotherhood." He presented his hand to Kihrin. "Come on, we have work to do."

"Wait!" Kihrin looked around the church, at the towering statue of Thaena and the dead and mourning clogging the aisles. "How did I end up here? What's going on? Where is everyone?"

Teraeth ticked off points on his fingers. "You were sacrificed to Xaltorath, but since Xaltorath didn't receive your entire soul, he's not technically under anyone's control. So Xaltorath is starting a Hellmarch,* summoning up every demon he can. High Lord Therin, Lady Miya, and General Milligreest have left to send him back to Hell. Galen went back to the Blue Palace to oversee the evacuation of your surviving family. Meanwhile, Gadrith was wearing the Stone of Shackles when Sandus killed him, so the Emperor is dead, and Gadrith is wearing his body like a fancy new cloak. Tyentso's gone to stop him."

Kihrin blinked. "Damn it, we had a plan."

"Which worked beautifully right up until the point where it didn't." Teraeth sighed. "Such is the way of plans. Nobody could have predicted Gadrith would be capable of responding so quickly."

Kihrin scowled. "Is Tyentso strong enough to kill him?"

---

*The last Hellmarch was twelve years ago, starting in Marakor, and cost incalculable lives. Jorat is still underpopulated.

A pained look crossed Teraeth's face. "She's counting on the fact that he won't be able to cast spells while he's adjusting to his new body."

"Remember what Tyentso said about possessing my body? He's been planning this for *years,* Teraeth. He knows how to cast spells in Sandus's body."

Teraeth made a face. "Doesn't matter anyway. He won't be alone."

"Thurvishar," Kihrin said, his chest growing tight. What were the odds that Jarith had been able to successfully arrest him? So poor even Kihrin wouldn't take that bet.

"Plus, we have no idea what powers the Crown and Scepter themselves will give him."

Kihrin nodded. "Okay. Let's go back her up." He took a step, stumbled, and sagged when he tried to catch himself.

Teraeth looked surprised and cursed under his breath. "You need to rest. You can barely walk."

Kihrin shook his head. "Being dead was rest enough. Wait, I need a sword." He cast his gaze around the room.

He stopped at Jarith's body and looked sick.

"The High General brought him in," Teraeth said as he saw Kihrin's expression. "Soul dead. He was probably killed by a demon."

"Damn it all." Kihrin walked over to the body, bent down, and pulled out the sword that was in Jarith's scabbard. The blade was Khorveshan, sharp along one edge and wickedly curved. It was nothing like a normal Quuros dueling blade, and four years before, Kihrin would have had no idea how to wield one. He did now.

His old weapons trainer, the Thriss lizard man Szzarus, would be so proud.

Kihrin leaned the dull end against one shoulder, holding the hilt with his other hand. "Okay, let's go."

Teraeth held out his hands. "Where? I don't know where Tyentso went." He didn't sound happy about that.

"We'll figure something out." Kihrin stumbled through the halls, managing not to curse as he tripped over dead bodies.

Teraeth put an arm under his to steady him. "You couldn't fight a leprous rabbit in this condition."

"Just give me a minute to catch my second wind," Kihrin said.

The two men paused on the steps of the cathedral. It seemed like most of the City was on fire, a hearth-like wind blowing ashes and smoke up into the sky. The noise as people screamed, fought, panicked, and died was an unintelligible roar.

There was a flash of purple light in the distance.

Kihrin pointed. "Did you see that? Magic . . . That came from the Culling Fields."

"Are you sure . . . ?" But as Teraeth asked, there was a flash of red, a flash of purple, and then lightning.

They looked at each other.

"Quite a trick you pulled there, brat," Darzin said as he stood up from the twisted, withered tree he'd been leaning against. Behind him, flashes of multicolored light brightened the sky. "I'd heard someone sacrificed to a demon couldn't be Returned."

Kihrin pushed Teraeth away from him so Kihrin was standing on his own, and the blond man cocked his head and regarded Darzin. "Yeah, funny thing about that. I suppose you should probably go ask Xaltorath if he really received an acceptable sacrifice. I've got a funny hunch he lied about having to do what you say."

Darzin pulled his sword from his scabbard. "Doesn't matter. We already have what we want. Who's your friend?"

"Doesn't matter," Kihrin said back. "Shall we end this?" He lowered the sword from his shoulder.

Thurvishar was looking past Darzin, toward the center of the Arena. He showed no interest in Kihrin or Teraeth, but was staring at the bright light flashes. Dread stole over Kihrin. If Thurvishar was still here, that meant Tyentso had been wrong about Gadrith's decline in power. She was fighting the man himself.

That was not a good sign.

"End this?" Darzin laughed outright. "Oh brat, you can hardly stand. Do you really think you'll be any good against me?" He waved the sword in front of him.

"Are you too afraid to find out?"

Darzin's nostrils flared. He stepped forward, nimble feet dodging the fallen branches and bleached white bones of the Culling Fields floor. He came in with a quick sword swing.

Kihrin blocked it easily and took a step to the side. "You need to work on your stance."

Darzin's eyes widened in surprise, but he didn't waste breath on a reply. He attacked again, slicing to Kihrin's off-side, feinting, and then sliding to the right to thrust the blade at Kihrin's thigh.

Kihrin again reacted, moving his sword to block the feint, then leaning back just enough so that Darzin's sword sliced through the fabric of his kef but no deeper. Darzin and Kihrin circled each other, until Kihrin's back was to the center of the park. Darzin lunged forward. Kihrin caught the inside of Darzin's blade against his own, and while the blades were trapped there, Darzin lashed out and punched Kihrin in the face.

Kihrin staggered back and wiped the blood from his nose.

Darzin shook his head. "Oh, come on, this isn't even a challenge. The least you can do is put some backbone into it."

Kihrin readied his blade again.

Thurvishar sighed as he watched the lights fade from the center of the Arena. "What a tragedy. She was magnificent."

"What?" Kihrin's eyes flickered to Thurvishar in horror, and Darzin saw his chance.

More than one person saw their chance. As Darzin swung at Kihrin, a wall of energy—fine deadly webs of glowing blue lines—spread out from Thurvishar. Teraeth vanished from where he had been standing and re-appeared, almost in position to slice his poisoned blades across Thurvishar's back. Almost, but not quite.

Teraeth flew back as if he'd run into an invisible wall.

Kihrin wasn't distracted. Too late, Darzin tried to stop himself, but he was already committed to the sword swing. Kihrin stepped inside Darzin's blade, holding his sword next to his body with one hand on the hilt and the other hand directing the back end of the sword. He sliced across Darzin's wrist, then in a single quicksilver-smooth motion lifted the sword and brought the blade up and across Darzin's throat.

Kihrin stepped backward as Darzin put his hand to his neck, shock widening his eyes as blood gushed outward. Kihrin didn't have to see beyond the First Veil to know what Darzin was doing.

He was healing himself.

"Not this time." Kihrin swung his sword in a tight arc with all his remaining strength.

Darzin's head and several of his fingers tumbled onto the grass.

"I'm sorry," Thurvishar whispered. "I have no choice. None."

Kihrin turned to him in time to see the branches and roots of trees twisting out of the ground to wrap around Teraeth—the real Teraeth—who struggled at the bonds with little success of freeing himself.

Kihrin held up his sword as he moved back to confront Thurvishar. "You're gaeshed."

The magus smiled. "If only I could answer."

"Notice how I didn't ask you."

"Yes, perhaps that's for the best."

Kihrin swallowed and looked past him into the center of the park. The darkness that lingered now was far more threatening than the colored light show had been earlier. "Settle a curiosity for me, would you? I get that you don't look like Sandus because you're half-vordreth, but the age thing has been bothering me. I think I've got it though: it's because you've spent time in that lighthouse, Shadrag Gor, isn't it? Time moves slower there, and that's why everyone thinks you're too old to be Sandus's son, even though you are. Truthfully, you're not any older than I am."

"Oh, I am older than you," Thurvishar corrected, looking impressed, even as he explained the details as much as the gaesh allowed. "I lived those years. I just didn't live them here."

"Kihrin!" Teraeth shouted. "Just run. Run! You can't take them both."

"And I can't run fast enough either," Kihrin said, looking past Thurvishar. "He's already here."

As if on command, Gadrith strode out of the darkness.

87: The Breaking of Oaths

Gadrith smiled as he walked forward, a look that had been foreign to Dead Man's face. It was in keeping with Sandus's sunny air, made more macabre for that false cheer.

It was like a sick joke, Kihrin thought as he watched him step toward the group. Gadrith, who had pretended to be Thurvishar's father, now possessing the body of Thurvishar's real father in an evil mockery of that memory. Kihrin saw the look of unrepentant hate on Thurvishar's face and knew that, if he had been able to, he would have destroyed Gadrith long ago.

"I'm curious how you Returned," Gadrith told Kihrin. "Still, I don't begrudge you Darzin's death. You were right back in the tombs: his usefulness came to an end the moment he sacrificed you to Xaltorath."

"I assume you killed Tyentso," Kihrin said, his expression grim.

Gadrith raised an eyebrow. "You may need to be more specific, young man."

"Raverí," Kihrin corrected. "Your wife."

"Ah!" Gadrith smiled again. "Yes. She acquitted herself admirably. I almost regret I had to slay her."

"Really?" Thurvishar asked, surprise coloring his voice.

"No. I was being polite."

"What happens now?" Thurvishar asked. "Do you want me to take care of these two while you search the tombs for Urthaenriel?"

Gadrith cocked his head and gave Thurvishar a look of intense dissatisfaction. ". . . yes."

Kihrin walked forward, trying not to stagger. He concentrated on pulling what strength he could from the ground, the trees, the surrounding grass. "Is that what this is all about? Recovering Kandor's sword, Godslayer?" Kihrin paused, and his eyes narrowed. "I had this wrong, didn't I? We all had this wrong. You weren't trying to become Emperor. You could have been Emperor years ago. You could have been Emperor whenever you wanted, but you didn't care about that crown until you realized it was the only way you could step a foot inside those ruins—

without the Empire's magic blasting you to pieces. This isn't a coup . . .
it's a . . . it's. . . ." Kihrin laughed. "This is a *burglary.*"

"Yes," Gadrith agreed in a flat, dry tone. He looked over at his "son."
"He's smarter than his brother."

Thurvishar nodded in agreement.

Gadrith walked toward the ruins. "Kill him. I have a sword to find
and then, many gods to slay. I think I'll start with Thaena."

Thurvishar's shoulders slumped. His earlier wording, "take care of,"
allowed him room to take prisoners. Gadrith's new orders did not.

Kihrin could see despair in the man's eyes as Thurvishar lifted his
hands. "I'm sorry," Thurvishar whispered.

"You have a choice," Kihrin told him.

"I really don't," Thurvishar replied.

"I've been where you are. You always have a choice."

Thurvishar responded by gesturing, and the Khorveshan sword in
Kihrin's hands turned red hot and slagged into molten metal.

The sword might have burned him, but Kihrin was good at protecting himself against fire. There was only a slight sting as he found the
molten metal pouring down his fingers.

"I don't want to kill you," Thurvishar said, "but I really don't see how
my death will allow you to kill Gadrith. It would be different if you were
a trained wizard. I even think you have the talent, but you don't have
the years of training you'd need to defeat a sorcerer of his caliber. Even
if you did, he's wearing the Crown and Scepter *and* the Stone of Shackles. He'll overpower you—and if you kill him, you still lose."

"Just give me a chance—"

Thurvishar shook his head. "You know how this works. I can't." He
raised a hand.

As Kihrin backed up, he tripped over an old rusted sword—straight,
narrow, and archaic in style. It wouldn't help him. The blade was dull
and pitted; it looked like it would break after a single good swing. But
Kihrin was a swordsman. He had the irrational urge to die with a blade
in his hand this time, if it was to be his fate to die twice in one day.

He wrapped his hand around the hilt and pulled the sword free of
the dark, wormy ground.

Thurvishar threw lightning at him, but Kihrin barely noticed. He batted the spell out of the air, so it crashed into the Arena forest. It lit a red
fire, snuffed by the odd magical distortions of the mutated trees. His
whole attention was focused on the sword, now an elegant and shimmering bar of silver white metal.

The blade was singing in his mind.

The harmonies of the sword were so beautiful that he felt tears at the
corners of his eyes; the sweet, rapturous raising of a single voice that

seemed to hold within it the promise of joy and a glimpse at Heaven. There was a danger, holding that sword, that it would consume him. It might be all he could hear or focus on, forever lost in the harmony of that perfect sound. There was something so familiar about the blade too. Kihrin was reminded of when he'd concentrated on the necklace that had contained his gaesh. He was holding something to which he was connected—something that was once part of him, once whole and now separate.

"You unbelievably lucky bastard," Thurvishar told him, his voice tinged with awe.

Kihrin focused enough through the singing to respond. "Yes," he told the wizard. "So I am. Call for Gadrith, please."

Thurvishar conjured a ball of fire and tossed it at Kihrin, mostly to buy himself and his gaesh-given order more time. Kihrin shoved the fire aside without it affecting him.

"Gadrith!" Thurvishar screamed. "I need you. I need you out here *right now.*"

Kihrin's strength returned to him. He felt as though he could run races, swim the Senlay, perform any feat. He crossed over to the unconscious Teraeth. He didn't think that the tree branches that were holding the assassin trapped were technically magical anymore, but here in this place he suspected everything was just a bit magical. He tried sliding his vision past the Veil to check but found it impossible: he couldn't concentrate through the sound of the sword's singing.

"What *is* it?" Gadrith snapped as he passed through the doorway of one of the ruined towers. He paused and frowned as he saw that Kihrin was still alive. "I told you to kill him."

"I *can't,*" Thurvishar admitted through gritted teeth, doubling over through the pain.

Kihrin knew the signs well enough. Gaesh feedback would kill the man if Kihrin didn't act.

"Can't? Why–" Gadrith's words cut off though, as he saw Kihrin advancing toward him, and the sword Kihrin held in his hand.

"It wasn't inside the buildings?" Gadrith was astonished. "All this time, and it was never inside the buildings at all?" He looked as though his whole world had just been upended. Perhaps it had.

"Yeah, kick in the crotch, isn't it? You've spent thirty years chasing something that anyone could have picked up," Kihrin agreed, "at any duel fought in the Arena. It was tangled in some roots, out in the open, lying in plain sight." Kihrin smiled in a wicked way. "You have enough toys. You don't get to keep this one."

"Impossible," Gadrith said. "I am the Thief of Souls. I am the King of Demons. *I* killed the Emperor. *I* will free the demons. It's *my* destiny to destroy the Empire, to remake the world. ME. NOT KAEN. NOT RELOS VAR. ME!" He growled and stretched his hands toward Kihrin, but whatever his intention, Kihrin intercepted the spell with the sword, and it died in the air.

How to deal with Gadrith? Kihrin couldn't just kill him. If he did, he'd only switch places with the man's soul, thus giving the necromancer exactly what he had truly desired from the beginning: Urthaenriel. Gadrith was upset and unsettled now, but if Kihrin gave the man time, the sorcerer might well come to the conclusions Tyentso had years before. Even someone immune to magic needed air to breathe and solid ground under their feet.

Then Kihrin remembered: he wielded a sword that could break the magic of gods.

So Gadrith was not his target.

The Stone of Shackles glittered on Gadrith's chest, a bouncing goal that shimmered with malice. Kihrin aimed for the gem and drove his sword forward. Gadrith moved to block the blow. He probably used a spell, but Urthaenriel paid no heed to spells. Time moved slowly as Urthaenriel first shattered the Stone of Shackles into tiny blue shards and then dove forward, slicing into Gadrith's chest and impaling his heart.

The dark mage gave Kihrin one look of terrific surprise. Then the circlet vanished from Gadrith's head, the wand from his grip. The men watching had exactly that long to appreciate what had just occurred before they felt a tremendous pressure that lifted them, ripped up the roots binding Teraeth, and pushed them all outside the boundaries of the Arena. They landed on the soft, wet grass just outside the Culling Fields inn.

The body Gadrith had stolen, still impaled on Kihrin's sword, came with them.

The rainbow soap-bubble force field that protected the Arena flickered back into existence. It reverted to its default state when waiting for the contest that would decide its new owner.

Gadrith the Twisted, briefly Emperor of Quur, was dead.

88: Miya's Gift

The City burned.

Little demons, large demons, fat demons, demons of every shape, color, and description imaginable destroyed and savaged whatever and whoever they could find. They basked in the warmth of the spreading City fires. They maliciously killed thousands and just as inexplicably left as many survivors unmolested to witnesses and remember their atrocities. They feasted on fear and dined well.

Even though Xaltorath had now been banished, it would still take months, if not years, to undo the damage he left behind.

"Is everyone here?" Therin asked Galen, as he walked up with Lady Miya at his side. The High Lord and his seneschal were both singed and dirty, with slashes and burns on their clothing that spoke of injuries received in the fighting.

"I've gathered everyone I could find," Galen said, "but a few people are still in the City overseeing the Blue Houses." The number of family brought together in the great hall seemed small, compared to the number of D'Mons who had existed just a day prior. It was too painful to contemplate some of those missing . . .

Galen clenched his teeth and refused to think about his father.

"Good," Therin said. "I'm sending you, your wife, and a small contingent of healers to the summer palace in Kirpis. Your job is to stay safe, do you understand?"

"What about–" Galen swallowed the question.

Therin's face was without expression. Someone who didn't know the D'Mons might make the mistake of interpreting it as without emotion. Galen knew better.

"Finish the question," Therin ordered.

He wanted to ask about Kihrin. He wanted to, but he didn't. Galen was flustered and upset. Not so long ago he had not only watched family members die, but remembered that Kihrin hadn't been willing to die for him. Kihrin had been willing to die for Lady Miya, had in fact died for Lady Miya, but not for Galen.

So, Galen asked, "What about my father?"

"Your father is a dead man or will be soon," Therin stated. "He will be forgotten, and his name will never be mentioned in this House again. I have disowned him. I can only pray it's enough to satisfy the gods."

He might not be dead yet, Galen thought, but he knew better than to say it out loud.

Behind Lord Therin, Lady Miya made a small noise.

"Do you understand me, Lord Heir?"

The title didn't register right away. Galen almost looked for his father. Even as Therin continued to frown at Galen, he still couldn't make himself believe the implications. "My lord?"

"You were his firstborn son. That makes you Lord Heir now. That is why you and Sheloran must leave. The House will have a very difficult road ahead of it. I need to make sure you are protected."

Galen could only blink. So, he hadn't heard wrong in the temple, when Therin had claimed Kihrin was *his* son. Not Darzin's son at all. Not Darzin's son, and not Galen's brother.

Galen's uncle.

"Yes, my lord. I understand."

"Good. Now–"

"Therin–" Lady Miya's voice was at once both shocked and jubilant. "Therin, the gaesh is *gone.*"

"What?" The man blinked at her as if he hadn't really understood the statement or its context. Therin raised his hand to examine the thin, tarnished silver chain looped several times around his wrist, a small pendant of a tree dangling at the end.

The pendant crumbled to ash and drifted away on the air.

Lady Miya put a hand to her neck. "I can breathe," she said. "After so long, I can draw breath."

"How is this possible?" Therin asked.

"I do not know," Lady Miya answered. "I cannot imagine, and yet, Therin, I can feel that it is gone."

All conversation in the great hall ceased.

"Lady Miya–" Galen crossed over to her, planning to offer her whatever support he could.

Galen's movement must have caught her attention, because she turned her stare back to him. That stare made him pause because there was nothing friendly about it. Miya didn't look at him with the blank indifference he expected from the House seneschal. No, this stare held *malice.*

"That is not my name," she corrected.

Galen felt himself lifted. A bar of invisible air, hard as steel, tightened around his neck. He choked, gasping, his sight darkening as he tried to draw in breath and failed.

Something gave way in his neck with a loud, hard snap.

Galen D'Mon fell to the ground, dead.

For a few eternal seconds, no one moved. Plenty in the room had never known a time when Lady Miya had not served the House and protected its members. Even then, watching her kill the new Lord Heir, witnesses wondered if she'd somehow been replaced by that mimic, or if someone had taken control of her mind.

Then they screamed and ran, but the large doors to the great hall slammed shut the moment anyone approached. For the second time in a day, they were prisoners to a sorcerer in their own home.

"You're not Lady Miya," Therin said, eyes wide. "You can't be."

She didn't smile at him. No hate or outrage shone from her eyes. She tilted her head as if to acknowledge a truth. "To be honest, I have *never* been Miya. The real Miya died before you and I ever met." The tiniest bitter smile graced the corners of her lips as she stepped over Galen's body. "I could not tell you who I really am. The gaesh prevented it."

"So, who are you?" Therin glanced down at Galen's body, then back at Miya. His experience as a former priest of Thaena told him Galen's condition was not necessarily permanent and so there was not yet reason to panic.

"Khaeriel." She smiled as Therin's eyes widened. "Khaeriel, queen of all the vané, daughter of Khaevatz, queen of the Manol vané, daughter of Khaemezra, of the Eight Guardians."*

Therin closed his eyes. "Let them go. It's me you want. Let them go."

"You are half-correct. It is you I want, but not for a reason so petty as revenge. However, I am also not going to let your family go. They are the tethers that shackle you to this House and this title as surely as that gaesh once chained me." She gestured again. On the far side of the room, where Galen's new widow banged against the door, Sheloran jerked as her neck snapped. She collapsed into an untidy heap on the floor.

Therin shook himself from his shock and attacked Khaeriel.

Khaeriel brushed aside whatever spell he attempted to cast—likely some enchantment meant to stun and incapacitate—before narrowing her eyes at Therin.

He flew backward against the wall, arms and legs spread like a pinned butterfly.

---

*This explains why King Terindel, of the Kirpis vané, thought that Queen Khaevatz was "unfit" to rule the vané—because of her voramer mother. Presumably since then, the Royal Family has come to terms with that bit of grafting onto the family tree. This is especially true since they probably know Khaemezra is actually the goddess Thaena. Also, technically, Kihrin and Teraeth aren't related to each other—only because Kihrin's *biological* mother is Miya (even if Miya's body is now possessed by Khaemezra's granddaughter Khaeriel). Were that not the case, Teraeth, who is Khaevatz's half-brother, would be Kihrin's great-uncle. Yes, it's complicated.

Therin grit his teeth together and tore himself free. He dropped to the ground, catching himself at the last moment before he stumbled. Therin gestured and said something under his breath.

The air around Khaeriel turned thick and choking.

The clouds ripped away from her, scattering into wispy tatters.

"A sound strategy," she said. "No talismans would protect me from breathing in poisonous vapors, but you chose the medium poorly, for air is mine. You should try enfolding my clothes in flame, turning the ground underneath me to acid, collapsing the roof on top of me. Mayhap you would have better luck."

"I will stop you," Therin hissed.

"No," Khaeriel said, "and truth be told, your heart does not want you to. Do you know that you are the grandson of usurped King Terindel, of the Kirpis vané? It is true. Your father Pedron's—"

"He was not my father . . ."

She dismissed his protest with a wave. "Yes, he was. We both know it. Your vané blood betrays your lineage. For Pedron's mother was Princess Valrashar, King Terindel's daughter. She was gaeshed and sold to the D'Mons by *my* father, King Kelindel. My father usurped the Kirpis vané crown. So your father Pedron—and your aunt Tishar—were by all rights the true rulers of the Kirpis vané. Since both are dead now . . . that leaves you. You are now heir to a throne that seemed so distant, that no one could have imagined you would claim it. Leave behind your human shackles, Therin. Shed them and join me."

He didn't answer her. Instead he concentrated.

Khaeriel screamed as blood streamed from the corners of her eyes. She fell down to her knees.

"I'm sorry," Therin said. "Your eyes will heal, but I can't let you do this." He walked toward her, steps unsteady from the damage he had taken when she had thrown him. "We'll hide you until you heal, help you somehow. I won't let the Council—"

Therin dropped to the ground, twitching, his eyes locked open in shock.

Khaeriel stood. She wiped the blood away from her eyes.

"I have targeted several specific nerve clusters. Painless, but you cannot move or organize your thoughts enough to channel magic. Lorgrin taught me that," she said. "Oh but I shall miss him. His was a most puissant skill with matters of medicine and anatomy." She bent down next to the shuddering High Lord. "I do not need you to protect me, Therin. And the Council will be the ones hiding from me before I have finished with them."

She reached out and stroked his hair. "I give to you this gift: the one thing you have always wanted, the one thing you have never been brave enough to admit is your true heart's desire." She straightened. "I shall free you of the D'Mons."

She turned back to the crowd.

Some fought. Others begged. Many did both, running or trying to hide, but the result was the same.

Finally, only two people remained alive in the hall.

Khaeriel returned to him when she was finished, stepping over the body of Bavrin D'Mon's youngest son, Thallis. His eyes stared forward, open but unseeing.

"I know you think you shall never forgive me for this, but in time you will." Khaeriel raised her hand, and Therin's body floated upward. "You shall never blame me even a quarter as much as you blame yourself. A part of you, and not a small part, believes you deserve to be punished for your crimes." Khaeriel smiled. "And when have I ever refused your commands, my lord?"

Therin couldn't struggle. He couldn't scream, or cry, or whisper. He was trapped inside his own body, a prisoner. All he could do was watch, impotent, as the former queen of the vané opened a portal, and ushered them both through.

89: PARTING

Kihrin would have laughed, shouted, danced a little on Gadrith's corpse, but there was the matter of Thurvishar drowning in a gaesh loop. He yanked Urthaenriel free from Gadrith's body and turned back to Thurvishar, unsure what he could do to help.

But Thurvishar was fine.

The wizard was standing up, out of breath and massaging his throat, but with no other sign of distress. He wasn't in fact dying.

Thurvishar gazed at Gadrith's body, really Sandus's body, with an unreadable expression.

"I–" Kihrin exhaled. "I'm sorry. I killed your father. Well, okay, I'm not exactly sorry–"

"You didn't kill my father," Thurvishar corrected. "You killed my father's murderer. For that I'm in your debt." He turned back toward Teraeth, still unconscious and wrapped in the remnants of tree roots that had pulled free when they were all expelled.

Kihrin gazed fondly at the unconscious vané. "I shouldn't rub this in," Kihrin said, "but where would be the fun in that?" He walked over and then frowned.

"You can't be affected by magic," Thurvishar said, "but neither can you perceive it or cast it." He stared over at the unconscious assassin and concentrated.

Teraeth opened his eyes and leapt to his feet, blades in each hand.

"You missed the excitement," Kihrin said. "We won."

Teraeth looked around, his gaze stopping at the body of the dead necromancer. "We won?"

Kihrin clapped Thurvishar on the shoulder. "You were gaeshed, and by Quuros law the man who holds your gaesh is responsible for your crimes. That man is dead. I'm sure once I explain the situation to the High General–"

Thurvishar pulled himself away from Kihrin. "No. No, I'll explain matters to the High General. I'll throw myself at his mercy. He will use magic, and the truth will come out. As you said, they will not hold me to account for Gadrith's crimes. You, however, must leave. Leave the City and leave immediately."

Kihrin blinked. "What? Why?"

Thurvishar scowled. "You have no idea what you've done, do you?"

Kihrin pointed to the corpse. "Yeah, I saved everyone, that's what I've done."

Thurvishar gave Teraeth an exasperated look.

"What did he do?" Teraeth asked, his tone more cautious.

Thurvishar swept the scene with his arm. "He killed the Emperor—"

"That wasn't the real Emperor!" Kihrin protested.

Thurvishar glared at Kihrin. "Gadrith was wearing the Crown and Scepter. He was wearing my father's body. He *was* the Emperor." Thurvishar returned his focus to Teraeth. "Kihrin killed the Emperor. Kihrin claimed Urthaenriel. And now . . . now he's destroyed—shattered—the Stone of Shackles."

Teraeth's expression froze in shock.

"Wait. Wait, why—" Kihrin paused. "I admit it wasn't ideal, but it was the only way I could kill him without our souls switching places—"

"And that was a clever solution to the problem," Thurvishar admitted. "If you hadn't, he would have ended up in your body, holding Urthaenriel. But . . ." He licked his lips and winced. "All the eight artifact Cornerstones have a sympathetic relationship to the element to which they are attuned. The Stone of Shackles is connected to gaeshe."

Kihrin felt light-headed. "That's why you didn't die. That's why you didn't die, even though you never obeyed Gadrith's last command. You're not gaeshed anymore."

"No one is gaeshed anymore," Thurvishar agreed. "No one in the *whole world* is gaeshed anymore. You've *freed* them."

Kihrin turned back toward the City. "Miya—"

"No." Teraeth's hand came down on Kihrin's shoulder. "You can't. She's fine. Your mother is a powerful sorceress. Believe she will be fine. But he's right—you won't be fine if you stay here. That sword only protects you from magic, not swords or arrows."

"It gets worse," Thurvishar said then.

"Really?" Kihrin said. "Because I already want to throw up."

"Do it later," Thurvishar replied. "The pacts that allow for the summoning of demons hinges on them being able to tap into the power of the Stone of Shackles to gaesh—if they can't do that, then the contracts are nullified. So someone has freed the demons, just as prophecy predicted, but it wasn't Gadrith or Kaen."

Kihrin stared at him. "What you're saying—" He shook his head. "No—"

"Give the sword to Teraeth," Thurvishar said. "Or to me. We'll hand it over to Milligreest so he may place it back in a vault, to wait on the choosing of the next Emperor. There are no witnesses but ourselves to tell the tale of how Gadrith died, and we can craft any story we choose. No one has to know it was your hand that held the Ruin of Kings."

"I like the way you think," Teraeth said with an approving note to his voice. He moved a hand toward Kihrin's sword arm. "Yes, give me—"

And paused, as Teraeth found a silver straight blade placed against his throat with all the neat precision of a shaving razor.

"I can't," Kihrin said. His throat worked with no sound and his eyes were bright and wet. "Please step back, Teraeth. You're my friend." There was a pleading note to the request.

Their eyes met. "I remember," Teraeth said. "She has a beautiful voice, doesn't she? It's hard to hear anything else." He stepped backward and let his hands fall to his sides.

Kihrin lowered the sword and stood there, shuddering.

"I gather the sword won't let you give it up," Thurvishar said, "but regardless, you must leave now. The High General has his own vows, and one of those is to protect the Empire from all threats. And you just became a threat to the Empire."

"Milligreest doesn't believe in the prophecies," Kihrin said. His voice was weak and tense.

Teraeth shook his head. He was back in ready mode, hands on his daggers and watching for anyone who might interrupt them. "I think he might change his mind after tonight. Come on. We can steal aboard a ship tonight and head out to sea with the tide."

"No," Kihrin said. He drew in a deep breath and seemed to recover some composure. "No, you go. Go by ship. The more of a chase we can lead them on the better. I'll leave by land." He walked over to Gadrith's body and bent down, working a ring off the dead man's finger—a red intaglio ruby. He held it up to Thurvishar. "Was this Gadrith's or Sandus's?"

Thurvishar inspected it. "It must have belonged to Sandus."

Kihrin handed him the ring. "You should have something that belonged to your real father." He turned toward the center of the Arena and his nostrils flared. "What about Tyentso?"

"Leave her," Teraeth blurted out.

"She'll come back, won't she?" Kihrin looked at Teraeth. "Thaena will bring her back?"

Teraeth's expression was grim. "I don't know. The rules inside the Arena are different."

"I've never heard of Thaena allowing anyone who died inside the Arena to Return," Thurvishar said.

When Kihrin turned to go back to reclaim Tyentso's body, Teraeth put himself in the way. "Go, Kihrin. If she doesn't Return, Thurvishar can send someone back for her body. She'll be buried in the D'Lorus crypts."

"I'm pretty sure she'd have hated the idea of being buried in the D'Lorus crypts," Kihrin snapped, but he didn't try to force his way past the vané a second time.

"Technically," Thurvishar said, "the D'Lorus family died tonight. The only true D'Lorus left is High Lord Cedric, and he's a sad, broken old man." He sounded like he couldn't quite decide how he felt about that.

"I won't tell if you don't," Kihrin said. He looked around, realizing he had nothing he could use to sheath the sword. "Good luck, both of you."

"Where are you going?" Teraeth asked.

Kihrin answered, "Jorat. I hear there's a knight there who's causing some trouble. I'm going to find him."

The Arena was quiet. The demon battles, so recently over, didn't touch those peaceful green fields. No wind breached the force field to ruffle the branches of twisted trees, no birds remained within its boundaries, no squirrels had ever feasted on nuts and berries there. If any had found their way inside in the brief time the field was dormant, they too were shunted outside when Gadrith breathed his last.

No living animal, two-legged or otherwise, could stay inside the boundaries of the Arena until the next contest—until the next battle that would end when one man fought all comers. The victor would be the one wearing the Crown and holding the Scepter when he left its boundaries. The ritual would be as it had always been: anyone who wished to take part would gather; the Voices would lower the barriers; the fighting would begin.

Normally.

Tyentso, once called Raverí, inhaled deeply and arched her back to suck in more sweet air as she Returned. She was still not entirely aware of where she was, or what had occurred around her. She only knew that she had lost and paid a price for that losing—a price not so final as it might have been for another. She lay in the field at the center of the Arena, looking up at a soap-bubble field of magical energy, while the rain sprinkled on her face.

Above her head, directly over her head, a glowing circle of light bisected by a white line floated. She stared at both in confusion for a moment before she realized what she was seeing.

Tyentso began to laugh.

No living thing could stay inside the Arena after the Emperor's death, but Tyentso had—at that singular perfect moment—not been alive, so her body hadn't moved.

She reached up with both hands to claim the Crown and Scepter of Quur.

90: Final Notes

Empress Tyentso,

A few notes are in order to wrap up this account.

The death toll to the Capital City was staggering. It's estimated that at least five thousand people died due to demon attacks that night. About thirty thousand more perished in the fires that erupted thanks to their chaos. Still more will die in the coming months of starvation or disease if immediate steps are not taken.

The body of the Emperor, Sandus, was recovered from the Culling Fields. It was interned in the Hall of Heroes in the Emperor's Palace to full state ceremony, next to the preserved body of his wife. According to official history, he was slain by an unknown assailant, possibly demonic, after bringing Gadrith D'Lorus to justice.

Xaltorath was "banished" by Qoran Milligreest, Therin D'Mon, and Therin's "slave" Miya. But the timing suggests that most of Xaltorath's demons actually returned to Hell of their own accord, a short time after the Stone of Shackles was destroyed. It is a faux reprieve; now that their chains are broken, the demons are free to begin their war against the physical races anew, without restriction.

Qoran returned to the Citadel and, it was assumed, Therin D'Mon and Lady Miya returned to the Blue Palace.

However, this is the last time anyone can document seeing High Lord Therin D'Mon or Lady Miya. Just a short time after the main part of the fighting ended, a physicker discovered the site of the D'Mon massacre. It had claimed almost all remaining D'Mon members. We must assume it was the work of Miya, freed of the gaesh and become Khaeriel, Queen-in-Exile, once more. She must have retaliated against the family who'd kept her imprisoned.

High Lord Therin's fate is unknown.

The D'Mon family has been devastated, reduced to a handful of members. And none of those remaining are easily available to petition Thaena for the Return of any others. With Therin missing and Darzin dead, their future is uncertain. Kihrin D'Mon's location is uncertain too: the last anyone saw, he left the north gates of the City with several D'Mon riding horses, a Joratese groom, and a gray Jorat fireblood.

Urthaenriel is now loose again in the world. No demon may be safely summoned lest they run amok, which means no slave may be gaeshed.

People are saying it's the end of the world.

My Empress, we know it's just the beginning.

ADDENDUM I:
GLOSSARY

A

Afterlife, the–a dark mirror of the living world; souls go to the Afterlife after death, hopefully to move on to the Land of Peace

agolé (a-GOAL-ay)–a piece of cloth worn draped around the shoulders and hips by both men and women in western Quur

Alavel (a-la-VEL)–home city of the wizard's school known as the Academy

Arena, the–a park in the center of the Capital City that serves as the battleground for the choosing of the Emperor

ariala (ah-rye-LAY)–a metal, known for its variety of color, mined in Kirpis

Attuleema, Landril–a merchant of the Copper Quarter

B

Baelosh (BAY-losh)–a dragon, best known for the size of his hoard of treasure

Bertok (BER-tok)–a god of war

Black Brotherhood, the–a group of assassins for hire

black lotus–a plant native to the Manol Jungle that is the source of a deadly poison of the same name

Butterbelly–a pawnshop owner and fence with the Shadowdancers

C

Calay Harbor (kal-LAY)–the harbor that shelters the Capital City

Caless (kal-LESS)–a goddess of physical love

Camarnith (kam-ARN-ith)–a god of healing, native to Zherias

Chainbreaker–a magical artifact associated with the Manol vané; has powers dealing with illusions

Cherthog (cher-THOG)–a god of winter and ice, primarily worshipped in Yor

Cimillion (seh-MIL-e-on)–Emperor Sandus's son, believed killed as an infant by Gadrith the Twisted

Citadel, the–headquarters of the Quuros Imperial Military

City, the, aka the Capital City—just called "the City"; originally a city-state under the control of the god-king Qhuaras, its original name (Quur) now applies to the whole Empire

Continuance—a royal practice of delaying the execution of a female member of the House until she has borne a child; usually done when there is no male heir

Copper Quarter, the—the mercantile district of the Lower Circle in the Capital City

Cornerstones, the—eight magical artifacts; the Stone of Shackles and Chainbreaker are two of these

Court of Gems, the—slang for the Royal Families of the Upper Circle, represented by twelve different kinds of gemstones

Crown and Scepter, the—famous artifacts that may only be wielded by the Emperor of Quur

Culling Fields, the—a tavern and inn situated just outside the Imperial Arena. Also a nickname for Arena Park.

D

Daakis (DAY-kis)—a god of sports, swordplay, and games

Dana (dan-AY)—god-queen of Eamithon, still worshipped as the goddess of wisdom and virtue

D'Aramarin (day-ar-a-MAR-in)
  Dorman (DOR-man)—a nobleman belonging to House D'Aramarin, cousin and friend of Galen D'Mon

Daughter of Laaka, aka kraken—an enormous immortal sea creature

Delon (DEL-on)—first mate aboard the slave ship *The Misery*

demons—an alien race from another dimension that can, through effort, gain access to the material world; famous for their cruelty and power. See: Hellmarch

D'Erinwa (day-er-in-WAY),
  Morvos (MOR-vos)—a nobleman of House D'Erinwa, fond of card games
  Phaellen (FAY-lan)—a nobleman of House D'Erinwa, murdered by Gadrith D'Lorus

Desolation, the—an island chain between Zherias and Khorvesh that poses a major shipping and navigational hazard because of the lack of currents on one side and the Maw on the other

Dethic (DETH-ik)—a eunuch slave trader operating out of Kishna-Farriga

D'Lorus (du-LOR-us)
  Cedric (KED-rik)—High Lord of House D'Lorus; father of Gadrith
  Gadrith (GAD-rith)—Lord Heir of House D'Lorus, convicted of treason and executed at the end of the Affair of the Voices; also known as Gadrith the Twisted

Raverí (rav-ear-EE)—wife of Gadrith D'Lorus; officially listed as mother of Thurvishar D'Lorus. She was believed executed after his birth for the charges of witchcraft and treason

Thurvishar (thur-vish-AR)—son of Gadrith and Raverí D'Lorus, Lord Heir of House D'Lorus after his father Gadrith's execution

D'Mon (day-MON)

Alshena (al-shen-AY)—wife of Darzin D'Mon, originally from House D'Aramarin

Bavrin (BAV-rin)—second living son of High Lord Therin D'Mon

Darzin (DAR-zin)—Lord Heir and eldest living son of High Lord Therin D'Mon

Devyeh (DEV-yeh)—third living son of High Lord Therin D'Mon

Galen (GAL-len)—second son of Lord Heir Darzin D'Mon

Kihrin (KEAR-rin)—eldest son of Lord Heir Darzin D'Mon by a slave, Lyrilyn. See: Rook

Saerá (SAY-ra)—eldest daughter of Darzin D'Mon

Therin (THER-rin)—High Lord of House D'Mon

Tishar (tish-AR)—younger sister of Pedron D'Mon, also half-vané

Devoran Prophecies, the—a many-book series of prophecies that are believed to foretell the end of the world

Devors (de-VORS)—island chain south of the Capital City, most famous as the home of the Devoran priests and their prophecies

Doc (Dok)—the owner and primary bartender of the Culling Fields, a tavern

Doltar (dol-TAR)—a country distant from Quur

Dragonspires, the—a mountain range running north–south through Quur, dividing the dominions of Kirpis, Kazivar, Eamithon, and Khorvesh from Raenena, Jorat, Marakor, and Yor

dreth (DRETH)—See: vordreth

drussian (deus-E-an)—a rare metal superior to iron that can only be created through super hot magical fires

Dyana (DEE-an-ah)—a vordreth woman, married to Emperor Sandus, murdered by Gadrith the Twisted

E

Eamithon (AY-mith-ON)—a dominion just north of the Capital City, the oldest of the Quuros dominions and considered the most tranquil

Empire of Quur—See: Quur

Esiné (eh-SIN-ah)—a Manol vané clan that communicated through hand movements

F

Faris (FAIR-is)—a member of the Shadowdancers criminal organization, formally code-named Ferret

firebloods—a race originally related to horses but modified by the god-king Korshal to possess extraordinary size, power, resilience, loyalty, and intelligence. Firebloods are omnivorous and although they do not possess opposable thumbs, some are capable of manipulating tenyé. They have an average life expectancy of eighty years or more.

Four Races, the—four immortal, powerful races that once existed; only the vané still exist in their original, immortal forms, with the other races having devolved into the morgage, dreth, and human races

G

gaesh (gaysh), pl. gaeshe (gash-ee)—an enchantment that forces the victim to follow all commands given by the person who physically possesses the totem focus, up to and including commands of suicide. Being unable or unwilling to perform a command results in death.

Galava (gal-a-VAY)—one of the Eight Immortals; goddess of life and nature

Galla Sea (GAL-la)—sea between the Devors island cluster and the Desolation

Gallthis (gal-THIS)—a garbage pit outside the Capital City, unofficially used by people who don't wish to pay the fees charged by the Junk Boys

Gendal (GEN-dal)—former Emperor of Quur, murdered by Gadrith D'Lorus

god-touched—a "gift" or "curse" (depending on who one asks) handed down by the Eight Immortals to the eight Royal Houses of Quur. The Royal Houses are forbidden on pain of death, from making laws. As a side effect of the curse, each House has a distinctive eye color.

Guarem (GOW-rem)—the primary language of Quur

Grizzst (GRIST)—falsely attributed to being one of the Eight Immortals; famous wizard, sometimes considered a god of magic, particularly demonology. Believed to be responsible for the binding of demons

H

Hell—distinct from the Land of Peace; where demons come from

Hellmarch—the result of a powerful demon gaining access to the physical world, freely summoning demons and possessing corpses. This usually results in a runaway path of death and devastation.

I

Ivory District, the—the temple district of the Upper Circle in the Capital City

J

Jorat (jor-AT)–a dominion in the middle of Quur with varying climate and wide reaches of grassy plains, known for its horses

Juval, Captain (JEW-val)–the Zheriaso captain of the slave ship *The Misery*

K

Kalindra (KAL-ind-rah)–a member of the Black Brotherhood, of Khorvesh and Zherias descent

Kame (KAY-me)–a prostitute working the harbor area of the Capital

Kandor (KAN-dor)

> Atrin (AT-rin)–an Emperor of Quur who significantly expanded the borders of the Empire; most famous for deciding to invade the Manol, which resulted in the destruction of virtually the entire Quuros army, leaving Quur defenseless against the subsequent morgage invasion. Also, the last known wielder of the Sword of Empire, Urthaenriel.

> Elana (eh-lan-AY)–Atrin Kandor's wife; after her husband's death, she returned to using her maiden name, Milligreest

Karolaen (KAR-o-lane)–former name of Kharas Gulgoth

Kazivar (KAZ-eh-var)–one of the dominions of Quur, north of Eamithon

Kelanis (KEL-a-nis)–son of Khaevatz and Kelindel, now king of the vané

Kelindel (KEL-in-del)–the Kirpis vané king who married the Manol vané queen Khaevatz and united the vané people

Key–a specialist burglar working for the Shadowdancers, trained at unlocking magical wards and enchantments; technically a witch. See: witch

Kirpis, the (KIR-pis)–a dominion to the north of Kazivar, primarily forest. Most famous for being the original home of one of the vané races, as well as the Academy. Also home of a number of very famous vineyards.

Kirpis vané–a fair-skinned, immortal race who once lived in the Kirpis forest before being driven south to eventually relocate into the Manol Jungle

Kishna-Farriga (KISH-na-fair-eh-GAH)–one of the Free States, independent city-states south of Quur, past the Manol Jungle; Kishna-Farriga is used as a trading entrepôt by many neighboring countries

Khaemezra (kay-MEZ-rah), aka Mother–the High Priestess of Thaena, and leader of the Black Brotherhood; Teraeth's mother

Khaeriel (kay-RE-el)–queen of the vané, deceased

Khaevatz (KAY-vatz)–Manol vané queen, famous for resisting Atrin Kandor's invasion; she later married Kirpis vané king Kelindel

Kharas Gulgoth (KAR-as GUL-goth)—a ruin in the middle of the Korthaen Blight; believed sacred (and cursed) by the morgage

Khored (KOR-ed)—one of the Eight Immortals, God of Destruction

Khoreval (KOR-e-val)—a magic spear wielded by Janel Theranon, particularly efficacious against demons

Khorsal (KOR-sal)—a god-king who ruled Jorat. He was particularly obsessed with horses, and modified a great many of the people and animals under his power. Responsible for the creation of the fireblood horse lines and centaurs.

Khorvesh (kor-VESH)—a dominion to the south of the Capital City, just north of the Manol Jungle

Korthaen Blight, the (Kor-THANE)—also called the Wastelands, a cursed and unlivable land that is (somehow) home to the morgage

L

Laaka (LAKE-ay)—goddess of storms, shipwrecks, and sea serpents

Land of Peace, the—Heaven, the place rewarded souls go after they die and are judged worthy by Thaena

Lorgrin (LOR-grin)—chief physicker of House D'Mon

Lower Circle—the area of the Capital City that exists outside of the safety of the tabletop mesa of the Upper Circle, thus making it vulnerable to flooding

Lyrilyn (LIR-il-in)—a slave girl owned by Pedron D'Mon

M

Maevanos (MAY-van-os)—1. an erotic dance; 2. a holy rite of the Black Gate, the church of Thaena

Magoq (mag-OK)—oar master on board *The Misery*

Manol, the (MAN-ol)—an area of dense jungle in the equatorial region of the known world; home to the Manol vané

Mataris, Baron (MAT-ar-is)—a nobleman from Eamithon who liked to live in the City

Maw, the—an area of ocean maelstrom to the south of the Desolation, near Zherias

Merit (MER-it)—a thief running with Faris in the Shadowdancers

Milligreest (mill-eh-GREEST)

Elana (e-lan-AY)—wife of Atrin Kandor, responsible for ending the morgage invasion of Khorvesh

Jarith (JAR-ith)—only son of Qoran Milligreest; like most Milligreests, serves in the military

Nikali (ni-KAL-i)—cousin of Qoran Milligreest, famous for his skill with a sword. See: Terindel

Qoran (KOR-an)—High General of the Quuros army, considered one of the most powerful people in the Empire

mimics—a mysterious shape-changing race that hide amongst humanity, typically selling their services as spies and assassins; infamous for their fondness for devouring brains

Misery, The—a slave ship

misha (MEESH-ah)—a long-sleeved shirt worn by men in Quur

Miyathreall (my-ah-threel), aka Miya—a handmaiden to Queen Khaeriel; gaeshed slave to Therin D'Mon

Morea (Mor-E-ah)—a slave girl owned by Ola Nathera; Talea's sister

morgage (mor-gah-GEE)—a wild and savage race that lives in the Korthaen Blight and makes constant war on its neighbors, mainly Khorvesh

Mouse—a Key in the Shadowdancers, deceased

N
Nathera, Ola (OH-la na-THER-ah), aka Raven—a former slave, now owner of the Shattered Veil Club in Velvet Town

O
Octagon, the—the main slave auction house of the Capital City

Ogenra (OH-jon-RAY)—an unrecognized bastard of one of the Royal Families. Far from being unwanted, Ogenra are considered an important part of the political process because of their ability to circumvent the god-touched curse.

Old Man, the—See: Sharanakal

ord—the main monetary unit of Kishna-Farriga

Q
Quur, the Great and Holy Empire of (koor)—a large empire originally expanded from a single city-state (also named Quur) that now serves as the Empire's capital

R
Raenena (RAY-nen-ah)—a dominion of Quur, nestled in the Dragonspire Mountains to the north

Roarin (RAY-or-in)—a morgage-blooded bouncer at the Shattered Veil Club

raisigi (RAY-sig-eye)—a tight-fitting bodice worn by women

Rava (ra-VAY)—Raverí's mother, executed for witchcraft

Raven—See: Nathera, Ola

Rook—See: D'Mon, Kihrin

S

sallí (sal-LEE)—a hooded, cloak-like garment designed to protect the wearer from the intense heat of the Capital City

Sandus (SAND-us)—a farmer from Marakor, later Emperor of Quur

S'arric (sar-RIC)—one of the Eight Immortals, mostly unknown (and deceased); god of sun, stars, and sky

Scandal—a fireblood mare from Jorat

Shadowdancers, the—an illegal criminal organization operating in the Lower Circle of the Capital City

Sharanakal (SHA-ran-a-KAL)—a dragon, associated with fire; also known as "the Old Man"

Shattered Veil Club, the—a velvet house and entertainment hall owned by Ola Nathera

Simillion (SIM-i-le-on)—first Emperor of Quur

Standing Keg, the—a tavern in the Lower Circle

Star—a Joratese horse trainer, enslaved for stealing horses

star tears—a kind of rare blue diamond

Stone of Shackles, the—one of the eight Cornerstones, ancient artifacts of unknown origin

Suless (SEW-less)—god-queen of Yor, associated with witchcraft, deception, treachery, and betrayal

Surdyeh (SUR-de-yeh)—a blind musician who lives and works in the Copper Quarter, Lower Circle, Capital City

T

Taja (TAJ-ah)—one of the Eight Immortals, Goddess of Luck

Talea (tal-E-ah)—Morea's sister, a slave girl formerly owned by Baron Mataris

talisman—a otherwise normal object whose tenyé has been modified to vibrate in sympathy with the owner, thus reinforcing the tenyé against enemies who might use magic to change it; this also means it's extremely dangerous to allow one's talismans to fall into enemy hands. Since talismans interfere with magical power, every talisman worn weakens the spell effectiveness of the wearer.

Talon—a mimic assassin and spy working for Darzin D'Mon

tenyé (ten-AY)—the true essence of an object, vital to all magic

Teraeth (ter-WRATHE)—hunter of Thaena; a Manol vané assassin and member of the Black Brotherhood; son of Khaemezra

Terindel (TER-in-del)—an infamous Kirpis vané who tried to assassinate Queen Khaevatz and usurp his brother's throne

Thaena (thane-AY)—one of the Eight Immortals, Goddess of Death

Theranon, Janel (jan-EL ther-a-NON)—a demon-tainted warrior who goes to the Afterlife when she sleeps

Three Sisters, the—either Taja, Tya, and Thaena, or Galava, Tya, and
   Thaena; also, the three moons in the night sky
tsali stone (zal-e)—a crystal created from the condensed soul of a person
Tya (tie-ah)—one of the Eight Immortals, Goddess of Magic
Tya's Veil (tie-ah)—an aurora borealis effect visible in the night sky
Tyentso (tie-EN-so)—a sea witch serving aboard the slave ship *The
   Misery*

U

Upper Circle—the mesa plateau in the center of the Capital City that is
   home to the Royal Houses, temples, government, and Arena
Urthaenriel (UR-thane-re-EL)—Godslayer, the Ruin of Kings, the Emperor's Sword. A powerful artifact that is believed to make its wielder
   completely immune to magic and thus is capable of killing gods
usigi (YOU-sig-eye)—undergarments, specifically underpants or loincloths

V

Valathea (val-a-THE-a)—a harp passed through the Milligreest family;
   also, a deceased queen of the Kirpis vané
Valrashar (val-ra-SHAR)—a vané princess, daughter of Kirpis vané King
   Terindel and Queen Valathea
Valrazi (val-RAH-zi)—Captain of the Guard for House D'Mon
vané (van-EH) aka vorfelané—an immortal, magically gifted race known
   for their exceptional beauty
Veil—1. the aurora borealis effect sometimes seen in the nighttime sky;
   2. the state of perception separating seeing the "normal" world from
   seeing the true essence or tenyé of the world, necessary for magic
Velvet Town—the red-light district of the Lower Circle. Those who engage in the sex trade are commonly described as "velvet," e.g., velvet
   boys or velvet girls
Vishai Mysteries, the (vish-AY)—an underground religion popular in parts
   of Eamithon, Jorat, and Marakor; little is known about their inner
   workings, but their religion seems to principally center around a solar deity; often pacifistic
Vol Karoth (VOL ka-ROTH), aka War Child—a demon offspring crafted
   by the demons to counter the Eight Guardians
voramer (vor-a-MEER), aka vormer—an extinct water-dwelling race believed to be the progenitors of the morgage and the ithlakor; of the
   two, only the ithlakor still live in water
voras (vor-AS), aka vorarras—an extinct race believed to have been the
   progenitors of humanity, who lost their immortality when Kharolaen
   was destroyed

vordreth (vor-DRETH), aka vordredd, dreth, dredd, dwarves—an underground-dwelling race known for their strength and intelligence; despite their nickname, not short. Believed to have been wiped out when Atrin Kandor conquered Raenena.

W

Watchmen—the guards tasked with policing the Capital City

Winding Sheet, the—a velvet house specializing in providing lethal entertainments for those with sufficient wealth to afford them

witch—anyone using magic who has not received formal, official training and licensing; although technically gender-neutral, usually only applied to women

X

Xalome (ZAL-o-may)—a dragon, associated with souls

Xaltorath (zal-tor-OTH)—a demon prince, who can only be summoned through the sacrifice of a family member; self-associated with lust and war

Y

Ynis (y-NIS)—a god-king who once ruled the area now known as Khorvesh; associated with death and snakes

Ynisthana (y-NIS-than-AY)—an island in the Desolation chain, used as a training grounds by the Black Brotherhood

Yor (Yor)—one of Quur's dominions, the most recently added

Z

Zherias (ZER-e-as)—a large island to the southwest of Quur. Independent from Quur, and anxious to stay that way; famous for their skill at piracy and trade

THE ROYAL HOUSES

House D'Aramarin

Gem: Emerald
Heraldic device: Kraken
Eyes: Green
Monopoly: The Gatekeepers. Transportation and teleportation.

House D'Evelin

Gem: Amethyst
Heraldic device: Cyclone
Eyes: Violet
Monopoly: The Junk Boys. Sewage, garbage, water treatment, brewing.

House D'Erinwa

Gem: Jacinth
Heraldic device: Elephant
Eyes: Amber
Monopoly: The Octagon. Slavery, private mercenaries.

House D'Jorax

Gem: Opal
Heraldic device: Lightning
Eyes: Multicolored green/purple, or red/blue (artificial)
Monopoly: Revelers. Minstrels and entertainers, courtesans, velvet.

House D'Kaje

Gem: Topaz
Heraldic device: Crocodile
Eyes: Yellow
Monopoly: Lamplighters, chandlers, cuisine.

House D'Kard

Gem: Jade
Heraldic device: Spider
Eyes: Dark green (artificial)
Monopoly: Masons, builders, carpentry, crafts.

House D'Laakar

Gem: Aquamarine
Heraldic device: Two fish
Eyes: Turquoise
Monopoly: The Ice Men. Refrigeration, food preservation, air-cooling.

House D'Lorus

Gem: Onyx
Heraldic device: Flower
Eyes: Black
Monopoly: The Binders. Magic, education, scholarly research, book- and mapmaking.

House D'Moló

Gem: Chrysoberyl
Heraldic device: Jaguar
Eyes: Cat's eyes (artificial)
Monopoly: Animal husbandry, leatherworking, weaving, tailoring.

House D'Mon

Gem: Blue sapphire
Heraldic device: Hawk
Eyes: Blue
Monopoly: The Blue Houses. Healing and medical arts.

House D'Nofra

Gem: Carnelian
Heraldic device: Tower
Eyes: Wolf-like (artificial)
Monopoly: Crops, herbs, spices, teas, coffee.

House D'Talus

Gem: Ruby
Heraldic device: Lion
Eyes: Red
Monopoly: The Red Men. Smelting, mining, and all metal craft.

ADDENDUM III:
PRONUNCIATION GUIDE

While there is no single hard rule to the pronunciation of names, a few common rules widely exist. Note that these guidelines are primarily for Quuros names. People from outside the Empire, or people from conquered nations, may have other pronunciation rules.

1. A single vowel at the end of a name is pronounced with a hard sound. For example, Alshena is pronounced al-shen-AY.
2. Vowels at the end with accents break this rule. Sallí, for example, is pronounced sal-LEE, not sal-LI. Norà is pronounced with a soft a.
3. Two vowels together in the middle of a word make the first vowel hard while the second becomes silent. For example: Khaemezra is pronounced kay-mez-RAY.
4. If two vowels are at the end of a word, only the vowel just after the consonant is made hard, but the second vowel is still pronounced. Example: Morea is pronounced mor-E-ah.
5. "C" is pronounced with a hard "k" sound.

The Ruling Families of the Vané

For purposes of genealogy, the biologically living body is considered the survivor for determining relationships in cases of soul switching because of the Stone of Shackles.

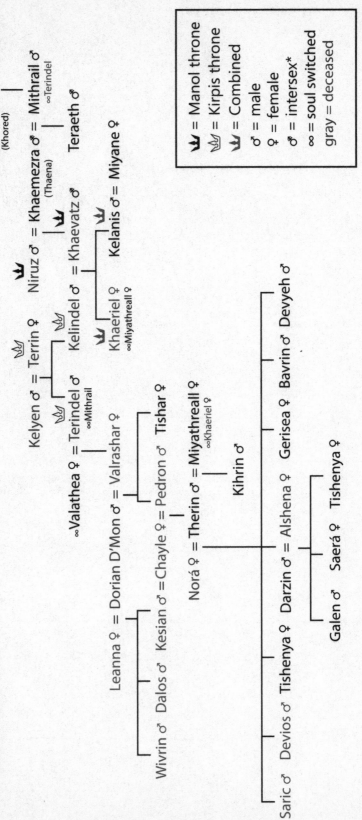

Legend:
- 👑 = Manol throne
- 👣 = Kirpis throne
- 👑 = Combined
- ♂ = male
- ♀ = female
- ⚥ = intersex*
- ∞ = soul switched
- gray = deceased

*All vorarmer are born male, and become female during the later part of their life cycle. They are capable of reproduction during both stages.